(3/2)   5.-

D0337883

PENGUIN BOOKS

STORIES OF THE OLD SOUTH

Ben Forkner is a professor of English and American literature at the University of Angers in France. A graduate of Stetson University in Florida, he received his M.A. and Ph.D. from the University of North Carolina in Chapel Hill. He has published articles on writers from Ireland and from the American South and has edited two anthologies of Irish short stories: *Modern Irish Short Stories* (Penguin) and *A New Book of Dubliners*. With Patrick Samway, S.J., he has co-edited two other anthologies of Southern literature, *Stories of the Modern South* (Penguin) and *A Modern Southern Reader*. He also edits the *Journal of the Short Story in English* published biannually by the University of Angers Press.

Patrick Samway, S.J., received his B.A. and M.A. from Fordham University, his M. Div. from Woodstock College, and his Ph.D. in English from the University of North Carolina at Chapel Hill. Father Samway taught for eight years at Le Moyne College in Syracuse, New York, and also has received two Fulbright lectureships to France (universities of Nantes and Paris VII), in addition to having been a Bannan Fellow at the University of Santa Clara in California and Visiting Associate Professor at Boston College. At present, he is Literary Editor of *America* and teaches American literature at Fordham University at Lincoln Center. He is the author of *Faulkner's "Intruder in the Dust": A Critical Study of the Typescripts* and co-editor with Michel Gresset of *Faulkner and Idealism: Perspectives From Paris*.

STORIES
OF THE
OLD SOUTH

❀

Edited by
Ben Forkner
and
Patrick Samway, S.J.

PENGUIN BOOKS

PENGUIN BOOKS
Published by the Penguin Group
Viking Penguin, a division of Penguin Books USA Inc.,
40 West 23rd Street, New York, New York 10010, U.S.A.
Penguin Books Ltd, 27 Wrights Lane,
London W8 5TZ, England
Penguin Books Australia Ltd, Ringwood,
Victoria, Australia
Penguin Books Canada Ltd, 2801 John Street,
Markham, Ontario, Canada L3R 1B4
Penguin Books (N.Z.) Ltd, 182–190 Wairau Road,
Auckland 10, New Zealand

Penguin Books Ltd, Registered Offices:
Harmondsworth, Middlesex, England

First published in simultaneous hardcover and paperback editions by
Viking Penguin, a division of Penguin Books USA Inc. 1989

1   3   5   7   9   10   8   6   4   2

Pages v and vi constitute an extension of this copyright page.

LIBRARY OF CONGRESS CATALOGING IN PUBLICATION DATA
Stories of the Old South / edited by Ben Forkner and Patrick Samway, S.J.
p.   cm.
ISBN 0 14 01.2006 8
1. Short stories, American—Southern States.   2. Southern States—
Fiction.   I. Forkner, Ben.   II. Samway, Patrick H.
PS551.S76   1989
813'.01'08975—dc19   88-38342

Printed in the United States of America
Set in Times Roman

COPYRIGHT NOTICES AND ACKNOWLEDGMENTS

CONTENTS

INTRODUCTION

Stories of the Old South covers a century of Southern short fiction, from roughly the 1830s on up through the early 1930s. The later dates, of course, point to the first full wave of the remarkable creative tide of Southern writing that even today, almost three generations later, gives little sign of faltering. The 1830s, however, mark perhaps an even more important transition in the history of the Southern imagination. After more than 200 years of colonial, revolutionary, and republican coexistence with the North, the South began to engage much of its intellectual and creative energy in an increasingly defiant process of self-definition.

The hypnotic resonances evoked by the term "Old South" reach back to the moment the collective spirit of the South, more and more conscious of its outside reputation as an unbudging, conservative plantation economy, decided to justify rather than dissolve its differences. The result of that choice is well known: increasing social and political entrenchment during the 30 years before the Civil War; the murderous war itself; the occupied Reconstruction times of ruined fields, impotent survival, and bitter bile; the emerging modern South confounded by all sorts of old memories and new divisions—and behind all this, the powerful, persistent elevation of the defeated, dying Confederacy into a mythic drama of apparently universal appeal. Though this is just one possible version of the "Old South," condensed a bit overemphatically, anyone who has even a passing acquaintance with the official records and the bare facts knows that an account of Southern history during the last century has little need of embellishment to make a narrative impact; and some idea of an echoing, overdetermined, dramatic, suffering past should be kept constantly in mind when approaching most of the major writers of the South, old and new.

This is not to argue that the best literature of a country, even when revealing powerful attachments, conforms in any narrow, hidebound way to the country's dominant myths. The war years of gore and glory are a different matter, but even then, as the rediscovery and publication in 1984 of Mary Boykin Chesnut's monumental diaries demonstrated, the waves of political propaganda and exuberant idealism did not smother all literary insight.

The forces that generate history and myth tend to leave a large measure of everyday reality and private life by the wayside, but the genuine artistic impulse is more often than not extremely reluctant to leave anything, however eccentric and out-of-the-way, wholly unaccounted for. And in the South, which Walker Percy once described as a large club, the writers have usually been among the most unruly and unclubbable members. Even during the Civil War, once the fires of rebellion were lit, at least two maverick Confederate writers—George Washington Cable and Mark Twain—did not hesitate to take rebelliousness a step further, logically claiming a right to independent thought even when directed against the blindspots and failures of the country they had fought for. Cable and Twain are, admittedly, very special cases, but only an unwise literary historian would attempt to fit each individual Southern writer into any sort of collective mold. This would apply equally to the Southern writers most fiercely sympathetic to the cause of the South: George Washington Harris, William Gilmore Simms, and Thomas Nelson Page. The reader of their stories, and of the stories of the other writers of the Old South collected here, should not be too surprised, then, that even early Southern fiction cannot help but intersect the rise and fall of Southern nationalism at some very odd angles.

Though scholars never cease to argue about the degrees of historical veracity underlying the images, characters, and plots of the fiction of George Washington Harris, Simms, and Page, among others, they do agree that the events leading up to the Civil War revealed serious disjunctions in American society that had been building up for years. To a large extent, the Southern way of life— particularly from 1820, when the Missouri Compromise was adopted and in which Congress declared that slavery should not extend in any state, except Missouri, formed from the Louisiana Territory north of the latitude 36°30′—depended both on slavery and on the production of cotton. It is good to recall, moreover, that the history of slavery, as contemporary scholars such as C. Vann Woodward and James M. McPherson have demonstrated, is long and complicated. At root, no one seems to deny that the proponents of slavery firmly grounded their views in the seriously erroneous belief commonly held in the 19th century that blacks were inferior to whites.

In the late 17th century, blacks made up 4 percent of the total population of Virginia. The majority of those "bound" to work in these new lands were whites who submitted to indentured servitude. By 1708, however, blacks in South Carolina had outnumbered whites, and by the middle of the 18th century, the black population in Virginia and Maryland had risen to somewhere between 30 and 40 percent. Though the Northern states began prohibiting slavery soon after the American Revolution, and the Northwest Ordinance, passed in 1787, declared that it was illegal to introduce slavery north and west of the Ohio River—Congress in 1808 forbade the importation of slaves—it is ironic that the South had more antislavery societies in 1820 than did the North. As of 1830, approximately one-fourth of the two million slaves in America lived in Virginia. Joel Williamson writes of this period: "Even as white society moved across to impose a more rigid police control over black people, it also moved across the race line to touch blacks with unprecedented intimacy. This era may well be called the 'hard-soft' period of slavery. On the one hand, white society elaborated and tightened the laws of dealing with the blacks, both slave and free, and revamped the police system for enforcing those laws. On the other side, white people went among black people in a new style. Whites strove hard to make a place for black people in the white-dominated world, to integrate them, as it were, into a harmonious order—almost to make them white. Ultimately, what had begun as an effort to change blacks ended in the reconstitution of the white society itself. Out of the labor of race control was born an altered Southern character."

For many, including John Jay, Thomas Jefferson, and James Monroe, the answer to the racial problem was to send blacks back to Africa, and in the 1820s and afterward thousands were shipped to Liberia. In 1831, when Nat Turner led a small band of black slaves in an open revolt, the potential hostility within the black communities became apparent as 57 whites were slaughtered. With this and similar rebellions, white Southerners knew deep down that their dreams could turn into nightmares, that the black families on their farms and plantations could turn on them and destroy them. Yet, as Bruce Catton, Shelby Foote, John Macdonald, Warren W. Hassler, Jr., and other Civil War historians have indicated one way or another, it was almost unthinkable that such an entrenched social organization and such habits of thought cherished in the South in the years before the war could eliminate a slave system that ensured the cultivation of raw materials and the mass production of crops, as well as afforded the dominant white society time and leisure to fabricate a way of life they deemed vital for their well-being.

As Southern planters and their families prospered, slavery became, especially during the era of Andrew Jackson, increasingly central to their economic development. Ironically, the rising status of these planters, who became more and more prominent, and thus open to public scrutiny, increased the odds against slavery's continued existence. And few would deny that by 1860 King Cotton did become a severe master these planters served, 10,000 of whom (or 50,000, if one counts all the members of these white households) owned 50 or more slaves each on various types of plantations from Maryland to Florida and from Texas to Arkansas.

In the pre-war decades after the 1830s, the odd divergences and full range of the Southern short story were apparent when the first stirrings of an "Old South" literature began to be clearly distinguishable. From the perspective of the 1850s and looking back, the three stories of John Pendleton Kennedy, William Elliott, and Augustus Baldwin Longstreet could not be more different, but not one of these men would have batted an eyelid at being referred to as a "Southern" writer. And they each would have recognized the Southern affiliations of the others, in man and in story, again without the slightest qualm of insincerity or confusion.

The colonial detective romance of Kennedy's "A Legend of Maryland," the plantation hunting parties of Elliott's "A Day at Chee-Ha," and the low-life entertainments of Longstreet's "The Horse-Swap" each exemplify a particular and relatively new Southern literary interest. The differences are due to many factors, the geographical origins of the authors themselves being perhaps the chief influence. But regional and social oppositions were going to persist all through the century, and not even the unifying powers of the Confederacy would succeed in breaking down inner divisions that existed all across the South, and often met, unfused, in the same writer.

Despite their own divisions and differences, Kennedy, Elliott, and Longstreet would have agreed that each of their stories displayed a recognizable Southern fascination: the retrospective probing and gentlemanly skepticism of Kennedy; Elliott's sheer narrative enjoyment of the storyteller's platform authority and rollicking freedom to perform; Longstreet's undisguised admiration for low cunning and raw native speech. In other words, they would have agreed on the logical existence of a Southern literature, even though they were not able to agree on the logical existence of a single, national South. With the arrival of the Civil War, Kennedy went with the Union; Elliott, after attacking secession, went with the South and lived just long enough to see his whole world crucified on the cross he had not wanted to plant; Longstreet agreed wholeheartedly with secession, survived the war, and ended his life peacefully unreconstructed in Oxford, Mississippi.

The usual approach to Southern fiction of the 19th century is to consider it according to well-defined categories: the colonial romance, the plantation novel or story, the Southern humorist stories and tales and, later, after the Civil War, the fiction of the local color movement. These categories certainly apply to the great bulk of fiction written during the century, and many of the stories in *Stories of the Old South* can be readily fitted into one or another of these categories and movements. In every case, the stories we have chosen do represent the best and most original writing done by the major Southern writers, but they are also representative of the prevailing literary tastes of the age. Certainly it would be a mistake to measure the early stories too narrowly by the standards of modern realism. Once classifications are made, however, as Edmund Wilson explained in his magisterial study *Patriotic Gore* (1962), there still remains a good deal to be said, for the simple reason that the most original and most accomplished work of any literary period may contain the typical and, at the same time, much more.

This is especially true when we turn to the group of humorous dialect stories popular in journals and anthologies during the decades just before the Civil War. They were the work of writers often called the Southern, or Southwestern, humorists—"Southwestern" referring to those Southern states just west of the older coastal settlements and including middle Georgia, Tennessee, Arkansas, Kentucky, Alabama, Mississippi, and Louisiana. These remarkable stories almost always draw on the ripe idioms, exaggerated comparisons, wildly inventive images, and coarse physical humor of the homegrown Southern back-country character, entirely unhampered by "literary" language or genteel inhibitions. Occasionally, as in the case of Sut Lovingood, the ribald narrator of George Washington Harris's stories, the speaker is aware of literary language, but scorns it, preferring the democratic freedom of "calling a hog a hog," especially when the "hog" is human. Usually, though, the rough dialect story is set apart by a presentation in the far-more-sophisticated voice of the actual writer —Longstreet, Johnson Jones Hooper, Thomas Bangs Thorpe, Madison Tensas—whose reputable social standing—lawyer, journalist, artist, doctor—helps make the outrageous credible by bringing it into the realm of observed reality.

The Southern-humorist story ranges over a wide territory of what was then largely Southern wilderness, from the Appalachian mountains through the barely settled middle South, and down to the lower Mississippi and isolated bayou wetlands. And they portray in masterly ways an astonishing number of what Mark Twain called the "fragrantly unwashed": raucus pranksters, fearless backwoodsmen, outright outlaws—and the most popular of all—the resilient tricksters, like Simon Suggs, who possessed ground-level cunning and quick-striking insight into the hidden vices of human nature. There are as many moods in these stories as there are types, though high spirits and low humor tend to prevail in them all. The Sut Lovingood stories have long been esteemed as the most remarkable of all; Sut is capable of suddenly igniting a brilliant, unexpected turn of phrase of his own invention. He was not the only narrator to show flashes of genius, however; it would be difficult for any modern comic writer to equal the complete absurdity of Mik-hootah's complaint in Tensas's "The Indefatigable Bear-Hunter." And Simms, not always recognized as a major Southern humorist, wrote one of the best stories in the tradition, "How Sharp Snaffles Got His Capital and Wife." Here are the ancestors of William Faulkner's tribe of Snopeses and of Flannery O'Connor's hired help.

Both the Tensas and the Simms stories are good examples of the popular hunting story that very often centers on bears. Thorpe's "The Big Bear of Arkansas" is the best known of the group, and deserves to be. It begins in the usual mode of tall-tale boasts, but once the narrative itself gets under way, the tone gradually shifts toward the reverential awe the Arkansas hunter feels when faced with the primitive, mysterious force of the "unhuntable" bear he finally kills. The line between Thorpe's story and Faulkner's masterpiece "The Bear" is a long one, but direct.

In reading the Southern humorists in the historical framework leading up to the Civil War, it is tempting to suggest that they may have been obeying a half-conscious impulse to defend Southern interests at the very time the South as a section of the country began affirming its own independent rights. The Southern character revealed in the humorist tradition might be coarse and cunning and even brutal, but no one could deny that the bear-hunter, for example, was a fiercely independent individual, more than willing to stand his ground. But the argument goes further. Most of such stories and tales were written by educated men from the Southeast, and by portraying the unruly elements of Southern society—in the interest of honest self-appraisal—these men may have been looking back toward the civilized Southern planter as a guiding force of stability and political responsibility. The contrast between the two worlds was too blatant to be missed, and thereby confirmed on the planter a special status that Northern criticism wanted nothing more than to reduce.

Running counter to the humorist tradition up to the Civil War, virtually submerging it afterward, was the popular Southern romance. The early Southern romance often concentrated on colonial or revolutionary adventures, especially in Virginia and South Carolina, and strongly emphasized the leading role these two states played in the early days of the nation's history. The plantation novel or story—going back to Kennedy's *Swallow Barn* (1832), one of the first, and best, of the group—derives from much of the same self-gratifying impulse, and is best represented in this anthology by "Marse Chan," Thomas Nelson Page's late-Confederate version of the genre.

The act of looking back in Kennedy's novels, including his fine colonial romance *Horse-Shoe Robinson* (1835), in which the title character epitomizes the ideal Southerner—half-Scotch-Irish-backwoodsman and half-chivalric-cavalier—should not be confused with the backward glance of the early modern Southern writer. The early plantation fiction expressed a strong regret that a better world was breaking up. Far more overtly than the Southern humorists, the writers of the colonial and plantation romance were certainly engaged—as William R. Taylor termed it in his valuable study *Cavalier and Yankee* (1961)—in a form of "defensive fiction."

The degree of engagement differed, of course, from writer to writer, and became stronger as the Civil War loomed nearer. Kennedy was not a Southern nationalist, for all his pro-plantation attachments, but the direction of his writing was very probably guided by a felt fear that the South was becoming isolated as a slave society in a world where slavery was rapidly disappearing. By looking back to an early period of plantation slavery, a writer could lessen criticism by lessening isolation, and thus the Southern colonial or plantation romance could offer a much more favorable portrait of the distinctive nature of Southern slavery as just one form of slave-based colonial society among others: English, French, Spanish, and Portuguese. In this company, the Southern writer could compel comparisons between the South and the much harsher slave regimes of the West Indies or South America. It was an effective diversionary stance, as was the argument that the English had forced slavery on the Southern colonies often against the expressed will of the colonial assemblies. As late as 1892, Page, in his polemical essay "The Old South," could marshal forth these same arguments.

One powerful Southern element missing in much of the early Southern writing—the reasons are unfortunately obvious enough—is the presence of the Southern black. Slaves and free blacks in

the South do exist in early fiction, and in fact appear quite frequently in American writing. But even in Harriet Beecher Stowe's
skillful and sympathetic characterizations in *Uncle Tom's Cabin*
(1852), the vivid voice and living culture of the Southern black do
not emerge in anything close to its full range and importance. With
the stories of Joel Chandler Harris, one of the first white writers
to appreciate fully the native culture of the Southern black—and
with the stories of the first wave of Southern black writers, Arna
Wendell Bontemps, Charles Waddell Chesnutt, Zora Neale Hurston, Jean Toomer, and Richard Wright—the black world of the
South injects new life into its literature. Before these writers, there
had been a considerable amount of writing by Southern blacks,
almost always in the form of the slave narrative. Two of the best
of these are *The Narrative of the Life of Frederick Douglass* (1845)
and *Twenty Years a Slave* (1853) by Solomon Northrup. Both are
powerful documents of almost unbearable suffering and injustice,
and they have had and will continue to have, along with hundreds
of other slave narratives, an enormous influence on later black
writing. But there is little in them—again, the reasons are obvious—to suggest the developing Southern black culture.

What the slave narrative could not, and did not intend to,
achieve was accomplished only when the problems of narrative
language and character development were solved. Too often, the
slave narrative, and even an antebellum novel by a Southern black,
William Wells Brown's *Clotel; or the President's Daughter* (1853),
relied on conventional Victorian prose that did far more to distort
than to reveal. Yet, the importance of the black voice and of black
culture in defining a specific Southern literature cannot be over-
emphasized. As Wilbur Cash explained in his *The Mind of the
South* (1941), blacks entered into the white man's society as profoundly as the white man entered into the black's—subtly influ-
encing every gesture, every word, every emotion and idea, every
attitude. As least half the stories in this volume, ranging from
Poe's "The Gold-Bug" through Joel Chandler Harris's "Free Joe
and the Rest of the World" and Grace King's "The Little Convent
Girl" to Chesnutt's "The Web of Circumstance" and Toomer's
"Blood-Burning Moon," testify to the force of Cash's argument,
and demonstrate, one after another, that the dual destinies of black
and white are two halves of a single Southern reality.

The enormous weight of the racial, social, political, and cultural
import of the stories in this volume cannot be felt without some
realization of the terrible breadth and scope of the Civil War itself
since the events leading up to the war, the actual experience of it,
and its aftermath help make much of this fiction distinctive. On

December 20, 1860, at a state convention in Charleston, South Carolina, a resolution was passed 169 to 0, which dissolved the union between South Carolina and the other states. Four days later, two documents, the "Declaration of the Immediate Causes which Induce and Justify the Secession of South Carolina from the Federal Union" and another addressed "To the People of the Slave-holding States of the United States," formulated by the same group of men, spelled out their firm intentions. The first document proclaimed that the benefits in the U.S. Constitution had been overturned by the actions of the Northern states: "Those States have assumed the right of deciding upon the propriety of our domestic institutions; and have denied the rights of property established in fifteen of the States recognized by the Constitution; they have denounced as sinful the institution of Slavery; they have permitted the open establishment among them of societies, whose avowed object is to disturb the peace and to eloign the property of the citizens of other States." These cryptic words undoubtedly encoded the views of the majority of white Southerners, though one always has to distinguish between the divergent views of those in the border states, the Upper South, and the Deep South; yet these same words became the basis for a four-year war between the 21 states of the U.S. Federal Government and the 11 states that constituted the Confederate States of America (South Carolina, Mississippi, Florida, Alabama, Georgia, Louisiana, Texas, Virginia, Arkansas, Tennessee, and North Carolina—the border states of Maryland, Kentucky, and Missouri stayed with the Union). They were also the catalyst that prompted, on April 12, 1861, the shelling of Fort Sumter, a solid but relatively obscure Federal outpost with five-foot-thick walls rising 40 feet out of the water in Charleston Harbor, located equidistant between the two Confederate strongholds, Fort Moultrie and Fort Johnson.

The initial bombardment on Fort Sumter ended 34 hours later when Robert Anderson, a Union officer who commanded 128 men, 43 of whom were civilians, surrendered to Pierre Gustave Toutant Beauregard, who had approximately 7,000 men in his charge. In her diaries, Mary Boykin Chesnut recorded on April 15, 1861, the following, almost breezy, recollections: "Saturday last was a great day. I saw my husband carried by a mob to tell Gen. Beauregard the news that Fort Sumter had surrendered—he followed Louis Wigfall to Fort Sumter after a few minutes' interval, then returned with the news of the surrender & carried fire Engines to Fort Sumter. Our men cheered madly when Anderson continued his firing after he was blazing with houses on fire. Mrs. Cheves McCord & I dined togethr in the evening. Mrs. Joe Heyward, Mrs. Preston,

Mrs. Wigfall & [I] drove on the battery in an open carriage. So gay it was—crowded & the tents & cannons." In a war filled with myriad ironies, it should be noted that Beauregard, the first brigadier general in the Confederate Army, was Anderson's former student at the U.S. Military Academy at West Point, New York, and for a short time its commandant until he resigned from there in 1861.

To show their resolve and determination in preserving their values and way of life, Southern leaders had prepared themselves for eventual hostile actions by electing, in February 1861, Jefferson Davis President of the Confederate States at Montgomery, Alabama. Davis, likewise a graduate from West Point who had fought in the Mexican War, a wealthy senator from Mississippi in 1847, and Secretary of War under President Franklin Pierce in 1853, had both many endearing qualities and serious faults, and was his own General in Chief until he passed the baton to Robert Edward Lee on February 6, 1865. To check these secessionists, President Abraham Lincoln called for a temporary militia of 75,000 and a blockade of the Confederate states, which had already summoned 100,000 soldiers and was soon to increase this number fourfold. The population of what is normally considered the South at that time was approximately nine million, of whom 3,500,000 were slaves, while the North, which had a system of government already in place and a superiority of 30-to-1 in the production of military arms, had over twice this population. The Deep South, to pinpoint the focus a bit more, had, in 1860—according to Bruce Collins—2,580,000 inhabitants and 2,310,000 slaves; in South Carolina, to cite but one example, the 301,000 whites were in a minority against the 402,000 slaves. At this time, there were over 1,470,000 white families in the Southern slave states, and of these, 150,000 people owned from five to nine slaves, and approximately 48,000 planters had 20 or more slaves. In defending itself, the South could count on the fact that it had already fought a good many wars of various types on different fronts, and could profit from a 3,500-mile coastline that was impossible to blockade.

For his part, President Lincoln could modestly boast of having served in the Illinois State Legislature and in the U.S. House of Representatives. His brief military record was limited to the Black Hawk War, and he had recently been elected President of the United States after gaining the Republican nomination in May 1860. In spite of a limited academic background and relatively short service in government, Lincoln was able to mature as a leader as he learned the tactics and strategies of warfare. Fortunately, the succession of Unionist military generals did not impede a final victory; Winfield Scott was General in Chief when the war began, and retired in November 1, 1861; George Brinton McClellan, a later opponent of Lincoln for the presidency in 1864, lasted until March 11, 1862; Henry Halleck held the post until March 9, 1864, when Ulysses Simpson Grant took charge until the end of the war.

The early battles of the war give some indication of its tremendous scope and the difficulties both sides faced. Lincoln initially forced his blue-clad soldiers to penetrate the South and take advantage of the initial period of the war, concentrating on the blockade; he also had troops descend the Mississippi River, a natural pathway into the heart of Dixie. In northwest Virginia, where some of the first battles took place, McClellan, an alumnus of West Point who graduated top in his class, led 20,000 soldiers in the summer of 1861 and won battles at Philippi, Rich Mountain, and Carrick's Ford. At this time, Lincoln had good reason to worry as the military leaders in the Confederate capital at Richmond, Virginia, were sending soldiers north toward Washington, D.C. On May 6, 1861, Robert E. Lee ordered a force to head for Manassas Junction, 26 miles southwest of Washington. Lincoln, in turn, ordered the untested soldiers of Irvin McDowell (promoted to brigadier general on May 14, 1861) to meet the enemy at Manassas, while it was planned that the forces in the Shenandoah Valley of Confederate Joseph Eggleston Johnston, an 1829 graduate of West Point, would be prevented from reinforcing the Southern troops amassing near Bull Run located close to Manassas. McDowell moved out from Washington in mid-July with nearly 35,000 men toward Bull Run. The First Battle of Bull Run took place on July 21, 1861, and McDowell found that Johnston had joined with Beauregard and had a combined army of 32,500 men. Brigadier General Thomas Jonathan "Stonewall" Jackson's troops (Jackson also was a graduate of West Point) rebuffed the exhausted Federal troops, who subsequently fled in the rain toward Washington. Both sides lost a total of 4,888 soldiers, heavy at that time, but comparatively light when put in the total context; this battle proved to be a dress rehearsal, and it was clear that a long and bloody war would ensue.

The names of some of the other principle battles and maneuvers of the Civil War (Second Battle of Bull Run, Antietam, Chancellorsville, Gettysburg, Shiloh, Vicksburg, the Battle of the Wilderness, Sherman's March Through Georgia) are well known. Those that took place on the Eastern front in 1862 alone might well serve as reminders of the devastation that took place in general during this war. When McClellan replaced Winfield Scott as General in Chief, he began to strengthen the Army of the Potomac, which grew at that time to over 100,000 men, even though Mc-

Clellan's health was precarious from bouts with typhoid fever. In March 1862, however, he was strong enough to commence his Peninsular Campaign between the York and James Rivers in Virginia. In the battle at Seven Pines (or Fair Oaks, as the North called it) in late May and early June, Johnston was wounded by a *minié*ball and General Lee, who had been at the battle site with President Davis, assumed the command of the Army of Northern Virginia. When McClellan counterattacked, he was able to push the Confederate troops farther south; together both sides lost over 11,000 men. As McClellan approached Richmond, Lee recalled Jackson's forces, and with about 90,000 soldiers, fought the Seven Days' Battles in late June and early July. Lee successfully defended Richmond and forced a stronger and better-equipped army to retreat, though not without both sides suffering over 35,000 casualties. McClellan, on Lincoln's orders, returned to Washington, and power was transferred to Halleck as General in Chief and to John Pope as the new Federal army commander.

Subsequently, Lee ordered Jackson to enjoin John Pope's Army of Virginia in what is called the Second Battle of Bull Run, beginning on August 29, 1862, during which Lee and Jackson forced the Northerners back to Washington. Lee split his army and sent Jackson to Manassas to encounter Pope's troops; with James Longstreet's forces, Lee took another route and this strategy proved successful. Jackson positioned his forces along an unfinished railroad track, and though outnumbered by three to one, the rebels managed to repel the attacks of Major General Pope's troops. The brave stand by Jackson so preoccupied Pope that Major General Longstreet's 25,000 men fell into position near Jackson. Next day, Pope resumed his efforts and unfortunately ignored reports of Longstreet's presence on the battlefield. When Jackson appealed to Lee for help, Longstreet moved in and reversed the course of the battle. Pope suffered 14,462 casualties and Lee 9,474 out of a combined force of over 117,000 men, and as a result Pope's star had faded and McClellan again resumed the command of the Army of the Potomac.

Confidently, Lee moved toward Frederick, Maryland, as McClellan was forced to look after the defense of Washington, as well, indeed, as that of Maryland. By September, McClellan met Lee's army at Antietam Creek, near Sharpsburg, Maryland. On September 17, the Civil War saw one of its bloodiest battles as Lee eventually was forced back into Virginia. At Antietam, Unionist McClellan lost over 12,000 men while Lee lost over 11,000 men. McClellan had turned away the Confederate troops, but had not won the victory expected of him, though *The New-York Times* of

September 21, 1862, in a burst of patriotism, had reported otherwise. At this point, McClellan was replaced by Major General Ambrose Everett Burnside, a graduate of West Point and formerly a corps commander at Antietam. It had been Lincoln's intention to hold the Union together by engaging in this war, though more and more his attention centered on the anti-abolition movement. He knew, too, that foreign leaders would be reluctant to enter into the war because that would indicate clearly that they were for slavery as a legal institution. Following the Confederate withdrawal after Antietam, Lincoln published his Emancipation Proclamation on September 22, 1862, in which he decreed that as of the beginning of the new year all slaves in those states that were in rebellion against the Union would be "then, thenceforward and forever free."

Lincoln, as other politicians of the time knew, especially Frederick Douglass, the future of the country lay westward, and that the balance of power would reside in those who could control its political—and racial—development. It did not escape his enemies, however, that Lincoln had no control over these Southern slaves, nor of those in the border states who remained faithful to the Union; the emancipation he hoped for would come with the Thirteenth Amendment to the Constitution, in 1865. As 1862 was drawing to a close, Burnside with an army of over 116,000 near Fredericksburg, Virginia, ordered a series of 16 assaults against Lee's 78,513-man army. Burnside lost over 12,000 men, while Lee lost less than half that number. On January 25, 1863, Burnside was replaced by Corps Commander Joseph "Fighting Joe" Hooker, as both armies sought winter quarters near Fredericksburg. Lincoln, always a shrewd moderate, knew that the will of the people would hold the country together, and though the Federal troops might suffer some defeats, he still had reason to be confident.

When Lee surrendered finally what was left of his Army of Northern Virginia at the McLean House at Appomattox Court House on April 9, 1865, the war had taken its toll. Such wars were not uncommon on our planet at that time; in the 1850s the Taiping Rebellion brought about the deaths of millions of Chinese, and 10 years later, Georges Clemenceau, who had been a French reporter in Washington during the American Civil War, noted that the French suppressed the Paris Commune uprising with such cruelty that half of France seemed to die at the hands of the other half. In all, during the Civil War, some 1,556,000 soldiers served in the Federal armies; of these, there were a total of 634,703 casualties (359,528 dead and 275,175 wounded). There were approximately

800,000 men in the Confederate forces, which sustained approximately 483,000 casualties (about 258,000 dead and 225,000 wounded).

After the trauma of the war, and after Reconstruction, the glamorous legend of the Lost Cause took hold on the popular imagination, North and South, and intruded on almost every form of literature: poetry, drama, and especially the long prose romance. The brutalities of the war itself, the perplexing contradictions and dramatic conflicts it hurled into private lives, the tragic effects felt long after the battles had ended—all these daily jolts were paradoxically seldom allowed to penetrate in any full way the popular fiction of the day. Understandably enough, the reader was given forgetful doses of pathos and selective nostalgia, usually presented in a refined genteel prose that was too starched and proper to stoop to the raging life of the real world.

Southern writers contributed mightily to the spread of an idealized vision of a prelapsarian South. One after another, year after year, the romanticized productions multiplied, and almost always they were composed in the inflated, awkwardly derivative style of the Sir Walter Scott cult that Mark Twain bitterly denounces in *Life on the Mississippi* (1883). It is difficult to read the popular best-sellers of John Esten Cooke or Augusta Jane Evans without losing consciousness halfway through. The pure Southern romance is probably best considered as part of a much more general cultural or social impulse whose low-grade vitality and stubborn survival place it outside the realm of an enduring literary art.

In *Life on the Mississippi*, when Twain comes to the end of his attack on the genteel evasions of popular Southern prose, he at once leaps to an admiring defense of his two favorite Southern contemporaries: George Washington Cable and Joel Chandler Harris. For Twain, they are the valuable voices of the modern South, and whenever he mentions their names, his praise knows no bounds. It is notable that though both Cable and Harris wrote novels, their best work was done in the short story, a form that tends to focus on a limited action and on the dramatically revealed, singularly odd character. It has little room to spare for the full panoply of social types, or for the droning digression and long-winded genealogy.

There are exceptions, however, and the 19th-century South had its share. There is such a thing as the short prose romance, and in *Stories of the Old South* the form is best exemplified by James Lane Allen's "Two Gentlemen of Kentucky." Once an immensely popular work, it exhibits all the genteel traditions, especially the esthetic conviction that all narrative action must cease when any ornate phrase happens to fly to mind. Yet Allen possessed an inventive lyrical flair and an old-time charm capable of humor and wit, and both these gifts are present in "Two Gentlemen of Kentucky." Perhaps he should have written more short stories, instead of the longer romances that invariably drift away from the dramatizations of individual character into exercises of literary impressionism.

The natural benefits of the short story form during the post-war period are best illustrated in the dialect stories of Page, whose collection of stories *In Ole Virginia* (1887) established him as the acknowledged leader of the Southern memorialist school that looked back to the high spirits and fine manners of an idealized plantation world "befo' the war." But unlike the long novels in this mode, including several written by Page himself, the stories *In Ole Virginia* are skillfully crafted and effective. In "Marse Chan," perhaps the best of the group, Page sets forth the popular formula of the plantation love match, complicated and cut short by the Civil War. Long before Margaret Mitchell's *Gone with the Wind* (1936), "Marse Chan" defines the fundamental structure and stock characters of the archetypal Confederate melodrama. But by presenting the story as spoken out in the wholly credible language of a devote old black who has survived his master and the vanished "good times" of the antebellum years, Page deepens the meaning of the narrative without in any way dividing it. The told tale thrives on stylized characterizations and a quick succession of dramatic situations. And perhaps even more important to the success of the story, the fact that it is told in a living black voice tends to turn the attention of the reader away from the remembered events toward the narrator himself and the deep current of genuine emotion he is able to convey.

No one could possibly argue that the black narrator of "Marse Chan" fully addresses the experience of the black Southerner: that process was a long one, and would not be realized until the first stories of Chesnutt, Hurston, Toomer, and Wright make their appearance in Southern letters. But it is interesting to note that the same year "Marse Chan" was published, in 1884, Mark Twain brought out *Huckleberry Finn*, the first significant Southern novel in which the cruel realities and brutal ironies of black slavery were openly dramatized. Part of the irresistible force of Twain's narrative lies in the gradual transformation of Jim—presented through the eyes and voice of Huck—from a childlike, minstrelized creation of slavery into a human being capable of a wide range of human expression, including love, wit, and indignation. *Huckleberry Finn* opened up the meaning of the South in a revolutionary, completely independent way, and most modern Southern writers look back on it as the foundation of modern Southern literature.

Three years after the publication of *Huckleberry Finn*, in 1887, Twain published his self-satiric, partly finished fictionalized account of his brief spell in the Confederate army: "The History of a Compaign That Failed." And that same year Twain's friend Joel Chandler Harris brought out his moving portrait of a free black in pre-war Georgia. Poe had been one of the first to introduce the free black in Southern fiction 40 years earlier, with Jupiter in "The Gold-Bug," but "Free Joe and the Rest of the World" is special in that Harris centers the whole story on Free Joe, and in that he writes this pre-war portrait precisely at the time—the mid-1880s—when the newly freed blacks around him were beginning to enter a new regime of discrimination and civic dispossession.

All three stories, "Marse Chan," "The History of a Campaign That Failed," and "Free Joe and the Rest of the World," offer evidence that the world of Southern fiction after the Civil War defied a single vision of the South just as emphatically as the Southern writers before the war, more so, in fact, now that the Southern black had finally been allowed a voice. These stories are good to remember, too, when we turn to the group of stories of the Old South written by modern Southern writers in the first half of the 20th century.

A new set of Southern divisions confronted the Southern writer at the beginning of the 20th century, at a time when the Civil War was still a part of the remembered past, when family members talked about events that had rocked and displaced their lives forever; when they could look up at the Confederate memorials and watch the annual parades of veterans; when, amid these reminders of a glorious, if embittered, era, they grew up, fascinated and attentive, but not all sure that it was their world as much as it was their fathers' and grandfathers', or mothers' or grandmothers' for that matter. William Faulkner, in his brilliant panoramic essay on the changing world of his South, "Mississippi" (1954), remembers with bemused fondness the "women, the indomitable, the undefeated, who never surrendered, refusing to allow the Yankee *minié*balls to be dug out of portico column or mantelpiece or linel, who seventy years later would get up and walk out of *Gone with the Wind* as soon as Sherman's name was mentioned; irreconcilable and enraged and still talking about it long after the weary exhausted men who had fought and lost it gave up trying to make them hush. . . ."

Like William Alexander Percy, author of *Lanterns on the Levee* (1941), the modern Southern writer enjoyed listening to familiar, exalted voices, but could not quite allow himself to be completely persuaded. Much of the Old South, of course, remained the same when the 20th century began; the small towns and rural ways were still largely governed by rhythms and duties that had not been much different several generations earlier. There were dependable realities among the modern changes, and the changes themselves, in fact, sharpened the awareness of young Southerners to their culture and language, and made them alert to details that their grandparents might not have considered so important. Yet these younger writers belonged to the wide modern world, too, especially after World War I, and their divided loyalties and inner debates, when they reflected on the South, could not help but be several degrees up the scale compared to the Southern writers they followed. And if they were black writers, born and raised in the South, but moving North as soon as they could, there was no degree anywhere on the scale to express how they felt about their home ground.

The title of our collection, *Stories of the Old South*, was chosen to reflect a deliberate double reference. It concentrates on Southern stories written during the 19th century, but it also includes a large group of early modern stories that center on the Old South. In every case, these more recent stories were written by Southerners who were born close enough to the Old South to witness personally its stubborn thrust into the 20th century. A few of these stories are widely known: Faulkner's "Mountain Victory," Toomer's "Blood-Burning Moon," and Eudora Welty's "First Love." These are astonishing masterpieces of modern fiction. The other stories of this group, by Bontemps, Glasgow, Hurston, Lytle, Porter, Roberts, Wolfe, and Wright, are not as well known, but deserve to be. Read as a group, all 11 of them—each one singular, indelibly of the South—go a long way toward demonstrating what we have felt for many years: The Old South received, even lasting up to a time before World War II, its most complete expression not in any single work, but in a wide-ranging family of independent fiction driven backward, by the common conviction that the past remained the chief custodian of hidden truth.

Understandably enough, living both within and without, the first generation of modern Southern writers began their careers with a prolonged meditation on the meaning of the Old South. The early members of the Fugitive group in Nashville wrote some of their best poetry while engaged in the backward glance that Allen Tate claimed later as the primary act of the modern Southern mind. The phrase "backward glance" must be approached as an example of Tate's natural love of ironic understatement, and does not do full justice to the extent and the intensity of the past's fascination for the Southerner. Three central poems of the Fugitive movement,

John Crowe Ransom's "Antique Harvesters," Donald Davidson's "Lee in the Mountains," and Tate's "Ode to the Confederate Dead," give a better idea of the complex, self-conscious, retrospective, compulsive probing Tate was thinking of.

The Fugitives/Agrarians carried their poetic themes into more theoretical forms of discourse as well. They published biographies of Confederate leaders (Tate and Andrew Lytle), histories of the Old South (Davidson), and essays—defensive and critical—touching on all aspects of Southern culture (Ransom, Davidson, Lytle, and Robert Penn Warren). Together with the Fugitive/Agrarian writing, the most powerful expression of the Old South in the modern mind is to be found in the prose fiction of the same period: Ellen Glasgow's Virginia novels, Thomas Wolfe's North Carolina chronicles, and towering above everyone, William Faulkner's long succession of Mississippi novels and stories set in his fictional Yoknapatawpha County. Faulkner's masterpiece, *Absalom, Absalom!* (1936), swells like a great organ recital as it relates the decline and fall of Thomas Sutpen's life, a Civil War avatar of King David, who lamented the tragic death of his beloved son as narrated in the Old Testament book of 2 Samuel. All of these modern works, especially Faulkner's, are deeply informed by a penetrating new vision of Southern history. Like the Fugitives, Glasgow, Wolfe, and Faulkner were well aware that their own identities owed as much to their Old South attachments as they did to the irresistible transformation of modern times. They were quite willing to itemize the contradictions of their Southern allegiances; they could attack the evasive idealism and cloying charm of much popular Southern fiction and raise the cry—as Ellen Glasgow did—for more "blood and irony"; but they knew, too, that their own creative source lay in the old deep wells of an unabandonable local origin.

Finally, it should be noted that in all cases we have provided, as we did in the companion volume *Stories of the Modern South*, authoritative editions of the stories and tales included in this volume, many of which represent the first printing of the various texts. In a very few cases, we have altered spelling and punctuation; we have done this only when necessary and when we felt that the texts would honestly be enhanced by such changes.

Ben Forkner
Patrick Samway, S.J.

STORIES
OF THE OLD
SOUTH

James Lane Allen

(1849–1925)

Born and raised in the bluegrass region of Kentucky, Allen spent the first 22 years of his life on his father's modest working farm. After his graduation from Kentucky University in 1872, he taught school for several years and helped support his family in the hard times after the Civil War. He turned to a career as a full-time writer in the 1880s, settled in New York, and lived there the rest of his life. His stories and novels almost always evoked, with ornate lyricism, his native rural Kentucky. Known particularly for his lush nature descriptions, he was called, apparently without irony, the Corot of Kentucky. A popular, even best-selling, writer in his day, especially with his short novel, A Kentucky Cardinal *(1894), he wrote in many modes: symbolic allegories in the manner of Hawthorne; nostalgic historical romances; and, increasingly, problem novels of religious doubt and crisis. Never able to fully free himself from a fashionable, genteel romantic style, he was far more independent in his choice of subjects, and restless or pessimistic enough to confront such unfashionable themes as honesty between a man and a woman. As a footnote to literary history, it is worth remembering that James Joyce admired Allen's psychological portraits and paid him the honor of borrowing from his* The Mettle of the Pasture *(1903) a key phrase in* Ulysses. *Among Allen's novels and collections are* Flute and Violin and Other Kentucky Tales and Romances *(1891),* John Gray: A Kentucky Tale of the Olden Time *(1893),* Aftermath *(1895),* Summer in Arcady: A Tale of Nature *(1896),* The Choir Invisible *(1897),* The Reign of Law: A Tale of the Kentucky Hemp Fields *(1900),* The Bride of the Mistletoe *(1909),* The Sword of Youth *(1915),* A Cathedral Singer *(1916),* The Kentucky Warbler *(1918),* The Alabaster Box *(1923), and* The Landmark *(1925). "Two Gentlemen of Kentucky," originally called "Two Gentlemen of the Old School," was first published in* The Century Magazine *(April 1888), and subsequently in Allen's* Flute and Violin and Other Kentucky Tales and Romances.*

1

TWO GENTLEMEN OF KENTUCKY

❀

"The woods are hushed, their music is no more:
The leaf is dead, the yearning passed away:
New leaf, new life—the days of frost are o'er:
New life, new love, to suit the newer day."

The Woods Are Hushed

It was near the middle of the afternoon of an autumnal day, on the wide, grassy plateau of Central Kentucky.

The Eternal Power seemed to have quitted the universe and left all nature folded in the calm of the Eternal Peace. Around the pale-blue dome of the heavens a few pearl-colored clouds hung motionless, as though the wind had been withdrawn to other skies. Not a crimson leaf floated downward through the soft, silvery light that filled the atmosphere and created the sense of lonely, unimaginable spaces. This light overhung the far-rolling landscape of field and meadow and wood, crowning with faint radiance the remoter low-swelling hill-tops and deepening into dreamy half-shadows on their eastern slopes. Nearer, it fell in a white flake on an unstirred sheet of water which lay along the edge of a mass of sombre-hued woodland, and nearer still it touched to spring-like brilliancy a level, green meadow on the hither edge of the water, where a group of Durham cattle stood with reversed flanks near the gleaming trunks of some leafless sycamores. Still nearer, it caught the top of the brown foliage of a little bent oak-tree and burned it into a silvery flame. It lit on the back and the wings of a crow flying heavily in the path of its rays, and made his blackness as white as the breast of a swan. In the immediate foreground, it sparkled in minute gleams along the stalks of the coarse, dead weeds that fell away from the legs and the flanks of a white horse, and slanted across the face of the rider and through the ends of his gray hair, which straggled from beneath his soft black hat.

The horse, old and patient and gentle, stood with low-stretched neck and closed eyes half asleep in the faint glow of the waning heat; and the rider, the sole human presence in all the field, sat looking across the silent autumnal landscape, sunk in reverie. Both horse and rider seemed but harmonious elements in the panorama of still-life, and completed the picture of a closing scene.

To the man it was a closing scene. From the rank, fallow field through which he had been riding he was now surveying, for the last time, the many features of a landscape that had been familiar to him from the beginning of memory. In the afternoon and the autumn of his age he was about to rend the last ties that bound him to his former life, and, like one who had survived his own destiny, turn his face towards a future that was void of everything he held significant or dear.

The Civil War had only the year before reached its ever-memorable close. From where he sat there was not a home in sight, as there was not one beyond the reach of his vision, but had felt its influence. Some of his neighbors had come home from its camps and prisons, aged or altered as though by half a lifetime of years. The bones of some lay whitening on its battlefields. Families, reassembled around their hearth-stones, spoke in low tones unceasingly of defeat and victory, heroism and death. Suspicion and distrust and estrangement prevailed. Former friends met each other on the turnpikes without speaking; brothers avoided each other in the streets of the neighboring town. The rich had grown poor; the poor had become rich. Many of the latter were preparing to move West. The negroes were drifting blindly hither and thither, deserting the country and flocking to the towns. Even the once united church of his neighborhood was jarred by the unstrung and discordant spirit of the times. At affecting passages in the sermons men grew pale and set their teeth fiercely; women suddenly lowered their black veils and rocked to and fro in their pews; for it is always at the bar of Conscience and before the very altar of God that the human heart is most wrung by a sense of its losses and the memory of its wrongs. The war had divided the people of Kentucky as the false mother would have severed the child.

It had not left the old man unscathed. His younger brother had fallen early in the conflict, borne to the end of his brief warfare by his impetuous valor; his aged mother had sunk under the tidings of the death of her latest-born; his sister was estranged from him by his political differences with her husband; his old family servants, men and women, had left him, and grass and weeds had already grown over the door-steps of the shut, noiseless cabins. Nay, the whole vast social system of the old régime had fallen, and he was henceforth but a useless fragment of the ruins.

All at once his mind turned from the cracked and smoky mirror of the times and dwelt fondly upon the scenes of the past. The

silent fields around him seemed again alive with the negroes, singing as they followed the ploughs down the corn-rows or swung the
cradles through the bearded wheat. Again, in a frenzy of merriment, the strains of the old fiddles issued from crevices of cabin-
doors to the rhythmic beat of hands and feet that shook the rafters
and the roof. Now he was sitting on his porch, and one little negro
was blacking his shoes, another leading his saddle-horse to the
stiles, a third bringing his hat, and a fourth handing him a glass
of ice-cold sangaree; or now he lay under the locust-trees in his
yard, falling asleep in the drowsy heat of the summer afternoon,
while one waved over him a bough of pungent walnut leaves, until
he lost consciousness and by-and-by awoke to find that they both
had fallen asleep side by side on the grass and that the abandoned
fly-brush lay full across his face.

From where he sat also were seen slopes on which picnics were
danced under the broad shade of maples and elms in June by those
whom death and war had scattered like the transitory leaves that
once had sheltered them. In this direction lay the district school-
house where on Friday evenings there were wont to be speeches
and debates; in that, lay the blacksmith's shop where of old he
and his neighbors had met on horseback of Saturday afternoons
to hear the news, get the mails, discuss elections, and pitch quoits.
In the valley beyond stood the church at which all had assembled
on calm Sunday mornings like the members of one united family.
Along with these scenes went many a chastened reminiscence of
bridal and funeral and simpler events that had made up the annals
of his country life.

The reader will have a clearer insight into the character and past
career of Colonel Romulus Fields by remembering that he represented a fair type of that social order which had existed in rank
perfection over the blue-grass plains of Kentucky during the final
decades of the old régime. Perhaps of all agriculturists in the
United States the inhabitants of that region had spent the most
nearly idyllic life, on account of the beauty of the climate, the
richness of the land, the spacious comfort of their homes, the
efficiency of their negroes, and the characteristic contentedness of
their dispositions. Thus nature and history combined to make them
a peculiar class, a cross between the aristocratic and the bucolic,
being as simple as shepherds and as proud as kings, and not seldom
exhibiting among both men and women types of character which
were as remarkable for pure, tender, noble states of feeling as
they were commonplace in powers and cultivation of mind.

It was upon this luxurious social growth that the war naturally
fell as a killing frost, and upon no single specimen with more

blighting power than upon Colonel Fields. For destiny had quarried and chiselled him, to serve as an ornament in the barbaric temple of human bondage. There *were* ornaments in that temple, and he was one. A slave-holder with Southern sympathies, a man educated not beyond the ideas of his generation, convinced that slavery was an evil, yet seeing no present way of removing it, he had of all things been a model master. As such he had gone on record in Kentucky, and no doubt in a Higher Court; and as such his efforts had been put forth to secure the passage of many of those milder laws for which his State was distinguished. Often, in those dark days, his face, anxious and sad, was to be seen amid the throng that surrounded the blocks on which slaves were sold at auction; and more than one poor wretch he had bought to save him from separation from his family or from being sold into the Southern plantations—afterwards riding far and near to find him a home on one of the neighboring farms.

But all those days were over. He had but to place the whole picture of the present beside the whole picture of the past to realize what the contrast meant for him.

At length he gathered the bridle reins from the neck of his old horse and turned his head homeward. As he rode slowly on, every spot gave up its memories. He dismounted when he came to the cattle and walked among them, stroking their soft flanks and feeling in the palm of his hand the rasp of their salt-loving tongues; on his sideboard at home was many a silver cup which told of premiums on cattle at the great fairs. It was in this very pond that as a boy he had learned to swim on a cherry rail. When he entered the woods, the sight of the walnut-trees and the hickory-nut trees, loaded on the topmost branches, gave him a sudden pang.

Beyond the woods he came upon the garden, which he had kept as his mother had left it—an old-fashioned garden with an arbor in the centre, covered with Isabella grape-vines on one side and Catawba on the other; with walks branching thence in four directions, and along them beds of jump-up-johnnies, sweet-williams, daffodils, sweet-peas, larkspur, and thyme, flags and the sensitive-plant, celestial and maiden's-blush roses. He stopped and looked over the fence at the very spot where he had found his mother on the day when the news of the battle came.

She had been kneeling, trowel in hand, driving away vigorously at the loamy earth, and, as she saw him coming, had risen and turned towards him her face with the ancient pink bloom on her clear cheeks and the light of a pure, strong soul in her gentle eyes. Overcome by his emotions, he had blindly faltered out the words, "Mother, John was among the killed!" For a moment she had looked at him as though stunned by a blow. Then a violent flush had overspread her features, and then an ashen pallor; after which, with a sudden proud dilating of her form as though with joy, she had sunk down like the tenderest of her lily-stalks, cut from its root.

Beyond the garden he came to the empty cabin and the great wood-pile. At this hour it used to be a scene of hilarious activity—the little negroes sitting perched in chattering groups on the top-most logs or playing leap-frog in the dust, while some picked up baskets of chips or dragged a back-log into the cabins.

At last he drew near the wooden stiles and saw the large house of which he was the solitary occupant. What darkened rooms and noiseless halls! What beds, all ready, that nobody now came to sleep in, and cushioned old chairs that nobody rocked! The house and the contents of its attic, presses, and drawers could have told much of the history of Kentucky from almost its beginning; for its foundations had been laid by his father near the beginning of the century, and through its doors had passed a long train of forms, from the veterans of the Revolution to the soldiers of the Civil War. Old coats hung up in closets; old dresses folded away in drawers; saddle-bags and buckskin-leggins; hunting-jackets, powder-horns, and militiamen hats; looms and knitting-needles; snuffboxes and reticules—what a treasure-house of the past it was! And now the only thing that had the springs of life within its bosom was the great, sweet-voiced clock, whose faithful face had kept unchanged amid all the swift pageantry of changes.

He dismounted at the stiles and handed the reins to a gray-haired negro, who had hobbled up to receive them with a smile and a gesture of the deepest respect.

"Peter," he said, very simply, "I am going to sell the place and move to town. I can't live here any longer."

With these words he passed through the yard-gate, walked slowly up the broad pavement, and entered the house.

Music No More

On the disappearing form of the colonel was fixed an ancient pair of eyes that looked out at him from behind a still more ancient pair of silver-rimmed spectacles with an expression of indescribable solicitude and love.

These eyes were set in the head of an old gentleman—for such he was—named Peter Cotton, who was the only one of the colonel's former slaves that had remained inseparable from his person and his altered fortunes. In early manhood Peter had been a wood-chopper; but he had one day had his leg broken by the limb of a falling tree, and afterwards, out of consideration for his limp, had been made supervisor of the wood-pile, gardener, and a sort of nondescript servitor of his master's luxurious needs.

Nay, in larger and deeper characters must his history be writ, he having been, in days gone by, one of those ministers of the gospel whom conscientious Kentucky masters often urged to the exercise of spiritual functions in behalf of their benighted people. In course of preparation for this august work, Peter had learned to read and had come to possess a well-chosen library of three several volumes—*Webster's Spelling-Book, The Pilgrim's Progress,* and the Bible. But even these unusual acquisitions he deemed not enough; for being touched with a spark of poetic fire from heaven, and fired by the African's fondness for all that is conspicuous in dress, he had conceived for himself the creation of a unique garment which should symbolize in perfection the claims and consolations of his apostolic office. This was nothing less than a sacred blue-jeans coat that he had had his old mistress make him, with very long and spacious tails, whereon, at his further direction, she embroidered sundry texts of Scripture which it pleased him to regard as the fit visible annunciations of his holy calling. And inasmuch as his mistress, who had had the coat woven on her own looms from the wool of her finest sheep, was, like other gentlewomen of her time, rarely skilled in the accomplishments of the needle, and was moreover in full sympathy with the piety of his intent, she wrought of these passages a border enriched with such intricate curves, marvellous flourishes, and harmonious letterings, that Solomon never reflected the glory in which Peter was arrayed whenever he put it on. For after much prayer that the Almighty wisdom would aid his reason in the difficult task of selecting the most appropriate texts, Peter had chosen seven—one for each day in the week—with such tact, and no doubt heavenly guidance, that when braided together they did truly constitute an eloquent epitome of Christian duty, hope, and pleading.

From first to last they were as follows: "Woe is unto me if I preach not the gospel"; "Servants, be obedient to them that are your masters according to the flesh"; "Come unto me, all ye that labour and are heavy laden"; "Consider the lilies of the field, how they grow; they toil not, neither do they spin"; "Now abideth faith, hope, and charity, these three; but the greatest of these is charity"; "I would not have you to be ignorant, brethren, concerning them which are asleep"; "For as in Adam all die, even so in Christ shall all be made alive." This concatenation of texts Peter wished to have duly solemnized, and therefore, when the work was finished, he further requested his mistress to close the entire chain with the word "Amen," introduced in some suitable place.

But the only spot now left vacant was one of a few square inches, located just where the coat-tails hung over the end of Peter's spine; so that when any one stood full in Peter's rear, he could but marvel at the sight of so solemn a word emblazoned in so unusual a locality.

Panoplied in this robe of righteousness, and with a worn leathern Bible in his hand, Peter used to go around of Sundays, and during the week, by night, preaching from cabin to cabin the gospel of his heavenly Master.

The angriest lightnings of the sultriest skies often played amid the darkness upon those sacred coat-tails and around that girdle of everlasting texts, as though the evil spirits of the air would fain have burned them and scattered their ashes on the roaring winds. The slow-sifting snows of winter whitened them as though to chill their spiritual fires; but winter and summer, year after year, in weariness of body, often in sore distress of mind, for miles along this lonely road and for miles across that rugged way, Peter trudged on and on, withal perhaps as meek a spirit as ever grew foot-sore in the paths of its Master. Many a poor over-burdened slave took fresh heart and strength from the sight of that celestial raiment; many a stubborn, rebellious spirit, whose flesh but lately quivered under the lash, was brought low by its humble teaching; many a worn-out old frame, racked with pain in its last illness, pressed a fevered lip to its hopeful hem; and many a dying eye closed in death peacefully fixed on its immortal pledges.

When Peter started abroad, if a storm threatened, he carried an old cotton umbrella of immense size; and as the storm burst, he gathered the tails of his coat carefully up under his armpits that they might be kept dry. Or if caught by a tempest without his umbrella, he would take his coat off and roll it up inside out, leaving his body exposed to the fury of the elements. No care, however, could keep it from growing old and worn and faded; and when the slaves were set free and he was called upon by the interposition of Providence to lay it finally aside, it was covered by many a patch and stain as proofs of its devoted usage.

One after another the colonel's old servants, gathering their children about them, had left him, to begin their new life. He bade them all a kind good-bye, and into the palm of each silently pressed some gift that he knew would soon be needed. But no inducement could make Peter or Phillis, his wife, budge from their cabin. "Go, Peter! Go, Phillis!" the colonel had said time and again. "No one is happier that you are free than I am; and you can call on me for what you need to set you up in business." But Peter and Phillis asked to stay with him. Then suddenly, several months before the time at which this sketch opens, Phillis had died, leaving the colonel and Peter as the only relics of that populous life which had once filled the house and the cabins. The colonel had succeeded in hiring a woman to do Phillis's work; but her presence was a strange note of discord in the old domestic harmony, and only saddened the recollections of its vanished peace.

Peter had a short, stout figure, dark-brown skin, smooth-shaven face, eyes round, deep-set and wide apart, and a short, stub nose which dipped suddenly into his head, making it easy for him to wear the silver-rimmed spectacles left him by his old mistress. A peculiar conformation of the muscles between the eyes and the nose gave him the quizzical expression of one who is about to sneeze, and this was heightened by a twinkle in the eyes which seemed caught from the shining of an inner sun upon his tranquil heart.

Sometimes, however, his face grew sad enough. It was sad on this afternoon while he watched the colonel walk slowly up the pavement, well overgrown with weeds, and enter the house, which the setting sun touched with the last radiance of the finished day.

New Life

About two years after the close of the war, therefore, the colonel and Peter were to be found in Lexington, ready to turn over a new leaf in the volumes of their lives, which already had an old-fashioned binding, a somewhat musty odor, and but few unwritten leaves remaining.

After a long, dry summer you may have seen two gnarled old apple-trees, that stood with interlocked arms on the western slope of some quiet hill-side, make a melancholy show of blooming out again in the autumn of the year and dallying with the idle buds that mock their sapless branches. Much the same was the belated, fruitless efflorescence of the colonel and Peter.

The colonel had no business habits, no political ambition, no wish to grow richer. He was too old for society, and without near family ties. For some time he wandered through the streets like one lost—sick with yearning for the fields and woods, for his cattle, for familiar faces. He haunted Cheapside and the courthouse square, where the farmers always assembled when they came to town; and if his eye lighted on one, he would button-hole him on the street-corner and lead him into a grocery and sit down for a quiet chat. Sometimes he would meet an aimless, melancholy wanderer like himself, and the two would go off and discuss over and over again their departed days; and several times he came unexpectedly upon some of his old servants who had fallen into bitter want, and who more than repaid him for the help he gave by contrasting the hardships of a life of freedom with the ease of their shackled years.

In the course of time, he could but observe that human life in the town was reshaping itself slowly and painfully, but with resolute energy. The colossal structure of slavery had fallen, scattering its ruins far and wide over the State; but out of the very débris was being taken the material to lay the deeper foundations of the new social edifice. Men and women as old as he were beginning life over and trying to fit themselves for it by changing the whole attitude and habit of their minds—by taking on a new heart and spirit. But when a great building falls, there is always some rubbish, and the colonel and others like him were part of this. Henceforth they possessed only an antiquarian sort of interest, like the stamped bricks of Nebuchadnezzar.

Nevertheless he made a show of doing something, and in a year or two opened on Cheapside a store for the sale of hardware and agricultural implements. He knew more about the latter than anything else, and, furthermore, he secretly felt that a business of this kind would enable him to establish in town a kind of headquarters for the farmers. His account-books were to be kept on a system of twelve months' credit; and he resolved that if one of his customers couldn't pay then, it would make no difference.

Business began slowly. The farmers dropped in and found a good lounging-place. On county-court days, which were great market-days for the sale of sheep, horses, mules, and cattle in front of the colonel's door, they swarmed in from the hot sun and sat around on the counter and the ploughs and machines till the entrance was blocked to other customers.

When a customer did come in, the colonel, who was probably talking with some old acquaintance, would tell him just to look around and pick out what he wanted and the price would be all right. If one of those acquaintances asked for a pound of nails, the colonel would scoop up some ten pounds and say, "I reckon that's about a pound, Tom." He had never seen a pound of nails in his life; and if one had been weighed on his scales, he would have said the scales were wrong.

He had no great idea of commercial despatch. One morning a lady came in for some carpet-tacks, an article that he had forgotten to lay in. But he at once sent off an order for enough to have tacked a carpet pretty well all over Kentucky, and when they came, two weeks later, he told Peter to take her up a dozen papers with his compliments. He had laid in, however, an ample and especially fine assortment of pocket-knives, for that instrument had always been to him one of gracious and very winning qualities. Then when a friend dropped in he would say, "General, don't you need a new pocket-knife?" and, taking out one, would open all the blades and commend the metal and the handle. The "general" would inquire the price, and the colonel, having shut the blades, would hand it to him, saying in a careless, fond way, "I reckon I won't charge you anything for that." His mind could not come down to the low level of such ignoble barter, and he gave away the whole case of knives.

These were the pleasanter aspects of his business life, which did not lack as well its tedium and crosses. Thus there were many dark stormy days when no one he cared to see came in; and he then became rather a pathetic figure, wandering absently around amid the symbols of his past activity, and stroking the ploughs, like dumb companions. Or he would stand at the door and look across at the old court-house, where he had seen many a slave sold and had listened to the great Kentucky orators.

But what hurt him most was the talk of the new farming and the abuse of the old which he was forced to hear; and he generally refused to handle the improved implements and mechanical devices by which labor and waste were to be saved.

Altogether he grew tired of "the thing," and sold out at the end of the year with a loss of over a thousand dollars, though he insisted he had done a good business.

As he was then seen much on the streets again and several times heard to make remarks in regard to the sidewalks, gutters, and crossings, when they happened to be in bad condition, the *Daily Press* one morning published a card stating that if Colonel Romulus Fields would consent to make the race for mayor he would receive the support of many Democrats, adding a tribute to his virtues and his influential past. It touched the colonel, and he walked down-town with a rather commanding figure the next morning. But it pained him to see how many of his acquaintances returned his salutations very coldly; and just as he was passing the Northern Bank he met the young opposition candidate—a little red-haired fellow, walking between two ladies, with a rose-bud in his button-hole—who refused to speak at all, but made the ladies laugh by some remark he uttered as the colonel passed. The card had been inserted humorously, but he took it seriously; and when his friends found this out, they rallied round him. The day of election drew

near. They told him he must buy votes. He said he wouldn't buy
a vote to be mayor of the New Jerusalem. They told him he must
"mix" and "treat." He refused. Foreseeing he had no chance, they
besought him to withdraw. He said he would not. They told him
he wouldn't poll twenty votes. He replied that *one* would satisfy
him, provided it was neither begged nor bought. When his defeat
was announced, he accepted it as another evidence that he had no
part in the present—no chance of redeeming his idleness.

A sense of this weighed heavily on him at times; but it is not
likely that he realized how pitifully he was undergoing a moral
shrinkage in consequence of mere disuse. Actually, extinction had
set in with him long prior to dissolution, and he was dead years
before his heart ceased beating. The very basic virtues on which
had rested his once spacious and stately character were now but
the mouldy corner-stones of a crumbling ruin.

It was a subtle evidence of deterioration in manliness that he
had taken to dress. When he had lived in the country, he had never
dressed up unless he came to town. When he had moved to town,
he thought he must remain dressed up all the time; and this fact
first fixed his attention on a matter which afterwards began to be
loved for its own sake. Usually he wore a Derby hat, a black
diagonal coat, gray trousers, and a white necktie. But the article
of attire in which he took chief pleasure was hose; and the better
to show the gay colors of these, he wore low-cut shoes of the finest
calfskin, turned up at the toes. Thus his feet kept pace with the
present, however far his head may have lagged in the past; and it
may be that this stream of fresh fashions, flowing perennially over
his lower extremities like water about the roots of a tree, kept him
from drying up altogether.

Peter always polished his shoes with too much blacking, perhaps
thinking that the more the blacking the greater the proof of love.
He wore his clothes about a season and a half—having several
suits—and then passed them on to Peter, who, foreseeing the joy
of such an inheritance, bought no new ones. In the act of transferring them the colonel made no comment until he came to the
hose, from which he seemed unable to part without a final tribute
of esteem, as: "These are fine, Peter"; or, "Peter, these are nearly
as good as new." Thus Peter, too, was dragged through the whims
of fashion. To have seen the colonel walking about his grounds
and garden followed by Peter, just a year and a half behind in
dress and a yard and a half behind in space, one might well have
taken the rear figure for the colonel's double, slightly the worse
for wear, somewhat shrunken, and cast into a heavy shadow.

Time hung so heavily on his hands at night that with a happy inspiration he added a dress suit to his wardrobe, and accepted the first invitation to an evening party.

He grew excited as the hour approached, and dressed in a great fidget for fear he should be too late.

"How do I look, Peter?" he inquired at length, surprised at his own appearance.

"Splendid, Marse Rom," replied Peter, bringing in the shoes with more blacking on them than ever before.

"I think," said the colonel, apologetically—"I think I'd look better if I'd put a little powder on. I don't know what makes me so red in the face."

But his heart began to sink before he reached his hostess's, and he had a fearful sense of being the observed of all observers as he slipped through the hall and passed rapidly up to the gentlemen's room. He stayed there after the others had gone down, bewildered and lonely, dreading to go down himself. By-and-by the musicians struck up a waltz, and with a little cracked laugh at his own performance he cut a few shines of an unremembered pattern; but his ankles snapped audibly, and he suddenly stopped with the thought of what Peter would say if he should catch him at these antics. Then he boldly went down-stairs.

He had touched the new human life around him at various points: as he now stretched out his arms towards its society, for the first time he completely realized how far removed it was from him. Here he saw a younger generation—the flowers of the new social order—sprung from the very soil of fraternal battlefields, but blooming together as the emblems of oblivious peace. He saw fathers who had fought madly on opposite sides talking quietly in corners as they watched their children dancing, or heard them toasting their old generals and their campaigns over their champagne in the supper-room. He was glad of it; but it made him feel, at the same time, that, instead of treading the velvety floors, he ought to step up and take his place among the canvases of old-time portraits that looked down from the walls.

The dancing he had done had been not under the blinding glare of gaslight, but by the glimmer of tallow-dips and star-candles and the ruddy glow of cavernous firesides—not to the accompaniment of an orchestra of wind-instruments and strings, but to a chorus of girls' sweet voices, as they trod simpler measures, or to the maddening sway of a gray-haired negro fiddler standing on a chair in the chimney-corner. Still, it is significant to note that his saddest thought, long after leaving, was that his shirt bosom had not lain down smooth, but stuck out like a huge cracked egg-shell, and that when, in imitation of the others, he had laid his white silk handkerchief across his bosom inside his vest, it had slipped out during the evening, and had been found by him, on confronting a mirror, flapping over his stomach like a little white masonic apron.

"Did you have a nice time, Marse Rom?" inquired Peter, as they drove home through the darkness.

"Splendid time, Peter, splendid time," replied the colonel, nervously.

"Did you dance any, Marse Rom?"

"I didn't *dance*. Oh, I *could* have danced if I'd *wanted* to; but I didn't."

Peter helped the colonel out of the carriage with pitying gentleness when they reached home. It was the first and only party.

Peter also had been finding out that his occupation was gone.

Soon after moving to town, he had tendered his pastoral services to one of the fashionable churches of the city—not because it was fashionable, but because it was made up of his brethren. In reply he was invited to preach a trial sermon, which he did with gracious unction.

It was a strange scene, as one calm Sunday morning he stood on the edge of the pulpit, dressed in a suit of the colonel's old clothes, with one hand in his trousers-pocket, and his lame leg set a little forward at an angle familiar to those who know the statues of Henry Clay.

How self-possessed he seemed, yet with what a rush of memories did he pass his eyes slowly over that vast assemblage of his emancipated people! With what feelings must he have contrasted those silk hats, and walking-canes, and broadcloths; those gloves and satins, laces and feathers, jewelry and fans—that whole many-colored panorama of life—with the weary, sad, and sullen audiences that had often heard him of old under the forest trees or by the banks of some turbulent stream!

In a voice husky, but heard beyond the flirtation of the uttermost pew, he took his text: "Consider the lilies of the field, how they grow; they toil not, neither do they spin." From this he tried to preach a new sermon, suited to the newer day. But several times the thoughts of the past were too much for him, and he broke down with emotion.

The next day a grave committee waited on him and reported that the sense of the congregation was to call a colored gentleman from Louisville. Private objections to Peter were that he had a broken leg, wore Colonel Fields's second-hand clothes, which were too big for him, preached in the old-fashioned way, and lacked self-control and repose of manner.

Peter accepted his rebuff as sweetly as Socrates might have done. Humming the burden of an old hymn, he took his righteous coat from a nail in the wall and folded it away in a little brass-nailed deer-skin trunk, laying over it the spelling-book and the *Pilgrim's Progress,* which he had ceased to read. Thenceforth his relations to his people were never intimate, and even from the other servants of the colonel's household he stood apart. But the colonel took Peter's rejection greatly to heart, and the next morning gave him the new silk socks he had worn at the party. In paying his servants the colonel would sometimes say, "Peter, I reckon I'd better begin to pay you a salary; that's the style now." But Peter would turn off, saying he didn't "have no use fur no salary."

Thus both of them dropped more and more out of life, but as they did so drew more and more closely to each other. The colonel had bought a home on the edge of the town, with some ten acres of beautiful ground surrounding. A high osage-orange hedge shut it in, and forest trees, chiefly maples and elms, gave to the lawn and house abundant shade. Wild-grape vines, the Virginia-creeper, and the climbing-oak swung their long festoons from summit to summit, while honeysuckles, clematis, and the Mexican-vine clambered over arbors and trellises, or along the chipped stone of the low, old-fashioned house. Just outside the door of the colonel's bedroom slept an ancient, broken sundial.

The place seemed always in half-shadow, with hedgerows of box, clumps of dark holly, darker firs half a century old, and aged, crape-like cedars.

It was in the seclusion of this retreat, which looked almost like a wild bit of country set down on the edge of the town, that the colonel and Peter spent more of their time as they fell farther in the rear of onward events. There were no such flower-gardens in the city, and pretty much the whole town went thither for its flowers, preferring them to those that were to be had for a price at the nurseries.

There was, perhaps, a suggestion of pathetic humor in the fact that it should have called on the colonel and Peter, themselves so nearly defunct, to furnish the flowers for so many funerals; but, it is certain, almost weekly the two old gentlemen received this chastening admonition of their all-but-spent mortality. The colonel cultivated the rarest fruits also, and had under glass varieties that were not friendly to the climate; so that by means of the fruits and flowers there was established a pleasant social bond with many who otherwise would never have sought them out.

But others came for better reasons. To a few deep-seeing eyes the colonel and Peter were ruined landmarks on a fading historic landscape, and their devoted friendship was the last steady burning-down of that pure flame of love which can never again shine out in the future of the two races. Hence a softened charm invested the drowsy quietude of that shadowy paradise in which the old master without a slave and the old slave without a master still kept up a brave pantomime of their obsolete relations. No one ever saw in their intercourse ought but the finest courtesy, the most delicate consideration. The very tones of their voices in addressing each other were as good as sermons on gentleness, their antiquated playfulness as melodious as the babble of distant water. To be near them was to be exorcised of evil passions.

The sun of their day had indeed long since set, but like twin clouds lifted high and motionless into some far quarter of the gray twilight skies, they were still radiant with the glow of the invisible orb.

Henceforth the colonel's appearances in public were few and regular. He went to church on Sundays, where he sat on the edge of the choir in the centre of the building, and sang an ancient bass of his own improvisation to the older hymns, and glanced furtively around to see whether any one noticed that he could not sing the new ones. At the Sunday-school picnics the committee of arrangements allowed him to carve the mutton, and after dinner to swing the smallest children gently beneath the trees. He was seen on Commencement Day at Morrison Chapel, where he always gave his bouquet to the valedictorian. It was the speech of that young gentleman that always touched him, consisting as it did of farewells.

In the autumn he might sometimes be noticed sitting high up in the amphitheatre at the fair, a little blue around the nose, and looking absently over into the ring where the judges were grouped around the music-stand. Once he had strutted around as a judge himself, with a blue ribbon in his button-hole, while the band played "Sweet Alice, Ben Bolt," and "Gentle Annie." The ring seemed full of young men now, and no one even thought of offering him the privileges of the grounds. In his day the great feature of the exhibition had been cattle; now everything was turned into a horse-show. He was always glad to get home again to Peter, his true yoke-fellow. For just as two old oxen—one white and one black—that have long toiled under the same yoke will, when turned out to graze at last in the widest pasture, come and put themselves horn to horn and flank to flank, so the colonel and Peter were never so happy as when ruminating side by side.

New Love

In their eventless life the slightest incident acquired the importance of a history. Thus, one day in June, Peter discovered a young couple love-making in the shrubbery, and with the deepest agitation reported the fact to the colonel.

Never before, probably, had the fluttering of the dear god's wings brought more dismay than to these ancient involuntary guardsmen of his hiding-place. The colonel was at first for breaking up what he considered a piece of underhand proceedings, but Peter reasoned stoutly that if the pair were driven out they would simply go to some other retreat; and without getting the approval of his conscience to this view, the colonel contented himself with merely repeating that they ought to go straight and tell the girl's parents. Those parents lived just across the street outside his grounds. The young lady he knew very well himself, having a few years before given her the privilege of making herself at home among his flowers. It certainly looked hard to drive her out now, just when she was making the best possible use of his kindness and her opportunity. Moreover, Peter walked down street and ascertained that the young fellow was an energetic farmer living a few miles from town, and son of one of the colonel's former friends; on both of which accounts the latter's heart went out to him. So when, a few days later, the colonel, followed by Peter, crept up breathlessly and peeped through the bushes at the pair strolling along the shady perfumed walks, and so plainly happy in that happiness which comes but once in a lifetime, they not only abandoned the idea of betraying the secret, but afterwards kept away from that part of the grounds, lest they should be an interruption.

"Peter," stammered the colonel, who had been trying to get the words out for three days, "do you suppose he has already—*asked* her?"

"Some's pow'ful quick on de trigger, en some's mighty slow," replied Peter, neutrally. "En some," he added, exhaustively, "don't use de trigger 't all!"

"I always thought there had to be asking done by *somebody*," remarked the colonel, a little vaguely.

"I nuver axed Phillis!" exclaimed Peter, with a certain air of triumph.

"Did Phillis ask *you*, Peter?" inquired the colonel, blushing and confidential.

"No, no, Marse Rom! I couldn't er stood dat from no 'oman!" replied Peter, laughing and shaking his head.

The colonel was sitting on the stone steps in front of the house, and Peter stood below, leaning against a Corinthian column, hat in hand, as he went on to tell his love-story.

"Hit all happ'n dis way, Marse Rom. We wuz gwine have pra'r-meetin', en I 'lowed to walk home wid Phillis en ax 'er on de road. I been 'lowin' to ax 'er heap o' times befo', but I ain' jes nuver done so. So I says to myse'f, says I, 'I jes mek my sermon to-night kiner lead up to whut I gwine tell Phillis on de road home.' So I tuk my tex' from de *lef'* tail o' my coat: 'De greates' o' dese is charity'; caze I knowed charity wuz same ez love. En all de time I wuz preachin' an' glorifyin' charity en identifyin' charity wid love, I couldn' he'p thinkin' 'bout what I gwine say to Phillis on de road home. Dat mek me feel better; en de better I *feel*, de better I *preach*, so hit boun' to mek my *heahehs* feel better likewise—Phillis 'mong um. So Phillis she jes sot dah listenin' en listenin' en lookin' like we wuz a'ready on de road home, till I got so wuked up in my feelin's I jes knowed de time wuz come. By-en-by, I had n' mo' 'n done preachin' en wuz lookin' roun' to git my Bible en my hat, 'fo' up popped dat big Charity Green, who been settin' 'long-side o' Phillis en tekin' ev'y las' thing I said to *her*se'f. En she tuk hole o' my han' en squeeze it, en say she felt mos' like shoutin'. En 'fo' I knowed it, I jes see Phillis wrap 'er shawl roun' 'er head en tu'n 'er nose up at me right quick en flip out de dooh. De dogs howl mighty mou'nful when I walk home by myse'f *dat* night," added Peter, laughing to himself, "en I ain' preach dat sermon no mo' tell atter me en Phillis wuz married.

"Hit wuz long time," he continued, " 'fo' Phillis come to heah me preach any mo'. But 'long 'bout de nex' fall we had big meetin', en heap mo' um j'ined. But Phillis, she ain't nuver j'ined yit. I preached mighty nigh all roun' my coat-tails till I say to myse'f, D' ain't but one tex' lef', en I jes got to fetch 'er wid dat! De tex' wuz on de *right* tail o' my coat: 'Come unto me, all ye dat labor en is heavy laden.' Hit wuz a ve'y momentous sermon, en all 'long I jes see Phillis wras'lin' wid 'erse'f, en I say, 'She *got* to come *dis* night, de Lohd he'pin' me.' En I had n' mo' 'n said de word, 'fo' she jes walked down en guv me 'er han'.

"Den we had de baptizin' in Elkhorn Creek, en de watter wuz deep en de curren' tol'ble swif'. Hit look to me like dere wuz five hundred uv um on de creek side. By-en-by I stood on de edge o' de watter, en Phillis she come down to let me baptize 'er. En me en 'er j'ined han's en waded out in the creek, mighty slow, caze Phillis didn' have no shot roun' de bottom uv 'er dress, en it kep' bobbin' on top de watter till I pushed it down. But by-en-by we got 'way out in de creek, en bof uv us wuz tremblin'. En I says to 'er ve'y kin'ly, 'When I put you un'er de watter, Phillis, you mus'

try en hole yo'se'f stiff, so I can lif' you up easy.' But I hadn't mo'
'n jes got 'er laid back over de watter ready to souze 'er un'er
when 'er feet flew up off de bottom uv de creek, en when I retched
out to fetch 'er up, I stepped in a hole; en 'fo' I knowed it, we
wuz flounderin' roun' in de watter, en de hymn dey was singin' on
de bank sounded mighty confused-like. En Phillis she swallowed
some watter, en all 't oncet she jes grap me right tight roun' de
neck, en say mighty quick, says she, 'I gwine marry whoever gits
me out'n dis yere watter!'

"En by-en-by, when me en 'er wuz walkin' up de bank o' de
creek, drippin' all over, I says to 'er, says I:

" 'Does you 'member what you said back yon'er in de watter,
Phillis?'

" 'I ain' out'n no watter yit,' says she, ve'y contemptuous.

" 'When does you consider yo'se'f out'n de watter?' says I, ve'y
humble.

" 'When I git dese soakin' clo'es off'n my back,' says she.

"Hit wuz good dark when we got home, en atter a while I crope
up to de dooh o' Phillis's cabin en put my eye down to de key-
hole, en see Phillis jes settin' 'fo' dem blazin' walnut logs dressed
up in 'er new red linsey dress, en 'er eyes shinin'. En I shuk so I
'mos' faint. Den I tap easy on de dooh, en say in a mighty tremblin'
tone, says I:

" 'Is you out'n de watter yit, Phillis?'

" 'I got on dry dress,' says she.

" 'Does you 'member what you said back yon'er in de watter,
Phillis?' says I.

" 'De latch-string on de outside de dooh,' says she, mighty sof'.
"En I walked in."

As Peter drew near the end of this reminiscence, his voice sank
to a key of inimitable tenderness; and when it was ended he stood
a few minutes, scraping the gravel with the toe of his boot, his
head dropped forward. Then he added, huskily:

"Phillis been dead heap o' years now"; and turned away.

This recalling of the scenes of a time long gone by may have
awakened in the breast of the colonel some gentle memory; for
after Peter was gone he continued to sit a while in silent musing.
Then getting up, he walked in the falling twilight across the yard
and through the gardens until he came to a secluded spot in the
most distant corner. There he stooped or rather knelt down and
passed his hands, as though with mute benediction, over a little
bed of old-fashioned China pinks. When he had moved in from
the country he had brought nothing away from his mother's garden
but these, and in all the years since no one had ever pulled them,

as Peter well knew; for one day the colonel had said, with his face turned away:

"Let them have all the flowers they want; but leave the pinks."

He continued kneeling over them now, touching them softly with his fingers, as though they were the fragrant, never-changing symbols of voiceless communion with his past. Still it may have been only the early dew of the evening that glistened on them when he rose and slowly walked away, leaving the pale moonbeams to haunt the spot.

Certainly after this day he showed increasing concern in the young lovers who were holding clandestine meetings in his grounds.

"Peter," he would say, "why, if they love each other, don't they get married? Something may happen."

"I been spectin' some'n' to happ'n fur some time, ez dey been quar'lin' right smart lately," replied Peter, laughing.

Whether or not he was justified in this prediction, before the end of another week the colonel read a notice of their elopement and marriage; and several days later he came up from down-town and told Peter that everything had been forgiven the young pair, who had gone to house-keeping in the country. It gave him pleasure to think he had helped to perpetuate the race of blue-grass farmers.

The Yearning Passed Away

It was in the twilight of a late autumn day in the same year that nature gave the colonel the first direct intimation to prepare for the last summons. They had been passing along the garden walks, where a few pale flowers were trying to flourish up to the very winter's edge, and where the dry leaves had gathered unswept and rustled beneath their feet. All at once the colonel turned to Peter, who was a yard and a half behind, as usual, and said:

"Give me your arm, Peter, I feel tired"; and thus the two, for the first time in all their lifetime walking abreast, passed slowly on.

"Peter," said the colonel, gravely, a minute or two later, "we are like two dried-up stalks of fodder. I wonder the Lord lets us live any longer."

"I reck'n He's managin' to use us *some* way, or we wouldn' be heah," said Peter.

"Well, all I have to say is, that if He's using me, He can't be in much of a hurry for his work," replied the colonel.

"He uses snails, en I *know* we ain' ez slow ez *dem*," argued Peter, composedly.

"I don't know. I think a snail must have made more progress since the war than I have."

The idea of his uselessness seemed to weigh on him, for a little later he remarked, with a sort of mortified smile:

"Do you think, Peter, that we would pass for what they call representative men of the New South?"

"We done *had* ou' day, Marse Rom," replied Peter. "We got to pass fur what we *wuz*. Mebbe de *Lohd's* got mo' use fur us yit 'n *people* has," he added, after a pause.

From this time on the colonel's strength gradually failed him; but it was not until the following spring that the end came.

A night or two before his death his mind wandered backward, after the familiar manner of the dying, and his delirious dreams showed the shifting, faded pictures that renewed themselves for the last time on his wasting memory. It must have been that he was once more amid the scenes of his active farm life, for his broken snatches of talk ran thus:

"Come, boys, get your cradles! Look where the sun is! You are late getting to work this morning. That is the finest field of wheat in the county. Be careful about the bundles! Make them the same size and tie them tight. That swath is too wide, and you don't hold your cradle right, Tom. . . .

"Sell *Peter! Sell Peter Cotton!* No, sir! You might buy *me* some day and work *me* in your cotton-field; but as long as he's mine, you can't buy Peter, and you can't buy any of *my* negroes. . . .

"Boys! boys! If you don't work faster, you won't finish this field to-day. . . . You'd better go in the shade and rest now. The sun's very hot. Don't drink too much ice-water. There's a jug of whisky in the fence-corner. Give them a good dram around, and tell them to work slow till the sun gets lower. . . ."

Once during the night a sweet smile played over his features as he repeated a few words that were part of an old rustic song and dance. Arranged, not as they came broken and incoherent from his lips, but as he once had sung them, they were as follows:

"O Sister Phœbe! How merry were we
　When we sat under the juniper-tree,
　　　The juniper-tree, heigho!
　Put this hat on your head! Keep your head warm;
　Take a sweet kiss! It will do you no harm,
　　　Do you no harm, I know!"

After this he sank into a quieter sleep, but soon stirred with a look of intense pain.

"Helen! Helen!" he murmured. "Will you break your promise? Have you changed in your feelings towards me? I have brought you the pinks. Won't you take the pinks, Helen?"

Then he sighed as he added, "It wasn't her fault. If she had only known—"

Who was the Helen of that far-away time? Was this the colonel's love-story?

But during all the night, whithersoever his mind wandered, at intervals it returned to the burden of a single strain—the harvesting. Towards daybreak he took it up again for the last time:

"O boys, boys, *boys!* If you don't work faster you won't finish the field to-day. Look how low the sun is! . . . I am going to the house. They can't finish the field to-day. Let them do what they can, but don't let them work late. I want Peter to go to the house with me. Tell him to come on. . . ."

In the faint gray of the morning, Peter, who had been watching by the bedside all night, stole out of the room, and going into the garden pulled a handful of pinks—a thing he had never done before—and, re-entering the colonel's bedroom, put them in a vase near his sleeping face. Soon afterwards the colonel opened his eyes and looked around him. At the foot of the bed stood Peter, and on one side sat the physician and a friend. The night-lamp burned low, and through the folds of the curtains came the white light of early day.

"Put out the lamp and open the curtains," he said, feebly. "It's day." When they had drawn the curtains aside, his eyes fell on the pinks, sweet and fresh with the dew on them. He stretched out his hand and touched them caressingly, and his eyes sought Peter's with a look of grateful understanding.

"I want to be alone with Peter for a while," he said, turning his face towards the others.

When they were left alone, it was some minutes before anything was said. Peter, not knowing what he did, but knowing what was coming, had gone to the window and hid himself behind the curtains, drawing them tightly around his form as though to shroud himself from sorrow.

At length the colonel said, "Come here!"

Peter, almost staggering forward, fell at the foot of the bed, and, clasping the colonel's feet with one arm, pressed his cheek against them.

"Come closer!"

Peter crept on his knees and buried his head on the colonel's thigh.

"Come up here—closer"; and putting one arm around Peter's

neck, he laid the other hand softly on his head, and looked long and tenderly into his eyes. "I've got to leave you, Peter. Don't you feel sorry for me?"

"Oh, Marse Rom!" cried Peter, hiding his face, his whole form shaken by sobs.

"Peter," added the colonel with ineffable gentleness, "if I had served my Master as faithfully as you have served yours, I should not feel ashamed to stand in his presence."

"If my Marseter is ez mussiful to me ez you have been—"

"I have fixed things so that you will be comfortable after I am gone. When your time comes, I should like you to be laid close to me. We can take the long sleep together. Are you willing?"

"That's whar I want to be laid."

The colonel stretched out his hand to the vase, and taking the bunch of pinks, said very calmly:

"Leave these in my hand; I'll carry them with me." A moment more, and he added:

"If I shouldn't wake up any more, good-bye, Peter!"

"Good-bye, Marse Rom!"

And they shook hands a long time. After this the colonel lay back on the pillows. His soft, silvery hair contrasted strongly with his child-like, unspoiled, open face. To the day of his death, as is apt to be true of those who have lived pure lives but never married, he had a boyish strain in him—a softness of nature, showing itself even now in the gentle expression of his mouth. His brown eyes had in them the same boyish look when, just as he was falling asleep, he scarcely opened them to say:

"Pray, Peter."

Peter, on his knees, and looking across the colonel's face towards the open door, through which the rays of the rising sun streamed in upon his hoary head, prayed, while the colonel fell asleep, adding a few words for himself now left alone.

Several hours later, memory led the colonel back again through the dim gate-way of the past, and out of that gate-way his spirit finally took flight into the future.

Peter lingered a year. The place went to the colonel's sister, but he was allowed to remain in his quarters. With much thinking of the past, his mind fell into a lightness and a weakness. Sometimes he would be heard crooning the burden of old hymns, or sometimes seen sitting beside the old brass-nailed trunk, fumbling with the spelling-book and *The Pilgrim's Progress*. Often, too, he walked out to the cemetery on the edge of the town, and each time could hardly find the colonel's grave amid the multitude of the dead.

One gusty day in spring, the Scotch sexton, busy with the blades of blue-grass springing from the animated mould, saw his familiar figure standing motionless beside the colonel's resting-place. He had taken off his hat—one of the colonel's last bequests—and laid it on the colonel's head-stone. On his body he wore a strange coat of faded blue, patched and weather-stained, and so moth-eaten that parts of the curious tails had dropped entirely away. In one hand he held an open Bible, and on a much-soiled page he was pointing with his finger to the following words:

"I would not have you ignorant, brethren, concerning them which are asleep."

It would seem that, impelled by love and faith, and guided by his wandering reason, he had come forth to preach his last sermon on the immortality of the soul over the dust of his dead master.

The sexton led him home, and soon afterwards a friend, who had loved them both, laid him beside the colonel.

It was perhaps fitting that his winding-sheet should be the vestment in which, years agone, he had preached to his fellow-slaves in bondage; for if it so be that the dead of this planet shall come forth from their graves clad in the trappings of mortality, then Peter should arise on the Resurrection Day wearing his old jeans coat.

Arna Wendell Bontemps

(1902–1973)

*Born in Alexandria, Louisiana, Bontemps moved with his family
to California when he was three years old. Though raised and educated in Los Angeles, he remained constantly in touch with the
Deep South through his family and other Southern-born transplants.
After graduating from Pacific Union College in 1923, he was attracted by the excitement of a black cultural renaissance in New
York City's Harlem. There he became close friends with Langston
Hughes, with whom he collaborated on several anthologies. In Harlem, Bontemps first made his name as a poet, but it was only in the
1960s that he became fully recognized as one of the important figures
of the Harlem Renaissance. After leaving New York City at the
beginning of the Depression, he lived for many years in the South,
working as a librarian at Fisk University, as a teacher, and later in
his life, as a popular lecturer. By the time of his death, largely
through his teaching and influential anthologies, he had become
known as one of the leading authorities of Southern black folkways.
His writing ranges over a number of literary forms, including poetry,
novels, short stories, essays, biographies, and social histories.
Among his books are* God Sends Sunday *(1931),* Black Thunder
(1936), Drums at Dusk *(1939),* Father of the Blues, the Autobiography of W. C. Handy *(1941),* They Seek a City *(1945; revised
as* Anyplace But Here, *1966 with Jack Conroy),* The Story of the
Negro *(1948),* The Poetry of the Negro: 1747–1949 *(1949, with
Langston Hughes),* George Washington Carver *(1950),* Lonesome
Boy *(1955),* Frederick Douglass: Slave Fighter *(1958),* The Book
of American Negro Folklore *(1958, with Langston Hughes),* American Negro Poetry *(1963),* Great Slave Narratives *(1969), and* The
Harlem Renaissance Remembered *(1972). "A Summer Tragedy,"
from* The Old South: "A Summer Tragedy" *and Other Stories of
the Thirties* (1973), *was first published in* Opportunity: A Journal
of Negro Life *(June 1933).*

A SUMMER TRAGEDY

❀

Old Jeff Patton, the black share farmer, fumbled with his bow tie. His fingers trembled, and the high, stiff collar pinched his throat. A fellow loses his hand for such vanities after thirty or forty years of simple life. Once a year, or maybe twice if there's a wedding among his kin-folks, he may spruce up; but generally fancy clothes do nothing but adorn the wall of the big room and feed the moths. That had been Jeff Patton's experience. He had not worn his stiff-bosomed shirt more than a dozen times in all his married life. His swallowtailed coat lay on the bed beside him, freshly brushed and pressed, but it was as full of holes as the overalls in which he worked on week days. The moths had used it badly. Jeff twisted his mouth into a hideous toothless grimace as he contended with the obstinate bow. He stamped his good foot and decided to give up the struggle.

"Jennie," he called.

"What's that, Jeff?" His wife's shrunken voice came out of the adjoining room like an echo. It was hardly bigger than a whisper.

"I reckon you'll have to he'p me wid this heah bow tie, baby," he said meekly. "Dog if I can hitch it up."

Her answer was not strong enough to reach him, but presently the old woman came to the door, feeling her way with a stick. She had a wasted, dead-leaf appearance. Her body, as scrawny and gnarled as a stringbean, seemed less than nothing in the ocean of frayed and faded petticoats that surrounded her. These hung an inch or two above the tops of her heavy, unlaced shoes and showed little grotesque piles where the stockings had fallen down from her negligible legs.

"You oughta could do a heap mo' wid a thing like that 'n me—beingst as you got yo' good sight."

"Looks like I *oughta* could," he admitted. "But ma fingers is gone democrat on me. I get all mixed up in the looking glass an' can't tell whicha way to twist the devilish thing."

Jennie sat on the side of the bed and old Jeff Patton got down on one knee while she tied the bow knot. It was a slow and painful ordeal for each of them in this position. Jeff's bones cracked, his knee ached, and it was only after a half dozen attempts that Jennie worked a semblance of a bow into the tie.

"I got to dress maself now," the old woman whispered. "These

26

is ma old shoes an' stockings, and I ain't so much as unwrapped ma dress."

"Well, don't worry 'bout me no mo', baby," Jeff said. "That 'bout finishes me. All I gotta do now is slip on that old coat 'n ves' an' I'll be fixed to leave."

Jennie disappeared again through the dim passage into the shed room. Being blind was no handicap to her in that black hole. Jeff heard the cane placed against the wall beside the door and knew that his wife was on easy ground. He put on his coat, took a battered top hat from the bed post, and hobbled to the front door. He was ready to travel. As soon as Jennie could get on her Sunday shoes and her old black silk dress, they would start.

Outside the tiny log house the day was warm and mellow with sunshine. A host of wasps was humming with busy excitement in the trunk of a dead sycamore. Grey squirrels were searching through the grass for hickory nuts and blue jays were in the trees, hopping from branch to branch. Pine woods stretched away to the left like a black sea. Among them were scattered scores of log houses like Jeff's, houses of black share farmers. Cows and pigs wandered freely among the trees. There was no danger of loss. Each farmer knew his own stock and knew his neighbor's as well as he knew his neighbor's children.

Down the slope to the right were the cultivated acres on which the colored folks worked. They extended to the river, more than two miles away, and they were today green with the unmade cotton crop. A tiny thread of a road, which passed directly in front of Jeff's place, ran through these green fields like a pencil mark.

Jeff, standing outside the door with his absurd hat in his left hand, surveyed the wide scene tenderly. He had been forty-five years on these acres. He loved them with the unexplained affection that others have for the countries to which they belong.

The sun was hot on his head, his collar still pinched his throat, and the Sunday clothes were intolerably hot. Jeff transferred the hat to his right hand and began fanning with it. Suddenly the whisper that was Jennie's voice came out of the shed room.

"You can bring the car round front whilst you's waitin'," it said feebly. There was a tired pause; then it added, "I'll soon be fixed to go."

"A'right, baby," Jeff answered. "I'll get it in a minute."

But he didn't move. A thought struck him that made his mouth fall open. The mention of the car brought to his mind, with new intensity, the trip he and Jennie were about to take. Fear came into his eyes; excitement took his breath. Lord, Jesus!

"Jeff . . . Oh Jeff," the old woman's whisper called.

He awakened with a jolt. "Hunh, baby?"

"What you doin'?"

"Nuthin. Jes studyin'. I jes been turnin' things round 'n round in ma mind."

"You could be gettin' the car," she said.

"Oh yes, right away, baby."

He started round to the shed, limping heavily on his bad leg. There were three frizzly chickens in the yard. All his other chickens had been killed or stolen recently. But the frizzly chickens had been saved somehow. That was fortunate indeed, for these curious creatures had a way of devouring "poison" from the yard and in that way protecting against conjure and bad luck and spells. But even the frizzly chickens seemed now to be in a stupor. Jeff thought they had some ailment; he expected all three of them to die shortly.

The shed in which the old model-T Ford stood was only a grass roof held up by four corner poles. It had been built by tremulous hands at a time when the little rattletrap car had been regarded as a peculiar treasure. And, miraculously, despite wind and downpour, it still stood.

Jeff adjusted the crank and put his weight on it. The engine came to life with a sputter and bang that rattled the old car from radiator to tail light. Jeff hopped into the seat and put his foot on the accelerator. The sputtering and banging increased. The rattling became more violent. That was good. It was good banging, good sputtering and rattling, and it meant that the aged car was still in running condition. She could be depended on for this trip.

Again Jeff's thought halted as if paralyzed. The suggestion of the trip fell into the machinery of his mind like a wrench. He felt dazed and weak. He swung the car out into the yard, made a half turn, and drove around to the front door. When he took his hands off the wheel, he noticed that he was trembling violently. He cut off the motor and climbed to the ground to wait for Jennie.

A few moments later she was at the window, her voice rattling against the pane like a broken shutter.

"I'm ready, Jeff."

He did not answer, but limped into the house and took her by the arm. He led her slowly through the big room, down the step, and across the yard.

"You reckon I'd oughta lock the do'?" he asked softly.

They stopped and Jennie weighed the question. Finally she shook her head.

"Ne' mind the do'," she said. "I don't see no cause to lock up things."

"You right," Jeff agreed. "No cause to lock up."

Jeff opened the door and helped his wife into the car. A quick shudder passed over him. Jesus! Again he trembled.

"How come you shaking so?" Jennie whispered.

"I don't know," he said.

"You mus' be scairt, Jeff."

"No, baby, I ain't scairt."

He slammed the door after her and went around to crank up again. The motor started easily. Jeff wished that it had not been so responsive. He would have liked a few more minutes in which to turn things around in his head. As it was, with Jennie chiding him about being afraid, he had to keep going. He swung the car into the little pencil-mark road and started off toward the river, driving very slowly, very cautiously.

Chugging across the green countryside, the small, battered Ford seemed tiny indeed. Jeff felt a familiar excitement, a thrill, as they came down the first slope to the immense levels on which the cotton was growing. He could not help reflecting that the crops were good. He knew what that meant, too; he had made forty-five of them with his own hands. It was true that he had worn out nearly a dozen mules, but that was the fault of old man Stevenson, the owner of the land. Major Stevenson had the odd notion that one mule was all a share farmer needed to work a thirty-acre plot. It was an expensive notion, the way it killed mules from overwork, but the old man held to it. Jeff thought it killed a good many share farmers as well as mules, but he had no sympathy for them. He had always been strong, and he had been taught to have no patience with weakness in men. Women or children might be tolerated if they were puny, but a weak man was a curse. Of course, his own children—

Jeff's thought halted there. He and Jennie never mentioned their dead children any more. And naturally he did not wish to dwell upon them in his mind. Before he knew it, some remark would slip out of his mouth and that would make Jennie feel blue. Perhaps she would cry. A woman like Jennie could not easily throw off the grief that comes from losing five grown children within two years. Even Jeff was still staggered by the blow. His memory had not been much good recently. He frequently talked to himself. And, although he had kept it a secret, he knew that his courage had left him. He was terrified by the least unfamiliar sound at night. He was reluctant to venture far from home in the daytime. And that habit of trembling when he felt fearful was now far beyond his control. Sometimes he became afraid and trembled without knowing what had frightened him. The feeling would just come over him like a chill.

The car rattled slowly over the dusty road. Jennie sat erect and silent, with a little absurd hat pinned to her hair. Her useless eyes seemed very large and very white in their deep sockets. Suddenly Jeff heard her voice, and he inclined his head to catch the words.

"Is we passed Delia Moore's house yet?" she asked.

"Not yet," he said.

"You must be drivin' mighty slow, Jeff."

"We jes as well take our time, baby."

There was a pause. A little puff of steam was coming out of the radiator of the car. Heat wavered above the hood. Delia Moore's house was nearly half a mile away. After a moment Jennie spoke again.

"You ain't really scairt, is you, Jeff?"

"Nah, baby, I ain't scairt."

"You know how we agreed—we gotta keep on goin'."

Jewels of perspiration appeared on Jeff's forehead. His eyes rounded, blinked, became fixed on the road.

"I don't know," he said with a shiver. "I reckon it's the only thing to do."

"Hm."

A flock of guinea fowls, pecking in the road, were scattered by the passing car. Some of them took to their wings; others hid under bushes. A blue jay, swaying on a leafy twig, was annoying a roadside squirrel. Jeff held an even speed till he came near Delia's place. Then he slowed down noticeably.

Delia's house was really no house at all, but an abandoned store building converted into a dwelling. It sat near a crossroads, beneath a single black cedar tree. There Delia, a catlike old creature of Jennie's age, lived alone. She had been there more years than anybody could remember, and long ago had won the disfavor of such women as Jennie. For in her young days Delia had been gayer, yellower, and saucier than seemed proper in those parts. Her ways with menfolks had been dark and suspicious. And the fact that she had had as many husbands as children did not help her reputation.

"Yonder's old Delia," Jeff said as they passed.

"What she doin'?"

"Jes sittin' in the do'," he said.

"She see us?"

"Hm," Jeff said. "Musta did."

That relieved Jennie. It strengthened her to know that her old enemy had seen her pass in her best clothes. That would give the old she-devil something to chew her gums and fret about, Jennie thought. Wouldn't she have a fit if she didn't find out? Old evil

Delia! This would be just the thing for her. It would pay her back for being so evil. It would also pay her, Jennie thought, for the way she used to grin at Jeff—long ago when her teeth were good.

The road became smooth and red, and Jeff could tell by the smell of the air that they were nearing the river. He could see the rise where the road turned and ran along parallel to the stream. The car chugged on monotonously. After a long silent spell, Jennie leaned against Jeff and spoke.

"How many bale o' cotton you think we got standin'?" she said.

Jeff wrinkled his forehead as he calculated.

" 'Bout twenty-five, I reckon."

"How many you make las' year?"

"Twenty-eight," he said. "How come you ask that?"

"I's jes thinkin'," Jennie said quietly.

"It don't make a speck o' diff'ence though," Jeff reflected. "If we get much or if we get little, we still gonna be in debt to old man Stevenson when he gets through counting up agin us. It's took us a long time to learn that."

Jennie was not listening to these words. She had fallen into a trance-like meditation. Her lips twitched. She chewed her gums and rubbed her old gnarled hands nervously. Suddenly, she leaned forward, buried her face in the nervous hands, and burst into tears. She cried aloud in a dry, cracked voice that suggested the rattle of fodder on dead stalks. She cried aloud like a child, for she had never learned to suppress a genuine sob. Her slight old frame shook heavily and seemed hardly able to sustain such violent grief.

"What's the matter, baby?" Jeff asked awkwardly. "Why you cryin' like all that?"

"I's jes thinkin'," she said.

"So you the one what's scairt now, hunh?"

"I ain't scairt, Jeff. I's jes thinkin' 'bout leavin' eve'thing like this—eve'thing we been used to. It's right sad-like."

Jeff did not answer, and presently Jennie buried her face again and continued crying.

The sun was almost overhead. It beat down furiously on the dusty wagon path road, on the parched roadside grass, and the tiny battered car. Jeff's hands, gripping the wheel, became wet with perspiration; his forehead sparkled. Jeff's lips parted and his mouth shaped a hideous grimace. His face suggested the face of a man being burned. But the torture passed and his expression softened again.

"You mustn't cry, baby," he said to his wife. "We gotta be strong. We can't break down."

Jennie waited a few seconds, then said, "You reckon we oughta do it, Jeff? You reckon we oughta go 'head an' do it really?"

Jeff's voice choked; his eyes blurred. He was terrified to hear Jennie say the thing that had been in his mind all morning. She had egged him on when he had wanted more than anything in the world to wait, to reconsider, to think things over a little longer. Now *she* was getting cold feet. Actually, there was no need of thinking the question through again. It would only end in making the same painful decision once more. Jeff knew that. There was no need of fooling around longer.

"We jes as well to do like we planned," he said. "They ain't nuthin else for us now—it's the bes' thing."

Jeff thought of the handicaps, the near impossibility, of making another crop with his leg bothering him more and more each week. Then there was always the chance that he would have another stroke, like the one that had made him lame. Another one might kill him. The least it could do would be to leave him helpless. Jeff gasped . . . Lord, Jesus! He could not bear to think of being helpless, like a baby, on Jennie's hands. Frail, blind Jennie.

The little pounding motor of the car worked harder and harder. The puff of steam from the cracked radiator became larger. Jeff realized that they were climbing a little rise. A moment later the road turned abruptly and he looked down upon the face of the river.

"Jeff."

"Hunh?"

"Is that the water I hear?"

"Hm. Tha's it."

"Well, which way you goin' now?"

"Down this-a way," he answered. "The road runs 'long-side o' the water a lil piece."

She waited a while calmly. Then she said, "Drive faster."

"A'right, baby," Jeff said.

The water roared in the bed of the river. It was fifty or sixty feet below the level of the road. Between the road and the water there was a long smooth slope, sharply inclined. The slope was dry; the clay had been hardened by prolonged summer heat. The water below, roaring in a narrow channel, was noisy and wild.

"Jeff."

"Hunh?"

"How far you goin'?"

"Jes a lil piece down the road."

"You ain't scairt is you, Jeff?"

"Nah, baby," he said trembling. "I ain't scairt."

"Remember how we planned it, Jeff. We gotta do it like we said. Brave-like."

"Hm."

Jeff's brain darkened. Things suddenly seemed unreal, like figures in a dream. Thoughts swam in his mind foolishly, hysterically, like little blind fish in a pool within a dense cave. They rushed, crossed one another, jostled, collided, retreated, and rushed again. Jeff soon became dizzy. He shuddered violently and turned to his wife.

"Jennie, I can't do it. I can't." His voice broke pitifully.

She did not appear to be listening. All the grief had gone from her face. She sat erect, her unseeing eyes wide open, strained and frightful. Her glossy black skin had become dull. She seemed as thin and as sharp and bony as a starved bird. Now, having suffered and endured the sadness of tearing herself away from beloved things, she showed no anguish. She was absorbed with her own thoughts, and she didn't even hear Jeff's voice shouting in her ear.

Jeff said nothing more. For an instant there was light in his cavernous brain. That chamber was, for less than a second, peopled by characters he knew and loved. They were simple, healthy creatures, and they behaved in a manner that he could understand. They had quality. But since he had already taken leave of them long ago, the remembrance did not break his heart again. Young Jeff Patton was among them, the Jeff Patton of fifty years ago who went down to New Orleans with a crowd of country boys to the Mardi Gras doings. The gay young crowd—boys with candy-striped shirts and rouged brown girls in noisy silks—was like a picture in his head. Yet it did not make him sad. On that very trip Slim Burns had killed Joe Beasley—the crowd had been broken up. Since then Jeff Patton's world had been the Greenbrier Plantation. If there had been other Mardi Gras carnivals, he had not heard of them. Since then there had been no time; the years had fallen on him like waves. Now he was old, worn out. Another paralytic stroke like the one he had already suffered would put him on his back for keeps. In that condition, with a frail blind woman to look after him, he would be worse off than if he were dead.

Suddenly Jeff's hands became steady. He actually felt brave. He slowed down the motor of the car and carefully pulled off the road. Below, the water of the stream boomed, a soft thunder in the deep channel. Jeff ran the car onto the clay slope, pointed it directly toward the stream, and put his foot heavily on the accelerator. The little car leaped furiously down the steep incline toward the water. The movement was nearly as swift and direct as a fall. The two old black folks, sitting quietly side by side, showed no excitement. In another instant the car hit the water and dropped immediately out of sight.

A little later it lodged in the mud of a shallow place. One wheel of the crushed and upturned little Ford became visible above the rushing water.

George Washington Cable

(1844–1925)

George Washington Cable was born in New Orleans, Louisiana, of New England and Virginia stock. His formal education ended when he was 14 years old, at his father's death. He worked as a clerk in New Orleans, the main support of his mother and sisters. When New Orleans was captured early in the Civil War, he and his family refused to sign the loyalty oath imposed by the Union forces and were made to leave the city. Cable, 19 years old, enlisted as a soldier in the Confederate army and was wounded twice. After the war, he resumed his work as a clerk, in the Cotton Exchange, but soon began writing columns for the New Orleans Picayune. He also began writing the stories of romantic, proud, declining Creole families that were collected in 1879 in Old Creole Days, and that made him famous as a leading member of the "local color" school of regionalist fiction. A perceptive, if sometimes sentimental, observer of traditional Louisiana society, its mixed-blood populations, and its odd marriage of French and American culture, he became an increasingly outspoken opponent of racial injustice. His public campaigns and unsparing arguments against segregation earned him such notoriety in New Orleans that he eventually moved to New England. During the winter before he left the South for good, he made a highly publicized reading tour with his friend Mark Twain. In some ways, Cable's divided attitude toward his native society anticipates tensions found in the major Southern writers of the 20th century. His stories, polemical essays, and two of his strongest novels, The Grandissimes (1880) and John March, Southerner (1894), give him an importance beyond—with the exceptions of Kate Chopin and Joel Chandler Harris—the other local colorists. Unfortunately, his later books, perhaps due to the long physical break with the South, show a falling off of social fervor and dramatic power as he turned more and more to the fashionable escapism of historical romance. His other fiction and essays include Madame

Delphine *(1881)*, The Creoles of Louisiana *(1884)*, Dr. Sevier *(1884)*, The Silent South *(1885)*, Bonaventure: A Prose Pastoral of Acadian Louisiana *(1888)*, The Negro Question *(1890)*, The Busy Man's Bible *(1891)*, Strong Hearts *(1899)*, The Cavalier *(1901)*, Bylow Hill *(1902)*, Kincaid's Battery *(1908)*, Gideon's Band: A Tale of the Mississippi *(1914)*, *and* Lovers of Louisiana *(1918)*. *"Jean-ah Poquelin," from* Old Creole Days, *was first published in* Scribner's Monthly *(May 1875)*.

JEAN-AH POQUELIN

�֎

In the first decade of the present century, when the newly established American Government was the most hateful thing in Louisiana—when the Creoles were still kicking at such vile innovations as the trial by jury, American dances, anti-smuggling laws, and the printing of the Governor's proclamation in English—when the Anglo-American flood that was presently to burst in a crevasse of immigration upon the delta had thus far been felt only as slippery seepage which made the Creole tremble for his footing—there stood, a short distance above what is now Canal Street, and considerably back from the line of villas which fringed the river-bank on Tchoupitoulas Road, an old colonial plantation-house half in ruin.

It stood aloof from civilization, the tracts that had once been its indigo fields given over to their first noxious wildness, and grown up into one of the horridest marshes within a circuit of fifty miles.

The house was of heavy cypress, lifted up on pillars, grim, solid, and spiritless, its massive build a strong reminder of days still earlier, when every man had been his own peace officer and the insurrection of the blacks a daily contingency. Its dark, weather-beaten roof and sides were hoisted up above the jungly plain in a distracted way, like a gigantic ammunition-wagon stuck in the mud and abandoned by some retreating army. Around it was a dense growth of low water willows, with half a hundred sorts of thorny or fetid bushes, savage strangers alike to the "language of flowers" and to the botanist's Greek. They were hung with countless strands of discolored and prickly smilax, and the impassable mud below bristled with *chevaux de frise* of the dwarf palmetto. Two lone forest-trees, dead cypresses, stood in the centre of the marsh, dotted with roosting vultures. The shallow strips of water were hid by myriads of aquatic plants, under whose coarse and spiritless flowers, could one have seen it, was a harbor of reptiles, great and small, to make one shudder to the end of his days.

The house was on a slightly raised spot, the levee of a draining canal. The waters of this canal did not run; they crawled, and were full of big, ravening fish and alligators, that held it against all comers.

Such was the home of old Jean Marie Poquelin, once an opulent indigo planter, standing high in the esteem of his small, proud circle of exclusively male acquaintances in the old city; now a hermit, alike shunned by and shunning all who had ever known him. "The last of his line," said the gossips. His father lies under the floor of the St. Louis Cathedral, with the wife of his youth on one side, and the wife of his old age on the other. Old Jean visits the spot daily. His half-brother—alas! there was a mystery; no one knew what had become of the gentle, young half-brother, more than thirty years his junior, whom once he seemed so fondly to love, but who, seven years ago, had disappeared suddenly, once for all, and left no clew of his fate.

They had seemed to live so happily in each other's love. No father, mother, wife to either, no kindred upon earth. The elder a bold, frank, impetuous, chivalric adventurer; the younger a gentle, studious, book-loving recluse; they lived upon the ancestral estate like mated birds, one always on the wing, the other always in the nest.

There was no trait in Jean Marie Poquelin, said the old gossips, for which he was so well known among his few friends as his apparent fondness for his "little brother." "Jacques said this," and "Jacques said that"; he "would leave this or that, or any thing to Jacques," for Jacques was a scholar, and "Jacques was good," or "wise," or "just," or "far-sighted," as the nature of the case required; and "he should ask Jacques as soon as he got home," since Jacques was never elsewhere to be seen.

It was between the roving character of the one brother, and the bookishness of the other, that the estate fell into decay. Jean Marie, generous gentleman, gambled the slaves away one by one, until none was left, man or woman, but one old African mute.

The indigo-fields and vats of Louisiana had been generally abandoned as unremunerative. Certain enterprising men had substituted the culture of sugar; but while the recluse was too apathetic to take so active a course, the other saw larger, and, at that time, equally respectable profits, first in smuggling, and later in the African slave-trade. What harm could he see in it? The whole people said it was vitally necessary, and to minister to a vital public necessity—good enough, certainly, and so he laid up many a doubloon, that made him none the worse in the public regard.

One day old Jean Marie was about to start upon a voyage that was to be longer, much longer, than any that he had yet made. Jacques had begged him hard for many days not to go, but he laughed him off, and finally said, kissing him:

"*Adieu, 'tit frère.*"

"No," said Jacques, "I shall go with you."

They left the old hulk of a house in the sole care of the African mute, and went away to the Guinea coast together.

Two years after, old Poquelin came home without his vessel. He must have arrived at his house by night. No one saw him come. No one saw "his little brother"; rumor whispered that he, too, had returned, but he had never been seen again.

A dark suspicion fell upon the old slave-trader. No matter that the few kept the many reminded of the tenderness that had ever marked his bearing to the missing man. The many shook their heads. "You know he has a quick and fearful temper"; and "why does he cover his loss with mystery?" "Grief would out with the truth."

"But," said the charitable few, "look in his face; see that expression of true humanity." The many did look in his face, and, as he looked in theirs, he read the silent question: "Where is thy brother Abel?" The few were silenced, his former friends died off, and the name of Jean Marie Poquelin became a symbol of witchery, devilish crime, and hideous nursery fictions.

The man and his house were alike shunned. The snipe and duck hunters forsook the marsh, and the wood-cutters abandoned the canal. Sometimes the hardier boys who ventured out there snake-shooting heard a low thumping of oar-locks on the canal. They would look at each other for a moment half in consternation, half in glee, then rush from their sport in wanton haste to assail with their gibes the unoffending, withered old man who, in rusty attire, sat in the stern of a skiff, rowed homeward by his white-headed African mute.

"O Jean-ah Poquelin! O Jean-ah! Jean-ah Poquelin!"

It was not necessary to utter more than that. No hint of wickedness, deformity, or any physical or moral demerit; merely the name and tone of mockery: "Oh, Jean-ah Poquelin!" and while they tumbled one over another in their needless haste to fly, he would rise carefully from his seat, while the aged mute, with downcast face, went on rowing, and rolling up his brown fist and extending it toward the urchins, would pour forth such an unholy broadside of French imprecation and invective as would all but craze them with delight.

Among both blacks and whites the house was the object of a thousand superstitions. Every midnight, they affirmed, the *feu follet* came out of the marsh and ran in and out of the rooms, flashing from window to window. The story of some lads, whose word in ordinary statements was worthless, was generally credited, that the night they camped in the woods, rather than pass the place after dark, they saw, about sunset, every window blood-red, and on each of the four chimneys an owl sitting, which turned his head three times round, and moaned and laughed with a human voice. There was a bottomless well, everybody professed to know, beneath the sill of the big front door under the rotten veranda; whoever set his foot upon that threshold disappeared forever in the depth below.

What wonder the marsh grew as wild as Africa! Take all the Faubourg Ste. Marie, and half the ancient city, you would not find one graceless dare-devil reckless enough to pass within a hundred yards of the house after nightfall.

The alien races pouring into old New Orleans began to find the few streets named for the Bourbon princes too strait for them. The wheel of fortune, beginning to whirl, threw them off beyond the ancient corporation lines, and sowed civilization and even trade upon the lands of the Graviers and Girods. Fields became roads, roads streets. Everywhere the leveller was peering through his glass, rodsmen were whacking their way through willow-brakes and rose-hedges, and the sweating Irishmen tossed the blue clay up with their long-handled shovels.

"Ha! that is all very well," quoth the Jean-Baptistes, feeling the reproach of an enterprise that asked neither co-operation nor advice of them, "but wait till they come yonder to Jean Poquelin's marsh; ha! ha! ha!" The supposed predicament so delighted them, that they put on a mock terror and whirled about in an assumed stampede, then caught their clasped hands between their knees in excess of mirth, and laughed till the tears ran; for whether the street-makers mired in the marsh, or contrived to cut through old "Jean-ah's" property, either event would be joyful. Meantime a line of tiny rods, with bits of white paper in their split tops, gradually extended its way straight through the haunted ground, and across the canal diagonally.

"We shall fill that ditch," said the men in mud-boots, and

brushed close along the chained and padlocked gate of the haunted mansion. Ah, Jean-ah Poquelin, those were not Creole boys, to be stampeded with a little hard swearing.

He went to the Governor. That official scanned the odd figure with no slight interest. Jean Poquelin was of short, broad frame, with a bronzed leonine face. His brow was ample and deeply furrowed. His eye, large and black, was bold and open like that of a war-horse, and his jaws shut together with the firmness of iron. He was dressed in a suit of Attakapas cottonade, and his shirt unbuttoned and thrown back from the throat and bosom, sailorwise, showed a herculean breast, hard and grizzled. There was no fierceness or defiance in his look, no harsh ungentleness, no symptom of his unlawful life or violent temper; but rather a peaceful and peaceable fearlessness. Across the whole face, not marked in one or another feature, but as it were laid softly upon the countenance like an almost imperceptible veil, was the imprint of some great grief. A careless eye might easily overlook it, but, once seen, there it hung—faint, but unmistakable.

The Governor bowed.

"Parlez-vous français?" asked the figure.

"I would rather talk English, if you can do so," said the Governor.

"My name, Jean Poquelin."

"How can I serve you, Mr. Poquelin?"

"My 'ouse is yond'; *dans le marais là-bas.*"

The Governor bowed.

"Dat *marais* billong to me."

"Yes, sir."

"To me; Jean Poquelin; I hown 'im meself."

"Well, sir?"

"He don't billong to you; I get him from me father."

"That is perfectly true, Mr. Poquelin, as far as I am aware."

"You want to make strit pass yond'?"

"I do not know, sir; it is quite probable; but the city will indemnify you for any loss you may suffer—you will get paid, you understand."

"Strit can't pass dare."

"You will have to see the municipal authorities about that, Mr. Poquelin."

A bitter smile came upon the old man's face.

"Pardon, Monsieur, you is not *le Gouverneur?"*

"Yes."

"Mais, yes. You har *le Gouverneur*—yes. Veh-well. I come to you. I tell you, strit can't pass at me 'ouse."

"But you will have to see—"

"I come to you. You is *le Gouverneur*. I know not the new laws. I ham a Fr-r-rench-a-man! Fr-rench-a-man have something *aller au contraire*—he come at his *Gouverneur*. I come at you. If me not had been bought from me king like *bossals* in the hold time, ze king gof—France would-a-show *Monsieur le Gouverneur* to take care his men to make strit in right places. *Mais,* I know; we billong to *Monsieur le Président.* I want you do somesin for me, eh?"

"What is it?" asked the patient Governor.

"I want you tell *Monsieur le Président,* strit—can't—pass—at—me—'ouse."

"Have a chair, Mr. Poquelin"; but the old man did not stir. The Governor took a quill and wrote a line to a city official, introducing Mr. Poquelin, and asking for him every possible courtesy. He handed it to him, instructing him where to present it.

"Mr. Poquelin," he said, with a conciliatory smile, "tell me, is it your house that our Creole citizens tell such odd stories about?"

The old man glared sternly upon the speaker, and with immovable features said:

"You don't see me trade some Guinea nigga'?"

"Oh, no."

"You don't see me make some smugglin'?"

"No, sir; not at all."

"But, I am Jean Marie Poquelin. I mine me hown bizniss. Dat all right? Adieu."

He put his hat on and withdrew. By and by he stood, letter in hand, before the person to whom it was addressed. This person employed an interpreter.

"He says," said the interpreter to the officer, "he come to make you the fair warning how you muz not make the street pas' at his 'ouse."

The officer remarked that "such impudence was refreshing"; but the experienced interpreter translated freely.

"He says: 'Why you don't want?' " said the interpreter.

The old slave-trader answered at some length.

"He says," said the interpreter, again turning to the officer, "the marass is a too unhealth' for peopl' to live."

"But we expect to drain his old marsh; it's not going to be a marsh."

"Il dit"—The interpreter explained in French.

The old man answered tersely.

"He says the canal is a private," said the interpreter.

"Oh! *that* old ditch; that's to be filled up. Tell the old man we're going to fix him up nicely."

Translation being duly made, the man in power was amused to
see a thunder-cloud gathering on the old man's face.

"Tell him," he added, "by the time we finish, there'll not be a
ghost left in his shanty."

The interpreter began to translate, but—

"*J' comprends, J' comprends,*" said the old man, with an impatient gesture, and burst forth, pouring curses upon the United
States, the President, the Territory of Orleans, Congress, the Governor and all his subordinates, striding out of the apartment as he
cursed, while the object of his maledictions roared with merriment
and rammed the floor with his foot.

"Why, it will make his old place worth ten dollars to one," said
the official to the interpreter.

" 'Tis not for de worse of de property," said the interpreter.

"I should guess not," said the other, whittling his chair,—"seems
to me as if some of these old Creoles would liever live in a crawfish
hole than to have a neighbor."

"You know what make old Jean Poquelin make like that? I will
tell you. You know—"

The interpreter was rolling a cigarette, and paused to light his
tinder; then, as the smoke poured in a thick double stream from
his nostrils, he said, in a solemn whisper:

"He is a witch."

"Ho, ho, ho!" laughed the other.

"You don't believe it? What you want to bet?" cried the interpreter, jerking himself half up and thrusting out one arm while he
bared it of its coat-sleeve with the hand of the other. "What you
want to bet?"

"How do you know?" asked the official.

"Dass what I goin' to tell you. You know, one evening I was
shooting some *grosbec*. I killed three; but I had trouble to find
them, it was becoming so dark. When I have them I start' to come
home; then I got to pas' at Jean Poquelin's house."

"Ho, ho, ho!" laughed the other, throwing his leg over the arm
of his chair.

"Wait," said the interpreter. "I come along slow, not making
some noises; still, still—"

"And scared," said the smiling one.

"*Mais,* wait. I get all pas' the 'ouse. 'Ah!' I say; 'all right!' Then
I see two thing' before! Hah! I get as cold and humide, and shake
like a leaf. You think it was nothing? There I see, so plain as
can be (though it was making nearly dark), I see Jean—Marie—
Po-que-lin walkin' right in front, and right there beside of him was
something like a man—but not a man—white like paint!—I dropp'

on the grass from scared—they pass'; so sure as I live 'twas the ghos' of Jacques Poquelin, his brother!"

"Pooh!" said the listener.

"I'll put my han' in the fire," said the interpreter.

"But did you never think," asked the other, "that that might be Jack Poquelin, as you call him, alive and well, and for some cause hid away by his brother?"

"But there har' no cause!" said the other, and the entrance of third parties changed the subject.

Some months passed and the street was opened. A canal was first dug through the marsh, the small one which passed so close to Jean Poquelin's house was filled, and the street, or rather a sunny road, just touched a corner of the old mansion's dooryard. The morass ran dry. Its venomous denizens slipped away through the bulrushes; the cattle roaming freely upon its hardened surface trampled the superabundant undergrowth. The bellowing frogs croaked to westward. Lilies and the flower-de-luce sprang up in the place of reeds; smilax and poison-oak gave way to the purple-plumed iron-weed and pink spiderwort; the bindweeds ran every-where, blooming as they ran, and on one of the dead cypresses a giant creeper hung its green burden of foliage and lifted its scarlet trumpets. Sparrows and red-birds flitted through the bushes, and dewberries grew ripe beneath. Over all these came a sweet, dry smell of salubrity which the place had not known since the sedi-ments of the Mississippi first lifted it from the sea.

But its owner did not build. Over the willow-brakes, and down the vista of the open street, bright new houses, some singly, some by ranks, were prying in upon the old man's privacy. They even settled down toward his southern side. First a wood-cutter's hut or two, then a market gardener's shanty, then a painted cottage, and all at once the faubourg had flanked and half surrounded him and his dried-up marsh.

Ah! then the common people began to hate him. "The old tyrant!" "You don't mean an old *tyrant?*" "Well, then, why don't he build when the public need demands it? What does he live in that unneighborly way for?" "The old pirate!" "The old kidnap-per!" How easily even the most ultra Louisianians put on the imported virtues of the North when they could be brought to bear against the hermit. "There he goes, with the boys after him! Ah! ha! ha! Jean-ah Poquelin! Ah! Jean-ah! Aha! aha! Jean-ah Marie! Jean-ah Poquelin! The old villain!" How merrily the swarming Américains echo the spirit of persecution! "The old fraud," they say—"pretends to live in a haunted house, does he? We'll tar and feather him some day. Guess we can fix him."

He cannot be rowed home along the old canal now; he walks.
He has broken sadly of late, and the street urchins are ever at his
heels. It is like the days when they cried: "Go up, thou bald-head,"
and the old man now and then turns and delivers ineffectual curses.

To the Creoles—to the incoming lower class of superstitious
Germans, Irish, Sicilians, and others—he became an omen and
embodiment of public and private ill-fortune. Upon him all the
vagaries of their superstitions gathered and grew. If a house caught
fire, it was imputed to his machinations. Did a woman go off in a
fit, he had bewitched her. Did a child stray off for an hour, the
mother shivered with the apprehension that Jean Poquelin had
offered him to strange gods. The house was the subject of every
bad boy's invention who loved to contrive ghostly lies. "As long
as that house stands we shall have bad luck. Do you not see our
pease and beans dying, our cabbages and lettuce going to seed and
our gardens turning to dust, while every day you can see it raining
in the woods? The rain will never pass old Poquelin's house. He
keeps a fetich. He has conjured the whole Faubourg St. Marie.
And why, the old wretch? Simply because our playful and innocent
children call after him as he passes."

A "Building and Improvement Company," which had not yet
got its charter, "but was going to," and which had not, indeed,
any tangible capital yet, but "was going to have some," joined the
"Jean-ah Poquelin" war. The haunted property would be such a
capital site for a market-house! They sent a deputation to the old
mansion to ask its occupant to sell. The deputation never got
beyond the chained gate and a very barren interview with the
African mute. The President of the Board was then empowered
(for he had studied French in Pennsylvania and was considered
qualified) to call and persuade M. Poquelin to subscribe to the
company's stock; but—

"Fact is, gentlemen," he said at the next meeting, "it would
take us at least twelve months to make Mr. Pokaleen understand
the rather original features of our system, and he wouldn't subscribe when we'd done; besides, the only way to see him is to stop
him on the street."

There was a great laugh from the Board; they couldn't help it.
"Better meet a bear robbed of her whelps," said one.

"You're mistaken as to that," said the President. "I did meet
him, and stopped him, and found him quite polite. But I could
get no satisfaction from him; the fellow wouldn't talk in French,
and when I spoke in English he hoisted his old shoulders up, and
gave the same answer to every thing I said."

"And that was—?" asked one or two, impatient of the pause.

"That it 'don't worse w'ile?' "

One of the Board said: "Mr. President, this market-house project, as I take it, is not altogether a selfish one; the community is to be benefited by it. We may feel that we are working in the public interest [the Board smiled knowingly], if we employ all possible means to oust this old nuisance from among us. You may know that at the time the street was cut through, this old Poquelann did all he could to prevent it. It was owing to a certain connection which I had with that affair that I heard a ghost story [smiles, followed by a sudden dignified check]—ghost story, which, of course, I am not going to relate; but I *may* say that my profound conviction, arising from a prolonged study of that story, is, that this old villain, John Poquelann, has his brother locked up in that old house. Now, if this is so, and we can fix it on him, I merely *suggest* that we can make the matter highly useful. I don't know," he added, beginning to sit down, "but that it is an action we owe to the community—hem!"

"How do you propose to handle the subject?" asked the President.

"I was thinking," said the speaker, "that, as a Board of Directors, it would be unadvisable for us to authorize any action involving trespass; but if you, for instance, Mr. President, should, as it were, for mere curiosity, *request* some one, as, for instance, our excellent Secretary, simply as a personal favor, to look into the matter—this is merely a suggestion."

The Secretary smiled sufficiently to be understood that, while he certainly did not consider such preposterous service a part of his duties as secretary, he might, notwithstanding, accede to the President's request; and the Board adjourned.

Little White, as the Secretary was called, was a mild, kind-hearted little man, who, nevertheless, had no fear of any thing, unless it was the fear of being unkind.

"I tell you frankly," he privately said to the President, "I go into this purely for reasons of my own."

The next day, a little after nightfall, one might have descried this little man slipping along the rear fence of the Poquelin place, preparatory to vaulting over into the rank, grass-grown yard, and bearing himself altogether more after the manner of a collector of rare chickens than according to the usage of secretaries.

The picture presented to his eye was not calculated to enliven his mind. The old mansion stood out against the western sky, black and silent. One long, lurid pencil-stroke along a sky of slate was all that was left of daylight. No sign of life was apparent; no light at any window, unless it might have been on the side of the house hidden from view. No owls were on the chimneys, no dogs were in the yard.

He entered the place, and ventured up behind a small cabin which stood apart from the house. Through one of its many crannies he easily detected the African mute crouched before a flickering pine-knot, his head on his knees, fast asleep.

He concluded to enter the mansion, and, with that view, stood and scanned it. The broad rear steps of the veranda would not serve him; he might meet some one midway. He was measuring, with his eye, the proportions of one of the pillars which supported it, and estimating the practicability of climbing it, when he heard a footstep. Some one dragged a chair out toward the railing, then seemed to change his mind and began to pace the veranda, his footfalls resounding on the dry boards with singular loudness. Little White drew a step backward, got the figure between himself and the sky, and at once recognized the short, broad-shouldered form of old Jean Poquelin.

He sat down upon a billet of wood, and, to escape the stings of a whining cloud of mosquitoes, shrouded his face and neck in his handkerchief, leaving his eyes uncovered.

He had sat there but a moment when he noticed a strange, sickening odor, faint, as if coming from a distance, but loathsome and horrid.

Whence could it come? Not from the cabin; not from the marsh, for it was as dry as powder. It was not in the air; it seemed to come from the ground.

Rising up, he noticed, for the first time, a few steps before him a narrow footpath leading toward the house. He glanced down it—ha! right there was some one coming—ghostly white!

Quick as thought, and as noiselessly, he lay down at full length against the cabin. It was bold strategy, and yet, there was no denying it, little White felt that he was frightened. "It is not a ghost," he said to himself. "I *know* it cannot be a ghost"; but the perspiration burst out at every pore, and the air seemed to thicken with heat. "It is a living man," he said in his thoughts. "I hear his footstep, and I hear old Poquelin's footsteps, too, separately, over on the veranda. I am not discovered; the thing has passed; there is that odor again; what a smell of death! Is it coming back? Yes. It stops at the door of the cabin. Is it peering in at the sleeping mute? It moves away. It is in the path again. Now it is gone." He shuddered. "Now, if I dare venture, the mystery is solved." He rose cautiously, close against the cabin, and peered along the path.

The figure of a man, a presence if not a body—but whether clad in some white stuff or naked, the darkness would not allow him to determine—had turned, and now, with a seeming painful gait, moved slowly from him. "Great Heaven! can it be that the dead do walk?" He withdrew again the hands which had gone to his eyes. The dreadful object passed between two pillars and under the house. He listened. There was a faint sound as of feet upon a staircase; then all was still except the measured tread of Jean Poquelin walking on the veranda, and the heavy respirations of the mute slumbering in the cabin.

The little Secretary was about to retreat; but as he looked once more toward the haunted house a dim light appeared in the crack of a closed window, and presently old Jean Poquelin came, dragging his chair, and sat down close against the shining cranny. He spoke in a low, tender tone in the French tongue, making some inquiry. An answer came from within. Was it the voice of a human? So unnatural was it—so hollow, so discordant, so unearthly—that the stealthy listener shuddered again from head to foot; and when something stirred in some bushes near by—though it may have been nothing more than a rat—and came scuttling through the grass, the little Secretary actually turned and fled. As he left the enclosure he moved with bolder leisure through the bushes; yet now and then he spoke aloud: "Oh, oh! I see, I understand!" and shut his eyes in his hands.

How strange that henceforth little White was the champion of Jean Poquelin! In season and out of season—wherever a word was uttered against him—the Secretary, with a quiet, aggressive force that instantly arrested gossip, demanded upon what authority the statement or conjecture was made; but as he did not condescend to explain his own remarkable attitude, it was not long before the disrelish and suspicion which had followed Jean Poquelin so many years fell also upon him.

It was only the next evening but one after his adventure that he made himself a source of sullen amazement to one hundred and fifty boys, by ordering them to desist from their wanton hallooing. Old Jean Poquelin, standing and shaking his cane, rolling out his long-drawn maledictions, paused and stared, then gave the Secretary a courteous bow and started on. The boys, save one, from pure astonishment, ceased; but a ruffianly little Irish lad, more daring than any had yet been, threw a big hurtling clod, that struck old Poquelin between the shoulders and burst like a shell. The enraged old man wheeled with uplifted staff to give chase to the scampering vagabond; and—he may have tripped, or he may not, but he fell full length. Little White hastened to help him up, but he waved him off with a fierce imprecation and staggering to his feet resumed his way homeward. His lips were reddened with blood.

Little White was on his way to the meeting of the Board. He would have given all he dared spend to have staid away, for he felt both too fierce and too tremulous to brook the criticisms that were likely to be made.

"I can't help it, gentlemen; I can't help you to make a case against the old man, and I'm not going to."

"We did not expect this disappointment, Mr. White."

"I can't help that, sir. No, sir; you had better not appoint any more investigations. Somebody'll investigate himself into trouble. No, sir; it isn't a threat, it is only my advice, but I warn you that whoever takes the task in hand will rue it to his dying day—which may be hastened, too."

The President expressed himself surprised.

"I don't care a rush," answered little White, wildly and foolishly. "I don't care a rush if you are, sir. No, my nerves are not disordered; my head's as clear as a bell. No, I'm *not* excited."

A Director remarked that the Secretary looked as though he had waked from a nightmare.

"Well, sir, if you want to know the fact, I have; and if you choose to cultivate old Poquelin's society you can have one, too."

"White," called a facetious member, but White did not notice. "White," he called again.

"What?" demanded White, with a scowl.

"Did you see the ghost?"

"Yes, sir; I did," cried White, hitting the table, and handing the President a paper which brought the Board to other business.

The story got among the gossips that somebody (they were afraid to say little White) had been to the Poquelin mansion by night and beheld something appalling. The rumor was but a shadow of the truth, magnified and distorted as is the manner of shadows. He had seen skeletons walking, and had barely escaped the clutches of one by making the sign of the cross.

Some madcap boys with an appetite for the horrible plucked up courage to venture through the dried marsh by the cattle-path, and come before the house at a spectral hour when the air was full of bats. Something which they but half saw—half a sight was enough—sent them tearing back through the willow-brakes and acacia bushes to their homes, where they fairly dropped down, and cried:

"Was it white?" "No—yes—nearly so—we can't tell—but we

saw it." And one could hardly doubt, to look at their ashen faces, that they had, whatever it was.

"If that old rascal lived in the country we come from," said certain Américains, "he'd have been tarred and feathered before now, wouldn't he, Sanders?"

"Well, now he just would."

"And we'd have rid him on a rail, wouldn't we?"

"That's what I allow."

"Tell you what you *could* do." They were talking to some rollicking Creoles who had assumed an absolute necessity for doing *something*. "What is it you call this thing where an old man marries a young girl, and you come out with horns and—"

"*Charivari?*" asked the Creoles.

"Yes, that's it. Why don't you shivaree him?" Felicitous suggestion.

Little White, with his wife beside him, was sitting on their door-steps on the sidewalk, as Creole custom had taught them, looking toward the sunset. They had moved into the lately-opened street. The view was not attractive on the score of beauty. The houses were small and scattered, and across the flat commons, spite of the lofty tangle of weeds and bushes, and spite of the thickets of acacia, they needs must see the dismal old Poquelin mansion, tilted awry and shutting out the declining sun. The moon, white and slender, was hanging the tip of its horn over one of the chimneys.

"And you say," said the Secretary, "the old black man has been going by here alone? Patty, suppose old Poquelin should be concocting some mischief; he don't lack provocation; the way that clod hit him the other day was enough to have killed him. Why, Patty, he dropped as quick as *that!* No wonder you haven't seen him. I wonder if they haven't heard something about him up at the drug-store. Suppose I go and see."

"Do," said his wife.

She sat alone for half an hour, watching that sudden going out of the day peculiar to the latitude.

"That moon is ghost enough for one house," she said, as her husband returned. "It has gone right down the chimney."

"Patty," said little White, "the drug-clerk says the boys are going to shivaree old Poquelin tonight. I'm going to try to stop it."

"Why, White," said his wife, "you'd better not. You'll get hurt."

"No, I'll not."

"Yes, you will."

"I'm going to sit out here until they come along. They're compelled to pass right by here."

"Why, White, it may be midnight before they start; you're not going to sit out here till then."

"Yes, I am."

"Well, you're very foolish," said Mrs. White in an undertone, looking anxious, and tapping one of the steps with her foot.

They sat a very long time talking over little family matters.

"What's that?" at last said Mrs. White.

"That's the nine-o'clock gun," said White, and they relapsed into a long-sustained, drowsy silence.

"Patty, you'd better go in and go to bed," said he at last.

"I'm not sleepy."

"Well, you're very foolish," quietly remarked little White, and again silence fell upon them.

"Patty, suppose I walk out to the old house and see if I can find out any thing."

"Suppose," said she, "you don't do any such—listen!"

Down the street arose a great hubbub. Dogs and boys were howling and barking; men were laughing, shouting, groaning, and blowing horns, whooping, and clanking cow-bells, whinnying, and howling, and rattling pots and pans.

"They are coming this way," said little White. "You had better go into the house, Patty."

"So had you."

"No. I'm going to see if I can't stop them."

"Why, White!"

"I'll be back in a minute," said White, and went toward the noise.

In a few moments the little Secretary met the mob. The pen hesitates on the word, for there is a respectable difference, measurable only on the scale of the half century, between a mob and a *charivari*. Little White lifted his ineffectual voice. He faced the head of the disorderly column, and cast himself about as if he were made of wood and moved by the jerk of a string. He rushed to one who seemed, from the size and clatter of his tin pan, to be a leader. *"Stop these fellows, Bienvenu, stop them just a minute, till I tell them something."* Bienvenu turned and brandished his instruments of discord in an imploring way to the crowd. They slackened their pace, two or three hushed their horns and joined the prayer of little White and Bienvenu for silence. The throng halted. The hush was delicious.

"Bienvenu," said little White, "don't shivaree old Poquelin to-night; he's—"

"My fwang," said the swaying Bienvenu, "who tail you I goin' to chahivahi somebody, eh? You sink bickause I make a little playfool wiz zis tin pan zat I am *dhonk?*"

"Oh, no, Bienvenu, old fellow, you're all right. I was afraid you might not know that old Poquelin was sick, you know, but you're not going there, are you?"

"My fwang, I vay soy to tail you zat you ah dhonk as de dev'. I am *shem* of you. I ham ze servan' of ze *publique.* Zese *citoyens* goin' to wickwest Jean Poquelin to give to the Ursuline' two hondred fifty dolla'—"

"Hé quoi!" cried a listener, *"Cinq cent piastres, oui!"*

"Oui!" said Bienvenu, "and if he wiffuse we make him some lit' *musique*; ta-ra-ta!" He hoisted a merry hand and foot, then frowning, added: "Old Poquelin got no bizniz dhink s'much w'isky."

"But, gentlemen," said little White, around whom a circle had gathered, "the old man is very sick."

"My faith!" cried a tiny Creole, "we did not make him to be sick. W'en we have say we going make *le charivari,* do you want that we hall tell a lie? My faith! 'sfools!"

"But you can shivaree somebody else," said desperate little White.

"Oui!" cried Bienvenu, *"et chahivahi* Jean-ah Poquelin tomo'w!"

"Let us go to Madame Schneider!" cried two or three, and amid huzzas and confused cries, among which was heard a stentorian Celtic call for drinks, the crowd again began to move.

"Cent piastres pour l'hôpital de charité!"

"Hurrah!"

"One hongred dolla' for Charity Hospital!"

"Hurrah!"

"Whang!" went a tin pan, the crowd yelled, and Pandemonium gaped again. They were off at a right angle.

Nodding, Mrs. White looked at the mantle-clock.

"Well, if it isn't away after midnight."

The hideous noise down street was passing beyond earshot. She raised a sash and listened. For a moment there was silence. Some one came to the door.

"Is that you, White?"

"Yes." He entered. "I succeeded, Patty."

"Did you?" said Patty, joyfully.

"Yes. They've gone down to shivaree the old Dutchwoman who married her step-daughter's sweetheart. They say she has got to pay a hundred dollars to the hospital before they stop."

The couple retired, and Mrs. White slumbered. She was awakened by her husband snapping the lid of his watch.

"What time?" she asked.

"Half-past three. Patty, I haven't slept a wink. Those fellows are out yet. Don't you hear them?"

"Why, White, they're coming this way!"

"I know they are," said White, sliding out of bed and drawing on his clothes, "and they're coming fast. You'd better go away from that window, Patty! My! what a clatter!"

"Here they are," said Mrs. White, but her husband was gone. Two or three hundred men and boys pass the place at a rapid walk straight down the broad, new street, toward the hated house of ghosts. The din was terrific. She saw little White at the head of the rabble brandishing his arms and trying in vain to make himself heard; but they only shook their heads, laughing and hooting the louder, and so passed, bearing him on before them.

Swiftly they pass out from among the houses, away from the dim oil lamps of the street, out into the broad starlit commons, and enter the willowy jungles of the haunted ground. Some hearts fail and their owners lag behind and turn back, suddenly remembering how near morning it is. But the most part push on, tearing the air with their clamor.

Down ahead of them in the long, thicket-darkened way there is—singularly enough—a faint, dancing light. It must be very near the old house; it is. It has stopped now. It is a lantern, and is under a well-known sapling which has grown up on the wayside since the canal was filled. Now it swings mysteriously to and fro. A goodly number of the more ghost-fearing give up the sport; but a full hundred move forward at a run, doubling their devilish howling and banging.

Yes; it is a lantern, and there are two persons under the tree. The crowd draws near—drops into a walk; one of the two is the old African mute; he lifts the lantern up so that it shines on the other; the crowd recoils; there is a hush of all clangor, and all at once, with a cry of mingled fright and horror from every throat, the whole throng rushes back, dropping every thing, sweeping past little White and hurrying on, never stopping until the jungle is left behind, and then to find that not one in ten has seen the cause of the stampede, and not one of the tenth is certain what it was.

There is one huge fellow among them who looks capable of any villany. He finds something to mount on, and, in the Creole *patois,* calls a general halt. Bienvenu sinks down, and, vainly trying to recline gracefully, resigns the leadership. The herd gather round the speaker; he assures them that they have been outraged. Their right peaceably to traverse the public streets has been trampled upon. Shall such encroachments be endured? It is now daybreak. Let them go now by the open light of day and force a free passage of the public highway!

A scattering consent was the response, and the crowd, thinned now and drowsy, straggled quietly down toward the old house. Some drifted ahead, others sauntered behind, but every one, as he again neared the tree, came to a stand-still. Little White sat upon a bank of turf on the opposite side of the way looking very stern and sad. To each newcomer he put the same question:

"Did you come here to go to old Poquelin's?"

"Yes."

"He's dead." And if the shocked hearer started away he would say: "Don't go away."

"Why not?"

"I want you to go to the funeral presently."

If some Louisianian, too loyal to dear France or Spain to understand English, looked bewildered, some one would interpret for him; and presently they went. Little White led the van, the crowd trooping after him down the middle of the way. The gate, that had never been seen before unchained, was open. Stern little White stopped a short distance from it; the rabble stopped behind him. Something was moving out from under the veranda. The many whisperers stretched upward to see. The African mute came very slowly toward the gate, leading by a cord in the nose a small brown bull, which was harnessed to a rude cart. On the flat body of the cart, under a black cloth, were seen the outlines of a long box.

"Hats off, gentlemen," said little White, as the box came in view, and the crowd silently uncovered.

"Gentlemen," said little White, "here come the last remains of Jean Marie Poquelin, a better man, I'm afraid, with all his sins,— yes, a better—a kinder man to his blood—a man of more self-forgetful goodness—than all of you put together will ever dare to be."

There was a profound hush as the vehicle came creaking through the gate; but when it turned away from them toward the forest, those in front started suddenly. There was a backward rush, then all stood still again staring one way; for there, behind the bier, with eyes cast down and labored step, walked the living remains— all that was left—of little Jacques Poquelin, the long-hidden brother—a leper, as white as snow.

Dumb with horror, the cringing crowd gazed upon the walking death. They watched, in silent awe, the slow *cortége* creep down the long, straight road and lessen on the view, until by and by it stopped where a wild, unfrequented path branched off into the undergrowth toward the rear of the ancient city.

"They are going to the *Terre aux Lépreux*," said one in the crowd. The rest watched them in silence.

The little bull was set free; the mute, with the strength of an ape, lifted the long box to his shoulder. For a moment more the mute and the leper stood in sight, while the former adjusted his heavy burden; then, without one backward glance upon the unkind human world, turning their faces toward the ridge in the depths of the swamp known as the Leper's Land, they stepped into the jungle, disappeared, and were never seen again.

Charles Waddell Chesnutt

(1858–1932)

America's first major black writer of fiction, Chesnutt was born in Cleveland, Ohio, two years after his free-black parents left Fayetteville, North Carolina, to escape the increasing tensions of the South just before the Civil War. When he was eight years old, he returned with his parents to Fayetteville, where his father opened a grocery store. Chesnutt attended a school established by the Freedman's Bureau, and eventually became a teacher himself, in Charlotte and in Fayetteville. Doubtful about his future in the post-Reconstruction South, he moved with his wife and children to Cleveland in 1884. There he worked as a court reporter, passed his bar exams, and started a legal stenography firm that made him a prosperous and well-known Cleveland citizen. His first important writing was a series of dialect stories narrated by ex-slave Uncle Julius, a more modern and more racially conscious version of Joel Chandler Harris's Uncle Remus. In other stories, Chesnutt turned away from black folklore and moved into the contemporary world of mixed-blood blacks, in both the North and the South, where miscegenation and life on the color line imposed permanent and often tragic difficulties. His two collections of stories were followed by three novels that dealt with the post-Civil War South and what Chesnutt perceived as the almost hopeless decline of black status in the early days of segregation. These were not as successful as his dialect stories, and he published little in the last decades of his life. Works by Chesnutt include The Conjure Woman (1899), Frederick Douglass (1899), The Wife of His Youth and Other Stories of the Color Line (1899), The House Behind the Cedars (1900), The Marrow of Tradition (1901), and The Colonel's Dream (1905). "The Web of Circumstance" first appeared in The Wife of His Youth and Other Stories of the Color Line.

THE WEB OF CIRCUMSTANCE

❀

1

Within a low clapboarded hut, with an open front, a forge was glowing. In front a blacksmith was shoeing a horse, a sleek, well-kept animal with the signs of good blood and breeding. A young mulatto stood by and handed the blacksmith such tools as he needed from time to time. A group of negroes were sitting around, some in the shadow of the shop, one in the full glare of the sunlight. A gentleman was seated in a buggy a few yards away, in the shade of a spreading elm. The horse had loosened a shoe, and Colonel Thornton, who was a lover of fine horseflesh, and careful of it, had stopped at Ben Davis's blacksmith shop, as soon as he discovered the loose shoe, to have it fastened on.

"All right, Kunnel," the blacksmith called out. "Tom," he said, addressing the young man, "he'p me hitch up."

Colonel Thornton alighted from the buggy, looked at the shoe, signified his approval of the job, and stood looking on while the blacksmith and his assistant harnessed the horse to the buggy.

"Dat's a mighty fine whip yer got dere, Kunnel," said Ben, while the young man was tightening the straps of the harness on the opposite side of the horse. "I wush I had one like it. Where kin yer git dem whips?"

"My brother brought me this from New York," said the Colonel. "You can't buy them down here."

The whip in question was a handsome one. The handle was wrapped with interlacing threads of variegated colors, forming an elaborate pattern, the lash being dark green. An octagonal ornament of glass was set in the end of the handle. "It cert'n'y is fine," said Ben; "I wish I had one like it." He looked at the whip longingly as Colonel Thornton drove away.

" 'Pears ter me Ben gittin' mighty blooded," said one of the bystanders, "drivin' a hoss an' buggy, an' wantin' a whip like Colonel Thornton's."

"What's de reason I can't hab a hoss an' buggy an' a whip like Kunnel Tho'nton's, ef I pay fer 'em?" asked Ben. "We colored folks never had no chance ter git nothin' befo' de wah, but ef eve'y nigger in dis town had a tuck keer er his money sence de wah, like

56

I has, an' bought as much lan' as I has, de niggers might 'a' got half de lan' by dis time," he went on, giving a finishing blow to a horseshoe, and throwing it on the ground to cool.

Carried away by his own eloquence, he did not notice the approach of two white men who came up the street from behind him.

"An' ef you niggers," he continued, raking the coals together over a fresh bar of iron, "would stop wastin' yo' money on 'scursions to put money in w'ite folks' pockets, an' stop buildin' fine chu'ches, an' buil' houses fer yo'se'ves, you'd git along much faster."

"You're talkin' sense, Ben," said one of the white men. "Yo'r people will never be respected till they've got property."

The conversation took another turn. The white men transacted their business and went away. The whistle of a neighboring steam sawmill blew a raucous blast for the hour of noon, and the loafers shuffled away in different directions.

"You kin go ter dinner, Tom," said the blacksmith. "An' stop at de gate w'en yer go by my house, and tell Nancy I'll be dere in 'bout twenty minutes. I got ter finish dis yer plough p'int fus'."

The young man walked away. One would have supposed, from the rapidity with which he walked, that he was very hungry. A quarter of an hour later the blacksmith dropped his hammer, pulled off his leather apron, shut the front door of the shop, and went home to dinner. He came into the house out of the fervent heat, and, throwing off his straw hat, wiped his brow vigorously with a red cotton handkerchief.

"Dem collards smells good," he said, sniffing the odor that came in through the kitchen door, as his good-looking yellow wife opened it to enter the room where he was. "I've got a monst'us good appetite ter-day. I feels good, too. I paid Majah Ransom de intrus' on de mortgage dis mawnin' an' a hund'ed dollahs besides, an' I spec's ter hab de balance ready by de fust of nex' Jiniwary; an' den we won't owe nobody a cent. I tell yer dere ain' nothin' like propputy ter make a pusson feel like a man. But w'at's de matter wid yer, Nancy? Is sump'n' skeered yer?"

The woman did seem excited and ill at ease. There was a heaving of the full bust, a quickened breathing, that betokened suppressed excitement.

"I—I—jes' seen a rattlesnake out in de gyahden," she stammered.

The blacksmith ran to the door. "Which way? Whar wuz he?" he cried.

He heard a rustling in the bushes at one side of the garden, and the sound of a breaking twig, and, seizing a hoe which stood by the door, he sprang toward the point from which the sound came.

"No, no," said the woman hurriedly, "it wuz over here," and she directed her husband's attention to the other side of the garden.

The blacksmith, with the uplifted hoe, its sharp blade gleaming in the sunlight, peered cautiously among the collards and tomato plants, listening all the while for the ominous rattle, but found nothing.

"I reckon he's got away," he said, as he set the hoe up again by the door. "Whar's de chillen?" he asked with some anxiety. "Is dey playin' in de woods?"

"No," answered his wife, "dey've gone ter de spring."

The spring was on the opposite side of the garden from that on which the snake was said to have been seen, so the blacksmith sat down and fanned himself with a palm-leaf fan until the dinner was served.

"Yer ain't quite on time ter-day, Nancy," he said, glancing up at the clock on the mantel, after the edge of his appetite had been taken off. "Got ter make time ef yer wanter make money. Didn't Tom tell yer I'd be heah in twenty minutes?"

"No," she said; "I seen him goin' pas'; he didn' say nothin'."

"I dunno w'at's de matter wid dat boy," mused the blacksmith over his apple dumpling. "He's gittin' mighty keerless heah lately; mus' hab sump'n' on 'is min',—some gal, I reckon."

The children had come in while he was speaking,—a slender, shapely boy, yellow like his mother, a girl several years younger, dark like her father: both bright-looking children and neatly dressed.

"I seen cousin Tom down by de spring," said the little girl, as she lifted off the pail of water that had been balanced on her head. "He come out er de woods jest ez we wuz fillin' our buckets."

"Yas," insisted the blacksmith, "he's got some gal on his min'."

2

The case of the State of North Carolina *vs*. Ben Davis was called. The accused was led into court, and took his seat in the prisoner's dock.

"Prisoner at the bar, stand up."

The prisoner, pale and anxious, stood up. The clerk read the indictment, in which it was charged that the defendant by force and arms had entered the barn of one G. W. Thornton, and feloniously taken therefrom one whip, of the value of fifteen dollars.

"Are you guilty or not guilty?" asked the judge.

"Not guilty, yo' Honah; not guilty, Jedge. I never tuck de whip."

The State's attorney opened the case. He was young and zealous. Recently elected to the office, this was his first batch of cases, and he was anxious to make as good a record as possible. He had no doubt of the prisoner's guilt. There had been a great deal of petty thieving in the county, and several gentlemen had suggested to him the necessity for greater severity in punishing it. The jury were all white men. The prosecuting attorney stated the case.

"We expect to show, gentlemen of the jury, the facts set out in the indictment,—not altogether by direct proof, but by a chain of circumstantial evidence which is stronger even than the testimony of eyewitnesses. Men might lie, but circumstances cannot. We expect to show that the defendant is a man of dangerous character, a surly, impudent fellow; a man whose views of property are prejudicial to the welfare of society, and who has been heard to assert that half the property which is owned in this county has been stolen, and that, if justice were done, the white people ought to divide up the land with the negroes; in other words, a negro nihilist, a communist, a secret devotee of Tom Paine and Voltaire, a pupil of the anarchist propaganda, which, if not checked by the stern hand of the law, will fasten its insidious fangs on our social system, and drag it down to ruin."

"We object, may it please your Honor," said the defendant's attorney. "The prosecutor should defer his argument until the testimony is in."

"Confine yourself to the facts, Major," said the court mildly.

The prisoner sat with half-open mouth, overwhelmed by this flood of eloquence. He had never heard of Tom Paine or Voltaire. He had no conception of what a nihilist or an anarchist might be, and could not have told the difference between a propaganda and a potato.

"We expect to show, may it please the court, that the prisoner had been employed by Colonel Thornton to shoe a horse; that the horse was taken to the prisoner's blacksmith shop by a servant of Colonel Thornton's; that, this servant expressing a desire to go somewhere on an errand before the horse had been shod, the prisoner volunteered to return the horse to Colonel Thornton's stable; that he did so, and the following morning the whip in question was missing; that, from circumstances, suspicion naturally fell upon the prisoner, and a search was made of his shop, where the whip was found secreted; that the prisoner denied that the whip was there, but when confronted with the evidence of his crime, showed by his confusion that he was guilty beyond a peradventure."

The prisoner looked more anxious; so much eloquence could not but be effective with the jury.

The attorney for the defendant answered briefly, denying the defendant's guilt, dwelling upon his previous good character for honesty, and begging the jury not to pre-judge the case, but to remember that the law is merciful, and that the benefit of the doubt should be given to the prisoner.

The prisoner glanced nervously at the jury. There was nothing in their faces to indicate the effect upon them of the opening statements. It seemed to the disinterested listeners as if the defendant's attorney had little confidence in his client's cause.

Colonel Thornton took the stand and testified to his ownership of the whip, the place where it was kept, its value, and the fact that it had disappeared. The whip was produced in court and identified by the witness. He also testified to the conversation at the blacksmith shop in the course of which the prisoner had expressed a desire to possess a similar whip. The cross-examination was brief, and no attempt was made to shake the Colonel's testimony.

The next witness was the constable who had gone with a warrant to search Ben's shop. He testified to the circumstances under which the whip was found.

"He wuz brazen as a mule at fust, an' wanted ter git mad about it. But when we begun ter turn over that pile er truck in the cawner, he kinder begun ter trimble; when the whip-handle stuck out, his eyes commenced ter grow big, an' when we hauled the whip out he turned pale ez ashes, an' begun to swear he didn' take the whip an' didn' know how it got thar."

"You may cross-examine," said the prosecuting attorney triumphantly.

The prisoner felt the weight of the testimony, and glanced furtively at the jury, and then appealingly at his lawyer.

"You say that Ben denied that he had stolen the whip," said the prisoner's attorney, on cross-examination. "Did it not occur to you that what you took for brazen impudence might have been but the evidence of conscious innocence?"

The witness grinned incredulously, revealing thereby a few blackened fragments of teeth.

"I've tuck up more'n a hundred niggers fer stealin', Kurnel, an' I never seed one yit that didn' 'ny it ter the las'."

"Answer my question. Might not the witness's indignation have been a manifestation of conscious innocence? Yes or no?"

"Yes, it mought, an' the moon mought fall—but it don't."

Further cross-examination did not weaken the witness's testimony, which was very damaging, and every one in the court room felt instinctively that a strong defense would be required to break down the State's case.

"The State rests," said the prosecuting attorney, with a ring in his voice which spoke of certain victory.

There was a temporary lull in the proceedings, during which a bailiff passed a pitcher of water and a glass along the line of jurymen. The defense was then begun.

The law in its wisdom did not permit the defendant to testify in his own behalf. There were no witnesses to the facts, but several were called to testify to Ben's good character. The colored witnesses made him out possessed of all the virtues. One or two white men testified that they had never known anything against his reputation for honesty.

The defendant rested his case, and the State called its witnesses in rebuttal. They were entirely on the point of character. One testified that he had heard the prisoner say that, if the negroes had their rights, they would own at least half the property. Another testified that he had heard the defendant say that the negroes spent too much money on churches, and that they cared a good deal more for God than God had ever seemed to care for them.

Ben Davis listened to this testimony with half-open mouth and staring eyes. Now and then he would lean forward and speak perhaps a word, when his attorney would shake a warning finger at him, and he would fall back helplessly, as if abandoning himself to fate; but for a moment only, when he would resume his puzzled look.

The arguments followed. The prosecuting attorney briefly summed up the evidence, and characterized it as almost a mathematical proof of the prisoner's guilt. He reserved his eloquence for the closing argument.

The defendant's attorney had a headache, and secretly believed his client guilty. His address sounded more like an appeal for mercy than a demand for justice. Then the State's attorney delivered the maiden argument of his office, the speech that made his reputation as an orator, and opened up to him a successful political career.

The judge's charge to the jury was a plain, simple statement of the law as applied to circumstantial evidence, and the mere statement of the law foreshadowed the verdict.

The eyes of the prisoner were glued to the jury-box, and he looked more and more like a hunted animal. In the rear of the crowd of blacks who filled the back part of the room, partly concealed by the projecting angle of the fireplace, stood Tom, the blacksmith's assistant. If the face is the mirror of the soul, then this man's soul, taken off its guard in this moment of excitement, was full of lust and envy and all evil passions.

The jury filed out of their box, and into the jury room behind the judge's stand. There was a moment of relaxation in the court room. The lawyers fell into conversation across the table. The judge beckoned to Colonel Thornton, who stepped forward, and they conversed together a few moments. The prisoner was all eyes and ears in this moment of waiting, and from an involuntary gesture on the part of the judge he divined that they were speaking of him. It is a pity he could not hear what was said.

"How do you feel about the case, Colonel?" asked the judge.

"Let him off easy," replied Colonel Thornton. "He's the best blacksmith in the county."

The business of the court seemed to have halted by tacit consent, in anticipation of a quick verdict. The suspense did not last long. Scarcely ten minutes had elapsed when there was a rap on the door, the officer opened it, and the jury came out.

The prisoner, his soul in his eyes, sought their faces, but met no reassuring glance; they were all looking away from him.

"Gentlemen of the jury, have you agreed upon a verdict?"

"We have," responded the foreman. The clerk of the court stepped forward and took the fateful slip from the foreman's hand.

The clerk read the verdict: "We, the jury impaneled and sworn to try the issues in this cause, do find the prisoner guilty as charged in the indictment."

There was a moment of breathless silence. Then a wild burst of grief from the prisoner's wife, to which his two children, not understanding it all, but vaguely conscious of some calamity, added their voices in two long, discordant wails, which would have been ludicrous had they not been heart-rending.

The face of the young man in the back of the room expressed relief and badly concealed satisfaction. The prisoner fell back upon the seat from which he had half risen in his anxiety, and his dark face assumed an ashen hue. What he thought could only be surmised. Perhaps, knowing his innocence, he had not believed conviction possible; perhaps, conscious of guilt, he dreaded the punishment, the extent of which was optional with the judge, within very wide limits. Only one other person present knew whether or not he was guilty, and that other had slunk furtively from the court room.

Some of the spectators wondered why there should be so much ado about convicting a negro of stealing a buggy-whip. They had forgotten their own interest of the moment before. They did not realize out of what trifles grow the tragedies of life.

It was four o'clock in the afternoon, the hour for adjournment, when the verdict was returned. The judge nodded to the bailiff.

"Oyez, oyez! this court is now adjourned until ten o'clock to-morrow morning," cried the bailiff in a singsong voice. The judge left the bench, the jury filed out of the box, and a buzz of conversation filled the court room.

"Brace up, Ben, brace up, my boy," said the defendant's lawyer, half apologetically. "I did what I could for you, but you can never tell what a jury will do. You won't be sentenced till to-morrow morning. In the meantime I'll speak to the judge and try to get him to be easy with you. He may let you off with a light fine."

The negro pulled himself together, and by an effort listened.

"Thanky, Majah," was all he said. He seemed to be thinking of something far away.

He barely spoke to his wife when she frantically threw herself on him, and clung to his neck, as he passed through the side room on his way to jail. He kissed his children mechanically, and did not reply to the soothing remarks made by the jailer.

3

There was a good deal of excitement in town the next morning. Two white men stood by the post office talking.

"Did yer hear the news?"

"No, what wuz it?"

"Ben Davis tried ter break jail las' night."

"You don't say so! What a fool! He ain't be'n sentenced yit."

"Well, now," said the other, "I've knowed Ben a long time, an' he wuz a right good nigger. I kinder found it hard ter b'lieve he did steal that whip. But what's a man's feelin's ag'in' the proof?"

They spoke on awhile, using the past tense as if they were speaking of a dead man.

"Ef I know Jedge Hart, Ben 'll wish he had slep' las' night, 'stidder tryin' ter break out'n jail."

At ten o'clock the prisoner was brought into court. He walked with shambling gait, bent at the shoulders, hopelessly, with downcast eyes, and took his seat with several other prisoners who had been brought in for sentence. His wife, accompanied by the children, waited behind him, and a number of his friends were gathered in the court room.

The first prisoner sentenced was a young white man, convicted several days before of manslaughter. The deed was done in the heat of passion, under circumstances of great provocation, during a quarrel about a woman. The prisoner was admonished of the sanctity of human life, and sentenced to one year in the penitentiary.

The next case was that of a young clerk, eighteen or nineteen years of age, who had committed a forgery in order to procure the means to buy lottery tickets. He was well connected, and the case would not have been prosecuted if the judge had not refused to allow it to be nolled, and, once brought to trial, a conviction could not have been avoided.

"You are a young man," said the judge gravely, yet not unkindly, "and your life is yet before you. I regret that you should have been led into evil courses by the lust for speculation, so dangerous in its tendencies, so fruitful of crime and misery. I am led to believe that you are sincerely penitent, and that, after such punishment as the law cannot remit without bringing itself into contempt, you will see the error of your ways and follow the strict path of rectitude. Your fault has entailed distress not only upon yourself, but upon your relatives, people of good name and good family, who suffer as keenly from your disgrace as you yourself. Partly out of consideration for their feelings, and partly because I feel that, under the circumstances, the law will be satisfied by the penalty I shall inflict, I sentence you to imprisonment in the county jail for six months, and a fine of one hundred dollars and the costs of this action."

"The jedge talks well, don't he?" whispered one spectator to another.

"Yes, and kinder likes ter hear hisse'f talk," answered the other.

"Ben Davis, stand up," ordered the judge.

He might have said "Ben Davis, wake up," for the jailer had to touch the prisoner on the shoulder to rouse him from his stupor. He stood up, and something of the hunted look came again into his eyes, which shifted under the stern glance of the judge.

"Ben Davis, you have been convicted of larceny, after a fair trial before twelve good men of this county. Under the testimony, there can be no doubt of your guilt. The case is an aggravated one. You are not an ignorant, shiftless fellow, but a man of more than ordinary intelligence among your people, and one who ought to know better. You have not even the poor excuse of having stolen to satisfy hunger or a physical appetite. Your conduct is wholly without excuse, and I can only regard your crime as the result of a tendency to offenses of this nature, a tendency which is only too common among your people; a tendency which is a menace to civilization, a menace to society itself, for society rests upon the sacred right of property. Your opinions, too, have been given a wrong turn; you have been heard to utter sentiments which, if disseminated among an ignorant people, would breed discontent, and give rise to strained relations between them and their best friends, their old masters, who understand their real nature and their real needs, and to whose justice and enlightened guidance they can safely trust. Have you anything to say why sentence should not be passed upon you?"

"Nothin', suh, cep'n dat I did n' take de whip."

"The law, largely, I think, in view of the peculiar circumstances of your unfortunate race, has vested a large discretion in courts as to the extent of the punishment for offenses of this kind. Taking your case as a whole, I am convinced that it is one which, for the sake of the example, deserves a severe punishment. Nevertheless, I do not feel disposed to give you the full extent of the law, which would be twenty years in the penitentiary,* but, considering the fact that you have a family, and have heretofore borne a good reputation in the community, I will impose upon you the light sentence of imprisonment for five years in the penitentiary at hard labor. And I hope that this will be a warning to you and others who may be similarly disposed, and that after your sentence has expired you may lead the life of a law-abiding citizen."

"O Ben! O my husband! O God!" moaned the poor wife, and tried to press forward to her husband's side.

"Keep back, Nancy, keep back," said the jailer. "You can see him in jail."

Several people were looking at Ben's face. There was one flash of despair, and then nothing but a stony blank, behind which he masked his real feelings, whatever they were.

Human character is a compound of tendencies inherited and hab-its acquired. In the anxiety, the fear of disgrace, spoke the nine-teenth century civilization with which Ben Davis had been more or less closely in touch during twenty years of slavery and fifteen years of freedom. In the stolidity with which he received this sentence for a crime which he had not committed, spoke who knows what trait of inherited savagery? For stoicism is a savage virtue.

4

One morning in June, five years later, a black man limped slowly along the old Lumberton plank road; a tall man, whose bowed shoulders made him seem shorter than he was, and a face from

---

*There are no degrees of larceny in North Carolina, and the penalty for any offense lies in the discretion of the judge, to the limit of twenty years.

which it was difficult to guess his years, for in it the wrinkles and flabbiness of age were found side by side with firm white teeth, and eyes not sunken,—eyes bloodshot, and burning with something, either fever or passion. Though he limped painfully with one foot, the other hit the ground impatiently, like the good horse in a poorly matched team. As he walked along, he was talking to himself:—

"I wonder what dey'll do w'en I git back? I wonder how Nancy's s'ported the fambly all dese years? Tuck in washin', I s'ppose,—she was a monst'us good washer an' ironer. I wonder ef de chillun 'll be too proud ter reco'nize deir daddy come back f'um de penetenchy? I 'spec' Billy must be a big boy by dis time. He won' b'lieve his daddy ever stole anything. I'm gwine ter slip roun' an' s'prise 'em."

Five minutes later a face peered cautiously into the window of what had once been Ben Davis's cabin,—at first an eager face, its coarseness lit up with the fire of hope; a moment later a puzzled face; then an anxious, fearful face as the man stepped away from the window and rapped at the door.

"Is Mis' Davis home?" he asked of the woman who opened the door.

"Mis' Davis don' live here. You er mistook in de house."

"Whose house is dis?"

"It b'longs ter my husban', Mr. Smith,—Primus Smith."

" 'Scuse me, but I knowed de house some years ago w'en I wuz here oncet on a visit, an' it b'longed ter a man name' Ben Davis."

"Ben Davis—Ben Davis?—oh yes, I 'member now. Dat wuz de gen'man w'at wuz sent ter de penitenchy fer sump'n er nuther,—sheep-stealin', I b'lieve. Primus," she called, "w'at wuz Ben Davis, w'at useter own dis yer house, sent ter de penitenchy fer?"

"Hoss-stealin'," came back the reply in sleepy accents, from the man seated by the fireplace.

The traveler went on to the next house. A neat-looking yellow woman came to the door when he rattled the gate, and stood looking suspiciously at him.

"W'at you want?" she asked.

"Please, ma'am, will you tell me whether a man name' Ben Davis useter live in dis neighborhood?"

"Useter live in de nex' house; wuz sent ter de penitenchy fer killin' a man."

"Kin yer tell me w'at went wid Mis' Davis?"

"Umph! I 's a 'spectable 'oman, I is, en don' mix wid dem kind er people. She wuz 'n' no better 'n her husban'. She tuk up wid a man dat useter wuk fer Ben, an' dey 're livin' down by de ole wagon-ya'd, where no 'spectable 'oman ever puts her foot."

"An' de chillen?"

"De gal's dead. Wuz 'n' no better 'n she oughter be'n. She fell in de crick an' got drown'; some folks say she wuz 'n' sober w'en it happen'. De boy tuck atter his pappy. He wuz 'rested las' week fer shootin' a w'ite man, an' wuz lynch' de same night. Dey wa'n't none of 'em no 'count after deir pappy went ter de penitenchy."

"What went wid de proputty?"

"Hit wuz sol' fer de mortgage, er de taxes, er de lawyer, er sump'n,—I don' know w'at. A w'ite man got it."

The man with the bundle went on until he came to a creek that crossed the road. He descended the sloping bank, and, sitting on a stone in the shade of a water-oak, took off his coarse brogans, unwound the rags that served him in lieu of stockings, and laved in the cool water the feet that were chafed with many a weary mile of travel.

After five years of unrequited toil, and unspeakable hardship in convict camps,—five years of slaving by the side of human brutes, and of nightly herding with them in vermin-haunted huts,—Ben Davis had become like them. For a while he had received occasional letters from home, but in the shifting life of the convict camp they had long since ceased to reach him, if indeed they had been written. For a year or two, the consciousness of his innocence had helped to make him resist the debasing influences that surrounded him. The hope of shortening his sentence by good behavior, too, had worked a similar end. But the transfer from one contractor to another, each interested in keeping as long as possible a good worker, had speedily dissipated any such hope. When hope took flight, its place was not long vacant. Despair followed, and black hatred of all mankind, hatred especially of the man to whom he attributed all his misfortunes. One who is suffering unjustly is not apt to indulge in fine abstractions, nor to balance probabilities. By long brooding over his wrongs, his mind became, if not unsettled, at least warped, and he imagined that Colonel Thornton had deliberately set a trap into which he had fallen. The Colonel, he convinced himself, had disapproved of his prosperity, and had schemed to destroy it. He reasoned himself into the belief that he represented in his person the accumulated wrongs of a whole race, and Colonel Thornton the race who had oppressed them. A burning desire for revenge sprang up in him, and he nursed it until his sentence expired and he was set at liberty. What he had learned since reaching home had changed his desire into a deadly purpose.

When he had again bandaged his feet and slipped them into his shoes, he looked around him, and selected a stout sapling from among the undergrowth that covered the bank of the stream. Taking from his pocket a huge clasp-knife, he cut off the length of an ordinary walking stick and trimmed it. The result was an ugly-looking bludgeon, a dangerous weapon when in the grasp of a strong man.

With the stick in his hand, he went on down the road until he approached a large white house standing some distance back from the street. The grounds were filled with a profusion of shrubbery. The negro entered the gate and secreted himself in the bushes, at a point where he could hear any one that might approach.

It was near midday, and he had not eaten. He had walked all night, and had not slept. The hope of meeting his loved ones had been meat and drink and rest for him. But as he sat waiting, outraged nature asserted itself, and he fell asleep, with his head on the rising root of a tree, and his face upturned.

And as he slept, he dreamed of his childhood; of an old black mammy taking care of him in the daytime, and of a younger face, with soft eyes, which bent over him sometimes at night, and a pair of arms which clasped him closely. He dreamed of his past,—of his young wife, of his bright children. Somehow his dreams all ran to pleasant themes for a while.

Then they changed again. He dreamed that he was in the convict camp, and, by an easy transition, that he was in hell, consumed with hunger, burning with thirst. Suddenly the grinning devil who stood over him with a barbed whip faded away, and a little white angel came and handed him a drink of water. As he raised it to his lips the glass slipped, and he struggled back to consciousness.

"Poo' man! Poo' man sick, an' sleepy. Dolly b'ing f'owers to cover poo' man up. Poo' man mus' be hungry. W'en Dolly get him covered up, she go b'ing poo' man some cake."

A sweet little child, as beautiful as a cherub escaped from Paradise, was standing over him. At first he scarcely comprehended the words the baby babbled out. But as they became clear to him, a novel feeling crept slowly over his heart. It had been so long since he had heard anything but curses and stern words of command, or the ribald songs of obscene merriment, that the clear tones of this voice from heaven cooled his calloused heart as the water of the brook had soothed his blistered feet. It was so strange, so unwonted a thing, that he lay there with half-closed eyes while the child brought leaves and flowers and laid them on his face and on his breast, and arranged them with little caressing taps.

She moved away, and plucked a flower. And then she spied

another farther on, and then another, and, as she gathered them, kept increasing the distance between herself and the man lying there, until she was several rods away.

Ben Davis watched her through eyes over which had come an unfamiliar softness. Under the lingering spell of his dream, her golden hair, which fell in rippling curls, seemed like a halo of purity and innocence and peace, irradiating the atmosphere around her. It is true the thought occurred to Ben, vaguely, that through harm to her he might inflict the greatest punishment upon her father; but the idea came like a dark shape that faded away and vanished into nothingness as soon as it came within the nimbus that surrounded the child's person.

The child was moving on to pluck still another flower, when there came a sound of hoof-beats, and Ben was aware that a horseman, visible through the shrubbery, was coming along the curved path that led from the gate to the house. It must be the man he was waiting for, and now was the time to wreak his vengeance. He sprang to his feet, grasped his club, and stood for a moment irresolute. But either the instinct of the convict, beaten, driven, and debased, or the influence of the child, which was still strong upon him, impelled him, after the first momentary pause, to flee as though seeking safety.

His flight led him toward the little girl, whom he must pass in order to make his escape, and as Colonel Thornton turned the corner of the path he saw a desperate-looking negro, clad in filthy rags, and carrying in his hand a murderous bludgeon, running toward the child, who, startled by the sound of footsteps, had turned and was looking toward the approaching man with wondering eyes. A sickening fear came over the father's heart, and drawing the ever-ready revolver, which according to the Southern custom he carried always upon his person, he fired with unerring aim. Ben Davis ran a few yards farther, faltered, threw out his hands, and fell dead at the child's feet.

Some time, we are told, when the cycle of years has rolled around, there is to be another golden age, when all men will dwell together in love and harmony, and when peace and righteousness shall prevail for a thousand years. God speed the day, and let not the shining thread of hope become so enmeshed in the web of circumstance that we lose sight of it; but give us here and there, and now and then, some little foretaste of this golden age, that we may the more patiently and hopefully await its coming!

Kate Chopin

(1851–1904)

*Born Katherine O'Flaherty in St. Louis, Missouri, Kate Chopin
was brought up in prosperous surroundings and educated at the
best Catholic schools. Her father was an Irishman, from Galway,
who had become a successful businessman in St. Louis. Her mother
came from an old French Creole family, and her maternal great-
grandmother lived at the O'Flaherty home and taught Kate French.
Her life as a girl and young woman was deeply saddened by a bitter
series of family tragedies: Her father was killed in a train accident
when she was four years old; her half-brother died of typhoid fever
after being imprisoned by the Union army during the Civil War, and
her other brother died not long after in a drowning accident. When
she was 19 years old she married Oscar Chopin, a cotton trader from
Louisiana. She moved with him to New Orleans, where they had six
children and played an active role in New Orleans society. In 1879,
the Chopins moved to Cloutierville, Louisiana, a small town in the
Cane River region in the Natchitoches Parish, home of the Chopin
family plantations and the setting for many of her short stories. Her
husband died of swamp fever in 1883, and a year later she left Louisiana and returned to St. Louis. There, influenced by her reading of
Maupassant, she began writing, chiefly stories of Creole Louisiana,
some of which were published in two collections:* Bayou Folk *(1894)
and* A Night in Acadie *(1897). Now recognized as one of the strongest, most important writers of her day, she has been praised for her
realistic descriptions of Louisiana life and for her original and convincing portraits of young women struggling to redefine themselves
when faced with the unforeseen constraints of marriage. Her best-
known work, the short novel* The Awakening *(1899), was condemned as immoral when first published, but today has taken its
place as one of the masterpieces of American fiction. "Athénaïse: A
Story of a Temperament" is taken from* A Night in Acadie *and was
first published in* The Atlantic Monthly *(August and September
1896).*

ATHÉNAÏSE: A STORY
OF A TEMPERAMENT

❁

1

Athénaïse went away in the morning to make a visit to her parents,
ten miles back on rigolet du Bon Dieu. She did not return in the
evening, and Cazeau, her husband, fretted not a little. He did not
worry much about Athénaïse, who, he suspected, was resting only
too content in the bosom of her family; his chief solicitude was
manifestly for the pony she had ridden. He felt sure those "lazy
pigs," her brothers, were capable of neglecting it seriously. This
misgiving Cazeau communicated to his servant, old Félicité, who
waited upon him at supper.

His voice was low pitched, and even softer than Félicité's. He
was tall, sinewy, swarthy, and altogether severe looking. His thick
black hair waved, and it gleamed like the breast of a crow. The
sweep of his mustache, which was not so black, outlined the broad
contour of the mouth. Beneath the under lip grew a small tuft
which he was much given to twisting, and which he permitted to
grow, apparently, for no other purpose. Cazeau's eyes were dark
blue, narrow and overshadowed. His hands were coarse and stiff
from close acquaintance with farming tools and implements, and
he handled his fork and knife clumsily. But he was distinguished
looking, and succeeded in commanding a good deal of respect,
and even fear sometimes.

He ate his supper alone, by the light of a single coal-oil lamp
that but faintly illumined the big room, with its bare floor and
huge rafters, and its heavy pieces of furniture that loomed dimly
in the gloom of the apartment. Félicité, ministering to his wants,
hovered about the table like a little, bent, restless shadow.

She served him a dish of sunfish fried crisp and brown. There
was nothing else set before him beside the bread and butter and
the bottle of red wine which she locked carefully in the buffet after
he had poured his second glass. She was occupied with her mistress's absence, and kept reverting to it after he had expressed his
solicitude about the pony.

71

"Dat beat me! on'y marry two mont', an' got de head turn' a'ready to go 'broad. Ce n'est pas Chrétien, ténez!"

Cazeau shrugged his shoulders for answer, after he had drained his glass and pushed aside his plate. Félicité's opinion of the unchristian-like behavior of his wife in leaving him thus alone after two months of marriage weighed little with him. He was used to solitude, and did not mind a day or a night or two of it. He had lived alone ten years, since his first wife died, and Félicité might have known better than to suppose that he cared. He told her she was a fool. It sounded like a compliment in his modulated, caressing voice. She grumbled to herself as she set about clearing the table, and Cazeau arose and walked outside on the gallery; his spur, which he had not removed upon entering the house, jangled at every step.

The night was beginning to deepen, and to gather black about the clusters of trees and shrubs that were grouped in the yard. In the beam of light from the open kitchen door a black boy stood feeding a brace of snarling, hungry dogs; further away, on the steps of a cabin, some one was playing the accordion; and in still another direction a little negro baby was crying lustily. Cazeau walked around to the front of the house, which was square, squat, and one-story.

A belated wagon was driving in at the gate, and the impatient driver was swearing hoarsely at his jaded oxen. Félicité stepped out on the gallery, glass and polishing-towel in hand, to investigate, and to wonder, too, who could be singing out on the river. It was a party of young people paddling around, waiting for the moon to rise, and they were singing "Juanita," their voices coming tempered and melodious through the distance and the night.

Cazeau's horse was waiting, saddled, ready to be mounted, for Cazeau had many things to attend to before bedtime; so many things that there was not left to him a moment in which to think of Athénaïse. He felt her absence, though, like a dull, insistent pain.

However, before he slept that night he was visited by the thought of her, and by a vision of her fair young face with its drooping lips and sullen and averted eyes. The marriage had been a blunder; he had only to look into her eyes to feel that, to discover her growing aversion. But it was a thing not by any possibility to be undone. He was quite prepared to make the best of it, and expected no less than a like effort on her part. The less she revisited the rigolet, the better. He would find means to keep her at home hereafter.

These unpleasant reflections kept Cazeau awake far into the

night, notwithstanding the craving of his whole body for rest and sleep. The moon was shining, and its pale effulgence reached dimly into the room, and with it a touch of the cool breath of the spring night. There was an unusual stillness abroad; no sound to be heard save the distant, tireless, plaintiff notes of the accordion.

2

Athénaïse did not return the following day, even though her husband sent her word to do so by her brother, Montéclin, who passed on his way to the village early in the morning.

On the third day Cazeau saddled his horse and went himself in search of her. She had sent no word, no message, explaining her absence, and he felt that he had good cause to be offended. It was rather awkward to have to leave his work, even though late in the afternoon,—Cazeau had always so much to do; but among the many urgent calls upon him, the task of bringing his wife back to a sense of her duty seemed to him for the moment paramount.

The Michés, Athénaïse's parents, lived on the old Gotrain place. It did not belong to them; they were "running" it for a merchant in Alexandria. The house was far too big for their use. One of the lower rooms served for the storing of wood and tools; the person "occupying" the place before Miché having pulled up the flooring in despair of being able to patch it. Upstairs, the rooms were so large, so bare, that they offered a constant temptation to lovers of the dance, whose importunities Madame Miché was accustomed to meet with amiable indulgence. A dance at Miché's and a plate of Madame Miché's gumbo filé at midnight were pleasures not to be neglected or despised, unless by such serious souls as Cazeau.

Long before Cazeau reached the house his approach had been observed, for there was nothing to obstruct the view of the outer road; vegetation was not yet abundantly advanced, and there was but a patchy, straggling stand of cotton and corn in Miché's field.

Madame Miché, who had been seated on the gallery in a rocking-chair, stood up to greet him as he drew near. She was short and fat, and wore a black skirt and loose muslin sack fastened at the throat with a hair brooch. Her own hair, brown and glossy, showed but a few threads of silver. Her round pink face was cheery, and her eyes were bright and good humored. But she was plainly perturbed and ill at ease as Cazeau advanced.

Montéclin, who was there too, was not ill at ease, and made no attempt to disguise the dislike with which his brother-in-law inspired him. He was a slim, wiry fellow of twenty-five, short of stature like his mother, and resembling her in feature. He was in shirt-sleeves, half leaning, half sitting, on the insecure railing of the gallery, and fanning himself with his broad-rimmed felt hat.

"Cochon!" he muttered under his breath as Cazeau mounted the stairs,—"sacré cochon!"

"Cochon" had sufficiently characterized the man who had once on a time declined to lend Montéclin money. But when this same man had had the presumption to propose marriage to his well-beloved sister, Athénaïse, and the honor to be accepted by her, Montéclin felt that a qualifying epithet was needed fully to express his estimate of Cazeau.

Miché and his oldest son were absent. They both esteemed Cazeau highly, and talked much of his qualities of head and heart, and thought much of his excellent standing with city merchants.

Athénaïse had shut herself up in her room. Cazeau had seen her rise and enter the house at perceiving him. He was a good deal mystified, but no one could have guessed it when he shook hands with Madame Miché. He had only nodded to Montéclin, with a muttered "Comment ça va?"

"Tiens! something tole me you were coming to-day!" exclaimed Madame Miché, with a little blustering appearance of being cordial and at ease, as she offered Cazeau a chair.

He ventured a short laugh as he seated himself.

"You know, nothing would do," she went on, with much gesture of her small, plump hands, "nothing would do but Athénaïse mus' stay las' night fo' a li'le dance. The boys wouldn' year to their sister leaving."

Cazeau shrugged his shoulders significantly, telling as plainly as words that he knew nothing about it.

"Comment! Montéclin didn' tell you we were going to keep Athénaïse?" Montéclin had evidently told nothing.

"An' how about the night befo'," questioned Cazeau, "an' las' night? It isn't possible you dance every night out yere on the Bon Dieu!"

Madame Miché laughed, with amiable appreciation of the sarcasm; and turning to her son, "Montéclin, my boy, go tell yo' sister that Monsieur Cazeau is yere."

Montéclin did not stir except to shift his position and settle himself more securely on the railing.

"Did you year me, Montéclin?"

"Oh yes, I yeard you plain enough," responded her son, "but you know as well as me it's no use to tell 'Thénaïse anything. You been talkin' to her yo'se'f since Monday; an' pa's preached himse'f hoa'se on the subject; an' you even had uncle Achille down yere

yesterday to reason with her. W'en 'Thénaïse said she wasn' goin'
to set her foot back in Cazeau's house, she meant it."

This speech, which Montéclin delivered with thorough uncon-
cern, threw his mother into a condition of painful but dumb embarrassment. It brought two fiery red spots to Cazeau's cheeks,
and for the space of a moment he looked wicked.

What Montéclin had spoken was quite true, though his taste in
the manner and choice of time and place in saying it were not of
the best. Athénaïse, upon the first day of her arrival, had announced that she came to stay, having no intention of returning
under Cazeau's roof. The announcement had scattered consternation, as she knew it would. She had been implored, scolded,
entreated, stormed at, until she felt herself like a dragging sail that
all the winds of heaven had beaten upon. Why in the name of God
had she married Cazeau? Her father had lashed her with the question a dozen times. Why indeed? It was difficult now for her to
understand why, unless because she supposed it was customary for
girls to marry when the right opportunity came. Cazeau, she knew,
would make life more comfortable for her; and again, she had
liked him, and had even been rather flustered when he pressed
her hands and kissed them, and kissed her lips and cheeks and
eyes, when she accepted him.

Montéclin himself had taken her aside to talk the thing over.
The turn of affairs was delighting him.

"Come, now, 'Thénaïse, you mus' explain to me all about it, so
we can settle on a good cause, an' secu' a separation fo' you. Has
he been mistreating an' abusing you, the sacré cochon?" They
were alone together in her room, whither she had taken refuge
from the angry domestic elements.

"You please to reserve yo' disgusting expressions, Montéclin.
No, he has not abused me in any way that I can think."

"Does he drink? Come, 'Thénaïse, think well over it. Does he
ever get drunk?"

"Drunk! Oh, mercy, no,—Cazeau never gets drunk."

"I see; it's jus' simply you feel like me: you hate him."

"No, I don't hate him," she returned reflectively; adding with
a sudden impulse, "It's jus' being married that I detes' an' despise.
I hate being Mrs. Cazeau, an' would want to be Athénaïse Miché
again. I can't stan' to live with a man: to have him always there;
his coats an' pantaloons hanging in my room; his ugly bare feet—
washing them in my tub, befo' my very eyes, ugh!" She shuddered
with recollections, and resumed, with a sigh that was almost a sob:
"Mon Dieu, mon Dieu! Sister Marie Angélique knew w'at she was
saying; she knew me better than myse'f w'en she said God had

sent me a vocation an' I was turning deaf ears. W'en I think of a blessed life in the convent, at peace! Oh, w'at was I dreaming of!" and then the tears came.

Montéclin felt disconcerted and greatly disappointed at having obtained evidence that would carry no weight with a court of justice. The day had not come when a young woman might ask the court's permission to return to her mamma on the sweeping grounds of a constitutional disinclination for marriage. But if there was no way of untying this Gordian knot of marriage, there was surely a way of cutting it.

"Well, 'Thénaïse, I'm mighty durn sorry you got no better groun's 'an w'at you say. But you can count on me to stan' by you w'atever you do. God knows I don' blame you fo' not wantin' to live with Cazeau."

And now there was Cazeau himself, with the red spots flaming in his swarthy cheeks, looking and feeling as if he wanted to thrash Montéclin into some semblance of decency. He arose abruptly, and approaching the room which he had seen his wife enter, thrust open the door after a hasty preliminary knock. Athénaïse, who was standing erect at a far window, turned at his entrance.

She appeared neither angry nor frightened, but thoroughly unhappy, with an appeal in her soft dark eyes and a tremor on her lips that seemed to him expressions of unjust reproach, that wounded and maddened him at once. But whatever he might feel, Cazeau knew only one way to act toward a woman.

"Athénaïse, you are not ready?" he asked in his quiet tones. "It's getting late; we havn' any time to lose."

She knew that Montéclin had spoken out, and she had hoped for a wordy interview, a stormy scene, in which she might have held her own as she had held it for the past three days against her family, with Montéclin's aid. But she had no weapon with which to combat subtlety. Her husband's looks, his tones, his mere presence, brought to her a sudden sense of hopelessness, an instinctive realization of the futility of rebellion against a social and sacred institution.

Cazeau said nothing further, but stood waiting in the doorway. Madame Miché had walked to the far end of the gallery, and pretended to be occupied with having a chicken driven from her parterre. Montéclin stood by, exasperated, fuming, ready to burst out.

Athénaïse went and reached for her riding-skirt that hung against the wall. She was rather tall, with a figure which, though not robust, seemed perfect in its fine proportions. "La fille de son père," she was often called, which was a great compliment to Miché. Her brown hair was brushed all fluffily back from her temples and low forehead, and about her features and expression lurked a softness, a prettiness, a dewiness, that were perhaps too childlike, that savored of immaturity.

She slipped the riding-skirt, which was of black alpaca, over her head, and with impatient fingers hooked it at the waist over her pink linen-lawn. Then she fastened on her white sunbonnet and reached for her gloves on the mantelpiece.

"If you don' wan' to go, you know w'at you got to do, 'Thénaïse," fumed Montéclin. "You don' set yo' feet back on Cane River, by God, unless you want to,—not w'ile I'm alive."

Cazeau looked at him as if he were a monkey whose antics fell short of being amusing.

Athénaïse still made no reply, said not a word. She walked rapidly past her husband, past her brother; bidding goodby to no one, not even to her mother. She descended the stairs, and without assistance from any one mounted the pony, which Cazeau had ordered to be saddled upon his arrival. In this way she obtained a fair start of her husband, whose departure was far more leisurely, and for the greater part of the way she managed to keep an appreciable gap between them. She rode almost madly at first, with the wind inflating her skirt balloon-like about her knees, and her sunbonnet falling back between her shoulders.

At no time did Cazeau make an effort to overtake her until traversing an old fallow meadow that was level and hard as a table. The sight of a great solitary oak-tree, with its seemingly immutable outlines, that had been a landmark for ages—or was it the odor of elderberry stealing up from the gully to the south? or what was it that brought vividly back to Cazeau, by some association of ideas, a scene of many years ago? He had passed that old live-oak hundreds of times, but it was only now that the memory of one day came back to him. He was a very small boy that day, seated before his father on horseback. They were proceeding slowly, and Black Gabe was moving on before them at a little dog-trot. Black Gabe had run away, and had been discovered back in the Gotrain Swamp. They had halted beneath this big oak to enable the negro to take breath; for Cazeau's father was a kind and considerate master, and every one had agreed at the time that Black Gabe was a fool, a great idiot indeed, for wanting to run away from him.

The whole impression was for some reason hideous, and to dispel it Cazeau spurred his horse to a swift gallop. Overtaking his wife, he rode the remainder of the way at her side in silence.

It was late when they reached home. Félicité was standing on the grassy edge of the road, in the moonlight, waiting for them.

Cazeau once more ate his supper alone; for Athénaïse went to her room, and there she was crying again.

3

Athénaïse was not one to accept the inevitable with patient resignation, a talent born in the souls of many women; neither was she the one to accept it with philosophical resignation, like her husband. Her sensibilities were alive and keen and responsive. She met the pleasurable things of life with frank, open appreciation, and against distasteful conditions she rebelled. Dissimulation was as foreign to her nature as guile to the breast of a babe, and her rebellious outbreaks, by no means rare, had hitherto been quite open and aboveboard. People often said that Athénaïse would know her own mind some day, which was equivalent to saying that she was at present unacquainted with it. If she ever came to such knowledge, it would be by no intellectual research, by no subtle analyses or tracing the motives of actions to their source. It would come to her as the song to the bird, the perfume and color to the flower.

Her parents had hoped—not without reason and justice—that marriage would bring the poise, the desirable pose, so glaringly lacking in Athénaïse's character. Marriage they knew to be a wonderful and powerful agent in the development and formation of a woman's character; they had seen its effect too often to doubt it.

"And if this marriage does nothing else," exclaimed Miché in an outburst of sudden exasperation, "it will rid us of Athénaïse; for I am at the end of my patience with her! You have never had the firmness to manage her,"—he was speaking to his wife,—"I have not had the time, the leisure, to devote to her training; and what good we might have accomplished, that maudit Montéclin— Well, Cazeau is the one! It takes just such a steady hand to guide a disposition like Athénaïse's, a master hand, a strong will that compels obedience."

And now, when they had hoped for so much, here was Athénaïse, with gathered and fierce vehemence, beside which her former outbursts appeared mild, declaring that she would not, and she would not, and she would *not* continue to enact the rôle of wife to Cazeau. If she had had a reason! as Madame Miché lamented; but it could not be discovered that she had any sane one. He had never scolded, or called names, or deprived her of comforts, or been guilty of any of the many reprehensible acts commonly attributed to objectionable husbands. He did not slight nor neglect her. Indeed, Cazeau's chief offense seemed to be that he loved her, and Athénaïse was not the woman to be loved against her will. She called marriage a trap set for the feet of unwary and unsuspecting girls, and in round, unmeasured terms reproached her mother with treachery and deceit.

"I told you Cazeau was the man," chuckled Miché, when his wife had related the scene that had accompanied and influenced Athénaïse's departure.

Athénaïse again hoped, in the morning, that Cazeau would scold or make some sort of a scene, but he apparently did not dream of it. It was exasperating that he should take her acquiescence so for granted. It is true he had been up and over the fields and across the river and back long before she was out of bed, and he may have been thinking of something else, which was no excuse, which was even in some sense an aggravation. But he did say to her at breakfast, "That brother of yo's, that Montéclin, is unbearable."

"Montéclin? Par exemple!"

Athénaïse, seated opposite to her husband, was attired in a white morning wrapper. She wore a somewhat abused, long face, it is true,—an expression of countenance familiar to some husbands,— but the expression was not sufficiently pronounced to mar the charm of her youthful freshness. She had little heart to eat, only playing with the food before her, and she felt a pang of resentment at her husband's healthy appetite.

"Yes, Montéclin," he reasserted. "He's developed into a firs'-class nuisance; an' you better tell him, Athénaïse,—unless you want me to tell him,—to confine his energies after this to matters that concern him. I have no use fo' him or fo' his interference in w'at regards you an' me alone."

This was said with unusual asperity. It was the little breach that Athénaïse had been watching for, and she charged rapidly: "It's strange, if you detes' Montéclin so heartily, that you would desire to marry his sister." She knew it was a silly thing to say, and was not surprised when he told her so. It gave her a little foothold for further attack, however. "I don't see, anyhow, w'at reason you had to marry me, w'en there were so many others," she complained, as if accusing him of persecution and injury. "There was Marianne running after you fo' the las' five years till it was disgraceful; an' any one of the Dortrand girls would have been glad to marry you. But no, nothing would do; you mus' come out on the rigolet fo' me." Her complaint was pathetic, and at the same time so amusing that Cazeau was forced to smile.

"I can't see w'at the Dortrand girls or Marianne have to do with it," he rejoined; adding, with no trace of amusement, "I married

you because I loved you; because you were the woman I wanted
to marry, an' the only one. I reckon I tole you that befo'. I
thought—of co'se I was a fool fo' taking things fo' granted—but
I did think that I might make you happy in making things easier
an' mo' comfortable fo' you. I expected—I was even that big a
fool—I believed that yo' coming yere to me would be like the sun
shining out of the clouds, an' that our days would be like w'at the
storybooks promise after the wedding. I was mistaken. But I can't
imagine w'at induced you to marry me. W'atever it was, I reckon
you foun' out you made a mistake, too. I don' see anything to do
but make the best of a bad bargain, an' shake han's over it." He
had arisen from the table, and, approaching, held out his hand to
her. What he had said was commonplace enough, but it was significant, coming from Cazeau, who was not often so unreserved
in expressing himself.

Athénaïse ignored the hand held out to her. She was resting her
chin in her palm, and kept her eyes fixed moodily upon the table.
He rested his hand, that she would not touch, upon her head for
an instant, and walked away out of the room.

She heard him giving orders to workmen who had been waiting
for him out on the gallery, and she heard him mount his horse
and ride away. A hundred things would distract him and engage
his attention during the day. She felt that he had perhaps put her
and her grievance from his thoughts when he crossed the threshold;
whilst she—

Old Félicité was standing there holding a shining tin pail, asking
for flour and lard and eggs from the storeroom, and meal for the
chicks.

Athénaïse seized the bunch of keys which hung from her belt
and flung them at Félicité's feet.

"Tiens! tu vas les garder comme tu as jadis fait. Je ne veux plus
de ce train là, moi!"

The old woman stooped and picked up the keys from the floor.
It was really all one to her that her mistress returned them to her
keeping, and refused to take further account of the ménage.

4

It seemed now to Athénaïse that Montéclin was the only friend
left to her in the world. Her father and mother had turned from
her in what appeared to be her hour of need. Her friends laughed
at her, and refused to take seriously the hints which she threw
out,—feeling her way to discover if marriage were as distasteful

to other women as to herself. Montéclin alone understood her. He alone had always been ready to act for her and with her, to comfort and solace her with his sympathy and support. Her only hope for rescue from her hateful surroundings lay in Montéclin. Of herself she felt powerless to plan, to act, even to conceive a way out of this pitfall into which the whole world seemed to have conspired to thrust her.

She had a great desire to see her brother, and wrote asking him to come to her. But it better suited Montéclin's spirit of adventure to appoint a meeting-place at the turn of the lane, where Athénaïse might appear to be walking leisurely for health and recreation, and where he might seem to be riding along, bent on some errand of business or pleasure.

There had been a shower, a sudden downpour, short as it was sudden, that had laid the dust in the road. It had freshened the pointed leaves of the live-oaks, and brightened up the big fields of cotton on either side of the lane till they seemed carpeted with green, glittering gems.

Athénaïse walked along the grassy edge of the road, lifting her crisp skirts with one hand, and with the other twirling a gay sun-shade over her bare head. The scent of the fields after the rain was delicious. She inhaled long breaths of their freshness and per-fume, that soothed and quieted her for the moment. There were birds splashing and spluttering in the pools, pluming themselves on the fence-rails, and sending out little sharp cries, twitters, and shrill rhapsodies of delight.

She saw Montéclin approaching from a great distance,—almost as far away as the turn of the woods. But she could not feel sure it was he; it appeared too tall for Montéclin, but that was because he was riding a large horse. She waved her parasol to him; she was so glad to see him. She had never been so glad to see Montéclin before; not even the day when he had taken her out of the convent, against her parents' wishes, because she had expressed a desire to remain there no longer. He seemed to her, as he drew near, the embodiment of kindness, of bravery, of chivalry, even of wisdom; for she had never known Montéclin at a loss to extricate himself from a disagreeable situation.

He dismounted, and, leading his horse by the bridle, started to walk beside her, after he had kissed her affectionately and asked her what she was crying about. She protested that she was not crying, for she was laughing, though drying her eyes at the same time on her handkerchief, rolled in a soft mop for the purpose.

She took Montéclin's arm, and they strolled slowly down the lane; they could not seat themselves for a comfortable chat, as they would have liked, with the grass all sparkling and bristling wet.

Yes, she was quite as wretched as ever, she told him. The week which had gone by since she saw him had in no wise lightened the burden of her discontent. There had even been some additional provocations laid upon her, and she told Montéclin all about them,—about the keys, for instance, which in a fit of temper she had returned to Félicité's keeping; and she told how Cazeau had brought them back to her as if they were something she had accidentally lost, and he had recovered; and how he had said, in that aggravating tone of his, that it was not the custom on Cane River for the negro servants to carry the keys, when there was a mistress at the head of the household.

But Athénaïse could not tell Montéclin anything to increase the disrespect which he already entertained for his brother-in-law; and it was then he unfolded to her a plan which he had conceived and worked out for her deliverance from this galling matrimonial yoke.

It was not a plan which met with instant favor, which she was at once ready to accept, for it involved secrecy and dissimulation, hateful alternatives both of them. But she was filled with admiration for Montéclin's resources and wonderful talent for contrivance. She accepted the plan; not with the immediate determination to act upon it, rather with the intention to sleep and to dream upon it.

Three days later she wrote to Montéclin that she had abandoned herself to his counsel. Displeasing as it might be to her sense of honesty, it would yet be less trying than to live on with a soul full of bitterness and revolt, as she had done for the past two months.

5

When Cazeau awoke, one morning, at his usual very early hour, it was to find the place at his side vacant. This did not surprise him until he discovered that Athénaïse was not in the adjoining room, where he had often found her sleeping in the morning on the lounge. She had perhaps gone out for an early stroll, he reflected, for her jacket and hat were not on the rack where she had hung them the night before. But there were other things absent,— a gown or two from the armoire; and there was a great gap in the piles of lingerie on the shelf; and her traveling-bag was missing, and so were her bits of jewelry from the toilet tray—and Athénaïse was gone!

But the absurdity of going during the night, as if she had been a prisoner, and he the keeper of a dungeon! So much secrecy and mystery, to go sojourning out on the Bon Dieu! Well, the Michés might keep their daughter after this. For the companionship of no woman on earth would he again undergo the humiliating sensation of baseness that had overtaken him in passing the old oak-tree in the fallow meadow.

But a terrible sense of loss overwhelmed Cazeau. It was not new or sudden; he had felt it for weeks growing upon him, and it seemed to culminate with Athénaïse's flight from home. He knew that he could again compel her return as he had done once before,—compel her return to the shelter of his roof, compel her cold and unwilling submission to his love and passionate transports; but the loss of self-respect seemed to him too dear a price to pay for a wife.

He could not comprehend why she had seemed to prefer him above others; why she had attracted him with eyes, with voice, with a hundred womanly ways, and finally distracted him with love which she seemed, in her timid, maidenly fashion, to return. The great sense of loss came from a realization of having missed a chance for happiness,—a chance that would come his way again only through a miracle. He could not think of himself loving any other woman, and could not think of Athénaïse ever—even at some remote date—caring for him.

He wrote her a letter, in which he disclaimed any further intention of forcing his commands upon her. He did not desire her presence ever again in his home unless she came of her free will, uninfluenced by family or friends; unless she could be the companion he had hoped for in marrying her, and in some measure return affection and respect for the love which he continued and would always continue to feel for her. This letter he sent out to the rigolet by a messenger early in the day. But she was not out on the rigolet, and had not been there.

The family turned instinctively to Montéclin, and almost literally fell upon him for an explanation; he had been absent from home all night. There was much mystification in his answers, and a plain desire to mislead in his assurances of ignorance and innocence.

But with Cazeau there was no doubt or speculation when he accosted the young fellow. "Montéclin, w'at have you done with Athénaïse?" he questioned bluntly. They had met in the open road on horseback, just as Cazeau ascended the river bank before his house.

"W'at have you done to Athénaïse?" returned Montéclin for answer.

"I don't reckon you've considered yo' conduct by any light of decency an' propriety in encouraging yo' sister to such an action, but let me tell you—"

"Voyons, you can let me alone with yo' decency an' morality an' fiddlesticks. I know you mus' 'a' done Athénaïse pretty mean that she can't live with you; an' fo' my part, I'm mighty durn glad she had the spirit to quit you."

"I ain't in the humor to take any notice of yo' impertinence, Montéclin; but let me remine you that Athénaïse is nothing but a chile in character; besides that, she's my wife, an' I hole you responsible fo' her safety an' welfare. If any harm of any description happens to her, I'll strangle you, by God, like a rat, and fling you in Cane River, if I have to hang fo' it!" He had not lifted his voice. The only sign of anger was a savage gleam in his eyes.

"I reckon you better keep yo' big talk fo' the women, Cazeau," replied Montéclin, riding away.

But he went doubly armed after that, and intimated that the precaution was not needless, in view of the threats and menaces that were abroad touching his personal safety.

6

Athénaïse reached her destination sound of skin and limb, but a good deal flustered, a little frightened, and altogether excited and interested by her unusual experiences.

Her destination was the house of Sylvie, on Dauphine Street, in New Orleans,—a three-story gray brick, standing directly on the banquette, with three broad stone steps leading to the deep front entrance. From the second-story balcony swung a small sign, conveying to passers-by the intelligence that within were "chambres garnies."

It was one morning in the last week of April that Athénaïse presented herself at the Dauphine Street house. Sylvie was expecting her, and introduced her at once to her apartment, which was in the second story of the back ell, and accessible by an open, outside gallery. There was a yard below, paved with broad stone flagging; many fragrant flowering shrubs and plants grew in a bed along the side of the opposite wall, and others were distributed about in tubs and green boxes.

It was a plain but large enough room into which Athénaïse was ushered, with matting on the floor, green shades and Nottingham-lace curtains at the windows that looked out on the gallery, and furnished with a cheap walnut suit. But everything looked exquisitely clean, and the whole place smelled of cleanliness.

Athénaïse at once fell into the rocking-chair, with the air of exhaustion and intense relief of one who has come to the end of her troubles. Sylvie, entering behind her, laid the big traveling-bag on the floor and deposited the jacket on the bed.

She was a portly quadroon of fifty or thereabout, clad in an ample volant of the old-fashioned purple calico so much affected by her class. She wore large golden hoop-earrings, and her hair was combed plainly, with every appearance of effort to smooth out the kinks. She had broad, coarse features, with a nose that turned up, exposing the wide nostrils, and that seemed to emphasize the loftiness and command of her bearing,—a dignity that in the presence of white people assumed a character of respectfulness, but never of obsequiousness. Sylvie believed firmly in maintaining the color-line, and would not suffer a white person, even a child, to call her "Madame Sylvie,"—a title which she exacted religiously, however, from those of her own race.

"I hope you be please' wid yo' room, madame," she observed amiably. "Dat's de same room w'at yo' brother, M'sieur Miché, all time like w'en he come to New Orlean'. He well, M'sieur Miché? I receive' his letter las' week, an' dat same day a gent'man want I give 'im dat room. I say, 'No, dat room already ingage'.' Ev'body like dat room on 'count it so quite [quiet]. M'sieur Gouvernail, dere in nax' room, you can't pay 'im! He been stay t'ree year' in dat room; but all fix' up fine wid his own furn'ture an' books, 'tel you can't see! I say to 'im plenty time', 'M'sieur Gouvernail, w'y you don' take dat t'ree-story front, now, long it's empty?' He tell me, 'Leave me 'lone, Sylvie; I know a good room w'en I fine it, me.' "

She had been moving slowly and majestically about the apartment, straightening and smoothing down bed and pillows, peering into ewer and basin, evidently casting an eye around to make sure that everything was as it should be.

"I sen' you some fresh water, madame," she offered upon retiring from the room. "An w'en you want an't'ing, you jus' go out on de gall'ry an' call Pousette: she year you plain,—she right down dere in de kitchen."

Athénaïse was really not so exhausted as she had every reason to be after that interminable and circuitous way by which Montéclin had seen fit to have her conveyed to the city.

Would she ever forget that dark and truly dangerous midnight ride along the "coast" to the mouth of Cane River! There Montéclin had parted with her, after seeing her aboard the St. Louis and Shreveport packet which he knew would pass there before dawn. She had received instructions to disembark at the mouth of Red River, and there transfer to the first southbound steamer for New Orleans: all of which instructions she had followed implicitly, even to making her way at once to Sylvie's upon her arrival in the city. Montéclin had enjoined secrecy and much caution; the clandestine nature of the affair gave it a savor of adventure which was highly pleasing to him. Eloping with his sister was only a little less engaging than eloping with some one else's sister.

But Montéclin did not do the grand seigneur by halves. He had paid Sylvie a whole month in advance for Athénaïse's board and lodging. Part of the sum he had been forced to borrow, it is true, but he was not niggardly.

Athénaïse was to take her meals in the house, which none of the other lodgers did; the one exception being that Mr. Gouvernail was served with breakfast on Sunday mornings.

Sylvie's clientèle came chiefly from the southern parishes; for the most part, people spending but a few days in the city. She prided herself upon the quality and highly respectable character of her patrons, who came and went unobtrusively.

The large parlor opening upon the front balcony was seldom used. Her guests were permitted to entertain in this sanctuary of elegance,—but they never did. She often rented it for the night to parties of respectable and discreet gentlemen desiring to enjoy a quiet game of cards outside the bosom of their families. The second-story hall also led by a long window out on the balcony. And Sylvie advised Athénaïse, when she grew weary of her back room, to go and sit on the front balcony, which was shady in the afternoon, and where she might find diversion in the sounds and sights of the street below.

Athénaïse refreshed herself with a bath, and was soon unpacking her few belongings, which she ranged neatly away in the bureau drawers and the armoire.

She had revolved certain plans in her mind during the past hour or so. Her present intention was to live on indefinitely in this big, cool, clean back room on Dauphine Street. She had thought seriously, for moments, of the convent, with all readiness to embrace the vows of poverty and chastity; but what about obedience? Later, she intended, in some roundabout way, to give her parents and her husband the assurance of her safety and welfare; reserving the right to remain unmolested and lost to them. To live on at the expense of Montéclin's generosity was wholly out of the question, and Athénaïse meant to look about for some suitable and agreeable employment.

The imperative thing to be done at present, however, was to go out in search of material for an inexpensive gown or two; for she found herself in the painful predicament of a young woman having almost literally nothing to wear. She decided upon pure white for one, and some sort of a sprigged muslin for the other.

7

On Sunday morning, two days after Athénaïse's arrival in the city, she went in to breakfast somewhat later than usual, to find two covers laid at table instead of the one to which she was accustomed. She had been to mass, and did not remove her hat, but put her fan, parasol, and prayer-book aside. The dining-room was situated just beneath her own apartment, and, like all the rooms of the house, was large and airy; the floor was covered with a glistening oil-cloth.

The small, round table, immaculately set, was drawn near the open window. There were some tall plants in boxes on the gallery outside; and Pousette, a little, old, intensely black woman, was splashing and dashing buckets of water on the flagging, and talking loud in her creole patois to no one in particular.

A dish piled with delicate river-shrimps and crushed ice was on the table; a caraffe of crystal-clear water, a few hors d'œuvres, beside a small golden-brown crusty loaf of French bread at each plate. A half-bottle of wine and the morning paper were set at the place opposite Athénaïse.

She had almost completed her breakfast when Gouvernail came in and seated himself at table. He felt annoyed at finding his cherished privacy invaded. Sylvie was removing the remains of a mutton-chop from before Athénaïse, and serving her with a cup of café au lait.

"M'sieur Gouvernail," offered Sylvie in her most insinuating and impressive manner, "you please leave me make you acquaint' wid Madame Cazeau. Dat's M'sieur Miché's sister; you meet 'im two t'ree time', you rec'lec', an' you been one day to de race wid 'im. Madame Cazeau, you please leave me make you acquaint' wid M'sieur Gouvernail."

Gouvernail expressed himself greatly pleased to meet the sister of Monsieur Miché, of whom he had not the slightest recollection. He inquired after Monsieur Miché's health, and politely offered Athénaïse a part of his newspaper—the part which contained the Woman's Page and the social gossip.

Athénaïse faintly remembered that Sylvie had spoken of a Monsieur Gouvernail occupying the room adjoining hers, living amid luxurious surroundings and a multitude of books. She had not thought of him further than to picture him a stout, middle-aged gentleman, with a bushy beard turning gray, wearing large gold-rimmed spectacles, and stooping somewhat from much bending over books and writing material. She had confused him in her mind with the likeness of some literary celebrity that she had run across in the advertising pages of a magazine.

Gouvernail's appearance was, in truth, in no sense striking. He looked older than thirty and younger than forty, was of medium height and weight, with a quiet, unobtrusive manner which seemed to ask that he be let alone. His hair was light brown, brushed carefully and parted in the middle. His mustache was brown, and so were his eyes, which had a mild, penetrating quality. He was neatly dressed in the fashion of the day; and his hands seemed to Athénaïse remarkably white and soft for a man's.

He had been buried in the contents of his newspaper, when he suddenly realized that some further little attention might be due to Miché's sister. He started to offer her a glass of wine, when he was surprised and relieved to find that she had quietly slipped away while he was absorbed in his own editorial on Corrupt Legislation.

Gouvernail finished his paper and smoked his cigar out on the gallery. He lounged about, gathered a rose for his buttonhole, and had his regular Sunday-morning confab with Pousette, to whom he paid a weekly stipend for brushing his shoes and clothes. He made a great pretense of haggling over the transaction, only to enjoy her uneasiness and garrulous excitement.

He worked or read in his room for a few hours, and when he quitted the house, at three in the afternoon, it was to return no more till late in the night. It was his almost invariable custom to spend Sunday evenings out in the American quarter, among a congenial set of men and women,—des esprits forts, all of them, whose lives were irreproachable, yet whose opinions would startle even the traditional "sapeur," for whom "nothing is sacred." But for all his "advanced" opinions, Gouvernail was a liberal-minded fellow; a man or woman lost nothing of his respect by being married.

When he left the house in the afternoon, Athénaïse had already ensconced herself on the front balcony. He could see her through the jalousies when he passed on his way to the front entrance. She had not yet grown lonesome or homesick; the newness of her surroundings made them sufficiently entertaining. She found it diverting to sit there on the front balcony watching people pass by, even though there was no one to talk to. And then the comforting, comfortable sense of not being married!

She watched Gouvernail walk down the street, and could find no fault with his bearing. He could hear the sound of her rockers for some little distance. He wondered what the "poor little thing" was doing in the city, and meant to ask Sylvie about her when he should happen to think of it.

8

The following morning, towards noon, when Gouvernail quitted his room, he was confronted by Athénaïse, exhibiting some confusion and trepidation at being forced to request a favor of him at so early a stage of their acquaintance. She stood in her doorway, and had evidently been sewing, as the thimble on her finger testified, as well as a long-threaded needle thrust in the bosom of her gown; and she held a stamped but unaddressed letter in her hand.

And would Mr. Gouvernail be so kind as to address the letter to her brother, Mr. Montéclin Miché? She would hate to detain him with explanations this morning,—another time, perhaps,—but now she begged that he would give himself the trouble.

He assured her that it made no difference, that it was no trouble whatever; and he drew a fountain pen from his pocket and addressed the letter at her dictation, resting it on the inverted rim of his straw hat. She wondered a little at a man of his supposed erudition stumbling over the spelling of "Montéclin" and "Miché."

She demurred at overwhelming him with the additional trouble of posting it, but he succeeded in convincing her that so simple a task as the posting of a letter would not add an iota to the burden of the day. Moreover, he promised to carry it in his hand, and thus avoid any possible risk of forgetting it in his pocket.

After that, and after a second repetition of the favor, when she had told him that she had had a letter from Montéclin, and looked as if she wanted to tell him more, he felt that he knew her better. He felt that he knew her well enough to join her out on the balcony, one night, when he found her sitting there alone. He was not one who deliberately sought the society of women, but he was not wholly a bear. A little commiseration for Athénaïse's aloneness, perhaps some curiosity to know further what manner of woman she was, and the natural influence of her feminine charm were equal unconfessed factors in turning his steps towards the balcony when he discovered the shimmer of her white gown through the open hall window.

It was already quite late, but the day had been intensely hot, and neighboring balconies and doorways were occupied by chattering groups of humanity, loath to abandon the grateful freshness of the outer air. The voices about her served to reveal to Athénaïse the feeling of loneliness that was gradually coming over her. Notwithstanding certain dormant impulses, she craved human sympathy and companionship.

She shook hands impulsively with Gouvernail, and told him how glad she was to see him. He was not prepared for such an admission, but it pleased him immensely, detecting as he did that the expression was as sincere as it was outspoken. He drew a chair up within comfortable conversational distance of Athénaïse, though he had no intention of talking more than was barely necessary to encourage Madame— He had actually forgotten her name!

He leaned an elbow on the balcony rail, and would have offered an opening remark about the oppressive heat of the day, but Athénaïse did not give him the opportunity. How glad she was to talk to some one, and how she talked!

An hour later she had gone to her room, and Gouvernail stayed smoking on the balcony. He knew her quite well after that hour's talk. It was not so much what she had said as what her half saying had revealed to his quick intelligence. He knew that she adored Montéclin, and he suspected that she adored Cazeau without being herself aware of it. He had gathered that she was self-willed, impulsive, innocent, ignorant, unsatisfied, dissatisfied; for had she not complained that things seemed all wrongly arranged in this world, and no one was permitted to be happy in his own way? And he told her he was sorry she had discovered that primordial fact of existence so early in life.

He commiserated her loneliness, and scanned his bookshelves next morning for something to lend her to read, rejecting everything that offered itself to his view. Philosophy was out of the question, and so was poetry; that is, such poetry as he possessed. He had not sounded her literary tastes, and strongly suspected she had none; that she would have rejected The Duchess as readily as Mrs. Humphry Ward. He compromised on a magazine.

It had entertained her passably, she admitted, upon returning it. A New England story had puzzled her, it was true, and a creole tale had offended her, but the pictures had pleased her greatly, especially one which had reminded her so strongly of Montéclin after a hard day's ride that she was loath to give it up. It was one

of Remington's Cowboys, and Gouvernail insisted upon her keeping it,—keeping the magazine.

He spoke to her daily after that, and was always eager to render
her some service or to do something towards her entertainment.

One afternoon he took her out to the lake end. She had been
there once, some years before, but in winter, so the trip was comparatively new and strange to her. The large expanse of water
studded with pleasure-boats, the sight of children playing merrily
along the grassy palisades, the music, all enchanted her. Gouvernail thought her the most beautiful woman he had ever seen. Even
her gown—the sprigged muslin—appeared to him the most charm-
ing one imaginable. Nor could anything be more becoming than
the arrangement of her brown hair under the white sailor hat, all
rolled back in a soft pluff from her radiant face. And she carried
her parasol and lifted her skirts and used her fan in ways that
seemed quite unique and peculiar to herself, and which he considered almost worthy of study and imitation.

They did not dine out there at the water's edge, as they might
have done, but returned early to the city to avoid the crowd.
Athénaïse wanted to go home, for she said Sylvie would have
dinner prepared and would be expecting her. But it was not difficult
to persuade her to dine instead in the quiet little restaurant that
he knew and liked, with its sanded floor, its secluded atmosphere,
its delicious menu, and its obsequious waiter wanting to know what
he might have the honor of serving to "monsieur et madame." No
wonder he made the mistake, with Gouvernail assuming such an
air of proprietorship. But Athénaïse was very tired after it all; the
sparkle went out of her face, and she hung draggingly on his arm
in walking home.

He was reluctant to part from her when she bade him good-
night at her door and thanked him for the agreeable evening. He
had hoped she would sit outside until it was time for him to regain
the newspaper office. He knew that she would undress and get
into her peignoir and lie upon her bed; and what he wanted to do,
what he would have given much to do, was to go and sit beside
her, read to her something restful, soothe her, do her bidding,
whatever it might be. Of course there was no use in thinking of
that. But he was surprised at his growing desire to be serving her.
She gave him an opportunity sooner than he looked for.

"Mr. Gouvernail," she called from her room, "will you be so
kine as to call Pousette an' tell her she fo'got to bring my ice-
water?"

He was indignant at Pousette's negligence, and called severely to her over the banisters. He was sitting before his own door, smoking. He knew that Athénaïse had gone to bed, for her room was dark, and she had opened the slats of the door and windows. Her bed was near a window.

Pousette came flopping up with the ice-water, and with a hundred excuses: "Mo pa oua vou à tab c'te lanuite, mo cri vou pé gagni déja là-bas; parole! Vou pas cri conté ça Madame Sylvie?" She had not seen Athénaïse at table, and thought she was gone. She swore to this, and hoped Madame Sylvie would not be informed of her remissness.

A little later Athénaïse lifted her voice again: "Mr. Gouvernail, did you remark that young man sitting on the opposite side from us, coming in, with a gray coat an' a blue ban' aroun' his hat?"

Of course Gouvernail had not noticed any such individual, but he assured Athénaïse that he had observed the young fellow particularly.

"Don't you think he looked something,—not *very* much, of co'se,—but don't you think he had a little faux-air of Montéclin?"

"I think he looked strikingly like Montéclin," asserted Gouvernail, with the one idea of prolonging the conversation. "I meant to call your attention to the resemblance, and something drove it out of my head."

"The same with me," returned Athénaïse. "Ah, my dear Montéclin! I wonder w'at he is doing now?"

"Did you receive any news, any letter from him to-day?" asked Gouvernail, determined that if the conversation ceased it should not be through lack of effort on his part to sustain it.

"Not to-day, but yesterday. He tells me that maman was so distracted with uneasiness that finally, to pacify her, he was fo'ced to confess that he knew w'ere I was, but that he was boun' by a vow of secrecy not to reveal it. But Cazeau has not noticed him or spoken to him since he threaten' to throw po' Montéclin in Cane River. You know Cazeau wrote me a letter the morning I lef', thinking I had gone to the rigolet. An' maman opened it, an' said it was full of the mos' noble sentiments, an' she wanted Montéclin to sen' it to me; but Montéclin refuse' poin'blank, so he wrote to me."

Gouvernail preferred to talk of Montéclin. He pictured Cazeau as unbearable, and did not like to think of him.

A little later Athénaïse called out, "Good-night, Mr. Gouvernail."

"Good-night," he returned reluctantly. And when he thought that she was sleeping, he got up and went away to the midnight pandemonium of his newspaper office.

9

Athénaïse could not have held out through the month had it not been for Gouvernail. With the need of caution and secrecy always uppermost in her mind, she made no new acquaintances, and she did not seek out persons already known to her; however, she knew so few, it required little effort to keep out of their way. As for Sylvie, almost every moment of her time was occupied in looking after her house; and, moreover, her deferential attitude towards her lodgers forbade anything like the gossipy chats in which Athénaïse might have condescended sometimes to indulge with her landlady. The transient lodgers, who came and went, she never had occasion to meet. Hence she was entirely dependent upon Gouvernail for company.

He appreciated the situation fully; and every moment that he could spare from his work he devoted to her entertainment. She liked to be out of doors, and they strolled together in the summer twilight through the mazes of the old French quarter. They went again to the lake end, and stayed for hours on the water; returning so late that the streets through which they passed were silent and deserted. On Sunday morning he arose at an unconscionable hour to take her to the French market, knowing that the sights and sounds there would interest her. And he did not join the intellectual coterie in the afternoon, as he usually did, but placed himself all day at the disposition and service of Athénaïse.

Notwithstanding all, his manner toward her was tactful, and evinced intelligence and a deep knowledge of her character, surprising upon so brief an acquaintance. For the time he was everything to her that she would have him; he replaced home and friends. Sometimes she wondered if he had ever loved a woman. She could not fancy him loving any one passionately, rudely, offensively, as Cazeau loved her. Once she was so naïve as to ask him outright if he had ever been in love, and he assured her promptly that he had not. She thought it an admirable trait in his character, and esteemed him greatly therefor.

He found her crying one night, not openly or violently. She was leaning over the gallery rail, watching the toads that hopped about in the moonlight, down on the damp flagstones of the courtyard. There was an oppressively sweet odor rising from the cape jessamine. Pousette was down there, mumbling and quarreling with some one, and seeming to be having it all her own way,—as well she might, when her companion was only a black cat that had come in from a neighboring yard to keep her company.

Athénaïse did admit feeling heart-sick, body-sick, when he questioned her; she supposed it was nothing but homesick. A letter from Montéclin had stirred her all up. She longed for her mother, for Montéclin; she was sick for a sight of the cotton-fields, the scent of the ploughed earth, for the dim, mysterious charm of the woods, and the old tumble-down home on the Bon Dieu.

As Gouvernail listened to her, a wave of pity and tenderness swept through him. He took her hands and pressed them against him. He wondered what would happen if he were to put his arms around her.

He was hardly prepared for what happened, but he stood it courageously. She twined her arms around his neck and wept outright on his shoulder; the hot tears scalding his cheek and neck, and her whole body shaken in his arms. The impulse was powerful to strain her to him; the temptation was fierce to seek her lips; but he did neither.

He understood a thousand times better than she herself understood it that he was acting as substitute for Montéclin. Bitter as the conviction was, he accepted it. He was patient; he could wait. He hoped some day to hold her with a lover's arms. That she was married made no particle of difference to Gouvernail. He could not conceive or dream of its making a difference. When the time came that she wanted him,—as he hoped and believed it would come,—he felt he would have a right to her. So long as she did not want him, he had no right to her,—no more than her husband had. It was very hard to feel her warm breath and tears upon his cheek, and her struggling bosom pressed against him, and her soft arms clinging to him, and his whole body and soul aching for her, and yet to make no sign.

He tried to think what Montéclin would have said and done, and to act accordingly. He stroked her hair, and held her in a gentle embrace, until the tears dried and the sobs ended. Before releasing herself she kissed him against the neck; she had to love somebody in her own way! Even that he endured like a stoic. But it was well he left her, to plunge into the thick of rapid, breathless, exacting work till nearly dawn.

Athénaïse was greatly soothed, and slept well. The touch of friendly hands and caressing arms had been very grateful. Henceforward she would not be lonely and unhappy, with Gouvernail there to comfort her.

10

The fourth week of Athénaïse's stay in the city was drawing to a close. Keeping in view the intention which she had of finding some suitable and agreeable employment, she had made a few tentatives in that direction. But with the exception of two little girls who had promised to take piano lessons at a price that it would be embarrassing to mention, these attempts had been fruitless. Moreover, the homesickness kept coming back, and Gouvernail was not always there to drive it away.

She spent much of her time weeding and pottering among the flowers down in the courtyard. She tried to take an interest in the black cat, and a mocking-bird that hung in a cage outside the kitchen door, and a disreputable parrot that belonged to the cook next door, and swore hoarsely all day long in bad French.

Besides, she was not well; she was not herself, as she told Sylvie. The climate of New Orleans did not agree with her. Sylvie was distressed to learn this, as she felt in some measure responsible for the health and well-being of Monsieur Miché's sister; and she made it her duty to inquire closely into the nature and character of Athénaïse's malaise.

Sylvie was very wise, and Athénaïse was very ignorant. The extent of her ignorance and the depth of her subsequent enlightenment were bewildering. She stayed a long, long time quite still, quite stunned, except for the short, uneven breathing that ruffled her bosom. Her whole being was steeped in a wave of ecstasy. When she finally arose from the chair in which she had been seated, and looked at herself in the mirror, a face met hers which she seemed to see for the first time, so transfigured was it with wonder and rapture.

One mood quickly followed another, in this new turmoil of her senses, and the need of action became uppermost. Her mother must know at once, and her mother must tell Montéclin. And Cazeau must know. As she thought of him, the first purely sensuous tremor of her life swept over her. She half whispered his name, and the sound of it brought red blotches into her cheeks. She spoke it over and over, as if it were some new, sweet sound born out of darkness and confusion, and reaching her for the first time. She was impatient to be with him. Her whole passionate nature was aroused as if by a miracle.

She seated herself to write to her husband. The letter he would get in the morning, and she would be with him at night. What would he say? How would he act? She knew that he would forgive her, for had he not written a letter?—and a pang of resentment toward Montéclin shot through her. What did he mean by with-holding that letter? How dared he not have sent it?

Athénaïse attired herself for the street, and went out to post the letter which she had penned with a single thought, a spontaneous impulse. It would have seemed incoherent to most people, but Cazeau would understand.

She walked along the street as if she had fallen heir to some magnificent inheritance. On her face was a look of pride and sat-isfaction that passers-by noticed and admired. She wanted to talk to some one, to tell some person; and she stopped at the corner and told the oyster-woman, who was Irish, and who God-blessed her, and wished prosperity to the race of Cazeaus for generations to come. She held the oyster-woman's fat, dirty little baby in her arms and scanned it curiously and observingly, as if a baby were a phenomenon that she encountered for the first time in life. She even kissed it!

Then what a relief it was to Athénaïse to walk the streets without dread of being seen and recognized by some chance acquaintance from Red River! No one could have said now that she did not know her own mind.

She went directly from the oyster-woman's to the office of Hard-ing & Offdean, her husband's merchants; and it was with such an air of partnership, almost proprietorship, that she demanded a sum of money on her husband's account, they gave it to her as unhesitatingly as they would have handed it over to Cazeau him-self. When Mr. Harding, who knew her, asked politely after her health, she turned so rosy and looked so conscious, he thought it a great pity for so pretty a woman to be such a little goose.

Athénaïse entered a dry-goods store and bought all manner of things,—little presents for nearly everybody she knew. She bought whole bolts of sheerest, softest, downiest white stuff; and when the clerk, in trying to meet her wishes, asked if she intended it for infant's use, she could have sunk through the floor, and wondered how he might have suspected it.

As it was Montéclin who had taken her away from her husband, she wanted it to be Montéclin who should take her back to him. So she wrote him a very curt note,—in fact it was a postal card,—asking that he meet her at the train on the evening following. She felt convinced that after what had gone before, Cazeau would await her at their own home; and she preferred it so.

Then there was the agreeable excitement of getting ready to leave, of packing up her things. Pousette kept coming and going, coming and going; and each time that she quitted the room it was with something that Athénaïse had given her,—a handkerchief, a petticoat, a pair of stockings with two tiny holes at the toes, some broken prayer-beads, and finally a silver dollar.

Next it was Sylvie who came along bearing a gift of what she called "a set of pattern',"—things of complicated design which never could have been obtained in any new-fangled bazaar or pattern-store, that Sylvie had acquired of a foreign lady of distinction whom she had nursed years before at the St. Charles Hotel. Athénaïse accepted and handled them with reverence, fully sensible of the great compliment and favor, and laid them religiously away in the trunk which she had lately acquired.

She was greatly fatigued after the day of unusual exertion, and went early to bed and to sleep. All day long she had not once thought of Gouvernail, and only did think of him when aroused for a brief instant by the sound of his foot falls on the gallery, as he passed in going to his room. He had hoped to find her up, waiting for him.

But the next morning he knew. Some one must have told him. There was no subject known to her which Sylvie hesitated to discuss in detail with any man of suitable years and discretion.

Athénaïse found Gouvernail waiting with a carriage to convey her to the railway station. A momentary pang visited her for having forgotten him so completely, when he said to her, "Sylvie tells me you are going away this morning."

He was kind, attentive, and amiable, as usual, but respected to the utmost the new dignity and reserve that her manner had developed since yesterday. She kept looking from the carriage window, silent, and embarrassed as Eve after losing her ignorance. He talked of the muddy streets and the murky morning, and of Montéclin. He hoped she would find everything comfortable and pleasant in the country, and trusted she would inform him whenever she came to visit the city again. He talked as if afraid or mistrustful of silence and himself.

At the station she handed him her purse, and he bought her ticket, secured for her a comfortable section, checked her trunk, and got all the bundles and things safely aboard the train. She felt very grateful. He pressed her hand warmly, lifted his hat, and left her. He was a man of intelligence, and took defeat gracefully; that was all. But as he made his way back to the carriage, he was thinking, "By Heaven, it hurts, it hurts!"

11

Athénaïse spent a day of supreme happiness and expectancy. The fair sight of the country unfolding itself before her was balm to her vision and to her soul. She was charmed with the rather unfamiliar, broad, clean sweep of the sugar plantations, with their monster sugar-houses, their rows of neat cabins like little villages of a single street, and their impressive homes standing apart amid clusters of trees. There were sudden glimpses of a bayou curling between sunny, grassy banks, or creeping sluggishly out from a tangled growth of wood, and brush, and fern, and poison-vines, and palmettos. And passing through the long stretches of monotonous woodlands, she would close her eyes and taste in anticipation the moment of her meeting with Cazeau. She could think of nothing but him.

It was night when she reached her station. There was Montéclin, as she had expected, waiting for her with a two-seated buggy, to which he had hitched his own swift-footed, spirited pony. It was good, he felt, to have her back on any terms; and he had no fault to find since she came of her own choice. He more than suspected the cause of her coming; her eyes and her voice and her foolish little manner went far in revealing the secret that was brimming over in her heart. But after he had deposited her at her own gate, and as he continued his way toward the rigolet, he could not help feeling that the affair had taken a very disappointing, an ordinary, a most commonplace turn, after all. He left her in Cazeau's keeping.

Her husband lifted her out of the buggy, and neither said a word until they stood together within the shelter of the gallery. Even then they did not speak at first. But Athénaïse turned to him with an appealing gesture. As he clasped her in his arms, he felt the yielding of her whole body against him. He felt her lips for the first time respond to the passion of his own.

The country night was dark and warm and still, save for the distant notes of an accordion which some one was playing in a cabin away off. A little negro baby was crying somewhere. As Athénaïse withdrew from her husband's embrace, the sound arrested her.

"Listen, Cazeau! How Juliette's baby is crying! Pauvre ti chou, I wonder w'at is the matter with it?"

Charles Egbert Craddock
(Mary Noailles Murfree)

(1850–1922)

Born on the large family plantation, Grantland, in middle Tennessee, near Murfreesboro—the town had been renamed to honor her great-grandfather—Mary Noailles Murfree was raised surrounded by the advantages of wealth and of parents who were well-read and cultivated. Her mother was a lover of music, and her father was a lawyer, a linguist, and a writer who encouraged her and helped her on her first stories. Slightly crippled by an early illness, she led a sheltered childhood, but traveled frequently around Tennessee with her parents. Her summers were spent in resorts in the Cumberlands and the Great Smokies, and there, as a familiar outsider, she observed the Tennessee mountain people who figure in most of her writing. She attended the Nashville Female Academy and the Chegary Institute in Philadelphia. During the Civil War, the colonial house at Grantland was destroyed in a battle whose aftermath she described in her novel Where the Battle Was Fought (1884). In the 1880s, she lived for several years in St. Louis—as always, with her parents and sister—before returning to Murfreesboro in 1890. Her first stories were published under the pseudonym, Charles Craddock, and she continued to be known by this name even after she created a national literary sensation by revealing her identity in 1885. She has been accused of some of the common weaknesses of the "local color" school: stock characters and an uneasy mixture of romance and realism, especially in the juxtaposition of a lush, literary narrative with a too-emphatic phonetic dialect. But many of the objections to her writing come from the fact that she repeated herself again and again. Despite this, she achieved memorable work in her four best books: In the Tennessee Mountains (1884), The Prophet of the Great Smoky Mountains (1885), In the Clouds (1886), and In the "Stranger People's" Country (1891). Extremely popular in the first years of her career, her reputation drifted more and more into obscurity as she turned to historical fiction. She died *an invalid, and almost destitute, in Murfreesboro. Her other books include* Down the Ravine *(1885)*, His Vanished Star *(1894)*, The Phantoms of the Foot-Bridge and Other Stories *(1895)*, The Juggler *(1897)*, The Young Mountaineers *(1897)*, The Story of Old Fort Loudon *(1899)*, The Frontiersmen *(1904)*, The Windfall *(1907)*, The Ordeal: A Mountain Romance of Tennessee *(1912)*, *and* The Raid of the Guerilla and Other Stories *(1912)*. *"The 'Harnt' That Walks Chilhowee" is taken from* In the Tennessee Mountains *and was first published in* The Atlantic Monthly *(May 1883)*.

THE "HARNT"
THAT WALKS CHILHOWEE

✿

June had crossed the borders of Tennessee. Even on the summit of Chilhowee Mountain the apples in Peter Giles's orchard were beginning to redden, and his Indian corn, planted on so steep a declivity that the stalks seemed to have much ado to keep their footing, was crested with tassels and plumed with silk. Among the dense forests, seen by no man's eye, the elder was flying its creamy banners in honor of June's coming, and, heard by no man's ear, the pink and white bells of the azalea rang out melodies of welcome.

"An' it air a toler'ble for'ard season. Yer wheat looks likely; an' yer gyarden truck air thrivin' powerful. Even that cold spell we-uns hed about the full o' the moon in May ain't done sot it back none, it 'pears like ter me. But, 'cording ter my way o' thinkin', ye hev got chickens enough hyar ter eat off every pea-bloom ez soon ez it opens." And Simon Burney glanced with a gardener's disapproval at the numerous fowls, lifting their red combs and tufted top-knots here and there among the thick clover under the apple-trees.

"Them's Clarsie's chickens,—my darter, ye know," drawled Peter Giles, a pale, listless, and lank mountaineer. "An' she hev been gin ter onderstand ez they hev got ter be kep' out 'n the gyarden; 'thout," he added indulgently,—" 'thout I'm a-plowin', when I lets 'em foller in the furrow ter pick up worms. But law!

Clarsie is so spry that she don't ax no better 'n ter be let ter run them chickens off'n the peas."

Then the two men tilted their chairs against the posts of the little porch in front of Peter Giles's log cabin, and puffed their pipes in silence. The panorama spread out before them showed misty and dreamy among the delicate spiral wreaths of smoke. But was that gossamer-like illusion, lying upon the far horizon, the magic of nicotian, or the vague presence of distant heights? As ridge after ridge came down from the sky in ever-graduating shades of intenser blue, Peter Giles might have told you that this parallel system of enchantment was only "the mountings": that here was Foxy, and there was Big Injun, and still beyond was another, which he had "hearn tell ran spang up into Virginny." The sky that bent to clasp this kindred blue was of varying moods. Floods of sunshine submerged Chilhowee in liquid gold, and revealed that dainty outline limned upon the northern horizon; but over the Great Smoky mountains clouds had gathered, and a gigantic rainbow bridged the valley.

Peter Giles's listless eyes were fixed upon a bit of red clay road, which was visible through a gap in the foliage far below. Even a tiny object, that ant-like crawled upon it, could be seen from the summit of Chilhowee. "I reckon that's my brother's wagon an' team," he said, as he watched the moving atom pass under the gorgeous triumphal arch. "He 'lowed he war goin' ter the Cross-Roads ter-day."

Simon Burney did not speak for a moment. When he did, his words seemed widely irrelevant. "That's a likely gal o' yourn," he drawled, with an odd constraint in his voice,—"a likely gal, that Clarsie."

There was a quick flash of surprise in Peter Giles's dull eyes. He covertly surveyed his guest, with an astounded curiosity rampant in his slow brains. Simon Burney had changed color; an expression of embarrassment lurked in every line of his honest, florid, hard-featured face. An alert imagination might have detected a deprecatory self-consciousness in every gray hair that striped the black beard raggedly fringing his chin.

"Yes," Peter Giles at length replied, "Clarsie air a likely enough gal. But she air mightily sot ter hevin' her own way. An' ef 't ain't give ter her peaceable-like, she jes' takes it, whether or no."

This statement, made by one presumably fully informed on the subject, might have damped the ardor of many a suitor,—for the monstrous truth was dawning on Peter Giles's mind that suitor was the position to which this slow, elderly widower aspired. But Simon Burney, with that odd, all-pervading constraint still prominently apparent, mildly observed, "Waal, ez much ez I hev seen of her goin's-on, it 'pears ter me ez her way air a mighty good way. An' it ain't comical that she likes it."

Urgent justice compelled Peter Giles to make some amends to the absent Clarissa. "That's a fac'," he admitted. "An' Clarsie ain't no hand ter jaw. She don't hev no words. But then," he qualified, truth and consistency alike constraining him, "she air a toler'ble hard-headed gal. That air a true word. Ye mought ez well try ter hender the sun from shining ez ter make that thar Clarsie Giles do what she don't want ter do."

To be sure, Peter Giles had a right to his opinion as to the hardness of his own daughter's head. The expression of his views, however, provoked Simon Burney to wrath; there was something astir within him that in a worthier subject might have been called a chivalric thrill, and it forbade him to hold his peace. He retorted: "Of course ye kin say that, ef so minded; but ennybody ez hev got eyes kin see the change ez hev been made in this hyar place sence that thar gal hev been growed. I ain't a-purtendin' ter know that thar Clarsie ez well ez you-uns knows her hyar at home, but I hev seen enough, an' a deal more 'n enough, of her goin's-on, ter know that what she does ain't done fur *herself*. An' ef she will hev her way, it air fur the good of the whole tribe of ye. It 'pears ter me ez thar ain't many gals like that thar Clarsie. An' she air a merciful critter. She air mighty savin' of the feelin's of everything, from the cow an' the mare down ter the dogs, an' pigs, an' chickens; always a-feedin' of 'em jes' ter the time, an' never draggin', an' clawin', an' beatin' of 'em. Why, that thar Clarsie can't put her foot out'n the door, that every dumb beastis on this hyar place ain't a-runnin' ter git nigh her. I hev seen them pigs mos' climb the fence when she shows her face at the door. 'Pears ter me ez that thar Clarsie could tame a b'ar, ef she looked at him a time or two, she's so savin' o' the critter's feelin's! An' thar's that old yaller dog o' yourn," pointing to an ancient cur that was blinking in the sun, "he's older 'n Clarsie, an' no 'count in the worl'. I hev hearn ye say forty times that ye would kill him, 'ceptin' that Clarsie purtected him, an' hed sot her heart on his a-livin' along. An' all the home-folks, an' everybody that kems hyar to sot an' talk awhile, never misses a chance ter kick that thar old dog, or poke him with a stick, or cuss him. But Clarsie!—I hev seen that gal take the bread an' meat off'n her plate, an' give it ter that old dog, ez 'pears ter me ter be the worst dispositionest dog I ever see, an' no thanks lef' in him. He hain't hed the grace ter wag his tail fur twenty year. That thar Clarsie air surely a merciful critter, an' a mighty spry, likely young gal, besides."

Peter Giles sat in stunned astonishment during this speech, which was delivered in a slow, drawling monotone, with frequent meditative pauses, but nevertheless emphatically. He made no reply, and as they were once more silent there rose suddenly the sound of melody upon the air. It came from beyond that tumultuous stream that raced with the wind down the mountain's side; a great log thrown from bank to bank served as bridge. The song grew momentarily more distinct; among the leaves there were fugitive glimpses of blue and white, and at last Clarsie appeared, walking lightly along the log, clad in her checked homespun dress, and with a pail upon her head.

She was a tall, lithe girl, with that delicately transparent complexion often seen among the women of these mountains. Her lustreless black hair lay along her forehead without a ripple or wave; there was something in the expression of her large eyes that suggested those of a deer,—something free, untamable, and yet gentle. " 'T ain't no wonder ter me ez Clarsie is all tuk up with the wild things, an' critters ginerally," her mother was wont to say. "She sorter looks like 'em, I'm a-thinkin'."

As she came in sight there was a renewal of that odd constraint in Simon Burney's face and manner, and he rose abruptly. "Waal," he said, hastily, going to his horse, a raw-boned sorrel, hitched to the fence, "it's about time I war a-startin' home, I reckons."

He nodded to his host, who silently nodded in return, and the old horse jogged off with him down the road, as Clarsie entered the house and placed the pail upon a shelf.

"Who d' ye think hev been hyar a-speakin' of complimints on ye, Clarsie?" exclaimed Mrs. Giles, who had overheard through the open door every word of the loud, drawling voice on the porch.

Clarsie's liquid eyes widened with surprise, and a faint tinge of rose sprang into her pale face, as she looked an expectant inquiry at her mother.

Mrs. Giles was a slovenly, indolent woman, anxious, at the age of forty-five, to assume the prerogatives of advanced years. She had placed all her domestic cares upon the shapely shoulders of her willing daughter, and had betaken herself to the chimney-corner and a pipe.

"Yes, thar hev been somebody hyar a-speakin' of complimints on ye, Clarsie," she reiterated, with chuckling amusement. "He war a mighty peart, likely boy,—that he war!"

Clarsie's color deepened.

"Old Simon Burney!" exclaimed her mother, in great glee at the incongruity of the idea. "*Old Simon Burney!*—jes' a-sittin' out thar, a-wastin' the time, an' a-burnin' of daylight—jes' ez perlite an' smilin' ez a basket of chips—a-speakin' of compli*mints* on ye!''

There was a flash of laughter among the sylvan suggestions of Clarsie's eyes,—a flash as of sudden sunlight upon water. But despite her mirth she seemed to be unaccountably disappointed. The change in her manner was not noticed by her mother, who continued banteringly,—

"Simon Burney air a mighty pore old man. Ye oughter be sorry fur him, Clarsie. Ye must n't think less of folks than ye does of the dumb beastis,—that ain't religion. Ye knows ye air sorry fur mos' everything; why not fur this comical old consarn? Ye oughter marry him ter take keer of him. He said ye war a merciful critter; now is yer chance ter show it! Why, air ye a-goin' ter weavin', Clarsie, jes' when I wants ter talk ter ye 'bout 'n old Simon Burney? But law! I knows ye kerry him with ye in yer heart.''

The girl summarily closed the conversation by seating herself before a great hand-loom; presently the persistent thump, thump, of the batten and the noisy creak of the treadle filled the room, and through all the long, hot afternoon her deft, practiced hands lightly tossed the shuttle to and fro.

The breeze freshened, after the sun went down, and the hop and gourd vines were all astir as they clung about the little porch where Clarsie was sitting now, idle at last. The rain clouds had disappeared, and there bent over the dark, heavily wooded ridges a pale blue sky, with here and there the crystalline sparkle of a star. A halo was shimmering in the east, where the mists had gathered about the great white moon, hanging high above the mountains. Noiseless wings flitted through the dusk; now and then the bats swept by so close as to wave Clarsie's hair with the wind of their flight. What an airy, glittering, magical thing was that gigantic spider-web suspended between the silver moon and her shining eyes! Ever and anon there came from the woods a strange, weird, long-drawn sigh, unlike the stir of the wind in the trees, unlike the fret of the water on the rocks. Was it the voiceless sorrow of the sad earth? There were stars in the night besides those known to astronomers: the stellular fireflies gemmed the black shadows with a fluctuating brilliancy; they circled in and out of the porch, and touched the leaves above Clarsie's head with quivering points of light. A steadier and an intenser gleam was advancing along the road, and the sound of languid footsteps came with it; the aroma of tobacco graced the atmosphere, and a tall figure walked up to the gate.

"Come in, come in," said Peter Giles, rising, and tendering the guest a chair. "Ye air Tom Pratt, ez well ez I kin make out by this light. Waal, Tom, we hain't furgot ye sence ye done been hyar.''

As Tom had been there on the previous evening, this might be considered a joke, or an equivocal compliment. The young fellow was restless and awkward under it, but Mrs. Giles chuckled with great merriment.

"An' how air ye a-comin' on, Mrs. Giles?" he asked propitiatorily.

"Jes' toler'ble, Tom. Air they all well ter yer house?"

"Yes, they're toler'ble well, too." He glanced at Clarsie, intending to address to her some polite greeting, but the expression of her shy, half-startled eyes, turned upon the far-away moon, warned him. "Thar never war a gal so skittish," he thought. "She'd run a mile, skeered ter death, ef I said a word ter her."

And he was prudently silent.

"Waal," said Peter Giles, "what's the news out yer way, Tom? Ennything a-goin' on?"

"Thar war a shower yander on the Backbone; it rained toler'ble hard fur a while, an' sot up the corn wonderful. Did ye git enny hyar?"

"Not a drap."

" 'Pears ter me ez I kin see the clouds a-circlin' round Chilhowee, an' a-rainin' on everybody's corn-field 'ceptin' ourn," said Mrs. Giles. "Some folks is the favored of the Lord, an' t' others hev ter work fur everything an' git nuthin'. Waal, waal; we-uns will see our reward in the nex' worl'. Thar's a better worl' than this, Tom."

"That's a fac'," said Tom, in orthodox assent.

"An' when we leaves hyar once, we leaves all trouble an' care behind us, Tom; fur we don't come back no more." Mrs. Giles was drifting into one of her pious moods.

"I dunno," said Tom. "Thar hev been them ez hev."

"Hev what?" demanded Peter Giles, startled.

"Hev come back ter this hyar yearth. Thar's a harnt that walks Chilhowee every night o' the worl'. I know them ez hev seen him."

Clarsie's great dilated eyes were fastened on the speaker's face. There was a dead silence for a moment, more eloquent with these looks of amazement than any words could have been.

"I reckons ye remember a puny, shriveled little man, named Reuben Crabb, ez used ter live yander, eight mile along the ridge ter that thar big sulphur spring," Tom resumed, appealing to Peter Giles. "He war born with only one arm."

"I 'members him," interpolated Mrs. Giles, vivaciously. "He war a mighty porely, sickly little critter, all the days of his life. 'T war a wonder he war ever raised ter be a man,—an' a pity, too. An' 't war powerful comical, the way of his takin' off; a stunted, one-armed little critter a-ondertakin' ter fight folks an' shoot pistols. He hed the use o' his one arm, sure."

"Waal," said Tom, "his house ain't thar now, 'kase Sam Grim's brothers burned it ter the ground fur his a-killin' of Sam. That warn't all that war done ter Reuben fur killin' of Sam. The sheriff run Reuben Crabb down this hyar road 'bout a mile from hyar,— mebbe less,—an' shot him dead in the road, jes' whar it forks. Waal, Reuben war in company with another evil-doer,—*he* war from the Cross-Roads, an' I furgits what he hed done, but he war a-tryin' ter hide in the mountings, too; an' the sheriff lef' Reuben a-lying thar in the road, while he tries ter ketch up with the t'other; but his horse got a stone in his hoof, an' he los' time, an' hed ter gin it up. An' when he got back ter the forks o' the road whar he had lef' Reuben a-lyin' dead, thar war nuthin' thar 'ceptin' a pool o' blood. Waal, he went right on ter Reuben's house, an' them Grim boys hed burnt it ter the ground; but he seen Reuben's brother Joel. An' Joel, he tole the sheriff that late that evenin' he hed tuk Reuben's body out'n the road an' buried it, 'kase it hed been lyin' thar in the road ever sence early in the mornin', an' he could n't leave it thar all night, an' he hed n't no shelter fur it, sence the Grim boys hed burnt down the house. So he war obleeged ter bury it. An' Joel showed the sheriff a new-made grave, an' Reuben's coat whar the sheriff's bullet hed gone in at the back an' kem out'n the breast. The sheriff 'lowed ez they'd fine Joel fifty dollars fur a-buryin' of Reuben afore the cor'ner kem; but they never done it, ez I knows on. The sheriff said that when the cor'ner kem the body would be tuk up fur a 'quest. But thar hed been a powerful big frishet, an' the river 'twixt the cor'ner's house an' Chilhowee could n't be forded fur three weeks. The cor'ner never kem, an' so thar it all stayed. That war four year ago."

"Waal," said Peter Giles, dryly, "I ain't seen no harnt yit. I knowed all that afore."

Clarsie's wondering eyes upon the young man's moonlit face had elicited these facts, familiar to the elders, but strange, he knew, to her.

"I war jes' a-goin' on ter tell," said Tom, abashed. "Waal, ever sence his brother Joel died, this spring, Reuben's harnt walks Chilhowee. He war seen week afore las', 'bout day-break, by Ephraim Blenkins, who hed been a-fishin', an' war a-goin' home. Eph happened ter stop in the laurel ter wind up his line, when all in a minit he seen the harnt go by, his face white, an' his eye-balls like fire, an' puny an' one-armed, jes' like he lived. Eph, he owed me a haffen day's work; I holped him ter plow las' month, an' so he kem ter-day an' hoed along cornsider'ble ter pay fur it. He say he believes the harnt never seen him, 'kase it went right by. He 'lowed ef the harnt hed so much ez cut one o' them blazin' eyes round at him he could n't but hev drapped dead. Waal, this mornin', 'bout sunrise, my brother Bob's little gal, three year old, strayed off from home while her mother war out milkin' the cow. An' we went a-huntin' of her, mightily worked up, 'kase thar hev been a b'ar prowlin' round our cornfield twict this summer. An' I went to the right, an' Bob went to the lef'. An' he say ez he war a-pushin' 'long through the laurel, he seen the bushes ahead of him a-rustlin'. An' he jes' stood still an' watched 'em. An' fur a while the bushes war still too; an' then they moved jes' a little, fust this way an' then that, till all of a suddint the leaves opened, like the mouth of hell mought hev done, an' thar he seen Reuben Crabb's face. He say he never seen sech a face! Its mouth war open, an' its eyes war a-startin' out 'n its head, an' its skin war white till it war blue; an' ef the devil hed hed it a-hangin' over the coals that minit it could n't hev looked no more skeered. But that war all that Bob seen, 'kase he jes' shet his eyes an' screeched an' screeched like he war *de*stracted. An' when he stopped a second ter ketch his breath he hearn su'thin' a-answerin' him back, sorter weak-like, an' thar war little Peggy a-pullin' through the laurel. Ye know she's too little ter talk good, but the folks down ter our house believes she seen the harnt, too."

"My Lord!" exclaimed Peter Giles. "I 'low I could n't live a minit ef I war ter see that thar harnt that walks Chilhowee!"

"I know *I* could n't," said his wife.

"Nor me, nuther," murmured Clarsie.

"Waal," said Tom, resuming the thread of his narrative, "we hev all been a-talkin' down yander ter our house ter make out the reason why Reuben Crabb's harnt hev sot out ter walk *jes' sence his brother Joel died,*—'kase it war never seen afore then. An' ez nigh ez we kin make it out, the reason is 'kase thar 's nobody lef' in this hyar worl' what believes he war n't ter blame in that thar killin' o' Sam Grim. Joel always swore ez Reuben never killed him no more 'n nuthin'; that Sam's own pistol went off in his own hand, an' shot him through the heart jes' ez he war a-drawin' of it ter shoot Reuben Crabb. An' I hev hearn other men ez war a-standin' by say the same thing, though them Grims tells another tale; but ez Reuben never owned no pistol in his life, nor kerried one, it don't 'pear ter me ez what them Grims say air reasonable. Joel always swore ez Sam Grim war a mighty mean man,—a great big feller like him a-rockin' of a deformed little critter, an' a-mockin' of him, an' a-hittin' of him. An' the day of the fight Sam jes' knocked him down fur nuthin' at all; an' afore ye could wink

Reuben jumped up suddint, an' flew at him like an eagle, an' struck him in the face. An' then Sam drawed his pistol, an' it went off in his own hand, an' shot him through the heart, an' killed him dead. Joel said that ef he could hev kep' that pore little critter Reuben still, an' let the sheriff arrest him peaceable-like, he war sure the jury would hev let him off; 'kase how war Reuben a-goin' ter shoot ennybody when Sam Grim never left a-holt of the only pistol between 'em, in life, or in death? They tells me they hed ter bury Sam Grim with that thar pistol in his hand; his grip war too tight fur death to unloose it. But Joel said that Reuben war sartain they 'd hang him. He hed n't never seen no jestice from enny one man, an' he could n't look fur it from twelve men. So he jes' sot out ter run through the woods, like a painter or a wolf, ter be hunted by the sheriff, an' he war run down an' kilt in the road. Joel said *he* kep' up arter the sheriff ez well ez he could on foot,—fur the Crabbs never hed no horse,—ter try ter beg fur Reuben, ef he war cotched, an' tell how little an' how weakly he war. I never seen a young man's head turn white like Joel's done; he said he reckoned it war his troubles. But ter the las' he stuck ter his rifle faithful. He war a powerful hunter; he war out rain or shine, hot or cold, in sech weather ez other folks would think thar war n't no use in tryin' ter do nuthin' in. I'm mightily afeard o' seein' Reuben, now, that's a fac'," concluded Tom, frankly; " 'kase I hev hearn tell, an' I believes it, that ef a harnt speaks ter ye, it air sartain ye 're bound ter die right then."

" 'Pears ter me," said Mrs. Giles, "ez many mountings ez thar air round hyar, he mought hev tuk ter walkin' some o' them, stiddier Chilhowee."

There was a sudden noise close at hand: a great inverted splint-basket, from which came a sound of flapping wings, began to move slightly back and forth. Mrs. Giles gasped out an ejaculation of terror, the two men sprang to their feet, and the coy Clarsie laughed aloud in an exuberance of delighted mirth, forgetful of her shyness. "I declar' ter goodness, you-uns air all skeered fur true! Did ye think it war the harnt that walks Chilhowee?"

"What's under that thar basket?" demanded Peter Giles, rather sheepishly, as he sat down again.

"Nuthin' but the duck-legged Dominicky," said Clarsie, "what air bein' broke up from settin'." The moonlight was full upon the dimpling merriment in her face, upon her shining eyes and parted red lips, and her gurgling laughter was pleasant to hear. Tom Pratt edged his chair a trifle nearer, as he, too, sat down.

"Ye ought n't never ter break up a duck-legged hen, nor a Dominicky, nuther," he volunteered, " 'kase they air sech a good kind o' hen ter kerry chickens; but a hen that is duck-legged an' Dominicky too oughter be let ter set, whether or no."

Had he been warned in a dream, he could have found no more secure road to Clarsie's favor and interest than a discussion of the poultry. "I'm a-thinkin'," she said, "that it air too hot fur hens ter set now, an' 't will be till the las' of August."

"It don't 'pear ter me ez it air hot much in June up hyar on Chilhowee,—thar's a differ, I know, down in the valley; but till July, on Chilhowee, it don't 'pear ter me ez it air too hot ter set a hen. An' a duck-legged Dominicky air mighty hard ter break up."

"That's a fac'," Clarsie admitted; "but I'll hev ter do it, some-how, 'kase I ain't got no eggs fur her. All my hens air kerryin' of chickens."

"Waal!" exclaimed Tom, seizing his opportunity, "I'll bring ye some ter-morrer night, when I come agin. We-uns hev got eggs ter our house."

"Thanky," said Clarsie, shyly smiling.

This unique method of courtship would have progressed very prosperously but for the interference of the elders, who are an element always more or less adverse to love-making. "Ye oughter turn out yer hen now, Clarsie," said Mrs. Giles, "ez Tom air a-goin' ter bring ye some eggs ter-morrer. I wonder ye don't think it's mean ter keep her up longer'n ye air obleeged ter. Ye oughter remember ye war called a merciful critter jes' ter-day."

Clarsie rose precipitately, raised the basket, and out flew the "duck-legged Dominicky," with a frantic flutter and hysterical cackling. But Mrs. Giles was not to be diverted from her purpose; her thoughts had recurred to the absurd episode of the afternoon, and with her relish of the incongruity of the joke she opened upon the subject at once.

"Waal, Tom," she said, "we'll be hevin' Clarsie married, afore long, I'm a-thinkin'." The young man sat bewildered. He, too, had entertained views concerning Clarsie's speedy marriage, but with a distinctly personal application; and this frank mention of the matter by Mrs. Giles had a sinister suggestion that perhaps her ideas might be antagonistic. "An' who d'ye think hev been hyar ter-day, a-speakin' of complimints on Clarsie?" He could not an-swer, but he turned his head with a look of inquiry, and Mrs. Giles continued, "He is a mighty peart, likely boy,—he is."

There was a growing anger in the dismay on Tom Pratt's face; he leaned forward to hear the name with a fiery eagerness, alto-gether incongruous with his usual lack-lustre manner.

"Old Simon Burney!" cried Mrs. Giles, with a burst of laughter. "*Old Simon Burney!* Jes' a-speakin' of complimints on Clarsie!"

The young fellow drew back with a look of disgust. "Why, he's a old man; he ain't no fit husband fur Clarsie."

"Don't ye be too sure ter count on that. I war jes' a-layin' off ter tell Clarsie that a gal oughter keep mighty clar o' widowers, 'thout she wants ter marry one. Fur I believes," said Mrs. Giles, with a wild flight of imagination, "ez them men hev got some sort'n trade with the Evil One, an' he gives 'em the power ter witch the gals, somehow, so's ter git 'em ter marry; 'kase I don't think that any gal that's got good sense air a-goin' ter be a man's second ch'ice, an' the mother of a whole pack of step-chil'ren, 'thout she air under some sort'n spell. But them men carries the day with the gals, ginerally, an' I'm a-thinkin' they're banded with the devil. Ef I war a gal, an' a smart, peart boy like Simon Burney kem around a-speakin' of compli*mints,* an' sayin' I war a merciful critter, I'd jes' give it up, an' marry him fur second ch'ice. Thar's one blessin'," she continued, contemplating the possibility in a cold-blooded fashion positively revolting to Tom Pratt: "he ain't got no tribe of chil'ren fur Clarsie ter look arter; nary chick nor child hev old Simon Burney got. He hed two, but they died."

The young man took leave presently, in great depression of spirit,—the idea that the widower was banded with the powers of evil was rather overwhelming to a man whose dependence was in merely mortal attractions; and after he had been gone a little while Clarsie ascended the ladder to a nook in the roof, which she called her room.

For the first time in her life her slumber was fitful and restless, long intervals of wakefulness alternating with snatches of fantastic dreams. At last she rose and sat by the rude window, looking out through the chestnut leaves at the great moon, which had begun to dip toward the dark uncertainty of the western ridges, and at the shimmering, translucent, pearly mists that filled the intermediate valleys. All the air was dew and incense; so subtle and penetrating an odor came from that fir-tree beyond the fence that it seemed as if some invigorating infusion were thrilling along her veins; there floated upward, too, the warm fragrance of the clover, and every breath of the gentle wind brought from over the stream a thousand blended, undistinguishable perfumes of the deep forests beyond. The moon's idealizing glamour had left no trace of the uncouthness of the place which the daylight revealed; the little log house, the great overhanging chestnut-oaks, the jagged precipice before the door, the vague outlines of the distant ranges, all suffused with a magic sheen, might have seemed a stupendous alto-rilievo in silver repoussé. Still, there came here and there the sweep of the bat's dusky wings; even they were a part of the night's witchery. A tiny owl perched for a moment or two amid the dew-tipped chestnut-leaves, and gazed with great round eyes at Clarsie as solemnly as she gazed at him.

"I'm thankful enough that ye hed the grace not ter screech while ye war hyar," she said, after the bird had taken his flight. "I ain't ready ter die yit, an' a screech-ow*el* air the sure sign."

She felt now and then a great impatience with her wakeful mood. Once she took herself to task: "Jes' a-sittin' up hyar all night, the same ez ef I war a fox, or that thar harnt that walks Chilhowee!"

And then her mind reverted to Tom Pratt, to old Simon Burney, and to her mother's emphatic and oracular declaration that widowers are in league with Satan, and that the girls upon whom they cast the eye of supernatural fascination have no choice in the matter. "I wish I knowed ef that thar sayin' war true," she murmured, her face still turned to the western spurs, and the moon sinking so slowly toward them.

With a sudden resolution she rose to her feet. She knew a way of telling fortunes which was, according to tradition, infallible, and she determined to try it, and ease her mind as to her future. Now was the propitious moment. "I hev always hearn that it won't come true 'thout ye try it jes' before daybreak, an' a-kneelin' down at the forks of the road." She hesitated a moment and listened intently. "They'd never git done a-laffin' at me, ef they fund it out," she thought.

There was no sound in the house, and from the dark woods arose only those monotonous voices of the night, so familiar to her ears that she accounted their murmurous iteration as silence too. She leaned far out of the low window, caught the wide-spreading branches of the tree beside it, and swung herself noiselessly to the ground. The road before her was dark with the shadowy foliage and dank with the dew; but now and then, at long intervals, there lay athwart it a bright bar of light, where the moonshine fell through a gap in the trees. Once, as she went rapidly along her way, she saw speeding across the white radiance, lying just before her feet, the ill-omened shadow of a rabbit. She paused, with a superstitious sinking of the heart, and she heard the animal's quick, leaping rush through the bushes near at hand; but she mustered her courage, and kept steadily on. " 'Tain't no use a-goin' back ter git shet o' bad luck," she argued. "Ef old Simon Burney air my fortune, he'll come whether or no,—ef all they say air true."

The serpentine road curved to the mountain's brink before it forked, and there was again that familiar picture of precipice, and far-away ridges, and shining mist, and sinking moon, which was visibly turning from silver to gold. The changing lustre gilded the feathery ferns that grew in the marshy dip. Just at the angle of the divergent paths there rose into the air a great mass of indistinct white blossoms, which she knew were the exquisite mountain azaleas, and all the dark forest was starred with the blooms of the laurel.

She fixed her eyes upon the mystic sphere dropping down the sky, knelt among the azaleas at the forks of the road, and repeated the time-honored invocation:—

"Ef I'm a-goin' ter marry a young man, whistle, Bird, whistle. Ef I'm a-goin' ter marry an old man, low, Cow, low. Ef I ain't a-goin' ter marry nobody, knock, Death, knock."

There was a prolonged silence in the matutinal freshness and perfume of the woods. She raised her head, and listened attentively. No chirp of half-awakened bird, no tapping of woodpecker, or the mysterious death-watch; but from far along the dewy aisles of the forest, the ungrateful Spot, that Clarsie had fed more faithfully than herself, lifted up her voice, and set the echoes vibrating. Clarsie, however, had hardly time for a pang of disappointment. While she still knelt among the azaleas her large, deer-like eyes were suddenly dilated with terror. From around the curve of the road came the quick beat of hastening footsteps, the sobbing sound of panting breath, and between her and the sinking moon there passed an attenuated, one-armed figure, with a pallid, sharpened face, outlined for a moment on its brilliant disk, and dreadful starting eyes, and quivering open mouth. It disappeared in an instant among the shadows of the laurel, and Clarsie, with a horrible fear clutching at her heart, sprang to her feet.

Her flight was arrested by other sounds. Before her reeling senses could distinguish them, a party of horsemen plunged down the road. They reined in suddenly as their eyes fell upon her, and their leader, an eager, authoritative man, was asking her a question. Why could she not understand him? With her nerveless hands feebly catching at the shrubs for support, she listened vaguely to his impatient, meaningless words, and saw with helpless deprecation the rising anger in his face. But there was no time to be lost. With a curse upon the stupidity of the mountaineer, who could n't speak when she was spoken to, the party sped on in a sweeping gallop, and the rocks and the steeps were hilarious with the sound.

When the last faint echo was hushed, Clarsie tremblingly made her way out into the road; not reassured, however, for she had a frightful conviction that there was now and then a strange stir in the laurel, and that she was stealthily watched. Her eyes were fixed upon the dense growth with a morbid fascination, as she moved away; but she was once more rooted to the spot when the leaves parted and in the golden moonlight the ghost stood before her. She could not nerve herself to run past him, and he was directly in her way homeward. His face was white, and lined, and thin; that pitiful quiver was never still in the parted lips; he looked at her with faltering, beseeching eyes. Clarsie's merciful heart was stirred. "What ails ye, ter come back hyar, an' foller me?" she cried out, abruptly. And then a great horror fell upon her. Was not one to whom a ghost should speak doomed to death, sudden and immediate?

The ghost replied in a broken, shivering voice, like a wail of pain, "I war a-starvin',—I war a-starvin'," with despairing iteration.

It was all over, Clarsie thought. The ghost had spoken, and she was a doomed creature. She wondered that she did not fall dead in the road. But while those beseeching eyes were fastened in piteous appeal on hers, she could not leave him. "I never hearn that 'bout ye," she said, reflectively. "I knows ye hed awful troubles while ye war alive, but I never knowed ez ye war starved."

Surely that was a gleam of sharp surprise in the ghost's prominent eyes, succeeded by a sly intelligence.

"Day is nigh ter breakin'," Clarsie admonished him, as the lower rim of the moon touched the silver mists of the west. "What air ye a-wantin' of me?"

There was a short silence. Mind travels far in such intervals. Clarsie's thoughts had overtaken the scenes when she should have died that sudden terrible death: when there would be no one left to feed the chickens; when no one would care if the pigs cried with the pangs of hunger, unless, indeed, it were time for them to be fattened before killing. The mare,—how often would she be taken from the plow, and shut up for the night in her shanty without a drop of water, after her hard day's work! Who would churn, or spin, or weave? Clarsie could not understand how the machinery of the universe could go on without her. And Towse, poor Towse! He was a useless cumberer of the ground, and it was hardly to be supposed that after his protector was gone he would be spared a blow or a bullet, to hasten his lagging death. But Clarsie still stood in the road, and watched the face of the ghost, as he, with his eager, starting eyes, scanned her open, ingenuous countenance.

"Ye do ez ye air bid, or it'll be the worse for ye," said the "harnt," in the same quivering, shrill tone. "Thar's hunger in the nex' worl' ez well ez in this, an' ye bring me some vittles hyar this time ter-morrer, an' don't ye tell nobody ye hev seen me, nuther, or it'll be the worse for ye."

There was a threat in his eyes as he disappeared in the laurel, and left the girl standing in the last rays of moonlight.

A curious doubt was stirring in Clarsie's mind when she reached home, in the early dawn, and heard her father talking about the sheriff and his posse, who had stopped at the house in the night, and roused its inmates, to know if they had seen a man pass that way.

"Clarsie never hearn none o' the noise, I'll be bound, 'kase she always sleeps like a log," said Mrs. Giles, as her daughter came in with the pail, after milking the cow. "Tell her 'bout'n it."

"They kem a-bustin' along hyar a while afore day-break, a-runnin' arter the man," drawled Mr. Giles, dramatically. "An' they knocked me up, ter know ef ennybody hed passed. An' one o' them men—I never seen none of 'em afore; they's all valley folks, I'm a-thinkin'—an' one of 'em bruk his saddle-girt' a good piece down the road, an' he kem back ter borrer mine; an' ez we war a-fixin' of it, he tole me what they war all arter. He said that word war tuk ter the sheriff down yander in the valley—'pears ter me them town-folks don't think nobody in the mountings hev got good sense—word war tuk ter the sheriff 'bout this one-armed harnt that walks Chilhowee; an' he sot it down that Reuben Crabb war n't dead at all, an' Joel jes' purtended ter hev buried him, an' it air Reuben hisself that walks Chilhowee. An' thar air two hunderd dollars blood-money reward fur ennybody ez kin ketch him. These hyar valley folks air powerful cur'ous critters,—two hunderd dollars blood-money reward fur that thar harnt that walks Chilhowee! I jes' sot myself ter laffin' when that thar cuss tole it so solemn. I jes' 'lowed ter him ez he could n't shoot a harnt nor hang a harnt, an' Reuben Crabb hed about got done with his persecutions in this worl'. An' he said that by the time they hed scoured this mounting, like they hed laid off ter do, they would find that that thar puny little harnt war nuthin' but a mortal man, an' could be kep' in a jail ez handy ez enny other flesh an' blood. He said the sheriff 'lowed ez the reason Reuben hed jes' taken ter walk Chilhowee sence Joel died is 'kase thar air nobody ter feed him, like Joel done, mebbe, in the nights; an' Reuben always war a pore, one-armed, weakly critter, what can't even kerry a gun, an' he air driv by hunger out'n the hole whar he stays, ter prowl round the cornfields an' hen-coops ter steal suthin',—an' that's how he kem ter be seen frequent. The sheriff 'lowed that Reuben can't find enough roots an' yerbs ter keep him up; but law!—a harnt eatin'! It jes' sot me off ter laffin'. Reuben Crabb hev been too busy in torment fur the las' four year ter be a-studyin' 'bout eatin'; an' it air his harnt that walks Chilhowee."

The next morning, before the moon sank, Clarsie, with a tin pail in her hand, went to meet the ghost at the appointed place. She understood now why the terrible doom that falls upon those to whom a spirit may chance to speak had not descended upon her, and that fear was gone; but the secrecy of her errand weighed heavily. She had been scrupulously careful to put into the pail only such things as had fallen to her share at the table, and which she had saved from the meals of yesterday. "A gal that goes a-robbin' fur a hongry harnt," was her moral reflection, "oughter be throwed bodaciously off'n the bluff."

She found no one at the forks of the road. In the marshy dip were only the myriads of mountain azaleas, only the masses of feathery ferns, only the constellated glories of the laurel blooms. A sea of shining white mist was in the valley, with glinting golden rays striking athwart it from the great cresset of the sinking moon; here and there the long, dark, horizontal line of a distant mountain's summit rose above the vaporous shimmer, like a dreary, sombre island in the midst of enchanted waters. Her large, dreamy eyes, so wild and yet so gentle, gazed out through the laurel leaves upon the floating gilded flakes of light, as in the deep coverts of the mountain, where the fulvous-tinted deer were lying, other eyes, as wild and as gentle, dreamily watched the vanishing moon. Overhead, the filmy, lace-like clouds, fretting the blue heavens, were tinged with a faint rose. Through the trees she caught a glimpse of the red sky of dawn, and the glister of a great lucent, tremulous star. From the ground, misty blue exhalations were rising, alternating with the long lines of golden light yet drifting through the woods. It was all very still, very peaceful, almost holy. One could hardly believe that these consecrated solitudes had once reverberated with the echoes of man's death-dealing ingenuity, and that Reuben Crabb had fallen, shot through and through, amid that wealth of flowers at the forks of the road. She heard suddenly the far-away baying of a hound. Her great eyes dilated, and she lifted her head to listen. Only the solemn silence of the woods, the slow sinking of the noiseless moon, the voiceless splendor of that eloquent day-star.

Morning was close at hand, and she was beginning to wonder that the ghost did not appear, when the leaves fell into abrupt commotion, and he was standing in the road, beside her. He did not speak, but watched her with an eager, questioning intentness, as she placed the contents of the pail upon the moss at the roadside. "I'm a-comin' agin ter-morrer," she said, gently. He made no reply, quickly gathered the food from the ground, and disappeared in the deep shades of the woods.

She had not expected thanks, for she was accustomed only to the gratitude of dumb beasts; but she was vaguely conscious of something wanting, as she stood motionless for a moment, and watched the burnished rim of the moon slip down behind the western mountains. Then she slowly walked along her misty way in the dim light of the coming dawn. There was a footstep in the road behind her; she thought it was the ghost once more. She turned, and met Simon Burney, face to face. His rod was on his shoulder, and a string of fish was in his hand.

"Ye air a-doin' wrongful, Clarsie," he said, sternly. "It air agin the law fur folks ter feed an' shelter them ez is a-runnin' from jestice. An' ye'll git yerself inter trouble. Other folks will find ye out, besides me, an' then the sheriff'll be up hyar arter ye."

The tears rose to Clarsie's eyes. This prospect was infinitely more terrifying than the awful doom which follows the horror of a ghost's speech.

"I can't help it," she said, however, doggedly swinging the pail back and forth. "I can't gin my consent ter starvin' of folks, even ef they air a-hidin' an' a-runnin' from jestice."

"They mought put ye in jail, too,—I dunno," suggested Simon Burney.

"I can't holp that, nuther," said Clarsie, the sobs rising, and the tears falling fast. "Ef they comes an' gits me, and puts me in the pen'tiary away down yander, somewhars in the valley, like they done Jane Simpkins, fur a-cuttin' of her step-mother's throat with a butcher-knife, while she war asleep,—though some said Jane war crazy,—I can't gin my consent ter starvin' of folks."

A recollection came over Simon Burney of the simile of "hendering the sun from shining."

"She hev done sot it down in her mind," he thought, as he walked on beside her and looked at her resolute face. Still he did not relinquish his effort.

"Doin' wrong, Clarsie, ter aid folks what air a-doin' wrong, an' mebbe *hev* done wrong, air powerful hurtful ter everybody, an' henders the law an' jestice."

"I can't holp it," said Clarsie.

"It 'pears toler'ble comical ter me," said Simon Burney, with a sudden perception of a curious fact which has proved a marvel to wiser men, "that no matter how good a woman is, she ain't got no respect fur the laws of the country, an' don't sot no store by jestice." After a momentary silence he appealed to her on another basis. "Somebody will ketch him arter a while, ez sure ez ye air born. The sheriff's a-sarchin' now, an' by the time that word gits around, all the mounting boys 'll turn out, 'kase thar air two hunderd dollars blood-money fur him. An' then he'll think, when they ketches him,—an' everybody 'll say so, too,—ez ye war constant in feedin' him jes' ter 'tice him ter comin' ter one place, so ez ye could tell somebody whar ter go ter ketch him, an' make them gin ye haffen the blood-money, mebbe. That's what the mounting will say, mos' likely."

"I can't holp it," said Clarsie, once more.

He left her walking on toward the rising sun, and retraced his way to the forks of the road. The jubilant morning was filled with the song of birds; the sunlight flashed on the dew; all the delicate enameled bells of the pink and white azaleas were swinging tremulously in the wind; the aroma of ferns and mint rose on the delicious fresh air. Presently he checked his pace, creeping stealthily on the moss and grass beside the road rather than in the beaten path. He pulled aside the leaves of the laurel with no more stir than the wind might have made, and stole cautiously through its dense growth, till he came suddenly upon the puny little ghost, lying in the sun at the foot of a tree. The frightened creature sprang to his feet with a wild cry of terror, but before he could move a step he was caught and held fast in the strong grip of the stalwart mountaineer beside him. "I hev kem hyar ter tell ye a word, Reuben Crabb," said Simon Burney. "I hev kem hyar ter tell ye that the whole mounting air a-goin' ter turn out ter sarch fur ye; the sheriff air a-ridin' now, an' ef ye don't come along with me they 'll hev ye afore night, 'kase thar air two hunderd dollars reward fur ye."

What a piteous wail went up to the smiling blue sky, seen through the dappling leaves above them! What a horror, and despair, and prescient agony were in the hunted creature's face! The ghost struggled no longer; he slipped from his feet down upon the roots of the tree, and turned that woful face, with its starting eyes and drawn muscles and quivering parted lips, up toward the unseeing sky.

"God A'mighty, man!" exclaimed Simon Burney, moved to pity. "Why n't ye quit this hyar way of livin' in the woods like ye war a wolf? Why n't ye come back an' stand yer trial? From all I've hearn tell, it 'pears ter me ez the jury air obleeged ter let ye off, an' I'll take keer of ye agin them Grims."

"I hain't got no place ter live in," cried out the ghost, with a keen despair.

Simon Burney hesitated. Reuben Crabb was possibly a murderer,—at the best could but be a burden. The burden, however, had fallen in his way, and he lifted it.

"I tell ye now, Reuben Crabb," he said, "I ain't a-goin' ter holp no man ter break the law an' hender jestice; but ef ye will go an' stand yer trial, I'll take keer of ye agin them Grims ez long ez I kin fire a rifle. An' arter the jury hev done let ye off, ye air welcome ter live along o' me at my house till ye die. Ye air no-'count ter work, I know, but I ain't a-goin' ter grudge ye fur a livin' at my house."

And so it came to pass that the reward set upon the head of the harnt that walked Chilhowee was never claimed.

With his powerful ally, the forlorn little spectre went to stand his trial, and the jury acquitted him without leaving the box. Then he came back to the mountains to live with Simon Burney. The cruel gibes of his burly mockers that had beset his feeble life from his childhood up, the deprivation and loneliness and despair and fear that had filled those days when he walked Chilhowee, had not improved the harnt's temper. He was a helpless creature, not able to carry a gun or hold a plow, and the years that he spent smoking his cob-pipe in Simon Burney's door were idle years and unhappy. But Mrs. Giles said she thought he was "a mighty lucky little critter: fust, he hed Joel ter take keer of him an' feed him, when he tuk ter the woods ter pertend he war a harnt; an' they do say now that Clarsie Pratt, afore she war married, used ter kerry him vittles, too; an' then old Simon Burney tuk him up an' fed him ez plenty ez ef he war a good workin' hand, an' gin him clothes an' house-room, an' put up with his jawin' jes' like he never hearn a word of it. But law! some folks dunno when they air well off."

There was only a sluggish current of peasant blood in Simon Burney's veins, but a prince could not have dispensed hospitality with a more royal hand. Ungrudgingly he gave of his best; valiantly he defended his thankless guest at the risk of his life; with a moral gallantry he struggled with his sloth, and worked early and late, that there might be enough to divide. There was no possibility of a recompense for him, not even in the encomiums of discriminating friends, nor the satisfaction of tutored feelings and a practiced spiritual discernment; for he was an uncouth creature, and densely ignorant.

The grace of culture is, in its way, a fine thing, but the best that art can do—the polish of a gentleman—is hardly equal to the best that Nature can do in her higher moods.

William Elliott

(1788–1863)

Born in Beaufort, South Carolina, to a family firmly established at the top of the planter aristocracy in the lower South, Elliott inherited immense wealth and an elevated social standing. His father was a well-known politician and gentleman farmer, and William Elliott followed in his father's footsteps. He attended Harvard College after an education that, for the most part, had been given to him by private tutors at home. When his father died in 1808, he became responsible, at 20 years of age, for the family plantations and fortunes. In 1817, he married a wealthy heiress from Charleston who brought five more plantations to his holdings. For almost 20 years he served in the South Carolina legislature, but he resigned in 1832 to oppose nullification. He became an authority on agricultural reform, and was in great demand as a lecturer, a writer of articles for agricultural papers, and as a spokesman for South Carolina planting interests. In 1855, he traveled to Paris to represent South Carolina at the Universal Exhibition. He set himself apart from the majority of his social class by opposing secession in 1861, but he did not hesitate to side with the Confederacy once the Civil War began. During the War, much of his property was confiscated, and he lived long enough to see his mansions destroyed and his world in ruins. His best-known work is the collection of hunting tales Carolina Sports by Land and Water, Including Incidents of Devil-Fishing, Wild Cat, Deer and Bear Hunting, Etc. (1846). These eccentric, rambling essay-stories look back to the English personal essay of the 18th century, and are best read as a spirited Southern version of a conventional, but fully engaging and demanding, genre. The two-part story on "Chee-Ha" is one of a group of journalistic pieces signed pseudonymously by Elliott as "Venator" and "Piscator" and first published in book form in Carolina Sports. Among his other writings are Fiesco: A Tragedy (1850), Letters of Agricola (1852), and a number of journalistic articles, chiefly on agricultural reform.

A Day at Chee-Ha

The traveller in South-Carolina, who passes along the road between the Ashepoo and Combahee rivers, will be struck by the appearance of two lofty white columns, rising among the pines that skirt the road. They are the only survivors of eight, which supported, in times anterior to our revolutionary war, a sylvan temple, erected by a gentleman who, to the higher qualities of a devoted patriot, united the taste and liberality of the sportsman. The spot was admirably chosen, being on the brow of a piney ridge, which slopes away at a long gun-shot's length into a thick swamp; and many a deer, has, we doubt not, in times past, been shot from the temple when it stood in its pride,—as we ourselves have struck them from its ruins. From this ruin, stretching eastwardly some twelve or fourteen miles, is a neck of land, known from the Indian name of the small river that waters and almost bisects it,—as Chee-Ha: or as it is incorrectly written Chy-haw! It is now the best hunting ground in Carolina,—for which the following reasons may be given. The lands are distributed in large tracts; there are therefore few proprietors. The rich land is confined to the belt of the rivers, and there remains a wide expanse of barrens, traversed by deep swamps, always difficult and sometimes impassable, in which the deer find a secure retreat.

At a small hunting lodge located in this region, it has often been my good fortune to meet a select body of hunting friends, and enjoy in their company the pleasures of the chase.

I give you one of my "days,"—not that the success was unusual, it was by no means so: but that it was somewhat more marked by incident, than most of its fellows. We turned out, *after breakfast,* on a fine day in February, with a pack of twelve hounds, and two whippers in, or drivers, as we call them. The field consisted of one old shot besides myself, and two sportsmen who had not yet "fleshed their maiden swords." When we reached the ground, we had to experience the fate which all tardy sportsmen deserve, and must often undergo: the fresh print of dogs' feet, and the deep impression of horses' hoofs, showed us that another party had anticipated us in the drive, and that the game had been started and was off. Two expedients suggested themselves,—we must either leave our ground, and in that case incur the risk of sharing the same fate in our next drive: or, we must beat up the ground now before us in a way which our predecessors in the field had probably neglected to do. We chose the latter part: and finding that the drive embraced two descriptions of ground,—first, the main wood, which we inferred had already been taken, and next, the briery thickets that skirted a contiguous old field:—into these thickets we pushed. Nor had we entered far, before the long, deep, querulous note of "Ruler" as he challenged on a trail, told us to expect the game. A few minutes later, and the whole pack announced the still more exciting fact,—"the game is up." The first move of the deer was into a back-water, which he crossed, while the pack half swimming, half wading, came yelping at his heels. He next dashed across an old field and made for a thicket, which he entered; it was a piece of briery and tangled ground, which the dogs could not traverse without infinite toil. By these two moves, he gained a great start of the hounds: if he kept on, we were thrown out, and our dogs lost for the day,—if he doubled, and the nature of the ground favored that supposition, there were two points, whereat he would be most likely to be intercepted. I consulted the wind, and made my choice. I was wrong. It proved to be a young deer, who did not heed the wind, and he made for the pass, I had *not selected*. The pack now turned; we found from their cry, that the deer had doubled, and our hearts beat high with expectation, as mounted on our respective hunters, we stretched ourselves across the old field which he must necessarily traverse, before he could regain the shelter of the wood. And now I saw my veteran comrade stretch his neck as if he spied something in the thicket; then with a sudden fling he brought his double barrel to his shoulder and fired. His horse admonished by the spur then fetched a caracole; from the new position, a new glimpse of the deer is gained,—and crack! goes the second barrel. In a few moments, I saw one of our recruits dismount and fire. Soon after, the deer made his appearance and approached the second, who descended from his horse and fired. The deer kept on seemingly untouched, and had gained the crown of the hill when his second barrel brought him to the ground in sight of the whole field. We all rode to the spot, to congratulate our novice on his first exploit in sylvan warfare,—when as he stooped to examine the direction of his shot, our friend Loveleap slipped his knife into the throat of the deer, and before his purpose could be guessed at, bathed his face with the blood of his victim. (This, you must know, *is hunter's law* with us, on the killing a first deer.) As our young sportsman started up from the ablution,—his face glaring like an Indian Chief's in all the splendor of war paint,—Robin the hunter touched his cap and thus accosted him.

"Maussa Tickle, if you wash off dat blood dis day,—you neber hab luck agen so long as you hunt."

"Wash it off!" cried we all with one accord,—"who ever heard of such a folly. He can be no true sportsman, who is ashamed of such a livery."

Thus beset, and moved thereunto, by other sage advices, showered upon him, by his companions in sport; he wore his bloody mask, to the close of that long day's sport, and sooth to say, returned to receive the congratulations of his young and lovely wife, his face still adorned with the stains of victory. Whether he was received, as victors are wont to be, returning from other fields of blood, is a point whereon I shall refuse to satisfy the impertinent curiosity of my reader; but I am bound, in deference to historic truth, to add,—that the claims of our novice, to the merit and penalties of this day's hunt, were equally incomplete: for it appeared on after inspection, that Loveleap had given the mortal wound, and that Tickle had merely given the "coup de grace" to a deer that if unfired on, would have fallen of itself, in a run of a hundred yards. It must be believed, however, that we were quite too generous to divulge this unpleasant discovery to our novice, in the first pride of his triumph!

And now we tried other grounds, which our precursors in the field had already beaten; so that the prime of the day was wasted before we made another start. At last, in the afternoon, a splendid burst from the whole pack made us aware that a second deer had suddenly been roused. I was riding to reach a pass, (or *stand* as we term it) when I saw a buck dashing along before the hounds at the top of his speed: the distance was seventy-five yards,—but I reined in my horse and let slip at him. To my surprise, he fell; but before I could reach the spot from which I was separated by a thick underwood, he had shuffled off, and disappeared. The hounds came roaring on, and showed me by their course that he had made for a marsh that lay hard by. For that, we all pushed in hopes of anticipating him. He was before us, we saw him plunge into the canal, and mount the opposite bank, tho' evidently in distress and crippled in one of his hind legs. The dogs rush furiously on (the scent of blood in their nostrils), plunge into the canal, sweep over the bank, and soon pursuers and pursued, are shut out from sight, as they wind among the thick covers that lie scattered over the face of the marsh.

"What use of horse now!" said Robin, as (sliding from his saddle where his horse instinctively made a dead halt at the edge of the impracticable Serbonian bog that lay before him), he began to climb a tree that overlooked the field of action,—"what use of horse now?"

From this "vantage ground," however, he looked in vain to catch a glimpse of the deer. The eye of a lynx could not penetrate the thick mass of grass, that stretched upwards six feet from the surface of the marsh. The cry of the hounds now grew faint from distance, and now again came swelling on the breeze; when suddenly our ears were saluted by a full burst from the whole pack, in that loud, open note, which tells a practised ear, that the cry comes from the water.

"Zounds, Robin," cried I, in the excitement of the moment,— "they have him at bay there,—there in the canal. Down from your perch my lad, or they'll eat him, horns and all, before you reach him."

Robin apparently, did not partake of this enthusiasm, for he maintained his perch on the tree, and coolly observed,—"What use maussa, fore I git dere, dem dog polish ebery bone."

"You are afraid you rascal! you have only to swim the canal and then,"

"Got, maussa," said Robin, as he looked ruefully over the field of his proposed missionary labors; "if he be water, I swim 'um,— if he be bog, I bog 'um,—if he be briar, I kratch tru um,—but who de debble, but otter, no so alligator, go tru all tree one time!"

The thought was just stealing its way into my mind, that under the excitement of my feelings, I was giving an order, that I might have hesitated personally to execute,—when the cry of the hounds lately so clamorous, totally ceased. "There," cried I, in the disappointed tone of a sportsman who had lost a fine buck,—"save your skin you loitering rascal! You may sleep where you sit, for by this time they have eaten him sure enough." This conclusion was soon overset by the solitary cry of Ruler, which was now heard, half a mile to the left of the scene of the late uproar.

"Again! What is this? *It is* the cry of Ruler! ho! I understand it,—the deer is not eaten,—but has taken the canal,—and the nose of that Prince of hounds, has scented him down the running stream.— Aye, aye, he makes for the wood,—and now to cut him off." No sooner said than done. I gave the spur to my horse, and shot off accordingly, but not in time to prevent the success of the masterly manœuvre by which the buck, baffling his pursuers, was now seen straining every nerve to regain the shelter of the wood. I made a desperate effort to cut him off, but reached the wood only in time to note the direction he had taken. It was now sunset,

and the white outspread tail of the deer, was my only guide in the
pursuit, as he glided among the trees. "Now for it, Boxer,—show
your speed, my gallant nag." The horse, as if he entered fully into
the purpose of his rider, stretched himself to the utmost, obedient
to the slightest touch of the reins, as he threaded the intricacies
of the forest; and was gaining rapidly on the deer, when plash! he
came to a dead halt,—his fore legs plunged in a quagmire, over
which the buck with his split hoofs had bounded in security. What
a baulk!—"but here goes"—and the gun was brought instantly to
the shoulder, and the left hand barrel fired. The distance was eighty
yards, and the shot ineffectual. Making a slight circuit to avoid the
bog, I again push at the deer and again approach,—"Ah, if I had
but reserved the charge, I had so idly wasted!" But no matter, I
must run him down,—and gaining a position on his flank, I spurred
my horse full upon his broad-side, to bear him to the ground. The
noble animal (he *was* a noble animal, for he traced, with some
baser admixture indeed, through Boxer, Medley, Gimcrack, to the
Godolphin Arabian), refused to trample on his fellow quadruped;
and, in spite of the goading spur, ranged up close along side of
the buck, as if his only pride lay in surpassing him in speed. This
brought me in close contact with the buck. Detaching my right
foot from the stirrup, I struck the armed heel of my boot full
against his head;—he reeled from the blow and plunged into a
neighboring thicket—too close for horse to enter. I fling myself
from my horse, and pursue on foot,—he gains on me: I dash down
my now useless gun, and, freed from all encumbrance, press after
the panting animal. A large fallen oak lies across his path; he
gathers himself up for the leap, and falls exhausted directly across
it. Before he could recover his legs, and while he lay thus poised
on the tree, I fling myself at full length upon the body of the
struggling deer,—my left hand clasps his neck, while my right
detaches the knife; whose fatal blade, in another moment, is buried
in his throat. There he lay in his blood, and I remained sole occupant of the field. I seize my horn, but am utterly breathless, and
incapable of sounding it: I strive to shout, but my voice is extinct
from fatigue and exhaustion. I retrace my steps, while the waning
light yet sufficed to show me the track of the deer,—recover my
horse and gun, and return to the tree where my victim lay. But
how apprise my comrades of my position? My last shot, however,
had not been unnoted,—and soon their voices are heard cheering
on "Ruler," while far in advance of the yet baffled pack, he follows
unerringly on the tracks of the deer. They came at last: but found
me still so exhausted from fatigue; that to wave my bloody knife,
and point to the victim where he lay at my feet,—were all the

history I could then give, of the spirit-stirring incidents I have just recorded. Other hunting matches have I been engaged in, wherein double the number of deer have been killed; but never have I engaged in one of deeper or more absorbing interest, than that which marked this "day at Chee-Ha."

The Last Day at Chee-Ha

The day was fine, and many a familiar face was noted at the gathering place. There was G——, of Port Royal, with his hunts-man Dick, and his famous pack, that, sweeping like a whirlwind over the land, dashed across an ordinary river, as if they scarcely counted it an impediment; nor checked their career, when their mettle was fairly roused, for any thing short of an arm of the sea. He was mounted on his gallant roan; his person, youthful and erect, though the frosts had prematurely settled on his head,— possibly from reflecting too bitterly on the perverseness of man,— possibly from the toil of circumventing and sacrificing whole hec-atombs of deer! Then came E. R——, of Beaufort. He had not laid aside his spectacles; but they no longer pored over the deci-sions of the Courts, nor glanced at the fees of clients, but rested unprofitably upon two polished barrels, which, yet, were pointed at nothing. He had his labor for his pains; yet he counted all labor as productive,—and was content! Then came C——, of Bray's Island, with "Big Thunder" sleeping on his thigh. It was anomalous thunder: it uttered no sound that day! Then came G. P. E——, of Smiiie's. He made no puns, but wore a serious visage; medi-tating, perhaps, how he might provide new subjects for his infir-mary! Then came T. R. S——, of the "Bluff" (the Loveleap of our former histories), a sportsman, accomplished in all the mys-teries of wood-craft,—yet not so resolved in sport, as to swim a river after a buck! Then came T. R. S. E——, of "Ball's,"—at that time a stripling, yet willing, like David, to encounter Goliath himself, if he came in the shape of a buck or a Devil-fish! And, lastly, came myself,—some time "Piscator," but now "Venator," if your courtesy will allow him the designation! Three drivers, and upwards of twenty hounds, completed the equipment for the hunt.

We assembled at "Social Hall"; and sending the drivers and hounds to enter the wood from the direction of "Smilie's," pro-ceeded to occupy all the prominent passes of the "White Oak," stretching along, at intervals, from the flood-gate dam to "Sandy Run." My own stand was taken at the head of a long pond, or chain of ponds, which, approaching closely to the "White Oak," stretched away towards the South-East, until it found its outlet in "Wright's Bay." I stood at the head of this pond, on a knoll that, piercing the swamp to the distance of one hundred and fifty yards, was flanked on either side by deep morasses, affording very thick cover. Standing among some dwarf trees that crowned the summit of this knoll, and which served as a partial screen, with my bridle reins thrown carelessly over my arm, I was listening to the cry of the hounds, as, at great distance, and at slow intervals, they challenged on a trail,—when I caught a glimpse of a large dark object moving on my right; a second object was perceived, but still indistinct, and covered by the thicket. Presently a third and fourth were seen, and as they emerged from the dense cover, I perceived, to my great surprise, that they were *bears*. They were crossing the foot of the knoll on which I stood, from the right to the left. I leaped into the saddle, and as the ground in front was favorable to a horse, dashed at them, to cut them off, if possible, before they had gained the cover on the left. I had not run more than half my career, when I reined in my horse; for I perceived that two of the bears had changed their course, and were coming towards me. Their object, I presume, was not *attack,* but *escape* from the hounds, whose distant baying they had heard. They ran straight for me, however, until they had approached within twenty yards; when the leading bear, a large one, stopped and looked me full in the face. A yearling bear followed, and, as if prompted by curiosity, reared himself on his hind legs and looked inquisitively over the shoulder of the leader. I seized the moment when their heads were thus brought in line, and almost in contact, and drew aim directly between the eyes of the larger bear. It occurred to me, at the instant, that my left hand barrel was charged with shot of unusually large size, and I accordingly touched the left hand trigger. Instantly the foremost bear disappeared, and the second uttering a cry of distress, rolled over among the bushes, so as to assure me of its being seriously hurt; but the glimpse I had of him was so imperfect, that I did not fire my second barrel. Riding to the spot, imagine my surprise at seeing the large bear motionless, and in the same upright posture which he maintained before I had fired; his head, only, had sunk upon his knees! *He was stone dead!*—two shot had pierced his brain. His death, apparently, had been instantaneous,—and the slight support of a fallen tree, had enabled him to retain a posture, by which he yet simulated life! In searching for his wounded companion, I was guided to the edge of the morass by the torn earth and trampled grass; but there, lost all trace of him in the tangled underwood. Diverging a little to the right, and following a faintly traced path that penetrated the thicket, I again came upon a trail. Evidently there were several that had taken this direction: here was the foot-print, freshly stamped in the muddy soil,—here were the logs which they had leaped, on their retreat, yet dripping with the water splashed on them,—but the bears had passed onward, and the ground became more and more difficult, until it prevented all further advance.

I was now in the heart of the swamp, and I sounded my horn to call around me the hunters and hounds, the first for consultation; the second for pursuit. No horn replied! I shouted,—no answer! I listened—and began to understand why my signals were unnoticed. The hounds had roused a deer, and were bearing down towards my left; and none of the field were willing, by leaving their stands, or answering a blast whose import they could not understand, to forfeit their own chance of sport. Nearer and nearer comes the cry,—they are skirting the thicket, and are driving directly for my stand!

"Well!—let them come! I have one barrel yet in reserve,"—and with this reflection, I make the best of my way back to the position I had just occupied! The chase turned to the left; presently a shot is fired in that direction, but no horn sounds the signal of success! "Ha! the dogs are gaining the pine ridge in the rear, and may soon be lost,—that must not be,"—and I dash away at full speed to intercept them. It was no easy task to beat them off, heated as they were in the chase, and stimulated by the report of the gun. I rode across their track, and shouted, and blew my horn: but all in vain,—when the drivers came up opportunely to my assistance! By dint of chiding, and smacking of whips, they at last succeed in drawing off the hounds, that were almost frantic with eagerness to pursue the deer! The horns then sound a call, and the hunters come dropping in.

"Why have you stopped the dogs?" said the Laird, with something of brusquerie in his manner.

"Because they are out of the drive; and, if not stopped, may be lost for the day."

"But I have shot a buck," said he.

"Where is he?"

"Gone on," said he; "but I'm sure they'll catch him in short order."

"So very sure!—found blood then?"

"No."

"How far off was he when you fired?"

"Oh, for that matter, he was jumping over me!"

"Then he carries shot bravely," said I; "but before we follow this buck,—who, by your shewing, cannot possibly go far—there is other business for the hounds: a nobler quarry is before us!—I have shot a bear!"

"A bear!" cried the hunters in astonishment. "You joke!—we never saw one in these woods!"

"True, nevertheless! Ride up with the hounds, and it will be hard but I will shew you blood!"

And away we went at a rattling pace for the scene of action: some faces expressing confidence, and some mistrust! As we neared the spot,—

"No joke, by gracious!" cried G—— (his piety forbidding any stronger exclamation). "Look at the dogs!—how the hair is bristling upon their backs; they smell the bear at this moment!"

And so, indeed, they did; for there he stood before them!—not fallen, but crouching, as if prepared to spring,—yet, as we have said, *stone dead!* It was pleasant to witness the surprise, and to receive the congratulations of my sporting friends, as they crowded around the bear,—the horses showing uneasiness, however, and the dogs mistrust, amounting almost to terror!

While the drivers were encouraging the hounds to approach and familiarize themselves with the scent of the bear,—which they were baying at a distance, as if they feared his quietude might be counterfeit,—I dismounted and re-loaded my left-hand barrel.

"And now, my friends," said I, on remounting, "we have glorious sport ahead!—a wounded bear is within fifty yards of us."

"Now we know you joke," said they in a breath; "you fired but one barrel!"

"But that," said I, "had bullets for two. I have shot another, as sure as a gun!—but *that* (glancing at him of the buck) is not always the highest assurance! look here, at these bushes, torn up by his struggles,—and this blood! He made his way into that thicket, and *there* we'll find him! Let us surround it,—set on the dogs, and then hurra! for the quickest shot and the surest marksman!—only take care, as we stand so close, that we do not shoot each other!"

The hounds were now brought to the trail, while we shout and clap our hands in encouragement. But they were panic stricken, and would not budge a foot in advance of the drivers.

"Let us ride in," said Loveleap!

"Done," said I; and we placed ourselves, with G—— and C——, in the first line, while the other hunters, moving on the flanks, were in position to give their fire, if he broke out.

"Here he is!" said C——, before we had advanced twenty yards into the thicket.

"Where?"

"Before me. I cannot see him, but my horse does, for he snorts and refuses to advance!"

We close our ranks, with finger on trigger, and hearts beating with expectation; but there was no room for chase, or fight,—*the bear lay dead before us!!* A grand hurra burst from us!—a grand flourish of horns!—and my hunting cap was whirled aloft on the muzzle of my gun!—while the drivers tore their way into the thicket on foot, and dragged out the second bear to keep company with the first. I was delighted,—exalted,—overmuch, perhaps!—but my pride was soon to have its rebuke.

"Well," said Splash, slapping his thigh with emphasis, and looking from the bears, which for some moments he had been eyeing, to the piece of ordnance which he had been carrying by way of gun, as if to *that* alone should have belonged the credit of such a shot,—"you *are the luckiest man I ever saw in my life!!*"

What a damper!—to tell a man who was priding himself on having made a magnificent shot, that it was nothing but luck.

"I'll tell you what, Splash," said I, "to have met the bears, was my good luck, I grant you; but to have disposed of them, thus artistically, excuse me!"—and my wounded self-love led me into a recital of incidents perfectly true, yet so nearly akin to vain glorious boasting, that *even now* I redden beneath my visor at the recollection! "It was by good luck then, that I once killed two bucks with one barrel! Loveleap, you saw this! By good luck, that, at another time, I killed two does with one barrel!—then, too, you were present. By good luck that I killed, in a two-days' hunt, five deer in five shots,—not missing a shot! By good luck that I killed thirty wild ducks at a fire! (but why speak of that; any one can shoot in a flock)! It is by good luck, I suppose, that I throw up a piece of silver coin, and batter it while in the air, into the shape of a pewter mug!—or, laying my gun upon a table before me, fling up two oranges successively before I touch the gun, then snatch it up, and strike them both before they reach the earth, one with each barrel! Luck,—luck,—nothing but luck! Be it so; but when you have beaten this shot, and killed three bears with one barrel, let me know it, I pray you, and I will try my luck again! But while we waste time in talk, the scent gets cold. There are two other bears which took that foot-path there; let us pursue them,—and *good luck* to the expertest sportsman in the field. I shall not fire another shot to day!"

We cheered on the hounds, but they would not respond. In vain the drivers brought them to the trail,—they would follow the horsemen, but would not advance a step before them,—such was the instinctive dread they entertained of the bears, which none of them had seen before that day. Oh, for a bull terrier, or some other dog of bolder nature!—even a cur of low degree, would have yelped in pursuit, and enabled us to add two more bears, perhaps, to the list of slain! But it was useless, and we gave it up when we had tracked them to "Sandy Run,"—feeling assured that, by this time, they had crossed the Ashepoo, and gained their fastnesses in the hammocks beyond.

We re-assembled at the spot, where we had left the bears (henceforward known as "The Bear Stand"); and sending one of the drivers to the plantation, for a cart to take them home, betook ourselves to tracking up the wounded buck, in whose favor the bears had unwittingly made so effectual a diversion. The Laird did not seem altogether so confident now, as he had been a few hours before: some slight misgivings as to the success of his shot appeared to be hanging about him, and his companions began to jeer!

"Show us the very spot," said one.

"There," said he; "I was standing behind this log, and as the deer leaped over both at once, I fired!"

"Singed him, no doubt," said one.

"Shot off one leg, at least!" said he, reassuring himself.

"Made capital use of the remainder, however!" bantered a third. "But come,—we burn day-light; look for blood, and put the dogs on the trail of the legless buck."

And away went the Laird, hunting for the hoof print, and turning over the leaves, to try and coax a show of blood.

"Here it is!" cried he, as he held up a leaf. "I told you so!"

"Blood?" enquired G——.

"No," said he, "the marrow of his leg!"

"Poh! poh!" said G——; "marrow without blood!—how would you get at it?"

"Marrow!" said he.

"Fudge!" said G——; "but put on the hounds, and they will soon tell who is right."

We brought them to the trail, and it was curious to observe how instantaneously they regained their confidence, when it was no longer a bear to be encountered, but a buck to be pulled down! Away they go for "Green Pond,"—and all the hunters are riding pell mell with the dogs, expecting to see the wounded buck, leap from every bush that lay in their way. At Green Pond, they turned and pushed into Wright's Bay. How the cry redoubled when they passed over the swampy soil, that had retained the scent more freshly than the high pine land!

"On for Washington's," said Loveleap; "he makes for the river,—take up the passes or we lose him!"

And we dash along at full speed, until we occupy the intended stands. We are far ahead of the hounds; but the deer was ahead of us,—and when the dogs came roaring by the place where we stood, they swept on in full career for the Chee-Ha. There was small chance of their turning, and we ordered our drivers to ride down to the marshes and recover the dogs, if possible, before they reached the river. They were too late. When they reached the bank, some dogs were swimming, some howling on the margin. The deer evidently had crossed, and the drivers sounded their horns in vain to re-assemble the pack.

We waited in the road until our patience was exhausted: when, after a weary interval, the drivers reappeared, with but a scanty following of hounds. Dick, in particular, with a subdued tone, reporting the entire Port Royal pack as missing.

"They crossed," he said, "to 'May's Folly,' and having put the river between themselves and him, would not mind his horn!"

"Any blood on the trail?"

"None, sir."

"*Any marrow?*" said another.

The drivers, smothering a laugh, wheel off to the rear, without reply; and, to this day, the spot where this remarkable shot was made (and the log is still there to mark it) is called, *the Marrow Stand!*

The high tone of excitement, that had thus far buoyed us up, was now gone. We could not descend from the chorus of the full band, to the piping of the thin straggling cry; nor stoop from bears, and bloodless bucks; to chase, perhaps, a raccoon or a fox!—so we adjourned to dinner!—when, though we eat not, nor drank, like Homer's heroes, we doubtless played our parts without reproach, until, at length (to use the strong antique expression), "the rage of hunger being satisfied," we set ourselves to muse, to speculate, and to jest, over the events of the day.

"Apropos of marrow!" said C.; "that buck must have been well supplied, or it would have leaked off in so long a run!"

"No more of that, Hal, if thou lovest me," said the Laird.

"His bones are marrowless!" said R.

"And his eyes lack speculation!" I rejoined; "and when I put this and that together, and reflect on these anomalous events, and these seemingly contradictory statements, I confess, gentlemen," said I, with a face composed to seriousness, "that I have strange misgivings about this same buck! His seeming to be shot, yet moving as if unhurt!—his losing a leg, yet running off without it!—his bloodlessness!—*his disappearance at 'May's Folly'!*—the confusion of the hounds,—and the unaccountable dispersion of the pack!—impress upon my mind the possibility of this being no deer of flesh and blood,—but the 'Spectre Buck', of which we have heard traditionally, but which I never supposed had been met by daylight!"

"The tradition!"—"the tradition!" cried several voices impatiently.

"It is simple enough," I rejoined, "and brief. Some forty or fifty years ago, there lived in this region, then thinly settled, a German, or man of German extraction, named May. He constructed, we are told (just at the place where we so mysteriously lost our dogs to-day), those embankments, of which the remains are yet visible; and which were intended to reclaim these extensive marshes from waste. They failed of their purpose,—involving him in pecuniary difficulty; and hence the name of 'May's Folly,' which the spot yet bears. He became, from this moment, a soured and discontented man: sometimes hunting the deer on these grounds that we have traversed to-day, with desperate energy, as if he would exterminate the very race,—and then relapsing into a state of moody listlessness. He grew still more unsocial and secluded, as he advanced in life; and men began to whisper strange stories of him. Some hinted that the poisonous influence of French revolutionary atheism, had tainted him even in these remote solitudes; that he had mocked at sacred things,—respected not the consecrated ground,—and even denied the authority and sanctity of the holy book! Others said, that in his moody fits, he had treated his slaves with barbarity; and had shrunk back from the public scorn, which such cowardice is sure to provoke, into the seclusion we have noticed. Be the cause what it may, he withdrew himself more and more from the public observation,—until, at last, he died. Then, it is said, that a few of his confidential slaves, to whom he had imparted his desire, complied with his dying injunctions; which were,—'to bury his body secretly, in the midst of these wild and melancholy barrens; to level the grave, and strew it over with leaves, so that no man might discover the place of his burial!' Whether he did this, to mark his scorn of consecrated ground, and of religious services over the departed; or whether he feared that the slaves whom he had maltreated, would offer indignities to his remains; it is useless to enquire. All that we know is,—that he died, and was buried as he had desired. No head-stone marked the spot of his grave: no prayer was breathed above it,—no requiem sung. At midnight,—stealthily, and by the glimmer of a torch,—was he returned to earth; and all was silent, but the sighing of the night-wind among the towering pines,—as if Nature moaned over the desolation of her perverse and misguided child!

"The negro looks on this as haunted ground: and hurries over it, after nightfall, with quickened step, and palpitating heart! Sometimes a gush of air, warm as from a furnace, passes fitfully across his face,—while a cold shivering seizes on his frame! What surer token than this, that a *spirit* is passing near? Sometimes a milk-white buck is seen, by glimpses of the moon, taking gigantic leaps,—then shrouded in a mist wreath, and changed, in a twinkling, into the likeness of a pale old man, swathed in his grave clothes,—then melting away slowly into air! At other times, the 'Spectre Buck' starts up before his eyes, pursued by phantom hounds, which rush maddening through the glades,—yet utter no sound, nor shake the leaves, while they flit by like meteors! It is the ghost of May, doing penance for the sins done in the flesh, under the form of the animal which he most persecuted when living!"

"You speak as earnestly as if you gave credit to the legend," said R. "Is it possible that you can believe in ghosts?"

"Doctor Johnson *did,*" said L.

"Aye; but he was eminently superstitious,—and strained himself into the opinion, because the Scriptures recognised spirits; and he would not be thought to gainsay them."

"Yet," said I, "it is clearly within the competency of God, to create ghosts as well as men; beings of vapor, as well as of flesh and blood;—sensible to sight, yet impalpable to touch; beings bearing the same relation to man, as the thin vapoury comet to the more solid planetary bodies of our system!"

"Yet, to what end," said R., "should they be created? God creates nothing in vain; and what authentic story is on record to show that ghosts, even if they exist, have ever exerted any agency, either for good or evil, on human affairs? Show me that they have served for warning, or for instruction,—and yield the point; but, until then, 'Nec Deus intersit nisi nodus vindice dignus,' is the safer maxim."

"There is great force in what you say," I rejoined; "but how can we reason against the evidence of our senses. If *I* have not seen ghosts, *I have seen those who have!*"

The hunters, who were seated loungingly about the table, playing with their glasses, started at this avowal, as if a ghost had taken a seat among them!

"Explain!—tell us what you mean!—can you be in earnest?"

But, before a word could be uttered,—

"Ho! ho! ho! ho!" interrupted the Laird, at this point. "Will you suffer him to gull you at this rate? 'Mark you how a plain tale shall set him down.' This romantic story is woven out of mere cobweb. This old May, whom he would invest with the dignity of a poetical personage, was nothing more than a sodden-headed sot, who loved his bottle better than any thing in life; and this is the clue to lead us to the understanding of a conduct, not otherwise easy to be explained. How do I know this? you will say. Don't bother me, and you shall hear. It happened that I was galloping after the hounds which were in pursuit of a deer, in an unfrequented part of these woods, when, slap! went my horse's legs into a hole, in which he sunk to his shoulder! while I took measure of a good slip of land beyond. Having shaken off the dust, I went to help the horse, who kept floundering about in the hole; and I then perceived that he had fallen *into a grave,* which had caved in under his weight.

" 'A treasure or old May!' said I, and soon began to dig; when I came to,—what do you think? At the bottom of the grave, among fragments of a decayed coffin, was stretched out a skeleton complete,—and, at its head and feet, by way of head-stone and footboard, lay—a bottle of *brandy,* and another of *rum,*—corked, sealed, and deposited for convenient use, in another world,—if, haply, in that world, *drinking* were a permitted enjoyment! And here we have the solution of the incident, so ingeniously mystified. The heathenish old reprobate preferred his bottle to his salvation,—and looked more to one than to the other, in his last moments!!"

"The spell is broken," cried I; "you have disenchanted 'old May' with a vengeance! You have a knack of your own, of getting at *the marrow* of a thing, you know!"

"Confound your marrow," said the Laird; and bounding from the table, he retired to bed; to dream of hounds that fled, while bears in packs pursued them,—of bucks that melted into air, while the death-dealing charge passed through them harmless,—of smoke wreaths, bodying forth the forms of men long dead and mouldering,—and such like "perilous stuff as dreams are made of!"

But what has become of our missing hounds all the while? *We* have run off, as *they* have done; and must now recover the track of our narrative. The night passed, and nothing was heard of them: the next day, and they did not come: on the second day, a mounted huntsman was sent across the river, to search for them on the opposite side. We have seen, that starting from the Ashepoo, they had crossed the Chee-Ha: taking up the search at this point, he traced them from plantation to plantation, until he reached Tar Bluff on the Combahee. At this spot (moistened by the last blood spilt in the revolutionary contest,—that of the gallant John Laurens, of South-Carolina), he lost all trace of the deer. Whether he swam the Combahee, as he had before swam the Chee-Ha; whether he here escaped from the hounds, or was devoured by them; whether he was a deer of flesh and blood, or the phantom buck of the legend,—we cannot decide. The data are before our readers; and each one can settle these questions for himself, according to his peculiar taste. As for the hounds, they were found (like veterans, as they were) quartered in couples, on the plantations that bordered on their line of march. They were recovered, and returned to their anxious master, who, we fancy, will think twice, before he halloos them off a second time, in chase of a phantom buck, or any buck,—whose blood is marrow!

William Faulkner

(1897–1962)

*William Faulkner is generally regarded as one of America's foremost modern writers. In his own lifetime he moved from relative obscurity to international prominence, and in 1949 was awarded the Nobel Prize for literature. He was born in New Albany, Mississippi, in 1897, and lived most of his life in nearby Oxford, Mississippi. His father's family was well established in north Mississippi, and included the almost legendary figure of Faulkner's great-grandfather, William Clark Falkner (1825–85), the "Old Colonel": a popular novelist (*The White Rose of Memphis*), Confederate hero, cofounder of the Ripley Railroad Company, and outspoken local leader who was shot and killed by a former business rival. Faulkner attended high school in Oxford, and the University of Mississippi, although he never graduated from either. During World War I, he enlisted with the British Royal Air Force in Canada, but saw no action. While living in New Orleans in the 1920s he met Sherwood Anderson, who encouraged him to write and helped him find a publisher. Faulkner's first two novels,* Soldiers' Pay *(1926) and* Mosquitoes *(1927), show an early mastery of narrative style, but it was with his third novel,* Sartoris *(1929), that he began to create his mythical Southern world, "Yoknapatawpha County," and to stamp his work with a voice and subject all his own. Among his many works, the following stand out as vital classics of American prose fiction:* The Sound and the Fury *(1929),* As I Lay Dying *(1930),* Light in August *(1932),* Absalom, Absalom! *(1936),* The Hamlet *(1940), and* Go Down, Moses *(1942). All his life Faulkner was a teller of tales, and many of his longer works are organized around short stories. His own collection of stories, which he selected and arranged himself, was published in 1950 as* Collected Stories of William Faulkner. *A. Walton Litz, editor of* Major American Short Stories, *calls the* Collected Stories *"one of the richest volumes in the history of the American short story." Toward the end of his* *life, Faulkner was writer-in-residence at the University of Virginia. He died July 6, 1962. Among his other books are* Sanctuary *(1931),* These Thirteen *(1931),* Doctor Martino and Other Stories *(1934),* The Unvanquished *(1938),* The Wild Palms *(1939),* Intruder in the Dust *(1948),* Knight's Gambit *(1949),* Requiem for a Nun *(1951),* A Fable *(1954),* Big Woods *(1955),* The Town *(1957),* The Mansion *(1959), and* The Reivers *(1962). "Mountain Victory," from* Collected Stories, *first appeared in* The Saturday Evening Post, *December 3, 1932, as "A Mountain Victory."*

MOUNTAIN VICTORY

⚜

1

Through the cabin window the five people watched the cavalcade toil up the muddy trail and halt at the gate. First came a man on foot, leading a horse. He wore a broad hat low on his face, his body shapeless in a weathered gray cloak from which his left hand emerged, holding the reins. The bridle was silvermounted, the horse a gaunt, mudsplashed, thoroughbred bay, wearing in place of saddle a navy blue army blanket bound on it by a piece of rope. The second horse was a shortbodied, bigheaded, scrub sorrel, also mudsplashed. It wore a bridle contrived of rope and wire, and an army saddle in which, perched high above the dangling stirrups, crouched a shapeless something larger than a child, which at that distance appeared to wear no garment or garments known to man.

One of the three men at the cabin window left it quickly. The others, without turning, heard him cross the room swiftly and then return, carrying a long rifle.

"No, you don't," the older man said.

"Don't you see that cloak?" the younger said. "That rebel cloak?"

"I wont have it," the other said. "They have surrendered. They have said they are whipped."

Through the window they watched the horses stop at the gate. The gate was of sagging hickory, in a rock fence which straggled down a gaunt slope sharp in relief against the valley and a still further range of mountains dissolving into the low, dissolving sky.

They watched the creature on the second horse descend and hand his reins also into the same left hand of the man in gray that held the reins of the thoroughbred. They watched the creature enter the gate and mount the path and disappear beyond the angle of the window. Then they heard it cross the porch and knock at the door. They stood there and heard it knock again.

After a while the older man said, without turning his head, "Go and see."

One of the women, the older one, turned from the window, her feet making no sound on the floor, since they were bare. She went to the front door and opened it. The chill, wet light of the dying April afternoon fell in upon her—upon a small woman with a gnarled expressionless face, in a gray shapeless garment. Facing her across the sill was a creature a little larger than a large monkey, dressed in a voluminous blue overcoat of a private in the Federal army, with, tied tentlike over his head and falling about his shoulders, a piece of oilcloth which might have been cut square from the hood of a sutler's wagon; within the orifice the woman could see nothing whatever save the whites of two eyes, momentary and phantomlike, as with a single glance the Negro examined the woman standing barefoot in her faded calico garment, and took in the bleak and barren interior of the cabin hall.

"Marster Major Soshay Weddel send he compliments en say he wishful fo sleeping room fo heself en boy en two hawses," he said in a pompous, parrot-like voice. The woman looked at him. Her face was like a spent mask. "We been up yonder a ways, fighting dem Yankees," the Negro said. "Done quit now. Gwine back home."

The woman seemed to speak from somewhere behind her face, as though behind an effigy or a painted screen: "I'll ask him."

"We ghy pay you," the Negro said.

"Pay?" Pausing, she seemed to muse upon him. "Hit aint near a ho-tel on the mou-tin."

The Negro made a large gesture. "Don't make no diffunce. We done stayed de night in worse places den whut dis is. You just tell um it Marse Soshay Weddel." Then he saw that the woman was looking past him. He turned and saw the man in the worn gray cloak already halfway up the path from the gate. He came on and mounted the porch, removing with his left hand the broad slouched hat bearing the tarnished wreath of a Confederate field officer. He had a dark face, with dark eyes and black hair, his face at once thick yet gaunt, and arrogant. He was not tall, yet he topped the

Negro by five or six inches. The cloak was weathered, faded about the shoulders where the light fell strongest. The skirts were bedraggled, frayed, mudsplashed: the garment had been patched again and again, and brushed again and again; the nap was completely gone.

"Goodday, madam," he said. "Have you stableroom for my horses and shelter for myself and my boy for the night?"

The woman looked at him with a static, musing quality, as though she had seen without alarm an apparition.

"I'll have to see," she said.

"I shall pay," the man said. "I know the times."

"I'll have to ask him," the woman said. She turned, then stopped. The older man entered the hall behind her. He was big, in jean clothes, with a shock of iron-gray hair and pale eyes.

"I am Saucier Weddel," the man in gray said. "I am on my way home to Mississippi from Virginia. I am in Tennessee now?"

"You are in Tennessee," the other said. "Come in."

Weddel turned to the Negro. "Take the horses on to the stable," he said.

The Negro returned to the gate, shapeless in the oilcloth cape and the big overcoat, with that swaggering arrogance which he had assumed as soon as he saw the woman's bare feet and the meagre, barren interior of the cabin. He took up the two bridle reins and began to shout at the horses with needless and officious vociferation, to which the two horses paid no heed, as though they were long accustomed to him. It was as if the Negro himself paid no attention to his cries, as though the shouting were merely concomitant to the action of leading the horses out of sight of the door, like an effluvium by both horses and Negro accepted and relegated in the same instant.

2

Through the kitchen wall the girl could hear the voices of the men in the room from which her father had driven her when the stranger approached the house. She was about twenty: a big girl with smooth, simple hair and big, smooth hands, standing barefoot in a single garment made out of flour sacks. She stood close to the wall, motionless, her head bent a little, her eyes wide and still and empty like a sleepwalker's, listening to her father and the guest enter the room beyond it.

The kitchen was a plank leanto built against the log wall of the cabin proper. From between the logs beside her the clay chinking, dried to chalk by the heat of the stove, had fallen away in places. Stooping, the movement slow and lush and soundless as the whispering of her bare feet on the floor, she leaned her eye to one of these cracks. She could see a bare table on which sat an earthenware jug and a box of musket cartridges stenciled *U. S. Army*. At the table her two brothers sat in splint chairs, though it was only the younger one, the boy, who looked toward the door, though she knew, could hear now, that the stranger was in the room. The older brother was taking the cartridges one by one from the box and crimping them and setting them upright at his hand like a mimic parade of troops, his back to the door where she knew the stranger was now standing. She breathed quietly. "Vatch would have shot him," she said, breathed, to herself, stooping. "I reckon he will yet."

Then she heard feet again and her mother came toward the door to the kitchen, crossing and for a moment blotting the orifice. Yet she did not move, not even when her mother entered the kitchen. She stooped to the crack, her breathing regular and placid, hearing her mother clattering the stovelids behind her. Then she saw the stranger for the first time and then she was holding her breath quietly, not even aware that she had ceased to breathe. She saw him standing beside the table in his shabby cloak, with his hat in his left hand. Vatch did not look up.

"My name is Saucier Weddel," the stranger said.

"Soshay Weddel," the girl breathed into the dry chinking, the crumbled and powdery wall. She could see him at full length, in his stained and patched and brushed cloak, with his head lifted a little and his face worn, almost gaunt, stamped with a kind of indomitable weariness and yet arrogant too, like a creature from another world with other air to breathe and another kind of blood to warm the veins. "Soshay Weddel," she breathed.

"Take some whiskey," Vatch said without moving.

Then suddenly, as it had been with the suspended breathing, she was not listening to the words at all, as though it were no longer necessary for her to hear, as though curiosity too had no place in the atmosphere in which the stranger dwelled and in which she too dwelled for the moment as she watched the stranger standing beside the table, looking at Vatch, and Vatch now turned in his chair, a cartridge in his hand, looking up at the stranger. She breathed quietly into the crack through which the voices came now without heat or significance out of that dark and smoldering and violent and childlike vanity of men:

"I reckon you know these when you see them, then?"

"Why not? We used them too. We never always had the time nor the powder to stop and make our own. So we had to use yours now and then. Especially during the last."

"Maybe you would know them better if one exploded in your face."

"Vatch." She now looked at her father, because he had spoken. Her younger brother was raised a little in his chair, leaning a little forward, his mouth open a little. He was seventeen. Yet still the stranger stood looking quietly down at Vatch, his hat clutched against his worn cloak, with on his face that expression arrogant and weary and a little quizzical.

"You can show your other hand too," Vatch said. "Don't be afraid to leave your pistol go."

"No," the stranger said. "I am not afraid to show it."

"Take some whiskey, then," Vatch said, pushing the jug forward with a motion slighting and contemptuous.

"I am obliged infinitely," the stranger said. "It's my stomach. For three years of war I have had to apologize to my stomach; now, with peace, I must apologize for it. But if I might have a glass for my boy? Even after four years, he cannot stand cold."

"Soshay Weddel," the girl breathed into the crumbled dust beyond which the voices came, not yet raised yet forever irreconcilable and already doomed, the one blind victim, the other blind executioner:

"Or maybe behind your back you would know it better."

"You, Vatch."

"Stop, sir. If he was in the army for as long as one year, he has run too, once. Perhaps oftener, if he faced the Army of Northern Virginia."

"Soshay Weddel," the girl breathed, stooping. Now she saw Weddel, walking apparently straight toward her, a thick tumbler in his left hand and his hat crumpled beneath the same arm.

"Not that way," Vatch said. The stranger paused and looked back at Vatch. "Where are you aiming to go?"

"To take this out to my boy," the stranger said. "Out to the stable. I thought perhaps this door—" His face was in profile now, worn, haughty, wasted, the eyebrows lifted with quizzical and arrogant interrogation. Without rising Vatch jerked his head back and aside. "Come away from that door." But the stranger did not stir. Only his head moved a little, as though he had merely changed the direction of his eyes.

"He's looking at paw," the girl breathed. "He's waiting for paw to tell him. He ain't skeered of Vatch. I knowed it."

"Come away from that door," Vatch said. "You damn nigra."

"So it's my face and not my uniform," the stranger said. "And you fought four years to free us, I understand."

Then she heard her father speak again. "Go out the front way and around the house, stranger," he said.

"Soshay Weddel," the girl said. Behind her her mother clattered at the stove. "Soshay Weddel," she said. She did not say it aloud. She breathed again, deep and quiet and without haste. "It's like a music. It's like a singing."

3

The Negro was squatting in the hallway of the barn, the sagging and broken stalls of which were empty save for the two horses. Beside him was a worn rucksack, open. He was engaged in polishing a pair of thin dancing slippers with a cloth and a tin of paste, empty save for a thin rim of polish about the circumference of the tin. Beside him on a piece of plank sat one finished shoe. The upper was cracked; it had a crude sole nailed recently and crudely on by a clumsy hand.

"Thank de Lawd folks cant see de bottoms of yo feets," the Negro said. "Thank de Lawd it's just dese hyer mountain trash. I'd even hate fo Yankees to see yo feets in dese things." He rubbed the shoe, squinted at it, breathed upon it, rubbed it again upon his squatting flank.

"Here," Weddel said, extending the tumbler. It contained a liquid as colorless as water.

The Negro stopped, the shoe and the cloth suspended. "Which?" he said. He looked at the glass. "Whut's dat?"

"Drink it," Weddel said.

"Dat's water. Whut you bringing me water fer?"

"Take it," Weddel said. "It's not water."

The Negro took the glass gingerly. He held it as if it contained nitroglycerin. He looked at it, blinking, bringing the glass slowly under his nose. He blinked. "Where'd you git dis hyer?" Weddel didn't answer. He had taken up the finished slipper, looking at it. The Negro held the glass under his nose. "It smell kind of like it ought to," he said. "But I be dawg ef it look like anything. Dese folks fixing to pizen you." He tipped the glass and sipped gingerly, and lowered the glass, blinking.

"I didn't drink any of it," Weddel said. He set the slipper down.

"You better hadn't," the Negro said. "When here I done been fo years trying to take care of you en git you back home like whut

Mistis tole me to do, and here you sleeping in folks' barns at night like a tramp, like a pater-roller nigger—" He put the glass to his lips, tilting it and his head in a single jerk. He lowered the glass, empty; his eyes were closed; he said, "Whuf!" shaking his head with a violent, shuddering motion. "It smells right, and it act right. But I be dawg ef it look right. I reckon you better let it alone, like you started out. When dey try to make you drink it you send um to me. I done already stood so much I reckon I can stand a little mo fer Mistis' sake."

He took up the shoe and the cloth again. Weddel stooped above the rucksack. "I want my pistol," he said.

Again the Negro ceased, the shoe and the cloth poised. "Whut fer?" He leaned and looked up the muddy slope toward the cabin. "Is dese folks Yankees?" he said in a whisper.

"No," Weddel said, digging in the rucksack with his left hand. The Negro did not seem to hear him.

"In Tennessee? You tole me we was in Tennessee, where Memphis is, even if you never tole me it was all disyer up-and-down land in de Memphis country. I know I never seed none of um when I went to Memphis wid yo paw dat time. But you says so. And now you telling me dem Memphis folks is Yankees?"

"Where is the pistol?" Weddel said.

"I done tole you," the Negro said. "Acting like you does. Letting dese folks see you come walking up de road, leading Caesar caze you think he tired; making me ride whilst you walks when I can outwalk you any day you ever lived and you knows it, even if I is fawty en you twenty-eight. I ghy tell yo maw. I ghy tell um."

Weddel rose, in his hand a heavy cap-and-ball revolver. He chuckled it in his single hand, drawing the hammer back, letting it down again. The Negro watched him, crouched like an ape in the blue Union army overcoat. "You put dat thing back," he said. "De war done wid now. Dey tole us back dar at Ferginny it was done wid. You dont need no pistol now. You put it back, you hear me?"

"I'm going to bathe," Weddel said. "Is my shirt—"

"Bathe where? In whut? Dese folks aint never seed a bathtub."

"Bathe at the well. Is my shirt ready?"

"Whut dey is of it. . . . You put dat pistol back, Marse Soshay. I ghy tell yo maw on you. I ghy tell um. I just wish Marster was here."

"Go to the kitchen," Weddel said. "Tell them I wish to bathe in the well house. Ask them to draw the curtain on that window there." The pistol had vanished beneath the grey cloak. He went to the stall where the thoroughbred was. The horse nuzzled at him,

its eyes rolling soft and wild. He patted its nose with his left hand.
It whickered, not loud, its breath sweet and warm.

4

The Negro entered the kitchen from the rear. He had removed the
oilcloth tent and he now wore a blue forage cap which, like the
overcoat, was much too large for him, resting upon the top of his
head in such a way that the unsupported brim oscillated faintly
when he moved as though with a life of its own. He was completely
invisible save for his face between cap and collar like a dried Dyak
trophy and almost as small and dusted lightly over as with a thin
pallor of wood ashes by the cold. The older woman was at the
stove on which frying food now hissed and sputtered; she did not
look up when the Negro entered. The girl was standing in the
middle of the room, doing nothing at all. She looked at the Negro,
watching him with a slow, grave, secret, unwinking gaze as he
crossed the kitchen with that air of swaggering caricatured assurance, and upended a block of wood beside the stove and sat
upon it.

"If disyer is de kind of weather yawl has up here all de time,"
he said, "I dont care ef de Yankees does has dis country." He
opened the overcoat, revealing his legs and feet as being wrapped,
shapeless and huge, in some muddy and anonymous substance
resembling fur, giving them the appearance of two muddy beasts
the size of halfgrown dogs lying on the floor; moving a little nearer
the girl, the girl thought quietly *Hit's fur. He taken and cut up a
fur coat to wrap his feet in* "Yes, suh," the Negro said. "Just yawl
let me git home again, en de Yankees kin have all de rest of it."

"Where do you-uns live?" the girl said.

The Negro looked at her. "In Miss'ippi. On de Domain. Aint
you never hyeard tell of Countymaison?"

"Countymaison?"

"Dat's it. His grandpappy named it Countymaison caze it's bigger den a county to ride over. You cant ride across it on a mule
betwixt sunup and sundown. Dat's how come." He rubbed his
hands slowly on his thighs. His face was now turned toward the
stove; he snuffed loudly. Already the ashy overlay on his skin had
disappeared, leaving his face dead black, wizened, his mouth a
little loose, as though the muscles had become slack with usage,
like rubber bands—not the eating muscles, the talking ones. "I
reckon we is gittin nigh home, after all. Leastways dat hawg meat
smell like it do down whar folks lives."

"Countymaison," the girl said in a rapt, bemused tone, looking at the Negro with her grave, unwinking regard. Then she turned her head and looked at the wall, her face perfectly serene, perfectly inscrutable, without haste, with a profound and absorbed deliberation.

"Dat's it," the Negro said. "Even Yankees is heard tell of Weddel's Countymaison en erbout Marster Francis Weddel. Maybe yawl seed um pass in de carriage dat time he went to Washn'ton to tell yawl's president how he aint like de way yawl's president wuz treating de people. He rid all de way to Washn'ton in de carriage, wid two niggers to drive en to heat de bricks to kept he foots warm, en de man done gone on ahead wid de wagon en de fresh hawses. He carried yawl's president two whole dressed bears en eight sides of smoked deer venison. He must a passed right out dar in front yawl's house. I reckon yo pappy or maybe his pappy seed um pass." He talked on, voluble, in soporific singsong, his face beginning to glisten, to shine a little with the rich warmth, while the mother bent over the stove and the girl, motionless, static, her bare feet cupped smooth and close to the rough puncheons, her big, smooth, young body cupped soft and richly mammalian to the rough garment, watching the Negro with her ineffable and unwinking gaze, her mouth open a little.

The Negro talked on, his eyes closed, his voice interminable, boastful, his air lazily intolerant, as if he were still at home and there had been no war and no harsh rumors of freedom and of change, and he (a stableman, in the domestic hierarchy a man of horses) were spending the evening in the quarters among field hands, until the older woman dished the food and left the room, closing the door behind her. He opened his eyes at the sound and looked toward the door and then back to the girl. She was looking at the wall, at the closed door through which her mother had vanished. "Dont dey lets you eat at de table wid um?" he said.

The girl looked at the Negro, unwinking. "Countymaison," she said. "Vatch says he is a nigra too."

"Who? Him? A nigger? Marse Soshay Weddel? Which un is Vatch?" The girl looked at him. "It's caze yawl aint never been nowhere. Ain't never seed nothing. Living up here on a nekkid hill whar you cant even see smoke. Him a nigger? I wish his maw could hear you say dat." He looked about the kitchen, wizened, his eyeballs rolling white, ceaseless, this way and that. The girl watched him.

"Do the girls there wear shoes all the time?" she said.

The Negro looked about the kitchen, "Where does yawl keep dat ere Tennessee spring water? Back here somewhere?"

"Spring water?"

The Negro blinked slowly. "Dat ere light-drinking kahysene."

"Kahysene?"

"Dat ere light colored lamp oil whut yawl drinks. Aint you got a little of it hid back here somewhere?"

"Oh," the girl said. "You mean corn." She went to a corner and lifted a loose plank in the floor, the Negro watching her, and drew forth another earthen jug. She filled another thick tumbler and gave it to the Negro and watched him jerk it down his throat, his eyes closed. Again he said, "Whuf!" and drew his back hand across his mouth.

"What wuz dat you axed me?" he said.

"Do the girls down there at Countymaison wear shoes?"

"De ladies does. If dey didn't have none, Marse Soshay could sell a hun'ed niggers en buy um some . . . Which un is it say Marse Soshay a nigger?"

The girl watched him. "Is he married?"

"Who married? Marse Soshay?" The girl watched him. "How he have time to git married, wid us fighting de Yankees for fo years? Aint been home in fo years now where no ladies to marry is." He looked at the girl, his eyewhites a little bloodshot, his skin shining in faint and steady highlights. Thawing, he seemed to have increased in size a little too. "Whut's it ter you, if he married or no?"

They looked at each other. The Negro could hear her breathing. Then she was not looking at him at all, though she had not yet even blinked nor turned her head. "I dont reckon he'd have any time for a girl that didn't have any shoes," she said. She went to the wall and stooped again to the crack. The Negro watched her. The older woman entered and took another dish from the stove and departed without having looked at either of them.

5

The four men, the three men and the boy, sat about the supper table. The broken meal lay on thick plates. The knives and forks were iron. On the table the jug still sat. Weddel was now cloakless. He was shaven, his still damp hair combed back. Upon his bosom the ruffles of the shirt frothed in the lamplight, the right sleeve, empty, pinned across his breast with a thin gold pin. Under the table the frail and mended dancing slippers rested among the brogans of the two men and the bare splayed feet of the boy.

"Vatch says you are a nigra," the father said.

Weddel was leaning a little back in his chair. "So that explains it," he said. "I was thinking that he was just congenitally illtempered. And having to be a victor, too."

"Are you a nigra?" the father said.

"No," Weddel said. He was looking at the boy, his weathered and wasted face a little quizzical. Across the back of his neck his hair, long, had been cut roughly as though with a knife or perhaps a bayonet. The boy watched him in complete and rapt immobility. *As if I might be an apparition,* he thought. *A hant. Maybe I am.* "No," he said. "I am not a Negro."

"Who are you?" the father said.

Weddel sat a little sideways in his chair, his hand lying on the table. "Do you ask guests who they are in Tennessee?" he said. Vatch was filling a tumbler from the jug. His face was lowered, his hands big and hard. His face was hard. Weddel looked at him. "I think I know how you feel," he said. "I expect I felt that way once. But it's hard to keep on feeling any way for four years. Even feeling at all."

Vatch said something, sudden and harsh. He clapped the tumbler on the table, splashing some of the liquor out. It looked like water, with a violent, dynamic odor. It seemed to possess an inherent volatility which carried a splash of it across the table and on to the foam of frayed yet immaculate linen on Weddel's breast, striking sudden and chill through the cloth against his flesh.

"Vatch!" the father said.

Weddel did not move; his expression arrogant, quizzical, and weary, did not change. "He did not mean to do that," he said.

"When I do," Vatch said, "it will not look like an accident."

Weddel was looking at Vatch. "I think I told you once," he said. "My name is Saucier Weddel. I am a Mississippian. I live at a place named Contalmaison. My father built it and named it. He was a Choctaw chief named Francis Weddel, of whom you have probably not heard. He was the son of a Choctaw woman and a French émigré of New Orleans, a general of Napoleon's and a knight of the Legion of Honor. His name was François Vidal. My father drove to Washington once in his carriage to remonstrate with President Jackson about the Government's treatment of his people, sending on ahead a wagon of provender and gifts and also fresh horses for the carriage, in charge of the man, the native overseer, who was a full blood Choctaw and my father's cousin. In the old days The Man was the hereditary title of the head of our clan; but after we became Europeanised like the white people, we lost the title to the branch which refused to become polluted, though we kept the slaves and the land. The Man now lives in a house a little larger than the cabins of the Negroes—an upper servant. It was in Washington that my father met and married my mother. He was killed in the Mexican War. My mother died two years ago, in '63, of a complication of pneumonia acquired while superintending the burying of some silver on a wet night when Federal troops entered the county, and of unsuitable food; though my boy refuses to believe that she is dead. He refuses to believe that the country would have permitted the North to deprive her of the imported Martinique coffee and the beaten biscuit which she had each Sunday noon and Wednesday night. He believes that the country would have risen in arms first. But then, he is only a Negro, member of an oppressed race burdened with freedom. He has a daily list of my misdoings which he is going to tell her on me when we reach home. I went to school in France, but not very hard. Until two weeks ago I was a major of Mississippi infantry in the corps of a man named Longstreet, of whom you may have heard."

"So you were a major," Vatch said.

"That appears to be my indictment; yes."

"I have seen a rebel major before," Vatch said. "Do you want me to tell you where I saw him?"

"Tell me," Weddel said.

"He was lying by a tree. We had to stop there and lie down, and he was lying by the tree, asking for water. 'Have you any water, friend?' he said. 'Yes. I have water,' I said. 'I have plenty of water.' I had to crawl; I couldn't stand up. I crawled over to him and I lifted him so that his head would be propped against the tree. I fixed his face to the front."

"Didn't you have a bayonet?" Weddel said. "But I forgot; you couldn't stand up."

"Then I crawled back. I had to crawl back a hundred yards, where—"

"Back?"

"It was too close. Who can do decent shooting that close? I had to crawl back, and then the damned musket—"

"Damn musket?" Weddel sat a little sideways in his chair, his hand on the table, his face quizzical and sardonic, contained.

"I missed, the first shot. I had his face propped up and turned, and his eyes open watching me, and then I missed. I hit him in the throat and I had to shoot again because of the damned musket."

"Vatch," the father said.

Vatch's hands were on the table. His head, his face, were like his father's, though without the father's deliberation. His face was furious, still, unpredictable. "It was that damn musket. I had to shoot three times. Then he had three eyes, in a row across his face propped against the tree, all three of them open, like he was watching me with three eyes. I gave him another eye, to see better with. But I had to shoot twice because of the damn musket."

"You, Vatch," the father said. He stood now, his hands on the table, propping his gaunt body. "Dont you mind Vatch, stranger. The war is over now."

"I dont mind him," Weddel said. His hand went to his bosom, disappearing into the foam of linen while he watched Vatch steadily with his alert, quizzical, sardonic gaze. "I have seen too many of him for too long a time to mind one of him any more."

"Take some whiskey," Vatch said.

"Are you just making a point?"

"Damn the pistol," Vatch said. "Take some whiskey."

Weddel laid his hand again on the table. But instead of pouring, Vatch held the jug poised over the tumbler. He was looking past Weddel's shoulder. Weddel turned. The girl was in the room, standing in the doorway with her mother just behind her. The mother said as if she were speaking to the floor under her feet: "I tried to keep her back, like you said. I tried to. But she is strong as a man; hardheaded like a man."

"You go back," the father said.

"Me to go back?" the mother said to the floor.

The father spoke a name; Weddel did not catch it; he did not even know that he had missed it. "You go back."

The girl moved. She was not looking at any of them. She came to the chair on which lay Weddel's worn and mended cloak and opened it, revealing the four ragged slashes where the sable lining had been cut out as though with a knife. She was looking at the cloak when Vatch grasped her by the shoulder, but it was at Weddel that she looked. "You cut hit out and gave hit to that nigra to wrap his feet in," she said. Then the father grasped Vatch in turn. Weddel had not stirred, his face turned over his shoulder; beside him the boy was upraised out of his chair by his arms, his young, slacked face leaned forward into the lamp. But save for the breathing of Vatch and the father there was no sound in the room.

"I am stronger than you are, still," the father said. "I am a better man still, or as good."

"You wont be always," Vatch said.

The father looked back over his shoulder at the girl. "Go back," he said. She turned and went back toward the hall, her feet silent as rubber feet. Again the father called that name which Weddel had not caught; again he did not catch it and was not aware again that he had not. She went out the door. The father looked at

Weddel. Weddel's attitude was unchanged, save that once more his hand was hidden inside his bosom. They looked at one another—the cold, Nordic face and the half Gallic half Mongol face thin and worn like a bronze casting, with eyes like those of the dead, in which only vision has ceased and not sight. "Take your horses, and go," the father said.

6

It was dark in the hall, and cold, with the black chill of the mountain April coming up through the floor about her bare legs and her body in the single coarse garment. "He cut the lining outen his cloak to wrap that nigra's feet in," she said. "He done hit for a nigra." The door behind her opened. Against the lamplight a man loomed, then the door shut behind him. "Is it Vatch or paw?" she said. Then something struck her across the back—a leather strap. "I was afeared it would be Vatch," she said. The blow fell again.

"Go to bed," the father said.

"You can whip me, but you cant whip him," she said.

The blow fell again: a thick, flat, soft sound upon her immediate flesh beneath the coarse sacking.

7

In the deserted kitchen the Negro sat for a moment longer on the upturned block beside the stove, looking at the door. Then he rose carefully, one hand on the wall.

"Whuf!" he said. "Wish us had a spring on de Domain whut run dat. Stock would git trompled to death, sho mon." He blinked at the door, listening, then he moved, letting himself carefully along the wall, stopping now and then to look toward the door and listen, his air cunning, unsteady, and alert. He reached the corner and lifted the loose plank, stooping carefully, bracing himself against the wall. He lifted the jug out, whereupon he lost his balance and sprawled on his face, his face ludicrous and earnest with astonishment. He got up and sat flat on the floor, carefully, the jug between his knees, and lifted the jug and drank. He drank a long time.

"Whuf!" he said. "On de Domain we'd give disyer stuff to de hawgs. But deseyer ign'unt mountain trash—" He drank again; then with the jug poised there came into his face an expression of concern and then consternation. He set the jug down and tried to get up, sprawling above the jug, gaining his feet at last, stooped, swaying, drooling, with that expression of outraged consternation on his face. Then he fell headlong to the floor, overturning the jug.

8

They stooped above the Negro, talking quietly to one another—Weddel in his frothed shirt, the father and the boy.

"We'll have to tote him," the father said.

They lifted the Negro. With his single hand Weddel jerked the Negro's head up, shaking him. "Jubal," he said.

The Negro struck out, clumsily, with one arm. "Le'm be," he muttered. "Le'm go."

"Jubal!" Weddel said.

The Negro thrashed, sudden and violent. "You le'm be," he said. "I ghy tell de Man. I ghy tell um." He ceased, muttering: "Field hands. Field niggers."

"We'll have to tote him," the father said.

"Yes," Weddel said. "I'm sorry for this. I should have warned you. But I didn't think there was another jug he could have gained access to." He stooped, getting his single hand under the Negro's shoulders.

"Get away," the father said. "Me and Hule can do it." He and the boy picked the Negro up. Weddel opened the door. They emerged into the high black cold. Below them the barn loomed. They carried the Negro down the slope. "Get them horses out, Hule," the father said.

"Horses?" Weddel said. "He cant ride now. He cant stay on a horse."

They looked at one another, each toward the other voice, in the cold, the icy silence.

"You wont go now?" the father said.

"I am sorry. You see I cannot depart now. I will have to stay until daylight, until he is sober. We will go then."

"Leave him here. Leave him one horse, and you ride on. He is nothing but a nigra."

"I am sorry. Not after four years." His voice was quizzical, whimsical almost, yet with that quality of indomitable weariness. "I've worried with him this far; I reckon I will get him on home."

"I have warned you," the father said.

"I am obliged. We will move at daylight. If Hule will be kind enough to help me get him into the loft."

The father had stepped back. "Put that nigra down, Hule," he said.

"He will freeze here," Weddel said. "I must get him into the loft." He hauled the Negro up and propped him against the wall and stooped to hunch the Negro's lax body onto his shoulder. The weight rose easily, though he did not understand why until the father spoke again:

"Hule. Come away from there."

"Yes; go," Weddel said quietly. "I can get him up the ladder." He could hear the boy's breathing, fast, young, swift with excitement perhaps. Weddel did not pause to speculate, nor at the faintly hysterical tone of the boy's voice:

"I'll help you."

Weddel didn't object again. He slapped the Negro awake and they set his feet on the ladder rungs, pushing him upward. Halfway up he stopped; again he thrashed out at them. "I ghy tell um. I ghy tell de Man. I ghy tell Mistis. Field hands. Field niggers."

9

They lay side by side in the loft, beneath the cloak and the two saddle blankets. There was no hay. The Negro snored, his breath reeking and harsh, thick. Below, in its stall, the Thoroughbred stamped now and then. Weddel lay on his back, his arm across his chest, the hand clutching the stub of the other arm. Overhead, through the cracks in the roof the sky showed—the thick chill, black sky which would rain again tomorrow and on every tomorrow until they left the mountains. "If I leave the mountains," he said quietly, motionless on his back beside the snoring Negro, staring upward. "I was concerned. I had thought that it was exhausted; that I had lost the privilege of being afraid. But I have not. And so I am happy. Quite happy." He lay rigid on his back in the cold darkness, thinking of home. "Contalmaison. Our lives are summed up in sounds and made significant. Victory. Defeat. Peace. Home. That's why we must do so much to invent meanings for the sounds, so damned much. Especially if you are unfortunate enough to be victorious: so damned much. It's nice to be whipped; quiet to be whipped. To be whipped and to lie under a broken roof, thinking of home." The Negro snored. "So damned much"; seeming to watch the words shape quietly in the darkness above his mouth. "What would happen, say, a man in the lobby of the Gayoso, in Memphis, laughing suddenly aloud. But I am quite happy—" Then he heard the sound. He lay utterly still then, his hand clutching the butt of the pistol warm beneath the stub of his right arm, hearing the quiet, almost infinitesimal sound as it mounted the ladder. But he made no move until he saw the dim orifice of the trap door blotted out. "Stop where you are," he said.

"It's me," the voice said; the voice of the boy, again with that swift, breathless quality which even now Weddel did not pause to designate as excitement or even to remark at all. The boy came on his hands and knees across the dry, sibilant chaff which dusted the floor. "Go ahead and shoot," he said. On his hands and knees he loomed above Weddel with his panting breath. "I wish I was dead. I so wish hit. I wish we was both dead. I could wish like Vatch wishes. Why did you uns have to stop here?"

Weddel had not moved. "Why does Vatch wish I was dead?"

"Because he can still hear you uns yelling. I used to sleep with him and he wakes up at night and once paw had to keep him from choking me to death before he waked up and him sweating, hearing you uns yelling still. Without nothing but unloaded guns, yelling, Vatch said, like scarecrows across a cornpatch, running." He was crying now, not aloud. "Damn you! Damn you to hell!"

"Yes," Weddel said. "I have heard them, myself. But why do you wish you were dead?"

"Because she was trying to come, herself. Only she had to—"

"Who? She? Your sister?"

"—had to go through the room to get out. Paw was awake. He said, 'If you go out that door, dont you never come back.' And she said, 'I dont aim to.' And Vatch was awake too and he said, 'Make him marry you quick because you are going to be a widow at daylight.' And she come back and told me. But I was awake too. She told me to tell you."

"Tell me what?" Weddel said. The boy cried quietly, with a kind of patient and utter despair.

"I told her if you was a nigra, and if she done that—I told her that I—"

"What? If she did what? What does she want you to tell me?"

"About the window into the attic where her and me sleep. There is a foot ladder I made to come back from hunting at night for you to get in. But I told her if you was a nigra and if she done that I would—"

"Now then," Weddel said sharply; "pull yourself together now. Dont you remember? I never even saw her but that one time when she came in the room and your father sent her out."

"But you saw her then. And she saw you."

"No," Weddel said.

The boy ceased to cry. He was quite still above Weddel. "No what?"

"I wont do it. Climb up your ladder."

For a while the boy seemed to muse above him, motionless, breathing slow and quiet now; he spoke now in a musing, almost dreamy tone: "I could kill you easy. You aint got but one arm, even if you are older. . . ." Suddenly he moved, with almost unbelievable quickness; Weddel's first intimation was when the boy's hard, overlarge hands took him by the throat. Weddel did not move. "I could kill you easy. And wouldn't none mind."

"Shhhhhh," Weddel said. "Not so loud."

"Wouldn't none care." He held Weddel's throat with hard, awkward restraint. Weddel could feel the choking and the shaking expend itself somewhere about the boy's forearms before it reached his hands, as though the connection between brain and hands was incomplete. "Wouldn't none care. Except Vatch would be mad."

"I have a pistol," Weddel said.

"Then shoot me with it. Go on."

"No."

"No what?"

"I told you before."

"You swear you wont do it? Do you swear?"

"Listen a moment," Weddel said; he spoke now with a sort of soothing patience, as though he spoke one-syllable words to a child: "I just want to go home. That's all. I have been away from home for four years. All I want is to go home. Dont you see? I want to see what I have left there, after four years."

"What do you do there?" The boy's hands were loose and hard about Weddel's throat, his arms still, rigid. "Do you hunt all day, and all night too if you want, with a horse to ride and nigras to wait on you, to shine your boots and saddle the horse, and you setting on the gallery, eating, until time to go hunting again?"

"I hope so. I haven't been home in four years, you see. So I dont know any more."

"Take me with you."

"I dont know what's there, you see. There may not be anything there: no horses to ride and nothing to hunt. The Yankees were there, and my mother died right afterward, and I dont know what we would find there, until I can go and see."

"I'll work. We'll both work. You can get married in Mayesfield. It's not far."

"Married? Oh. Your . . . I see. How do you know I am not

already married?" Now the boy's hands shut on his throat, shaking him. "Stop it!" he said.

"If you say you have got a wife, I will kill you," the boy said.

"No," Weddel said. "I am not married."

"And you dont aim to climb up that foot ladder?"

"No. I never saw her but once. I might not even know her if I saw her again."

"She says different. I dont believe you. You are lying."

"No," Weddel said.

"Is it because you are afraid to?"

"Yes. That's it."

"Of Vatch?"

"Not Vatch. I'm just afraid. I think my luck has given out. I know that it has lasted too long; I am afraid that I shall find that I have forgot how to be afraid. So I cant risk it. I cant risk finding that I have lost touch with truth. Not like Jubal here. He believes that I still belong to him; he will not believe that I have been freed. He wont even let me tell him so. He does not need to bother about truth, you see."

"We would work. She might not look like the Miss'ippi women that wear shoes all the time. But we would learn. We would not shame you before them."

"No," Weddel said. "I cannot."

"Then you go away. Now."

"How can I? You see that he cannot ride, cannot stay on a horse." The boy did not answer at once; an instant later Weddel could almost feel the tenseness, the utter immobility, though he himself had heard no sound; he knew that the boy, crouching, not breathing, was looking toward the ladder. "Which one is it?" Weddel whispered.

"It's paw."

"I'll go down. You stay here. You keep my pistol for me."

10

The dark air was high, chill, cold. In the vast invisible darkness the valley lay, the opposite cold and invisible range black on the black sky. Clutching the stub of his missing arm across his chest, he shivered slowly and steadily.

"Go," the father said.

"The war is over," Weddel said. "Vatch's victory is not my trouble."

"Take your horses and nigra, and ride on."

"If you mean your daughter, I never saw her but once and I never expect to see her again."

"Ride on," the father said. "Take what is yours, and ride on."

"I cannot." They faced one another in the darkness. "After four years I have bought immunity from running."

"You have till daylight."

"I have had less than that in Virginia for four years. And this is just Tennessee." But the other had turned; he dissolved into the black slope. Weddel entered the stable and mounted the ladder. Motionless above the snoring Negro the boy squatted.

"Leave him here," the boy said. "He aint nothing but a nigra. Leave him, and go."

"No," Weddel said.

The boy squatted above the snoring Negro. He was not looking at Weddel, yet there was between them, quiet and soundless, the copse, the sharp dry report, the abrupt wild thunder of upreared horse, the wisping smoke. "I can show you a short cut down to the valley. You will be out of the mountains in two hours. By daybreak you will be ten miles away."

"I cant. He wants to go home too. I must get him home too." He stooped; with his single hand he spread the cloak awkwardly, covering the Negro closer with it. He heard the boy creep away, but he did not look. After a while he shook the Negro. "Jubal," he said. The Negro groaned; he turned heavily, sleeping again. Weddel squatted above him as the boy had done. "I thought that I had lost it for good," he said. "—The peace and the quiet; the power to be afraid again."

11

The cabin was gaunt and bleak in the thick cold dawn when the two horses passed out the sagging gate and into the churned road, the Negro on the Thoroughbred, Weddel on the sorrel. The Negro was shivering. He sat hunched and high, with updrawn knees, his face almost invisible in the oilcloth hood.

"I tole you dey wuz fixing to pizen us wid dat stuff," he said. "I tole you. Hillbilly rednecks. En you not only let um pizen me, you fotch me de pizen wid yo own hand. O Lawd, O Lawd! If we ever does git home."

Weddel looked back at the cabin, at the weathered, blank house where there was no sign of any life, not even smoke. "She has a young man, I suppose—a beau." He spoke aloud, musing, quizzical. "And that boy. Hule. He said to come within sight of a laurel copse where the road disappears, and take a path to the left. He said we must not pass that copse."

"Who says which?" the Negro said. "I aint going nowhere. I going back to dat loft en lay down."

"All right," Weddel said. "Get down."

"Git down?"

"I'll need both horses. You can walk on when you are through sleeping."

"I ghy tell yo maw," the Negro said. "I ghy tell um. Ghy tell how after four years you aint got no more sense than to not know a Yankee when you seed um. To stay de night wid Yankees en let um pizen one of Mistis' niggers. I ghy tell um."

"I thought you were going to stay here," Weddel said. He was shivering too. "Yet I am not cold," he said. "I am not cold."

"Stay here? Me? How in de world you ever git home widout me? Whut I tell Mistis when I come in widout you en she ax me whar you is?"

"Come," Weddel said. He lifted the sorrel into motion. He looked quietly back at the house, then rode on. Behind him on the Thoroughbred the Negro muttered and mumbled to himself in woebegone singsong. The road, the long hill which yesterday they had toiled up, descended now. It was muddy, rockchurned, scarred across the barren and rocky land beneath the dissolving sky, jolting downward to where the pines and laurel began. After a while the cabin had disappeared.

"And so I am running away," Weddel said. "When I get home I shall not be very proud of this. Yes, I will. It means that I am still alive. Still alive, since I still know fear and desire. Since life is an affirmation of the past and a promise to the future. So I am still alive—Ah." It was the laurel copse. About three hundred yards ahead it seemed to have sprung motionless and darkly secret in the air which of itself was mostly water. He drew rein sharply, the Negro, hunched, moaning, his face completely hidden, overriding him unawares until the Thoroughbred stopped of its own accord. "But I dont see any path—" Weddel said; then a figure emerged from the copse, running toward them. Weddel thrust the reins beneath his groin and withdrew his hand inside his cloak. Then he saw that it was the boy. He came up trotting. His face was white, strained, his eyes quite grave.

"It's right yonder," he said.

"Thank you," Weddel said. "It was kind of you to come and show us, though we could have found it, I imagine."

"Yes," the boy said as though he had not heard. He had already taken the sorrel's bridle. "Right tother of the brush. You cant see hit until you are in hit."

"In whut?" the Negro said. "I ghy tell um. After four years you aint got no more sense. . . ."

"Hush," Weddel said. He said to the boy, "I am obliged to you. You'll have to take that in lieu of anything better. And now you get on back home. We can find the path. We will be all right now."

"They know the path too," the boy said. He drew the sorrel forward. "Come on."

"Wait," Weddel said, drawing the sorrel up. The boy still tugged at the bridle, looking on ahead toward the copse. "So we have one guess and they have one guess. Is that it?"

"Damn you to hell, come on!" the boy said, in a kind of thin frenzy. "I am sick of hit. Sick of hit."

"Well," Weddel said. He looked about, quizzical, sardonic, with his gaunt, weary, wasted face. "But I must move. I cant stay here, not even if I had a house, a roof to live under. So I have to choose between three things. That's what throws a man off—that extra alternative. Just when he has come to realize that living consists in choosing wrongly between two alternatives, to have to choose among three. You go back home."

The boy turned and looked up at him. "We'd work. We could go back to the house now, since paw and Vatch are . . . We could ride down the mou-tin, two on one horse and two on tother. We could go back to the valley and get married at Mayesfield. We would not shame you."

"But she has a young man, hasn't she? Somebody that waits for her at church on Sunday and walks home and takes Sunday dinner, and maybe fights the other young men because of her?"

"You wont take us, then?"

"No. You go back home."

For a while the boy stood, holding the bridle, his face lowered. Then he turned; he said quietly: "Come on, then. We got to hurry."

"Wait," Weddel said; "what are you going to do?"

"I'm going a piece with you. Come on." He dragged the sorrel forward, toward the roadside.

"Here," Weddel said, "you go on back home. The war is over now. Vatch knows that."

The boy did not answer. He led the sorrel into the underbrush. The Thoroughbred hung back. "Whoa, you Caesar!" the Negro said. "Wait, Marse Soshay. I aint gwine ride down no. . . ."

The boy looked over his shoulder without stopping. "You keep back there," he said. "You keep where you are."

The path was a faint scar, doubling and twisting among the brush. "I see it now," Weddel said. "You go back."

"I'll go a piece with you," the boy said; so quietly that Weddel discovered that he had been holding his breath, in a taut, strained alertness. He breathed again, while the sorrel jolted stiffly downward beneath him. "Nonsense," he thought. "He will have me playing Indian also in five minutes more. I had wanted to recover the power to be afraid, but I seem to have outdone myself." The path widened; the Thoroughbred came alongside, the boy walking between them; again he looked at the Negro.

"You keep back, I tell you," he said.

"Why back?" Weddel said. He looked at the boy's wan, strained face; he thought swiftly, "I dont know whether I am playing Indian or not." He said aloud: "Why must he keep back?"

The boy looked at Weddel; he stopped, pulling the sorrel up. "We'd work," he said. "We wouldn't shame you."

Weddel's face was now as sober as the boy's. They looked at one another. "Do you think we have guessed wrong? We had to guess. We had to guess one out of three."

Again it was as if the boy had not heard him. "You wont think hit is me? You swear hit?"

"Yes. I swear it." He spoke quietly, watching the boy; they spoke now as two men or two children. "What do you think we ought to do?"

"Turn back. They will be gone now. We could . . ." He drew back on the bridle; again the Thoroughbred came abreast and forged ahead.

"You mean, it could be along here?" Weddel said. Suddenly he spurred the sorrel, jerking the clinging boy forward. "Let go," he said. The boy held onto the bridle, swept forward until the two horses were again abreast. On the Thoroughbred the Negro perched, highkneed, his mouth still talking, flobbed down with ready speech, easy and worn with talk like an old shoe with walking.

"I done tole him en tole him," the Negro said.

"Let go!" Weddel said, spurring the sorrel, forcing its shoulder into the boy. "Let go!"

"You wont turn back?" the boy said. "You wont?"

"Let go!" Weddel said. His teeth showed a little beneath his mustache; he lifted the sorrel bodily with the spurs. The boy let go of the bridle and ducked beneath the Thoroughbred's neck;

Weddel, glancing back as the sorrel leaped, saw the boy surge upward and on to the Thoroughbred's back, shoving the Negro back along its spine until he vanished.

"They think you will be riding the good horse," the boy said in a thin, panting voice; "I told them you would be riding . . . Down the mou-tin!" he cried as the Thoroughbred swept past; "the horse can make hit! Git outen the path! Git outen the. . . ." Weddel spurred the sorrel; almost abreast the two horses reached the bend where the path doubled back upon itself and into a matted shoulder of laurel and rhododendron. The boy looked back over his shoulder. "Keep back!" he cried. "Git outen the path!" Weddel rowelled the sorrel. On his face was a thin grimace of exasperation and anger almost like smiling.

It was still on his dead face when he struck the earth, his foot still fast in the stirrup. The sorrel leaped at the sound and dragged Weddel to the path side and halted and whirled and snorted once, and began to graze. The Thoroughbred however rushed on past the curve and whirled and rushed back, the blanket twisted under its belly and its eyes rolling, springing over the boy's body where it lay in the path, the face wrenched sideways against a stone, the arms backsprawled, openpalmed, like a woman with lifted skirts springing across a puddle. Then it whirled and stood above Weddel's body, whinnying, with tossing head, watching the laurel copse and the fading gout of black powder smoke as it faded away.

The Negro was on his hands and knees when the two men emerged from the copse. One of them was running. The Negro watched him run forward, crying monotonously, "The durned fool! The durned fool! The durned fool!" and then stop suddenly and drop the gun; squatting, the Negro saw him become stone still above the fallen gun, looking down at the boy's body with an expression of shock and amazement like he was waking from a dream. Then the Negro saw the other man. In the act of stopping, the second man swung the rifle up and began to reload it. The Negro did not move. On his hands and knees he watched the two white men, his irises rushing and wild in the bloodshot whites. Then he too moved and, still on hands and knees, he turned and scuttled to where Weddel lay beneath the sorrel and crouched over Weddel and looked again and watched the second man backing slowly away up the path, loading the rifle. He watched the man stop; he did not close his eyes nor look away. He watched the rifle elongate and then rise and diminish slowly and become a round spot against the white shape of Vatch's face like a period on a page. Crouching, the Negro's eyes rushed wild and steady and red, like those of a cornered animal.

Ellen Glasgow

(1874–1945)

Born in Richmond, Virginia, Ellen Glasgow was raised by a father who was a rigid authoritarian from Scotch Presbyterian stock, and by a mother who was a fragile and long-suffering descendant of Tidewater Episcopalians. The constant tension between her parents made her childhood an unhappy one, and her later novels revolt against what she considered the equally destructive inheritances of blinding authoritarianism and blind fatalism. One of many children, she was educated for the most part at home, in her father's library. Her readings of Darwin, Spencer, and Mill gave her a taste of intellectual independence at an early age, and before she was 20 she had begun to write. A resident of Richmond for most of her life, she made Richmond and Virginia the subjects of almost all her writing. Her first two novels were portraits of New York bohemian life, but her third, The Voice of the People *(1900), began the long series of her Virginia novels. They would include an unsentimental Civil War novel,* The Battle-Ground *(1902),* The Deliverance *(1904), a story of a strong woman willing to affirm herself against social convention, and* Virginia *(1913), another story of a strong woman, though in this case, strong in her self-sacrifice. Her two masterpieces are* Barren Ground *(1925), a searing treatment of independence and revenge in the life of Dorinda Oakley, and* The Sheltered Life *(1932), the last, and best, of her Richmond comedies of manners, a trilogy that also included* The Romantic Comedians *(1926) and* They Stooped to Folly *(1929). Glasgow's long career spans the transition between Southern literature of the late 19th century, and the new uncompromising Southern writing that her own novels, especially her later ones, exemplify. Asserting that Southern fiction needed more "blood and irony," she strongly opposed the genteel romance and evasive idealism of the popular literary South, though in many ways she remained, as she herself admitted, held by these same traditions in her struggle against them.*

Among her many books are The Descendant *(1897),* The Ancient
Law *(1908),* The Romance of a Plain Man *(1909),* The Miller of
Old Church *(1911),* The Shadowy Third and Other Stories *(1923),*
Vein of Iron *(1935), and* In This Our Life *(1941). Her autobiography* The Woman Within *(1954) was not published, in accordance
with her instructions, until after her death. "Jordan's End" is taken
from* The Shadowy Third and Other Stories.

JORDAN'S END

❀

At the fork of the road there was the dead tree where buzzards
were roosting, and through its boughs I saw the last flare of the
sunset. On either side the November woods were flung in broken
masses against the sky. When I stopped they appeared to move
closer and surround me with vague, glimmering shapes. It seemed
to me that I had been driving for hours; yet the ancient negro who
brought the message had told me to follow the Old Stage Road
till I came to Buzzard's Tree at the fork. "F'om dar on hit's
moughty nigh ter Marse Jur'dn's place," the old man had assured
me, adding tremulously, "en young Miss she sez you mus' come
jes' ez quick ez you kin." I was young then (that was more than
thirty years ago), and I was just beginning the practice of medicine
in one of the more remote counties of Virginia.

My mare stopped, and leaning out, I gazed down each winding
road, where it branched off, under half bared boughs, into the
autumnal haze of the distance. In a little while the red would fade
from the sky, and the chill night would find me still hesitating
between those dubious ways which seemed to stretch into an immense solitude. While I waited uncertainly there was a stir in the
boughs overhead, and a buzzard's feather floated down and settled
slowly on the robe over my knees. In the effort to drive off depression, I laughed aloud and addressed my mare in a jocular tone:

"We'll choose the most God-forsaken of the two, and see where
it leads us."

To my surprise the words brought an answer from the trees at
my back. "If you're goin' to Isham's store, keep on the Old Stage
Road," piped a voice from the underbrush.

Turning quickly, I saw the dwarfed figure of a very old man, with a hunched back, who was dragging a load of pine knots out of the woods. Though he was so stooped that his head reached scarcely higher than my wheel, he appeared to possess unusual vigour for one of his age and infirmities. He was dressed in a rough overcoat of some wood brown shade, beneath which I could see his overalls of blue jeans. Under a thatch of grizzled hair his shrewd little eyes twinkled cunningly, and his bristly chin jutted so far forward that it barely escaped the descending curve of his nose. I remember thinking that he could not be far from a hundred; his skin was so wrinkled and weather-beaten that, at a distance, I had mistaken him for a negro.

I bowed politely. "Thank you, but I am going to Jordan's End," I replied.

He cackled softly. "Then you take the bad road. Thar's Jur'dn's turn-out." He pointed to the sunken trail, deep in mud, on the right. "An' if you ain't objectin' to a little comp'ny, I'd be obleeged if you'd give me a lift. I'm bound thar on my own o' count, an' it's a long ways to tote these here lightwood knots."

While I drew back my robe and made room for him, I watched him heave the load of resinous pine into the buggy, and then scramble with agility to his place at my side.

"My name is Peterkin," he remarked by way of introduction. "They call me Father Peterkin along o' the gran'child'en." He was a garrulous soul, I suspected, and would not be averse to imparting the information I wanted.

"There's not much travel this way," I began, as we turned out of the cleared space into the deep tunnel of the trees. Immediately the twilight enveloped us, though now and then the dusky glow in the sky was still visible. The air was sharp with the tang of autumn; with the effluvium of rotting leaves, the drift of wood smoke, the ripe flavour of crushed apples.

"Thar's nary a stranger, thoughten he was a doctor, been to Jur'dn's End as fur back as I kin recollect. Ain't you the new doctor?"

"Yes, I am the doctor." I glanced down at the gnomelike shape in the wood brown overcoat. "Is it much farther?"

"Naw, suh, we're all but thar jest as soon as we come out of Whitten woods."

"If the road is so little travelled, how do you happen to be going there?"

Without turning his head, the old man wagged his crescent shaped profile. "Oh, I live on the place. My son Tony works a slice of the farm on shares, and I manage to lend a hand at the harvest or corn shuckin', and, now-and-agen, with the cider. The old gentleman used to run the place that away afore he went deranged, an' now that the young one is laid up, thar ain't nobody to look arter the farm but Miss Judith. Them old ladies don't count. Thar's three of 'em, but they're all addle-brained an' look as if the buzzards had picked 'em. I reckon that comes from bein' shut up with crazy folks in that thar old tumbledown house. The roof ain't been patched fur so long that the shingles have most rotted away, an' thar's times, Tony says, when you kin skearcely hear yo' years fur the rumpus the wrens an' rats are makin' overhead.''

"What is the trouble with them—the Jordans, I mean?"

"Jest run to seed, suh, I reckon."

"Is there no man of the family left?"

For a minute Father Peterkin made no reply. Then he shifted the bundle of pine knots, and responded warily. "Young Alan, he's still livin' on the old place, but I hear he's been took now, an' is goin' the way of all the rest of 'em. 'Tis a hard trial for Miss Judith, po' young thing, an' with a boy nine year old that's the very spit an' image of his pa. Wall, wall, I kin recollect away back yonder when old Mr. Timothy Jur'dn was the proudest man anywhar aroun' in these parts; but arter the War things sorter begun to go down hill with him, and he was obleeged to draw in his horns.''

"Is he still living?"

The old man shook his head. "Mebbe he is, an' mebbe he ain't. Nobody knows but the Jur'dn's, an' they ain't tellin' fur the axin'.''

"I suppose it was this Miss Judith who sent for me?"

" 'Twould most likely be she, suh. She was one of the Yardlys that lived over yonder at Yardly's Field; an' when young Mr. Alan begun to take notice of her, 'twas the first time sence way back that one of the Jur'dn's had gone courtin' outside the family. That's the reason the blood went bad like it did, I reckon. Thar's a sayin' down aroun' here that Jur'dn an' Jur'dn won't mix.'' The name was invariably called Jurdin by all classes; but I had already discovered that names are rarely pronounced as they are spelled in Virginia.

"Have they been married long?"

"Ten year or so, suh. I remember as well as if 'twas yestiddy the day young Alan brought her home as a bride, an' thar warn't a soul besides the three daft old ladies to welcome her. They drove over in my son Tony's old buggy, though 'twas spick an' span then. I was goin' to the house on an arrant, an' I was standin' right down thar at the ice pond when they come by. She hadn't been much in these parts, an' none of us had ever seed her afore. When she

looked up at young Alan her face was pink all over and her eyes
war shinin' bright as the moon. Then the front do' opened an'
them old ladies, as black as crows, flocked out on the po'ch. Thar
never was anybody as peart-lookin' as Miss Judith was when she
come here; but soon arterwards she begun to peak an' pine, though
she never lost her sperits an' went mopin' roun' like all the other
women folks at Jur'dn's End. They married sudden, an' folks do
say she didn't know nothin' about the family, an' young Alan didn't
know much mo' than she did. The old ladies had kep' the secret
away from him, sorter believin' that what you don't know cyarn'
hurt you. Anyways they never let it leak out tell arter his chile
was born. Thar ain't never been but that one, an' old Aunt Jerusly
declars he was born with a caul over his face, so mebbe things will
be all right fur him in the long run."

"But who are the old ladies? Are their husbands living?"

When Father Peterkin answered the question he had dropped
his voice to a hoarse murmur. "Deranged. All gone deranged,"
he replied.

I shivered, for a chill depression seemed to emanate from the
November woods. As we drove on, I remembered grim tales of
enchanted forests filled with evil faces and whispering voices. The
scents of wood earth and rotting leaves invaded my brain like a
magic spell. On either side the forest was as still as death. Not a
leaf quivered, not a bird moved, not a small wild creature stirred
in the underbrush. Only the glossy leaves and the scarlet berries
of the holly appeared alive amid the bare interlacing branches of
the trees. I began to long for an autumn clearing and the red light
of the afterglow.

"Are they living or dead?" I asked presently.

"I've hearn strange tattle," answered the old man nervously,
"but nobody kin tell. Folks do say as young Alan's pa is shut up
in a padded place, and that his gran'pa died thar arter thirty years.
His uncles went crazy too, an' the daftness is beginnin' to crop out
in the women. Up tell now it has been mostly the men. One time
I remember old Mr. Peter Jur'dn tryin' to burn down the place in
the dead of the night. Thar's the end of the wood, suh. If you'll
jest let me down here, I'll be gittin' along home across the oldfield, an' thanky too."

At last the woods ended abruptly on the edge of an abandoned
field which was thickly sown with scrub pine and broomsedge. The
glow in the sky had faded now to a thin yellow-green, and a melancholy twilight pervaded the landscape. In this twilight I looked
over the few sheep huddled together on the ragged lawn, and saw

the old brick house crumbling beneath its rank growth of ivy. As I drew nearer I had the feeling that the surrounding desolation brooded there like some sinister influence.

Forlorn as it appeared at this first approach, I surmised that Jordan's End must have possessed once charm as well as distinction. The proportions of the Georgian front were impressive, and there was beauty of design in the quaint doorway, and in the steps of rounded stone which were brocaded now with a pattern of emerald moss. But the whole place was badly in need of repair. Looking up, as I stopped, I saw that the eaves were falling away, that crumbled shutters were sagging from loosened hinges, that odd scraps of hemp sacking or oil cloth were stuffed into windows where panes were missing. When I stepped on the floor of the porch, I felt the rotting boards give way under my feet.

After thundering vainly on the door, I descended the steps, and followed the beaten path that led round the west wing of the house. When I had passed an old boxwood tree at the corner, I saw a woman and a boy of nine years or so come out of a shed, which I took to be the smoke-house, and begin to gather chips from the woodpile. The woman carried a basket made of splits on her arm, and while she stooped to fill this, she talked to the child in a soft musical voice. Then, at a sound that I made, she put the basket aside, and rising to her feet, faced me in the pallid light from the sky. Her head was thrown back, and over her dress of some dark calico, a tattered gray shawl clung to her figure. That was thirty years ago; I am not young any longer; I have been in many countries since then, and looked on many women; but her face, with that wan light on it, is the last one I shall forget in my life. Beauty! Why, that woman will be beautiful when she is a skeleton, was the thought that flashed into my mind.

She was very tall, and so thin that her flesh seemed faintly luminous, as if an inward light pierced the transparent substance. It was the beauty, not of earth, but of triumphant spirit. Perfection, I suppose, is the rarest thing we achieve in this world of incessant compromise with inferior forms; yet the woman who stood there in that ruined place appeared to me to have stepped straight out of legend or allegory. The contour of her face was Italian in its pure oval; her hair swept in wings of dusk above her clear forehead; and, from the faintly shadowed hollows beneath her brows, the eyes that looked at me were purple-black, like dark pansies.

"I had given you up," she began in a low voice, as if she were afraid of being overheard. "You are the doctor?"

"Yes, I am the doctor. I took the wrong road and lost my way. Are you Mrs. Jordan?"

She bowed her head. "Mrs. Alan Jordan. There are three Mrs. Jordans besides myself. My husband's grandmother and the wives of his two uncles."

"And it is your husband who is ill?"

"My husband, yes. I wrote a few days ago to Doctor Carstairs." (Thirty years ago Carstairs, of Baltimore, was the leading alienist in the country.) "He is coming to-morrow morning; but last night my husband was so restless that I sent for you to-day." Her rich voice, vibrating with suppressed feeling, made me think of stained glass windows and low organ music.

"Before we go in," I asked, "will you tell me as much as you can?"

Instead of replying to my request, she turned and laid her hand on the boy's shoulder. "Take the chips to Aunt Agatha, Benjamin," she said, "and tell her that the doctor has come."

While the child picked up the basket and ran up the sunken steps to the door, she watched him with breathless anxiety. Not until he had disappeared into the hall did she lift her eyes to my face again. Then, without answering my question, she murmured, with a sigh which was like the voice of that autumn evening, "We were once happy here." She was trying, I realized, to steel her heart against the despair that threatened it.

My gaze swept the obscure horizon, and returned to the mouldering woodpile where we were standing. The yellow-green had faded from the sky, and the only light came from the house where a few scattered lamps were burning. Through the open door I could see the hall, as bare as if the house were empty, and the spiral staircase which crawled to the upper story. A fine old place once, but repulsive now in its abject decay, like some young blood of former days who has grown senile.

"Have you managed to wring a living out of the land?" I asked, because I could think of no words that were less compassionate.

"At first a poor one," she answered slowly. "We worked hard, harder than any negro in the fields, to keep things together, but we were happy. Then three years ago this illness came, and after that everything went against us. In the beginning it was simply brooding, a kind of melancholy, and we tried to ward it off by pretending that it was not real, that we imagined it. Only of late, when it became so much worse, have we admitted the truth, have we faced the reality—"

This passionate murmur, which had almost the effect of a chant rising out of the loneliness, was addressed, not to me, but to some abstract and implacable power. While she uttered it her composure was like the tranquillity of the dead. She did not lift her hand to hold her shawl, which was slipping unnoticed from her shoulders, and her eyes, so like dark flowers in their softness, did not leave my face.

"If you will tell me all, perhaps I may be able to help you," I said.

"But you know our story," she responded. "You must have heard it."

"Then it is true? Heredity, intermarriage, insanity?"

She did not wince at the bluntness of my speech. "My husband's grandfather is in an asylum, still living after almost thirty years. His father—my husband's, I mean—died there a few years ago. Two of his uncles are there. When it began I don't know, or how far back it reaches. We have never talked of it. We have tried always to forget it— Even now I cannot put the thing into words— My husband's mother died of a broken heart, but the grandmother and the two others are still living. You will see them when you go into the house. They are old women now, and they feel nothing."

"And there have been other cases?"

"I do not know. Are not four enough?"

"Do you know if it has assumed always the same form?" I was trying to be as brief as I could.

She flinched, and I saw that her unnatural calm was shaken at last. "The same, I believe. In the beginning there is melancholy, moping, Grandmother calls it, and then—" She flung out her arms with a despairing gesture, and I was reminded again of some tragic figure of legend.

"I know, I know." I was young, and in spite of my pride, my voice trembled. "Has there been in any case partial recovery, recurring at intervals?"

"In his grandfather's case, yes. In the others none. With them it has been hopeless from the beginning."

"And Carstairs is coming?"

"In the morning. I should have waited, but last night—" Her voice broke, and she drew the tattered shawl about her with a shiver. "Last night something happened. Something happened," she repeated, and could not go on. Then, collecting her strength with an effort which made her tremble like a blade of grass in the wind, she continued more quietly, "To-day he has been better. For the first time he has slept, and I have been able to leave him. Two of the hands from the fields are in the room." Her tone changed suddenly, and a note of energy passed into it. Some obscure resolution brought a tinge of colour to her pale cheek. "I must know," she added, "if this is as hopeless as all the others."

I took a step toward the house. "Carstairs's opinion is worth as much as that of any man living," I answered.

"But will he tell me the truth?"

I shook my head. "He will tell you what he thinks. No man's judgment is infallible."

Turning away from me, she moved with an energetic step to the house. As I followed her into the hall the threshold creaked under my tread, and I was visited by an apprehension, or, if you prefer, by a superstitious dread of the floor above. Oh, I got over that kind of thing before I was many years older; though in the end I gave up medicine, you know, and turned to literature as a safer outlet for a suppressed imagination.

But the dread was there at that moment, and it was not lessened by the glimpse I caught, at the foot of the spiral staircase, of a scantily furnished room, where three lean black-robed figures, as impassive as the Fates, were grouped in front of a wood fire. They were doing something with their hands. Knitting, crocheting, or plaiting straw?

At the head of the stairs the woman stopped and looked back at me. The light from the kerosene lamp on the wall fell over her, and I was struck afresh not only by the alien splendour of her beauty, but even more by the look of consecration, of impassioned fidelity that illumined her face.

"He is very strong," she said in a whisper. "Until this trouble came on him he had never had a day's illness in his life. We hoped that hard work, not having time to brood, might save us; but it has only brought the thing we feared sooner."

There was a question in her eyes, and I responded in the same subdued tone. "His health, you say, is good?" What else was there for me to ask when I understood everything?

A shudder ran through her frame. "We used to think that a blessing, but now—" She broke off and then added in a lifeless voice, "We keep two field hands in the room day and night, lest one should forget to watch the fire, or fall asleep."

A sound came from a room at the end of the hall, and, without finishing her sentence, she moved swiftly toward the closed door. The apprehension, the dread, or whatever you choose to call it, was so strong upon me, that I was seized by an impulse to turn and retreat down the spiral staircase. Yes, I know why some men turn cowards in battle.

"I have come back, Alan," she said in a voice that wrung my heartstrings.

The room was dimly lighted; and for a minute after I entered,

I could see nothing clearly except the ruddy glow of the wood fire in front of which two negroes were seated on low wooden stools. They had kindly faces, these men; there was a primitive humanity in their features, which might have been modelled out of the dark earth of the fields.

Looking round the next minute, I saw that a young man was sitting away from the fire, huddled over in a cretonne-covered chair with a high back and deep wings. At our entrance the negroes glanced up with surprise; but the man in the winged chair neither lifted his head nor turned his eyes in our direction. He sat there, lost within the impenetrable wilderness of the insane, as remote from us and from the sound of our voices as if he were the inhabitant of an invisible world. His head was sunk forward; his eyes were staring fixedly at some image we could not see; his fingers, moving restlessly, were plaiting and unplaiting the fringe of a plaid shawl. Distraught as he was, he still possessed the dignity of mere physical perfection. At his full height he must have measured not under six feet three; his hair was the colour of ripe wheat, and his eyes, in spite of their fixed gaze, were as blue as the sky after rain. And this was only the beginning, I realized. With that constitution, that physical frame, he might live to be ninety.

"Alan!" breathed his wife again in her pleading murmur.

If he heard her voice, he gave no sign of it. Only when she crossed the room and bent over his chair, he put out his hand, with a gesture of irritation, and pushed her away, as if she were a veil of smoke which came between him and the object at which he was looking. Then his hand fell back to its old place, and he resumed his mechanical plaiting of the fringe.

The woman lifted her eyes to mine. "His father did that for twenty years," she said in a whisper that was scarcely more than a sigh of anguish.

When I had made my brief examination, we left the room as we had come, and descended the stairs together. The three old women were still sitting in front of the wood fire. I do not think they had moved since we went upstairs; but, as we reached the hall below, one of them, the youngest, I imagine, rose from her chair, and came out to join us. She was crocheting something soft and small, an infant's sacque, I perceived as she approached, of pink wool. The ball had rolled from her lap as she stood up, and it trailed after her now, like a woolen rose, on the bare floor. When the skein pulled at her, she turned back and stooped to pick up the ball, which she rewound with caressing fingers. Good God, an infant's sacque in that house!

"Is it the same thing?" she asked.

"Hush!" responded the younger woman kindly. Turning to me she added, "We cannot talk here," and opening the door, passed out on the porch. Not until we had reached the lawn, and walked in silence to where my buggy stood beneath an old locust tree, did she speak again.

Then she said only, "You know now?"

"Yes, I know," I replied, averting my eyes from her face while I gave my directions as briefly as I could. "I will leave an opiate," I said. "To-morrow, if Carstairs should not come, send for me again. If he does come," I added, "I will talk to him and see you afterward."

"Thank you," she answered gently; and taking the bottle from my hand, she turned away and walked quickly back to the house.

I watched her as long as I could; and then getting into my buggy, I turned my mare's head toward the woods, and drove by moonlight, past Buzzard's Tree and over the Old Stage Road, to my home. "I will see Carstairs to-morrow," was my last thought that night before I slept.

But, after all, I saw Carstairs only for a minute as he was taking the train. Life at its beginning and its end had filled my morning; and when at last I reached the little station, Carstairs had paid his visit, and was waiting on the platform for the approaching express. At first he showed a disposition to question me about the shooting, but as soon as I was able to make my errand clear, his jovial face clouded.

"So you've been there?" he said. "They didn't tell me. An interesting case, if it were not for that poor woman. Incurable, I'm afraid, when you consider the predisposing causes. The race is pretty well deteriorated, I suppose. God! what isolation! I've advised her to send him away. There are three others, they tell me, at Staunton."

The train came; he jumped on it, and was whisked away while I gazed after him. After all, I was none the wiser because of the great reputation of Carstairs.

All that day I heard nothing more from Jordan's End; and then, early next morning, the same decrepit negro brought me a message.

"Young Miss, she tole me ter ax you ter come along wid me jes' ez soon ez you kin git ready."

"I'll start at once, Uncle, and I'll take you with me."

My mare and buggy stood at the door. All I needed to do was to put on my overcoat, pick up my hat, and leave word, for a possible patient, that I should return before noon. I knew the road now, and I told myself, as I set out, that I would make as quick a trip as I could. For two nights I had been haunted by the memory of that man in the armchair, plaiting and unplaiting the fringe of the plaid shawl. And his father had done that, the woman had told me, for twenty years!

It was a brown autumn morning, raw, windless, with an overcast sky and a peculiar illusion of nearness about the distance. A high wind had blown all night, but at dawn it had dropped suddenly, and now there was not so much as a ripple in the broomsedge. Over the fields, when we came out of the woods, the thin trails of blue smoke were as motionless as cobwebs. The lawn surrounding the house looked smaller than it had appeared to me in the twilight, as if the barren fields had drawn closer since my last visit. Under the trees, where the few sheep were browsing, the piles of leaves lay in windrifts along the sunken walk and against the wings of the house.

When I knocked the door was opened immediately by one of the old women, who held a streamer of black cloth or rusty crape in her hands.

"You may go straight upstairs," she croaked; and, without waiting for an explanation, I entered the hall quickly, and ran up the stairs.

The door of the room was closed, and I opened it noiselessly, and stepped over the threshold. My first sensation, as I entered, was one of cold. Then I saw that the windows were wide open, and that the room seemed to be full of people, though, as I made out presently, there was no one there except Alan Jordan's wife, her little son, the two old aunts, and an aged crone of a negress. On the bed there was something under a yellowed sheet of fine linen (what the negroes call "a burial sheet," I suppose), which had been handed down from some more affluent generation.

When I went over, after a minute, and turned down one corner of the covering, I saw that my patient of the other evening was dead. Not a line of pain marred his features, not a thread of gray dimmed the wheaten gold of his hair. So he must have looked, I thought, when she first loved him. He had gone from life, not old, enfeebled and repulsive, but enveloped still in the romantic illusion of their passion.

As I entered, the two old women, who had been fussing about the bed, drew back to make way for me, but the witch of a negress did not pause in the weird chant, an incantation of some sort, which she was mumbling. From the rag carpet in front of the empty fireplace, the boy, with his father's hair and his mother's eyes, gazed at me silently, broodingly, as if I were trespassing; and by the open window, with her eyes on the ashen November day, the young wife stood as motionless as a statue. While I looked at her a redbird flew out of the boughs of a cedar, and she followed it with her eyes.

"You sent for me?" I said to her.

She did not turn. She was beyond the reach of my voice, of any voice, I imagine; but one of the palsied old women answered my question.

"He was like this when we found him this morning," she said. "He had a bad night, and Judith and the two hands were up with him until daybreak. Then he seemed to fall asleep, and Judith sent the hands, turn about, to get their breakfast."

While she spoke my eyes were on the bottle I had left there. Two nights ago it had been full, and now it stood empty, without a cork, on the mantelpiece. They had not even thrown it away. It was typical of the pervading inertia of the place that the bottle should still be standing there awaiting my visit.

For an instant the shock held me speechless; when at last I found my voice it was to ask mechanically.

"When did it happen?"

The old woman who had spoken took up the story. "Nobody knows. We have not touched him. No one but Judith has gone near him." Her words trailed off into unintelligible muttering. If she had ever had her wits about her, I dare-say fifty years at Jordan's End had unsettled them completely.

I turned to the woman at the window. Against the gray sky and the black intersecting branches of the cedar, her head, with its austere perfection, was surrounded by that visionary air of legend. So Antigone might have looked on the day of her sacrifice, I reflected. I had never seen a creature who appeared so withdrawn, so detached, from all human associations. It was as if some spiritual isolation divided her from her kind.

"I can do nothing," I said.

For the first time she looked at me, and her eyes were unfathomable. "No, you can do nothing," she answered. "He is safely dead."

The negress was still crooning on; the other old women were fussing helplessly. It was impossible in their presence, I felt, to put in words the thing I had to say.

"Will you come downstairs with me?" I asked. "Outside of this house?"

Turning quietly, she spoke to the boy. "Run out and play, dear. He would have wished it."

Then, without a glance toward the bed, or the old women gathered about it, she followed me over the threshold, down the stairs, and out on the deserted lawn. The ashen day could not touch her,

I saw then. She was either so remote from it, or so completely a part of it, that she was impervious to its sadness. Her white face did not become more pallid as the light struck it; her tragic eyes did not grow deeper; her frail figure under the thin shawl did not shiver in the raw air. She felt nothing, I realized suddenly.

Wrapped in that silence as in a cloak, she walked across the windrifts of leaves to where my mare was waiting. Her step was so slow, so unhurried, that I remember thinking she moved like one who had all eternity before her. Oh, one has strange impressions, you know, at such moments!

In the middle of the lawn, where the trees had been stripped bare in the night, and the leaves were piled in long mounds like double graves, she stopped and looked in my face. The air was so still that the whole place might have been in a trance or asleep. Not a branch moved, not a leaf rustled on the ground, not a sparrow twittered in the ivy; and even the few sheep stood motionless, as if they were under a spell. Farther away, beyond the sea of broom-sedge, where no wind stirred, I saw the flat desolation of the landscape. Nothing moved on the earth, but high above, under the leaden clouds, a buzzard was sailing.

I moistened my lips before I spoke. "God knows I want to help you!" At the back of my brain a hideous question was drumming. How had it happened? Could she have killed him? Had that delicate creature nerved her will to the unspeakable act? It was incredible. It was inconceivable. And yet. . . .

"The worst is over," she answered quietly, with that tearless agony which is so much more terrible than any outburst of grief. "Whatever happens, I can never go through the worst again. Once in the beginning he wanted to die. His great fear was that he might live too long, until it was too late to save himself. I made him wait then. I held him back by a promise."

So she had killed him, I thought. Then she went on steadily, after a minute, and I doubted again.

"Thank God, it was easier for him than he feared it would be," she murmured.

No, it was not conceivable. He must have bribed one of the negroes. But who had stood by and watched without intercepting? Who had been in the room? Well, either way! "I will do all I can to help you," I said.

Her gaze did not waver. "There is so little that any one can do now," she responded, as if she had not understood what I meant. Suddenly, without the warning of a sob, a cry of despair went out of her, as if it were torn from her breast. "He was my life," she cried, "and I must go on!"

So full of agony was the sound that it seemed to pass like a gust of wind over the broomsedge. I waited until the emptiness had opened and closed over it. Then I asked as quietly as I could:

"What will you do now?"

She collected herself with a shudder of pain. "As long as the old people live, I am tied here. I must bear it out to the end. When they die, I shall go away and find work. I am sending my boy to school. Doctor Carstairs will look after him, and he will help me when the time comes. While my boy needs me, there is no release."

While I listened to her, I knew that the question on my lips would never be uttered. I should always remain ignorant of the truth. The thing I feared most, standing there alone with her, was that some accident might solve the mystery before I could escape. My eyes left her face and wandered over the dead leaves at our feet. No, I had nothing to ask her.

"Shall I come again?" That was all.

She shook her head. "Not unless I send for you. If I need you, I will send for you," she answered; but in my heart I knew that she would never send for me.

I held out my hand, but she did not take it; and I felt that she meant me to understand, by her refusal, that she was beyond all consolation and all companionship. She was nearer to the bleak sky and the deserted fields than she was to her kind.

As she turned away, the shawl slipped from her shoulders to the dead leaves over which she was walking; but she did not stoop to recover it, nor did I make a movement to follow her. Long after she had entered the house I stood there, gazing down on the garment that she had dropped. Then climbing into my buggy, I drove slowly across the field and into the woods.

George Washington Harris

(1814–1869)

Harris always considered Knoxville, Tennessee, his hometown. Though born in Allegheny City, Pennsylvania, he was taken to Knoxville when he was five years old to be raised by his half-brother. He was trained as a metalworker, had almost no formal schooling, and began to work for a living at an early age. Attracted by life on the river, he became captain of the Mississippi steamboat Knoxville when he was 21. Thereafter he was always known as Captain Harris. In 1843, he left steamboating and returned to Knoxville to open his own metalworking shop. That same year he began contributing to William T. Porter's New York paper Spirit of the Times, the leading publication of Southern—then called Southwestern—humorists. In 1854, Harris published the first of his Sut Lovingood stories, partly based on a man he had met in the copper mines at Ducktown, Tennessee. With Sut Lovingood, Harris introduced into Southern letters a vigorous, earthy character who has few equals in 19th-century fiction. Telling his own stories in a vivid, ribald, inventive mountain dialect, Sut freely exposes the hypocrisies and greed of the world while at the same time he expresses just as freely his own considerable failings, and his large appetite for food, drink, and energetic women. When the collection of Lovingood stories, Sut Lovingood. Yarns Spun by a "Nat'ral Born Durn'd Fool," was published in 1867, Mark Twain became one of the first of many admirers among American writers, including, in our century, William Faulkner, Edmund Wilson, and Robert Penn Warren. Before the Civil War, Harris had become an ardent secessionist, and the defeat of the South filled him with a bitterness that he never lost. Though he continued to write and had prepared a second collection of tales—never found—just before his death, the 1867 collection remained his only book during his lifetime. Despite the small body of his work, his reputation continues to grow, and he is now widely recognized as an original and influential master of the dialect nar-

rative. "Mrs. Yardley's Quilting" first appeared in book form in
Sut Lovingood. Yarns Spun by a "Nat'ral Born Durn'd Fool."
Warped and Wove for Public Wear *(1867).*

MRS. YARDLEY'S QUILTING

❀

"Thar's one durn'd nasty muddy job, an' I is jis' glad enuf tu take
a ho'n ur two, on the straingth ove hit."

"What have you been doing, Sut?"

"Helpin tu salt ole Missis Yardley down."

"What do you mean by that?"

"Fixin her fur rotten cumfurtably, kiverin her up wif sile, tu
keep the buzzards frum cheatin the wurms."

"Oh, you have been helping to bury a woman."

"That's hit, by golly! Now why the devil can't I 'splain mysef
like yu? I ladles out my words at random, like a calf kickin at
yaller-jackids; yu jis' rolls em out tu the pint, like a feller a-layin
bricks—every one fits. How is it that bricks fits so clost enyhow?
Rocks won't ni du hit."

"Becaze they'se all ove a size," ventured a man with a wen over
his eye.

"The devil yu say, hon'ey-head! haint reapin-mersheens ove a
size? I'd like tu see two ove em fit clost. Yu wait ontil yu sprouts
tuther ho'n, afore yu venters tu 'splain mix'd questions. George,
did yu know ole Missis Yardley?"

"No."

"Well, she wer a curious 'oman in her way, an' she wore shiney
specks. Now jis' listen: Whenever yu see a ole 'oman ahine a par
ove *shiney* specks, yu keep yer eye skinn'd; they am dang'rus in
the extreme. Thar is jis' no knowin what they ken du. I hed one
a-stradil ove me onst, fur kissin her gal. She went fur my har, an'
she went fur my skin, ontil I tho't she ment tu kill me, an' wud a-
dun hit, ef my hollerin hadent fotch ole Dave Jordan, a *bacheler,*
tu my aid. He, like a durn'd fool, cotch her by the laig, an' drug
her back'ards ofen me. She jis' kivered him, an' I run, by golly!
The nex time I seed him he wer bald headed, an' his face looked
like he'd been a-fitin wild-cats.

"Ole Missis Yardley wer a great noticer ove littil things, that nobody else ever seed. She'd say right in the middil ove sumbody's serious talk: 'Law sakes! thar goes that yaller slut ove a hen, a-flingin straws over her shoulder; she's arter settin now, an' haint laid but seven aigs. I'll disapint *her,* see ef I don't; I'll put a punkin in her ne's, an' a feather in her nose. An' bless my soul! jis' look at that cow wif the wilted ho'n, a-flingin up dirt an' a-smellin the place whar hit cum frum, wif the rale ginuine still-wurim twis' in her tail, too; what upon the face ove the yeath kin she be arter now, the ole fool? watch her, Sally. An' sakes alive! jis' look at that ole sow; she's a-gwine in a fas' trot, wif her empty bag a-floppin agin her sides. Thar, she hes stop't, an's a-listenin! massy on us! what a long yearnis grunt she gin; hit cum frum way back ove her kidneys. Thar she goes agin; she's arter no good, sich kerryin on means no good.'

"An' so she wud gabble, no odds who wer a-listenin. She looked like she mout been made at fust 'bout four foot long, an' the common thickness ove wimen when they's at tharsefs, an' then had her har tied tu a stump, a par ove steers hitched to her heels, an' then straiched out a-mos' two foot more—mos' ove the straichin cumin outen her laigs an' naik. Her stockins, a-hangin on the clothes-line tu dry, looked like a par ove sabre scabbards, an' her naik looked like a dry beef shank smoked, an' mout been ni ontu es tough. I never felt hit mysef, I didn't, I jis' jedges by looks. Her darter Sal wer bilt at fust 'bout the laingth ove her mam, but wer never straiched eny by a par ove steers an' she wer fat enuf tu kill; she wer taller lyin down than she wer a-standin up. Hit wer her who gin me the 'hump shoulder.' Jis' look at me; haint I'se got a tech ove the dromedary back thar bad? haint I humpy? Well, a-stoopin tu kiss that squatty lard-stan ove a gal is what dun hit tu me. She wer the fairest-lookin gal I ever seed. She allers wore thick woolin stockins 'bout six inches too long fur her laig; they rolled down over her garters, lookin like a par ove life-presarvers up thar. I tell yu she wer a tarin gal enyhow. Luved kissin, wrastlin, an' biled cabbige, an' hated tite clothes, hot weather, an' suckit-riders. B'leved strong in married folk's ways, cradles, an' the remishun ove sins, an' didn't b'leve in corsets, fleas, peaners, nur the fashun plates."

"What caused the death of Mrs. Yardley, Sut?"

"Nuffin, only her heart stop't beatin 'bout losin a nine dimunt quilt. True, she got a skeer'd hoss tu run over her, but she'd a-got over that ef a quilt hadn't been mix'd up in the catastrophy. Yu see quilts wer wun ove her speshul gifts; she run strong on the bed-kiver question. Irish chain, star ove Texas, sun-flower, nine dimunt, saw teeth, checker board, an' shell quilts; blue, an' white,

an' yaller an' black coverlids, an' callickercumfurts reigned trium-
phan' 'bout her hous'. They wer packed in drawers, layin in shelfs
full, wer hung four dubbil on lines in the lof, packed in chists,
piled on cheers, an' wer everywhar, even ontu the beds, an' wer
changed every bed-makin. She told everybody she cud git tu listen
tu hit that she ment tu give every durn'd one ove them tu Sal when
she got married. Oh, lordy! what es fat a gal es Sal Yardley cud
ever du wif half ove em, an' sleepin wif a husbun at that, is more
nor I ever cud see through. Jis' think ove her onder twenty layer
ove quilts in July, an' yu in thar too. Gewhillikins! George, look
how I is sweatin' now, an' this is December. I'd 'bout es lief be
shet up in a steam biler wif a three hundred pound bag ove lard,
es tu make a bisiness ove sleepin wif that gal—'twould kill a glass-
blower.

"Well, tu cum tu the serious part ove this conversashun, that is
how the old quilt-mersheen an' coverlid-loom cum tu stop oper-
ashuns on this yeath. She hed narrated hit thru the neighborhood
that nex Saterday she'd gin a quiltin—three quilts an' one cumfurt
tu tie. 'Goblers, fiddils, gals, an' whisky,' wer the words she sent
tu the men-folk, an' more tetchin ur wakenin words never drap't
ofen an 'oman's tongue. She sed tu the gals, 'Sweet toddy, huggin,
dancin, an' huggers in 'bundunce.' Them words struck the gals rite
in the pit ove the stumick, an' spread a ticklin sensashun bof ways,
ontil they scratched thar heads wif one han, an' thar heels wif
tuther.

"Everybody, he an' she, what wer baptized b'levers in the righ-
teousnes ove quiltins wer thar, an' hit jis' so happen'd that everybody in them parts, frum fifteen summers tu fifty winters, wer
unannamus b'levers. Strange, warn't hit? Hit wer the bigges' 'quiltin ever Missis Yardley hilt, an' she hed hilt hundreds; everybody
wer thar, 'scept the constibil an' suckit-rider, two dam easily-spared
pussons; the numbers ni ontu even too; jis' a few more boys nur
gals; that made hit more exhitin, fur hit gin the gals a chance tu
kick an' squeal a littil, wifout runnin eny risk ove not gittin kissed
at all, an' hit gin reasonabil grouns fur a few scrimmages amung
the he's. Now es kissin an' fitin am the pepper an' salt ove all
soshul getherins, so hit wer more espishully wif this ove ours. Es
I swung my eyes over the crowd, George, I thought quiltins, managed in a morril an' sensibil way, truly am good things—good fur
free drinkin, good fur free eatin, good fur free huggin, good fur
free dancin, good fur free fitin, an' goodest ove all fur poperlatin
a country fas'.

"Thar am a fur-seein wisdum in quiltins, ef they hes proper
trimmins: 'vittils, fiddils, an' sperrits in 'bundunce.' One holesum

quiltin am wuf three old pray'r-meetins on the poperlashun pint, purtickerly ef hits hilt in the dark ove the moon, an' runs intu the night a few hours, an' April ur May am the time chosen. The moon don't suit quiltins whar everybody is well acquainted an' already fur along in courtin. She dus help pow'ful tu begin a courtin match onder, but when hit draws ni ontu a head, nobody wants a moon but the ole mammys.

"The mornin cum, still, saft, sunshiney; cocks crowin, hens singin, birds chirpin, tuckeys gobblin—jis' the day tu sun quilts, kick, kiss, squeal, an' make love.

"All the plow-lines an' clothes-lines wer straiched tu every post an' tree. Quilts purvailed. Durn my gizzard ef two acres roun that ar house warn't jis' one solid quilt, all out a-sunnin, an' tu be seed. They dazzled the eyes, skeered the hosses, gin wimen the heart-burn, an' perdominated.

"To'ards sundown the he's begun tu drap in. Year-nis' needil-drivin cummenced tu lose groun; threads broke ofen, thimbils got los', an' quilts needed anuther roll. Gigglin, winkin, whisperin, smoofin ove har, an' gals a-ticklin one anuther, wer a-gainin every inch ove groun what the needils los'. Did yu ever notis, George, at all soshul getherins, when the he's begin tu gather, that the young she's begin tu tickil one anuther an' the ole maids swell thar tails, roach up thar backs, an' sharpen thar nails ontu the bed-posts an' door jams, an' spit an' groan sorter like cats a-courtin? Dus hit mean *rale* rath, ur is hit a dare tu the he's, sorter kivered up wif the outside signs ove danger? I honestly b'leve that the young she's' ticklin means, 'Cum an' take this job ofen our hans.' But that swellin I jis' don't onderstan; dus yu? Hit looks skeery, an' I never tetch one ove em when they am in the swellin way. I may be mistaken'd 'bout the ticklin bisiness too; hit may be dun like a feller chaws poplar bark when he haint got eny terbacker, a-sorter better nur nun make-shif. I dus know one thing tu a cer-tainty: that is, when the he's take hold the ticklin quits, an' ef yu gits one ove the ole maids out tu hersef, then she subsides an' is the smoofes, sleekes, saft thing yu ever seed, an' dam ef yu can't hear her purr, jis' es plain!

"But then, George, gals an' ole maids haint the things tu fool time away on. Hits widders, by golly, what am the rale sensibil, steady-goin, never-skeerin, never-kickin, willin, sperrited, smoof pacers. They cum clost up tu the hoss-block, standin still wif thar purty silky years playin, an' the naik-veins a-throbbin, an' waits fur the word, which ove course yu gives, arter yu finds yer feet well in the stirrup, an' away they moves like a cradil on cushioned rockers, ur a spring buggy runnin in damp san'. A tetch ove the bridil, an' they knows yu wants em tu turn, an' they dus hit es willin es ef the idear wer thar own. I be dod rabbited ef a man can't 'propriate happiness by the skinful ef he is in contack wif sumbody's widder, an' is smart. Gin me a willin widder, the yeath over: what they don't know, haint worth larnin. They hes all been tu Jamakey an' larnt how sugar's made, an' knows how tu sweeten wif hit; an' by golly, they is always ready tu use hit. All yu hes tu du is tu find the spoon, an' then drink cumfort till yer blind. Nex tu good sperrits an' my laigs, I likes a twenty-five year ole widder, wif roun ankils, an' bright eyes, honestly an' squarly lookin intu yurn, an' sayin es plainly es a partrige sez 'Bob White,' 'Don't be afraid ove me; I hes been thar; yu know hit ef yu hes eny sense, an' thar's no use in eny humbug, ole feller—cum ahead!'

"Ef yu onderstans widder nater, they ken save yu a power ove troubil, onsartinty, an' time, an' ef yu is interprisin yu gits mons'rous well paid fur hit. The very soun ove thar littil shoe-heels speak full trainin, an' hes a knowin click as they tap the floor; an' the rustil ove thar dress sez, 'I dar yu tu ax me.'

"When yu hes made up yer mind tu court one, jis' go at hit like hit wer a job ove rail-maulin. Ware yer workin close, use yer common, every-day moshuns an' words, an' abuv all, fling away yer cinamint ile vial an' burn all yer love songs. No use in tryin tu fool em, fur they sees plum thru yu, a durn'd sight plainer than they dus thru thar veils. No use in a pasted shut; she's been thar. No use in borrowin a cavortin fat hoss; she's been thar. No use in har-dye; she's been thar. No use in cloves, tu kill whisky breff; she's been thar. No use in buyin clost curtains fur yer bed, fur she has been thar. Widders am a speshul means, George, fur ripenin green men, killin off weak ones, an makin 'ternally happy the soun ones.

"Well, es I sed afore, I flew the track an' got ontu the widders. The fellers begun tu ride up an' walk up, sorter slow, like they warn't in a hurry, the durn'd 'saitful raskils, hitchin thar critters tu enything they cud find. One red-comb'd, long-spurr'd, domi-necker feller, frum town, in a red an' white grid-iron jackid an' patent leather gaiters, hitched his hoss, a wild, skeery, wall-eyed devil, inside the yard palins, tu a cherry tree lim'. Thinks I, that hoss hes a skeer intu him big enuf tu run intu town, an' perhaps beyant hit, ef I kin only tetch hit off; so I sot intu thinkin.

"One aind ove a long clothes-line, wif nine dimunt quilts ontu hit, wer tied tu the same cherry tree that the hoss wer. I tuck my knife and socked hit thru every quilt, 'bout the middil, an' jis' below the rope, an' tied them thar wif bark, so they cudent slip. Then I went tu the back aind, an' ontied hit frum the pos', knottin

in a hoe-handil, by the middil, tu keep the quilts frum slippin off
ef my bark strings failed, an' laid hit on the groun. Then I went
tu the tuther aind: thar wer 'bout ten foot tu spar, a-lyin on the
groun arter tyin tu the tree. I tuck hit atwix Wall-eye's hine laigs,
an' tied hit fas' tu bof stirrups, an' then cut the cherry tree lim'
betwix his bridil an' the tree, almos' off. Now, mine yu thar wer
two ur three uther ropes full ove quilts atween me an' the hous',
so I wer purty well hid frum thar. I jis' tore off a palin frum the
fence, an' tuck hit in bof hans, an' arter raisin hit 'way up yander,
I fotch hit down, es hard es I cud, flatsided to'ards the groun, an'
hit acksidentally happen'd tu hit Wall-eye, 'bout nine inches ahead
ove the root ove his tail. Hit landed so hard that hit made my hans
tingle, an' then busted intu splinters. The first thing I did, wer tu
feel ove mysef, on the same spot whar hit hed hit the hoss. I cudent
help duin hit tu save my life, an' I swar I felt sum ove Wall-eye's
sensashun, jis' es plain. The fust thing he did, wer tu tare down
the lim' wif a twenty foot jump, his head to'ards the hous'. Thinks
I, now yu hev dun hit, yu durn'd wall-eyed fool! tarin down that
lim' wer the beginin ove all the troubil, an' the hoss did hit hissef;
my conshuns felt clar es a mountin spring, an' I wer in a frame
ove mine tu obsarve things es they happen'd, an' they soon begun
tu happen purty clost arter one anuther rite then, an' thar, an'
tharabouts, clean ontu town, thru hit, an' still wer a-happenin, in
the woods beyant thar ni ontu eleven mile frum ole man Yardley's
gate, an' four beyant town.

"The fust line ove quilts he tried tu jump, but broke hit down;
the nex one he ran onder; the rope cotch ontu the ho'n ove the
saddil, broke at bof ainds, an' went along wif the hoss, the cherry
tree lim' an' the fust line ove quilts, what I hed proverdensally
tied fas' tu the rope. That's what I calls foresight, George. Right
furnint the frunt door he cum in contack wif ole Missis Yardley
hersef, an' anuther ole 'oman; they wer a-holdin a nine dimunt
quilt spread out, a-'zaminin hit, an' a-praisin hits purfeckshuns.
The durn'd onmanerly, wall-eyed fool run plum over Missis Yardley, frum ahine, stompt one hine foot through the quilt, takin hit
along, a-kickin ontil he made hits corners snap like a whip. The
gals screamed, the men hollered wo! an' the ole 'oman wer toted
intu the hous' limber es a wet string, an' every word she sed wer,
'Oh, my preshus nine dimunt quilt!'

"Wall-eye busted thru the palins, an' Dominicker sed 'im, made
a mortal rush fur his bitts, wer too late fur them, but in good time
fur the strings ove flyin quilts, got tangled amung 'em, an' the
gridiron jackid patren wer los' tu my sight amung star an' Irish
chain quilts; he went frum that quiltin at the rate ove thuty miles

tu the hour. Nuffin lef on the lot ove the hole consarn, but a nine biler hat, a par ove gloves, an' the jack ove hearts.

"What a onmanerly, suddin way ove leavin places sum folks hev got, enyhow.

"Thinks I, well, that fool hoss, tarin down that cherry tree lim', hes dun sum good, enyhow; hit hes put the ole 'oman outen the way fur the balance ove the quiltin, an' tuck Dominicker outen the way an' outen danger, fur that gridiron jackid wud a-bred a scab on his nose afore midnite; hit wer morrily boun tu du hit.

"Two months arterwards, I tracked the route that hoss tuck in his kalamatus skeer, by quilt rags, tufts ove cotton, bunches ove har, (human an' hoss,) an' scraps ove a gridiron jackid stickin ontu the bushes, an' plum at the aind ove hit, whar all signs gin out, I foun a piece ove watch chain an' a hosses head. The places what know'd Dominicker, know'd 'im no more.

"Well, arter they'd tuck the ole 'oman up stairs an' camfired her tu sleep, things begun tu work agin. The widders broke the ice, an' arter a littil gigglin, goblin, an' gabblin, the kissin begun. *Smack!*—'Thar, now,' a widder sed that. *Pop!*—'Oh, don't!' *Pfip!*—'Oh, yu quit!' *Plosh!*—'Go *way* yu awkerd critter, yu kissed me in the eye!' anuther widder sed that. *Bop!* 'Now yu ar satisfied, I recon, big mouf!' *Vip!*—'That haint fair!' *Spat!*—'Oh, lordy! May, cum pull Bill away; he's a-tanglin my har.' *Thut!*—'I jis' d-a-r-e yu tu du that agin!' a widder sed that, too. Hit sounded all 'roun that room like poppin co'n in a hot skillet, an' wer pow'ful sujestif.

"Hit kep on ontil I be durn'd ef *my* bristils didn't begin tu rise, an' sumthin like a cold buckshot wud run down the marrow in my back-bone 'bout every ten secons, an' then run up agin, tolerabil hot. I kep a swallerin wif nuthin tu swaller, an' my face felt swell'd; an' yet I wer fear'd tu make a bulge. Thinks I, I'll ketch one out tu hersef torreckly, an' then I guess we'll rastil. Purty soon Sal Yardley started fur the smoke-'ous, so I jis' gin my head I few short shakes, let down one ove my wings a-trailin, an' sirkiled roun her wif a side twis' in my naik, steppin sidewise, an' a-fetchin up my hinmos' foot wif a sorter jerkin slide at every step. Sez I, 'Too coo-took a-too.' She onderstood hit, an' stopt, sorter spreadin her shoulders. An' jis' es I hed pouch'd out my mouf, an' wer a-reachin forrid wif hit, fur the article hitsef, sunthin interfared wif me, hit did. George, wer yu ever ontu yer hans an' knees, an' let a hell-tarin big, mad ram, wif a ten-yard run, but yu yearnis'ly, jis' onst, right squar ontu the pint ove yer back-bone?"

"No, you fool; why do you ask?"

"Kaze I wanted tu know ef yu cud hev a realizin' noshun ove my shock. Hits scarcely worth while tu try tu make yu onderstan the case by words only, onless yu hev been tetched in that way. Gr-eat golly! the fust thing I felt, I tuck hit tu be a back-ackshun yeathquake; an' the fust thing I seed wer my chaw'r terbacker a-flyin over Sal's head like a skeer'd bat. My mouf wer pouch'd out, ready fur the article hitsef, yu know, an' hit went outen the roun hole like the wad outen a pop-gun—thug! an' the fust thing I know'd, I wer a flyin over Sal's head too, an' a-gainin on the chaw'r terbacker fast. I wer straitened out strait, toes hinemos', middil finger-nails foremos', an' the fust thing I hearn wer, 'Yu dam Shanghi!' Great Jerus-a-lam! I lit ontu my all fours jis' in time tu but the yard gate ofen hits hinges, an' skeer loose sum more hosses—kep on in a four-footed gallop, clean acrost the lane afore I cud straiten up, an' yere I cotch up wif my chaw'r terbacker, stickin flat agin a fence-rail. I hed got so good a start that I thot hit a pity tu spile hit, so I jis' jump'd the fence an' tuck thru the orchurd. I tell yu I dusted these yere close, fur I tho't hit wer arter me.

"Arter runnin a spell, I ventered tu feel roun back thar, fur sum signs ove what hed happened tu me. George, arter two pow'ful hardtugs, I pull'd out the vamp an' sole ove one ove ole man Yardley's big brogans, what he hed los' amung my coat-tails. Dre'-ful! dre'ful! Arter I got hit away frum thar, my flesh went fas' asleep, frum abuv my kidneys tu my knees; about now, fur the fust time, the idear struck me, what hit wer that hed interfar'd wif me, an' los' me the kiss. Hit wer ole Yardley hed kicked me. I walked fur a month like I wer straddlin a thorn hedge. Sich a shock, at sich a time, an' on sich a place—jis' think ove hit! hit am tremenjus, haint hit? The place feels num, right now."

"Well, Sut, how did the quilting come out?"

"How the hell du yu 'speck me tu know? I warn't thar eny more."

Joel Chandler Harris

(1848–1908)

Born in Eatonton, Georgia, Harris lived on familiar terms with
hard times through much of his childhood. His father was an Irish
laborer who disappeared when Harris was born, and his unmarried
mother eked out a living as a seamstress. When he was 13, he left
home to work as a typesetter on a weekly paper published on the
Turnwold plantation, an experience that launched him on a life-
long career as a newspaper man. After the Civil War, he worked
on a number of Southern papers, and, in 1873, he married Esther
La Rose with whom he had eight children. In 1876, he took a job
with the Atlanta Constitution, a leading Southern newspaper that
became, fired and fueled by editor Henry Grady, a beacon of New
South progressivism. Harris remained with the Constitution for 24
years, and developed in its pages his famous character Uncle Remus,
an old plantation black who related with a shrewd combination of
good humor and philosophy stories of the "old days" when animals
could talk. Harris fashioned these animal fables from folktales he
had heard from blacks in his youth. One of the first writers in any
country to admire and to make use of traditional black culture, he
helped open up to other writers, among them his admirers Mark
Twain and Rudyard Kipling, a whole new world of literary cross-
fertilization. Most of the Uncle Remus tales center on the ruses of
Brer Rabbit to outsmart larger animals ready to trap him on all
sides. Harris himself was conscious that the tales only barely disguised the human predicament of the slave needing all his wits to
survive against the stronger forces around him. When the first collection of Uncle Remus stories appeared in 1880, Harris became a
national figure, though he himself always made light of his literary
importance. In the 20th century he has sometimes been faulted for
presenting an overly romantic view of plantation life, but he is more
often praised for the accuracy of his black dialect, and for his sensitive appreciation of black folklore. In addition to his Uncle Remus

collections, Harris wrote over 20 other books, uneven in quality, dealing with a full range of Southern subjects. He was particularly interested in the farms and communities of Georgia back country, and created a Georgia "cracker," Billy Sanders, to narrate a number of rural stories. Harris's own favorite among his stories was "Free Joe and the Rest of the World," a striking work that shows him quite capable of confronting the injustices of the antebellum South. Among his many works are Uncle Remus: His Songs and Sayings *(1880),* Nights With Uncle Remus: Myths and Legends of the Old Plantation *(1883),* Mingo and Other Sketches in Black and White *(1884),* Free Joe and Other Georgian Sketches *(1887),* Balaam and His Master and Other Sketches and Stories *(1891), and* Gabriel Tolliver: A Story of Reconstruction *(1902). "Free Joe and the Rest of the World" first appeared in* The Century Magazine *(November 1884).*

FREE JOE AND THE REST OF THE WORLD

❀

The name of Free Joe strikes humorously upon the ear of memory. It is impossible to say why, for he was the humblest, the simplest, and the most serious of all God's living creatures, sadly lacking in all those elements that suggest the humorous. It is certain, moreover, that in 1850 the sober-minded citizens of the little Georgian village of Hillsborough were not inclined to take a humorous view of Free Joe, and neither his name nor his presence provoked a smile. He was a black atom, drifting hither and thither without an owner, blown about by all the winds of circumstance, and given over to shiftlessness.

The problems of one generation are the paradoxes of a succeeding one, particularly if war, or some such incident, intervenes to clarify the atmosphere and strengthen the understanding. Thus, in 1850, Free Joe represented not only a problem of large concern, but, in the watchful eyes of Hillsborough, he was the embodiment of that vague and mysterious danger that seemed to be forever lurking on the outskirts of slavery, ready to sound a shrill and ghostly signal in the impenetrable swamps, and steal forth under the midnight stars to murder, rapine, and pillage,—a danger always threatening, and yet never assuming shape; intangible, and yet real; impossible, and yet not improbable. Across the serene and smiling front of safety, the pale outlines of the awful shadow of insurrection sometimes fell. With this invisible panorama as a background, it was natural that the figure of Free Joe, simple and humble as it was, should assume undue proportions. Go where he would, do what he might, he could not escape the finger of observation and the kindling eye of suspicion. His lightest words were noted, his slightest actions marked.

Under all the circumstances it was natural that his peculiar condition should reflect itself in his habits and manners. The slaves laughed loudly day by day, but Free Joe rarely laughed. The slaves sang at their work and danced at their frolics, but no one ever heard Free Joe sing or saw him dance. There was something painfully plaintive and appealing in his attitude, something touching in his anxiety to please. He was of the friendliest nature, and seemed to be delighted when he could amuse the little children who had made a playground of the public square. At times he would please them by making his little dog Dan perform all sorts of curious tricks, or he would tell them quaint stories of the beasts of the field and birds of the air; and frequently he was coaxed into relating the story of his own freedom. That story was brief, but tragical.

In the year of our Lord 1840, when a negro-speculator of a sportive turn of mind reached the little village of Hillsborough on his way to the Mississippi region, with a caravan of likely negroes of both sexes, he found much to interest him. In that day and at that time there were a number of young men in the village who had not bound themselves over to repentance for the various misdeeds of the flesh. To these young men the negro-speculator (Major Frampton was his name) proceeded to address himself. He was a Virginian, he declared; and, to prove the statement, he referred all the festively inclined young men of Hillsborough to a barrel of peach-brandy in one of his covered wagons. In the minds of these young men there was less doubt in regard to the age and quality of the brandy than there was in regard to the negro-trader's birthplace. Major Frampton might or might not have been born in the Old Dominion,—that was a matter for consideration and inquiry,—but there could be no question as to the mellow pungency of the peach-brandy.

In his own estimation, Major Frampton was one of the most accomplished of men. He had summered at the Virginia Springs; he had been to Philadelphia, to Washington, to Richmond, to

Lynchburg, and to Charleston, and had accumulated a great deal of experience which he found useful. Hillsborough was hid in the woods of Middle Georgia, and its general aspect of innocence impressed him. He looked on the young men who had shown their readiness to test his peach-brandy, as overgrown country boys who needed to be introduced to some of the arts and sciences he had at his command. Thereupon the major pitched his tents, figuratively speaking, and became, for the time being, a part and parcel of the innocence that characterized Hillsborough. A wiser man would doubtless have made the same mistake.

The little village possessed advantages that seemed to be providentially arranged to fit the various enterprises that Major Frampton had in view. There was the auction-block in front of the stuccoed court-house, if he desired to dispose of a few of his negroes; there was a quarter-track, laid out to his hand and in excellent order, if he chose to enjoy the pleasures of horse-racing; there were secluded pine thickets within easy reach, if he desired to indulge in the exciting pastime of cock-fighting; and various lonely and unoccupied rooms in the second story of the tavern, if he cared to challenge the chances of dice or cards.

Major Frampton tried them all with varying luck, until he began his famous game of poker with Judge Alfred Wellington, a stately gentleman with a flowing white beard and mild blue eyes that gave him the appearance of a benevolent patriarch. The history of the game in which Major Frampton and Judge Alfred Wellington took part is something more than a tradition in Hillsborough, for there are still living three or four men who sat around the table and watched its progress. It is said that at various stages of the game Major Frampton would destroy the cards with which they were playing, and send for a new pack, but the result was always the same. The mild blue eyes of Judge Wellington, with few exceptions, continued to overlook "hands" that were invincible—a habit they had acquired during a long and arduous course of training from Saratoga to New Orleans. Major Frampton lost his money, his horses, his wagons, and all his negroes but one, his body-servant. When his misfortune had reached this limit, the major adjourned the game. The sun was shining brightly, and all nature was cheerful. It is said that the major also seemed to be cheerful. However this may be, he visited the court-house, and executed the papers that gave his body-servant his freedom. This being done, Major Frampton sauntered into a convenient pine thicket, and blew out his brains.

The negro thus freed came to be known as Free Joe. Compelled, under the law, to choose a guardian, he chose Judge Wellington, chiefly because his wife Lucinda was among the negroes won from Major Frampton. For several years Free Joe had what may be called a jovial time. His wife Lucinda was well provided for, and he found it a comparatively easy matter to provide for himself; so that, taking all the circumstances into consideration, it is not matter for astonishment that he became somewhat shiftless.

When Judge Wellington died, Free Joe's troubles began. The judge's negroes, including Lucinda, went to his half-brother, a man named Calderwood, who was a hard master and a rough customer generally,—a man of many eccentricities of mind and character. His neighbors had a habit of alluding to him as "Old Spite"; and the name seemed to fit him so completely, that he was known far and near as "Spite" Calderwood. He probably enjoyed the distinction the name gave him, at any rate, he never resented it, and it was not often that he missed an opportunity to show that he deserved it. Calderwood's place was two or three miles from the village of Hillsborough, and Free Joe visited his wife twice a week, Wednesday and Saturday nights.

One Sunday he was sitting in front of Lucinda's cabin, when Calderwood happened to pass that way.

"Howdy, marster?" said Free Joe, taking off his hat.

"Who are you?" exclaimed Calderwood abruptly, halting and staring at the negro.

"I'm name' Joe, marster. I'm Lucindy's ole man."

"Who do you belong to?"

"Marse John Evans is my gyardeen, marster."

"Big name—gyardeen. Show your pass."

Free Joe produced that document, and Calderwood read it aloud slowly, as if he found it difficult to get at the meaning:—

"To whom it may concern: This is to certify that the boy Joe Frampton has my permission to visit his wife Lucinda."

This was dated at Hillsborough, and signed *"John W. Evans."*

Calderwood read it twice, and then looked at Free Joe, elevating his eyebrows, and showing his discolored teeth.

"Some mighty big words in that there. Evans owns this place, I reckon. When's he comin' down to take hold?"

Free Joe fumbled with his hat. He was badly frightened.

"Lucindy say she speck you wouldn't min' my comin', long ez I behave, marster."

Calderwood tore the pass in pieces and flung it away.

"Don't want no free niggers 'round here," he exclaimed. "There's the big road. It'll carry you to town. Don't let me catch you here no more. Now, mind what I tell you."

Free Joe presented a shabby spectacle as he moved off with his little dog Dan slinking at his heels. It should be said in behalf of Dan, however, that his bristles were up, and that he looked back and growled. It may be that the dog had the advantage of insignificance, but it is difficult to conceive how a dog bold enough to raise his bristles under Calderwood's very eyes could be as insignificant as Free Joe. But both the negro and his little dog seemed to give a new and more dismal aspect to forlornness as they turned into the road and went toward Hillsborough.

After this incident Free Joe appeared to have clearer ideas concerning his peculiar condition. He realized the fact that though he was free he was more helpless than any slave. Having no owner, every man was his master. He knew that he was the object of suspicion, and therefore all his slender resources (ah! how pitifully slender they were!) were devoted to winning, not kindness and appreciation, but toleration; all his efforts were in the direction of mitigating the circumstances that tended to make his condition so much worse than that of the negroes around him,—negroes who had friends because they had masters.

So far as his own race was concerned, Free Joe was an exile. If the slaves secretly envied him his freedom (which is to be doubted, considering his miserable condition), they openly despised him, and lost no opportunity to treat him with contumely. Perhaps this was in some measure the result of the attitude which Free Joe chose to maintain toward them. No doubt his instinct taught him that to hold himself aloof from the slaves would be to invite from the whites the toleration which he coveted, and without which even his miserable condition would be rendered more miserable still.

His greatest trouble was the fact that he was not allowed to visit his wife; but he soon found a way out of this difficulty. After he had been ordered away from the Calderwood place, he was in the habit of wandering as far in that direction as prudence would permit. Near the Calderwood place, but not on Calderwood's land, lived an old man named Micajah Staley and his sister Becky Staley. These people were old and very poor. Old Micajah had a palsied arm and hand; but, in spite of this, he managed to earn a precarious living with his turning-lathe.

When he was a slave Free Joe would have scorned these representatives of a class known as poor white trash, but now he found them sympathetic and helpful in various ways. From the back door of their cabin he could hear the Calderwood negroes singing at night, and he sometimes fancied he could distinguish Lucinda's shrill treble rising above the other voices. A large poplar grew in the woods some distance from the Staley cabin, and at the foot of this tree Free Joe would sit for hours with his face turned toward Calderwood's. His little dog Dan would curl up in the leaves near by, and the two seemed to be as comfortable as possible.

One Saturday afternoon Free Joe, sitting at the foot of this friendly poplar, fell asleep. How long he slept, he could not tell; but when he awoke little Dan was licking his face, the moon was shining brightly, and Lucinda his wife stood before him laughing. The dog, seeing that Free Joe was asleep, had grown somewhat impatient, and he concluded to make an excursion to the Calderwood place on his own account. Lucinda was inclined to give the incident a twist in the direction of superstition.

"I 'uz settin' down front er de fireplace," she said, "cookin' me some meat, w'en all of a sudden I year sumpin at de do'—scratch, scratch. I tuck'n tu'n de meat over, en make out I aint year it. Bimeby it come dar 'gin—scratch, scratch. I up en open de do', I did, en, bless de Lord! dar wuz little Dan, en it look like ter me dat his ribs done grow tergeer. I gin 'im some bread, en den, w'en he start out, I tuck'n foller 'im, kaze, I say ter myse'f, maybe my nigger man mought be some'rs 'roun'. Dat ar little dog got sense, mon."

Free Joe laughed and dropped his hand lightly on Dan's head. For a long time after that he had no difficulty in seeing his wife. He had only to sit by the poplar-tree until little Dan could run and fetch her. But after a while the other negroes discovered that Lucinda was meeting Free Joe in the woods, and information of the fact soon reached Calderwood's ears. Calderwood was what is called a man of action. He said nothing; but one day he put Lucinda in his buggy, and carried her to Macon, sixty miles away. He carried her to Macon, and came back without her; and nobody in or around Hillsborough, or in that section, ever saw her again.

For many a night after that Free Joe sat in the woods and waited. Little Dan would run merrily off and be gone a long time, but he always came back without Lucinda. This happened over and over again. The "willis-whistlers" would call and call, like phantom huntsmen wandering on a far-off shore; the screech-owl would shake and shiver in the depths of the woods; the night-hawks, sweeping by on noiseless wings, would snap their beaks as though they enjoyed the huge joke of which Free Joe and little Dan were the victims; and the whip-poor-wills would cry to each other through the gloom. Each night seemed to be lonelier than the preceding, but Free Joe's patience was proof against loneliness. There came a time, however, when little Dan refused to go after Lucinda. When Free Joe motioned him in the direction of the

Calderwood place, he would simply move about uneasily and whine; then he would curl up in the leaves and make himself comfortable.

One night, instead of going to the poplar-tree to wait for Lucinda, Free Joe went to the Staley cabin, and, in order to make his welcome good, as he expressed it, he carried with him an armful of fat-pine splinters. Miss Becky Staley had a great reputation in those parts as a fortune-teller, and the schoolgirls, as well as older people, often tested her powers in this direction, some in jest and some in earnest. Free Joe placed his humble offering of light-wood in the chimney-corner, and then seated himself on the steps, dropping his hat on the ground outside.

"Miss Becky," he said presently, "whar in de name er gracious you reckon Lucindy is?"

"Well, the Lord he'p the nigger!" exclaimed Miss Becky, in a tone that seemed to reproduce, by some curious agreement of sight with sound, her general aspect of peakedness. "Well, the Lord he'p the nigger! haint you been a-seein' her all this blessed time? She's over at old Spite Calderwood's, if she's anywheres, I reckon."

"No'm, dat I aint, Miss Becky. I aint seen Lucindy in now gwine on mighty nigh a mont'."

"Well, it haint a-gwine to hurt you," said Miss Becky, somewhat sharply. "In my day an' time it wuz allers took to be a bad sign when niggers got to honeyin' 'roun' an' gwine on."

"Yessum," said Free Joe, cheerfully assenting to the proposition—"yessum, dat's so, but me an' my ole 'oman, we 'uz raise tergeer, en dey aint bin many days w'en we 'uz 'way fum one 'n'er like we is now."

"Maybe she's up an' took up wi' some un else," said Micajah Staley from the corner. "You know what the sayin' is, 'New master, new nigger.' "

"Dat's so, dat's de sayin', but tain't wid my ole 'oman like 'tis wid yuther niggers. Me en her wuz des natally raise up tergeer. Dey's lots likelier niggers dan w'at I is," said Free Joe, viewing his shabbiness with a critical eye, "but I knows Lucindy mos' good ez I does little Dan dar—dat I does."

There was no reply to this, and Free Joe continued,—

"Miss Becky, I wish you please, ma'am, take en run yo' kyards en see sump'n n'er 'bout Lucindy; kaze ef she sick, I'm gwine dar. Dey ken take en take me up en gimme a stroppin', but I'm gwine dar."

Miss Becky got her cards, but first she picked up a cup, in the bottom of which were some coffee-grounds. These she whirled slowly round and round, ending finally by turning the cup upside down on the hearth and allowing it to remain in that position.

"I'll turn the cup first," said Miss Becky, "and then I'll run the cards and see what they say."

As she shuffled the cards the fire on the hearth burned low, and in its fitful light the gray-haired, thin-featured woman seemed to deserve the weird reputation which rumor and gossip had given her. She shuffled the cards for some moments, gazing intently in the dying fire; then, throwing a piece of pine on the coals, she made three divisions of the pack, disposing them about in her lap. Then she took the first pile, ran the cards slowly through her fingers, and studied them carefully. To the first she added the second pile. The study of these was evidently not satisfactory. She said nothing, but frowned heavily; and the frown deepened as she added the rest of the cards until the entire fifty-two had passed in review before her. Though she frowned, she seemed to be deeply interested. Without changing the relative position of the cards, she ran them all over again. Then she threw a larger piece of pine on the fire, shuffled the cards afresh, divided them into three piles, and subjected them to the same careful and critical examination.

"I can't tell the day when I've seed the cards run this a-way," she said after a while. "What is an' what aint, I'll never tell you; but I know what the cards sez."

"W'at does dey say, Miss Becky?" the negro inquired, in a tone the solemnity of which was heightened by its eagerness.

"They er runnin' quare. These here that I'm a-lookin' at," said Miss Becky, "they stan' for the past. Them there, they er the present; and the t'others, they er the future. Here's a bundle,"— tapping the ace of clubs with her thumb,—"an' here's a journey as plain as the nose on a man's face. Here's Lucinda—"

"Whar she, Miss Becky?"

"Here she is—the queen of spades."

Free Joe grinned. The idea seemed to please him immensely.

"Well, well, well!" he exclaimed. "Ef dat don't beat my time! De queen er spades! W'en Lucindy year dat hit'll tickle 'er, sho'!"

Miss Becky continued to run the cards back and forth through her fingers.

"Here's a bundle an' a journey, and here's Lucinda. An' here's ole Spite Calderwood."

She held the cards toward the negro and touched the king of clubs.

"De Lord he'p my soul!" exclaimed Free Joe with a chuckle. "De faver's dar. Yesser, dat's him! W'at de matter 'long wid all un um, Miss Becky?"

The old woman added the second pile of cards to the first, and then the third, still running them through her fingers slowly and critically. By this time the piece of pine in the fireplace had wrapped itself in a mantle of flame, illuminating the cabin and throwing into strange relief the figure of Miss Becky as she sat studying the cards. She frowned ominously at the cards and mumbled a few words to herself. Then she dropped her hands in her lap and gazed once more into the fire. Her shadow danced and capered on the wall and floor behind her, as if, looking over her shoulder into the future, it could behold a rare spectacle. After a while she picked up the cup that had been turned on the hearth. The coffee-grounds, shaken around, presented what seemed to be a most intricate map.

"Here's the journey," said Miss Becky, presently; "here's the big road, here's rivers to cross, here's the bundle to tote." She paused and sighed. "They haint no names writ here, an' what it all means I'll never tell you. Cajy, I wish you'd be so good as to han' me my pipe."

"I haint no hand wi' the kyards," said Cajy, as he handed the pipe, "but I reckon I can patch out your misinformation, Becky, bekaze the other day, whiles I was a-finishin' up Mizzers Perdue's rollin'-pin, I hearn a rattlin' in the road. I looked out, an' Spite Calderwood was a-drivin' by in his buggy, an' thar sot Lucinda by him. It'd in-about drapt out er my min'."

Free Joe sat on the door-sill and fumbled at his hat, flinging it from one hand to the other.

"You aint see um gwine back, is you, Mars Cajy?" he asked after a while.

"Ef they went back by this road," said Mr. Staley, with the air of one who is accustomed to weigh well his words, "it must 'a' bin endurin' of the time whiles I was asleep, bekaze I haint bin no furder from my shop than to yon bed."

"Well, sir!" exclaimed Free Joe in an awed tone, which Mr. Staley seemed to regard as a tribute to his extraordinary powers of statement.

"Ef it's my beliefs you want," continued the old man, "I'll pitch 'em at you fair and free. My beliefs is that Spite Calderwood is gone an' took Lucindy outen the county. Bless your heart and soul! when Spite Calderwood meets the Old Boy in the road they'll be a turrible scuffle. You mark what I tell you."

Free Joe, still fumbling with his hat, rose and leaned against the door-facing. He seemed to be embarrassed. Presently he said,—

"I speck I better be gittin' 'long. Nex' time I see Lucindy, I'm gwine tell 'er w'at Miss Becky say 'bout de queen er spades—dat

I is. Ef dat don't tickle 'er, dey ain't no nigger 'oman never bin tickle'."

He paused a moment, as though waiting for some remark or comment, some confirmation of misfortune, or, at the very least, some indorsement of his suggestion that Lucinda would be greatly pleased to know that she had figured as the queen of spades; but neither Miss Becky nor her brother said any thing.

"One minnit ridin' in the buggy 'longside er Mars Spite, en de nex' highfalutin' 'roun' playin' de queen er spades. Mon, deze yer nigger gals gittin' up in de pictur's; dey sholy is."

With a brief "Good-night, Miss Becky, Mars Cajy," Free Joe went out into the darkness, followed by little Dan. He made his way to the poplar, where Lucinda had been in the habit of meeting him, and sat down. He sat there a long time; he sat there until little Dan, growing restless, trotted off in the direction of the Calderwood place. Dozing against the poplar, in the gray dawn of the morning, Free Joe heard Spite Calderwood's fox-hounds in full cry a mile away.

"Shoo!" he exclaimed, scratching his head, and laughing to himself, "dem ar dogs is des a-warmin' dat old fox up."

But it was Dan the hounds were after, and the little dog came back no more. Free Joe waited and waited, until he grew tired of waiting. He went back the next night and waited, and for many nights thereafter. His waiting was in vain, and yet he never regarded it as in vain. Careless and shabby as he was, Free Joe was thoughtful enough to have his theory. He was convinced that little Dan had found Lucinda, and that some night when the moon was shining brightly through the trees, the dog would rouse him from his dreams as he sat sleeping at the foot of the poplar-tree, and he would open his eyes and behold Lucinda standing over him, laughing merrily as of old; and then he thought what fun they would have about the queen of spades.

How many long nights Free Joe waited at the foot of the poplar-tree for Lucinda and little Dan, no one can ever know. He kept no account of them, and they were not recorded by Micajah Staley nor by Miss Becky. The season ran into summer and then into fall. One night he went to the Staley cabin, cut the two old people an armful of wood, and seated himself on the door-steps, where he rested. He was always thankful—and proud, as it seemed— when Miss Becky gave him a cup of coffee, which she was sometimes thoughtful enough to do. He was especially thankful on this particular night.

"You er still layin' off for to strike up wi' Lucindy out thar in the woods, I reckon," said Micajah Staley, smiling grimly. The situation was not without its humorous aspects.

"Oh, dey er comin', Mars Cajy, dey er comin', sho," Free Joe replied. "I boun' you dey'll come; en w'en dey does come, I'll des take en fetch um yer, whar you kin see um wid you own eyes, you en Miss Becky."

"No," said Mr. Staley, with a quick and emphatic gesture of disapproval. "Don't! don't fetch 'em anywheres. Stay right wi' 'em as long as may be."

Free Joe chuckled, and slipped away into the night, while the two old people sat gazing in the fire. Finally Micajah spoke.

"Look at that nigger; look at 'im. He's pine-blank as happy now as a killdee by a mill-race. You can't 'faze 'em. I'd in-about give up my t'other hand ef I could stan' flat-footed, an' grin at trouble like that there nigger."

"Niggers is niggers," said Miss Becky, smiling grimly, "an' you can't rub it out; yit I lay I've seed a heap of white people lots meaner'n Free Joe. He grins,—an' that's nigger,—but I've ketched his under jaw a-tremblin' when Lucindy's name uz brung up. An' I tell you," she went on, bridling up a little, and speaking with almost fierce emphasis, "the Old Boy's done sharpened his claws for Spite Calderwood. You'll see it."

"Me, Rebecca?" said Mr. Staley, hugging his palsied arm; "me? I hope not."

"Well, you'll know it then," said Miss Becky, laughing heartily t her brother's look of alarm.

The next morning Micajah Staley had occasion to go into the woods after a piece of timber. He saw Free Joe sitting at the foot of the poplar, and the sight vexed him somewhat.

"Git up from there," he cried, "an' go an' arn your livin'. A mighty purty pass it's come to, when great big buck niggers can lie a-snorin' in the woods all day, when t'other folks is got to be up an' a-gwine. Git up from there!"

Receiving no response, Mr. Staley went to Free Joe, and shook him by the shoulder; but the negro made no response. He was dead. His hat was off, his head was bent, and a smile was on his face. It was as if he had bowed and smiled when death stood before him, humble to the last. His clothes were ragged; his hands were rough and callous; his shoes were literally tied together with strings; he was shabby in the extreme. A passer-by, glancing at him, could have no idea that such a humble creature had been summoned as a witness before the Lord God of Hosts.

O. Henry
(William Sydney Porter)
(1862–1910)

Born in Greensboro, North Carolina, Porter quit school when he was 15 and went to work in his uncle's drugstore. Five years later he left Greensboro, traveled to Texas, and worked at various jobs, including a stint as a ranch hand. He also married into a prominent Austin family, wrote sketches of frontier life, and edited a weekly comic magazine, Rolling Stone. *Accused in 1896 of embezzling funds from the bank where he worked to help support his writing, he fled the country. He returned when he learned of his wife's terminal illness, was tried and convicted, and sentenced to serve time in the Ohio Federal Penitentiary. He remained there over three years, working as a clerk in the prison pharmacy, and writing stories. In 1902, two years after his release, he moved to New York, and began pouring out commercial magazine stories under the pseudonym, O. Henry, he had adopted while in prison. In the remaining eight years of his life, he published hundreds of stories and became famous for his technical skills, his trick endings, and his fascination with the poor and the eccentric on the streets of New York. At the time of his death, Porter was the most popular short-story writer in America. He compared his writing to the arts of vaudeville, and the comparison may help explain both the pleasures and the limitations of his continual search to entertain, and his constant juggling of conventional types and situations. He wrote a handful of stories dealing with his Southern background, including "The Guardian of the Accolade," "Best-Seller," and "A Blackjack Bargainer." "A Municipal Report" is by far the best of his Southern stories, and one of the best stories he ever wrote. His satirical portrait of "Major" Wentworth Caswell is a fine study of a certain type of professional Southerner. Among his many collections are* Cabbages and Kings *(1904),* The Four Million *(1906),* The Voice of the City *(1908),* Roads of Destiny *(1909),* Strictly Business *(1910), and* Whirligigs *(1910). "A Municipal Report" is taken from* Strictly Business, *and was originally published in the Nashville* Hampton's Magazine *(November 1909).*

A MUNICIPAL REPORT

❀

The cities are full of pride,
   Challenging each to each—
This from her mountainside,
   That from her burthened beach.
          R. KIPLING

Fancy a novel about Chicago or Buffalo, let us say, or Nashville, Tennessee! There are just three big cities in the United States that are "story cities"—New York, of course, New Orleans, and, best of the lot, San Francisco.—FRANK NORRIS.

East is East, and West is San Francisco, according to Californians. Californians are a race of people; they are not merely inhabitants of a State. They are the Southerners of the West. Now, Chicagoans are no less loyal to their city; but when you ask them why, they stammer and speak of lake fish and the new Odd Fellows Building. But Californians go into detail.

Of course they have, in the climate, an argument that is good for half an hour while you are thinking of your coal bills and heavy underwear. But as soon as they come to mistake your silence for conviction, madness comes upon them, and they picture the city of the Golden Gate as the Bagdad of the New World. So far, as a matter of opinion, no refutation is necessary. But dear cousins all (from Adam and Eve descended), it is a rash one who will lay his finger on the map and say: "In this town there can be no romance—what could happen here?" Yes, it is a bold and a rash deed to challenge in one sentence history, romance, and Rand and McNally.

NASHVILLE.—A city, port of delivery, and the capital of the State of Tennessee, is on the Cumberland River and on the N. C. & St. L. and the L. & N. railroads. This city is regarded as the most important educational centre in the South.

I stepped off the train at 8 P.M. Having searched thesaurus in vain for adjectives, I must, as a substitution, hie me to comparison in the form of a recipe.

198

Take of London fog 30 parts; malaria 10 parts; gas leaks 20 parts; dewdrops gathered in a brick yard at sunrise, 25 parts; odor of honeysuckle 15 parts. Mix.

The mixture will give you an approximate conception of a Nashville drizzle. It is not so fragrant as a moth-ball nor as thick as pea-soup; but 'tis enough—'twill serve.

I went to a hotel in a tumbril. It required strong self-suppression for me to keep from climbing to the top of it and giving an imitation of Sidney Carton. The vehicle was drawn by beasts of a bygone era and driven by something dark and emancipated.

I was sleepy and tired, so when I got to the hotel I hurriedly paid it the fifty cents it demanded (with approximate lagniappe, I assure you). I knew its habits; and I did not want to hear it prate about its old "marster" or anything that happened "befo' de wah."

The hotel was one of the kind described as "renovated." That means $20,000 worth of new marble pillars, tiling, electric lights and brass cuspidors in the lobby, and a new L. & N. time table and a lithograph of Lookout Mountain in each one of the great rooms above. The management was without reproach, the attention full of exquisite Southern courtesy, the service as slow as the progress of a snail and as good-humored as Rip Van Winkle. The food was worth traveling a thousand miles for. There is no other hotel in the world where you can get such chicken livers *en brochette*.

At dinner I asked a Negro waiter if there was anything doing in town. He pondered gravely for a minute, and then replied: "Well, boss, I don't really reckon there's anything at all doin' after sundown."

Sundown had been accomplished; it had been drowned in the drizzle long before. So that spectacle was denied me. But I went forth upon the streets in the drizzle to see what might be there.

It is built on undulating grounds; and the streets are lighted by electricity at a cost of $32,470 per annum.

As I left the hotel there was a race riot. Down upon me charged a company of freedmen, or Arabs, or Zulus, armed with—no, I saw with relief that they were not rifles, but whips. And I saw dimly a caravan of black, clumsy vehicles; and at the reassuring shouts, "Kyar you anywhere in the town, boss, fuh fifty cents," I reasoned that I was merely a "fare" instead of a victim.

I walked through long streets, all leading uphill. I wondered how those streets ever came down again. Perhaps they didn't until they were "graded." On a few of the "main streets" I saw lights in stores here and there; saw street cars go by conveying worthy burghers hither and yon; saw people pass engaged in the art of conversation, and heard a burst of semi-lively laughter issuing from a soda-water and ice-cream parlor. The streets other than "main" seemed to have enticed upon their borders houses consecrated to peace and domesticity. In many of them lights shone behind discreetly drawn window shades, in a few pianos tinkled orderly and irreproachable music. There was, indeed, little "doing." I wished I had come before sundown. So I returned to my hotel.

In November, 1864, the Confederate General Hood advanced against Nashville, where he shut up a National force under General Thomas. The latter then sallied forth and defeated the Confederates in a terrible conflict.

All my life I have heard of, admired, and witnessed the fine marksmanship of the South in its peaceful conflicts in the tobacco-chewing regions. But in my hotel a surprise awaited me. There were twelve bright, new, imposing, capacious brass cuspidors in the great lobby, tall enough to be called urns and so wide-mouthed that the crack pitcher of a lady baseball team should have been able to throw a ball into one of them at five paces distant. But, although a terrible battle had raged and was still raging, the enemy had not suffered. Bright, new, imposing, capacious, untouched, they stood. But, shades of Jefferson Brick! the tile floor—the beautiful tile floor! I could not avoid thinking of the battle of Nashville and trying to draw, as is my foolish habit, some deductions about hereditary marksmanship.

Here I first saw Major (by misplaced courtesy) Wentworth Caswell. I knew him for a type the moment my eyes suffered from the sight of him. A rat has no geographical habitat. My old friend, A. Tennyson, said, as he so well said almost everything:

> Prophet, curse me the blabbing lip,
> And curse me the British vermin, the rat.

Let us regard the word "British" as interchangeable *ad lib*. A rat is a rat.

This man was hunting about the hotel lobby like a starved dog that had forgotten where he had buried a bone. He had a face of great acreage, red, pulpy, and with a kind of sleepy massiveness like that of Buddha. He possessed one single virtue—he was very smoothly shaven. The mark of the beast is not indelible upon a man until he goes about with a stubble. I think that if he had not used his razor that day I would have repulsed his advances, and the criminal calendar of the world would have been spared the addition of one murder.

I happened to be standing within five feet of a cuspidor when Major Caswell opened fire upon it. I had been observant enough to perceive that the attacking force was using Gatlings instead of squirrel rifles, so I sidestepped so promptly that the major seized the opportunity to apologize to a noncombatant. He had the blabbing lip. In four minutes he had become my friend and had dragged me to the bar.

I desire to interpolate here that I am a Southerner. But I am not one by profession or trade. I eschew the string tie, the slouch hat, the Prince Albert, the number of bales of cotton destroyed by Sherman, and plug chewing. When the orchestra plays "Dixie" I do not cheer. I slide a little lower on the leather-cornered seat and, well, order another Würzburger and wish that Longstreet had—but what's the use?

Major Caswell banged the bar with his fist, and the first gun at Fort Sumter re-echoed. When he fired the last one at Appomattox I began to hope. But then he began on family trees, and demonstrated that Adam was only a third cousin of a collateral branch of the Caswell family. Genealogy disposed of, he took up, to my distaste, his private family matters. He spoke of his wife, traced her descent back to Eve, and profanely denied any possible rumor that she may have had relations in the land of Nod.

By this time I began to suspect that he was trying to obscure by noise the fact that he had ordered the drinks, on the chance that I would be bewildered into paying for them. But when they were down he crashed a silver dollar loudly upon the bar. Then, of course, another serving was obligatory. And when I had paid for that I took leave of him brusquely; for I wanted no more of him. But before I had obtained my release he had prated loudly of an income that his wife received, and showed a handful of silver money.

When I got my key at the desk the clerk said to me courteously: "If that man Caswell has annoyed you, and if you would like to make a complaint, we will have him ejected. He is a nuisance, a loafer, and without any known means of support, although he seems to have some money most the time. But we don't seem to be able to hit upon any means of throwing him out legally."

"Why, no," said I, after some reflection; "I don't see my way clear to making a complaint. But I would like to place myself on record as asserting that I do not care for his company. Your town," I continued, "seems to be a quiet one. What manner of entertainment, adventure, or excitement, have you to offer to the stranger within your gates?"

"Well, sir," said the clerk, "there will be a show here next Thursday. It is—I'll look it up and have the announcement sent up to your room with the ice water. Good-night."

After I went up to my room I looked out the window. It was only about ten o'clock, but I looked upon a silent town. The drizzle continued, spangled with dim lights, as far apart as currants in a cake sold at the Ladies' Exchange.

"A quiet place," I said to myself, as my first shoe struck the ceiling of the occupant of the room beneath mine. "Nothing of the life here that gives color and good variety to the cities in the East and West. Just a good, ordinary, hum-drum, business town."

Nashville occupies a foremost place among the manufacturing centres of the country. It is the fifth boot and shoe market in the United States, the largest candy and cracker manufacturing city in the South, and does an enormous wholesale drygoods, grocery, and drug business.

I must tell you how I came to be in Nashville, and I assure you the digression brings as much tedium to me as it does to you. I was traveling elsewhere on my own business, but I had a commission from a Northern literary magazine to stop over there and establish a personal connection between the publication and one of its contributors, Azalea Adair.

Adair (there was no clue to the personality except the handwriting) had sent in some essays (lost art!) and poems that had made the editors swear approvingly over their one o'clock luncheon. So they had commissioned me to round up said Adair and corner by contract his or her output at two cents a word before some other publisher offered her ten or twenty.

At nine o'clock the next morning, after my chicken livers *en brochette* (try them if you can find that hotel), I strayed out into the drizzle, which was still on for an unlimited run. At the first corner I came upon Uncle Cæsar. He was a stalwart Negro, older than the pyramids, with gray wool and a face that reminded me of Brutus, and a second afterwards of the late King Cettiwayo. He wore the most remarkable coat that I ever had seen or expect to see. It reached to his ankles and had once been a Confederate gray in colors. But rain and sun and age had so variegated it that Joseph's coat, beside it, would have faded to a pale monochrome. I must linger with that coat, for it has to do with the story—the story that is so long in coming, because you can hardly expect anything to happen in Nashville.

Once it must have been the military coat of an officer. The cape of it had vanished, but all adown its front it had been frogged and tasseled magnificently. But now the frogs and tassels were gone. In their stead had been patiently stitched (I surmised by some surviving "black mammy") new frogs made of cunningly twisted common hempen twine. This twine was frayed and disheveled. It must have been added to the coat as a substitute for vanished splendors, with tasteless but painstaking devotion, for it followed faithfully the curves of the long-missing frogs. And, to complete the comedy and pathos of the garment, all its buttons were gone save one. The second button from the top alone remained. The coat was fastened by other twine strings tied through the button-holes and other holes rudely pierced in the opposite side. There was never such a weird garment so fantastically bedecked and of so many mottled hues. The lone button was the size of a half-dollar, made of yellow horn and sewed on with coarse twine.

This Negro stood by a carriage so old that Ham himself might have started a hack line with it after he left the ark with the two animals hitched to it. As I approached he threw open the door, drew out a feather duster, waved it without using it, and said in deep, rumbling tones:

"Step right in, suh; ain't a speck of dust in it—jus' got back from a funeral, suh."

I inferred that on such gala occasions carriages were given an extra cleaning. I looked up and down the street and perceived that there was little choice among the vehicles for hire that lined the curb. I looked in my memorandum book for the address of Azalea Adair.

"I want to go to 861 Jessamine Street," I said, and was about to step into the hack. But for an instant the thick, long, gorilla-like arm of the Negro barred me. On his massive and saturnine face a look of sudden suspicion and enmity flashed for a moment. Then, with quickly returning conviction, he asked, blandishingly: "What are you gwine there for, boss?"

"What is that to you?" I asked, a little sharply.

"Nothin', suh, jus' nothin'. Only it's a lonesome kind of part of town and few folks ever has business out there. Step right in. The seats is clean—jes' got back from a funeral, suh."

A mile and a half it must have been to our journey's end. I could hear nothing but the fearful rattle of the ancient hack over the uneven brick paving; I could smell nothing but the drizzle, now further flavored with coal smoke and something like a mixture of tar and oleander blossoms. All I could see through the streaming windows were two rows of dim houses.

The city has an area of 10 square miles; 181 miles of streets, of which 137 miles are paved; a system of waterworks that cost $2,000,000 with 77 miles of mains.

Eight-sixty-one Jessamine Street was a decayed mansion. Thirty yards back from the street it stood, outmerged in a splendid grove of trees and untrimmed shrubbery. A row of box bushes overflowed and almost hid the paling fence from sight; the gate was kept closed by a rope noose that encircled the gate post and the first paling of the gate. But when you got inside you saw that 861 was a shell, a shadow, a ghost of former grandeur and excellence. But in the story, I have not yet got inside.

When the hack had ceased from rattling and the weary quadrupeds came to a rest I handed my jehu his fifty cents with an additional quarter, feeling a glow of conscious generosity as I did so. He refused it.

"It's two dollars, suh," he said.

"How's that?" I asked. "I plainly heard you call out at the hotel. 'Fifty cents to any part of the town.'"

"It's two dollars, suh," he repeated obstinately. "It's a long ways from the hotel."

"It is within the city limits and well within them," I argued. "Don't think that you have picked up a greenhorn Yankee. Do you see those hills over there?" I went on, pointing toward the east (I could not see them, myself, for the drizzle); "well, I was born and raised on their other side. You old fool nigger, can't you tell people from other people when you see 'em?"

The grim face of King Cettiwayo softened. "Is you from the South, suh? I reckon it was them shoes of yourn fooled me. They is somethin' sharp in the toes for a Southern gen'l'man to wear."

"Then the charge is fifty cents, I suppose?" said I, inexorably.

His former expression, a mingling of cupidity and hostility, returned, remained ten seconds, and vanished.

"Boss," he said, "fifty cents is right; but I *needs* two dollars, suh; I'm *obleeged* to have two dollars. I ain't *demandin'* it now, suh; after I knows whar you's from; I'm jus sayin' that I *has* to have two dollars to-night and business is mighty po'."

Peace and confidence settled upon his heavy features. He had been luckier than he had hoped. Instead of having picked up a greenhorn, ignorant of rates, he had come upon an inheritance.

"You confounded old rascal," I said, reaching down to my pocket, "you ought to be turned over to the police."

For the first time I saw him smile. He knew; *he knew;* HE KNEW.

I gave him two one-dollar bills. As I handed them over I noticed that one of them had seen parlous times. Its upper right-hand corner was missing, and it had been torn through in the middle, but joined again. A strip of blue tissue paper, pasted over the split, preserved its negotiability.

Enough of the African bandit for the present: I left him happy, lifted the rope, and opened the creaky gate.

The house, as I said, was a shell. A paint brush had not touched it in twenty years. I could not see why a strong wind should not have bowled it over like a house of cards until I looked again at the trees that hugged it close—the trees that saw the battle of Nashville and still drew their protecting branches around it against storm and enemy and cold.

Azalea Adair, fifty years old, white-haired, a descendant of the cavaliers, as thin and frail as the house she lived in, robed in the cheapest and cleanest dress I ever saw, with an air as simple as a queen's, received me.

The reception room seemed a mile square, because there was nothing in it except some rows of books, on unpainted white-pine bookshelves, a cracked marble-topped table, a rag rug, a hairless horsehair sofa, and two or three chairs. Yes, there was a picture on the wall, a colored crayon drawing of a cluster of pansies. I looked around for the portrait of Andrew Jackson and the pine-cone hanging basket but they were not there.

Azalea Adair and I had conversation, a little of which will be repeated to you. She was a product of the old South, gently nurtured in the sheltered life. Her learning was not broad, but was deep and of splendid originality in its somewhat narrow scope. She had been educated at home, and her knowledge of the world was derived from inference and by inspiration. Of such is the precious, small group of essayists made. While she talked to me I kept brushing my fingers, trying, unconsciously, to rid them guiltily of the absent dust from the half-calf backs of Lamb, Chaucer, Hazlitt, Marcus Aurelius, Montaigne, and Hood. She was exquisite, she was a valuable discovery. Nearly everybody nowadays knows too much—oh, so much too much—of real life.

I could perceive clearly that Azalea Adair was very poor. A house and a dress she had, not much else, I fancied. So, divided between my duty to the magazine and my loyalty to the poets and essayists who fought Thomas in the valley of the Cumberland, I listened to her voice which was like a harpsichord's, and found that I could not speak of contracts. In the presence of the nine Muses and the three Graces one hesitated to lower the topic to two cents. There would have to be another colloquy after I had regained my commercialism. But I spoke of my mission, and three o'clock of the next afternoon was set for the discussion of the business proposition.

"Your town," I said, as I began to make ready to depart (which is the time for smooth generalities) "seems to be a quiet, sedate place. A home town, I should say, where few things out of the ordinary ever happen."

It carries on an extensive trade in stoves and hollow ware with the West and South, and its flouring mills have a daily capacity of more than 2,000 barrels.

Azalea Adair seemed to reflect.

"I have never thought of it that way," she said, with a kind of sincere intensity that seemed to belong to her. "Isn't it in the still, quiet places that things do happen? I fancy that when God began to create the earth on the first Monday morning one could have leaned out one's window and heard the drops of mud splashing from His trowel as He built up the everlasting hills. What did the noisiest project in the world—I mean the building of the tower of Babel—result in finally? A page and a half of Esperanto in the *North American Review*."

"Of course," said I, platitudinously, "human nature is the same everywhere; but there is more color—er—more drama and movement and—er—romance in some cities than in others."

"On the surface," said Azalea Adair. "I have traveled many times around the world in a golden airship wafted on two wings—print and dreams. I have seen (on one of my imaginary tours) the

Sultan of Turkey bowstring with his own hands one of his wives who had uncovered her face in public. I have seen a man in Nashville tear up his theatre tickets because his wife was going out with her face covered—with rice powder. In San Francisco's Chinatown I saw the slave girl Sing Yee dipped slowly, inch by inch, in boiling almond oil to make her swear she would never see her American lover again. She gave in when the boiling oil had reached three inches above her knee. At a euchre party in East Nashville the other night I saw Kitty Morgan cut dead by seven of her schoolmates and lifelong friends because she had married a house painter. The boiling oil was sizzling as high as her heart; but I wish you could have seen the fine little smile that she carried from table to table. Oh, yes, it is a hum-drum town. Just a few miles of red brick houses and mud and stores and lumber yards."

Some one had knocked hollowly at the back of the house. Azalea Adair breathed a soft apology and went to investigate the sound. She came back in three minutes with brightened eyes, a faint flush on her cheeks, and ten years lifted from her shoulders.

"You must have a cup of tea before you go," she said, "and a sugar cake."

She reached and shook a little iron bell. In shuffled a small Negro girl about twelve, barefoot, not very tidy, glowering at me with thumb in mouth and bulging eyes.

Azalea Adair opened a tiny, worn purse and drew out a dollar bill, a dollar bill with the upper right-hand corner missing, torn in two pieces and pasted together again with a strip of blue tissue paper. It was one of those bills I had given the piratical Negro—there was no doubt of it.

"Go up to Mr. Baker's store on the corner, Impy," she said, handing the girl the dollar bill, "and get a quarter of a pound of tea—the kind he always sends me—and ten cents' worth of sugar cakes. Now, hurry. The supply of tea in the house happens to be exhausted," she explained to me.

Impy left by the back way. Before the scrape of her hard, bare feet had died away on the back porch, a wild shriek—I was sure it was hers—filled the hollow house. Then the deep, gruff tones of an angry man's voice mingled with the girl's further squeals and unintelligible words.

Azalea Adair rose without surprise or emotion and disappeared. For two minutes I heard the hoarse rumble of the man's voice; then something like an oath and a slight scuffle, and she returned calmly to her chair.

"This is a roomy house," she said, "and I have a tenant for part of it. I am sorry to have to rescind my invitation to tea. It is impossible to get the kind I always use at the store. Perhaps to-morrow Mr. Baker will be able to supply me."

I was sure that Impy had not had time to leave the house. I inquired concerning street-car lines and took my leave. After I was well on my way I remembered that I had not learned Azalea Adair's name. But to-morrow would do.

That same day I started in on the course of iniquity that this uneventful city forced upon me. I was in the town only two days, but in that time I managed to lie shamelessly by telegraph, and to be an accomplice—after the fact, if that is the correct legal term—to a murder.

As I rounded the corner nearest my hotel the Afrite coachman of the polychromatic, nonpareil coat seized me, swung open the dungeony door of his peripatetic sarcophagus, flirted his feather duster and began his ritual: "Step right in, boss. Carriage is clean—jus' got back from a funeral. Fifty cents to any—"

And then he knew me and grinned broadly. " 'Scuse me, boss; you is de gen'l'man what rid out with me dis mawnin'. Thank you kindly, suh."

"I am going out to 861 again to-morrow afternoon at three," said I, "and if you will be here, I'll let you drive me. So you know Miss Adair?" I concluded, thinking of my dollar bill.

"I belonged to her father, Judge Adair, suh," he replied.

"I judge that she is pretty poor," I said. "She hasn't much money to speak of, has she?"

For an instant I looked again at the fierce countenance of King Cettiwayo, and then he changed back to an extortionate old Negro hack driver.

"She ain't gwine to starve, suh," he said, slowly. "She has reso'ces, suh; she has reso'ces."

"I shall pay you fifty cents for the trip," said I.

"Dat is puffeckly correct, suh," he answered, humbly. "I jus' *had* to have dat two dollars dis mawnin', boss."

I went to the hotel and lied by electricity. I wired the magazine: "A. Adair holds out for eight cents a word."

The answer that came back was: "Give it to her quick, you duffer."

Just before dinner "Major" Wentworth Caswell bore down upon me with the greetings of a long-lost friend. I have seen few men whom I have so instantaneously hated, and of whom it was so difficult to be rid. I was standing at the bar when he invaded me; therefore I could not wave the white ribbon in his face. I would have paid gladly for the drinks, hoping thereby, to escape another; but he was one of those despicable, roaring, advertising bibbers who must have brass bands and fireworks attend upon every cent that they waste in their follies.

With an air of producing millions he drew two one-dollar bills from a pocket and dashed one of them upon the bar. I looked once more at the dollar bill with the upper right-hand corner missing, torn through the middle, and patched with a strip of blue tissue paper. It was my dollar again. It could have been no other.

I went up to my room. The drizzle and the monotony of a dreary, eventless Southern town had made me tired and listless. I remember that just before I went to bed I mentally disposed of the mysterious dollar bill (which might have formed the clue to a tremendously fine detective story of San Francisco) by saying to myself sleepily: "Seems as if a lot of people here own stock in the Hack-Drivers' Trust. Pays dividends promptly, too. Wonder if—" Then I fell asleep.

King Cettiwàyo was at his post the next day, and rattled my bones over the stones out to 861. He was to wait and rattle me back again when I was ready.

Azalea Adair looked paler and cleaner and frailer than she had looked on the day before. After she had signed the contract at eight cents per word she grew still paler and began to slip out of her chair. Without much trouble I managed to get her up on the antediluvian horsehair sofa and then I ran out to the sidewalk and yelled to the coffee-colored Pirate to bring a doctor. With a wisdom that I had not suspected in him, he abandoned his team and struck off up the street afoot, realizing the value of speed. In ten minutes he returned with a grave, gray-haired, and capable man of medicine. In a few words (worth much less than eight cents each) I explained to him my presence in the hollow house of mystery. He bowed with stately understanding, and turned to the old Negro.

"Uncle Cæsar," he said, calmly, "run up to my house and ask Miss Lucy to give you a cream pitcher full of fresh milk and half a tumbler of port wine. And hurry back. Don't drive—run. I want you to get back sometime this week."

It occurred to me that Mr. Merriman also felt a distrust as to the speeding powers of the land-pirate's steeds. After Uncle Cæsar was gone, lumberingly, but swiftly, up the street, the doctor looked me over with great politeness and as much careful calculation until he had decided that I might do.

"It is only a case of insufficient nutrition," he said. "In other words, the result of poverty, pride, and starvation. Mrs. Caswell has many devoted friends who would be glad to aid her, but she will accept nothing except from that old Negro, Uncle Cæsar, who was once owned by her family."

"Mrs. Caswell!" said I, in surprise. And then I looked at the contract and saw that she had signed it "Azalea Adair Caswell."

"I thought she was Miss Adair," I said.

"Married to a drunken, worthless loafer, sir," said the doctor. "It is said that he robs her even of the small sums that her old servant contributes toward her support."

When the milk and wine had been brought the doctor soon revived Azalea Adair. She sat up and talked of the beauty of the autumn leaves that were then in season and their height of color. She referred lightly to her fainting seizure as the outcome of an old palpitation of the heart. Impy fanned her as she lay on the sofa. The doctor was due elsewhere, and I followed him to the door. I told him that it was within my power and intentions to make a reasonable advance of money to Azalea Adair on future contributions to the magazine, and he seemed pleased.

"By the way," he said, "perhaps you would like to know that you have had royalty for a coachman. Old Cæsar's grandfather was a king in Congo. Cæsar himself has royal ways, as you may have observed."

As the doctor was moving off I heard Uncle Cæsar's voice inside: "Did he git bofe of dem two dollars from you, Mis' Zalea?"

"Yes, Cæsar," I heard Azalea Adair answer, weakly. And then I went in and concluded business negotiations with our contributor. I assumed the responsibility of advancing fifty dollars, putting it as a necessary formality in binding our bargain. And then Uncle Cæsar drove me back to the hotel.

Here ends all of the story as far as I can testify as a witness. The rest must be only bare statements of facts.

At about six o'clock I went out for a stroll. Uncle Cæsar was at his corner. He threw open the door of his carriage, flourished his duster, and began his depressing formula: "Step right in, suh. Fifty cents to anywhere in the city—hack's puffickly clean, suh—jus' got back from a funeral—"

And then he recognized me. I think his eyesight was getting bad. His coat had taken on a few more faded shades of color, the twine strings were more frayed and ragged, the last remaining button—the button of yellow horn—was gone. A motley descendant of kings was Uncle Cæsar!

About two hours later I saw an excited crowd besieging the front of the drug store. In a desert where nothing happens this was manna; so I wedged my way inside. On an extemporized couch of empty boxes and chairs was stretched the mortal corporeality of Major Wentworth Caswell. A doctor was testing him for the mortal ingredient. His decision was that it was conspicuous by its absence.

The erstwhile Major had been found dead on a dark street and brought by curious and ennuied citizens to the drug store. The late human being had been engaged in terrific battle—the details showed that. Loafer and reprobate though he had been, he had been also a warrior. But he had lost. His hands were yet clinched so tightly that his fingers would not be opened. The gentle citizens who had known him stood about and searched their vocabularies to find some good words, if it were possible, to speak of him. One kind-looking man said, after much thought: "When 'Cas' was about fo'teen he was one of the best spellers in the school."

While I stood there the fingers of the right hand of "the man that was," which hung down the side of a white pine box, relaxed, and dropped something at my feet. I covered it with one foot quietly, and a little later on I picked it up and pocketed it. I reasoned that in his last struggle his hand must have seized that object unwittingly and held it in a death grip.

At the hotel that night the main topic of conversation, with the possible exceptions of politics and prohibition, was the demise of Major Caswell. I heard one man say to a group of listeners:

"In my opinion, gentlemen, Caswell was murdered by some of these no-account niggers for his money. He had fifty dollars this afternoon which he showed to several gentlemen in the hotel. When he was found the money was not on his person."

I left the city the next morning at nine, and as the train was crossing the bridge over the Cumberland River I took out of my pocket a yellow horn overcoat button the size of a fifty-cent piece, with frayed ends of coarse twine hanging from it, and cast it out of the window into the slow, muddy waters below.

I wonder what's doing in Buffalo!

Johnson Jones Hooper

(1815–1862)

Born in Wilmington, North Carolina, Hooper came from a distin-guished family whose resources had dwindled considerably by the time he was a young man. His father—a lawyer, plantation owner, and newspaper editor—was unable to provide for his education, and when Hooper was 20 he left North Carolina to join his lawyer brother in La Fayette, Alabama, a small frontier town. There he studied law and became a lawyer himself. His chief occupation, however, was as a newspaper editor and publisher, beginning with the La Fayette East Alabamian *in 1842. In 1843, he wrote a hu-morous piece entitled "Taking the Census in Alabama." It was later reprinted in William T. Porter's humor magazine* Spirit of the Times. *During the same period, Hooper created the character Simon Suggs, a frontier rogue who stands out as one of the most vivid and comic characters in early Southern fiction. Many Simon Suggs sketches were published by Porter, who admired Hooper above almost all his other contributors. In 1845, Porter helped Hooper secure a New York publisher for his book* Some Adventures of Captain Simon Suggs, *a picaresque novel, or group of related sto-ries, presented as a "campaign biography" to help elect Suggs sher-iff. Obviously a satire of the popular political biographies that were widely circulated at the time,* Adventures *shows how Captain Suggs—relying on his frontier philosophy that "it is good to be shifty in a new country"—outshifts and outcheats almost everyone, in-cluding his own father. The model for Suggs was apparently a Georgian named Bird Young, who had moved to Alabama when he was 16. For much of his adult life, Hooper was active in politics, and, in fact, he increasingly felt that his popularity as a humorist detracted from his political prospects. He continued to write, but not as much as his admirers would have wished. An enthusiastic secessionist, he became Secretary to the Confederate Provisional Congress in 1861 and remained so until the reorganization of the Congress in 1862. Just before his death, he was engaged in editing the records of the Provisional Congress. Hooper's works include* Some Adventures of Captain Simon Suggs, Late of the Tallapoosa Volunteers; Together with "Taking the Census," and Other Alabama Sketches *(1845),* The Widow Rugby's Husband, A Night at the Ugly Man's, and Other Tales of Alabama *(1851); and* Dog and Gun: A Few Loose Chapters on Shooting *(1856). "The Captain Attends a Camp-Meeting" first appeared in book form in* Some Adventures of Captain Simon Suggs.

THE CAPTAIN ATTENDS
A CAMP-MEETING

❈

Captain Suggs found himself as poor at the conclusion of the Creek war, as he had been at its commencement. Although no "arbitrary," "despotic," "corrupt," and "unprincipled" judge had fined him a thousand dollars for his proclamation of martial law at Fort Suggs, or the enforcement of its rules in the case of Mrs. Haycock; yet somehow—the thing is alike inexplicable to him and to us— the money which he had contrived, by various shifts to obtain, melted away and was gone for ever. To a man like the Captain, of intense domestic affections, this state of destitution was most distressing. "He could stand it himself—didn't care a d—n for it, no way," he observed, "but the old woman and the children; *that* bothered him!"

As he sat one day, ruminating upon the unpleasant condition of his "financial concerns," Mrs. Suggs informed him that "the sugar and coffee was nigh about out," and that there were not "a dozen j'ints and middlins, *all put together,* in the smoke-house." Suggs bounced up on the instant, exclaiming, "D—n it! *somebody* must suffer!" But whether this remark was intended to convey the idea that he and his family were about to experience the want of the necessaries of life; or that some other, and as yet unknown individual should "suffer" to prevent that prospective exigency, must be left to the commentators, if perchance any of that ingenious class of persons should hereafter see proper to write notes for this history. It is enough for us that we give all the facts in this connection, so that ignorance of the subsequent conduct of Captain Suggs may not lead to an erroneous judgment in respect to his words.

Having uttered the exclamation we have repeated—and perhaps, hurriedly walked once or twice across the room—Captain Suggs drew on his famous old green-blanket overcoat, and ordered his horse, and within five minutes was on his way to a camp-meeting, then in full blast on Sandy creek, twenty miles distant, where he hoped to find amusement, at least. When he arrived there, he found the hollow square of the encampment filled with people, listening to the mid-day sermon and its dozen accompanying "exhortations." A half-dozen preachers were dispensing the word; the one in the pulpit, a meek-faced old man, of great simplicity and benevolence. His voice was weak and cracked, notwithstanding which, however, he contrived to make himself heard occasionally, above the din of the exhorting, the singing, and the shouting which were going on around him. The rest were walking to and fro, (engaged in the other exercises we have indicated,) among the "mourners"—a host of whom occupied the seat set apart for their especial use—or made personal appeals to the mere spectators. The excitement was intense. Men and women rolled about on the ground, or lay sobbing or shouting in promiscuous heaps. More than all, the negroes sang and screamed and prayed. Several, under the influence of what is technically called "the jerks," were plunging and pitching about with convulsive energy. The great object of all seemed to be, to see who could make the greatest noise—

> "And each—for madness ruled the hour—
> Would try his own expressive power."

"Bless my poor old soul!" screamed the preacher in the pulpit; "ef yonder aint a squad in that corner that we aint got one outen yet! It'll never do"—raising his voice—"you must come outen that! Brother Fant, fetch up that youngster in the blue coat! I see the Lord's a-workin' upon him! Fetch him along—glory—yes!—hold to him!"

"Keep the thing warm!" roared a sensual seeming man, of stout mould and florid countenance, who was exhorting among a bevy of young women, upon whom he was lavishing caresses. "Keep the thing warm, breethring!—come to the Lord, honey!" he added, as he vigorously hugged one of the damsels he sought to save.

"Oh, I've got him!" said another in exulting tones, as he led up a gawky youth among the mourners—"I've got him—he tried to git off, but—ha! Lord!"—shaking his head as much as to say, it took a smart fellow to escape him—"ha' Lord!"—and he wiped the perspiration from his face with one hand, and with the other, patted his neophyte on the shoulder—"he couldn't do it! No! Then he tried to argy wi' me—but bless the Lord!—he couldn't do that nother! Ha! Lord! I tuk him, fust in the Old Testament—bless the Lord!—and I argyed him all thro' Kings—then I throwed him into Proverbs—and from that, here we had it up and down, kleer down to the New Testament, and then I begun to see it work him!—then we got into Matthy, and from Matthy right straight along to Acts; and *thar* I throwed him! Y–e–s L–o–r–d!"—assuming the nasal twang and high pitch which are, in some parts, considered the perfection of rhetorical art—"Y-e-s L–o–r–d! and h–e–r–e he is! Now g–i–t down thar," addressing the subject, "and s–e–e ef the L–o–r–d won't do somethin' f–o–r you!" Having thus deposited his charge among the mourners, he started out, summarily to convert another soul!

"Gl–o–*ree!*" yelled a huge, greasy negro woman, as in a fit of the jerks, she threw herself convulsively from her feet, and fell "like a thousand of brick," across a diminutive old man in a little round hat, who was squeaking consolation to one of the mourners.

"Good Lord, have mercy!" ejaculated the little man earnestly and unaffectedly, as he strove to crawl from under the sable mass which was crushing him.

In another part of the square a dozen old women were singing. They were in a state of absolute extasy, as their shrill pipes gave forth,

> "I rode on the sky,
> Quite ondestified I,
> And the moon it was under my feet!"

Near these last, stood a delicate woman in that hysterical condition in which the nerves are incontrollable, and which is vulgarly—and almost blasphemously—termed the "holy laugh." A hideous grin distorted her mouth, and was accompanied with a maniac's chuckle; while every muscle and nerve of her face twitched and jerked in horrible spasms.*

*The reader is requested to bear in mind, that the scenes described in this chapter are not *now* to be witnessed. Eight or ten years ago, all classes of population of the Creek country were very different from what they now are. Of course, no disrespect is intended to any denomination of Christians. We believe that camp-meetings are not peculiar to any church, though most usual in the Methodist—a denomination whose respectability in Alabama is attested by the fact, that *very many* of its worthy clergymen and lay members, hold honourable and profitable offices in the gift of the state legislature; of which, indeed, almost a controlling portion are themselves Methodists.

Amid all this confusion and excitement Suggs stood unmoved. He viewed the whole affair as a grand deception—a sort of "opposition line" running against his own, and looked on with a sort of professional jealousy. Sometimes he would mutter running comments upon what passed before him.

"Well now," said he, as he observed the full-faced brother who was "officiating" among the women, "that ere feller takes *my* eye!—thar he's een this half-hour, a-figurin amongst them galls, and's never said the fust word to nobody else. Wonder what's the reason these here preachers never hugs up the old, ugly women? Never seed one do it in my life—the sperrit never moves 'em that way! It's nater tho'; and the women, *they* never flocks round one o' the old dried-up breethring—bet two to one old splinter-legs thar,"—nodding at one of the ministers—"won't git a chance to say turkey to a good-lookin gal to-day! Well! who blames 'em? Nater will be nater, all the world over; and I judge ef I was a preacher, I should save the purtiest souls fust, myself!"

While the Captain was in the middle of this conversation with himself, he caught the attention of the preacher in the pulpit, who inferring from an indescribable something about his appearance that he was a person of some consequence, immediately determined to add him at once to the church if it could be done; and to that end began a vigorous, direct personal attack.

"Breethring," he exclaimed, "I see yonder a man that's a sinner; I *know* he's a sinner! Thar he stands," pointing at Simon, "a missubble old crittur, with his head a-blossomin for the grave! A few more short years, and d–o–w–n he'll go to perdition, lessen the Lord have mer–cy on him! Come up here, you old hoary-headed sinner, a–n–d git down upon your knees, a–n–d put up your cry for the Lord to snatch you from the bottomless pit! You're ripe for the devil—you're b–o–u–n–d for hell, and the Lord only knows what'll become on you!"

"D—n it," thought Suggs, "*ef* I only had you down in the krick swamp for a minit or so, *I'd* show you who's *old! I'd* alter your tune *mighty* sudden, you sassy, 'saitful old rascal!" But he judiciously held his tongue and gave no utterance to the thought.

The attention of many having been directed to the Captain by the preacher's remarks, he was soon surrounded by numerous well-meaning, and doubtless very pious persons, each one of whom seemed bent on the application of his own particular recipe for the salvation of souls. For a long time the Captain stood silent, or answered the incessant stream of exhortation only with a sneer; but at length, his countenance began to give token of inward emotion. First his eye-lids twitched—then his upper lip quivered—next a transparent drop formed on one of his eye-lashes, and a similar one on the tip of his nose—and, at last, a sudden bursting of air from nose and mouth, told that Captain Suggs was overpowered by his emotions. At the moment of the explosion, he made a feint as if to rush from the crowd, but he was in experienced hands, who well knew that the battle was more than half won.

"Hold to him!" said one—"it's a-workin in him as strong as a Dick horse!"

"Pour it into him," said another, "it'll all come right directly!"

"That's the way I love to see 'em do," observed a third; "when you begin to draw the water from their eyes, taint gwine to be long afore you'll have 'em on their knees!"

And so they clung to the Captain manfully, and half dragged, half led him to the mourner's bench; by which he threw himself down, altogether unmanned, and bathed in tears. Great was the rejoicing of the brethren, as they sang, shouted, and prayed around him—for by this time it had come to be generally known that the "convicted" old man was Captain Simon Suggs, the very "chief of sinners" in all that region.

The Captain remained grovelling in the dust during the usual time, and gave vent to even more than the requisite number of sobs, and groans, and heart-piercing cries. At length, when the proper time had arrived, he bounced up, and with a face radiant with joy, commenced a series of vaultings and tumblings, which "laid in the shade" all previous performances of the sort at that camp-meeting. The brethren were in extasies at this demonstrative evidence of completion of the work; and whenever Suggs shouted "Gloree!" at the top of his lungs, every one of them shouted it back, until the woods rang with echoes.

The effervescence having partially subsided, Suggs was put upon his pins to relate his experience, which he did somewhat in this style—first brushing the tear-drops from his eyes, and giving the end of his nose a preparatory wring with his fingers, to free it of the superabundant moisture:

"Friends," he said, "it don't take long to curry a short horse, accordin' to the old sayin', and I'll give you the perticklers of the way I was 'brought to a knowledge' "—here the Captain wiped his eyes, brushed the tip of his nose and snuffled a little—"in less'n no time."

"Praise the Lord!" ejaculated a bystander.

"You see I come here full o' romancin' and devilment, and jist to make game of all the purceedins. Well, sure enough, I done so for some time, and was a-thinkin how I should play some trick—"

"Dear soul alive! *don't* he talk sweet!" cried an old lady in black silk—"Whar's John Dobbs? You Sukey!" screaming at a negro woman on the other side of the square—"ef you don't hunt up your mass John in a minute, and have him here to listen to his 'sperience, I'll tuck you up when I git home and give you a hundred and fifty lashes, madam!—see ef I don't! Blessed Lord!"—referring again to the Captain's relation—"aint it a *precious* 'scource!"

"I was jist a-thinkin' how I should play some trick to turn it all into redecule, when they began to come round me and talk. Long at fust I didn't mind it, but arter a little that brother"—pointing to the reverend gentlemen who had so successfully carried the unbeliever through the Old and New Testaments, and who Simon was convinced was the "big dog of the tanyard"—"that brother spoke a word that struck me kleen to the heart, and run all over me, like fire in dry grass—"

"*I—I—I* can bring 'em!" cried the preacher alluded to, in a tone of exultation—"Lord thou knows ef thy servant can't stir 'em up, nobody else needn't try—but the glory aint mine! I'm a poor worrum of the dust," he added, with ill-managed affectation.

"And so from that I felt somethin' a-pullin' me inside—"

"Grace! grace! nothin' but grace!" exclaimed one; meaning that "grace" had been operating in the Captain's gastric region.

"And then," continued Suggs, "I wanted to git off, but they hilt me, and bimeby I felt so missuble, I had to go yonder"—pointing to the mourners' seat—"and when I lay down thar it got wuss and wuss, and 'peared like somethin' was a-mashin' down on my back—"

"That was his load o' sin," said one of the brethren—"never mind, it'll tumble off presently, see ef it don't!" and he shook his head professionally and knowingly.

"And it kept a-gittin heavier and heavier, ontwell it looked like it might be a four year old steer, or a big pine log, or somethin' of that sort—"

"Glory to my soul," shouted Mrs. Dobbs, "it's the sweetest talk I *ever* hearn! You Sukey! aint you got John yit? never mind, my lady, *I'll* settle wi' you!" Sukey quailed before the finger which her mistress shook at her.

"And arter awhile," Suggs went on, " 'peared like I fell into a trance, like, and I seed—"

"Now we'll git the good on it!" cried one of the sanctified.

"And I seed the biggest, longest, rip-roarenest, blackest, scaliest—" Captain Suggs paused, wiped his brow, and ejaculated "Ah, L—o—r—d!" so as to give full time for curiosity to become impatience to know what he saw.

"*Sarpent!* warn't it?" asked one of the preachers.

"No, not a sarpent," replied Suggs, blowing his nose.

"Do tell us *what* it war, soul alive!—whar *is* John?" said Mrs. Dobbs.

"Allegator!" said the Captain.

"Alligator!" repeated every woman present, and screamed for very life.

Mrs. Dobbs's nerves were so shaken by the announcement, that after repeating the horrible word, she screamed to Sukey, "you Sukey, I say, you Su–u–ke–e–y! ef you let John come a-nigh this way, whar the dreadful alliga—shaw! what am I thinkin' 'bout? 'Twarn't nothin' but a vishin!"

"Well," said the Captain in continuation, "the allegator kept a-comin' and a-comin' to'ards me, with his great long jaws a-gapin' open like a ten-foot pair o' tailors' shears—"

"Oh! oh! oh! Lord! gracious above!" cried the women.

"SATAN!" was the laconic ejaculation of the oldest preacher present, who thus informed the congregation that it was the devil which had attacked Suggs in the shape of an alligator.

"And then I concluded the jig was up, 'thout I could block his game some way; for I seed his idee was to snap off my head—"

The women screamed again.

"So I fixed myself jist like I was purfectly willin' for him to take my head, and rather he'd do it as not"—here the women shuddered perceptibly—"and so I hilt my head straight out"—the Captain illustrated by elongating his neck—"and when he come up and was a gwine to *shet down* on it, I jist pitched in a big rock which choked him to death, and that minit I felt the weight slide off, and I had the best feelins—sorter like you'll have from *good* sperrits—any body ever had!"

"Didn't I *tell* you so? Didn't I *tell* you so?" asked the brother who had predicted the off-tumbling of the load of sin. "Ha, Lord! fool *who!* I've been *all* along thar!—yes, *all along thar!* and I know every inch of the way jist as good as I do the road home!"—and then he turned round and round, and looked at all, to receive a silent tribute to his superior penetration.

Captain Suggs was now the "lion of the day." Nobody could pray so well, or exhort so movingly, as "brother Suggs." Nor did his natural modesty prevent the proper performance of appropriate exercises. With the reverend Bela Bugg (him to whom, under providence, he ascribed his conversion), he was a most especial favourite. They walked, sang, and prayed together for hours.

"Come, come up; thar's room for all!" cried brother Bugg, in his evening exhortation. "Come to the 'seat,' and ef you won't pray yourselves, let *me* pray for you!"

"Yes!" said Simon, by way of assisting his friend; "it's a game that all can win at! Ante up! ante up, boys—friends I mean—don't back out!"

"Thar aint a sinner here," said Bugg, "no matter ef his soul's black as a nigger, but what thar's room for him!"

"No matter what sort of a hand you've got," added Simon in the fulness of his benevolence; "take stock! Here am *I*, the wickedest and blindest of sinners—has spent my whole life in the sarvice of the devil—has now come in on *narry pair* and won a *pile!*" and the Captain's face beamed with holy pleasure.

"D–o–n–'t be afeard!" cried the preacher; "come along! the meanest won't be turned away! humble yourselves and come!"

"No!" said Simon, still indulging in his favourite style of metaphor; "the bluff game aint played here! No runnin' of a body off! Every body holds four aces, and when you bet, you win!"

And thus the Captain continued, until the services were concluded, to assist in adding to the number at the mourners' seat; and up to the hour of retiring, he exhibited such enthusiasm in the cause, that he was unanimously voted to be the most efficient addition the church had made during that meeting.

The next morning, when the preacher of the day first entered the pulpit, he announced that "brother Simon Suggs," mourning over his past iniquities, and desirous of going to work in the cause as speedily as possible, would take up a collection to found a church in his own neighbourhood, at which he hoped to make himself useful as soon as he could prepare himself for the ministry, which the preacher didn't doubt, would be in a very few weeks, as brother Suggs was "a man of mighty good judge*ment,* and of *a great discorse.*" The funds were to be collected by "brother Suggs," and held in trust by brother Bela Bugg, who was the financial officer of the circuit, until some arrangement could be made to build a suitable house.

"Yes, breethring," said the Captain, rising to his feet; "I want to start a little 'sociation close to me, and I want you all to help. I'm mighty poor myself, as poor as any of you—don't leave breethring"—observing that several of the well-to-do were about to go off—"don't leave; ef you aint able to afford any thing, jist give us your blessin' and it'll be all the same!"

This insinuation did the business, and the sensitive individuals re-seated themselves.

"It's mighty little of this world's goods I've got," resumed Suggs, pulling off his hat and holding it before him; "but I'll bury *that* in the cause any how," and he deposited his last five-dollar bill in the hat.

There was a murmur of approbation at the Captain's liberality throughout the assembly.

Suggs now commenced collecting, and very prudently attacked first the gentlemen who had shown a disposition to escape. These, to exculpate themselves from anything like poverty, contributed handsomely.

"Look here, breethring," said the Captain, displaying the bank-notes thus received, "brother Snooks has drapt a five wi' me, and brother Snodgrass a ten! In course 'taint expected that you *that aint as well off as them,* will give *as much;* let every one give *accordin'* to ther means."

This was another chain-shot that raked as it went! "Who so low" as not to be able to contribute as much as Snooks and Snodgrass?

"Here's all the *small* money I've got about me," said a burly old fellow, ostentatiously handing to Suggs, over the heads of a half dozen, a ten dollar bill.

"That's what I call maganimus!" exclaimed the Captain; "that's the way *every* rich man ought to do!"

These examples were followed, more or less closely, by almost all present, for Simon had excited the pride of purse of the congregation, and a very handsome sum was collected in a very short time.

The reverend Mr. Bugg, as soon as he observed that our hero had obtained all that was to be had at that time, went to him and inquired what amount had been collected. The Captain replied that it was still uncounted, but that it couldn't be much under a hundred.

"Well, brother Suggs, you'd better count it and turn it over to me now. I'm goin' to leave presently."

"No!" said Suggs—"can't do it!"

"Why?—what's the matter?" inquired Bugg.

"It's got to be *prayed over,* fust!" said Simon, a heavenly smile illuminating his whole face.

"Well," replied Bugg, "less go one side and do it!"

"No!" said Simon, solemnly.

Mr. Bugg gave a look of inquiry.

"You see that krick swamp?" asked Suggs—"I'm gwine down in *thar,* and I'd gwine to lay this money down *so*"—showing how he would place it on the ground—"and I'm gwine to git on these here knees"—slapping the right one—"and I'm *n–e–v–e–r* gwine to quit the grit ontwell I feel it's got the blessin'! And nobody aint got to be thar but me!"

Mr. Bugg greatly admired the Captain's fervent piety, and bidding him God-speed, turned off.

Captain Suggs "struck for" the swamp sure enough, where his horse was already hitched. "Ef them fellers aint done to a cracklin," he muttered to himself as he mounted, "*I*'ll never bet on two pair agin! They're peart at the snap game, theyselves; but they're badly lewed this hitch! Well! Live and let live is a good old motter, and it's my sentiments adzactly!" And giving the spur to his horse, off he cantered.

Zora Neale Hurston

(1891–1960)

Now recognized as one of the major black writers of her time, Hurston was born and raised in Eatonville, Florida, a small, all-black community in the middle of the state. Her father was a Baptist preacher, a carpenter, and mayor of Eatonville, and her mother a former teacher. After her mother's death in 1912, Hurston lived with various relatives before she set out on her own as a wardrobe assistant with a Gilbert & Sullivan repertory group, to earn money for her studies. When her job ended, she entered Morgan Academy in Maryland, and, in 1918, she began studying at Howard University in Washington, D.C. During the early 1920s, she established herself in New York, where she became known as a writer of short stories right at the high tide of the Harlem Renaissance. In New York, she worked for a period as a live-in secretary to Fannie Hurst. Aided by Mrs. Annie Nathan Meyer, the first of several patrons, she received a scholarship at Barnard College. One of the first black students to be enrolled at Barnard, she finished her B.A. in 1928. Shortly after graduating, and with the encouragement of the Columbia University anthropologist Franz Boas, she won a grant to study black folklore in the South. She traveled to Florida and to Louisiana, and collected the pieces for her remarkable book of folklore, Mules and Men, *published in 1935. During the 1930s, she wrote three highly praised novels,* Jonah's Gourd Vine *(1934),* Their Eyes Were Watching God *(1937), and* Moses, Man of the Mountain *(1939). The first was based on her life in Eatonville, and all three display her extraordinary knowledge of black culture and black speech. Despite her considerable accomplishments, as a novelist, folklorist, and journalist, and despite her high standing among other members of the "Renaissance," she was hounded by problems of money and recognition. In her later years, almost penniless, and largely ignored, even by her former friends, she lived in Florida, became an ardent political conservative, and went from one odd*

223

*job to another. Her last home was in Fort Pierce, Florida, where
she attempted to return to her writing, and where she was befriended
by several local sympathizers, including the Florida artist A. E.
Backus and journalists Marjorie Silver Adler and Anne Wilder. She
died in the St. Lucie Welfare Home. Her autobiography,* Dust
Tracks on a Road *(1942), is a fine introduction to her life and
works. "The Gilded Six-Bits" first appeared in* Story *(August 1933).*

THE GILDED SIX-BITS

❊

It was a Negro yard around a Negro house in a Negro settlement
that looked to the payroll of the G and G Fertilizer works for its
support.

But there was something happy about the place. The front yard
was parted in the middle by a sidewalk from gate to door-step, a
sidewalk edged on either side by quart bottles driven neck down
into the ground on a slant. A mess of homey flowers planted
without a plan but blooming cheerily from their helter-skelter
places. The fence and house were whitewashed. The porch and
steps scrubbed white.

The front door stood open to the sunshine so that the floor of
the front room could finish drying after its weekly scouring. It was
Saturday. Everything clean from the front gate to the privy house.
Yard raked so that the strokes of the rake would make a pattern.
Fresh newspaper cut in fancy edge on the kitchen shelves.

Missie May was bathing herself in the galvanized washtub in the
bedroom. Her dark-brown skin glistened under the soapsuds that
skittered down from her wash rag. Her stiff young breasts thrust
forward aggressively like broad-based cones with the tips lacquered
in black.

She heard men's voices in the distance and glanced at the dollar
clock on the dresser.

"Humph! Ah'm way behind time t'day! Joe gointer be heah
'fore Ah git mah clothes on if Ah don't make haste."

She grabbed the clean meal sack at hand and dried herself hurriedly and began to dress. But before she could tie her slippers,
there came the ring of singing metal on wood. Nine times.

Missie May grinned with delight. She had not seen the big tall man come stealing in the gate and creep up the walk grinning happily at the joyful mischief he was about to commit. But she knew that it was her husband throwing silver dollars in the door for her to pick up and pile beside her plate at dinner. It was this way every Saturday afternoon. The nine dollars hurled into the open door, he scurried to a hiding place behind the cape jasmine bush and waited.

Missie May promptly appeared at the door in mock alarm.

"Who dat chunkin' money in mah do'way?" she demanded. No answer from the yard. She leaped off the porch and began to search the shrubbery. She peeped under the porch and hung over the gate to look up and down the road. While she did this, the man behind the jasmine darted to the china berry tree. She spied him and gave chase.

"Nobody ain't gointer be chunkin' money at me and Ah not do 'em nothin'," she shouted in mock anger. He ran around the house with Missie May at his heels. She overtook him at the kitchen door. He ran inside but could not close it after him before she crowded in and locked with him in a rough and tumble. For several minutes the two were a furious mass of male and female energy. Shouting, laughing, twisting, turning, tussling, tickling each other in the ribs; Missie May clutching onto Joe and Joe trying, but not too hard, to get away.

"Missie May, take yo' hand out mah pocket!" Joe shouted out between laughs.

"Ah ain't, Joe, not lessen you gwine gimme whateve' it is good you got in yo' pocket. Turn it go, Joe, do Ah'll tear yo' clothes."

"Go on tear 'em. You de one dat pushes de needles round heah. Move yo' hand Missie May."

"Lemme git dat paper sack out yo' pocket. Ah bet its candy kisses."

"Tain't. Move yo' hand. Woman ain't got no business in a man's clothes nohow. Go way."

Missie May gouged way down and gave an upward jerk and triumphed.

"Unhhunh! Ah got it. It 'tis so candy kisses. Ah knowed you had somethin' for me in yo' clothes. Now Ah got to see whut's in every pocket you got."

Joe smiled indulgently and let his wife go through all of his pockets and take out the things that he had hidden there for her to find. She bore off the chewing gum, the cake of sweet soap, the pocket handkerchief as if she had wrested them from him, as if they had not been bought for the sake of this friendly battle.

"Whew! dat play-fight done got me all warmed up," Joe exclaimed. "Got me some water in de kittle?"

"Yo' water is on de fire and yo' clean things is cross de bed. Hurry up and wash yo'self and git changed so we kin eat. Ah'm hongry." As Missie said this, she bore the steaming kettle into the bedroom.

"You ain't hongry, sugar," Joe contradicted her. "Youse jes' a little empty. Ah'm de one whut's hongry. Ah could eat up camp meetin', back off 'ssociation, and drink Jurdan dry. Have it on de table when Ah git out de tub."

"Don't you mess wid mah business, man. You git in yo' clothes. Ah'm a real wife, not no dress and breath. Ah might not look lak one, but if you burn me, you won't git a thing but wife ashes."

Joe splashed in the bedroom and Missie May fanned around in the kitchen. A fresh red and white checked cloth on the table. Big pitcher of buttermilk beaded with pale drops of butter from the churn. Hot fried mullet, crackling bread, ham hock atop a mound of string beans and new potatoes, and perched on the window-sill a pone of spicy potato pudding.

Very little talk during the meal but that little consisted of banter that pretended to deny affection but in reality flaunted it. Like when Missie May reached for a second helping of the tater pone. Joe snatched it out of her reach.

After Missie May had made two or three unsuccessful grabs at the pan, she begged, "Aw, Joe gimme some mo' dat tater pone."

"Nope, sweetenin' is for us men-folks. Y'all pritty lil frail eels don't need nothin' lak dis. You too sweet already."

"Please, Joe."

"Naw, naw. Ah don't want you to git no sweeter than whut you is already. We goin' down de road a lil piece t'night so you go put on yo' Sunday-go-to-meetin' things."

Missie May looked at her husband to see if he was playing some prank. "Sho nuff, Joe?"

"Yeah. We goin' to de ice cream parlor."

"Where de ice cream parlor at, Joe?"

"A new man done come heah from Chicago and he done got a place and took and opened it up for a ice cream parlor, and bein' as it's real swell, Ah wants you to be one de first ladies to walk in dere and have some set down."

"Do Jesus, Ah ain't knowed nothin' 'bout it. Who de man done it?"

"Mister Otis D. Slemmons, of spots and places—Memphis, Chicago, Jacksonville, Philadelphia and so on."

"Dat heavy-set man wid his mouth full of gold teethes?"

"Yeah. Where did you see 'im at?"

"Ah went down to de sto' tuh git a box of lye and Ah seen 'im standin' on de corner talkin' to some of de mens, and Ah come on back and went to scrubbin' de floor, and he passed and tipped his hat whilst Ah was scourin' de steps. Ah thought Ah never seen *him* befo'."

Joe smiled pleasantly. "Yeah, he's up to date. He got de finest clothes Ah ever seen on a colored man's back."

"Aw, he don't look no better in his clothes than you do in yourn. He got a puzzlegut on 'im and he so chuckle-headed, he got a pone behind his neck."

Joe looked down at his own abdomen and said wistfully, "Wisht Ah had a build on me lak he got. He ain't puzzle-gutted, honey. He jes' got a corperation. Dat make 'm look lak a rich white man. All rich mens is got some belly on 'em."

"Ah seen de pitchers of Henry Ford and he's a spare-built man and Rockefeller look lak he ain't got but one gut. But Ford and Rockefeller and dis Slemmons and all de rest kin be as many-gutted as dey please, Ah'm satisfied wid you jes' lak you is, baby. God took pattern after a pine tree and built you noble. Youse a pritty man, and if Ah knowed any way to make you mo' pritty still Ah'd take and do it."

Joe reached over gently and toyed with Missie May's ear. "You jes' say dat cause you love me, but Ah know Ah can't hold no light to Otis D. Slemmons. Ah ain't never been nowhere and Ah ain't got nothin' but you."

Missie May got on his lap and kissed him and he kissed back in kind. Then he went on. "All de womens is crazy 'bout 'im every-where he go."

"How you know dat, Joe?"

"He tole us so hisself."

"Dat don't make it so. His mouf is cut cross-ways, ain't it? Well, he kin lie jes' lak anybody else."

"Good Lawd, Missie! You womens sho is hard to sense into things. He's got a five-dollar gold piece for a stick-pin and he got a ten-dollar gold piece on his watch chain and his mouf is jes' crammed full of gold teethes. Sho wisht it wuz mine. And whut make it so cool, he got money 'cumulated. And womens give it all to 'im."

"Ah don't see whut de womens see on 'im. Ah wouldn't give 'im a wink if de sheriff wuz after 'im."

"Well, he tole us how de white womens in Chicago give 'im all dat gold money. So he don't 'low nobody to touch it at all. Not even put dey finger on it. Dey tole 'im not to. You kin make 'miration at it, but don't tetch it.''

"Whyn't he stay up dere where dey so crazy 'bout 'im?"

"Ah reckon dey done made 'im vast-rich and he wants to travel some. He say dey wouldn't leave 'im hit a lick of work. He got mo' lady people crazy 'bout him than he kin shake a stick at.''

"Joe, Ah hates to see you so dumb. Dat stray nigger jes' tell y'all anything and y'all b'lieve it.''

"Go 'head on now, honey and put on yo' clothes. He talkin' 'bout his pritty womens—Ah want 'im to see *mine*.''

Missie May went off to dress and Joe spent the time trying to make his stomach punch out like Slemmons' middle. He tried the rolling swagger of the stranger, but found that his tall bone-and-muscle stride fitted ill with it. He just had time to drop back into his seat before Missie May came in dressed to go.

On the way home that night Joe was exultant. "Didn't Ah say ole Otis was swell? Can't he talk Chicago talk? Wuzn't dat funny whut he said when great big fat ole Ida Armstrong come in? He asted me, 'Who is dat broad wid de forte shake?' Dat's a new word. Us always thought forty was a set of figgers but he showed us where it means a whole heap of things. Sometimes he don't say forty, he jes' say thirty-eight and two and dat mean de same thing. Know whut he tole me when Ah wuz payin' for our ice cream? He say, 'Ah have to hand it to you, Joe. Dat wife of yours is jes' thirty-eight and two. Yessuh, she's forte!' Ain't he killin'?''

"He'll do in case of a rush. But he sho is got uh heap uh gold on 'im. Dat's de first time Ah ever seed gold money. It lookted good on him sho nuff, but it'd look a whole heap better on you.''

"Who, me? Missie May youse crazy! Where would a po' man lak me git gold money from?''

Missie May was silent for a minute, then she said, "Us might find some goin' long de road some time. Us could.''

"Who would be losin' gold money round heah? We ain't even seen none dese white folks wearin' no gold money on dey watch chain. You must be figgerin' Mister Packard or Mister Cadillac goin' pass through heah.''

"You don't know whut been lost 'round heah. Maybe somebody way back in memorial times lost they gold money and went on off and it ain't never been found. And then if we wuz to find it, you could wear some 'thout havin' no gang of womens lak dat Slemmons say he got.''

Joe laughed and hugged her. "Don't be so wishful 'bout me. Ah'm satisfied de way Ah is. So long as Ah be yo' husband, Ah don't keer 'bout nothin' else. Ah'd ruther all de other womens in de world to be dead than for you to have de toothache. Less we go to bed and git our night rest.''

It was Saturday night once more before Joe could parade his wife in Slemmons' ice cream parlor again. He worked the night shift and Saturday was his only night off. Every other evening around six o'clock he left home, and dying dawn saw him hustling home around the lake where the challenging sun flung a flaming sword from east to west across the trembling water.

That was the best part of life—going home to Missie May. Their white-washed house, the mock battle on Saturday, the dinner and ice cream parlor afterwards, church on Sunday nights when Missie out-dressed any woman in town—all, everything was right.

One night around eleven the acid ran out at the G and G. The foreman knocked off the crew and let the steam die down. As Joe rounded the lake on his way home, a lean moon rode the lake in a silver boat. If anybody had asked Joe about the moon on the lake, he would have said he hadn't paid it any attention. But he saw it with his feelings. It made him yearn painfully for Missie. Creation obsessed him. He thought about children. They had been married more than a year now. They had money put away. They ought to be making little feet for shoes. A little boy child would be about right.

He saw a dim light in the bedroom and decided to come in through the kitchen door. He could wash the fertilizer dust off himself before presenting himself to Missie May. It would be nice for her not to know that he was there until he slipped into his place in bed and hugged her back. She always liked that.

He eased the kitchen door open slowly and silently, but when he went to set his dinner bucket on the table he bumped it into a pile of dishes, and something crashed to the floor. He heard his wife gasp in fright and hurried to reassure her.

"Iss me, honey. Don't git skeered."

There was a quick, large movement in the bedroom. A rustle, a thud, and a stealthy silence. The light went out.

What? Robbers? Murderers? Some varmint attacking his help-less wife, perhaps. He struck a match, threw himself on guard and stepped over the door-sill into the bedroom.

The great belt on the wheel of Time slipped and eternity stood still. By the match light he could see the man's legs fighting with his breeches in his frantic desire to get them on. He had both chance and time to kill the intruder in his helpless condition—half in and half out of his pants—but he was too weak to take action. The shapeless enemies of humanity that live in the hours of Time had waylaid Joe. He was assaulted in his weakness. Like Samson awakening after his haircut. So he just opened his mouth and laughed.

The match went out and he struck another and lit the lamp. A howling wind raced across his heart, but underneath its fury he heard his wife sobbing and Slemmons pleading for his life. Offering to buy it with all that he had. "Please, suh, don't kill me. Sixty-two dollars at de sto'. Gold money."

Joe just stood. Slemmons looked at the window, but it was screened. Joe stood out like a rough-backed mountain between him and the door. Barring him from escape, from sunrise, from life.

He considered a surprise attack upon the big clown that stood there laughing like a chessy cat. But before his fist could travel an inch, Joe's own rushed out to crush him like a battering ram. Then Joe stood over him.

"Git into yo' damn rags, Slemmons, and dat quick."

Slemmons scrambled to his feet and into his vest and coat. As he grabbed his hat, Joe's fury overrode his intentions and he grabbed at Slemmons with his left hand and struck at him with his right. The right landed. The left grazed the front of his vest. Slemmons was knocked a somersault into the kitchen and fled through the open door. Joe found himself alone with Missie May, with the golden watch charm clutched in his left fist. A short bit of broken chain dangled between his fingers.

Missie May was sobbing. Wails of weeping without words. Joe stood, and after awhile he found out that he had something in his hand. And then he stood and felt without thinking and without seeing with his natural eyes. Missie May kept on crying and Joe kept on feeling so much and not knowing what to do with all his feelings, he put Slemmons' watch charm in his pants pocket and took a good laugh and went to bed.

"Missie May, whut you cryin' for?"

"Cause Ah love you so hard and Ah know you don't love *me* no mo'."

Joe sank his face into the pillow for a spell then he said huskily, "You don't know de feelings of dat yet, Missie May."

"Oh Joe, honey, he said he wuz gointer give me dat gold money and he jes' kept on after me—"

Joe was very still and silent for a long time. Then he said, "Well, don't cry no mo', Missie May. Ah got yo' gold piece for you."

The hours went past on their rusty ankles. Joe still and quiet on one bed-rail and Missie May wrung dry of sobs on the other. Finally the sun's tide crept upon the shore of night and drowned all its hours. Missie May with her face stiff and streaked towards the window saw the dawn come into her yard. It was day. Nothing more. Joe wouldn't be coming home as usual. No need to fling open the front door and sweep off the porch, making it nice for Joe. Never no more breakfast to cook; no more washing and starching of Joe's jumper-jackets and pants. No more nothing. So why get up?

With this strange man in her bed, she felt embarrassed to get up and dress. She decided to wait till he had dressed and gone. Then she would get up, dress quickly and be gone forever beyond reach of Joe's looks and laughs. But he never moved. Red light turned to yellow, then white.

From beyond the no-man's land between them came a voice. A strange voice that yesterday had been Joe's.

"Missie May, ain't you gonna fix me no breakfus'?"

She sprang out of bed. "Yeah, Joe. Ah didn't reckon you wuz hongry."

No need to die today. Joe needed her for a few more minutes anyhow.

Soon there was a roaring fire in the cook stove. Water bucket full and two chickens killed. Joe loved fried chicken and rice. She didn't deserve a thing and good Joe was letting her cook him some breakfast. She rushed hot biscuits to the table as Joe took his seat.

He ate with his eyes in his plate. No laughter, no banter.

"Missie May, you ain't eatin' yo' breakfus'."

"Ah don't choose none, Ah thank yuh."

His coffee cup was empty. She sprang to refill it. When she turned from the stove and bent to set the cup beside Joe's plate, she saw the yellow coin on the table between them.

She slumped into her seat and wept into her arms.

Presently Joe said calmly, "Missie May, you cry too much. Don't look back lak Lot's wife and turn to salt."

The sun, the hero of every day, the impersonal old man that beams as brightly on death as on birth, came up every morning and raced across the blue dome and dipped into the sea of fire every evening. Water ran down hill and birds nested.

Missie knew why she didn't leave Joe. She couldn't. She loved him too much, but she could not understand why Joe didn't leave her. He was polite, even kind at times, but aloof.

There were no more Saturday romps. No ringing silver dollars to stack beside her plate. No pockets to rifle. In fact the yellow coin in his trousers was like a monster hiding in the cave of his pockets to destroy her.

She often wondered if he still had it, but nothing could have induced her to ask nor yet to explore his pockets to see for herself. Its shadow was in the house whether or no.

One night Joe came home around midnight and complained of pains in the back. He asked Missie to rub him down with liniment. It had been three months since Missie had touched his body and it all seemed strange. But she rubbed him. Grateful for the chance. Before morning, youth triumphed and Missie exulted. But the next day, as she joyfully made up their bed, beneath her pillow she found the piece of money with the bit of chain attached.

Alone to herself, she looked at the thing with loathing, but look she must. She took it into her hands with trembling and saw first thing that it was no gold piece. It was a gilded half dollar. Then she knew why Slemmons had forbidden anyone to touch his gold. He trusted village eyes at a distance not to recognize his stick-pin as a gilded quarter, and his watch charm as a four-bit piece.

She was glad at first that Joe had left it there. Perhaps he was through with her punishment. They were man and wife again. Then another thought came clawing at her. He had come home to buy from her as if she were any woman in the long house. Fifty cents for her love. As if to say that he could pay as well as Slemmons. She slid the coin into his Sunday pants pocket and dressed herself and left his house.

Half way between her house and the quarters she met her husband's mother, and after a short talk she turned and went back home. Never would she admit defeat to that woman who prayed for it nightly. If she had not the substance of marriage she had the outside show. Joe must leave *her*. She let him see she didn't want his old gold four-bits too.

She saw no more of the coin for some time though she knew that Joe could not help finding it in his pocket. But his health kept poor, and he came home at least every ten days to be rubbed.

The sun swept around the horizon, trailing its robes of weeks and days. One morning as Joe came in from work, he found Missie May chopping wood. Without a word he took the ax and chopped a huge pile before he stopped.

"You ain't got no business choppin' wood, and you know it."

"How come? Ah been choppin' it for de last longest."

"Ah ain't blind. You makin' feet for shoes."

"Won't you be glad to have a lil baby chile, Joe?"

"You know dat 'thout astin' me."

"Iss gointer be a boy chile and de very spit of you."

"You reckon, Missie May?"

"Who else could it look lak?"

Joe said nothing, but he thrust his hand deep into his pocket and fingered something there.

It was almost six months later Missie May took to bed and Joe went and got his mother to come wait on the house.

Missie May was delivered of a fine boy. Her travail was over when Joe came in from work one morning. His mother and the old women were drinking great bowls of coffee around the fire in the kitchen.

The minute Joe came into the room his mother called him aside.

"How did Missie May make out?" he asked quickly.

"Who, dat gal? She strong as a ox. She gointer have plenty mo'. We done fixed her wid de sugar and lard to sweeten her for de nex' one."

Joe stood silent awhile.

"You ain't ast 'bout de baby, Joe. You oughter be mighty proud cause he sho is de spittin' image of yuh, son. Dat's yourn all right, if you never git another one, dat un is yourn. And you know Ah'm mighty proud too, son, cause Ah never thought well of you marryin' Missie May cause her ma used tuh fan her foot round right smart and Ah been mighty skeered dat Missie May wuz gointer git misput on her road."

Joe said nothing. He fooled around the house till late in the day then just before he went to work, he went and stood at the foot of the bed and asked his wife how she felt. He did this every day during the week.

On Saturday he went to Orlando to make his market. It had been a long time since he had done that.

Meat and lard, meal and flour, soap and starch. Cans of corn and tomatoes. All the staples. He fooled around town for awhile and bought bananas and apples. Way after while he went around to the candy store.

"Hello, Joe," the clerk greeted him. "Ain't seen you in a long time."

"Nope, Ah ain't been heah. Been round in spots and places."

"Want some of them molasses kisses you always buy?"

"Yessuh." He threw the gilded half dollar on the counter. "Will dat spend?"

"Whut is it, Joe? Well, I'll be doggone! A gold-plated four-bit piece. Where'd you git it, Joe?"

"Offen a stray nigger dat come through Eatonville. He had it on his watch chain for a charm—goin' round making out iss gold money. Ha ha! He had a quarter on his tie pin and it wuz all golded up too. Tryin' to fool people. Makin' out he so rich and everything. Ha! Ha! Tryin' to tole off folkses wives from home."

"How did you git it, Joe? Did he fool you, too?"

"Who, me? Naw suh! He ain't fooled me none. Know whut Ah done? He come round me wid his smart talk. Ah hauled off and knocked 'im down and took his old four-bits way from 'im. Gointer buy my wife some good ole lasses kisses wid it. Gimme fifty cents worth of dem candy kisses."

"Fifty cents buys a mighty lot of candy kisses, Joe. Why don't you split it up and take some chocolate bars, too. They eat good, too."

"Yessuh, dey do, but Ah wants all dat in kisses. Ah got a lil boy chile home now. Tain't a week old yet, but he kin suck a sugar tit and maybe eat one them kisses hisself."

Joe got his candy and left the store. The clerk turned to the next customer. "Wisht I could be like these darkies. Laughin' all the time. Nothin' worries 'em."

Back in Eatonville, Joe reached his own front door. There was the ring of singing metal on wood. Fifteen times. Missie May couldn't run to the door, but she crept there as quickly as she could.

"Joe Banks, Ah hear you chunkin' money in mah do'way. You wait till Ah got mah strength back and Ah'm gointer fix you for dat."

John Pendleton Kennedy

(1795–1870)

Born in Baltimore, Maryland, Kennedy was able to look at the South from both within and without. His mother came from a family of Virginia planters, and Kennedy spent his summers among his Virginia relatives on their farms and plantations. His Irish-born father was a wealthy merchant whose business failed while Kennedy was preparing himself for the university. Abandoning his plans to enter Princeton, he attended college in Baltimore instead. He fought briefly in the War of 1812 and on his return to Baltimore he finished his law studies. For the rest of his life, he was to earn his living as a lawyer and as a state and national legislator. His career as a writer—though he never considered himself a full-time profes-sional—began with a series of satirical pieces in a local paper The Red Book, *which he edited and published with a friend. His major works were written during the 1830s, when sectional politics began to dominate American life. His first book,* Swallow Barn *(1832), a leisurely narration of plantation life in the form of impressions sent home by a Northern visitor, combines the genial irony Kennedy admired in 18th-century English writers with a frank appreciation of the planter's old-fashioned independence and good humor.* Swal-low Barn *is sometimes considered the first of the "plantation school" of popular Southern fiction, but it is far superior to later works by such writers as William Alexander Caruthers and John Esten Cooke, and never sinks to their levels of chivalrous mannerism and cloying charm. In 1835, Kennedy published* Horse-Shoe Robinson, *a his-torical romance of the American Revolution, and, in 1838,* Rob of the Bowl, *another historical romance, this time of colonial Mary-land of the 17th century. Thereafter, his political life overshadowed his writing, though he remained a well-known literary figure until his death. He was a good friend of Washington Irving and of William Makepeace Thackeray, and he helped Thackeray with his novel* The Virginians. *He also befriended Edgar Allan Poe and found him a*

235

job on The Southern Literary Messenger. *In 1840, Kennedy published* Quodlibet, *a satire on Jacksonian democracy, and, in 1842, he finished his biographical study* Memoirs of the Life of William Wirt. *In the years before the Civil War, Kennedy spoke out against the secessionist movement, and he sided with the Union when the hostilities began. Other than the works already mentioned, his books include:* The Defense of the Whigs *(1844),* Mr. Ambrose's Letters on the Rebellion *(1865), and three posthumous collections—*At Home and Abroad *(1872),* Occasional Addresses *(1872), and* Political and Official Papers *(1872). "A Legend of Maryland" was first read before the Maryland Institute, then published in* The Southern Literary Messenger *in March 1857. In final form, it appeared in* The Atlantic Monthly *(July and August 1860).*

A LEGEND OF MARYLAND

❁

"An Owre True Tale"

The framework of modern history is, for the most part, constructed out of the material supplied by national transactions described in official documents and contemporaneous records. Forms of government and their organic changes, the succession of those who have administered them, their legislation, wars, treaties, and the statistics demonstrating their growth or decline,—these are the elements that furnish the outlines of history. They are the dry timbers of a vast old edifice; they impose a dry study upon the antiquary, and are still more dry to his reader.

But that which makes history the richest of philosophies and the most genial pursuit of humanity is the spirit that is breathed into it by the thoughts and feelings of former generations, interpreted in actions and incidents that disclose the passions, motives, and ambition of men, and open to us a view of the actual life of our forefathers. When we can contemplate the people of a past age employed in their own occupations, observe their habits and manners, comprehend their policy and their methods of pursuing it, our imagination is quick to clothe them with the flesh and blood of human brotherhood and to bring them into full sympathy with

our individual nature. History then becomes a world of living figures,—a theatre that presents to us a majestic drama, varied by
alternate scenes of the grandest achievements and the most touching episodes of human existence.

In the composing of this drama the author has need to seek his
material in many a tangled thicket as well as in many an open
field. Facts accidentally encountered, which singly have but little
perceptible significance, are sometimes strangely discovered to il-
lustrate incidents long obscured and incapable of explanation.
They are like the lost links of a chain, which, being found, supply
the means of giving cohesion and completeness to the heretofore
useless fragments. The scholar's experience is full of these reunions
of illustrative incidents gathered from regions far apart in space,
and often in time. The historian's skill is challenged to its highest
task in the effort to draw together those tissues of personal and
local adventure which, at first without seeming or suspected dependence, prove, when brought into their proper relationship with
each other, to be unerring exponents of events of highest concern.

It is pleasant to fall upon the course of one of these currents of
adventure,—to follow a solitary rivulet of tradition, such as by
chance we now and then find modestly flowing along through the
obscure coverts of time, and to be able to trace its progress to
the confidence of other streams,—and finally to see it grow, by
the aid of these tributaries, to the proportions of an ample river,
which waters the domain of authentic history and bears upon its
bosom a clear testimony to the life and character of a people.

The following legend furnishes a striking and attractive exem-
plification of such a growth, in the unfolding of a romantic passage
of Maryland history, of which no annalist has ever given more than
an ambiguous and meagre hint. It refers to a deed of bloodshed,
of which the only trace that was not obliterated from living rumor
so long as a century ago was to be found in a vague and misty relic
of an old memory of the provincial period of the State. The facts
by which I have been enabled to bring it to the full light of an
historical incident, it will be seen in the perusal of this narrative,
have successively, and by most curious process of development,
risen into view through a series of accidental discoveries, which
have all combined, with singular coincidence and adaptation, to
furnish an unquestionable chapter of Maryland history, altogether
worthy of recital for its intrinsic interest, and still more worthy of
preservation for the elements it supplies towards a correct estimate
of the troubles which beset the career and formed the character
and manners of the forefathers of the State.

1

TALBOT'S CAVE

It is now many years ago,—long before I had reached manhood,—that, through my intimacy with a friend, then venerable for his years and most attractive to me by his store of historical knowledge, I became acquainted with a tradition touching a strange incident that had reference to a mysterious person connected with a locality on the Susquehanna River near Havre de Grace. In that day the tradition was repeated by a few of the oldest inhabitants who dwelt in the region. I dare say it has now entirely run out of all remembrance amongst their descendants, and that I am, perhaps, the only individual in the State who has preserved any traces of the facts to which I allude.

There was, until not long ago, a notable cavern at the foot of a rocky cliff about a mile below the town of Port Deposit. It was of small compass, yet sufficiently spacious to furnish some rude shelter against the weather to one who might seek refuge within its solitary chamber. It opened upon the river just where a small brook comes brattling down the bank, along the base of a hill of some magnitude that yet retains the stately name of Mount Ararat. The visitor of this cavern might approach it by a boat from the river, or by a rugged path along the margin of the brook and across the ledges of the rock. This rough shelter went by the name of Talbot's Cave down to a very recent period, and would still go by that name, if it were yet in existence. But it happened, not many years since, that Port Deposit was awakened to a sudden notion of the value of the granite of the cliff, and, as commerce is a most ruthless contemner of all romance, and never hesitates between a speculation of profit and a speculation of history, Talbot's Cave soon began to figure conspicuously in the Price Current, and in a very little while disappeared, like a witch from the stage, in blasts of sulphur fire and rumbling thunder, under the management of those effective scene-shifters, the quarrymen. A government contract, more potent than the necromancy of the famed wizard Michael Scott, lifted this massive rock from its base, and, flying with it full two hundred miles, buried it fathoms below the surface of the Atlantic, at the Rip Raps, near Hampton Roads; and thus it happens that I cannot vouch the ocular proof of the Cave to certify the legend I am about to relate.

The tradition attached to this spot had nothing but a misty and spectral outline. It was indefinite in the date, uncertain as to persons, mysterious as to the event,—just such a tradition as to whet the edge of one's curiosity and to leave it hopeless of gratification. I may relate it in a few words.

Once upon a time, somewhere between one and two hundred years ago, there was a man by the name of Talbot, a kinsman of Lord Baltimore, who had committed some crime, for which he fled and became an outlaw and was pursued by the authorities of the Province. To escape these, he took refuge in the wilderness on the Susquehanna, where he found this cave, and used it for concealment and defence for some time,—how long, the tradition does not say. This region was then inhabited by a fierce tribe of Indians, who are described on Captain John Smith's map as the "Sasquesahannocks," and who were friendly to the outlaw and supplied him with provisions. To these details was added another, which threw an additional interest over the story,—that Talbot had a pair of beautiful English hawks, such as were most prized in the sport of falconry, and that these were the companions of his exile, and were trained by him to pursue and strike the wild duck that abounded, then as now, on this part of the river; and he thus found amusement to beguile his solitude, as well as sustenance in a luxurious article of food, which is yet the pride of gastronomic science, and the envy of *bons vivants* throughout this continent.

These hawks my aged friend had often himself seen, in his own boyish days, sweeping round the cliffs and over the broad expanse of the Susquehanna. They were easily distinguished, he said, by the residents of that district, by their peculiar size and plumage, being of a breed not known to our native ornithology, and both being males. For many years, it was affirmed,—long after the outlaw had vanished from the scene,—these gallant old rovers of the river still pursued their accustomed game, a solitary pair, without kindred or acquaintance in our woods. They had survived their master,—no one could tell how long,—but had not abandoned the haunts of his exile. They still for many a year saw the wilderness beneath their daily flight giving place to arable fields, and learned to exchange their wary guard against the Indian's arrow for a sharper watch of the Anglo-Saxon rifle. Up to the last of their appearance the country-people spoke of them as Talbot's hawks.

This is a summary of the story, as it was told to me. No inquiry brought me any addition to these morsels of narrative. Who this Talbot was,—what was his crime,—how long he lived in this cave, and at what era,—were questions upon which the oracle of my tradition was dumb.

Such a story would naturally take hold of the fancy of a lover of romance, and kindle his zeal for an enterprise to learn something more about it; and I may reasonably suppose that this short sketch has already stirred the bosoms of the novel-reading portion, at least, of my readers with a desire that I should tell them what, in my later researches, I have found to explain this legend of the Cave. Even the outline I have given is suggestive of inferences to furnish quite a plausible chapter of history.

First, it is clear, from the narrative, that Talbot was a gentleman of rank in the old Province,—for he was kinsman to the Lord Proprietary; and there is one of the oldest counties of Maryland that bears the name of his family,—perhaps called so in honor of himself. Then he kept his hawks, which showed him to be a man of condition, and fond of the noble sport which figures so gracefully in the annals of Chivalry.

Secondly, this hawking carries the period of the story back to the time of one of the early Lords Baltimore; for falconry was not common in the eighteenth century: and yet the date could not have been much earlier than that century, because the hawks had been seen by old persons of the last generation somewhere about the period of our Revolution; and this bird does not live much over a hundred years. So we fix a date not far from sixteen hundred and eighty for Talbot's sojourn on the river.

Thirdly, the crime for which he was outlawed could scarcely have been a mean felony, perpetrated for gain, but more likely some act of passion,—a homicide, probably, provoked by a quarrel, and enacted in hot blood. This Talbot was too well conditioned for a sordid crime; and his flight to the wilderness and his abode there would seem to infer a man of strong purpose and self-reliance.

And, lastly, as he must have had friends and confederates on the frontier, to aid him in his concealment, and to screen him from the pursuit of the government officers, and, moreover, had made himself acceptable to the Indians, to whose power he had committed himself, we may conclude that he possessed some winning points of character; and I therefore assume him to have been of a brave, frank, and generous nature, capable of attracting partisans and enlisting the sympathies and service of bold men for his personal defence.

So, with the help of a little obvious speculation, founded upon the circumstantial evidence, we weave the network of quite a natural story of Talbot; and our meagre tradition takes on the form, and something of the substance, of an intelligible incident.

2

STRANGE REVELATIONS

At this point I leave the hero of my narrative for a while, in order that I may open another chapter.

Many years elapsed, during which the tradition remained in this unsatisfactory state, and I had given up all hope of further elucidation of it, when an accidental discovery brought me once more upon the track of inquiry.

There was published in the city of Baltimore, in the year 1808, a book whose title was certainly as little adapted to awaken the attention of one in quest of a picturesque legend as a treatise on Algebra. It was called "The Landholder's Assistant," and was intended, as its name imported, to assist that lucky portion of mankind who possessed the soil of Maryland in their pursuit of knowledge touching the mysteries of patents, warrants, surveys, and such like learning, necessary to getting land or keeping what they had. The character and style of this book, in its exterior aspect, were as unpromising as its title. It was printed by Messrs. Dobbin & Murphy, on rather dark paper, in a muddy type,—such as no Mr. Dobbin nor Mr. Murphy of this day would allow to bear his imprimatur,—though in 1808, I doubt not, it was considered a very creditable piece of Baltimore typography. This unpretending volume was compiled by Chancellor Kilty. It is a very instructive book, containing much curious matter, is worthy of better adornment in the form of its presentation to the world, and ought to have a title more suggestive of its antiquarian lore. I should call it "Fossil Remains of Old Maryland Law, with Notes by an Antiquary."

It fell into my hands by a purchase at auction, some twenty years after I had abandoned the Legend of the Cave and the Hawks as a hopeless quest. In running over its contents, I found that a Colonel George Talbot was once the Surveyor-General of Maryland; and in two short marginal notes (the substance of which I afterwards found in Chalmers's "Annals") it was said that "he was noted in the Province for the murder committed by him on Christopher Rousby, Collector of the Customs,"—the second note adding that this was done on board a vessel in Patuxent River, and that Talbot "was conveyed for trial to Virginia, from whence he made his escape; and after being retaken, and" (as the author expresses his belief) "tried and convicted, was finally pardoned by King James the Second."

These marginal notes, though bringing no clear support to the story of the Cave, were embers, however, of some old fire not entirely extinct, which emitted a feeble gleam upon the path of inquiry. The name of the chief actor coincided with that of the tradition; the time, that of James the Second, conformed pretty nearly to my conjecture derived from the age of the hawks; and the nature of the crime was what I had imagined. There was just enough in this brief revelation to revive the desire for further investigation. But where was the search to be made? No history that I was aware of, no sketch of our early time that I had ever seen, nothing in print was known to be in existence that could furnish a clue to the story of the Outlaw's Cave.

And here the matter rested again for some years. But after this lapse, chance brought me upon the highway of further development, which led me in due time to a strange realization of the old proverb that "Murder will out,"—though, in this case, its discovery could bring no other retribution than the settlement of an historical doubt, and give some posthumous fame to the subject of the disclosure.

In the month of May, 1836, I had a motive and an opportunity to make a visit to the County of St. Mary's. I had been looking into the histories of our early Maryland settlement, as they are recounted in the pages of Bozman, Chalmers, and Grahame, and found there some inducements to persuade me to make an exploration of the whereabouts of the old city which was planted near the Potomac by our first pilgrims. Through the kindness of a much valued friend, whose acquirements and taste—both highly cultivated—rendered him a most effective auxiliary in my enterprise, I was supplied with an opportunity to spend a week under the hospitable roof of Mr. Carberry, the worthy Superior of the Jesuit House of St. Inigoes on the St. Mary's River, within a short distance of the plain of the ancient city.

Mr. Campbell and myself were invited by our host to meet him, on an appointed day, at the Church of St. Nicholas on the Patuxent, near the landing at Town Creek, and we were to travel from there across to St. Inigoes in his carriage,—a distance of about fifteen miles.

Upon our arrival at St. Nicholas, we found a full day at our disposal to look around the neighborhood, which, being the scene of much historical interest in our older annals, presented a pleasant temptation to our excursion. Our friendly guide, Mr. Carberry, took us to Drum Point, the southern headland of the Patuxent at its entrance into Chesapeake Bay. Here was, at that time, and perhaps still is, the residence of the Carroll family, whose ancestors occupied the estate for many generations. The dwelling-house was a comfortable wooden building of the style and character of the present day, with all the appurtenances proper to a convenient and pleasant country homestead. Immediately in its neighborhood—so near that it might be said to be almost within the curtilage of the dwelling—stood an old brick ruin of what had apparently been a substantial mansion-house. Such a monument of the past as this, of course, could not escape our special attention, and, upon inquiry, we were told that it was once, a long time ago, the family home of the Rousbys, the ancestors of the present occupants of the estate; that several generations of this family, dating back to the early days of the Province, had resided in it; and that when it had fallen into decay, the modern building was erected, and the old one suffered to crumble into the condition in which we saw it. I could easily understand and appreciate the sentiment that preserved it untouched as part and parcel in the family associations of the place, and as a relic of the olden time which no one was willing to disturb.

The mention of the name of the Rousbys, here on the Patuxent River, was a sudden and vivid remembrancer to me of the old story of Talbot, and gave new encouragement to an almost abandoned hope of solving this mystery.

3

A GRAVEYARD AND AN EPITAPH

Within a short distance of this spot, perhaps not a mile from Drum Point, there is a small creek which opens into the river and bears the name of Mattapony. In early times there was a notable fort here, and connected with it a stately mansion, built by Charles Calvert, Lord Baltimore, for his own occasional residence. The fort and mansion are often mentioned in the Provincial records as the place where the Council sometimes met to transact business; and accordingly many public acts are dated from Mattapony.

Calvert was doubtless attracted to this spot by the pleasant scenery of the headland which here looks out upon the noble waterview of the Chesapeake, and by its breezy position as an agreeable refuge from the heats of summer.

Our party, therefore, determined to set out upon a search for some relics of the mansion and fort; and as a guide in this enterprise, we engaged an old negro who seemed to have a fair claim in his own conceit to be regarded both as the Solomon and the Methuselah of the plantation. He was a wrinkled, wise-looking old fellow, with a watery eye and a grizzled head, and might, perhaps, have been about eighty; but, from his own account, he left us to infer that he was not much behind that great patriarch of Scripture whose years are described as one hundred and threescore and fifteen.

Finding that he was native to the estate, and had lived here all his life, we interrogated him with some confidence in his ability to contribute something useful to the issue of our pursuit. Amongst all the Solomons of this world, there is not one so consciously impressed with the unquestionable verity of his wisdom and the intensity of his knowledge as one of these veterans of an old family-estate upon which he has spent his life. He is always an aristocrat of the most uncompromising stamp, and has a contemptuous disdain and intolerance for every form of democracy. Poor white people have not the slightest chance of his good opinion. The pedigree and history of his master's family possess an epic dignity in his imagination; and the liberty he takes with facts concerning them amounts to a grand poetical hyperbole. He represents their wealth in past times to have amounted to something of a fabulous superfluity, and their magnificence so unbounded, that he stares at you in describing it, as if its excess astonished himself.

When we now questioned our venerable conductor, to learn what he could tell us of the old Proprietary Mansion, he said, in his way, he "membered it, as if it was built only yesterday: he was fotch up so near it, that he could see it now as if it was standing before him: if *he* couldn't pint out where it stood, it was time for him to give up: it was a mighty grand brick house,"—laying an emphasis on *brick,* as a special point in his notion of its grandeur; and then he added, with all the gravity of which his very solemn visage was a copious index, that "Old Master Baltimore, who built it, was a real fine gentleman. He knowed him so well! He never gave anything but gold to the servants for tending on him. Bless you! he wouldn't even think of silver! Many a time has he given me a guinea for waiting on him."

This account of Old Master Baltimore, and his magnificent contempt of silver, and the intimacy of our patriarch with him, rather startled us, and I began to fear that the story of the house might turn out to be as big a lie as the acquaintance with the Lord Proprietary,—for Master Baltimore had then been dead just one hundred and twenty-one years. But we went on with him, and were pleasantly disappointed when he brought us upon a hill that sloped down to the Mattapony, and there traced out for us, by the depression of the earth, the visible lines of an old foundation of a large building, the former existence of which was further demonstrated by some scattered remains of the old imported brick of the edifice which were imbedded in the soil.

This spot had a fine outlook upon the Bay, and every advantage of locality to recommend its choice for a domestic establishment. We could find nothing to indicate the old fort except the commanding character of the hill with reference to the river, which might warrant a conjecture as to its position. I believe that the house was included within the ramparts of the fortification, as I perceive in some of the old records that the fortification itself was called the Mattapony House, which was once beleaguered and taken by Captain John Coode and Colonel Jowles.

After we had examined all that was to be seen here, our next point of interest was a graveyard, which, we had been informed by some of the household at Mrs. Carroll's, had been preserved upon the estate from a very early period. Our old gossip professed to know all about this, from its very first establishment. It was in another direction from the mansion-house, about a mile distant, on the margin of an inlet from the Bay, called Harper's Creek; and thither we accordingly went. Before we reached the spot, the old negro stopped at a cabin that lay in our route and provided himself with a hoe, which, borne upon his shoulder, gave a somewhat mysterious significance to the office he had assumed. He did not explain the purpose of this equipment to us, and we forbore to question him. After descending to the level of the tide and passing through some thickets of wild shrubbery, we arrived upon a grassy plain immediately upon the border of the creek; and there, in a quiet, sequestered nook of rural landscape, the smooth and sluggish little inlet begirt with water-lilies and reflecting wood and sky and the green hill-side upon its surface, was the chosen resting-place of the departed generations of the family. A few simple tombstones—some of them darkened by the touch of Time—lay clustered within an old inclosure. The brief memorials engraved upon them told us how inveterately Death had pursued his ancient vocation and gathered in his relentless tribute from young and old in times past as he does to-day.

Here was a theme for a sermon from the patriarch, who now leaned upon his hoe and shook his head with a slow ruminative motion, as if he hoped by this action to disengage from it some profound moral reflections, and then began to enumerate how many of these good people he had helped to bury; but before he had well begun this discourse we had turned away and were about leaving the place, when he recalled us by saying, "I have got one tombstone yet to show you, as soon as I can clear it off with the hoe: it belongs to old Master Rousby, who was stobbed aboard ship, and is, besides that, the grandest tombstone here."

Here was another of those flashes of light by which my story seemed to be preordained to a prosperous end. We eagerly encouraged the old man to this task, and he went to work in removing the green sod from a large slab which had been entirely hidden under the soil, and in a brief space revealed to us a tombstone fully six feet long, upon which we were able to read, in plainly chiselled letters, an inscription surmounted by a carved heraldic shield with its proper quarterings and devices.

Our group at this moment would have made a fine artistic study. There was this quiet landscape around us garnished with the beauty of May; there were the rustic tombs,—the old negro, with a countenance surcharged with the expression of solemn satisfaction at his employment, bending his aged figure over the broad, carved stone, and scraping from it the grass which had not been disturbed perhaps for a quarter of a century; and there was our own party looking on with eager interest, as the inscription every moment became more legible. That interest may be imagined, on reading the inscription, which, when brought to the full light of day, revealed these words:—

"Here lyeth the body of Xph^r Rousbie Esquire, who was taken out of this world by a violent death received on board his Majesty's ship The Quaker Ketch, Capt. Thos. Allen Commander, the last day of October 1684. And also of M^r. John Rousbie, his brother, who departed this naturall life on board the Ship Baltimore, being arrived in Patuxen the first day of February 1685."

This was a picturesque incident in its scenic character, but a still more engaging one as an occurrence in the path of discovery. Here was most unexpectedly brought to view a new link in the chain of our story. It was a pleasant surprise to have such a fact as this breaking upon us from an ambuscade, to help out a half-formed narrative which I had feared was hopeless of completion. The inscription is a necessary supplement to the marginal notes. As an insulated monument, it is meagre in its detail, and stands in need of explanation. It does not describe Christopher Rousby as the Collector of the Customs; it does not affirm that he was murdered; it makes no allusion to Talbot: but it gives the name of the ship and its commander, along with the date of the death. "The Landholder's Assistant" supplies all the facts that are wanting in this brief statement. These two memorials help each other and enlarge the common current of testimony, like two confluent streams coming from opposite sources. From the two together we learn that

Colonel Talbot, the Surveyor-General in 1684, killed Mr. Christopher Rousby on board of a ship of war; and we are apprised that Rousby was a gentleman of rank and authority in the Province, holding an important commission from the King. The place at which the tomb is found shows also that he was the owner of a considerable landed estate and a near neighbor of the Lord Proprietary.

The story, however, requires much more circumstance to give it the interest which we hope yet to find in it.

4

DRYASDUST

I have now to change my scene, and to pursue in another quarter more important investigations. I break off with some regret from my visit to St. Mary's, because it had many attractions of its own, which would form a pleasant theme for description. Some of the results of that visit I embodied, several years ago, in a fiction which I fear the world will hardly credit me in saying has as much history in it as invention.* But my journey had no further connection with the particular subject before us, after the discovery of the tomb. I therefore take my leave, at this juncture, of good Father Carberry and St. Inigoes, and also of my companion in this adventure,—pausing but a moment to say, that the Superior of St. Inigoes has, some time since, gone to his account, and that I am not willing to part with him in my narrative without a grateful recognition of the esteem I have for his memory, in which I share with all who were acquainted with him,—an esteem won by the simple, unostentatious merit of his character, his liberal religious sentiment, and his frank and cordial hospitality, which had the best flavor of the good old housekeeping of St. Mary's,—a commendation which every one conversant with that section of Maryland will understand to imply what the Irish schoolmaster, in one of Carleton's tales, calls "the hoighth of good living."

After my return from this excursion, I resolved to make a search amongst the records at Annapolis, to ascertain whether any memorials existed which might furnish further information in regard to the events to which I had now got a clue. And here comes in a morsel of official history which will excuse a short digression.

The Legislature had, about this time, directed the Executive to

---

*Rob of the Bowl.

cause a search through the government buildings, with a view to the discovery of old state papers and manuscripts, which, having been consigned, time out of mind, to neglect and oblivion, were known only as heaps of promiscuous lumber, strewed over the floors of damp cellars and unfrequented garrets. The careless and unappreciative spirit of the proper guardians of our archives in past years had suffered many precious folios and separate papers to be disposed of as mere rubbish; and the not less culpable and incurious indolence of their successors, in our own times, had treated them with equal indifference. The attention of the Legislature was awakened to the importance of this investigation by Mr. David Ridgely, the State Librarian, and he was appointed by the Executive to undertake the labor. Never did beagle pursue the chase with more steady foot than did this eager and laudable champion of the ancient fame of the State his chosen duty. He rummaged old cuddies, closets, vaults, and cocklofts, and pried into every recess of the Chancery, the Land Office, the Committee-Rooms, and the Council-Chamber, searching up-stairs and down-stairs, wherever a truant paper was supposed to lurk. Groping with lantern in hand and body bent, he made his way through narrow passages, startling the rats from their fastnesses, where they had been intrenched for half a century, and breaking down the thick drapery—the Gobelin tapestry I might call it—woven by successive families of spiders from the days of the last Lord Proprietary. The very dust which was kicked up in Annapolis, as the old newspapers tell us, at the passage of the Stamp Act, was once more set in motion by the foot of this resolute and unwearied invader, and everywhere something was found to reward the toil of the search. But the most valuable discoveries were made in the old Treasury,— made, alas! too late for the full fruition of the Librarian's labor. The Treasury, one of the most venerable structures in the State, is that lowly and quaint little edifice of brick which the visitor never fails to notice within the inclosure of the State-House grounds. It was originally designed for the accommodation of the Governor and his Council, and for the sessions of the Upper House of the Provincial Legislature; the Burgesses, at that time, holding their meetings in the old State House, which occupied the site of the present more imposing and capacious building: this latter having been erected about the year 1772.

In some dark recess of the Treasury Office Mr. Ridgely struck upon a mine of wealth, in a mouldy wooden box, which was found to contain many missing Journals of the Provincial Council, some of which bore date as far back as 1666. It was a sad disappointment to him, when his eye was greeted with the sight of these folios, to see them crumble, like the famed Dead-Sea Apples, into powder, upon every attempt to handle them. The form of the books was preserved and the character of the writing distinctly legible, but, from the effect of moisture, the paper had lost its cohesion, and fell to pieces at every effort to turn a leaf. I was myself a witness to this tantalizing deception, and, with the Librarian, read enough to show the date and character of the perishing record.

Through this accident, the Council Journals of a most interesting period, embracing several years between 1666 and 1692, were irretrievably lost. Others sustained less damage, and were partially preserved. Some few survived in good condition.

Our Maryland historians have had frequent occasion to complain of the deficiency of material for the illustration of several epochs in the Provincial existence, owing to the loss of official records. No research has supplied the means of describing the public events of these intervals, beyond some few inferences, which are only sufficient to show that these silent periods were marked by incidents of important interest. The most striking of these privations occurs towards the end of the seventeenth century,—precisely that period to which the crumbling folios had reference.

This loss of the records has been ascribed to their frequent removals during periods of trouble, and to the havoc made in the rage of parties. The Province, like the great world from which it was so far remote, was distracted with what are sometimes called religious quarrels, but what I prefer to describe as exceedingly irreligious quarrels, carried on by men professing to be Christians, and generated in the heat of disputes concerning the word of the great Teacher of "peace on earth." Out of these grew any quantity of rebellion and war, tinctured with their usual flavor of persecution. For at this era the wars of Christendom were chiefly waged in support of dogmas and creeds, and took a savage hue from the fury of religious bigotry. The wars of Europe since that period have arisen upon commercial and political questions, and religion has been freed from the dishonor of promoting these bloody strifes so incompatible with its high office. In these quarrels of the fathers of Maryland, the archives of government were seized more than once, and, perhaps, destroyed. On one occasion they were burnt. And so, amongst all these disorders, it has fallen out that the full development of the State history has been rendered impossible.

Mr. Ridgely's foray, however, into this domain of dust and darkness has happily rescued much useful matter to aid the future chronicler in supplying the deficiency of past attempts to trace the path of our modest annals through these silent intervals. Incidentally the Librarian's work has assisted my story; for, although the recovered folios did not touch the exact year of my search, the pursuit of them led me to what I may claim as a discovery of my own. I found what I could not say was wholly lost, but what, until Mr. Ridgely's exploration drew attention to the records, might have been said to have shrunk from all notice of the present generation, and to be fast falling a prey to the tooth of time and the visit of the worm. A few years more of neglect and the ill usage of careless custodians, and it would have passed to that depository of things lost upon the earth, which fable has placed in the moon. It was my good fortune, in this upturning of relics of the past, to lay my hand upon a sadly tattered and decayed MS. volume,— unbound, without beginning and without end, coated with the dust which had been gathering upon it ever since Chalmers and Bozman had done their work of deciphering its quaint old text. It lay in the state of rubbish, in an old case, where many documents of the same kind had been consigned to the same oblivion, and with it had been sleeping for as many years, perhaps, as the Beauty in the fairy tale,—happily destined, at last, to be awakened, as she was, by one who by his perseverance had won a title to herself.

This manuscript was now, in this day of revival, brought out from its hiding-place, and, upon inspection, proved to be a Journal of the Council for some few years including the very date of the death of the Collector on the Patuxent.

The record was complete, neatly written in the peculiar manuscript character of that age, so difficult for a modern reader to decipher. Its queer old-fashioned spelling suggested the idea that our ancestors considered both consonants and vowels too weak to stand alone, and that therefore they doubled them as often as they could; and there was such an actual identification of its antiquity in its exterior aspect as well as in its forms of speech, that, when I have sat poring over it alone at midnight in my study, as I have often done, I have turned my eye over my shoulder, expecting to see the apparition of Master John Llewellin—who subscribes his name with a very energetic flourish as Clerk of the Council— standing behind me in grave-colored doublet and trunk-hose, with a starched ruff, a wide-awake hat drawn over his brow, and a short black feather falling amongst the locks of his dark hair towards his back.

This Journal lets in a blaze of light upon the old tradition of Talbot's Cave. The narrative of what it discloses it is now my purpose to make as brief as is compatible with common justice to my subject.

5

A FRAGMENT OF HISTORY

Charles Calvert, Lord Baltimore, the son of Cecilius, was, according to the testimony of all our annalists, a worthy gentleman and an upright ruler. He was governor of Maryland, by the appointment of his father, from 1662 to 1675, and after that became the Lord Proprietary by inheritance, and administered the public affairs in person. His prudence and judgment won him the esteem of the best portion of his people, and the Province prospered in his hands.

All our histories tell of the troubles that beset the closing years of his residence in Maryland. They arose partly out of his religion, and in part out of the jealousy of the crown concerning the privileges of his charter.

He was a Roman Catholic; but, like his father, liberal and tolerant in opinion, and free from sectarian bias in the administration of his government. Apart from the influence of his father's example, the training of his education, his real attachment to the interests of the Province, and his own natural inclination,—all of which pointed out to him the duty as well as the advantage of affording the utmost security to the freedom of religious opinion,—the conditions under which he held his proprietary rights rendered a departure from this policy the most improbable accusation that could be made against him. The public mind of England at that period was fevered to a state of madness by the domestic quarrel that raged within the kingdom against the Catholics. The people were distracted with constant alarms of Popish plots for the overthrow of the government. The King, a heartless profligate, absorbed in frivolous pleasures, scarcely entertained any grave question of state affairs that had not some connection with his hatreds and his fears of Catholics and Dissenters. Then, also, the Province itself was composed, in far the greater part, of a Protestant population,—computed by some contemporary writers at the proportion of thirty to one,—a population who were guarantied freedom of conscience by the Charter, and who possessed all necessary power both legal and physical to enforce it.

Under such circumstances as these, how is it possible to impute designs against the old established toleration, which had marked the history of Maryland from its first settlement to that day, to so prudent and careful a ruler as Charles Calvert, without imputing to him, at the same time, a folly so absurd as to belie every opinion that has ever been uttered to his advantage?

Yet, notwithstanding these improbabilities, the accusation was made and affected to be believed by the King and his Council; the result of which was that a royal order was sent to the Proprietary, commanding him to dismiss every Catholic from employment in the Province, and to supply their places by the appointment of Protestants.

The most plausible theory upon which I can account for this harsh proceeding is suggested by the fact that parties in the Province took the same complexion with those in the mother country and ran parallel with them,—that the same excitements which agitated the minds of the people in England were industriously fomented here, where no similar reason for them existed, as the volunteer work of demagogues who saw in them the means of promoting their own interest,—that, in fact, this opposition to the Proprietary grew out of a failing in our ancestors which has not yet been cured in their descendants, a weakness in favor of the loaves and fishes. The party in the majority carried the elections, and felt, of course, as all parties do who perform such an exploit, that they had made a very gigantic sacrifice for the good of the country and deserved to be remunerated for such an act of heroism, and thereupon set up and asserted that venerable doctrine which has been erroneously and somewhat vaingloriously claimed as the conception of a modern statesman, namely,—"that to the victors belong the spoils." I rejoice in the discovery that a dogma so profound and so convenient has the sanction of antiquity to commend it to the platform of the patriots of our own time.

I must in a few words notice another charge against Lord Baltimore, which was even more serious than the first, and to which the cupidity of the King lent a willing ear. Parliament had passed an act for levying certain duties on the trade of the Southern Colonies, which were very oppressive to the commerce of Maryland. These duties were gathered by Collectors specially appointed for the occasion, who held their commissions from the Crown, and who were stationed at the several ports of entry of the Province. The frequent evasion of these duties gave rise to much ill-will between the Collectors and the people. Lord Baltimore was charged with having connived at these evasions, and with obstructing the collection of the royal revenue. His chief accusers were the Collectors, who, being Crown officers, seemed naturally to array themselves against him. Although there was really no foundation for this complaint, yet the King, who never threw away a chance to replenish his purse, compelled the Proprietary to pay by way of retribution a large sum into the Exchequer.

I have no need to dwell upon this subject, and have referred to it only because it explains the relation between Lord Baltimore and Christopher Rousby, and has therefore some connection with my story. Rousby was an enemy to the Proprietary; and from a letter preserved by Chalmers it appears there was no love lost between them. Lord Baltimore writes to the Earl of Anglesey, the President of the King's Council, in 1681,—"I have already written twice to your Lordship about Christopher Rousby, who I desired might be removed from his place of Collector of his Majesty's Customs,—he having been a great knave, and a disturber of the trade and peace of the Province"; which letter, it seems, had no effect,—as Christopher Rousby was continued in his post. He was doubtless emboldened by the failure of this remonstrance against him to exhibit his ill-will towards the Proprietary in more open and more vexatious modes of annoyance.

All these embarrassments threw a heavy shadow over the latter years of Lord Baltimore's life, and now drove him to the necessity of making a visit to England for the purpose of personal explanation and defence before the King. He accordingly took his departure in the month of June, 1684, intending to return in a few months; but a tide of misfortune that now set in upon him prevented that wish, and he never saw Maryland again.

In about half a year after Calvert's arrival in England, King Charles the Second was gathered to his fathers, and his brother, the Duke of York, a worse man, a greater hypocrite, and a more crafty despot, reigned in his stead.

James the Second was a Roman Catholic, and Calvert, on that score alone, might have expected some sympathy and favor: he might, at least, have expected justice. But James was heartless and selfish. The Proprietary found nothing but cold neglect, and a contemptible jealousy of the prerogatives and power conferred by his charter. James himself claimed to be a proprietary on this continent by virtue of extensive royal grants, and was directly interested with William Penn in defeating the claims of the Baltimore family to the country upon the Delaware; he was, therefore, in fact, the secret and prepossessed enemy of Calvert. Instead of protection from the Crown, Calvert found proceedings instituted in the King's Bench to annul his charter, which, but for the abrupt termination of this short, disgraceful reign in abdication and flight, would have been consummated under James's own direction. The Revolution of 1688 brought up other influences more hostile still to the Proprietary; and the Province, which was always sedulous to follow the fashions of London, was not behindhand on this occasion, but made, also, its revolution, in imitation of the great one. The end of all was the utter subversion of the Charter, and a new government of Maryland under a royal commission. How this was accomplished our historians are not able to tell. From 1688 to 1692 is one of our dark intervals of which I have spoken. It begins with a domestic revolution and ends with the appointment of a Royal Governor, and that is pretty nearly all we know about it. After this, there was no Proprietary dominion in Maryland, until it was restored upon the accession of George the First in 1715, when it reappears in the second Charles Calvert, a minor, the grandson of the late Proprietary. This gentleman was the son of Benedict Leonard Calvert, and was educated in the Protestant faith, which his father had adopted as more consonant with the prosperity of the family and the hopes of the Province.

Before Lord Baltimore took his departure, he made all necessary arrangements for the administration of the government during his absence. The chief authority he invested in his son Benedict Leonard, to whom I referred just now,—at that time a youth of twelve or fourteen years of age. My old record contains the commission issued on this occasion, which is of the most stately and royal breadth of phrase, and occupies paper enough to make a deed for the route of the Pacific Railroad. In this document "our dearly beloved son Benedict Leonard Calvert" is ordained and appointed to be "Lieutenant General, Chief Captain, Chief Governor and Commander, Chief Admiral both by sea and land, of our Province of Maryland, and of all our Islands, Territories, and Dominions whatsoever, and of all and singular our Castles, Forts, Fortresses, Fortifications, Munitions, Ships, and Navies in our said Province, Islands, Territories, and Dominions aforesaid."

I hope to be excused for the particularity of my quotation of this young gentleman's titles, which I have given at full length only by way of demonstration of the magnificence of our old Palatine Province of Maryland, and to excite in the present generation a becoming pride at having fallen heirs to such a principality; albeit Benedict Leonard's more recent successors to these princely prerogatives may have reason to complain of that relentless spirit of democracy which has shorn them of so many worshipful honors. But we republicans are philosophical, and can make sacrifices with a good grace.

As it was quite impossible for this young Lieutenant General to go alone under such a staggering weight of dignities, the same commission puts him in leading-strings by the appointment of nine Deputy or Lieutenant Governors who are charged with the execution of all his duties. The first-named of these deputies is "our dearly beloved Cousin," Colonel George Talbot, who is associated with "our well-beloved Counsellor," Thomas Tailler, Colonel Vincent Low, Colonel Henry Darnall, Colonel William Digges, Colonel William Stevens, Colonel William Burgess, Major Nicholas Sewall, and John Darnall, Esquire. These same gentlemen, with Edward Pye and Thomas Truman, are also commissioned to be of the Privy Council, "for and in relation to all matters of State."

These appointments being made and other matters disposed of, Charles Calvert took leave of his beautiful and favorite Maryland, never to see this fair land again.

6

A BORDER CHIEFTAIN

I have now to pursue the narrative of my story as I find the necessary material in the old Council Journal. I shall not incumber this narrative with literal extracts from these proceedings, but give the substance of what I find there, with such illustration as I have been able to glean from other sources.

Colonel George Talbot, whom we recognize as the first-named in the commission of the nine Deputy Governors and of the Privy Council, seems to have been a special favorite of the Proprietary. He was the grandson of the first Baron of Baltimore, the Secretary of State of James the First. His father was an Irish baronet, Sir George Talbot, of Cartown in Kildare, who had married Grace, one of the younger sisters of Cecilius, the second Proprietary and father of Charles Calvert. He was, therefore, as the commission describes him, the cousin of Lord Baltimore, who had now invested him with a leading authority in the administration of the government.

He was born in Ireland, and from some facts connected with his history I infer that he did not emigrate to Maryland until after his marriage, his wife being an Irish lady.

That he was a man of consideration in the Province, with large experience in its affairs, is shown by the character of the employments that were intrusted to him. He had been, for some years before the departure of Lord Baltimore on his visit to England, a conspicuous member of his Council. He had, for an equal length of time, held the post of Surveyor-General, an office of high responsibility and trust. But his chief employment was of a military nature, in which his discretion, courage, and conduct were in constant requisition. He had the chief command, with the title and commission of Deputy Governor, over the northern border of the

Province, a region continually exposed to the inroads of the fierce and warlike tribe of the "Sasquesahannocks."

The country lying between the Susquehanna and the Delaware, that which now coincides with parts of Harford and Cecil Counties in Maryland and the upper portion of the State of Delaware, was known in those days as New Ireland, and was chiefly settled by emigrants from the old kingdom whose name it bore. This region was included within the range of Talbot's command, and was gradually increasing in population and in farms and houses scattered over a line of some seventy or eighty miles from east to west, and slowly encroaching upon the thick wilderness to the north, where surly savages lurked and watched the advance of the white man with jealous anger.

The tenants of this tract held their lands under the Proprietary grants, coupled with a condition, imposed as much by their own necessities as by the law, to render active service in the defence of the frontier as a local militia. They were accordingly organized on a military establishment, and kept in a state of continual preparation to repel the unwelcome visits of their hostile neighbors.

A dispute between Lord Baltimore and William Penn, founded upon the claim of the former to a portion of the territory bounding on the Delaware, had given occasion to border feuds, which had imposed upon our Proprietary the necessity of building and maintaining a fort on Christiana Creek, near the present city of Wilmington; and there were also some few block-houses or smaller fortified strongholds along the line of settlement towards the Susquehanna. These forts were garrisoned by a small force of musketeers maintained by the government. The Province was also at the charge of a regiment of cavalry, of which Talbot was the Colonel, and parts of which were assigned to the defence of this frontier.

If we add to these a corps of rangers, who were specially employed in watching and arresting all trespassers upon the territory of the Province, it will complete our sketch of the military organization of the frontier over which Talbot had the chief command. The whole or any portion of this force could be assembled in a few hours to meet the emergencies of the time. Signals were established for the muster of the border. Beacon fires on the hills, the blowing of horns, and the despatch of runners were familiar to the tenants, and often called the ploughman away from the furrow to the appointed gathering-place. Three musket-shots fired in succession from a lonely cabin, at dead of night, awakened the sleeper in the next homestead; the three shots, repeated from house to house, across this silent waste of forest and field, carried the alarm onward; and before break of day a hundred stout yeomen, armed with cutlass and carbine, were on foot to check and punish the stealthy foray of the Sasquesahannock against the barred and bolted dwellings where mothers rocked their children to sleep, confident in the protection of this organized and effective system of defence.

In this region Talbot himself held a manor which was called New Connaught, and here he had his family mansion, and kept hospitality in rude woodland state, as a man of rank and command, with his retainers and friends gathered around him. This establishment was seated on Elk River, and was, doubtless, a fortified position. I picture to my mind a capacious dwelling-house built of logs from the surrounding forest; its ample hall furnished with implements of war, pikes, carbines, and basket-hilted swords, mingled with antlers of the buck, skins of wild animals, plumage of birds, and other trophies of the hunter's craft; the large fireplace surrounded with hardy woodsmen, and the tables furnished with venison, wild fowl, and fish, the common luxuries of the region, in that prodigal profusion to which our forefathers were accustomed, and which their descendants still regard as the essential condition of hearty and honest housekeeping. This mansion I fancy surrounded by a spacious picketed rampart, presenting its bristling points to the four quarters of the compass, and accessible only through a gateway of ponderous timber studded thick with nails: the whole offering defiance to the grim savage who might chance to prowl within the frown of its midnight shadow.

Here Talbot spent the greater portion of the year with his wife and children. Here he had his yacht or shallop on the river, and often skimmed this beautiful expanse of water in pursuit of its abundant game,—those hawks of which tradition preserves the memory his companions and auxiliaries in this pastime. Here, too, he had his hounds and other hunting-dogs to beat up the game for which the banks of Elk River are yet famous.

This sylvan lodge was cheered and refined by the presence of his wife and children, whose daily household occupations were assisted by numerous servants chosen from the warm-hearted people who had left their own Green Isle to find a home in this wilderness.

Amidst such scenes and the duties of her station we may suppose that Mrs. Talbot, a lady who could not but have relinquished many comforts in her native land for this rude life of the forest, found sufficient resource to quell the regrets of many fond memories of the home and friends she had left behind, and to reconcile her to the fortunes of her husband, to whom, as we shall see, she was devoted with an ardor that no hardship or danger could abate.

Being the dispenser of her husband's hospitality,—the bread-giver, in the old Saxon phrase,—the frequent companion of his pastime, and the bountiful friend, not only of the families whose cottages threw up their smoke within view of her dwelling, but of all who came and went on the occasions of business or pleasure in the common intercourse of the frontier, we may conceive the sentiment of respect and attachment she inspired in this insulated district, and the service she was thus enabled to command.

This is but a fancy picture, it is true, of the home of Talbot, which, for want of authentic elements of description, I am forced to draw. It is suggested by the few scattered glimpses we get in the records of his position and circumstances, and may, I think, be received at least as near the truth in its general aspect and characteristic features.

He was undoubtedly a bold, enterprising man,—impetuous, passionate, and harsh, as the incidents of his story show. He was, most probably, a soldier trained to the profession, and may have served abroad, as nearly all gentlemen of that period were accustomed to do. That he was an ardent and uncompromising partisan of the Proprietary in the dissensions of the Province seems to be evident. I suppose him, also, to have been warm-hearted, proud in spirit, and hasty in temper,—a man to be loved or hated by friend or foe with equal intensity. It is material to add to this sketch of him, that he was a Roman Catholic,—as we have record proof that all the Deputy Governors named in the recent commission were, I believe, without exception,—and that he was doubtless imbued with the dislike and indignation which naturally fired the gentlemen of his faith against those who were then supposed to be plotting the overthrow of the Proprietary government, by exciting religious prejudice against the Baltimore family.

7

THE OLD CITY

Let me now once more shift the scene. In the summer of 1684, the peaceful little port of St. Mary's was visited by a phenomenon of rare occurrence in those days. A ship of war of the smaller class, with the Cross of St. George sparkling on her broad flag, came gliding to an anchorage abreast the town. The fort of St. Inigoes gave the customary salute, which I have reason to believe was not returned. Not long after this, a bluff, swaggering, vulgar captain came on shore. He made no visit of respect or business to any member of the Council. He gave no report of his character or the purpose of his visit, but strolled to the tavern,—I suppose to that kept by Mr. Cordea, who, in addition to his calling of keeper of the ordinary, was the most approved shoemaker of the city,—and here regaled himself with a potation of strong waters. It is likely that he then repaired to Mr. Blakiston's, the King's Collector,— a bitter and relentless enemy of the Lord Proprietary,—and there may have met Kenelm Chiseldine, John Coode, Colonel Jowles, and others noted for their hatred of the Calvert family, and in such company as this indulged himself in deriding Lord Baltimore and his government. During his stay in the port, his men came on shore, and, imitating their captain's unamiable temper, roamed in squads about the town and its neighborhood, conducting themselves in a noisy, hectoring manner towards the inhabitants, disturbing the repose of the quiet burghers, and shocking their ears with ribald abuse of the authorities. These roystering sailors—I mention it as a point of historical interest—had even the audacity to break into Alderman Garret Van Swearingen's garden, and to pluck up and carry away his cabbages and other vegetables, and— according to the testimony of Mr. Cordea, whose indignation was the more intense from his veneration for the Alderman, and from the fact that he made his Worship's shoes—they would have killed one of his Worship's sheep, if his (Cordea's) man had not prevented them; and after this, as if on purpose more keenly to lacerate his feelings, they brought these cabbages to Cordea's house, and there boiled them before his eyes,—he being sick and not able to drive them away.

After a few days spent in this manner, the swaggering captain— whose name, it was soon bruited about, was Thomas Allen, of his Majesty's Navy—went on board of his ketch,—or brig, as we should call it,—the Quaker, weighed anchor, and set sail towards the Potomac, and thence stood down the Bay upon the coast of Virginia. Every now and then, after his departure, there came reports to the Council of insults offered by Captain Allen to the skippers of sundry Bay craft and other peaceful traders on the Chesapeake; these insults consisting generally in wantonly compelling them to heave to and submit to his search, in vexatiously detaining them, overhauling their papers, and offending them with coarse vituperation of themselves, as well as of the Lord Proprietary and his Council.

About a month later the Quaker was observed to enter the Patuxent River, and cast anchor just inside of the entrance, near the Calvert County shore, and opposite Christopher Rousby's house at Drum Point. This was—says my chronicle—on Thursday, the 30th of October, in this year 1684. As yet Captain Allen had not condescended to make any report of his arrival in the Province to any officer of the Proprietary.

On Sunday morning, the 2d of November, the city was thrown into a state of violent ebullition—like a little red-hot tea-kettle— by the circulation of a rumor that got wind about the hour the burghers were preparing to go to church. It was brought from Patuxent late in the previous night, and was now whispered from one neighbor to another, and soon came to boil with an extraordinary volume of steam. Stripping it of the exaggeration natural to such an excitement, the rumor was substantially this: That Colonel Talbot, hearing of the arrival of Captain Allen in the Patuxent on Thursday, and getting no message or report from him, set off on Friday morning, in an angry state of mind, and rode over to Patuxent, determined to give the unmannerly captain a lesson upon his duty. That as soon as he reached Mattapony House, he took his boat and went on board the ketch. That there he found Christopher Rousby, the King's Collector, cronying with Captain Allen, and upholding him in his disrespect to the government. That Colonel Talbot was very sharp upon Rousby, not liking him for old grudges, and more moved against him now; and that he spoke his mind both to Captain Allen and Christopher Rousby, and so got into a high quarrel with them. That when he had said all he desired to say to them, he made a move to leave the ketch in his boat, intending to return to Mattapony House; but they who were in the cabin prevented him, and would not let him go. That thereupon the quarrel broke out afresh, and became more bitter; and it being now in the night, and all in a great heat of passion, the parties having already come from words to blows, Talbot drew his skean, or dagger, and stabbed Rousby to the heart. That nothing was known on shore of the affray till Saturday evening, when the body was brought to Rousby's house; after which it became known to the neighborhood; and one of the men of Major Sewall's plantation, which adjoined Rousby's, having thus heard of it, set out and rode that night over to St. Mary's with the news, which he gave to the Major before midnight. It was added, that Colonel Talbot was now detained on board of the ketch, as a prisoner, by Captain Allen.

This was the amount of the dreadful story over which the gossips of St. Mary's were shaking their wise heads and discoursing on "crowner's quest law" that Sunday morning.

As soon as Major Sewall received these unhappy midnight tidings, he went instantly to his colleague, Colonel Darnall, and communicated them to him; and they, being warm friends of Talbot's, were very anxious to get him out of the custody of this Captain Allen. They therefore, on Sunday morning, issued a writ directed to Roger Brooke, the sheriff of Calvert County, commanding him to arrest the prisoner and bring him before the Council. Their next move was to ride over—the same morning—to Patuxent, taking with them Mr. Robert Carvil, and John Llewellin, their secretary. Upon reaching the river, all four went on board the ketch to learn the particulars of the quarrel. These particulars are not preserved in the record; and we have nothing better than our conjectures as to what they disclosed. We know nothing specific of the cause or character of the quarrel. The visitors found Talbot loaded with irons, and Captain Allen in a brutal state of exasperation, swearing that he would not surrender his prisoner to the authorities of the Province, but would carry him to Virginia and deliver him to the government there, to be dealt with as Lord Effingham should direct. He was grossly insulting to the two members of the Council who had come on this inquiry; and after they had left his vessel, in the pinnace, to return to the shore, he affected to believe that they had some concealed force lying in wait to seize the pinnace and its crew, and so ordered them back on board, but after a short detention thought better of it, and suffered them again to depart.

The contumacy of the captain, and the declaration of his purpose to carry away Talbot out of the jurisdiction of the Province within which the crime was committed, and to deliver him to the Governor of Virginia, was a grave assault upon the dignity of the government and a gross contempt of the public authorities, which required the notice of the Council. A meeting of this body was therefore held on the Patuxent, at Rich Neck, on the morning of the 4th of November. I find that five members were present on that occasion. Besides Colonel Darnall and Major Sewall, there were Counsellor Tailler and Colonels Digges and Burgess. Here the matter was debated and ended in a feeble resolve,—that, if this Captain Allen should persist in his contumacy and take Talbot to Virginia, the Council should immediately demand of Lord Effingham his redelivery into this Province. Alas, they could only scold! This resolution was all they could oppose to the bullying captain and the guns of the troublesome little Quaker.

Allen, after hectoring awhile in this fashion, and raising the wrath of the Colonels of the Council until they were red in the cheeks, defiantly took his departure, carrying with him his prisoner, in spite of the vehement indignation of the liegemen of the Province.

We may imagine the valorous anger of our little metropolis at this act or crime of lese-majesty. I can see the group of angry burghers, collected on the porch of Cordea's tavern, in a fume as they listen to Master John Llewellin's account of what had taken place,—Llewellin himself as peppery as his namesake when he made Ancient Pistol eat his leek; and I fancy I can hear Alderman Van Swearingen's choleric explosion against Lord Effingham, supposing his Lordship should presume to slight the order of the Council in respect to Talbot's return.

But these fervors were too violent to last. Christopher Rousby was duly deposited under the greensward upon the margin of Harper's Creek, where I found him safe, if not sound, more than a hundred and fifty years afterwards. The metropolis gradually ceased to boil, and slowly fell to its usual temperature of repose, and no more disturbed itself with thoughts of the terrible captain. Talbot, upon being transferred to the dominion of Virginia, was confined in the jail of Gloucester County, in the old town of Gloucester, on the northern bank of York River.

The Council now opened their correspondence with Lord Effingham, demanding the surrender of their late colleague. On their part, it was marked by a deferential respect, which, it is evident, they did not feel, and which seems to denote a timid conviction of the favor of Virginia and the disgrace of Maryland in the personal feelings of the King. It is manifest they were afraid of giving offence to the lordly governor of the neighboring Province. On the part of Lord Effingham, the correspondence is cavalier, arrogant, and peremptory.

The Council write deploringly to his Lordship. They "pray"— as they phrase it—"in humble, civil, and obliging terms, to have the prisoner safely returned to this government." They add,— "Your Excellency's great wisdom, prudence, and integrity, as well as neighborly affection and kindness for this Province, manifested and expressed, will, we doubt not, spare us the labor of straining for arguments to move your Excellency's consideration to this our so just and reasonable demand." Poor Colonel Darnall, Poor Colonel Digges, and the rest of you Colonels and Majors,—to write such whining hypocrisy as this! George Talbot would not have written to Lord Effingham in such phrase, if one of you had been unlawfully transported to his prison and Talbot were your pleader!

The nobleman to whom this servile language was addressed was a hateful despot, who stands marked in the history of Virginia for his oppressive administration, his arrogance, and his faithlessness.

To give this beseeching letter more significance and the flattery it contained more point, it was committed to the charge of two gentlemen who were commissioned to deliver it in person to his

Lordship. These were Mr. Clement Hill and Mr. Anthony Underwood.

Effingham's answer was cool, short, and admonitory. The essence of it is in these words:—"We do not think it warrantable to comply with your desires, but shall detain Talbot prisoner until his Majesty's particular commands be known therein." A postscript is added of this import:—"I recommend to your consideration, that you take care, as far as in you lies, that, in the matter of the Customs, his Majesty receive no further detriment by this unfortunate accident."

One almost rejoices to read such an answer to the fulsome language which drew it out. This correspondence runs through several such epistles. The Council complain of the rudeness and coarse behavior of Captain Allen, and particularly of his traducing Lord Baltimore's government and attempting to excite the people against it. Lord Effingham professes to disbelieve such charges against "an officer who has so long served his King with fidelity, and who could not but know what was due to his superiors."

Occasionally this same faithful officer, Captain Allen himself, reappears upon the stage. We catch him at a gentleman's house in Virginia, boasting over his cups—for he seems to have paid habitual tribute to a bowl of punch—that he will break up the government of Maryland, and annex this poor little Province of ours to Virginia: a fact worth notice just now, as it makes it clear that annexation is not the new idea of the Nineteenth Century, but lived in very muddy brains a long time ago. I now quit this correspondence to look after a bit of romance in a secret adventure.

8

A PLOT

We must return to the Manor of New Connaught upon the Elk River.

There we shall find a sorrowful household. The Lord of the Manor is in captivity; his people are dejected with a presentiment that they are to see him no more; his wife is lamenting with her children, and counting the weary days of his imprisonment.

> "His hounds they all run masterless,
>   His hawks they flee from tree to tree."

Everything in the hospitable woodland home is changed. November, December, January had passed by since Talbot was lodged in the Gloucester prison, and still no hope dawned upon the afflicted lady. The forest around her howled with the rush of the winter wind, but neither the wilderness nor the winter was so desolate as her own heart. The fate of her husband was in the hands of his enemies. She trembled at the thought of his being forced to a trial for his life in Virginia, where he would be deprived of that friendly sympathy so necessary even to the vindication of innocence, and where he ran the risk of being condemned without defence, upon the testimony of exasperated opponents.

But she was a strong-hearted and resolute woman, and would not despair. She had many friends around her,—friends devoted to her husband and herself. Amongst these was Phelim Murray, a cornet of cavalry under the command of Talbot,—a brave, reckless, true-hearted comrade, who had often shared the hospitality, the adventurous service, and the sports of his commander.

To Murray I attribute the planning of the enterprise I am now about to relate. He had determined to rescue his chief from his prison in Virginia. His scheme required the coöperation of Mrs. Talbot and one of her youngest children,—the pet boy, perhaps, of the family, some two or three years old,—I imagine, the special favorite of the father. The adventure was a bold one, involving many hardships and perils. Towards the end of January, the lady, accompanied by her boy with his nurse, and attended by two Irish men-servants, repaired to St. Mary's, where she was doubtless received as a guest in the mansion of the Proprietary, now the residence of young Benedict Leonard and those of the family who had not accompanied Lord Baltimore to England.

Whilst Mrs. Talbot tarried here, the Cornet was busy in his preparations. He had brought the Colonel's shallop from Elk River to the Patuxent, and was here concerting a plan to put the little vessel under the command of some ostensible owner who might appear in the character of its master to any over-curious or inopportune questioner. He had found a man exactly to his hand in a certain Roger Skreene, whose name might almost be thought to be adopted for the occasion and to express the part he had to act. He was what we may call the sloop's husband, but was bound to do whatever Murray commanded, to ask no questions, and to be profoundly ignorant of the real objects of the expedition. This pliant auxiliary had, like many thrifty—or more probably thriftless—persons of that time, a double occupation. He was amphibious in his habits, and lived equally on land and water. At home he was a tailor, and abroad a seaman, frequently plying his craft

as a skipper on the Bay, and sufficiently known in the latter vocation to render his present employment a matter to excite no
suspicious remark. It will be perceived in the course of his present
adventure that he was quite innocent of any avowed complicity in
the design which he was assisting.

Murray had a stout companion with him, a good friend to Talbot,
probably one of the familiar frequenters of the Manor House of
New Connaught,—a bold fellow, with a hand and a heart both
ready for any perilous service. He may have been a comrade of
the Cornet's in his troop. His name was Hugh Riley,—a name that
has been traditionally connected with dare-devil exploits ever since
the days of Dermot McMorrogh. There have been, I believe, but
few hard fights in the world, to which Irishmen have had anything
to say, without a Hugh Riley somewhere in the thickest part of
them.

The preparations being now complete, Murray anchored his
shallop near a convenient landing,—perhaps within the Mattapony
Creek.

In the dead of winter, about the 30th of January, 1685, Mrs.
Talbot, with her servants, her child, and nurse, set forth from the
Proprietary residence in St. Mary's, to journey over to the Patuxent,—a cold, bleak ride of fifteen miles. The party were all on
horseback: the young boy, perhaps, wrapped in thick coverings,
nestling in the arms of one of the men: Mrs. Talbot braving the
sharp wind in hood and cloak, and warmed by her own warm
heart, which beat with a courageous pulse against the fierce blasts
that swept and roared across her path. Such a cavalcade, of course,
could not depart from St. Mary's without observation at any season; but at this time of the year so unusual a sight drew every
inhabitant to the windows, and set in motion a current of gossip
that bore away all other topics from every fireside. The gentlemen
of the Council, too, doubtless had frequent conference with the
unhappy wife of their colleague, during her sojourn in the Government House, and perhaps secretly counselled with her on her
adventure. Whatever outward or seeming pretext may have been
adopted for this movement, we can hardly suppose that many
friends of the Proprietary were ignorant of its object. We have,
indeed, evidence that the enemies of the Proprietary charged the
Council with a direct connivance in the scheme of Talbot's escape,
and made it a subject of complaint against Lord Baltimore that he
afterwards approved of it.

Upon her arrival at the Patuxent, Mrs. Talbot went immediately
on board of the sloop, with her attendants. There she found the
friendly cornet and his comrade, Hugh Riley, on the alert to dis-

tinguish their loyalty in her cause. The amphibious Master Skreene
was now at the head of a picked crew,—the whole party consisting
of five stout men, with the lady, her child, and nurse. All the men
but Skreene were sons of the Emerald Isle,—of a race whose
historical boast is the faithfulness of their devotion to a friend in
need and their chivalrous courtesy to woman, but still more their
generous and gallant championship of woman in distress. On this
occasion this national sentiment was enhanced when it was called
into exercise in behalf of the sorrowful lady of the chief of their
border settlements.

They set sail from the Patuxent on Saturday, the 31st of January.
On Wednesday, the fifth day afterwards, they landed on the southern bank of the Rappahannock, at the house of Mr. Ralph Wormeley, near the mouth of the river. This long voyage of five days
over so short a distance would seem to indicate that they departed
from the common track of navigation to avoid notice.

The next morning Mr. Wormeley furnished them horses and a
servant, and Mrs. Talbot, with the nurse and child, under the
conduct of Cornet Murray, set out for Gloucester,—a distance of
some twenty miles. The day following,—that is, on Friday,—the
servant returned with the horses, having left the party behind.
Saturday passed and part of Sunday, when, in the evening, Mrs.
Talbot and the Cornet reappeared at Mr. Wormeley's. The child
and nurse had been left behind; and this was accounted for by
Mrs. Talbot's saying she had left the child with his father, to remain
with him until she should return to Virginia. I infer that the child
was introduced into this adventure to give some seeming to the
visit which might lull suspicion and procure easier access to the
prisoner; and the leaving of him in Gloucester proves that Mrs.
Talbot had friends, and probably confederates there, to whose
care he was committed.

As soon as the party had left the shallop, upon their first arrival
at Mr. Wormeley's, the wily Master Skreene discovered that he
had business at a landing farther up the river; and thither he
straightway took his vessel,—Wormeley's being altogether too suspicious a place for him to frequent. And now, when Mrs. Talbot
had returned to Wormeley's, Roger's business above, of course,
was finished, and he dropped down again opposite the house on
Monday evening; and the next morning took the Cornet and the
lady on board. Having done this, he drew out into the river. This
brings us to Tuesday, the 10th of February.

As soon as Mrs. Talbot was once more embarked in the shallop,
Murray and Riley (I give Master Skreene's own account of the
facts, as I find it in his testimony subsequently taken before the

Council) made a pretext to go on shore, taking one of the men with them. They were going to look for a cousin of this man,—so they told Skreene,—and besides that, intended to go to a tavern to buy a bottle of rum: all of which Skreene gives the Council to understand he verily believed to be the real object of their visit.

The truth was, that, as soon as Murray and Riley and their companion had reached the shore, they mounted on horseback and galloped away in the direction of Gloucester prison. From the moment they disappeared on this gallop until their return, we have no account of what they did. Roger Skreene's testimony before the Council is virtuously silent on this point.

After this party was gone, Mrs. Talbot herself took command, and, with a view to more privacy, ordered Roger to anchor near the opposite shore of the river, taking advantage of the concealment afforded by a small inlet on the northern side. Skreene says he did this at her request, because she expressed a wish to taste some of the oysters from that side of the river, which he, with his usual facility, believed to be the only reason for getting into this unobserved harbor; and, merely to gratify this wish, he did as she desired.

The day went by slowly to the lady on the water. Cold February, a little sloop, and the bleak roadstead at the mouth of the Rappahannock brought but few comforts to the anxious wife, who sat muffled upon that unstable deck, watching the opposite shore, whilst the ceaseless plash of the waves breaking upon her ear numbered the minutes that marked the weary hours, and the hours that marked the still more weary day. She watched for the party who had galloped into the sombre pine-forest that sheltered the road leading to Gloucester, and for the arrival of that cousin of whom Murray spoke to Master Skreene.

But if the time dragged heavily with her, it flew with the Cornet and his companions. We cannot tell when the twenty miles to Gloucester were thrown behind them, but we know that the whole forty miles of going and coming were accomplished by sunrise the next morning. For the deposition tells us that Roger Skreene had become very impatient at the absence of his passengers,—at least, so he swears to the Council; and he began to think, just after the sun was up, that, as they had not returned, they must have got into a revel at the tavern, and forgotten themselves; which careless demeanor of theirs made him think of recrossing the river and of going ashore to beat them up; when, lo! all of a sudden, he spied a boat coming round the point within which he lay. And here arises a pleasant little dramatic scene, of some interest to our story.

Mrs. Talbot had been up at the dawn, and watched upon the

deck, straining her sight, until she could see no more for tears; and at length, unable to endure her emotion longer, had withdrawn to the cabin. Presently Skreene came hurrying down to tell her that the boat was coming,—and, what surprised him, there were *four* persons in it. "Who is this fourth man?" he asked her, with his habitual simplicity, "and how are we to get him back to the shore again?"—a very natural question for Roger to ask, after all that had passed in his presence! Mrs. Talbot sprang to her feet,— her eyes sparkling, as she exclaimed, with a cheery voice, "Oh, his cousin has come!"—and immediately ran upon the deck to await the approaching party. There were pleasant smiling faces all around, as the four men came over the sloop's side; and although the testimony is silent as to the fact, there might have been some little kissing on the occasion. The new-comer was in a rough dress, and had the exterior of a servant; and our skipper says in his testimony, that "Mrs. Talbot spoke to him in the Irish language": very volubly, I have no doubt, and that much was said that was never translated. When they came to a pause in this conversation, she told Skreene, by way of interpretation, "he need not be uneasy about the stranger's going on shore, nor delay any longer, as this person had made up his mind to go with them to Maryland."

So the boat was made fast, the anchor was weighed, the sails were set, and the little sloop bent to the breeze and kissed the wave, as she rounded the headland and stood up the Bay, with Colonel George Talbot encircling with his arm his faithful wife, and with the gallant Cornet Murray sitting at his side.

They had now an additional reason for caution against search. So Murray ordered the skipper to shape his course over to the eastern shore, and to keep in between the islands and the main. This is a broad circuit outside of their course; but Roger is promised a reward by Mrs. Talbot, to compensate him for his loss of time; and the skipper is very willing. They had fetched a compass, as the Scripture phrase is, to the shore of Dorset County, and steered inside of Hooper's Island, into the mouth of Hungary River. Here it was part of the scheme to dismiss the faithful Roger from further service. With this view they landed on the island and went to Mr. Hooper's house, where they procured a supply of provisions, and immediately afterwards reëmbarked,—having clean forgotten Roger, until they were once more under full sail up the Bay, and too far advanced to turn back!

The deserted skipper bore his disappointment like a Christian; and being asked, on Hungary River, by a friend who met him there, and who gave his testimony before the Council, "What brought him there?" he replied, "He had been left on the island by Madam Talbot." And to another, "Where Madam Talbot was?" he answered, "She had gone up the Bay to her own house." Then, to a third question, "How he expected his pay?" he said, "He was to have it of Colonel Darnall and Major Sewall; and that Madam Talbot had promised him a hogshead of tobacco extra, for putting ashore at Hooper's Island." The last question was, "What news of Talbot?" and Roger's answer, "He had not been within twenty miles of him; neither did he know anything about the Colonel"!! But, on further discourse, he let fall, that "he knew the Colonel never would come to a trial,"—"that *he* knew this; but neither man, woman, nor child should know it, but those who knew it already."

So Colonel George Talbot is out of the hands of the proud Lord Effingham, and up the Bay with his wife and friends; and is buffeting the wintry head-winds in a long voyage to the Elk River, which, in due time, he reaches in safety.

9

TROUBLES IN COUNCIL

Let us now turn back to see what is doing at St. Mary's.

On the 17th of February comes to the Council a letter from Lord Effingham. It has the superscription, "These, with the greatest care and speed." It is dated on the 11th of February from Poropotanck, an Indian point on the York River above Gloucester, and memorable as being in the neighborhood of the spot where, some sixty years before these events, Pocahontas saved the life of that mirror of chivalry, Captain John Smith.

The letter brings information "that last night [the 10th of February] Colonel Talbot escaped out of prison,"—a subsequent letter says, "by the corruption of his guard,"—and it is full of admonition, which has very much the tone of command, urging all strenuous efforts to recapture him, and particularly recommending a proclamation of "hue and cry."

And now, for a month, there is a great parade in Maryland of proclamation, and hue and cry, and orders to sheriffs and county colonels to keep a sharp look-out everywhere for Talbot. But no person in the Province seems to be anxious to catch him, except Mr. Nehemiah Blakiston, the Collector, and a few others, who seem to have been ministering to Lord Effingham's spleen against the Council for not capturing him. His Lordship writes several letters of complaint at the delay and ill success of this pursuit, and some of them in no measured terms of courtesy. "I admire," he says in one of these, "at any slow proceedings in service wherein his Majesty is so concerned, and hope you will take off all occasions of future trouble, both unto me and you, of this nature, by manifesting yourselves zealous for his Majesty's service." They answer, that all imaginable care for the apprehending of Talbot has been taken by issuing proclamations, etc.,—but all have proved ineffectual, because Talbot upon all occasions flies and takes refuge "in the remotest parts of the woods and deserts of this Province."

At this point we get some traces of Talbot. There is a deposition of Robert Kemble of Cecil County, and some other papers, that give us a few particulars by which I am enabled to construct my narrative.

Colonel Talbot got to his own house about the middle of February,—nearly at the same time at which the news of his escape reached St. Mary's. He there lay warily watching the coming hue and cry for his apprehension. He collected his friends, armed them, and set them at watch and ward, at all his outposts. He had a disguise provided, in which he occasionally ventured abroad. Kemble met him, on the 19th of February, at George Oldfield's, on Elk River; and although the Colonel was disguised in a flaxen wig, and in other ways, Kemble says he knew him by hearing him cough in the night, in a room adjoining that in which Kemble slept. Whilst this witness was at Oldfield's, "Talbot's shallop," he says, "was busking and turning before Oldfield's landing for several hours." The roads leading towards Talbot's house were all guarded by his friends, and he had a report made to him of every vessel that arrived in the river. By way of more permanent concealment, until the storm should blow over, he had made preparations to build himself a cabin, somewhere in the woods out of the range of the thoroughfares of the district. When driven by a pressing emergency which required more than ordinary care to prevent his apprehension, he betook himself to the cave on the Susquehanna, where, most probably, with a friend or two,—Cornet Murray I hope was one of them,—he lay perdu for a few days at a time, and then ventured back to speak a word of comfort and encouragement to the faithful wife who kept guard at home.

In this disturbed and anxious alternation of concealment and flight Talbot passed the winter, until about the 25th of April, when, probably upon advice of friends, he voluntarily surrendered himself to the Council at St. Mary's, and was committed for trial in the provincial Court. The fact of the surrender was communicated to Lord Effingham by the Council, with a request that he would send the witnesses to Maryland to appear at his trial. Hereupon arose another correspondence with his Lordship, which is worthy of a moment's notice. Lord Effingham has lost nothing of his arrogance. He says, on the 12th of May, 1685, "I am so far from answering your desires, that I do hereby demand Colonel Talbot as my prisoner, in the King of England's name, and that you do forthwith convey him into Virginia. And to this my demand I expect your ready performance and compliance, upon your allegiance to his Majesty."

I am happy to read the answer to this insolent letter, in which it will be seen that the spirit of Maryland was waked up on the occasion to its proper voice.—It is necessary to say, by way of explanation to one point in this answer, that the Governor of Virginia had received the news of the accession and proclamation of James the Second, and had not communicated it to the Council in Maryland. The Council give an answer at their leisure, having waited till the 1st of June, when they write to his Lordship, protesting against Virginia's exercising any superintendence over Maryland, and peremptorily refusing to deliver Talbot. They tell him "that we are desirous and conclude to await his Majesty's resolution, [in regard to the prisoner,] which we question not will be agreeable to his Lordship's Charter, and, consequently, contrary to your expectations. In the mean time we cannot but resent in some measure, for we are willing to let you see that we observe, the small notice you seem to take of this Government, (contrary to that amicable correspondence so often promised, and expected by us,) in not holding us worthy to be advised of his Majesty's being proclaimed, without which, certainly, we have not been enabled to do our duty in that particular. Such advice would have been gratefully received by your Excellency's humble servants." Thanks, Colonels Darnall and Digges and you other Colonels and Majors, for this plain outspeaking of the old Maryland heart against the arrogance of the "Right Honorable Lord Howard, Baron of Effingham, Captain General and Chief Governor of his Majesty's Colony of Virginia," as he styles himself! I am glad to see this change of tone, since that first letter of obsequious submission.

Perhaps this change of tone may have had some connection with the recent change on the throne, in which the accession of a Catholic monarch may have given new courage to Maryland, and abated somewhat the confidence of Virginia. If so, it was but a transitory hope, born to a sad disappointment.

The documents afford but little more information.

Lord Baltimore, being in London, appears to have interceded with the King for some favor to Talbot, and writes to the Council on the third of July, "that it formerly was and still is the King's pleasure, that Talbot shall be brought over, in the Quaker Ketch, to England, to receive his trial there; and that, in order thereto, his Majesty had sent his commands to the Governor of Virginia to deliver him to Captain Allen, commander of said ketch, who is to bring him over." The Proprietary therefore directs his Council to send the prisoner to the Governor of Virginia, "to the end that his Majesty's pleasure may be fulfilled."

This letter was received on the 7th of October, 1685, and Talbot was accordingly sent, under the charge of Gilbert Clarke and a proper guard, to Lord Effingham, who gives Clarke a regular business receipt, as if he had brought him a hogshead of tobacco, and appends to it a short apologetic explanation of his previous rudeness, which we may receive as another proof of his distrust of the favor of the new monarch. "I had not been so urgent," he says, "had I not had advices from England, last April, of the measures that were taken there concerning him."

After this my chronicle is silent. We have no further tidings of Talbot. The only hint for a conjecture is the marginal note of "The Landholder's Assistant," got from Chalmers: "He was, I believe," says the note, "tried and convicted, and finally pardoned by James the Second."

This is probably enough. For I suppose him to have been of the same family with that Earl of Tyrconnel equally distinguished for his influence with James the Second as for his infamous life and character, who held at this period unbounded sway at the English Court. I hope, for the honor of our hero, that he preserved no family-likeness to that false-hearted, brutal, and violent favorite, who is made immortal in Macaulay's pages as Lying Dick Talbot. Through his intercession his kinsman may have been pardoned, or even never brought to trial.

10

CONCLUSION

This is the end of my story. But, like all stories, it requires that some satisfaction should be given to the reader in regard to the dramatic proprieties. We have our several heroes to dispose of. Phelim Murray and Hugh Riley, who had both been arrested by the Council to satisfy public opinion as to their complicity in the plot for the escape, were both honorably discharged,—I suppose being found entirely innocent! Roger Skreene swore himself black and blue, as the phrase is, that he had not the least suspicion of the business in which he was engaged; and so he was acquitted! I am also glad to be able to say that our gallant Cornet Murray, in the winding-up of this business, was promoted by the Council to a captaincy of cavalry, and put in command of Christiana Fort and its neighborhood, to keep that formidable Quaker, William Penn, at a respectful distance. It would gratify me still more, if I could find warrant to add, that the Cornet enjoyed himself, and married the lady of his choice, with whom he has, unknown to us, been violently in love during these adventures, and that they lived happily together for many years. I hope this was so,—although the chronicle does not allow one to affirm it,—it being but a proper conclusion to such a romance as I have plucked out of our history.

And so I have traced the tradition of the Cave to the end. What I have been able to certify furnishes the means of a shrewd estimate of the average amount of truth which popular traditions generally contain. There is always a fact at the bottom, lying under a superstructure of fiction,—truth enough to make the pursuit worth following. Talbot did not live in the Cave, but fled there occasionally for concealment. He had no hawks with him, but bred them in his own mews on the Elk River. The birds seen in after times were some of this stock, and not the solitary pair they were supposed to be. I dare say an expert naturalist would find many specimens of the same breed now in that region. But let us not be too critical on the tradition, which has led us into a quest through which I have been able to supply what I hope will be found to be a pleasant insight into that little world of action and passion,— with its people, its pursuits, and its gossips,—that, more than one hundred and seventy years ago, inhabited the beautiful banks of St. Mary's River, and wove the web of our early Maryland history.

POSTSCRIPT

I have another link in the chain of Talbot's history, furnished me by a friend in Virginia. It comes since I have completed my narrative, and very accurately confirms the conjecture of Chalmers, quoted in the note of "The Landholder's Assistant." "As for Colonel Talbot, he was conveyed for trial to Virginia, from whence he made his escape, and, after being retaken, and, *I believe,* tried and convicted, was finally pardoned by King James II." This is an extract from the note. It is now ascertained that Talbot was not taken to England for trial, as Lord Baltimore, in his letter of the 6th of July, 1685, affirmed it was the King's pleasure he should be; but that he was tried and convicted in Virginia on the 22d of April, 1686, and, on the 26th of the same month, reprieved by order of the King; after which we may presume he received a full pardon, and perhaps was taken to England in obedience to the royal command, to await it there. The conviction and reprieve are recorded in a folio of the State Records of Virginia at Richmond, on a mutilated and scarcely legible sheet,—a copy of which I present to my reader with all its obliterations and broken syllables and sad gashes in the text, for his own deciphering. The MS. is in keeping with the whole story, and may be looked upon as its appropriate emblem.

The story has been brought to light by chance, and has been rendered intelligible by close study and interpretation of fragmentary and widely separated facts, capable of being read only by one conversant with the text of human affairs, and who has the patience to grope through the trackless intervals of time, and the skill to supply the lost words and syllables of history by careful collation with those which are spared. How faithfully this accidentally found MS. typifies such a labor, the reader may judge from the literal copy of it I now offer to his perusal.

"By his Excellency

"Whereas his most Sacred Majesty has been Graciously pleased by his Royall Com'ands to Direct and Com'and Me ffrancis Lord Howard of Effingham his Maj^{ties} Lieut and Govr. Gen^{ll}. of Virginia that if George Talbott Esqr. upon his Tryall should be found Guilty of Killing Mr Christopher Rowsby, that Execution should be suspended untill his Majesties pleasure should be further signified unto Me; And forasmuch as the sd George Talbott was Indicted upon the Statute of Stabbing and hath Received a full and Legall Tryall in open Court on ye Twentieth and One and Twentieth dayes of this Instant Aprill, before his Majesties Justices of Oyer and Terminer, and found Guilty of ye aforesaid fact and condemned for the Same, I, therefore, ffrancis Lord Howard, Baron of Effingham, his Majesties Lieu^t and Govr. Gen^{ll}. of Virginia, by Virtue of   aj^{ties} Royall Com'ands to Me given there   doe hereby Suspend   tion of the Sentence of death   his Maj^{ties} Justices

        Terminer on the   till his Majesties
            erein be   nor any
              fail as yo   uttmost
          and for y^r soe doing this sh
                    Given under my   and Seale

the 26th day of Apri

                              EFFINGHAM

To his Majesties Justices
of Oyer and Terminer.

                    Recordatur E Chillon Gen[l] Car

    [Endorsed]
            Talbott's Repreif
              from L[d] Howard
                1686 for Killing Ch[r]. Rousby
                      Examined Sept. 24th
            26th Aprill 1686
                      Sentence of
                          ag[t] Col Ta
                            Suspended
                                Aprill 26 1 86"

Grace King

(1852–1932)

Grace King's literary reputation is bound up closely with her birthplace, New Orleans, Louisiana. Though she traveled frequently as an adult, especially to France, she never left New Orleans except for her trips, and her books deal almost exclusively with local society and history. Though she herself was a Presbyterian, she was educated at convent schools, and had an intimate knowledge of the old Catholic Creole families. Her father was a prominent lawyer whose fortunes collapsed when the Civil War forced him to move his family away from New Orleans to a remote family plantation. After the surrender, and during the Reconstruction, the King family was back in New Orleans, though now living in a modest house and struggling through hard times, like many of their friends. One of their best friends, and one who suffered more than most, was the lawyer-planter Charles Gayarré, the well-known historian of Louisiana. In her stories and novels King often draws on her girlhood experiences, and on the suffering and humiliation surrounding the Southern defeat. Her first published work was the story "Monsieur Motte" (1886), *written soon after an angry conversation with Richard Watson Gilder, editor of* The Century Illustrated Magazine. *He had challenged her to write something better than Cable after she had expressed agreement with Gayarré's criticism—shared by many inhabitants of New Orleans—that Cable's treatment of Creole society was unfair. Her two collections of stories,* Tales of a Time and Place (1892) *and* Balcony Stories (1893), *established her as a promising "local color" writer. She went on to write more fiction, and several historical accounts of New Orleans, but she never fulfilled her early promise. Her novel,* The Pleasant Ways of St. Médard (1916) *is considered by many to be her most accomplished work. It was based on her family's privations during Reconstruction. Though too much of her fiction depends complacently on a folklore simplicity of charracterization and on sentimental resolutions, at her best she is ca-*

pable of striking a deeply personal note of human loss, and her knowledge of the New Orleans world is always apparent. Edmund Wilson admiringly singled out "The Little Convent Girl" in his book Patriotic Gore *(1962). Among her books are* Monsieur Motte *(1888),* Jean Baptiste le Moyne, Sieur de Bienville *(1892),* New Orleans: The Place and the People *(1895),* De Soto and His Men in the Land of Florida *(1898),* Creole Families of New Orleans *(1921), and* Memories of a Southern Woman of Letters *(1932). "The Little Convent Girl," from* Balcony Stories, *first appeared in* The Century Magazine *(August 1893).*

THE LITTLE CONVENT GIRL

❀

She was coming down on the boat from Cincinnati, the little convent girl. Two sisters had brought her aboard. They gave her in charge of the captain, got her a state-room, saw that the new little trunk was put into it, hung the new little satchel up on the wall, showed her how to bolt the door at night, shook hands with her for good-by (good-bys have really no significance for sisters), and left her there. After a while the bells all rang, and the boat, in the awkward elephantine fashion of boats, got into midstream. The chambermaid found her sitting on the chair in the state-room where the sisters had left her, and showed her how to sit on a chair in the saloon. And there she sat until the captain came and hunted her up for supper. She could not do anything of herself; she had to be initiated into everything by some one else.

She was known on the boat only as "the little convent girl." Her name, of course, was registered in the clerk's office, but on a steamboat no one thinks of consulting the clerk's ledger. It is always the little widow, the fat madam, the tall colonel, the parson, etc. The captain, who pronounced by the letter, always called her the little con*vent* girl. She was the beau-ideal of the little convent girl. She never raised her eyes except when spoken to. Of course she never spoke first, even to the chambermaid, and when she did speak it was in the wee, shy, furtive voice one might imagine a just-budding violet to have; and she walked with such soft, easy, carefully calculated steps that one naturally felt the penalties that must have secured them—penalties dictated by a black code of deportment.

She was dressed in deep mourning. Her black straw hat was trimmed with stiff new crape, and her stiff new bombazine dress had crape collar and cuffs. She wore her hair in two long plaits fastened around her head tight and fast. Her hair had a strong inclination to curl, but that had been taken out of it as austerely as the noise out of her footfalls. Her hair was as black as her dress; her eyes, when one saw them, seemed blacker than either, on account of the bluishness of the white surrounding the pupil. Her eyelashes were almost as thick as the black veil which the sisters had fastened around her hat with an extra pin the very last thing before leaving. She had a round little face, and a tiny pointed chin; her mouth was slightly protuberant from the teeth, over which she tried to keep her lips well shut, the effort giving them a pathetic little forced expression. Her complexion was sallow, a pale sallow, the complexion of a brunette bleached in darkened rooms. The only color about her was a blue taffeta ribbon from which a large silver medal of the Virgin hung over the place where a breastpin should have been. She was so little, so little, although she was eighteen, as the sisters told the captain; otherwise they would not have permitted her to travel all the way to New Orleans alone.

Unless the captain or the clerk remembered to fetch her out in front, she would sit all day in the cabin, in the same place, crocheting lace, her spool of thread and box of patterns in her lap, on the handkerchief spread to save her new dress. Never leaning back—oh, no! always straight and stiff, as if the conventual back board were there within call. She would eat only convent fare at first, notwithstanding the importunities of the waiters, and the jocularities of the captain, and particularly of the clerk. Every one knows the fund of humor possessed by a steamboat clerk, and what a field for display the table at meal-times affords. On Friday she fasted rigidly, and she never began to eat, or finished, without a little Latin movement of the lips and a sign of the cross. And always at six o'clock of the evening she remembered the angelus, although there was no church bell to remind her of it.

She was in mourning for her father, the sisters told the captain, and she was going to New Orleans to her mother. She had not seen her mother since she was an infant, on account of some disagreement between the parents, in consequence of which the father had brought her to Cincinnati, and placed her in the convent. There she had been for twelve years, only going to her father for vacations and holidays. So long as the father lived he would never let the child have any communication with her mother. Now that he was dead all that was changed, and the first thing that the girl herself wanted to do was to go to her mother.

The mother superior had arranged it all with the mother of the girl, who was to come personally to the boat in New Orleans, and receive her child from the captain, presenting a letter from the mother superior, a facsimile of which the sisters gave the captain.

It is a long voyage from Cincinnati to New Orleans, the rivers doing their best to make it interminable, embroidering themselves *ad libitum* all over the country. Every five miles, and sometimes oftener, the boat would stop to put off or take on freight, if not both. The little convent girl, sitting in the cabin, had her terrible frights at first from the hideous noises attendant on these landings—the whistles, the ringings of the bells, the running to and fro, the shouting. Every time she thought it was shipwreck, death, judgment, purgatory; and her sins! her sins! She would drop her crochet, and clutch her prayer-beads from her pocket, and relax the constraint over her lips, which would go to rattling off prayers with the velocity of a relaxed windlass. That was at first, before the captain took to fetching her out in front to see the boat make a landing. Then she got to liking it so much that she would stay all day just where the captain put her, going inside only for her meals. She forgot herself at times so much that she would draw her chair a little closer to the railing, and put up her veil, actually, to see better. No one ever usurped her place, quite in front, or intruded upon her either with word or look; for every one learned to know her shyness, and began to feel a personal interest in her, and all wanted the little convent girl to see everything that she possibly could.

And it was worth seeing—the balancing and *chasséeing* and waltzing of the cumbersome old boat to make a landing. It seemed to be always attended with the difficulty and the improbability of a new enterprise; and the relief when it did sidle up anywhere within rope's-throw of the spot aimed at! And the roustabout throwing the rope from the perilous end of the dangling gangplank! And the dangling roustabouts hanging like drops of water from it—dropping sometimes twenty feet to the land, and not infrequently into the river itself. And then what a rolling of barrels, and shouldering of sacks, and singing of Jim Crow songs, and pacing of Jim Crow steps; and black skins glistening through torn shirts, and white teeth gleaming through red lips, and laughing, and talking and—bewildering! entrancing! Surely the little convent girl in her convent walls never dreamed of so much unpunished noise and movement in the world!

The first time she heard the mate—it must have been like the

first time woman ever heard man—curse and swear, she turned
pale, and ran quickly, quickly into the saloon, and—came out
again? No, indeed! not with all the soul she had to save, and all
the other sins on her conscience. She shook her head resolutely,
and was not seen in her chair on deck again until the captain not
only reassured her, but guaranteed his reassurance. And after that,
whenever the boat was about to make a landing, the mate would
first glance up to the guards, and if the little convent girl was sitting
there he would change his invective to sarcasm, and politely request
the colored gentlemen not to hurry themselves—on no account
whatever; to take their time about shoving out the plank; to send
the rope ashore by post-office—write him when it got there; begging them not to strain their backs; calling them mister, colonel,
major, general, prince, and your royal highness, which was vastly
amusing. At night, however, or when the little convent girl was
not there, language flowed in its natural curve, the mate swearing
like a pagan to make up for lost time.

The captain forgot himself one day: it was when the boat ran
aground in the most unexpected manner and place, and he went
to work to express his opinion, as only steamboat captains can, of
the pilot, mate, engineer, crew, boat, river, country, and the world
in general, ringing the bell, first to back, then to head, shouting
himself hoarser than his own whistle—when he chanced to see the
little black figure hurrying through the chaos on the deck; and the
captain stuck as fast aground in midstream as the boat had done.

In the evening the little convent girl would be taken on the upper
deck, and going up the steep stairs there was such confusion, to
keep the black skirts well over the stiff white petticoats; and, coming down, such blushing when suspicion would cross the unpre-
pared face that a rim of white stocking might be visible; and the
thin feet, laced so tightly in the glossy new leather boots, would
cling to each successive step as if they could never, never make
another venture; and then one boot would (there is but that word)
hesitate out, and feel and feel around, and have such a pause of
helpless agony as if indeed the next step must have been wilfully
removed, or was nowhere to be found on the wide, wide earth.

It was a miracle that the pilot ever got her up into the pilot-
house; but pilots have a lonely time, and do not hesitate even at
miracles when there is a chance for company. He would place a
box for her to climb to the tall bench behind the wheel, and he
would arrange the cushions, and open a window here to let in air,
and shut one there to cut off a draft, as if there could be no tenderer
consideration in life for him than her comfort. And he would talk
of the river to her, explain the chart, pointing out eddies, whirl-

pools, shoals, depths, new beds, old beds, cut-offs, caving banks, and making banks, as exquisitely and respectfully as if she had been the River Commission.

It was his opinion that there was as great a river as the Mississippi flowing directly under it—an underself of a river, as much a counterpart of the other as the second story of a house is of the first; in fact, he said they were navigating through the upper story. Whirlpools were holes in the floor of the upper river, so to speak; eddies were rifts and cracks. And deep under the earth, hurrying toward the subterranean stream, were other streams, small and great, but all deep, hurrying to and from that great mother-stream underneath, just as the small and great overground streams hurry to and from their mother Mississippi. It was almost more than the little convent girl could take in: at least such was the expression of her eyes; for they opened as all eyes have to open at pilot stories. And he knew as much of astronomy as he did of hydrology, could call the stars by name, and define the shapes of the constellations; and she, who had studied astronomy at the convent, was charmed to find that what she had learned was all true. It was in the pilot-house, one night, that she forgot herself for the first time in her life, and stayed up until after nine o'clock. Although she appeared almost intoxicated at the wild pleasure, she was immediately overwhelmed at the wickedness of it, and observed much more rigidity of conduct thereafter. The engineer, the boiler-men, the firemen, the stokers, they all knew when the little convent girl was up in the pilot-house: the speaking-tube became so mild and gentle.

With all the delays of river and boat, however, there is an end to the journey from Cincinnati to New Orleans. The latter city, which at one time to the impatient seemed at the terminus of the never, began, all of a sudden, one day to make its nearingness felt; and from that period every other interest paled before the interest in the immanence of arrival into port, and the whole boat was seized with a panic of preparation, the little convent girl with the others. Although so immaculate was she in person and effects that she might have been struck with a landing, as some good people might be struck with death, at any moment without fear of results, her trunk was packed and repacked, her satchel arranged and rearranged, and, the last day, her hair was brushed and plaited and smoothed over and over again until the very last glimmer of a curl disappeared. Her dress was whisked, as if for microscopic inspection; her face was washed; and her finger-nails were scrubbed with the hard convent nail-brush, until the disciplined little tips ached with a pristine soreness. And still there were hours to wait, and still the boat added up delays. But she arrived at last, after all, with not more than the usual and expected difference between the actual and the advertised time of arrival.

There was extra blowing and extra ringing, shouting, commanding, rushing up the gangway and rushing down the gangway. The clerks, sitting behind tables on the first deck, were plied, in the twinkling of an eye, with estimates, receipts, charges, countercharges, claims, reclaims, demands, questions, accusations, threats, all at topmost voices. None but steamboat clerks could have stood it. And there were throngs composed of individuals every one of whom wanted to see the captain first and at once: and those who could not get to him shouted over the heads of the others; and as usual he lost his temper and politeness, and began to do what he termed "hustle."

"Captain! Captain!" a voice called him to where a hand plucked his sleeve, and a letter was thrust toward him. "The cross, and the name of the convent." He recognized the envelop of the mother superior. He read the duplicate of the letter given by the sisters. He looked at the woman—the mother—casually, then again and again.

The little convent girl saw him coming, leading some one toward her. She rose. The captain took her hand first, before the other greeting, "Good-by, my dear," he said. He tried to add something else, but seemed undetermined what. "Be a good little girl—" It was evidently all he could think of. Nodding to the woman behind him, he turned on his heel, and left.

One of the deck-hands was sent to fetch her trunk. He walked out behind them, through the cabin, and the crowd on deck, down the stairs, and out over the gangway. The little convent girl and her mother went with hands tightly clasped. She did not turn her eyes to the right or left, or once (what all passengers do) look backward at the boat which, however slowly, had carried her surely over dangers that she wot not of. All looked at her as she passed. All wanted to say good-by to the little convent girl, to see the mother who had been deprived of her so long. Some expressed surprise in a whistle; some in other ways. All exclaimed audibly, or to themselves, "Colored!"

It takes about a month to make the round trip from New Orleans to Cincinnati and back, counting five days' stoppage in New Orleans. It was a month to a day when the steamboat came puffing and blowing up to the wharf again, like a stout dowager after too long a walk; and the same scene of confusion was enacted, as it had been enacted twelve times a year, at almost the same wharf for twenty years; and the same calm, a death calmness by contrast, followed as usual the next morning.

The decks were quiet and clean; one cargo had just been delivered, part of another stood ready on the levee to be shipped. The captain was there waiting for his business to begin, the clerk was in his office getting his books ready, the voice of the mate could be heard below, mustering the old crew out and a new crew in; for if steamboat crews have a single principle,—and there are those who deny them any,—it is never to ship twice in succession on the same boat. It was too early yet for any but roustabouts, marketers, and church-goers; so early that even the river was still partly mist-covered; only in places could the swift, dark current be seen rolling swiftly along.

"Captain!" A hand plucked at his elbow, as if not confident that the mere calling would secure attention. The captain turned. The mother of the little convent girl stood there, and she held the little convent girl by the hand. "I have brought her to see you," the woman said. "You were so kind—and she is so quiet, so still, all the time, I thought it would do her a pleasure."

She spoke with an accent, and with embarrassment; otherwise one would have said that she was bold and assured enough.

"She don't go nowhere, she don't do nothing but make her crochet and her prayers, so I thought I would bring her for a little visit of 'How d' ye do' to you."

There was, perhaps, some inflection in the woman's voice that might have made known, or at least awakened, the suspicion of some latent hope or intention, had the captain's ear been fine enough to detect it. There might have been something in the little convent girl's face, had his eye been more sensitive—a trifle paler, maybe, the lips a little tighter drawn, the blue ribbon a shade faded. He may have noticed that, but— And the visit of "How d' ye do" came to an end.

They walked down the stairway, the woman in front, the little convent girl—her hand released to shake hands with the captain—following, across the bared deck, out to the gangway, over to the middle of it. No one was looking, no one saw more than a flutter of white petticoats, a show of white stockings, as the little convent girl went under the water.

The roustabout dived, as the roustabouts always do, after the drowning, even at the risk of their good-for-nothing lives. The mate himself jumped overboard; but she had gone down in a whirlpool. Perhaps, as the pilot had told her whirlpools always did, it may have carried her through to the underground river, to that vast, hidden, dark Mississippi that flows beneath the one we see; for her body was never found.

Augustus Baldwin Longstreet

(1790–1870)

*Born in Augusta, Georgia, Longstreet grew up at a time when the
raw Southern frontier still included much of the state. He himself
enjoyed a comfortable childhood and a privileged education. He
attended Dr. Moses Waddel's elite academy in Willington, South
Carolina, and then entered Yale College, graduating in 1813. After
studying law in Connecticut, he returned to Georgia, became a
lawyer, and spent the first years of his career practicing law and
riding the circuit court. This latter experience provided him the
material for his best-known stories. He was elected representative
to the Georgia State Assembly, and, in 1822, was elected judge of
the Superior Court of Ocmulgee District. In 1827, he failed in his
reelection bid, and turned once more to private law practice in
Augusta. He later became an ardent convert to the Methodist
Church, and for a short time served as a Methodist preacher. In
the 1830s, he began publishing humorous anecdotes in the Mil-
ledgeville* Southern Recorder, *a weekly, and later in his own Augusta newspaper,* The States' Rights Sentinel. *In 1835, the* Sentinel
published a collection of these stories as a book, Georgia Scenes,
Characters, Incidents, &c., in the First Half Century of the Republic. *It was an immediate success. Edgar Allan Poe, not an easy
man to please, wrote an almost worshipful review, praising certain
stories of Georgia low-life, including "The Horse-Swap," as comic
masterpieces inspired by a "penetrating understanding" of the
Southern character. Harper & Brothers reprinted the book in 1840
to even greater acclaim, and it has seldom been out of print since.
Judge Longstreet's "amateur" status as a writer, and his morally
superior narrative distance from his subject, allowed him freedom
to dwell at length on the coarse habits, violent entertainments, and
ripe dialect of a type of Southerner who had been outlawed from
the pages of most professional fiction. Longstreet injected a vitalizing
dose of native realism into Southern letters at a time when romantic*

idealism prevailed, and his influence on later Southern writers has been powerful and healthy. In the pre-Civil War South, Georgia Scenes *helped launch the "Southwestern humorist" school of writing, which included such writers as George Washington Harris and Johnson Jones Hooper. Unfortunately, apart from* Georgia Scenes, *Longstreet wrote little else of lasting value. As an outspoken secessionist, he defended the South in two small polemical books, and toward the end of his life he wrote a moralistic temperance novel better forgotten. Four years after he published* Georgia Scenes, *he was made president of Emory College. He became well-known as an administrator and educator, and at the time of his death had served as president of three other Southern colleges. "The Horse-Swap," from* Georgia Scenes, *first appeared in the* Southern Recorder *(November 1833).*

THE HORSE-SWAP

❀

During the session of the Supreme Court, in the village of ——, about three weeks ago, when a number of people were collected in the principal street of the village, I observed a young man riding up and down the street, as I supposed, in a violent passion. He galloped this way, then that, and then the other; spurred his horse to one group of citizens, then to another; then dashed off at half speed, as if fleeing from danger; and, suddenly checking his horse, returned first in a pace, then in a trot, and then in a canter. While he was performing these various evolutions, he cursed, swore, whooped, screamed, and tossed himself in every attitude which man could assume on horseback. In short, he *cavorted* most magnanimously (a term which, in our tongue, expresses all that I have described, and a little more), and seemed to be setting all creation at defiance. As I like to see all that is passing, I determined to take a position a little nearer to him, and to ascertain, if possible, what it was that affected him so sensibly. Accordingly, I approached a crowd before which he had stopped for a moment, and examined it with the strictest scrutiny. But I could see nothing in it that seemed to have anything to do with the cavorter. Every man appeared to be in good humour, and all minding their own business. Not one so much as noticed the principal figure. Still he went on. After a semicolon pause, which my appearance seemed to produce (for he eyed me closely as I approached), he fetched a whoop, and swore that "he could out-swap any live man, woman, or child that ever walked these hills, or that ever straddled horse-flesh since the days of old daddy Adam. Stranger," said he to me, "did you ever see the *Yellow* Blossom from Jasper?"

"No," said I, "but I have often heard of him."

"I'm the boy," continued he; "perhaps a *leetle,* jist a *leetle,* of the best man at a horse-swap that ever trod shoe-leather."

I began to feel my situation a little awkward, when I was relieved by a man somewhat advanced in years, who stepped up and began to survey the *"Yellow Blossom's"* horse with much apparent interest. This drew the rider's attention, and he turned the conversation from me to the stranger.

"Well, my old coon," said he, "do you want to swap *hosses?"*

"Why, I don't know," replied the stranger; "I believe I've got a beast I'd trade with you for that one, if you like him."

"Well, fetch up your nag, my old cock; you're jist the lark I wanted to get hold of. I am perhaps a *leetle,* just a *leetle,* of the best man at a horse-swap that ever stole *cracklins* out of his mammy's fat gourd. Where's your *hoss?"*

"I'll bring him presently; but I want to examine your horse a little."

"Oh! look at him," said the Blossom, alighting and hitting him a cut; "look at him. He's the best piece of *hoss*flesh in the thirteen united univarsal worlds. There's no sort o' mistake in little Bullet. He can pick up miles on his feet, and fling 'em behind him as fast as the next man's *hoss,* I don't care where he comes from. And he can keep at it as long as the sun can shine without resting."

During this harangue, little Bullet looked as if he understood it all, believed it, and was ready at any moment to verify it. He was a horse of goodly countenance, rather expressive of vigilance than fire; though an unnatural appearance of fierceness was thrown into it by the loss of his ears, which had been cropped pretty close to his head. Nature had done but little for Bullet's head and neck; but he managed, in a great measure, to hide their defects by bowing perpetually. He had obviously suffered severely for corn; but if his ribs and hip bones had not disclosed the fact, *he* never would have done it; for he was in all respects as cheerful and happy as if he commanded all the corn-cribs and fodder-stacks in Georgia. His height was about twelve hands; but as his shape partook somewhat of that of the giraffe, his haunches stood much lower. They were short, strait, peaked, and concave. Bullet's tail, however, made amends for all his defects. All that the artist could do to beautify it had been done; and all that horse could do to compliment the artist, Bullet did. His tail was nicked in superior style, and exhibited the line of beauty in so many directions, that it could not fail to hit the most fastidious taste in some of them. From the root it dropped into a graceful festoon; then rose in a handsome curve; then resumed its first direction; and then mounted suddenly upward like a cypress knee to a perpendicular of about two and a half inches. The whole had a careless and bewitching inclination to the right. Bullet obviously knew where his beauty lay, and took all occasions to display it to the best advantage. If a stick cracked, or if any one moved suddenly about him, or coughed, or hawked, or spoke a little louder than common, up went Bullet's tail like lightning; and if the *going up* did not please, the *coming down* must of necessity, for it was as different from the other movement as was its direction. The first was a bold and rapid flight upward, usually to an angle of forty-five degrees. In this position he kept his interesting appendage until he satisfied himself that nothing in particular was to be done; when he commenced dropping it by half inches, in second beats, then in triple time, then faster and shorter, and faster and shorter still, until it finally died away imperceptibly into its natural position. If I might compare sights to sounds, I should say its *settling* was more like the note of a locust than anything else in nature.

Either from native sprightliness of disposition, from uncontrollable activity, or from an unconquerable habit of removing flies by the stamping of the feet, Bullet never stood still; but always kept up a gentle fly-scaring movement of his limbs, which was peculiarly interesting.

"I tell you, man," proceeded the Yellow Blossom, "he's the best live hoss that ever trod the grit of Georgia. Bob Smart knows the hoss. Come here, Bob, and mount this hoss, and show Bullet's motions." Here Bullet bristled up, and looked as if he had been hunting for Bob all day long, and had just found him. Bob sprang on his back. "Boo-oo-oo!" said Bob, with a fluttering noise of the lips; and away went Bullet, as if in a quarter race, with all his beauties spread in handsome style.

"Now fetch him back," said Blossom. Bullet turned and came in pretty much as he went out.

"Now trot him by." Bullet reduced his tail to *"customary;"* sidled to the right and left airily, and exhibited at least three varieties of trot in the short space of fifty yards.

"Make him pace!" Bob commenced twitching the bridle and kicking at the same time. These inconsistent movements obviously (and most naturally) disconcerted Bullet; for it was impossible for

him to learn, from them, whether he was to proceed or stand still.
He started to trot, and was told that wouldn't do. He attempted
a canter, and was checked again. He stopped, and was urged to
go on. Bullet now rushed into the wide field of experiment, and
struck out a gait of his own, that completely turned the tables upon
his rider, and certainly deserved a patent. It seemed to have derived its elements from the jig, the minuet, and the cotillon. If it
was not a pace, it certainly had *pace* in it, and no man would
venture to call it anything else; so it passed off to the satisfaction
of the owner.

"Walk him!" Bullet was now at home again; and he walked as
if money was staked on him.

The stranger, whose name, I afterward learned, was Peter
Ketch, having examined Bullet to his heart's content, ordered his
son Neddy to go and bring up Kit. Neddy soon appeared upon
Kit; a well-formed sorrel of the middle size, and in good order.
His *tout ensemble* threw Bullet entirely in the shade, though a
glance was sufficient to satisfy any one that Bullet had the decided
advantage of him in point of intellect.

"Why, man," said Blossom, "do you bring such a hoss as that
to trade for Bullet? Oh, I see you've no notion of trading."

"Ride him off, Neddy!" said Peter. Kit put off at a handsome
lope.

"Trot him back!" Kit came in at a long, sweeping trot, and
stopped suddenly at the crowd.

"Well," said Blossom, "let me look at him; maybe he'll do to
plough."

"Examine him!" said Peter, taking hold of the bridle close to
the mouth; "he's nothing but a tacky. He an't as *pretty* a horse as
Bullet, I know; but he'll do. Start 'em together for a hundred and
fifty *mile;* and if Kit an't twenty mile ahead of him at the coming
out, any man may take Kit for nothing. But he's a monstrous mean
horse, gentleman; any man may see that. He's the scariest horse,
too, you ever saw. He won't do to hunt on, no how. Stranger, will
you let Neddy have your rifle to shoot off him? Lay the rifle between his ears, Neddy, and shoot at the blaze in that stump. Tell
me when his head is high enough."

Ned fired, and hit the blaze; and Kit did not move a hair's
breadth.

"Neddy, take a couple of sticks, and beat on that hogshead at
Kit's tail."

Ned made a tremendous rattling, at which Bullet took fright,
broke his bridle, and dashed off in grand style; and would have
stopped all farther negotiations by going home in disgust, had not

a traveller arrested him and brought him back; but Kit did not move.

"I tell you, gentlemen," continued Peter, "he's the scariest horse you ever saw. He an't as gentle as Bullet, but he won't do any harm if you watch him. Shall I put him in a cart, gig, or wagon for you, stranger? He'll cut the same capers there he does here. He's a monstrous mean horse."

During all this time Blossom was examining him with the nicest scrutiny. Having examined his frame and limbs, he now looked at his eyes.

"He's got a curious look out of his eyes," said Blossom.

"Oh yes, sir," said Peter, "just as blind as a bat. Blind horses always have clear eyes. Make a motion at his eyes, if you please, sir."

Blossom did so, and Kit threw up his head rather as if something pricked him under the chin than as if fearing a blow. Blossom repeated the experiment, and Kit jerked back in considerable astonishment.

"Stone blind, you see, gentlemen," proceeded Peter; "but he's just as good to travel of a dark night as if he had eyes."

"Blame my buttons," said Blossom, "if I like them eyes."

"No," said Peter, "nor I neither. I'd rather have 'em made of diamonds; but they'll do, if they don't show as much white as Bullet's."

"Well," said Blossom, "make a pass at me."

"No," said Peter; "you made the banter, now make your pass."

"Well, I'm never afraid to price my hosses. You must give me twenty-five dollars boot."

"Oh, certainly; say fifty, and my saddle and bridle in. Here, Neddy, my son, take away daddy's horse."

"Well," said Blossom, "I've made my pass, now you make yours."

"I'm for short talk in a horse-swap, and therefore always tell a gentleman at once what I mean to do. You must give me ten dollars."

Blossom swore absolutely, roundly, and profanely, that he never would give boot.

"Well," said Peter, "I didn't care about trading; but you cut such high shines, that I thought I'd like to back you out, and I've done it. Gentlemen, you see I've brought him to a hack."

"Come, old man," said Blossom, "I've been joking with you. I begin to think you do want to trade; therefore, give me five dollars and take Bullet. I'd rather lose ten dollars any time than not make a trade, though I hate to fling away a good hoss."

"Well," said Peter, "I'll be as clever as you are. Just put the five dollars on Bullet's back, and hand him over; it's a trade."

Blossom swore again, as roundly as before, that he would not give boot; and, said he, "Bullet wouldn't hold five dollars on his back, no how. But, as I bantered you, if you say an even swap, here's at you."

"I told you," said Peter, "I'd be as clever as you; therefore, here goes two dollars more, just for trade sake. Give me three dollars, and it's a bargain."

Blossom repeated his former assertion; and here the parties stood for a long time, and the by-standers (for many were now collected) began to taunt both parties. After some time, however, it was pretty unanimously decided that the old man had backed Blossom out.

At length Blossom swore he "never would be backed out for three dollars after bantering a man;" and, accordingly, they closed the trade.

"Now," said Blossom, as he handed Peter the three dollars, "I'm a man that, when he makes a bad trade, makes the most of it until he can make a better. I'm for no rues and after-claps."

"That's just my way," said Peter; "I never goes to law to mend my bargains."

"Ah, you're the kind of boy I love to trade with. Here's your hoss, old man. Take the saddle and bridle off him, and I'll strip yours; but lift up the blanket easy from Bullet's back, for he's a mighty tender-backed hoss."

The old man removed the saddle, but the blanket stuck fast. He attempted to raise it, and Bullet bowed himself, switched his tail, danced a little, and gave signs of biting.

"Don't hurt him, old man," said Blossom, archly; "take it off easy. I am, perhaps, a leetle of the best man at a horse-swap that ever catched a coon."

Peter continued to pull at the blanket more and more roughly, and Bullet became more and more *cavortish:* insomuch that, when the blanket came off, he had reached the *kicking* point in good earnest.

The removal of the blanket disclosed a sore on Bullet's backbone that seemed to have defied all medical skill. It measured six full inches in length and four in breadth, and had as many features as Bullet had motions. My heart sickened at the sight; and I felt that the brute who had been riding him in that situation deserved the halter.

The prevailing feeling, however, was that of mirth. The laugh became loud and general at the old man's expense, and rustic witticisms were liberally bestowed upon him and his late purchase. These Blossom continued to provoke by various remarks. He asked the old man "if he thought Bullet would let five dollars lie on his back." He declared most seriously that he had owned that horse three months, and had never discovered before that he had a sore back, "or he never should have thought of trading him," &c., &c.

The old man bore it all with the most philosophic composure. He evinced no astonishment at his late discovery, and made no replies. But his son Neddy had not disciplined his feelings quite so well. His eyes opened wider and wider from the first to the last pull of the blanket; and, when the whole sore burst upon his view, astonishment and fright seemed to contend for the mastery of his countenance. As the blanket disappeared, he stuck his hands in his breeches pockets, heaved a deep sigh, and lapsed into a profound revery, from which he was only roused by the cuts at his father. He bore them as long as he could; and, when he could contain himself no longer, he began, with a certain wildness of expression which gave a peculiar interest to what he uttered: "His back's mighty bad off; but dod drot my soul if he's put it to daddy as bad as he thinks he has, for old Kit's both blind and *deef*, I'll be dod drot if he eint."

"The devil he is," said Blossom.

"Yes dod drot my soul if he *eint*. You walk him, and see if he *eint*. His eyes don't look like it; but he'd *jist as leve go agin* the house with you, or in a ditch, as any how. Now you go try him." The laugh was now turned on Blossom; and many rushed to test the fidelity of the little boy's report. A few experiments established its truth beyond controversy.

"Neddy," said the old man, "you oughtn't to try and make people discontented with their things. Stranger, don't mind what the little boy says. If you can only get Kit rid of them little failings, you'll find him all sorts of a horse. You are a *leetle* the best man at a horse-swap that ever I got hold of; but don't fool away Kit. Come, Neddy, my son, let's be moving; the stranger seems to be getting snappish."

Andrew Nelson Lytle

(1902–   )

Andrew Lytle was born in Murfreesboro, Tennessee. Both his mother and father came from families with deep roots in Tennessee history. His father farmed cotton and dealt in timber, and Lytle himself worked his father's farm Cornsilk for a year after graduating from Vanderbilt. His early education was completed at the Sewanee Military Academy. In 1921, he entered Vanderbilt, studied under John Crowe Ransom, and became friends with several members of the Fugitive poetry group. Within a few years he was to join these same friends when they regrouped as the Agrarians. After the year on his father's farm, Lytle studied playwriting at Yale in George Pierce Baker's School of Drama and tried acting in New York. Dissatisfied with life in New York, Lytle returned to Tennessee, in 1929, and to a long career in Southern letters and at Southern universities. He became a passionate defender of the Agrarian position, and his contribution "The Hind Tit" to the Agrarian manifesto I'll Take My Stand *(1930) is a powerful argument in favor of Southern small-farm economy. In everything he has written, Lytle has demonstrated a deep involvement with the history of the South. His first book was the Civil War biography,* Bedford Forrest and His Critter Company *(1931), and one of his most recent is the remarkable memoir-chronicle of his Tennessee relatives and forebears* A Wake for the Living *(1975). He has also written a small body of some of the best fiction written by a Southern writer this century. His first short stories, including "Mister McGregor" and "Jericho, Jericho, Jericho," were written in the 1930s. His four novels have received considerable praise from critics, and one novel,* The Velvet Horn *(1957), is now recognized as a modern classic. Lytle has managed to combine his writing of fiction with a highly successful career as university teacher, editor, and literary critic. He taught at the universities of Iowa and Florida, and at the University of the South, where during 12 years he edited* The Sewanee Review *and made it one of the best literary journals of his generation. Now retired, he continues to write essays and criticism in the radical conservative spirit of his first collection,* The Hero with the Private Parts *(1966). Among his books are* The Long Night *(1936),* At the Moon's Inn *(1941),* A Name for Evil *(1947),* A Novel, A Novella and Four Stories *(1958), and* Southerners and Europeans, Essays in a Time of Disorder *(1988). "Mister McGregor" first appeared in* The Virginia Quarterly Review *(April 1935).*

MISTER McGREGOR

❀

"I want to speak to Mister McGregor."

Yes, sir, that's what he said. Not marster, but MISTER Mc-GREGOR. If I live to be a hundred, and I don't think I will, account of my kidneys, I'll never forget the feelen that come over the room when he said them two words: Mister McGregor. The air shivered into a cold jelly; and all of us, me, ma, and pa, sort of froze in it. I remember thinken how much we favored one of them waxwork figures Sis Lou had learnt to make at Doctor Price's Female Academy. There I was, a little shaver of eight, standen by the window a-blowen my breath on it so's I could draw my name, like chillun'll do when they're kept to the house with a cold. The knock come sudden and sharp, I remember, as I was crossen a T. My heart flopped down in my belly and commenced to flutter around in my breakfast; then popped up to my ears and drawed all the blood out'n my nose except a little sack that got left in the point to swell and tingle. It's a singular thing, but the first time that nigger's fist hit the door I knowed it was the knock of death. I can smell death. It's a gift, I reckon, one of them no-count gifts like good conversation that don't do you no good no more. Once Cousin John Mebane come to see us, and as he leaned over to pat me on the head—he was polite and hog-friendly to everybody, chillun and poverty-wropped kin especial—I said, Cousin John, what makes you smell so funny? Ma all but took the hide off'n me; but four days later they was dressen him in his shroud. Then I didn't know what it was I'd smelled, but by this time I'd got better acquainted with the meanen.

Ma was rollen tapers for the mantel. She stiffened a spell like she was listenen for the North wind to rise; rolled out a taper and laid it down. She went to the door and put her hand square on the knob; hesitated like she knew what was comen; then opened it. There stood Rhears. He was the coachman. Him and his wife Della was ma's pets. The both of'm was give to ma by her pa at the marryen; and in a way that folks don't understand no more, they somehow become a part of her. Ma liked horses that wanted to run away all the time, and Rhears was the only nigger on the place that could manage'm. He was a powerful, dangerous feller. He'd killed the blacksmith and two free niggers in the other county before ma brought him to Long Gourd. His shoulders jest but stretched across the opening, as he stood there in a respectful-arrogant sort of way with a basket-knife in his hand.

"What do you want, Rhears?" his mistress asked.

"I want to speak to Mister McGregor," he said.

Pa had been scratchen away at his secretary. At "Mister" the scratchen stopped. That last scratch made more noise in my ears than the guns at Shiloh. Without a word, without even looken behind him, pa stood up and reached for his gun. The secretary was close to the fireplace and had a mirror over it. He didn't waste no time, but he didn't hurry none either. He just got up, took off his specs, and laid them as careful on the secretary, just like he meant to set'm in one special place and no other place would do. He reached for the gun and turned.

Rhears warn't no common field hand. He was proud, black like the satin in widow-women's shirt-waists, and spoiled. And his feel-ens was bad hurt. The day before, pa had whupped Della, and Rhears had had all night to fret and sull over it and think about what was be-en said in the quarters and how glad the field hands was she'd been whupped. He didn't mean to run away from his home like any blue-gum nigger. He jest come a-marchen straight to the house to settle with pa before them hot night thoughts had had time to git cooled down by the frost.

Pa turned and walked towards him. He still moved as steady and solemn. I watched the even distance each boot-heel made and calculated that two more steps would put him up to the threshold. Just to look at him you might have thought he was a-goen towards the courthouse to pay his taxes or walken down the aisle to his pew. All of a sudden he come to a stop. Ma's brown silk skirt had spread out before him. I looked up. There she was, one hand tight around the gun stock, the othern around the barrel. Her left little finger, plunged like a hornet's needle where the skin drew tight over pa's knuckles, made the blood drop on the bristly hairs along his hand; hang there; then spring to the floor. She held there the time it took three drops to bounce down and splatter. That blood put a spell on me.

A gold shiver along ma's dress made me look quick at their faces. Her hair was a shade darker than the dress she was wearen and slicked down around her ears. There wasn't no direct sun on it, but a light sorghum color slipped up and down as if it was playen on grease. The light might have come from her eyes, for they was afire. She was always fine to look at, although her face wasn't soft enough to rightly claim her beautiful. But she would have taken the breeches away from any ordinary man, I tell you. She'd rather manage folks than eat. Pa ought to have let her do a sight more of it than he did. She was happier than I ever seen her the time he went to the legislature. But he didn't take to politics somehow. He said the government rooms smelled too strong of tobacco and stale sweat. He couldn't abide the smell of tobacco. He was a mighty clean man, the cleanest I ever come across. Took a washen once a day reg'lar. When I come to think about ma, I see her a-studyen about somethen, with a wrinkle in her eyes. She didn't have to tell the servants not to bother her then. They stayed out of her way or went tippen around if their work took'm near her.

Well, pa saw he couldn't get his gun out of her grip without acting ungentlemanly. He gave her a curious look and a low bow; then turned it loose. Taken off his coat and folden it, he laid it across a chair. Ma was marbly-pale when she stepped out of the way, but she moved easy and steady.

For a long time I never could make out the meanen of them looks, nor why ma done what she done. And she never set us right about it. She wasn't the explainen kind, and you can bet nobody ever asked. I'd just as soon've asked the devil to pop his tail. It's bothered me a heap in my time, more'n it's had any right to. I reckon it's because I always think about it when I'm taperen off. That's a time when a man gits melancholy and thinks about how he come not to be president and sich-like concerns. Well, sir, when I'd run through all my mistakes and seen where if I'd a-done this instead of that how much better off I'd be today, and cuss myself for drinken up my kidneys, I'd always end up by asken myself why that woman acted like that. I've knowed a sight of women in my day, knowed'm as the Bible saints knowed'm, as well as in a social and business way; and I'm here to say, sir, they are stuffed with dynamite, the puniest of'm.

It was a question of authority, and a time when whuppen was out of the argyment. All you had to do was look at Rhears and that basket-knife sharpened thin like a dagger, a-hangen as innocent agen his pant leg, to see he didn't mean to take no whuppen.

He must have felt in his Afrykin way that pa had betrayed him. Folks jest didn't whup their house servants, and Rhears was a-meanen to teach pa his manners. Niggers can think straight up to a certain point, and beyond that the steadiest of'm let their senses fly like buckshot, high to scatter. It never struck him that Della needed her whuppen. No, sir, he was jest a-standen in the door tellen pa he warn't his marster.

Now ma might have thought that pa ought, with his proper strength, to show him who his marster was. There ain't no doubt but what he had to show it in some way, or he might as well have sold all his niggers for any work he could a got out'n them. Still it was a powerful big risk to run. And it was plain she was a-meanen for him to run it.

Anyway, that was the construction the kin put on it, and it was natural they would. But it never satisfied me. I got it in my head that Rhears warn't the only person on Long Gourd who didn't claim pa his marster. Before I tell you what I mean, give me a little taste of that shuck juice—half a glass'll do, jest enough to settle the dust in my belly. I'm about to choke to death with the drought.

Aah . . . that's sweet to the taste. Now, sir. You'll excuse me if I lean over and whisper this. *That other body was ma.* I know it ain't a-goen to sound right, for she and pa had the name of been a mighty loven couple. But a man and woman can fight and still love. Most of'm enjoy fighten. I ain't never seen one get wore out with it. They can go on with a fight for years. Can git fat on it. When they win out, they put the man down amongst the chillun and give him a whuppen when he forgits his manners or sasses back. But if he's stout enough to put her and keep her in her place, she don't hold it agin him. She's proud to think she picked such a game one. That's how come I never married. I'm peaceful by nature. Ain't but one thing ever gits me fighten mad: that's putten salt in my whiskey. That riles me. I'll fight a elyphant then.

Well, sir, that morning Della was late. Ma had had to send for her twice, and she come in looken like the hornets stung her. She fluffed down to her sewen and went to work in a sullen way, her lip stuck out so far it looked swole. And they ain't nothen meaner-looken than a blue-black, shiney lip of a sullen nigger woman. It looks like a devil's pillow.

Directly ma said, "Della, take out that seam and do it over again."

"Take it out yourself, if it don't suit," she flounced back.

In a second pa was on his feet: "Woman, lay down that sewen and come with me."

Them was his words; and if a nigger can git pale, Della done it. She seen right away what a mistake she'd made. She fell on the floor and commenced to grab at ma's skirts. "Don't let him whup me, mistiss. Don't let him." For a while ma didn't say a word.

"Get up off that floor and come with me," said pa again.

"Mister McGregor, what are you going to do with this girl?"

Pa never made her no answer. He walked over and lifted Della up by the arm.

"Don't you tech me; you don't dare tech me. I belongs to mistiss."

Pa shuck her till her teeth rattled; then she stopped her jumpen and goen on and stood there a-tremblen like a scared horse.

"Mister McGregor," come ma's even tones, "you're not going to punish that girl. She's mine."

And with that pa turned and said in a hard, polite way he never used before to ma: "And so are you mine, my dear." Then he nodded to Della to go before him, and she went.

When he came back, ma was standen in the middle of the floor just where he had left her. She hadn't moved a peg. She just stood there, stiff as a poker, her head thrown up and her eyes as wide as a hawk's.

"I have whipped Della and sent her to the field for six months. If at the end of that time she has learned not to forget her manners, she may take up again her duties here. In the meantime, so you will not want, I've sent for P'niny. If you find her too old or in any way unsuitable, you may take your choice of the young girls."

He waited a breath for her answer and when it didn't come, got on his horse and went runnen over the back road down to the fields. No other words passed between them that day. At supper the meal went off in quick order. There wasn't no good old-fashioned table talk. Everybody was as polite to one another as if they was visiten. Ma sat at the foot, froze to her chair. Pa at the head like a judge expecten shooten in the court. We knew some-then was bound to blow up and bust; and I do believe if somebody had tromped on a hog bladder, we chillun'd a jumped under the table.

Next mornen it come. That bow of pa's, as he let go of the gun, was his answer to the challenge. For you might almost say pa had whupped ma by proxy. And here was Rhears, agen by proxy, to make him answer for it . . . a nigger and a slave, his mistress's gallant, a-callen her husband and his marster to account for her. I don't reckon they'd been any such mixed-up arrangement as that before that time; and I know they ain't since.

I scrouched back in the corner and watched, so scared my eyes turned loose in their sockets. If Jesus Christ had a touched me on the shoulder and said, "Come on, little boy, and git your harp," I'd a no more looked at him than if he'd a been my dog come to lick me. For pa and Rhears was a-eyen one another. This fight was to be accorden to no rules. I saw straight off it would start fist and skull and work into stomp and gouge. If pa didn't manage to git that knife away from the nigger, it would be cut and grunt as well.

Pa was the slimberer of the two, but he wouldn't a looked it away from Rhears. From neckèd heel up he was six feet—no, six feet four—and his boots raised him an ench higher. Right away he took a quick easy step forward, and both of'm tied their muscles together. Rhears tightened his fingers around the knife. I looked at pa's breeches. They fit him tight; and the meat rolled up, snapped, then quivered under the cloth. His butt give in at the sides and squeezed away its sitten-down softness. His waist drawed in and pumped the wind into his chest, a-pushen out his shoulders just as easy and slow. I don't believe you could have found a man in the whole cotton country hung together any purtier.

Pa, quick-like, sunk his hand in and around the black flesh of Rhears' neck. The knife swung backwards, but pa grabbed it with his left hand before it could do its damage. A breath, and Rhears was a-spinnen round the room. The basket-knife lay in the door as still as any of the pine floor boards. This rattled the nigger some. He had figured on gitten Mister McGregor in the door, where he could a used the knife to advantage. Fighten in his mistress's room, a place he didn't feel at home in, rattled him some more. So before he could come to himself good, pa lambed a blow into his black jaw. It was a blow fit to down a mule, but Rhears shook his head and run in to close; changed quick; dropped low and butted. Four quick butts jambed pa agen the wall, where he saved his guts by grabben Rhears' shoulders—to hold. That kinky hunk of iron slowed down. Both men shook under the strain. The noise of destruction held up. All you could hear was a heavy, pumpen blowen, like two wind-broke horses drawen a killen load . . . then a rippen cry from Rhears' coat—and it was good broadcloth—as it split both ways from the small of his back. Both men drawed in their breaths for a long second.

Sudden-like pa's head and chest went down and forward. His feet pressed agen the wall. Slow as candy pullen he broke the nigger's holt on the front muscles of his thighs. But that nigger's grip never give. No, sir. What give was two drippen hunks of leg meat. Just the second that holt was broke pa shifted neat and shoved hard. Rhears smashed a sewen table top into kindlen wood before he hit the wall. That table saved his neck, or I'm as good a man as I used to be. Before he could get his bearens, pa was a-pounden his head into the hard pine floor. I looked for the brains to go a-splatteren any time, and I begun to wonder how far they would slide on the floor's smooth polish. But God never made but one thing tougher'n a nigger's head—and that's ironwood. Slowly Rhears raised up and, with a beautiful strain of muscles, got to his feet. Then him and pa went round the room. It looked like that bangen had set the nigger crazy. A stranger comen into the room would a thought he was set on breaken up ever stick of furniture, a-usen pa for his mallet. Once the two of'm come close to ma, so close the wind they made blowed her skirts; but never a peg did she move. She held as rigid as a conjure woman.

Directly the nigger begun to wear some. All that crazy spurt of energy hadn't done him no good. Gradually pa's feet touched the floor more and more; then they didn't leave it. The panten got heavier, more like bellows. A chair got in their way. They went over it. They did a sight of rollen—up to the door crowded with house servants, all a-looken like they had fell in the ash-hopper. You could follow how far they'd rolled by the sweat on the floor. It looked like a wet mop had been run by a triflen hand. Then, sir, my hairs straightened up and drawed in to hide under the scalp. Rhears had ended up on top and was a-shiften to gouge. Pa looked all wore down. I tried to holler to ma to shoot, but my throat was as parched as it is right this minute. . . . Thank you, sir. You are very generous.

Have you ever seen a long dead limb stretched between sky and droppen sun? Well, that's how still ma held on to that gun of pa's. I couldn't stand to see them black thumbs go down. As I turned my head, I heard the nigger holler. Pa had jerked up his knee and hit him in a tender spot. He fell back and grabbed himself. It must have been an accident, for pa made no move to take advantage of the break. He just lay there and let Rhears take hold of himself and git at pa's throat. I never seen such guts in nobody, nigger or white man. Bump went pa's head on the floor. Bump and agen. Ever time he lifted pa, he squeezed tighter. Ever time he come down he pushed him forward.

It had been one of them frosty December mornens, and a fire had been burnen in the chimney since first light. The front stick had been burned in two and left between it and the back stick a heap of red and blue hickory coals. They don't make no hotter fire than that. I saw right away what Rhears had in mind. Every time he bumped my father's head against the floor, he was that much nearer the hearth. Pa wriggled and jerked, but his wind was cut and the black blood ran into his eyes. Those heavy black hands growed deep in the red, greasy flesh of pa's neck.

They moved slower towards the fire, for pa had at last clamped his legs in a way to slow'm down. Then I saw him reach for his pocket. Rhears didn't see this move. His eyes was bucked on what they had in mind to do, and the heat from the hickory logs made'm swell with a dark, dry look of battle luck. After some fumblen pa finally brought out his knife. He opened it in a feeble way over the nigger's back, and let it rip and tear through his ribs. The blood first oozed; then spouted. It fell back from the knife like dirt from a turnen plow. Then pa made a jab back of the kidneys. That done for him. He grunted; turned loose and rolled over like a hunk of meat.

Staggering to his feet, pa went over and leaned agen the mantel. Directly Rhears spoke up, so low you could hardly hear him:

"Marster, if you hadn't got me, I'd a got you."

Then he shook with a chill, straightened out, and rolled back his eyes. Mister McGregor looked at him a minute before he turned to his wife. And then no words passed his mouth. He reached out his hand and she walked over and handed him the gun. He reached over the mantel and, his arms a-tremblen, set the gun back in its rack.

"Bring me a pan of warm water, the turpentine, and the things out of my medicine chest." That was ma speaken, sharp and peremptory, to the servants in the doorway. "And take this body out of here," she added in a tone she used when the girl Sally failed to dust behind the furniture.

"Sit down in that chair, Mister McGregor, so I can dress your wounds."

Pa done what she told him. She worked away at him with deft, quick fingers. Directly I heard her in a off-hand way, her head benden over and her hands busy wrappen:

"Colonel Winston will be through here on his way South. I think it would be best to sell him Della."

"I think that, my dear," said pa, "would be the most sensible thing to do."

Thomas Nelson Page

(1853–1922)

Born and brought up on his grandparents' plantation, Oakland, not far from Richmond, Virginia, Page spent his childhood watching the decline and collapse of the old plantation regime. Both his mother and father came from distinguished Virginia families, going back to two colonial governors. His father fought for the Confederacy, even though he had strongly opposed secession and war, and Page as a boy followed the Virginia campaigns through reports sent back by his father's body-servant. After the war, Page attended Washington College at a time when Robert E. Lee had become its president. He then studied law at the University of Virginia, and settled down in Richmond to practice law. He achieved his first literary success with the publication of "Marse Chan" in 1884. "Marse Chan" struck a powerful sympathetic chord in both North and South, and remains today the archetypal story of the fallen glories of the Old South. Long before Margaret Mitchell's Gone With the Wind (1936), "Marse Chan" introduced most of the stock features of the tragic and glamorous Southern legend, but made these same features almost credible by treating them in the form of an "oral narrative" and in the convincing voice of an old black haunted by memories of his former master. "Marse Chan" was collected with five other stories in Page's best-known book, In Ole Virginia, in 1887. Page became a national figure, and a popular spokesman for the Old South. His first wife died in 1886, two years after their marriage, and in 1893 he remarried, abandoned his law practice, moved to Washington, D.C., and devoted himself to his writing. In 1913, he was appointed Ambassador to Italy by Woodrow Wilson. He returned to the United States after the war, and died at Oakland. During his adult life, he produced an almost steady flow of fiction, essays, journalism, and social histories of the South, most of which were aimed at demonstrating his conviction that the virtues of the Old South far outweighed its faults. His novels have

*never received the critical respect accorded his early dialect stories,
though two of them,* Red Rock: A Chronicle of Reconstruction
(1898) and Gordon Keith *(1903), were popular successes. Despite
his shortcomings when it came to longer fictional forms, and despite
his highly selective "befo' the war" nostalgia, Page was a gifted
craftsman of the dialect story, and a powerful distiller of popular
attitudes about the Old South. His many books include* Two Little
Confederates *(1888),* The Old South: Essays Social and Political
(1892), Social Life in Old Virginia Before the War *(1897),* The
Negro: The Southerner's Problem *(1904),* Robert E. Lee, the
Southerner *(1908),* John Marvel, Assistant *(1909), and* Italy and
the World War *(1920). "Marse Chan: A Tale of Old Virginia" first
appeared in* The Century Magazine *(April 1884).*

MARSE CHAN

❀

A Tale of Old Virginia

One afternoon, in the autumn of 1872, I was riding leisurely down
the sandy road that winds along the top of the water-shed between
two of the smaller rivers of eastern Virginia. The road I was trav-
elling, following "the ridge" for miles, had just struck me as most
significant of the character of the race whose only avenue of communication with the outside world it had formerly been. Their
once splendid mansions, now fast falling to decay, appeared to
view from time to time, set back far from the road, in proud
seclusion, among groves of oak and hickory, now scarlet and gold
with the early frost. Distance was nothing to this people; time was
of no consequence to them. They desired but a level path in life,
and that they had, though the way was longer, and the outer world
strode by them as they dreamed.

I was aroused from my reflections by hearing some one ahead
of me calling, "Heah!—heah—whoo-oop, heah!"

Turning the curve in the road, I saw just before me a negro
standing, with a hoe and a watering-pot in his hand. He had evidently just gotten over the "worm-fence" into the road, out of the
path which led zigzag across the "old field" and was lost to sight

in the dense growth of sassafras. When I rode up, he was looking anxiously back down this path for his dog. So engrossed was he that he did not even hear my horse, and I reined in to wait until he should turn around and satisfy my curiosity as to the handsome old place half a mile off from the road.

The numerous out-buildings and the large barns and stables told that it had once been the seat of wealth, and the wild waste of sassafras that covered the broad fields gave it an air of desolation that greatly excited my interest. Entirely oblivious of my proximity, the negro went on calling "Whoo-oop, heah!" until along the path, walking very slowly and with great dignity, appeared a noble-looking old orange and white setter, gray with age, and corpulent with excessive feeding. As soon as he came in sight, his master began:

"Yes, dat you! You gittin' deaf as well as bline, I s'pose! Kyarnt heah me callin', I reckon? Whyn't yo' come on, dawg?"

The setter sauntered slowly up to the fence and stopped, without even deigning a look at the speaker, who immediately proceeded to take the rails down, talking meanwhile:

"Now, I got to pull down de gap, I s'pose! Yo' so sp'ilt yo' kyahn hardly walk. Jes' ez able to git over it as I is! Jes' like white folks—think 'cuz you's white and I's black, I got to wait on yo' all de time. Ne'm mine, I ain' gwi' do it!"

The fence having been pulled down sufficiently low to suit his dogship, he marched sedately through, and, with a hardly perceptible lateral movement of his tail, walked on down the road. Putting up the rails carefully, the negro turned and saw me.

"Sarvent, marster," he said, taking his hat off. Then, as if apologetically for having permitted a stranger to witness what was merely a family affair, he added: "He know I don' mean nothin' by what I sez. He's Marse Chan's dawg, an' he's so ole he kyahn git long no pearter. He know I'se jes' prodjickin' wid 'im."

"Who is Marse Chan?" I asked; "and whose place is that over there, and the one a mile or two back—the place with the big gate and the carved stone pillars?"

"Marse Chan," said the darky, "he's Marse Channin'—my young marster; an' dem places—dis one's Weall's, an' de one back dyar wid de rock gate-pos's is ole Cun'l Chahmb'lin's. Dey don' nobody live dyar now, 'cep' niggers. Arfter de war some one or nurr bought our place, but his name done kind o' slipped me. I nuver hearn on 'im befo'; I think dey's half-strainers. I don' ax none on 'em no odds. I lives down de road heah, a little piece, an' I jes' steps down of a evenin' and looks arfter de graves."

"Well, where is Marse Chan?" I asked.

"Hi! don' you know? Marse Chan, he went in de army. I was wid im. Yo' know he warn' gwine an' lef' Sam."

"Will you tell me all about it?" I said, dismounting.

Instantly, and as if by instinct, the darky stepped forward and took my bridle. I demurred a little; but with a bow that would have honored old Sir Roger, he shortened the reins, and taking my horse from me, led him along.

"Now tell me about Marse Chan," I said.

"Lawd, marster, hit's so long ago, I'd a'most forgit all about it, ef I hedn' been wid him ever sence he wuz born. Ez 'tis, I remembers it jes' like 'twuz yistiddy. Yo' know Marse Chan an' me—we wuz boys togerr. I wuz older'n he wuz, jes' de same ez he wuz whiter'n me. I wuz born plantin' corn time, de spring arfter big Jim an' de six steers got washed away at de upper ford right down dyar b'low de quarters ez he wuz a bringin' de Chris'mas things home; an' Marse Chan, he warn' born tell mos' to de harves' arfter my sister Nancy married Cun'l Chahmb'lin's Torm, 'bout eight years arfterwoods.

"Well, when Marse Chan wuz born, dey wuz de grettes' doin's at home you ever did see. De folks all hed holiday, jes' like in de Chris'mas. Ole marster (we didn' call 'im *ole* marster tell arfter Marse Chan wuz born—befo' dat he wuz jes' de marster, so)—well, ole marster, his face fyar shine wid pleasure, an' all de folks wuz mighty glad, too, 'cause dey all loved ole marster, and aldo' dey did step aroun' right peart when ole marster was lookin' at 'em, dyar warn' nyar han' on de place but what, ef he wanted anythin', would walk up to de back poach, an' say he warn' to see de marster. An' ev'ybody wuz talkin' 'bout de young marster, an' de maids an' de wimmens 'bout de kitchen wuz sayin' how 'twuz de purties' chile dey ever see; an' at dinner-time de mens (all on 'em hed holiday) come roun' de poach an' ax how de missis an' de young marster wuz, an' ole marster come out on de poach an' smile wus'n a 'possum, an' sez, 'Thankee! Bofe doin' fust rate, boys;' an' den he stepped back in de house, sort o' laughin' to hisse'f, an' in a minute he come out ag'in wid de baby in he arms, all wrapped up in flannens an' things, an' sez, 'Heah he is, boys.' All de folks den, dey went up on de poach to look at 'im, drappin' dey hats on de steps, an' scrapin' dey feets ez dey went up. An' pres'n'y ole marster, lookin' down at we all chil'en all packed togerr down dyah like a parecel o' sheep-burrs, cotch sight o' *me* (he knowed my name, 'cause I use' to hold he hoss fur 'im sometimes; but he didn' know all de chil'en by name, dey wuz so many on 'em), an' he sez, 'Come up heah.' So up I goes tippin', skeered like, an' old marster sez, 'Ain' you Mymie's son?' 'Yass, seh,' sez

I. 'Well,' sez he, 'I'm gwine to give you to yo' young Marse Chan-nin' to be his body-servant,' an' he put de baby right in my arms (it's de truth I'm tellin' yo'!), an' yo' jes' ought to a-heard de folks sayin', 'Lawd! marster, dat boy'll drap dat chile!' 'Naw, he won't,' sez marster; 'I kin trust 'im.' And den he sez: 'Now, Sam, from dis time you belong to yo' young Marse Channin'; I wan' you to tek keer on 'im ez long ez he lives. You are to be his boy from dis time. An' now,' he sez, 'carry 'im in de house.' An' he walks arfter me an' opens de do's fur me, an' I kyars 'im in my arms, an' lays 'im down on de bed. An from dat time I was tooken in de house to be Marse Channin's body-servant.

"Well, you nuver see a chile grow so. Pres'n'y he growed up right big, an' ole marster sez he must have some edication. So he sont 'im to school to ole Miss Lawry down dyar, dis side o' Cun'l Chahmb'lin's, an' I use' to go 'long wid 'im an' tote he books an' we all's snacks; an' when he larnt to read an' spell right good, an' got 'bout so-o big, ole Miss Lawry she died, an' ole marster said he mus' have a man to teach 'im an' trounce 'im. So we all went to Mr. Hall, whar kep' de school-house beyant de creek, an' dyar we went ev'y day, 'cep Sat'd'ys of co'se, an' sich days ez Marse Chan din' warn' go, an' ole missis begged 'im off.

"Hit wuz down dyar Marse Chan fust took notice o' Miss Anne. Mr. Hall, he taught gals ez well ez boys, an' Cun'l Chahmb'lin he sont his daughter (dat's Miss Anne I'm talkin' about). She wuz a leetle bit o' gal when she fust come. Yo' see, her ma wuz dead, an' ole Miss Lucy Chahmb'lin, she lived wid her brurr an' kep' house for 'im; an' he wuz so busy wid politics, he didn' have much time to spyar, so he sont Miss Anne to Mr. Hall's by a 'ooman wid a note. When she come dat day in de school-house, an' all de chil'en looked at her so hard, she tu'n right red, an' tried to pull her long curls over her eyes, an' den put bofe de backs of her little han's in her two eyes, an' begin to cry to herse'f. Marse Chan he was settin' on de een' o' de bench nigh de do', an' he jes' reached out an' put he arm roun' her an' drawed her up to 'im. An' he kep' whisperin' to her, an' callin' her name, an' coddlin' her; an' pres'n'y she took her han's down an' begin to laugh.

"Well, dey 'peared to tek' a gre't fancy to each urr from dat time. Miss Anne she warn' nuthin' but a baby hardly, an' Marse Chan he wuz a good big boy 'bout mos' thirteen years ole, I reckon. Hows'ever, dey sut'n'y wuz sot on each urr an' (yo' heah me!) ole marster an' Cun'l Chahmb'lin dey 'peared to like it 'bout well ez de chil'en. Yo' see, Cun'l Chahmb'lin's place j'ined ourn, an' it looked jes' ez natural fur dem two chil'en to marry an' mek it one plantation, ez it did fur de creek to run down de bottom from our place into Cun'l Chahmb'lin's. I don' rightly think de chil'en thought 'bout gittin' *married,* not den, no mo'n I thought 'bout marryin' Judy when she wuz a little gal at Cun'l Chahmb'lin's, runnin' 'bout de house, huntin' fur Miss Lucy's spectacles; but dey wuz good frien's from de start. Marse Chan he use' to kyar Miss Anne's books fur her ev'y day, an' ef de road wuz muddy or she wuz tired, he use' to tote her; an' 'twarn' hardly a day passed dat he didn' kyar her some'n' to school—apples or hick'y nuts, or some'n'. He wouldn't let none o' de chil'en tease her, nurr. Heh! One day, one o' de boys poked he finger at Miss Anne, and arfter school Marse Chan he axed 'im 'roun' hine de school-house out o' sight, an' ef he didn' whop 'im!

"Marse Chan, he wuz de peartes' scholar ole Mr. Hall hed, an' Mr. Hall he wuz mighty proud o' 'im. I don' think he use' to beat 'im ez much ez he did de urrs, aldo' he wuz de head in all debilment dat went on, jes' ez he wuz in sayin' he lessons.

"Heh! one day in summer, jes' fo' de school broke up, dyah come up a storm right sudden, an' riz de creek (dat one yo' cross' back yonder), an' Marse Chan he toted Miss Anne home on he back. He ve'y off'n did dat when de parf wuz muddy. But dis day when dey come to de creek, it had done washed all de logs 'way. 'Twuz still mighty high, so Marse Chan he put Miss Anne down, an' he took a pole an' waded right in. Hit took 'im long up to de shoulders. Den he waded back, an' took Miss Anne up on his head an' kyared her right over. At fust she wuz skeered; but he tol' her he could swim an' wouldn' let her git hu't, an' den she let 'im kyar her 'cross, she hol'in' his han's. I warn' 'long dat day, but he sut'n'y did dat thing.

"Ole marster he wuz so pleased 'bout it, he giv' Marse Chan a pony; an' Marse Chan rode 'im to school de day arfter he come, so proud, an' sayin' how he wuz gwine to let Anne ride behine 'im; an' when he come home dat evenin' he wuz walkin'. 'Hi! where's yo' pony?' said ole marster. 'I give 'im to Anne,' says Marse Chan. 'She liked 'im, an'—I kin walk.' 'Yes,' sez ole marster, laughin', 'I s'pose you's already done giv' her yo'se'f, an' nex' thing I know you'll be givin' her this plantation and all my niggers.'

"Well, about a fortnight or sich a matter arfter dat, Cun'l Chahmb'lin sont over an' invited all o' we all over to dinner, an' Marse Chan wuz 'spressly named in de note whar Ned brought; an' arfter dinner he made ole Phil, whar wuz his ker'ige-driver, bring roun' Marse Chan's pony wid a little side-saddle on 'im, an' a beautiful little hoss wid a bran'-new saddle an' bridle on 'im; an' he gits up an' meks Marse Chan a gre't speech, an' presents 'im de little hoss; an' den he calls Miss Anne, an' she comes out on de poach in a little ridin' frock, an' dey puts her on her pony, an' Marse Chan mounts his hoss, an' dey goes to ride, while de grown folks is a-laughin' an' chattin' an' smokin' dey cigars.

"Dem wuz good ole times, marster—de bes' Sam ever see! Dey wuz, in fac'! Niggers didn' hed nothin' 't all to do—jes' hed to 'ten' to de feedin' an' cleanin' de hosses, an' doin' what de marster tell 'em to do; an' when dey wuz sick, dey had things sont 'em out de house, an' de same doctor come to see 'em whar 'ten' to de white folks when dey wuz po'ly. Dyar warn' no trouble nor nothin'.

"Well, things tuk a change arfter dat. Marse Chan he went to de bo'din' school, whar he use' to write to me constant. Ole missis use' to read me de letters, an' den I'd git Miss Anne to read 'em ag'in to me when I'd see her. He use' to write to her too, an' she use' to write to him too. Den Miss Anne she wuz sont off to school too. An' in de summer time dey'd bofe come home, an' yo' hardly knowed whether Marse Chan lived at home or over at Cun'l Chahmb'lin's. He wuz over dyah constant. 'Twuz always ridin' or fishin' down dyah in de river; or sometimes he' go over dyah, an' 'im an' she'd go out an' set in de yard onder de trees; she settin' up mekin' out she wuz knittin' some sort o' bright-cullored some'n', wid de grarss growin all up 'g'inst her, an' her hat th'owed back on her neck, an' he readin' to her out books; an' sometimes dey'd bofe read out de same book, fust one an' den todder. I use' to see 'em! Dat wuz when dey wuz growin' up like.

"Den ole marster he run for Congress, an' ole Cun'l Chahmb'lin he wuz put up to run 'g'inst ole marster by de Dimicrats; but ole marster he beat 'im. Yo' know he wuz gwine do dat! Co'se he wuz! Dat made ole Cun'l Chahmb'lin mighty mad, and dey stopt visitin' each urr reg'lar, like dey had been doin' all 'long. Den Cun'l Chahmb'lin he sort o' got in debt, an' sell some o' he niggers, an' dat's de way de fuss begun. Dat's whar de lawsuit cum from. Ole marster he didn' like nobody to sell niggers, an' knowin' dat Cun'l Chahmb'lin wuz sellin' o' his, he writ an' offered to buy his M'ria an' all her chil'en, 'cause she hed married our Zeek'yel. An' don' yo' think, Cun'l Chahmb'lin axed ole marster mo' 'n th'ee niggers wuz wuth fur M'ria! Befo' old marster bought her, dough, de sheriff cum an' levelled on M'ria an' a whole parecel o' urr niggers. Ole marster he went to de sale, an' bid for 'em; but Cun'l Chahmb'lin he got some one to bid 'g'inst ole marster. Dey wuz knocked out to ole marster dough, an' den dey hed a big lawsuit, an' ole marster wuz agwine to co't, off an' on, fur some years, till at lars' de co't decided dat M'ria belonged to ole marster. Ole Cun'l Chahmb'lin den wuz so mad he sued ole marster for a little strip o' lan' down dyah on de line fence, whar he said belonged

to 'im. Evy'body knowed hit belonged to ole marster. Ef yo' go
down dyah now, I kin show it to yo', inside de line fence, whar it
hed done bin ever since long befo' Cun'l Chahmb'lin wuz born.
But Cun'l Chahmb'lin wuz a mons'us perseverin' man, an' ole
marster he wouldn' let nobody run over 'im. No, dat he wouldn'!
So dey wuz agwine down to co't about dat, fur I don' know how
long, till ole marster beat 'im.

"All dis time, yo' know, Marse Chan wuz agoin' back'ads an'
for'ads to college, an' wuz growed up a ve'y fine young man. He
wuz a ve'y likely gent'man! Miss Anne she hed done mos' growed
up too—wuz puttin' her hyar up like ole missis use' to put hers
up, an' 't wuz jes' ez bright ez de sorrel's mane when de sun cotch
on it, an' her eyes wuz gre't big dark eyes, like her pa's, on'y bigger
an' not so fierce, an' 'twarn' none o' de young ladies ez purty ez
she wuz. She an' Marse Chan still set a heap o' sto' by one 'nurr,
but I don' think dey wuz easy wid each urr ez when he used to
tote her home from school on his back. Marse Chan he use' to
love de ve'y groun' she walked on, dough, in my 'pinion. Heh!
His face 'twould light up whenever she come into chu'ch, or anywhere, jes' like de sun hed come th'oo a chink on it suddenly.

"Den ole marster lost he eyes. D' yo' ever heah 'bout dat? Heish!
Didn' yo'? Well, one night de big barn cotch fire. De stables, yo'
know, wuz under de big barn, an' all de hosses wuz in dyah. Hit
'peared to me like 'twarn' no time befo' all de folks an' de neighbors
dey come, an' dey wuz a-totin' water, an' a-tryin' to save de po'
critters, and dey got a heap on 'em out; but de ker'ige-hosses dey
wouldn' come out, an' dey wuz a-runnin' back'ads an' for'ads inside
de stalls, a-nikerin' an' a-screamin', like dey knowed dey time hed
come. Yo' could heah 'em so pitiful, an' pres'n'y old marster said
to Ham Fisher (he wuz de ker'ige-driver), 'Go in dyah an' try to
save 'em; don' let 'em bu'n to death.' An' Ham he went right in.
An' jest arfter he got in, de shed whar it hed fus' cotch fell in, an'
de sparks shot 'way up in de air; an' Ham didn' come back, an'
de fire begun to lick out under de eaves over whar de ker'ige-
hosses' stalls wuz, an' all of a sudden ole marster tu'ned an' kissed
ole missis, who wuz standin' nigh him, wid her face jes' ez white
ez a sperit's, an', befo' anybody knowed what he wuz gwine do,
jumped right in de do', an' de smoke come po'in' out behine 'im.
Well, seh, I nuver 'spects to heah tell Judgment sich a soun' ez de
folks set up! Ole missis she jes' drapt down on her knees in de
mud an' prayed out loud. Hit 'peared like her pra'r wuz heard;
for in a minit, right out de same do', kyarin' Ham Fisher in his
arms, come ole marster, wid his clo's all blazin'. Dey flung water

on 'im, an' put 'im out; an', ef you b'lieve me, yo' wouldn' a-knowed 'twuz ole marster. Yo' see, he hed find Ham Fisher done fall down in de smoke right by de ker'ige-hoss' stalls, whar he sont him, an' he hed to tote 'im back in his arms th'oo de fire what hed done cotch de front part o' de stable, and to keep de flame from gittin' down Ham Fisher's th'ote he hed tuk off his own hat and mashed it all over Ham Fisher's face, an' he hed kep' Ham Fisher from bein' so much bu'nt; but *he* wuz bu'nt dreadful! His beard an' hyar wuz all nyawed off, an' his face an' han's an' neck wuz scorified terrible. Well, he jes' laid Ham Fisher down, an' then he kind o' staggered for'ad, an' ole missis ketch' 'im in her arms. Ham Fisher, he warn' bu'nt so bad, an' he got out in a month or two; an' arfter a long time, ole marster he got well, too; but he wuz always stone blind arfter that. He nuver could see none from dat night.

"Marse Chan he comed home from college toreckly, an' he sut'n'y did nuss ole marster faithful—jes' like a 'ooman. Den he took charge of de plantation arfter dat; an' I use' to wait on 'im jes' like when we wuz boys togedder; an' sometimes we'd slip off an' have a fox-hunt, an' he'd be jes' like he wuz in ole times, befo' ole marster got bline, an' Miss Anne Chahmb'lin stopt comin' over to our house, an' settin' onder de trees, readin' out de same book.

"He sut'n'y wuz good to me. Nothin' nuver made no diffunce 'bout dat. He nuver hit me a lick in his life—an' nuver let nobody else do it, nurr.

"I 'members one day, when he wuz a leetle bit o' boy, ole marster hed done tole we all chil'en not to slide on de straw-stacks; an' one day me an' Marse Chan thought ole marster hed done gone 'way from home. We watched him git on he hoss an' ride up de road out o' sight, an' we wuz out in de field a-slidin' an a-slidin', when up comes ole marster. We started to run; but he hed done see us, an' he called us to come back; an' sich a whuppin' ez he did gi' us!

"Fust he took Marse Chan, an' den he teched me up. He nuver hu't me, but in co'se I wuz a-hollerin' ez hard ez I could stave it, 'cause I knowed dat wuz gwine mek him stop. Marse Chan he hed'n open he mouf long ez ole marster wuz tunin' 'im; but soon ez he commence warmin' me an' I begin to holler, Marse Chan he bu'st out cryin', an' stept right in befo' ole marster, an' ketchin' de whup, sed:

" 'Stop, seh! Yo' sha'n't whup 'im; he b'longs to me, an' ef you hit 'im another lick I'll set 'im free!'

"I wish yo' hed see ole marster. Marse Chan he warn' mo'n

eight years ole, an' dyah dey wuz—old marster stan'in' wid he whup raised up, an' Marse Chan red an' cryin', hol'in' on to it, an' sayin' I b'longst to 'im.

"Ole marster, he raise' de whup, an' den he drapt it, an' broke out in a smile over he face, an' he chuck' Marse Chan onder de chin, an' tu'n right roun' an' went away, laughin' to hisse'f, an' I heah' 'im tellin' ole missis dat evenin', an' laughin' 'bout it.

"'Twan' so mighty long arfter dat when dey fust got to talkin' 'bout de war. Dey wuz a-dictatin' back'ads an' for'ds 'bout it fur two or th'ee years 'fo' it come sho' nuff, you know. Ole marster, he was a Whig, an' of co'se Marse Chan he tuk after he pa. Cun'l Chahmb'lin, he wuz a Dimicrat. He wuz in favor of de war, an' ole marster and Marse Chan dey wuz agin' it. Dey wuz a-talkin' 'bout it all de time, an' purty soon Cun'l Chahmb'lin he went about ev'vywhar speakin' an' noratin' 'bout Ferginia ought to secede; an' Marse Chan he wuz picked up to talk agin' 'im. Dat wuz de way dey come to fight de duil. I sut'n'y wuz skeered fur Marse Chan dat mawnin', an' he was jes' ez cool! Yo' see, it happen so: Marse Chan he wuz a-speakin' down at de Deep Creek Tavern, an' he kind o' got de bes' of ole Cun'l Chahmb'lin. All de white folks laughed an' hoorawed, an' ole Cun'l Chahmb'lin—my Lawd! I t'ought he'd 'a' bu'st, he was so mad. Well, when it come to his time to speak, he jes' light into Marse Chan. He call 'im a traitor, an' a ab'litionis', an' I don' know what all. Marse Chan, he jes' kep' cool till de ole Cun'l light into he pa. Ez soon ez he name ole marster, I seen Marse Chan sort o' lif' up he head. D' yo' ever see a hoss rar he head up right sudden at night when he see somethin' comin' to'ds 'im from de side an' he don' know what 'tis? Ole Cun'l Chahmb'lin he went right on. He said ole marster hed taught Marse Chan; dat ole marster wuz a wuss ab'litionis' dan he son. I looked at Marse Chan, an' sez to myse'f: 'Fo' Gord! ole Cun'l Chahmb'lin better min',' an' I hedn' got de wuds out, when ole Cun'l Chahmb'lin 'cuse' ole marster o' cheatin' 'im out o' he niggers, an' stealin' piece o' he lan'—dat's de lan' I tole you 'bout. Well, seh, nex' thing I knowed, I heahed Marse Chan—hit all happen right 'long togerr, like lightnin' and thunder when they hit right at you—I heah 'im say:

" 'Cun'l Chahmb'lin, what you say is false, an' yo' know it to be so. You have wilfully slandered one of de pures' an' nobles' men Gord ever made, an' nothin' but yo' gray hyars protects you.'

"Well, ole Cun'l Chahmb'lin, he ra'ed an' he pitch'd. He said he wan' too ole, an' he'd show 'im so.

" 'Ve'y well,' says Marse Chan.

"De meetin broke up den. I wuz hol'in' de hosses out dyar in de road by de een' o' de poach, an' I see Marse Chan talkin' an' talkin' to Mr. Gordon an' anudder gent'man, and den he come out an' got on de sorrel an' galloped off. Soon ez he got out o' sight he pulled up, an' we walked along tell we come to de road whar leads off to'ds Mr. Barbour's. He wuz de big lawyer o' de country. Dar he tu'ned off. All dis time he hedn' sed a wud, 'cep' to kind o' mumble to hisse'f now and den. When we got to Mr. Barbour's, he got down an' went in. Dat wuz in de late winter; de folks wuz jes' beginnin' to plough fur corn. He stayed dyar 'bout two hours, an' when he come out Mr. Barbour come out to de gate wid 'im an' shake han's arfter he got up in de saddle. Den we all rode off. 'Twuz late den—good dark; an' we rid ez hard ez we could, tell we come to de ole school-house at ole Cun'l Chahmb'lin's gate. When we got dar, Marse Chan got down an' walked right slow 'roun' de house. Arfter lookin' roun' a little while an' tryin' de do' to see ef it wuz shet, he walked down de road tell he got to de creek. He stop' dyar a little while an' picked up two or three little rocks an' frowed 'em in, an' pres'n'y he got up an' we come on home. Ez he got down, he tu'ned to me an', rubbin' de sorrel's nose, said: 'Have 'em well fed, Sam; I'll want 'em early in de mawnin'.'

"Dat night at supper he laugh an' talk, an' he set at de table a long time. Arfter ole marster went to bed, he went in de charmber an' set on de bed by 'im talkin' to 'im an' tellin' 'im 'bout de meetin' an' e'vything; but he nuver mention ole Cun'l Chahmb'lin's name. When he got up to come out to de office in de yard, whar he slept, he stooped down an' kissed 'im jes' like he wuz a baby layin' dyar in de bed, an' he'd hardly let ole missis go at all. I knowed some'n wuz up, an' nex mawnin' I called 'im early befo' light, like he tole me, an' he dressed an' come out pres'n'y jes' like he wuz goin' to church. I had de hosses ready, an' we went out de back way to'ds de river. Ez we rode along, he said:

" 'Sam, you an' I wuz boys togedder, wa'n't we?'

" 'Yes,' sez I, 'Marse Chan, dat we wuz.'

" 'You have been ve'y faithful to me,' sez he, 'an' I have seen to it that you are well provided fur. You want to marry Judy, I know, an' you'll be able to buy her ef you want to.'

"Den he tole me he wuz goin' to fight a duil, an' in case he should git shot, he had set me free an' giv' me nuff to tek keer o' me an' my wife ez long ez we lived. He said he'd like me to stay an' tek keer o' ole marster an' ole missis ez long ez dey lived, an' he said it wouldn' be very long, he reckoned. Dat wuz de on'y time he voice broke—when he said dat; an' I couldn' speak a wud, my th'oat choked me so.

"When we come to de river, we tu'ned right up de bank, an' arfter ridin' 'bout a mile or sich a matter, we stopped whar dey wuz a little clearin' wid elder bushes on one side an' two big gum-trees on de urr, an' de sky wuz all red, an' de water down to'ds whar the sun wuz comin' wuz jes' like de sky.

"Pres'n'y Mr. Gordon he come, wid a 'hogany box 'bout so big 'fore 'im, an' he got down, an' Marse Chan tole me to tek all de hosses an' go 'roun' behine de bushes whar I tell you 'bout—off to one side; an' 'fore I got 'roun' dar, ole Cun'l Chahmb'lin an' Mr. Hennin an' Dr. Call come ridin' from t'urr way, to'ds ole Cun'l Chahmb'lin's. When dey hed tied dey hosses, de urr gent'mens went up to whar Mr. Gordon wuz, an' arfter some chattin' Mr. Hennin step' off 'bout fur ez 'cross dis road, or mebbe it mout be a little furder; an' den I seed 'em th'oo de bushes loadin' de pistils, an' talk a little while; an' den Marse Chan an' ole Cun'l Chahmb'lin walked up wid de pistils in dey han's, an' Marse Chan he stood wid his face right to'ds de sun. I seen it shine on him jes' ez it come up over de low groun's, an' he look like he did sometimes when he come out of church. I wuz so skeered I couldn' say nothin'. Ole Cun'l Chahmb'lin could shoot fust rate, an' Marse Chan he never missed.

"Den I heared Mr. Gordon say, 'Gent'mens, is yo' ready?' and bofe of 'em sez, 'Ready,' jes' so.

"An' he sez, 'Fire, one, two'—an' ez he said 'one,' ole Cun'l Chahmb'lin raised he pistil an' shot right at Marse Chan. De ball went th'oo his hat. I seen he hat sort o' settle on he head ez de bullit hit it, an' *he* jes' tilted his pistil up in de a'r an' shot—*bang*; an' ez de pistil went *bang*, he sez to Cun'l Chahmb'lin, 'I mek you a present to yo' fam'ly, seh!'

"Well, dey had some talkin' arfter dat. I didn't git rightly what it wuz; but it 'peared like Cun'l Chahmb'lin he warn't satisfied, an' wanted to have anurr shot. De seconds dey wuz talkin', an' pres'n'y dey put de pistils up, an' Marse Chan an' Mr. Gordon shook han's wid Mr. Hennin an' Dr. Call, an' come an' got on dey hosses. An' Cun'l Chahmb'lin he got on his horse an' rode away wid de urr gent'mens, lookin' like he did de day befo' when all de people laughed at 'im.

"I b'lieve ole Cun'l Chahmb'lin wan' to shoot Marse Chan, anyway!

"We come on home to breakfast, I totin' de box wid de pistils befo' me on de roan. Would you b'lieve me, seh, Marse Chan he nuver said a wud 'bout it to ole marster or nobody. Ole missis didn' fin' out 'bout it for mo'n a month, an' den, Lawd! how she did cry and kiss Marse Chan; an' ole marster, aldo' he never say much, he wuz jes' ez please' ez ole missis. He call' me in de room an' made me tole 'im all 'bout it, an' when I got th'oo he gi' me five dollars an' a pyar of breeches.

"But ole Cun'l Chahmb'lin he nuver did furgive Marse Chan, an' Miss Anne she got mad too. Wimmens is mons'us onreasonable nohow. Dey's jes' like a catfish: you can n' tek hole on 'em like udder folks, an' when you gits 'm yo' can n' always hole 'em.

"What meks me think so? Heaps o' things—dis: Marse Chan he done gi' Miss Anne her pa jes' ez good ez I gi' Marse Chan's dawg sweet 'taters, an' she git mad wid 'im ez if he hed kill 'im 'stid o' sen'in' 'im back to her dat mawnin' whole an' soun'. B'lieve me! she wouldn' even speak to him arfter dat!

"Don' I 'member dat mawnin'!

"We wuz gwine fox-huntin', 'bout six weeks or sich a matter arfter de duil, an' we met Miss Anne ridin' 'long wid anurr lady an' two gent'mens whar wuz stayin' at her house. Dyar wuz always some one or nurr dyar co'ting her. Well, dat mawnin' we meet 'em right in de road. 'Twuz de fust time Marse Chan had see her sence de duil, an' he raises he hat ez he pahss, an' she looks right at 'im wid her head up in de yair like she nuver see 'im befo' in her born days; an' when she comes by me, she sez, 'Good-mawnin', Sam!' Gord! I nuver see nuthin' like de look dat come on Marse Chan's face when she pahss 'im like dat. He gi' de sorrel a pull dat fotch 'im back settin' down in de san' on he hanches. He ve'y lips wuz white. I tried to keep up wid 'im, but 'twarn' no use. He sont me back home pres'n'y, an' he rid on. I sez to myself, 'Cun'l Chahmb'lin, don' yo' meet Marse Chan dis mawnin'. He ain' bin lookin' 'roun' de ole school-house, whar he an' Miss Anne use' to go to school to ole Mr. Hall together, fur nuffin'. He won' stan' no prodjickin' to-day.'

"He nuver come home dat night tell 'way late, an' ef he'd been fox-huntin' it mus' ha' been de ole red whar lives down in de greenscum mashes he'd been chasin'. De way de sorrel wuz gormed up wid sweat an' mire sut'n'y did hu't me. He walked up to de stable wid he head down all de way, an' I'se seen 'im go eighty miles of a winter day, an' prance into de stable at night ez fresh ez ef he hed jes' cantered over to ole Cun'l Chahmb'lin's to supper. I nuver seen a hoss beat so sence I knowed de fetlock from de fo'lock, an' bad ez he wuz he wan' ez bad ez Marse Chan.

"Whew! he didn' git over dat thing, seh—he nuver did git over it.

"De war come on jes' den, an Marse Chan wuz elected cap'n; but he wouldn' tek it. He said Firginia hadn' seceded, an' he wuz gwine stan' by her. Den dey 'lected Mr. Gordon cap'n.

"I sut'n'y did wan' Marse Chan to tek de place, cuz I knowed he wuz gwine tek me wid 'im. He wan' gwine widout Sam. An', beside, he look so po' an' thin, I thought he wuz gwine die.

"Of co'se, ole missis she heared 'bout it, an' she met Miss Anne in de road, an' cut her jes' like Miss Anne cut Marse Chan.

"Ole missis, she wuz proud ez anybody! So we wuz mo' strangers dan ef we hadn' live' in a hunderd miles of each urr. An' Marse Chan he wuz gittin' thinner an' thinner, an' Firginia she come out, an' den Marse Chan he went to Richmond an' listed, an' come back an' sey he wuz a private, an' he didn' know whe'r he could tek me or not. He writ to Mr. Gordon, hows'ever, an' 'twuz 'cided dat when he went I wuz to go 'long an' wait on him an' de cap'n too. I didn' min' dat, yo' know, long ez I could go wid Marse Chan, an' I like' Mr. Gordon, anyways.

"Well, one night Marse Chan come back from de offis wid a telegram dat say, 'Come at once,' so he wuz to start nex' mawnin'. He uniform wuz all ready, gray wid yaller trimmin's, an' mine wuz ready too, an' he had ole marster's sword, whar de State gi' 'im in de Mexikin war; an' he trunks wuz all packed wid ev'rything in 'em, an' my chist was packed too, an' Jim Rasher he druv 'em over to de depo' in de waggin, an' we wuz to start nex' mawnin' 'bout light. Dis wuz 'bout de las' o' spring, you know. Dat night ole missis made Marse Chan dress up in he uniform, an' he sut'n'y did look splendid, wid he long mustache an' he wavin' hyar an' he tall figger.

"Arfter supper he come down an' sez: 'Sam, I wan' you to tek dis note an' kyar it over to Cun'l Chahmb'lin's, an' gi' it to Miss Anne wid yo' own han's, an' bring me wud what she sez. Don' let any one know 'bout it, or know why you've gone.' 'Yes, seh,' sez I.

"Yo' see, I knowed Miss Anne's maid over at ole Cun'l Chahmb'lin's—dat wuz Judy whar is my wife now—an' I knowed I could wuk it. So I tuk de roan an' rid over, an' tied 'im down de hill in de cedars, an' I wen' 'roun' to de back yard. 'Twuz a right blowy sort o' night; de moon wuz jes' risin', but de clouds wuz so big it didn' shine 'cep' th'oo a crack now an' den. I soon foun' my gal, an' arfter tellin' her two or three lies 'bout herse'f, I got her to go in an' ax Miss Anne to come to de do'. When she come, I gi' her de note, an' arfter a little while she bro't me anurr, an' I tole her good-by, an' she gi' me a dollar, an' I come home an' gi' de letter to Marse Chan. He read it, an' tole me to have de hosses ready at twenty minits to twelve at de corner of de garden. An' jes' befo' dat he come out ez ef he wuz gwine to bed, but instid he come, an' we all struck out to'ds Cun'l Chahmb'lin's.

When we got mos' to de gate, de hosses got sort o' skeered, an' I see dey wuz some'n or somebody standin' jes' inside; an' Marse Chan he jumpt off de sorrel an' flung me de bridle and he walked up.

"She spoke fust ('twuz Miss Anne had done come out dyar to meet Marse Chan), an' she sez, jes' ez cold ez a chill, 'Well, seh, I granted your favor. I wished to relieve myse'f of de obligations you placed me under a few months ago, when you made me a present of my father, whom you fust insulted an' then prevented from gittin' satisfaction.'

"Marse Chan he didn' speak fur a minit, an' den he said: 'Who is with you?' (Dat wuz ev'y wud.)

" 'No one,' sez she; 'I came alone.'

" 'My God!' sez he, 'you didn' come all through those woods by yourse'f at this time o' night?'

" 'Yes, I'm not afraid,' sez she. (An' heah dis nigger! I don' b'lieve she wuz.)

"De moon come out, an' I cotch sight o' her stan'in' dyar in her white dress, wid de cloak she had wrapped herse'f up in drapped off on de groun', an' she didn' look like she wuz 'feared o' nuthin'. She wuz mons'us purty ez she stood dyar wid de green bushes behine her, an' she hed jes' a few flowers in her breas'—right hyah—and some leaves in her sorrel hyar; an' de moon come out an' shined down on her hyar an' her frock, an' 'peared like de light wuz jes' stan'in' off it ez she stood dyar lookin' at Marse Chan wid her head tho'd back, jes' like dat mawnin' when she pahss Marse Chan in de road widout speakin' to 'im, an' sez to me, 'Good mawnin', Sam.'

"Marse Chan, he den tole her he hed come to say good-by to her, ez he wuz gwine 'way to de war nex' mawnin'. I wuz watchin' on her, an' I tho't, when Marse Chan tole her dat, she sort o' started an' looked up at 'im like she wuz mighty sorry, an' 'peared like she didn' stan' quite so straight arfter dat. Den Marse Chan he went on talkin' right fars' to her; an' he tole her how he had loved her ever sence she wuz a little bit o' baby mos', an' how he nuver 'membered de time when he hedn' 'spected to marry her. He tole her it wuz his love for her dat hed made 'im stan' fust at school an' collige, an' hed kep' 'im good an' pure; an' now he wuz gwine 'way, wouldn' she let it be like 'twuz in ole times, an' ef he come back from de war wouldn' she try to think on him ez she use' to do when she wuz a little guirl?

"Marse Chan he had done been talkin' so serious, he hed done tuk Miss Anne's han', an' wuz lookin' down in her face like he wuz list'nin' wid his eyes.

"Arfter a minit Miss Anne she said somethin', an' Marse Chan he cotch her urr han' an' sez:

" 'But if you love me, Anne?'

"When he said dat, she tu'ned her head 'way from 'im, an' wait' a minit, an' den she said—right clear:

" 'But I don' love yo'.' (Jes' dem th'ee wuds!) De wuds fall right slow—like dirt falls out a spade on a coffin when yo's buryin' anybody, an' seys, 'Uth to uth.' Marse Chan he jes' let her hand drap, an' he stiddy hisse'f 'g'inst de gate-pos', an' he didn' speak torekly. When he did speak, all he sez wuz:

" 'I mus' see you home safe.'

"I 'clar, marster, I didn' know 'twuz Marse Chan's voice tell I look at 'im right good. Well, she wouldn' let 'im go wid her. She jes' wrap' her cloak 'roun' her shoulders, an' wen' 'long back by herse'f, widout doin' more'n jes' look up once at Marse Chan leanin' dyah 'g'inst de gate-pos' in he sodger clo's, wid he eyes on de groun'. She said 'Good-by' sort o' sorf, an' Marse Chan, widout lookin' up, shake han's wid her, an' she wuz done gone down de road. Soon ez she got 'mos' 'roun de curve, Marse Chan he followed her, keepin' under de trees so ez not to be seen, an' I led de hosses on down de road behine 'im. He kep' 'long behine her tell she wuz safe in de house, an' den he come an' got on he hoss, an' we all come home.

"Nex' mawnin' we all come off to j'ine de army. An' dey wuz a-drillin' an' a-drillin' all 'bout for a while an' dey went 'long wid all de res' o' de army, an' I went wid Marse Chan an' clean he boots, an' look arfter de tent, an' tek keer o' him an' de hosses. An' Marse Chan, he wan' a bit like he use' to be. He wuz so solum an' moanful all de time, at leas' 'cep' when dyah wuz gwine to be a fight. Den he'd peartin' up, an' he alwuz rode at de head o' de company, 'cause he wuz tall; an' hit wan' on'y in battles whar all his company wuz dat *he* went, but he use' to volunteer whenever de cun'l wanted anybody to fine out anythin', an' 'twuz so dangersome he didn' like to mek one man go no sooner'n anurr, yo' know, an' ax'd who'd volunteer. *He* 'peared to like to go prowlin' aroun' 'mong dem Yankees, an' he use' to tek me wid 'im whenever he could. Yes, seh, he sut'n'y wuz a good sodger! He didn' mine bullets no more'n he did so many draps o' rain. But I use' to be pow'ful skeered sometimes. It jes' use' to 'pear like fun to 'im. In camp he use' to be so sorrerful he'd hardly open he mouf. You'd 'a' tho't he wuz seekin', he used to look so moanful; but jes' le' 'im git into danger, an' he use' to be like ole times—jolly an' laughin' like when he wuz a boy.

"When Cap'n Gordon got he leg shot off, dey mek Marse Chan

cap'n on de spot, 'cause one o' de lieutenants got kilt de same day, an' turr one (named Mr. Ronny) wan' no 'count, an' all de company said Marse Chan wuz de man.

"An' Marse Chan he wuz jes' de same. He didn' never mention Miss Anne's name, but I knowed he wuz thinkin' on her constant. One night he wuz settin' by de fire in camp, an' Mr. Ronny—he wuz de secon' lieutenant—got to talkin' 'bout ladies, an' he say all sorts o' things 'bout 'em, an' I see Marse Chan kinder lookin' mad; an' de lieutenant mention Miss Anne's name. He hed been courtin' Miss Anne 'bout de time Marse Chan fit de duil wid her pa, an' Miss Anne hed kicked 'im, dough he wuz mighty rich, 'cause he warn' nuthin' but a half-strainer, an' 'cause she like Marse Chan, I believe, dough she didn' speak to 'im; an' Mr. Ronny he got drunk, an' 'cause Cun'l Chahmb'lin tole 'im not to come dyah no more, he got mighty mad. An' dat evenin' I'se tellin' yo' 'bout, he wuz talkin', an' he mention' Miss Anne's name. I see Marse Chan tu'n he eye 'roun' on 'im an' keep it on he face, and pres'n'y Mr. Ronny said he wuz gwine hev some fun dyah yit. He didn' mention her name dat time; but he said dey wuz all on 'em a parecel of stuckup 'risticrats, an' her pa wan' no gent'man anyway, an'—I don' know what he wuz gwine say (he nuver said it), fur ez he got dat far Marse Chan riz up an' hit 'im a crack, an' he fall like he hed been hit wid a fence-rail. He challenged Marse Chan to fight a duil, an' Marse Chan he excepted de challenge, an' dey wuz gwine fight; but some on 'em tole 'im Marse Chan wan' gwine mek a present o' him to his fam'ly, an' he got somebody to bre'k up de duil; twan' nuthin' dough, but he wuz 'fred to fight Marse Chan. An' purty soon he lef' de comp'ny.

"Well, I got one o' de gent'mens to write Judy a letter for me, an' I tole her all 'bout de fight, an' how Marse Chan knock Mr. Ronny over fur speakin' discontemptuous o' Cun'l Chahmb'lin, an' I tole her how Marse Chan wuz a-dyin' fur love o' Miss Anne. An' Judy she gits Miss Anne to read de letter fur her. Den Miss Anne she tells her pa, an'—you mind, Judy tells me all dis arfterwards, an' she say when Cun'l Chahmb'lin hear 'bout it, he wuz settin' on de poach, an' he set still a good while, an' den he sey to hisse'f:

" 'Well, he carn' he'p bein' a Whig.'

"An' den he gits up an' walks up to Miss Anne an' looks at her right hard; an' Miss Anne she hed done tu'n away her haid an' wuz makin' out she wuz fixin' a rose-bush 'g'inst de poach; an' when her pa kep' lookin' at her, her face got jes' de color o' de roses on de bush, and pres'n'y her pa sez:

" 'Anne!'

"An' she tu'ned roun', an' he sez:

" 'Do yo' want 'im?'

"An' she sez, 'Yes,' an' put her head on he shoulder an' begin to cry; an' he sez:

" 'Well, I won' stan' between yo' no longer. Write to 'im an' say so.'

"We didn' know nuthin' 'bout dis den. We wuz a-fightin' an' a-fightin' all dat time; an' come one day a letter to Marse Chan, an' I see 'im start to read it in his tent, an' he face hit look so cu'ious, an' he han's trembled so I couldn' mek out what wuz de matter wid 'im. An' he fol' de letter up an' wen' out an' wen' way down 'hine de camp, an' stayed dyah 'bout nigh an hour. Well, seh, I wuz on de lookout for 'im when he come back, an', fo' Gord, ef he face didn' shine like a angel's! I say to myse'f, 'Um'm! ef de glory o' Gord ain' done shine on 'im!' An' what yo' 'spose 'twuz?

"He tuk me wid 'im dat evenin', an' he tell me he hed done git a letter from Miss Anne, an' Marse Chan he eyes look like gre't big stars, an' he face wuz jes' like 'twuz dat mawnin' when de sun riz up over de low groun', an' I see 'im stan'in' dyah wid de pistil in he han', lookin' at it, an' not knowin' but what it mout be de lars' time, an' he done mek up he mine not to shoot ole Cun'l Chahmb'lin fur Miss Anne's sake, what writ 'im de letter.

"He fol' de letter wha' was in his han' up, an' put it in he inside pocket—right dyar on de lef' side; an' den he tole me he tho't mebbe we wuz gwine hev some warm wuk in de nex' two or th'ee days, an' arfter dat ef Gord speared 'im he'd git a leave o' absence fur a few days, an' we'd go home.

"Well, dat night de orders come, an' we all hed to git over to'ds Romney; an' we rid all night till 'bout light; an' we halted right on a little creek, an' we stayed dyah till mos' breakfas' time, an' I see Marse Chan set down on de groun' 'hine a bush an' read dat letter over an' over. I watch 'im, an' de battle wuz a-goin' on, but we had orders to stay 'hine de hill, an' ev'y now an' den de bullets would cut de limbs o' de trees right over us, an' one o' dem big shells what goes '*Awhar—awhar—awhar!*' would fall right 'mong us; but Marse Chan he didn' mine it no mo'n nuthin'! Den it 'peared to git closer an' thicker, and Marse Chan he calls me, an' I crep' up, an' he sez:

" 'Sam, we'se goin' to win in dis battle, an' den we'll go home an' git married; an' I'se goin' home wid a star on my collar.' An' den he sez, 'Ef I'm wounded, kyar me home, yo' hear?' An' I sez, 'Yes, Marse Chan.'

"Well, jes' den dey blowed boots an' saddles, 'an we mounted;

an' de orders come to ride 'roun' de slope, an' Marse Chan's comp'ny wuz de secon', an' when we got 'roun' dyah, we wuz right in it. Hit wuz de wust place ever dis nigger got in. An' dey said, 'Charge 'em!' an' my king! ef ever you see bullets fly, dey did dat day. Hit wuz jes' like hail; an' we wen' down de slope (I long wid de res') an' up de hill right to'ds de cannons, an' de fire wuz so strong dyar (dey hed a whole rigiment o' infintrys layin' down dyar onder de cannons) our lines sort o' broke an' stop; de cun'l was kilt, an' I b'lieve dey wuz jes' 'bout to bre'k all to pieces, when Marse Chan rid up an' cotch hol' de fleg an' hollers, 'Foller me!' an' rid strainin' up de hill 'mong de cannons. I seen 'im when he went, de sorrel four good lengths ahead o' ev'y urr hoss, jes' like he use' to be in a fox-hunt, an' de whole rigiment right arfter 'im. Yo' ain' nuver hear thunder! Fust thing I knowed, de roan roll' head over heels an' flung me up 'g'inst de bank, like yo' chuck a nubbin over 'g'inst de foot o' de corn pile. An dat's what kep' me from bein' kilt, I 'spects. Judy she say she think 'twuz Providence, but I think 'twuz de bank. O' co'se, Providence put de bank dyah, but how come Providence nuver saved Marse Chan? When I look' 'roun', de roan wuz layin' dyah by me, stone dead, wid a cannon-ball gone 'mos' th'oo him, an our men hed done swep' dem on t'urr side from de top o' de hill. 'Twan' mo'n a minit, de sorrel come gallupin' back wid his mane flyin', an' de rein hangin' down on one side to his knee. 'Dyar!' says I, 'fo' Gord! I 'specks dey done kill Marse Chan, an' I promised to tek care on him.'

"I jumped up an' run over de bank, an' dyar, wid a whole lot o' dead men, an' some not dead yit, onder one o' de guns wid de fleg still in he han', an' a bullet right th'oo he body, lay Marse Chan. I tu'n 'im over an' call 'im, 'Marse Chan!' but 'twan' no use, he wuz done gone home, sho' 'nuff. I pick' 'im up in my arms wid de fleg still in he han's, an' toted 'im back jes' like I did dat day when he wuz a baby, an' ole marster gin 'im to me in my arms, an' sez he could trus' me, an' tell me to tek keer on 'im long ez he lived. I kyar'd 'im 'way off de battlefiel' out de way o' de balls, an' I laid 'im down onder a big tree till I could git somebody to ketch de sorrel for me. He wuz cotched arfter a while, an' I hed some money, so I got some pine plank an' made a coffin dat evenin', an' wrapt Marse Chan's body up in de fleg, an' put 'im in de coffin; but I didn' nail de top on strong, 'cause I knowed ole missis wan' see 'im; an' I got a' ambulance an' set out for home dat night. We reached dyar de nex' evein', arfter travellin' all dat night an' all nex' day.

"Hit 'peared like somethin' hed tole ole missis we wuz comin' so; for when we got home she wuz waitin' for us—done drest up in her best Sunday-clo'es, an' stan'n' at de head o' de big steps, an' ole marster settin' in his big cheer—ez we druv up de hill to'ds de house, I drivin' de ambulance an' de sorrel leadin' 'long behine wid de stirrips crost over de saddle.

"She come down to de gate to meet us. We took de coffin out de ambulance an' kyar'd it right into de big parlor wid de pictures in it, whar dey use' to dance in ole times when Marse Chan wuz a schoolboy, an' Miss Anne Chahmb'lin use' to come over, an' go wid ole missis into her chamber an' tek her things off. In dyar we laid de coffin on two o' de cheers, an' ole missis nuver said a wud; she jes' looked so ole an' white.

"When I had tell 'em all 'bout it, I tu'ned right 'roun' an' rid over to Cun'l Chahmb'lin's, 'cause I knowed dat wuz what Marse Chan he'd 'a' wanted me to do. I didn' tell nobody whar I wuz gwine, 'cause yo' know none on 'em hadn' nuver speak to Miss Anne, not sence de duil, an' dey didn' know 'bout de letter.

"When I rid up in de yard, dyar wuz Miss Anne a-stan'in' on de poach watchin' me ez I rid up. I tied my hoss to de fence, an' walked up de parf. She knowed by de way I walked dyar wuz somethin' de motter, an' she wuz mighty pale. I drapt my cap down on de een' o' de steps an' went up. She nuver opened her mouf; jes' stan' right still an' keep her eyes on my face. Fust, I couldn' speak; den I cotch my voice, an' I say, 'Marse Chan, he done got he furlough.'

"Her face was mighty ashy, an' she sort o' shook, but she didn' fall. She tu'ned roun' an' said, 'Git me de ker'ige!' Dat wuz all.

"When de ker'ige come 'roun', she hed put on her bonnet, an' wuz ready. Ez she got in, she sey to me, 'Hev yo' brought him home?' an' we drove 'long, I ridin' behine.

"When we got home, she got out, an' walked up de big walk—up to de poach by herse'f. Ole missis hed done fin' de letter in Marse Chan's pocket, wid de love in it, while I wuz 'way, an' she wuz a-waitin' on de poach. Dey sey dat wuz de fust time ole missis cry when she find de letter, an' dat she sut'n'y did cry over it, pintedly.

"Well, seh, Miss Anne she walks right up de steps, mos' up to ole missis stan'in' dyar on de poach, an' jes' falls right down mos' to her, on her knees fust, an' den flat on her face right on de flo', ketchin' at ole missis' dress wid her two han's—so.

"Ole missis stood for 'bout a minit lookin' down at her, an' den she drapt down on de flo' by her, an' took her in bofe her arms.

"I couldn' see, I wuz cryin' so myse'f, an' ev'ybody wuz cryin'. But dey went in arfter a while in de parlor, an' shet de do'; an' I heahd 'em say, Miss Anne she tuk de coffin in her arms an' kissed

it, an' kissed Marse Chan, an' call 'im by his name, an' her darlin',
an' ole missis lef' her cryin' in dyar tell some on 'em went in, an'
found her done faint on de flo'.

"Judy (she's my wife) she tell me she heah Miss Anne when she
axed ole missis mout she wear mo'nin' fur 'im. I don' know how
dat is; but when we buried 'im nex' day, she wuz de one whar
walked arfter de coffin, holdin' ole marster, an' ole missis she
walked next to 'em.

"Well, we buried Marse Chan dyar in de ole grabeyard, wid de
fleg wrapped roun' 'im, an' he face lookin' like it did dat mawnin'
down in de low groun's, wid de new sun shinin' on it so peaceful.

"Miss Anne she nuver went home to stay arfter dat; she stay
wid ole marster an' ole missis ez long ez dey lived. Dat warn' so
mighty long, 'cause ole marster he died dat fall, when dey wuz
fallerin' fur wheat—I had jes' married Judy den—an' ole missis
she warn' long behine him. We buried her by him next summer.
Miss Anne she went in de hospitals toreckly arfter ole missis died;
an' jes' fo' Richmond fell she come home sick wid de fever. Yo'
nuver would 'a' knowed her fur de same ole Miss Anne. She wuz
light ez a piece o' peth, an' so white, 'cep' her eyes an' her sorrel
hyar, an' she kep' on gittin' whiter an' weaker. Judy she sut'n'y
did nuss her faithful. But she nuver got no betterment! De fever
an' Marse Chan's bein' kilt hed done strain her, an' she died jes'
fo' de folks wuz sot free.

"So we buried Miss Anne right by Marse Chan, in a place whar
ole missis hed tole us to leave, an' dey's bofe on 'em sleep side
by side over in de ole grabeyard at home.

"An' will yo' please tell me, marster? Dey tells me dat de Bible
sey dyar won' be marryin' nor givin' in marriage in heaven, but I
don' b'lieve it signifies dat—does you?"

I gave him the comfort of my earnest belief in some other interpretation, together with several spare "eighteen-pences," as he
called them, for which he seemed humbly grateful. And as I rode
away I heard him calling across the fence to his wife, who was
standing in the door of a small white-washed cabin, near which we
had been standing for some time:

"Judy, have Marse Chan's dawg got home?"

Edgar Allan Poe

(1809–1849)

The most original and far-reaching writer to emerge out of the antebellum South, Poe is recognized today as one of the early masters of the modern short story. He liked to present himself as a "Virginian," and spent over half his life in Virginia, Maryland, and South Carolina, but only a handful of his stories directly address his Southern background. From the very beginning, Poe was haunted by insecurity and a confusing choice of identities. His parents were itinerant actors who toured the theatrical circuits. Poe was born in Boston, but after his mother's death three years later in Richmond, Virginia, he was taken into the Richmond household of John Allan, a Scottish tobacco merchant. Poe was well educated, and well treated, but his relationship with his foster father was always strained. The situation became critical in 1827, when Poe was forced to leave the University of Virginia after only one year because of gambling debts. After two years as an enlisted soldier in South Carolina, and less than eight months as a cadet at West Point, Poe had himself dismissed from West Point, and broke with Allan for good. With three published volumes of poetry to his credit, he moved to his real father's hometown of Baltimore, and set out on a life-long struggle to survive by writing. He would work as a magazine editor (beginning with The Southern Literary Messenger), literary critic, and short-story writer. He wrote most of his major fiction during this period, but could not escape from a falling spiral of depression, poverty, and personal tragedy. He had married his young cousin, Virginia Clemm, in 1836, and when she died of tuberculosis in 1847, Poe's own life took a final desperate spin that ended with his death in Baltimore, after being found half-conscious in the streets. Poe has always been recognized as a gifted lyric poet. His belief in the sacred role of the artist gained him a worshipful following among the French symbolists who considered him the archetypal poet of the age. His modern reputation, however, is based *more on the powerful symbolism and brilliant inventiveness of his short fiction. His stories range through an astonishing variety, including tales of horror and obsession, humorous burlesques and outrageous satires, and a whole new narrative genre of detection and ratiocination. Though there is little that is deliberately Southern in his work, Poe expressed strong affinities with certain shared convictions of Southern culture, and was one of the first critics to praise the new school of "Southwestern humorists." "The Gold-Bug," his most popular story during his lifetime, is his most emphatically Southern work. Its Southern locale—Sullivan's Island—is less important than the characterizations of Jupiter, a free black, and his former master, the ruined Southerner Legrand. Poe's works include* Tamerlane and Other Poems *(1827),* Poems *(1831),* The Narrative of Arthur Gordon Pym *(1838),* Tales of the Grotesque and Arabesque *(1840), and* Eureka: A Prose Poem *(1848). "The Gold-Bug" was first published in the* Dollar Newspaper *of Philadelphia (June 1843).*

THE GOLD-BUG

❀

What ho! what ho! this fellow is dancing mad!
He hath been bitten by the Tarantula.
All in the Wrong

Many years ago, I contracted an intimacy with a Mr. William Legrand. He was of an ancient Huguenot family, and had once been wealthy; but a series of misfortunes had reduced him to want. To avoid the mortification consequent upon his disasters, he left New Orleans, the city of his forefathers, and took up his residence at Sullivan's Island, near Charleston, South Carolina.

This Island is a very singular one. It consists of little else than the sea sand, and is about three miles long. Its breadth at no point exceeds a quarter of a mile. It is separated from the main land by a scarcely perceptible creek, oozing its way through a wilderness of reeds and slime, a favorite resort of the marsh-hen. The vegetation, as might be supposed, is scant, or at least dwarfish. No trees of any magnitude are to be seen. Near the western extremity, where Fort Moultrie stands, and where are some miserable frame buildings, tenanted, during summer, by the fugitives from Charleston dust and fever, may be found, indeed, the bristly palmetto; but the whole island, with the exception of this western point, and a line of hard, white beach on the seacoast, is covered with a dense undergrowth of the sweet myrtle, so much prized by the horticulturists of England. The shrub here often attains the height of fifteen or twenty feet, and forms an almost impenetrable coppice, burthening the air with its fragrance.

In the inmost recesses of this coppice, not far from the eastern or more remote end of the island, Legrand had built himself a small hut, which he occupied when I first, by mere accident, made his acquaintance. This soon ripened into friendship—for there was much in the recluse to excite interest and esteem. I found him well educated, with unusual powers of mind, but infected with misanthropy, and subject to perverse moods of alternate enthusiasm and melancholy. He had with him many books, but rarely employed them. His chief amusements were gunning and fishing, or sauntering along the beach and through the myrtles, in quest of shells or entomological specimens;—his collection of the latter might have been envied by a Swammerdamm. In these excursions he was usually accompanied by an old negro, called Jupiter, who had been manumitted before the reverses of the family, but who could be induced, neither by threats nor by promises, to abandon what he considered his right of attendance upon the footsteps of his young "Massa Will." It is not improbable that the relatives of Legrand, conceiving him to be somewhat unsettled in intellect, had contrived to instil this obstinacy into Jupiter, with a view to the supervision and guardianship of the wanderer.

The winters in the latitude of Sullivan's Island are seldom very severe, and in the fall of the year it is a rare event indeed when a fire is considered necessary. About the middle of October, 18—, there occurred, however, a day of remarkable chilliness. Just before sunset I scrambled my way through the evergreens to the hut of my friend, whom I had not visited for several weeks— my residence being, at that time, in Charleston, a distance of nine miles from the Island, while the facilities of passage and re-passage were very far behind those of the present day. Upon reaching the hut I rapped, as was my custom, and getting no reply, sought for the key where I knew it was secreted, unlocked the door and went in. A fine fire was blazing upon the hearth. It was a novelty, and by no means an ungrateful one. I threw off an overcoat, took an armchair by the crackling logs, and awaited patiently the arrival of my hosts.

Soon after dark they arrived, and gave me a most cordial welcome. Jupiter, grinning from ear to ear, bustled about to prepare some marsh-hens for supper. Legrand was in one of his fits—how else shall I term them?—of enthusiasm. He had found an unknown bivalve, forming a new genus, and, more than this, he had hunted down and secured, with Jupiter's assistance, a *scarabaeus* which he believed to be totally new, but in respect to which he wished to have my opinion on the morrow.

"And why not to-night?" I asked, rubbing my hands over the blaze, and wishing the whole tribe of *scarabaei* at the devil.

"Ah, if I had only known you were here!" said Legrand, "but it's so long since I saw you; and how could I foresee that you would pay me a visit this very night of all others? As I was coming home I met Lieutenant G——, from the fort, and, very foolishly, I lent him the bug; so it will be impossible for you to see it until the morning. Stay here to-night, and I will send Jup down for it at sunrise. It is the loveliest thing in creation!"

"What?—sunrise?"

"Nonsense! no!—the bug. It is of a brilliant gold color—about the size of a large hickory-nut—with two jet black spots near one extremity of the back, and another, somewhat longer, at the other. The *antennae* are—"

"Dey aint *no* tin in him, Massa Will, I keep a tellin on you," here interrupted Jupiter; "de bug is a goole bug, solid, ebery bit of him, inside and all, sep him wing—neber feel half so hebby a bug in my life."

"Well, suppose it is, Jup," replied Legrand, somewhat more earnestly, it seemed to me, than the case demanded, "is that any reason for your letting the birds burn? The color"—here he turned to me—"is really almost enough to warrant Jupiter's idea. You never saw a more brilliant metallic lustre than the scales emit—but of this you cannot judge till to-morrow. In the mean time I can give you some idea of the shape." Saying this, he seated himself at a small table, on which were a pen and ink, but no paper. He looked for some in a drawer, but found none.

"Never mind," said he at length, "this will answer;" and he drew from his waistcoat pocket a scrap of what I took to be very dirty foolscap, and made upon it a rough drawing with the pen. While he did this, I retained my seat by the fire, for I was still chilly. When the design was complete, he handed it to me without rising. As I received it, a loud growl was heard, succeeded by a scratching at the door. Jupiter opened it, and a large Newfoundland, belonging to Legrand, rushed in, leaped upon my shoulders, and loaded me with caresses; for I had shown him much attention during previous visits. When his gambols were over, I looked at the paper, and, to speak the truth, found myself not a little puzzled at what my friend had depicted.

"Well!" I said, after contemplating it for some minutes, "this *is* a strange *scarabaeus,* I must confess: new to me: never saw anything like it before—unless it was a skull, or a death's-head—which it more nearly resembles than anything else that has come under *my* observation."

"A death's-head!" echoed Legrand—"Oh—yes—well, it has something of that appearance upon paper, no doubt. The two upper black spots look like eyes, eh? and the longer one at the bottom like a mouth—and then the shape of the whole is oval."

"Perhaps so," said I; "but, Legrand, I fear you are no artist. I must wait until I see the beetle itself, if I am to form any idea of its personal appearance."

"Well, I don't know," said he, a little nettled, "I draw tolerably—*should* do it at least—have had good masters, and flatter myself that I am not quite a blockhead."

"But, my dear fellow, you are joking then," said I, "this is a very passable *skull*—indeed, I may say that it is a very *excellent* skull, according to the vulgar notions about such specimens of physiology—and your *scarabaeus* must be the queerest *scarabaeus* in the world if it resembles it. Why, we may get up a very thrilling bit of superstition upon this hint. I presume you will call the bug *scarabaeus caput hominis,* or something of that kind—there are many similar titles in the Natural Histories. But where are the *antennae* you spoke of?"

"The *antennae!*" said Legrand, who seemed to be getting unaccountably warm upon the subject; "I am sure you must see the *antennae.* I made them as distinct as they are in the original insect, and I presume that is sufficient."

"Well, well," I said, "perhaps you have—still I don't see them;" and I handed him the paper without additional remark, not wishing to ruffle his temper; but I was much surprised at the turn affairs had taken; his ill humor puzzled me—and, as for the drawing of the beetle, there were positively *no antennae* visible, and the whole *did* bear a very close resemblance to the ordinary cut of a death's-head.

He received the paper very peevishly, and was about to crumple it, apparently to throw it in the fire, when a casual glance at the design seemed suddenly to rivet his attention. In an instant his face grew violently red—in another as excessively pale. For some minutes he continued to scrutinize the drawing minutely where he sat. At length he arose, took a candle from the table, and proceeded to seat himself upon a sea-chest in the farthest corner of the room. Here again he made an anxious examination of the paper; turning it in all directions. He said nothing, however, and his conduct greatly astonished me; yet I thought it prudent not to exacerbate the growing moodiness of his temper by any comment. Presently he took from his coat pocket a wallet, placed the paper carefully in it, and deposited both in a writing-desk, which he locked. He now grew more composed in his demeanor; but his original air of enthusiasm had quite disappeared. Yet he seemed not so much sulky as abstracted. As the evening wore away he became more and more absorbed in reverie, from which no sallies of mine could arouse him. It had been my intention to pass the night at the hut, as I had frequently done before, but, seeing my host in this mood, I deemed it proper to take leave. He did not press me to remain, but, as I departed, he shook my hand with even more than his usual cordiality.

It was about a month after this (and during the interval I had seen nothing of Legrand) when I received a visit, at Charleston, from his man, Jupiter. I had never seen the good old negro look so dispirited, and I feared that some serious disaster had befallen my friend.

"Well, Jup," said I, "what is the matter now?—how is your master?"

"Why, to speak de troof, massa, him not so berry well as mought be."

"Not well! I am truly sorry to hear it. What does he complain of?"

"Dar! dat's it—him neber plain of notin—but him berry sick for all dat."

"*Very* sick, Jupiter!—why didn't you say so at once? Is he confined to bed?"

"No, dat he aint!—he aint find nowhar—dat's just whar de shoe pinch—my mind is got to be berry hebby bout poor Massa Will."

"Jupiter, I should like to understand what it is you are talking about. You say your master is sick. Hasn't he told you what ails him?"

"Why, massa, taint worf while for to git mad bout de matter—Massa Will say noffin at all aint de matter wid him—but den what make him go about looking dis here way, wid he head down and he soldiers up, and as white as a gose? And den he keep a syphon all de time—"

"Keeps a what, Jupiter?"

"Keeps a syphon wid de figgurs on de slate—de queerest figgurs I ebber did see. Ise gitting to be skeered, I tell you. Hab for to keep mighty tight eye pon him noovers. Todder day he gib me slip fore de sun up and was gone de whole ob de blessed day. I had a big stick ready cut for to gib him d——d good beating when he did come—but Ise sich a fool dat I hadn't de heart arter all—he look so berry poorly."

"Eh?—what?—ah yes!—upon the whole I think you had better not be too severe with the poor fellow—don't flog him, Jupiter—he can't very well stand it—but can you form no idea of what has occasioned this illness, or rather this change of conduct? Has anything unpleasant happened since I saw you?"

"No, massa, dey aint bin noffin onpleasant *since* den—'twas *fore* den I'm feared—'twas de berry day you was dare."

"How? what do you mean?"

"Why, massa, I mean de bug—dare now."

"The what?"

"De bug—I'm berry sartain dat Massa Will bin bit somewhere bout de head by dat goole-bug."

"And what cause have you, Jupiter, for such a supposition?"

"Claws enuff, massa, and mouff too. I nebber did see sich a d——d bug—he kick and he bite ebery ting what cum near him. Massa Will cotch him fuss, but had for to let him go gin mighty quick, I tell you—den was de time he must ha got de bite. I didn't like de look ob de bug mouff, myself, no how, so I wouldn't take hold ob him wid my finger, but I cotch him wid a piece ob paper dat I found. I rap him up in de paper and stuff piece ob it in he mouff—dat was de way."

"And you think, then, that your master was really bitten by the beetle, and that the bite made him sick?"

"I don't tink noffin about it—I nose it. What make him dream bout de goole so much, if taint cause he bit by de goole-bug? Ise heerd bout dem goole-bugs fore dis."

"But how do you know he dreams about gold?"

"How I know? why cause he talk about it in he sleep—dat's how I nose."

"Well, Jup, perhaps you are right; but to what fortunate circumstance am I to attribute the honor of a visit from you to-day?"

"What de matter, massa?"

"Did you bring any message from Mr. Legrand?"

"No, massa, I bring dis here pissel;" and here Jupiter handed me a note which ran thus:

MY DEAR——
Why have I not seen you for so long a time? I hope you have not been so foolish as to take offence at any little *brus-querie* of mine; but no, that is improbable.

Since I saw you I have had great cause for anxiety. I have something to tell you, yet scarcely know how to tell it, or whether I should tell it at all.

I have not been quite well for some days past, and poor old Jup annoys me, almost beyond endurance, by his well-meant attentions. Would you believe it?—he had prepared a huge stick, the other day, with which to chastise me for giving him the slip, and spending the day, *solus,* among the hills on the main land. I verily believe that my ill looks alone saved me a flogging.

I have made no addition to my cabinet since we met.

If you can, in any way, make it convenient, come over with Jupiter. *Do* come. I wish to see you *to-night,* upon business of importance. I assure you that it is of the *highest* importance.

Ever yours,   WILLIAM LEGRAND.

There was something in the tone of this note which gave me great uneasiness. Its whole style differed materially from that of Legrand. What could he be dreaming of? What new crotchet possessed his excitable brain? What "business of the highest importance" could *he* possibly have to transact? Jupiter's account of him boded no good. I dreaded lest the continued pressure of misfortune had, at length, fairly unsettled the reason of my friend. Without a moment's hesitation, therefore, I prepared to accompany the negro.

Upon reaching the wharf, I noticed a scythe and three spades, all apparently new, lying in the bottom of the boat in which we were to embark.

"What is the meaning of all this, Jup?" I inquired.

"Him syfe, massa, and spade."

"Very true; but what are they doing here?"

"Him de syfe and de spade what Massa Will sis pon my buying for him in de town, and de debbil's own lot of money I had to gib for em."

"But what, in the name of all that is mysterious, is your 'Massa Will' going to do with scythes and spades?"

"Dat's more dan *I* know, and debbil take me if I don't blieve 'tis more dan he know, too. But it's all cum ob de bug."

Finding that no satisfaction was to be obtained of Jupiter, whose whole intellect seemed to be absorbed by "de bug," I now stepped into the boat and made sail. With a fair and strong breeze we soon ran into the little cove to the northward of Fort Moultrie, and a walk of some two miles brought us to the hut. It was about three in the afternoon when we arrived. Legrand had been awaiting us in eager expectation. He grasped my hand with a nervous *empressement* which alarmed me and strengthened the suspicions already entertained. His countenance was pale even to ghastliness, and his deep-set eyes glared with unnatural lustre. After some inquiries respecting his health, I asked him, not knowing what better to say, if he had yet obtained the *scarabaeus* from Lieutenant G——.

"Oh, yes," he replied, coloring violently, "I got it from him the next morning. Nothing should tempt me to part with that *scarabaeus*. Do you know that Jupiter is quite right about it?"

"In what way?" I asked, with a sad foreboding at heart.

"In supposing it to be a bug of *real gold*." He said this with an air of profound seriousness, and I felt inexpressibly shocked.

"This bug is to make my fortune," he continued, with a triumphant smile, "to reinstate me in my family possessions. Is it any wonder, then, that I prize it? Since Fortune has thought fit to bestow it upon me, I have only to use it properly and I shall arrive at the gold of which it is the index. Jupiter, bring me that *scarabaeus!*"

"What! de bug, massa? I'd rudder not go fer trubble dat bug—you mus git him for your own self." Hereupon Legrand arose, with a grave and stately air, and brought me the beetle from a glass case in which it was enclosed. It was a beautiful *scarabaeus,* and, at that time, unknown to naturalists—of course a great prize in a scientific point of view. There were two round, black spots near one extremity of the back, and a long one near the other. The scales were exceedingly hard and glossy, with all the appearance of burnished gold. The weight of the insect was very remarkable, and, taking all things into consideration, I could hardly blame Jupiter for his opinion respecting it; but what to make of Legrand's agreement with that opinion, I could not, for the life of me, tell.

"I sent for you," said he, in a grandiloquent tone, when I had completed my examination of the beetle, "I sent for you, that I might have your counsel and assistance in furthering the views of Fate and of the bug"—

"My dear Legrand," I cried, interrupting him, "you are certainly unwell, and had better use some little precautions. You shall go to bed, and I will remain with you a few days, until you get over this. You are feverish and"—

"Feel my pulse," said he.

I felt it, and, to say the truth, found not the slightest indication of fever.

"But you may be ill and yet have no fever. Allow me this once to prescribe for you. In the first place, go to bed. In the next"—

"You are mistaken," he interposed, "I am as well as I can expect to be under the excitement which I suffer. If you really wish me well, you will relieve this excitement."

"And how is this to be done?"

"Very easily. Jupiter and myself are going upon an expedition into the hills, upon the main land, and, in this expedition, we shall need the aid of some person in whom we can confide. You are the only one we can trust. Whether we succeed or fail, the excitement which you now perceive in me will be equally allayed."

"I am anxious to oblige you in any way," I replied; "but do you mean to say that this infernal beetle has any connection with your expedition into the hills?"

"It has."

"Then, Legrand, I can become a party to no such absurd proceeding."

"I am sorry—very sorry—for we shall have to try it by ourselves."

"Try it by yourselves! The man is surely mad!—but stay!—how long do you propose to be absent?"

"Probably all night. We shall start immediately, and be back, at all events, by sunrise."

"And will you promise me, upon your honor, that when this freak of yours is over, and the bug business (good God!) settled to your satisfaction, you will then return home and follow my advice implicitly, as that of your physician?"

"Yes; I promise; and now let us be off, for we have no time to lose."

With a heavy heart I accompanied my friend. We started about four o'clock—Legrand, Jupiter, the dog, and myself. Jupiter had with him the scythe and spades—the whole of which he insisted upon carrying—more through fear, it seemed to me, of trusting either of the implements within reach of his master, than from any excess of industry or complaisance. His demeanor was dogged in the extreme, and "dat d—d bug" were the sole words which escaped his lips during the journey. For my own part, I had charge of a couple of dark lanterns, while Legrand contented himself with the *scarabaeus,* which he carried attached to the end of a bit of whip-cord; twirling it to and fro, with the air of a conjuror, as he went. When I observed this last, plain evidence of my friend's aberration of mind, I could scarcely refrain from tears. I thought it best, however, to humor his fancy, at least for the present, or until I could adopt some more energetic measures with a chance of success. In the mean time I endeavored, but all in vain, to sound him in regard to the object of the expedition. Having succeeded in inducing me to accompany him, he seemed unwilling to hold conversation upon any topic of minor importance, and to all my questions vouchsafed no other reply than "we shall see!"

We crossed the creek at the head of the island by means of a skiff, and, ascending the high grounds on the shore of the main land, proceeded in a northwesterly direction, through a tract of country excessively wild and desolate, where no trace of a human footstep was to be seen. Legrand led the way with decision; pausing only for an instant, here and there, to consult what appeared to be certain landmarks of his own contrivance upon a former occasion.

In this manner we journeyed for about two hours, and the sun was just setting when we entered a region infinitely more dreary than any yet seen. It was a species of table land, near the summit of an almost inaccessible hill, densely wooded from base to pinnacle, and interspersed with huge crags that appeared to lie loosely upon the soil, and in many cases were prevented from precipitating themselves into the valleys below, merely by the support of the trees against which they reclined. Deep ravines, in various directions, gave an air of still sterner solemnity to the scene.

The natural platform to which we had clambered was thickly overgrown with brambles, through which we soon discovered that it would have been impossible to force our way but for the scythe; and Jupiter, by direction of his master, proceeded to clear for us a path to the foot of an enormously tall tulip-tree, which stood, with some eight or ten oaks, upon the level, and far surpassed them all, and all other trees which I had then ever seen, in the beauty of its foliage and form, in the wide spread of its branches, and in the general majesty of its appearance. When we reached this tree, Legrand turned to Jupiter, and asked him if he thought he could climb it. The old man seemed a little staggered by the question, and for some moments made no reply. At length he approached the huge trunk, walked slowly around it, and examined it with minute attention. When he had completed his scrutiny, he merely said,

"Yes, massa, Jup climb any tree he ebber see in he life."

"Then up with you as soon as possible, for it will soon be too dark to see what we are about."

"How far mus go up, massa?" inquired Jupiter.

"Get up the main trunk first, and then I will tell you which way to go—and here—stop! take this beetle with you."

"De bug, Massa Will!—de goole bug!" cried the negro, drawing

back in dismay—"what for mus tote de bug way up de tree?—
d—n if I do!"

"If you are afraid, Jup, a great big negro like you, to take hold
of a harmless little dead beetle, why you can carry it up by this
string—but, if you do not take it up with you in some way, I shall
be under the necessity of breaking your head with this shovel."

"What de matter now, massa?" said Jup, evidently shamed into
compliance; "always want for to raise fuss wid old nigger. Was
only funnin any how. *Me* feered de bug! what I keer for de bug?"
Here he took cautiously hold of the extreme end of the string,
and, maintaining the insect as far from his person as circumstances
would permit, prepared to ascend the tree.

In youth, the tulip-tree, or *Liriodendron Tulipiferum,* the most
magnificent of American foresters, has a trunk peculiarly smooth,
and often rises to a great height without lateral branches; but, in
its riper age, the bark becomes gnarled and uneven, while many
short limbs make their appearance on the stem. Thus the difficulty
of ascension, in the present case, lay more in semblance than in
reality. Embracing the huge cylinder, as closely as possible, with
his arms and knees, seizing with his hands some projections, and
resting his naked toes upon others, Jupiter, after one or two narrow
escapes from falling, at length wriggled himself into the first great
fork, and seemed to consider the whole business as virtually accomplished. The *risk* of the achievement was, in fact, now over,
although the climber was some sixty or seventy feet from the
ground.

"Which way mus go now, Massa Will?" he asked.

"Keep up the largest branch—the one on this side," said Legrand. The negro obeyed him promptly, and apparently with but
little trouble; ascending higher and higher, until no glimpse of his
squat figure could be obtained through the dense foliage which
enveloped it. Presently his voice was heard in a sort of halloo.

"How much fudder is got for go?"

"How high up are you?" asked Legrand.

"Ebber so fur," replied the negro; "can see de sky fru de top
of de tree."

"Never mind the sky, but attend to what I say. Look down the
trunk and count the limbs below you on this side. How many limbs
have you passed?"

"One, two, tree, four, fibe—I done pass fibe big limb, massa,
pon dis side."

"Then go one limb higher."

In a few minutes the voice was heard again, announcing that
the seventh limb was attained.

"Now, Jup," cried Legrand, evidently much excited, "I want you to work your way out upon that limb as far as you can. If you see anything strange, let me know."

By this time what little doubt I might have entertained of my poor friend's insanity, was put finally at rest. I had no alternative but to conclude him stricken with lunacy, and I became seriously anxious about getting him home. While I was pondering upon what was best to be done, Jupiter's voice was again heard.

"Mos feerd for to ventur pon dis limb berry far—tis dead limb putty much all de way."

"Did you say it was a *dead* limb, Jupiter?" cried Legrand in a quavering voice.

"Yes, massa, him dead as de door-nail—done up for sartain—done departed dis here life."

"What in the name of heaven shall I do?" asked Legrand, seemingly in the greatest distress.

"Do!" said I, glad of an opportunity to interpose a word, "why come home and go to bed. Come now!—that's a fine fellow. It's getting late, and, besides, you remember your promise."

"Jupiter," cried he, without heeding me in the least, "do you hear me?"

"Yes, Massa Will, hear you ebber so plain."

"Try the wood well, then, with your knife, and see if you think it *very* rotten."

"Him rotten, massa, sure nuff," replied the negro in a few moments, "but not so berry rotten as mought be. Mought ventur out leetle way pon de limb by myself, dat's true."

"By yourself!—what do you mean?"

"Why I mean de bug. 'Tis *berry* hebby bug. Spose I drop him down fuss, and den de limb won't break wid just de weight ob one nigger."

"You infernal scoundrel!" cried Legrand, apparently much relieved, "what do you mean by telling me such nonsense as that? As sure as you let that beetle fall I'll break your neck. Look here, Jupiter!—do you hear me?"

"Yes, massa, needn't hollo at poor nigger dat style."

"Well! now listen!—if you will venture out on the limb as far as you think safe, and not let go the beetle, I'll make you a present of a silver dollar as soon as you get down."

"I'm gwine, Massa Will—deed I is," replied the negro very promptly—"mos out to the eend now."

"*Out to the end!*" here fairly screamed Legrand, "do you say you are out to the end of that limb?"

"Soon be to de eend, massa,—o-o-o-o-oh! Lor-gol-a-marcy! what *is* dis here pon de tree?"

"Well!" cried Legrand, highly delighted, "what is it?"

"Why taint noffin but a skull—somebody bin lef him head up de tree, and de crows done gobble ebery bit ob de meat off."

"A skull, you say!—very well!—how is it fastened to the limb?—what holds it on?"

"Sure nuff, massa; mus look. Why dis berry curous sarcumstance, pon my word—dare's a great big nail in de skull, what fastens ob it on to de tree."

"Well now, Jupiter, do exactly as I tell you—do you hear?"

"Yes, massa."

"Pay attention, then!—find the left eye of the skull."

"Hum! hoo! dat's good! why dar aint no eye lef at all."

"Curse your stupidity! do you know your right hand from your left?"

"Yes, I nose dat—nose all bout dat—tis my lef hand what I chops de wood wid."

"To be sure! you are left-handed; and your left eye is on the same side as your left hand. Now, I suppose, you can find the left eye of the skull, or the place where the left eye has been. Have you found it?"

Here was a long pause. At length the negro asked,

"Is de lef eye of de skull pon de same side as de lef hand of de skull, too?—cause de skull aint got not a bit ob a hand at all—nebber mind! I got de lef eye now—here de lef eye! what mus do wid it?"

"Let the beetle drop through it, as far as the string will reach—but be careful and not let go your hold of the string."

"All dat done, Massa Will; mighty easy ting for to put de bug fru de hole—look out for him dar below!"

During this colloquy no portion of Jupiter's person could be seen; but the beetle, which he had suffered to descend, was now visible at the end of the string, and glistened, like a globe of burnished gold, in the last rays of the setting sun, some of which still faintly illumined the eminence upon which we stood. The *scarabaeus* hung quite clear of any branches, and, if allowed to fall, would have fallen at our feet. Legrand immediately took the scythe, and cleared with it a circular space, three or four yards in diameter, just beneath the insect, and, having accomplished this, ordered Jupiter to let go the string and come down from the tree.

Driving a peg, with great nicety, into the ground, at the precise spot where the beetle fell, my friend now produced from his pocket a tape-measure. Fastening one end of this at that point of the trunk of the tree which was nearest the peg, he unrolled it till it reached the peg, and thence farther unrolled it, in the direction already established by the two points of the tree and the peg, for the distance of fifty feet—Jupiter clearing away the brambles with the scythe. At the spot thus attained a second peg was driven, and about this, as a centre, a rude circle, about four feet in diameter, described. Taking now a spade himself, and giving one to Jupiter and one to me, Legrand begged us to set about digging as quickly as possible.

To speak the truth, I had no especial relish for such amusement at any time, and, at that particular moment, would most willingly have declined it; for the night was coming on, and I felt much fatigued with the exercise already taken; but I saw no mode of escape, and was fearful of disturbing my poor friend's equanimity by a refusal. Could I have depended, indeed, upon Jupiter's aid, I would have had no hesitation in attempting to get the lunatic home by force; but I was too well assured of the old negro's disposition, to hope that he would assist me, under any circumstances, in a personal contest with his master. I made no doubt that the latter had been infected with some of the innumerable Southern superstitions about money buried, and that his phantasy had received confirmation by the finding of the *scarabaeus,* or, perhaps, by Jupiter's obstinacy in maintaining it to be "a bug of real gold." A mind disposed to lunacy would readily be led away by such suggestions—especially if chiming in with favorite preconceived ideas—and then I called to mind the poor fellow's speech about the beetle's being "the index of his fortune." Upon the whole, I was sadly vexed and puzzled, but, at length, I concluded to make a virtue of necessity—to dig with a good will, and thus the sooner to convince the visionary, by ocular demonstration, of the fallacy of the opinions he entertained.

The lanterns having been lit, we all fell to work with a zeal worthy a more rational cause; and, as the glare fell upon our persons and implements, I could not help thinking how picturesque a group we composed, and how strange and suspicious our labors must have appeared to any interloper who, by chance, might have stumbled upon our whereabouts.

We dug very steadily for two hours. Little was said; and our chief embarrassment lay in the yelpings of the dog, who took exceeding interest in our proceedings. He, at length, became so obstreperous that we grew fearful of his giving the alarm to some stragglers in the vicinity;—or, rather, this was the apprehension of Legrand;—for myself, I should have rejoiced at any interruption which might have enabled me to get the wanderer home. The noise was, at length, very effectually silenced by Jupiter, who, getting out of the hole with a dogged air of deliberation, tied the brute's mouth up with one of his suspenders, and then returned, with a grave chuckle, to his task.

When the time mentioned had expired, we had reached a depth of five feet, and yet no signs of any treasure became manifest. A general pause ensued, and I began to hope that the farce was at an end. Legrand, however, although evidently much disconcerted, wiped his brow thoughtfully and recommenced. We had excavated the entire circle of four feet diameter, and now we slightly enlarged the limit, and went to the farther depth of two feet. Still nothing appeared. The gold-seeker, whom I sincerely pitied, at length clambered from the pit, with the bitterest disappointment imprinted upon every feature, and proceeded, slowly and reluctantly, to put on his coat, which he had thrown off at the beginning of his labor. In the mean time I made no remark. Jupiter, at a signal from his master, began to gather up his tools. This done, and the dog having been unmuzzled, we turned in profound silence towards home.

We had taken, perhaps, a dozen steps in this direction, when, with a loud oath, Legrand strode up to Jupiter, and seized him by the collar. The astonished negro opened his eyes and mouth to the fullest extent, let fall the spades, and fell upon his knees.

"You scoundrel," said Legrand, hissing out the syllables from between his clenched teeth—"you infernal black villain!—speak, I tell you!—answer me this instant, without prevarication!—which—which is your left eye?"

"Oh, my golly, Massa Will! ain't dis here my lef eye for sartain?" roared the terrified Jupiter, placing his hand upon his *right* organ of vision, and holding it there with a desperate pertinacity, as if in immediate dread of his master's attempt at a gouge.

"I thought so!—I knew it!—hurrah!" vociferated Legrand, letting the negro go, and executing a series of curvets and caracols, much to the astonishment of his valet, who, arising from his knees, looked, mutely, from his master to myself, and then from myself to his master.

"Come! we must go back," said the latter, "the game's not up yet;" and he again led the way to the tulip-tree.

"Jupiter," said he, when we reached its foot, "come here! was the skull nailed to the limb with the face outward, or with the face to the limb?"

"De face was out, massa, so dat de crows could get at de eyes good, widout any trouble."

"Well, then, was it this eye or that through which you let fall the beetle?"—here Legrand touched each of Jupiter's eyes.

"'Twas dis eye, massa—de lef eye—jis as you tell me," and here it was his right eye that the negro indicated.

"That will do—we must try it again."

Here my friend, about whose madness I now saw, or fancied that I saw, certain indications of method, removed the peg which marked the spot where the beetle fell, to a spot about three inches to the westward of its former position. Taking, now, the tape-measure from the nearest point of the trunk to the peg, as before, and continuing the extension in a straight line to the distance of fifty feet, a spot was indicated, removed, by several yards, from the point at which we had been digging.

Around the new position a circle, somewhat larger than in the former instance, was now described, and we again set to work with the spades. I was dreadfully weary, but, scarcely understanding what had occasioned the change in my thoughts, I felt no longer any great aversion from the labor imposed. I had become most unaccountably interested—nay, even excited. Perhaps there was something, amid all the extravagant demeanor of Legrand—some air of forethought, or of deliberation, which impressed me. I dug eagerly, and now and then caught myself actually looking, with something that very much resembled expectation, for the fancied treasure, the vision of which had demented my unfortunate companion. At a period when such vagaries of thought most fully possessed me, and when we had been at work perhaps an hour and a half, we were again interrupted by the violent howlings of the dog. His uneasiness, in the first instance, had been, evidently, but the result of playfulness or caprice, but he now assumed a bitter and serious tone. Upon Jupiter's again attempting to muzzle him, he made furious resistance, and, leaping into the hole, tore up the mould frantically with his claws. In a few seconds he had uncovered a mass of human bones, forming two complete skeletons, intermingled with several buttons of metal, and what appeared to be the dust of decayed woollen. One or two strokes of a spade upturned the blade of a large Spanish knife, and, as we dug farther, three or four loose pieces of gold and silver coin came to light.

At sight of these the joy of Jupiter could scarcely be restrained, but the countenance of his master wore an air of extreme disappointment. He urged us, however, to continue our exertions, and the words were hardly uttered when I stumbled and fell forward, having caught the toe of my boot in a large ring of iron that lay half buried in the loose earth.

We now worked in earnest, and never did I pass ten minutes of more intense excitement. During this interval we had fairly unearthed an oblong chest of wood, which, from its perfect preservation and wonderful hardness, had plainly been subjected to some mineralizing process—perhaps that of the Bi-chloride of Mercury. This box was three feet and a half long, three feet broad, and two and a half feet deep. It was firmly secured by bands of wrought iron, riveted, and forming a kind of trellis-work over the whole. On each side of the chest, near the top, were three rings of iron—six in all—by means of which a firm hold could be obtained by six persons. Our utmost united endeavors served only to disturb the coffer very slightly in its bed. We at once saw the impossibility of removing so great a weight. Luckily, the sole fastenings of the lid consisted of two sliding bolts. These we drew back—trembling and panting with anxiety. In an instant, a treasure of incalculable value lay gleaming before us. As the rays of the lanterns fell within the pit, there flashed upwards from a confused heap of gold and of jewels, a glow and a glare that absolutely dazzled our eyes.

I shall not pretend to describe the feelings with which I gazed. Amazement was, of course, predominant. Legrand appeared exhausted with excitement, and spoke very few words. Jupiter's countenance wore, for some minutes, as deadly a pallor as it is possible, in the nature of things, for any negro's visage to assume. He seemed stupified—thunderstricken. Presently he fell upon his knees in the pit, and, burying his naked arms up to the elbows in gold, let them there remain, as if enjoying the luxury of a bath. At length, with a deep sigh, he exclaimed, as if in a soliloquy,

"And dis all cum ob de goole-bug! de putty goole-bug! de poor little goole-bug, what I boosed in dat sabage kind ob style! Aint you shamed ob yourself, nigger?—answer me dat!"

It became necessary, at last, that I should arouse both master and valet to the expediency of removing the treasure. It was growing late, and it behooved us to make exertion, that we might get every thing housed before daylight. It was difficult to say what should be done; and much time was spent in deliberation—so confused were the ideas of all. We, finally, lightened the box by removing two thirds of its contents, when we were enabled, with some trouble, to raise it from the hole. The articles taken out were deposited among the brambles, and the dog left to guard them, with strict orders from Jupiter neither, upon any pretence, to stir from the spot, nor to open his mouth until our return. We then hurriedly made for home with the chest; reaching the hut in safety, but after excessive toil, at one o'clock in the morning. Worn out as we were, it was not in human nature to do more just then. We rested until two, and had supper; starting for the hills immediately afterwards, armed with three stout sacks, which, by good luck, were upon the premises. A little before four we arrived at the pit, divided the remainder of the booty, as equally as might be, among us, and, leaving the holes unfilled, again set out for the hut, at which, for the second time, we deposited our golden burthens, just as the first streaks of the dawn gleamed from over the tree-tops in the East.

We were now thoroughly broken down; but the intense excite-ment of the time denied us repose. After an unquiet slumber of some three or four hours' duration, we arose, as if by preconcert, to make examination of our treasure.

The chest had been full to the brim, and we spent the whole day, and the greater part of the next night, in a scrutiny of its contents. There had been nothing like order or arrangement. Every thing had been heaped in promiscuously. Having assorted all with care, we found ourselves possessed of even vaster wealth than we had at first supposed. In coin there was rather more than four hundred and fifty thousand dollars—estimating the value of the pieces, as accurately as we could, by the tables of the period. There was not a particle of silver. All was gold of antique date and of great variety—French, Spanish, and German money, with a few English guineas, and some counters, of which we had never seen specimens before. There were several very large and heavy coins, so worn that we could make nothing of their inscriptions. There was no American money. The value of the jewels we found more difficulty in estimating. There were diamonds—some of them ex-ceedingly large and fine—a hundred and ten in all, and not one of them small; eighteen rubies of remarkable brilliancy;—three hundred and ten emeralds, all very beautiful; and twenty-one sap-phires, with an opal. These stones had all been broken from their settings and thrown loose in the chest. The settings themselves, which we picked out from among the other gold, appeared to have been beaten up with hammers, as if to prevent identification. Be-sides all this, there was a vast quantity of solid gold ornaments;—nearly two hundred massive finger and ear rings;—rich chains—thirty of these, if I remember;—eighty-three very large and heavy crucifixes;—five gold censers of great value;—a prodigious golden punch-bowl, ornamented with richly chased vine-leaves and Bac-chanalian figures; with two sword-handles exquisitely embossed, and many other smaller articles which I cannot recollect. The weight of these valuables exceeded three hundred and fifty pounds avoirdupois; and in this estimate I have not included one hundred and ninety-seven superb gold watches; three of the number being worth each five hundred dollars, if one. Many of them were very old, and as time keepers valueless; the works having suffered, more or less, from corrosion—but all were richly jewelled and in cases of great worth. We estimated the entire contents of the chest, that night, at a million and a half of dollars; and, upon the subsequent disposal of the trinkets and jewels (a few being retained for our own use), it was found that we had greatly undervalued the treasure.

When, at length, we had concluded our examination, and the intense excitement of the time had, in some measure, subsided, Legrand, who saw that I was dying with impatience for a solution of this most extraordinary riddle, entered into a full detail of all the circumstances connected with it.

"You remember," said he, "the night when I handed you the rough sketch I had made of the *scarabaeus*. You recollect also, that I became quite vexed at you for insisting that my drawing resembled a death's-head. When you first made this assertion I thought you were jesting; but afterwards I called to mind the peculiar spots on the back of the insect, and admitted to myself that your remark had some little foundation in fact. Still, the sneer at my graphic powers irritated me—for I am considered a good artist—and, therefore, when you handed me the scrap of parchment, I was about to crumple it up and throw it angrily into the fire."

"The scrap of paper, you mean," said I.

"No; it had much of the appearance of paper, and at first I supposed it to be such, but when I came to draw upon it, I discovered it, at once, to be a piece of very thin parchment. It was quite dirty, you remember. Well, as I was in the very act of crumpling it up, my glance fell upon the sketch at which you had been looking, and you may imagine my astonishment when I perceived, in fact, the figure of a death's-head just where, it seemed to me, I had made the drawing of the beetle. For a moment I was too much amazed to think with accuracy. I knew that my design was very different in detail from this—although there was a certain similarity in general outline. Presently I took a candle, and seating myself at the other end of the room, proceeded to scrutinize the parchment more closely. Upon turning it over, I saw my own sketch upon the reverse, just as I had made it. My first idea, now, was mere surprise at the really remarkable similarity of outline—at the singular coincidence involved in the fact, that unknown to me, there should have been a skull upon the other side of the parchment, immediately beneath my figure of the *scarabaeus,* and that this skull, not only in outline, but in size, should so closely resemble my drawing. I say the singularity of this coincidence absolutely stupified me for a time. This is the usual effect of such coincidences. The mind struggles to establish a connexion—a sequence of cause and effect—and, being unable to do so, suffers a species of temporary paralysis. But, when I recovered from this stupor, there dawned upon me gradually a conviction which startled me even far more than the coincidence. I began distinctly, positively, to remember that there had been *no* drawing on the parchment when I made my sketch of the *scarabaeus*. I became perfectly certain of this; for I recollected turning up first one side and then the other, in search of the cleanest spot. Had the skull been then there, of course I could not have failed to notice it. Here was indeed a mystery which I felt it impossible to explain; but, even at that early moment, there seemed to glimmer, faintly, within the most remote and secret chambers of my intellect, a glow-worm-like conception of that truth which last night's adventure brought to so magnificent a demonstration. I arose at once, and putting the parchment securely away, dismissed all farther reflection until I should be alone.

"When you had gone, and when Jupiter was fast asleep, I betook myself to a more methodical investigation of the affair. In the first place I considered the manner in which the parchment had come into my possession. The spot where we discovered the *scarabaeus* was on the coast of the main land, about a mile eastward of the island; and but a short distance above high water mark. Upon my taking hold of it, it gave me a sharp bite, which caused me to let it drop. Jupiter, with his accustomed caution, before seizing the insect, which had flown towards him, looked about him for a leaf, or something of that nature, by which to take hold of it. It was at this moment that his eyes, and mine also, fell upon the scrap of parchment, which I then supposed to be paper. It was lying half buried in the sand, a corner sticking up. Near the spot where we found it, I observed the remnants of the hull of what appeared to have been a ship's long boat. The wreck seemed to have been there for a very great while; for the resemblance to boat timbers could scarcely be traced.

"Well, Jupiter picked up the parchment, wrapped the beetle in it, and gave it to me. Soon afterwards we turned to go home, and on the way met Lieutenant G——. I showed him the insect, and he begged me to let him take it to the fort. On my consenting, he thrust it forthwith into his waistcoat pocket, without the parchment in which it had been wrapped, and which I had continued to hold in my hand during his inspection. Perhaps he dreaded my changing my mind, and thought it best to make sure of the prize at once—you know how enthusiastic he is on all subjects connected with

Natural History. At the same time, without being conscious of it, I must have deposited the parchment in my own pocket.

"You remember that when I went to the table, for the purpose of making a sketch of the beetle, I found no paper where it was usually kept. I looked in the drawer, and found none there. I searched my pockets, hoping to find an old letter—and then my hand fell upon the parchment. I thus detail the precise mode in which it came into my possession; for the circumstances impressed me with peculiar force.

"No doubt you will think me fanciful—but I had already established a kind of *connexion*. I had put together two links of a great chain. There was a boat lying on a sea-coast, and not far from the boat was a parchment—*not a paper*—with a skull depicted on it. You will, of course, ask 'where is the connexion?' I reply that the skull, or death's-head, is the well-known emblem of the pirate. The flag of the death's-head is hoisted in all engagements.

"I have said that the scrap was parchment, and not paper. Parchment is durable—almost imperishable. Matters of little moment are rarely consigned to parchment; since, for the mere ordinary purposes of drawing or writing, it is not nearly so well adapted as paper. This reflection suggested some meaning—some relevancy—in the death's-head. I did not fail to observe, also, the *form* of the parchment. Although one of its corners had been, by some accident, destroyed, it could be seen that the original form was oblong. It was just such a slip, indeed, as might have been chosen for a memorandum—for a record of something to be long remembered and carefully preserved."

"But," I interposed, "you say that the skull was *not* upon the parchment when you made the drawing of the beetle. How then do you trace any connexion between the boat and the skull—since this latter, according to your own admission, must have been designed (God only knows how or by whom) at some period subsequent to your sketching the *scarabaeus?*"

"Ah, hereupon turns the whole mystery; although the secret, at this point, I had comparatively little difficulty in solving. My steps were sure, and could afford but a single result. I reasoned, for example, thus: When I drew the *scarabaeus,* there was no skull apparent on the parchment. When I had completed the drawing, I gave it to you, and observed you narrowly until you returned it. *You,* therefore, did not design the skull, and no one else was present to do it. Then it was not done by human agency. And nevertheless it was done.

"At this stage of my reflections I endeavored to remember, and *did* remember, with entire distinctness, every incident which occurred about the period in question. The weather was chilly (oh rare and happy accident!), and a fire was blazing on the hearth. I was heated with exercise and sat near the table. You, however, had drawn a chair close to the chimney. Just as I placed the parchment in your hand, and as you were in the act of inspecting it, Wolf, the Newfoundland, entered, and leaped upon your shoulders. With your left hand you caressed him and kept him off, while your right, holding the parchment, was permitted to fall listlessly between your knees, and in close proximity to the fire. At one moment I thought the blaze had caught it, and was about to caution you, but, before I could speak, you had withdrawn it, and were engaged in its examination. When I considered all these particulars, I doubted not for a moment that *heat* had been the agent in bringing to light, on the parchment, the skull which I saw designed on it. You are well aware that chemical preparations exist, and have existed time out of mind, by means of which it is possible to write on either paper or vellum, so that the characters shall become visible only when subjected to the action of fire. Zaffre, digested in *aqua regia,* and diluted with four times its weight of water, is sometimes employed; a green tint results. The regulus of cobalt, dissolved in spirit of nitre, gives a red. These colors disappear at longer or shorter intervals after the material written on cools, but again become apparent upon the reapplication of heat.

"I now scrutinized the death's-head with care. Its outer edges—the edges of the drawing nearest the edge of the vellum—were far more *distinct* than the others. It was clear that the action of the caloric had been imperfect or unequal. I immediately kindled a fire, and subjected every portion of the parchment to a glowing heat. At first, the only effect was the strengthening of the faint lines in the skull; but, on persevering in the experiment, there became visible, at the corner of the slip, diagonally opposite to the spot in which the death's-head was delineated, the figure of what I at first supposed to be a goat. A closer scrutiny, however, satisfied me that it was intended for a kid."

"Ha! ha!" said I, "to be sure I have no right to laugh at you—a million and a half of money is too serious a matter for mirth—but you are not about to establish a third link in your chain—you will not find any especial connexion between your pirates and a goat—pirates, you know, have nothing to do with goats; they appertain to the farming interest."

"But I have just said that the figure was *not* that of a goat."

"Well, a kid then—pretty much the same thing."

"Pretty much, but not altogether," said Legrand. "You may

have heard of one *Captain* Kidd. I at once looked on the figure of the animal as a kind of punning or hieroglyphical signature. I say signature; because its position on the vellum suggested this idea. The death's-head at the corner diagonally opposite, had, in the same manner, the air of a stamp, or seal. But I was sorely put out by the absence of all else—of the body to my imagined instrument—of the text for my context."

"I presume you expected to find a letter between the stamp and the signature."

"Something of that kind. The fact is, I felt irresistibly impressed with a presentiment of some vast good fortune impending. I can scarcely say why. Perhaps, after all, it was rather a desire than an actual belief;—but do you know that Jupiter's silly words, about the bug being of solid gold, had a remarkable effect on my fancy? And then the series of accidents and coincidences—these were so *very* extraordinary. Do you observe how mere an accident it was that these events should have occurred on the *sole* day of all the year in which it has been, or may be, sufficiently cool for fire, and that without the fire, or without the intervention of the dog at the precise moment in which he appeared, I should never have become aware of the death's-head, and so never the possessor of the treasure?"

"But proceed—I am all impatience."

"Well; you have heard, of course, the many stories current— the thousand vague rumors afloat about money buried, somewhere on the Atlantic coast, by Kidd and his associates. These rumors must have had some foundation in fact. And that the rumors have existed so long and so continuously, could have resulted, it appeared to me, only from the circumstance of the buried treasure still *remaining* entombed. Had Kidd concealed his plunder for a time, and afterwards reclaimed it, the rumors would scarcely have reached us in their present unvarying form. You will observe that the stories told are all about money-seekers, not about money-finders. Had the pirate recovered his money, there the affair would have dropped. It seemed to me that some accident—say the loss of a memorandum indicating its locality—had deprived him of the means of recovering it, and that this accident had become known to his followers, who otherwise might never have heard that treasure had been concealed at all, and who, busying themselves in vain, because unguided attempts, to regain it, had given first birth, and then universal currency, to the reports which are now so common. Have you ever heard of any important treasure being unearthed along the coast?"

"Never."

"But that Kidd's accumulations were immense, is well known. I took it for granted, therefore, that the earth still held them; and you will scarcely be surprised when I tell you that I felt a hope, nearly amounting to certainty, that the parchment so strangely found, involved a lost record of the place of deposit."

"But how did you proceed?"

"I held the vellum again to the fire, after increasing the heat; but nothing appeared. I now thought it possible that the coating of dirt might have something to do with the failure; so I carefully rinsed the parchment by pouring warm water over it, and, having done this, I placed it in a tin pan, with the skull downwards, and put the pan upon a furnace of lighted charcoal. In a few minutes, the pan having become thoroughly heated, I removed the slip, and, to my inexpressible joy, found it spotted, in several places, with what appeared to be figures arranged in lines. Again I placed it in the pan, and suffered it to remain another minute. On taking it off, the whole was just as you see it now."

Here Legrand, having re-heated the parchment, submitted it to my inspection. The following characters were rudely traced, in a red tint, between the death's-head and the goat:

53‡‡†305))6*;4826)4‡.)4‡);806*;48†8¶60))85;;]8*;:‡*
8†83(88)5*†;46(;88*96*?;8)*‡(;485);5*†2:*‡(;4956*2(5
—4)8¶8;4069285);)6†8)4‡‡;1(‡9;48081;8:8‡1;48†8
5;4)485†528806*81(‡9;48;(88;4(‡?34;48)4‡;161;:188;‡?;

"But," said I, returning him the slip, "I am as much in the dark as ever. Were all the jewels of Golconda awaiting me on my solution of this enigma, I am quite sure that I should be unable to earn them."

"And yet," said Legrand, "the solution is by no means so difficult as you might be led to imagine from the first hasty inspection of the characters. These characters, as any one might readily guess, form a cipher—that is to say, they convey a meaning; but then, from what is known of Kidd, I could not suppose him capable of constructing any of the more abstruse cryptographs. I made up my mind, at once, that this was of a simple species—such, however, as would appear, to the crude intellect of the sailor, absolutely insoluble without the key."

"And you really solved it?"

"Readily; I have solved others of an abstruseness ten thousand times greater. Circumstances, and a certain bias of mind, have led me to take interest in such riddles, and it may well be doubted whether human ingenuity can construct an enigma of the kind which human ingenuity may not, by proper application, resolve. In fact, having once established connected and legible characters, I scarcely gave a thought to the mere difficulty of developing their import.

"In the present case—indeed in all cases of secret writing—the first question regards the *language* of the cipher; for the principles of solution, so far, especially, as the more simple ciphers are concerned, depend upon, and are varied by, the genius of the particular idiom. In general, there is no alternative but experiment (directed by probabilities) of every tongue known to him who attempts the solution, until the true one be attained. But, with the cipher now before us, all difficulty is removed by the signature. The pun on the word 'Kidd' is appreciable in no other language than the English. But for this consideration I should have begun my attempts with the Spanish and French, as the tongues in which a secret of this kind would most naturally have been written by a pirate of the Spanish main. As it was, I assumed the cryptograph to be English.

"You observe there are no divisions between the words. Had there been divisions, the task would have been comparatively easy. In such case I should have commenced with a collation and analysis of the shorter words, and, had a word of a single letter occurred, as is most likely, (*a* or *I*, for example,) I should have considered the solution as assured. But, there being no division, my first step was to ascertain the predominant letters, as well as the least frequent. Counting all, I constructed a table, thus:

Of the character 8 there are 33.

;	"	26.
4	"	19.
‡)	"	16.
*	"	13.
5	"	12.
6	"	11.
†1	"	8.
0	"	6.
92	"	5.
:3	"	4.
?	"	3.
¶	"	2.
]—.	"	1.

"Now, in English, the letter which most frequently occurs is *e*. Afterwards, the succession runs thus: *a o i d h n r s t u y c f g l m w b k p q x z.* E, however, predominates so remarkably that an individual sentence of any length is rarely seen, in which it is not the prevailing character.

"Here, then, we have, in the very beginning, the ground-work for something more than a mere guess. The general use which may be made of the table is obvious—but, in this particular cipher, we shall only very partially require its aid. As our predominant character is 8, we will commence by assuming it as the *e* of the natural alphabet. To verify the supposition, let us observe if the 8 be seen often in couples—for *e* is doubled with great frequency in English—in which words, for example, as 'meet,' 'fleet,' 'speed,' 'seen,' 'been,' 'agree,' &c. In the present instance we see it doubled no less than five times, although the cryptograph is brief.

"Let us assume 8, then, as *e*. Now, of all *words* in the language, 'the' is most usual; let us see, therefore, whether there are not repetitions of any three characters, in the same order of collocation, the last of them being 8. If we discover repetitions of such letters, so arranged, they will most probably represent the word 'the.' On inspection, we find no less than seven such arrangements, the characters being ;48. We may, therefore, assume that the semicolon represents *t*, that 4 represents *h*, and that 8 represents *e*—the last being now well confirmed. Thus a great step has been taken.

"But, having established a single word, we are enabled to establish a vastly important point; that is to say, several commencements and terminations of other words. Let us refer, for example, to the last instance but one, in which the combination ;48 occurs—not far from the end of the cipher. We know that the semicolon immediately ensuing is the commencement of a word, and, of the six characters succeeding this 'the,' we are cognizant of no less than five. Let us set these characters down, thus, by the letters we know them to represent, leaving a space for the unknown—

t eeth.

"Here we are enabled, at once, to discard the '*th*,' as forming no portion of the word commencing with the first *t*; since, by experiment of the entire alphabet for a letter adapted to the vacancy, we perceive that no word can be formed of which this *th* can be a part. We are thus narrowed into t ee,

and, going through the alphabet, if necessary, as before, we arrive at the word 'tree,' as the sole possible reading. We thus gain another letter, *r*, represented by (, with the words 'the tree' in juxtaposition.

"Looking beyond these words, for a short distance, we again see the combination ;48, and employ it by way of *termination* to what immediately precedes. We have thus this arrangement:

the tree ;4(‡?34 the,

or, substituting the natural letters, where known, it reads thus:

the tree thr‡?3h the.

"Now, if, in place of the unknown characters, we leave blank spaces, or substitute dots, we read thus:

the tree thr. . .h the,

when the word *'through'* makes itself evident at once. But this discovery gives us three new letters, *o, u* and *g*, represented by ‡ ? and 3.

"Looking now, narrowly, through the cipher for combinations of known characters, we find, not very far from the beginning, this arrangement,

83(88, or egree,

which, plainly, is the conclusion of the word 'degree,' and gives us another letter, *d*, represented by †.

"Four letters beyond the word 'degree,' we perceive the combination

;46(;88*

"Translating the known characters, and representing the unknown by dots, as before, we read thus:

th . rtee.

an arrangement immediately suggestive of the word 'thirteen,' and again furnishing us with two new characters, *i* and *n*, represented by 6 and *.

"Referring, now, to the beginning of the cryptograph, we find the combination,

53‡‡†.

"Translating, as before, we obtain

.good,

which assures us that the first letter is *A*, and that the first two words are 'A good.'

"To avoid confusion, it is now time that we arrange our key, as far as discovered, in a tabular form. It will stand thus:

5	represents	a
†	"	d
8	"	e
3	"	g
4	"	h
6	"	i
*	"	n
‡	"	o
(	"	r
;	"	t

"We have, therefore, no less than ten of the most important letters represented, and it will be unnecessary to proceed with the details of the solution. I have said enough to convince you that ciphers of this nature are readily soluble, and give you some insight into the *rationale* of their development. But be assured that the specimen before us appertains to the very simplest species of cryptograph. It now only remains to give you the full translation of the characters upon the parchment, as unriddled. Here it is:

" *'A good glass in the bishop's hostel in the devil's seat twenty-one degrees and thirteen minutes northeast and by north main branch seventh limb east side shoot from the left eye of the death's-head a bee line from the tree through the shot fifty feet out.'* "

"But," said I, "the enigma seems still in as bad a condition as ever. How is it possible to extort a meaning from all this jargon about 'devil's seats,' 'death's-heads,' and 'bishop's hotels?' "

"I confess," replied Legrand, "that the matter still wears a serious aspect, when regarded with a casual glance. My first endeavor was to divide the sentence into the natural division intended by the cryptographist."

"You mean, to punctuate it?"

"Something of that kind."

"But how was it possible to effect this?"

"I reflected that it had been a *point* with the writer to run his words together without division, so as to increase the difficulty of solution. Now, a not over-acute man, in pursuing such an object, would be nearly certain to overdo the matter. When, in the course of his composition, he arrived at a break in his subject which would naturally require a pause, or a point, he would be exceedingly apt to run his characters, at this place, more than usually close together. If you will observe the M.S., in the present instance, you will easily detect five such cases of unusual crowding. Acting on this hint, I made the division thus:

" '*A good glass in the Bishop's hostel in the Devil's seat—twenty-one degrees and thirteen minutes—northeast and by north—main branch seventh limb east side—shoot from the left eye of the death's-head—a bee-line from the tree through the shot fifty feet out.*' "

"Even this division," said I, "leaves me still in the dark."

"It left me also in the dark," replied Legrand, "for a few days; during which I made diligent inquiry, in the neighborhood of Sullivan's Island, for any building which went by the name of the 'Bishop's Hotel;' for, of course, I dropped the obsolete word 'hostel.' Gaining no information on the subject, I was on the point of extending my sphere of search, and proceeding in a more systematic manner, when, one morning, it entered into my head, quite suddenly, that this 'Bishop's Hostel' might have some reference to an old family, of the name of Bessop, which, time out of mind, had held possession of an ancient manor-house, about four miles to the northward of the Island. I accordingly went over to the plantation, and re-instituted my inquiries among the older negroes of the place. At length one of the most aged of the women said that she had heard of such a place as *Bessop's Castle*, and thought that she could guide me to it, but that it was not a castle, nor a tavern, but a high rock.

"I offered to pay her well for her trouble, and, after some demur, she consented to accompany me to the spot. We found it without much difficulty, when, dismissing her, I proceeded to examine the place. The 'castle' consisted of an irregular assemblage of cliffs

and rocks—one of the latter being quite remarkable for its height
as well as for its insulted and artificial appearance. I clambered to
its apex, and then felt much at a loss as to what should be next
done.

"While I was busied in reflection, my eyes fell upon a narrow
ledge in the eastern face of the rock, perhaps a yard below the
summit on which I stood. This ledge projected about eighteen
inches, and was not more than a foot wide, while a niche in the
cliff just above it, gave it a rude resemblance to one of the hollow-
backed chairs used by our ancestors. I made no doubt that here
was the 'devil's-seat' alluded to in the MS., and now I seemed to
grasp the full secret of the riddle.

"The 'good glass,' I knew, could have reference to nothing but
a telescope; for the word 'glass' is rarely employed in any other
sense by seamen. Now here, I at once saw, was a telescope to be
used, and a definite point of view, *admitting no variation*, from
which to use it. Nor did I hesitate to believe that the phrases,
'twenty-one degrees and thirteen minutes,' and 'northeast and by
north,' were intended as directions for the levelling of the glass.
Greatly excited by these discoveries, I hurried home, procured a
telescope, and returned to the rock.

"I let myself down to the ledge, and found that it was impossible
to retain a seat on it unless in one particular position. This fact
confirmed my preconceived idea. I proceeded to use the glass. Of
course, the 'twenty-one degrees and thirteen minutes' could allude
to nothing but elevation above the visible horizon, since the horizontal direction was clearly indicated by the words, 'northeast and
by north.' This latter direction I at once established by means of
a pocket-compass; then, pointing the glass as nearly at an angle
of twenty-one degrees of elevation as I could do it by guess, I
moved it cautiously up or down, until my attention was arrested
by a circular rift or opening in the foliage of a large tree that
overtopped its fellows in the distance. In the centre of this rift I
perceived a white spot, but could not, at first, distinguish what it
was. Adjusing the focus of the telescope, I again looked, and now
made it out to be a human skull.

"On this discovery I was so sanguine as to consider the enigma
solved; for the phrase 'main branch, seventh limb, east side,' could
refer only to the position of the skull on the tree, while 'shoot
from the left eye of the death's-head' admitted, also, of but one
interpretation, in regard to a search for buried treasure. I perceived
that the design was to drop a bullet from the left eye of the skull,
and that a bee-line, or, in other words, a straight line, drawn from

the nearest point of the trunk through 'the shot,' (or the spot where the bullet fell,) and thence extended to a distance of fifty feet, would indicate a definite point—and beneath this point I thought it at least *possible* that a deposit of value lay concealed."

"All this," I said, "is exceedingly clear, and, although ingenious, still simple and explicit. When you left the Bishop's Hotel, what then?"

"Why, having carefully taken the bearings of the tree, I turned homewards. The instant that I left 'the devil's seat,' however, the circular rift vanished; nor could I get a glimpse of it afterwards, turn as I would. What seems to me the chief ingenuity in this whole business, is the fact (for repeated experiment has convinced me it *is* a fact) that the circular opening in question is visible from no other attainable point of view than that afforded by the narrow ledge on the face of the rock.

"In this expedition to the 'Bishop's Hotel' I had been attended by Jupiter, who had, no doubt, observed, for some weeks past, the abstraction of my demeanor, and took especial care not to leave me alone. But, on the next day, getting up very early, I contrived to give him the slip, and went into the hills in search of the tree. After much toil I found it. When I came home at night my valet proposed to give me a flogging. With the rest of the adventure I believe you are as well acquainted as myself."

"I suppose," said I, "you missed the spot, in the first attempt at digging, through Jupiter's stupidity in letting the bug fall through the right instead of through the left eye of the skull."

"Precisely. This mistake made a difference of about two inches and a half in the 'shot'—that is to say, in the position of the peg nearest the tree; and had the treasure been *beneath* the 'shot,' the error would have been of little moment; but 'the shot,' together with the nearest point of the tree, were merely two points for the establishment of a line of direction; of course the error, however trivial in the beginning, increased as we proceeded with the line, and by the time we had gone fifty feet, threw us quite off the scent. But for my deep-seated conviction that treasure was here somewhere actually buried, we might have had all our labor in vain."

"I presume the fancy of *the skull*—of letting fall a bullet through the skull's-eye—was suggested to Kidd by the piratical flag. No doubt he felt a kind of poetical consistency in recovering his money through this ominous insignium."

"Perhaps so; still I cannot help thinking that common-sense had quite as much to do with the matter as poetical consistency. To be visible from the Devil's seat, it was necessary that the object, if small, should be *white*; and there is nothing like your human skull for retaining and even increasing its whiteness under exposure to all vicissitudes of weather."

"But your grandiloquence, and your conduct in swinging the beetle—how excessively odd! I was sure you were mad. And why did you insist on letting fall the bug, instead of a bullet, from the skull?"

"Why, to be frank, I felt somewhat annoyed by your evident suspicions touching my sanity, and so resolved to punish you quietly, in my own way, by a little bit of sober mystification. For this reason I swung the beetle, and for this reason I let it fall from the tree. An observation of yours about its great weight suggested the latter idea."

"Yes, I perceive; and now there is only one point which puzzles me. What are we to make of the skeletons found in the hole?"

"That is a question I am no more able to answer than yourself. There seems, however, only one plausible way of accounting for them—and yet it is dreadful to believe in such atrocity as my suggestion would imply. It is clear that Kidd—if Kidd indeed secreted this treasure, which I doubt not—it is clear that he must have had assistance in the labor. But, the worst of this labor concluded, he may have thought it expedient to remove all participants in his secret. Perhaps a couple of blows with a mattock were sufficient, while his coadjutors were busy in the pit; perhaps it required a dozen—who shall tell?"

Katherine Anne Porter

(1890–1980)

Born in Indian Creek, Texas, to a family whose attachments to the rural South were deep and strong, Porter was raised by her paternal grandmother in Kyle, Texas. Her mother had died when Porter was two years old, and her father was unable to care for his five children after the death of his wife. Porter received little formal education, though she spent some time in a boarding school in San Antonio. She married John Henry Koonzt, the first of four husbands, when she was 16. After eight years of marriage, she left Koonzt and moved to Chicago, where she attempted a career in the movies. During the next few years she abandoned her movie career, moved to Louisiana to be with her sister, moved back to Texas, fell sick with tuberculosis, and spent a year in a Texas sanatorium. At this point she turned to writing as a full-time profession, first as a journalist in Denver, and then as both journalist and short-story writer. She settled for a time in New York, traveled to Mexico, married and divorced her second husband, and wrote her first group of major stories, published in 1930 as the collection Flowering Judas and Other Stories. In 1930 she returned to Mexico where she met—and eventually married— Eugene Pressley, a career officer in the American foreign service. With Pressley, she traveled all over Europe, and lived in Germany, Switzerland, and France. The marriage ended in divorce, and in 1937, in New Orleans, she married Albert Erskine, the well-known editor and publisher. The marriage was an unhappy one, and they were separated and finally divorced after her second collection of stories, Pale Horse, Pale Rider, was published in 1939. With this collection, Porter established herself as one of the finest short-story writers alive. Unfortunately, throughout her life she was troubled by the fear—encouraged by her publishers—that only a full-scale novel would confirm her reputation, and she spent over 20 years working on her single novel, Ship of Fools (1962). During this time, she supported herself by working for a brief period in Hollywood, *and by teaching in universities. After* Ship of Fools *was published, she finally secured the financial well-being and national popularity her short stories had failed to bring. Critics, however, found little to praise in* Ship of Fools, *and were right in esteeming her short stories, especially the Southern ones, above everything else she wrote. In 1965, her* Collected Stories *won the National Book Award. Among her other books are* The Leaning Tower and Other Stories *(1944),* The Collected Essays and Occasional Writings *(1970), and* The Never-Ending Wrong *(1977). "The Old Order" first appeared in* The Southern Review *(Winter 1936).*

THE OLD ORDER

In their later years, the Grandmother and old Nannie used to sit together for some hours every day over their sewing. They shared a passion for cutting scraps of the family finery, hoarded for fifty years, into strips and triangles, and fitting them together again in a carefully disordered patchwork, outlining each bit of velvet or satin or taffeta with a running briar stitch in clear lemon-colored silk floss. They had contrived enough bed and couch covers, table spreads, dressing table scarfs, to have furnished forth several households. Each piece as it was finished was lined with yellow silk, folded, and laid away in a chest, never again to see the light of day. The Grandmother was the great-granddaughter of Kentucky's most famous pioneer: he had, while he was surveying Kentucky, hewed out rather competently a rolling pin for his wife. This rolling pin was the Grandmother's irreplaceable treasure. She covered it with an extraordinarily complicated bit of patchwork, added golden tassels to the handles, and hung it in a conspicuous place in her room. She was the daughter of a notably heroic captain in the War of 1812. She had his razors in a shagreen case and a particularly severe-looking daguerreotype taken in his old age, with his chin in a tall stock and his black satin waistcoat smoothed over a still-handsome military chest. So she fitted a patchwork case over the shagreen and made a sort of envelope of cut velvet and violet satin, held together with briar stitching, to contain the portrait. The rest of her handiwork she put away, to the relief of her grandchildren, who had arrived at the awkward age when Grandmother's quaint old-fashioned ways caused them acute discomfort.

In the summer the women sat under the mingled trees of the side garden, which commanded a view of the east wing, the front and back porches, a good part of the front garden and a corner of the small fig grove. Their choice of this location was a part of their domestic strategy. Very little escaped them: a glance now and then would serve to keep them fairly well informed as to what was going on in the whole place. It is true they had not seen Miranda the day she pulled up the whole mint bed to give to a pleasant strange young woman who stopped and asked her for a sprig of fresh mint. They had never found out who stole the giant pomegranates growing too near the fence: they had not been in time to stop Paul from setting himself on fire while experimenting with a miniature blowtorch, but they had been on the scene to extinguish him with rugs, to pour oil on him, and lecture him. They never saw Maria climbing trees, a mania she had to indulge or pine away, for she chose tall ones on the opposite side of the house. But such casualties were so minor a part of the perpetual round of events that they did not feel defeated nor that their strategy was a failure. Summer, in many ways so desirable a season, had its drawbacks. The children were everywhere at once and the Negroes loved lying under the hackberry grove back of the barns playing seven-up, and eating watermelons. The summer house was in a small town a few miles from the farm, a compromise between the rigorously ordered house in the city and the sprawling old farmhouse which Grandmother had built with such pride and pains. It had, she often said, none of the advantages of either country or city, and all the discomforts of both. But the children loved it.

During the winters in the city, they sat in Grandmother's room, a large squarish place with a small coal grate. All the sounds of life in the household seemed to converge there, echo, retreat, and return. Grandmother and Aunt Nannie knew the whole complicated code of sounds, could interpret and comment on them by an exchange of glances, a lifted eyebrow, or a tiny pause in their talk.

They talked about the past, really—always about the past. Even the future seemed like something gone and done with when they spoke of it. It did not seem an extension of their past, but a repetition of it. They would agree that nothing remained of life as they had known it, the world was changing swiftly, but by the mysterious logic of hope they insisted that each change was probably the last; or if not, a series of changes might bring them, blessedly, back full-circle to the old ways they had known. Who knows why they loved their past? It had been bitter for them both, they had questioned the burdensome rule they lived by every day of their lives, but without rebellion and without expecting an answer. This unbroken thread of inquiry in their minds contained no doubt as to the utter rightness and justice of the basic laws of human existence, founded as they were on God's plan; but they wondered perpetually, with only a hint now and then to each other of the uneasiness of their hearts, how so much suffering and confusion could have been built up and maintained on such a foundation. The Grandmother's rôle was authority, she knew that; it was her duty to portion out activities, to urge or restrain where necessary, to teach morals, manners, and religion, to punish and reward her own household according to a fixed code. Her own doubts and hesitations she concealed, also, she reminded herself, as a matter of duty. Old Nannie had no ideas at all as to her place in the world. It had been assigned to her before birth, and for her daily rule she had all her life obeyed the authority nearest to her.

So they talked about God, about heaven, about planting a new hedge of rose bushes, about the new ways of preserving fruit and vegetables, about eternity and their mutual hope that they might pass it happily together, and often a scrap of silk under their hands would start them on long trains of family reminiscences. They were always amused to notice again how the working of their memories differed in such important ways. Nannie could recall names to perfection; she could always say what the weather had been like on all important occasions, what certain ladies had worn, how handsome certain gentlemen had been, what there had been to eat and drink. Grandmother had masses of dates in her mind, and no memories attached to them: her memories of events seemed detached and floating beyond time. For example, the 26th of August, 1871, had been some sort of red-letter day for her. She had said to herself then that never would she forget that date; and indeed, she remembered it well, but she no longer had the faintest notion what had happened to stamp it on her memory. Nannie was no help in the matter; she had nothing to do with dates. She did not know the year of her birth, and would never have had a birthday to celebrate if Grandmother had not, when she was still Miss Sophia Jane, aged ten, opened a calendar at random, closed her eyes, and marked a date unseen with a pen. So it turned out that Nannie's birthday thereafter fell on June 11, and the year, Miss Sophia Jane decided, should be 1827, her own birth-year, making Nannie just three months younger than her mistress. Sophia Jane then made an entry of Nannie's birth-date in the family Bible, inserting it just below her own. "Nannie Gay," she wrote, in stiff careful letters, "(black)," and though there was some uproar when this was discovered, the ink was long since sunk deeply into the paper, and besides no one was really upset enough to have it scratched out. There it remained, one of their pleasantest points of reference.

They talked about religion, and the slack way the world was going nowadays, the decay of behavior, and about the younger children, whom these topics always brought at once to mind. On these subjects they were firm, critical, and unbewildered. They had received educations which furnished them an assured habit of mind about all the important appearances of life, and especially about the rearing of young. They relied with perfect acquiescence on the dogma that children were conceived in sin and brought forth in iniquity. Childhood was a long state of instruction and probation for adult life, which was in turn a long, severe, unde- viating devotion to duty, the largest part of which consisted in bringing up children. The young were difficult, disobedient, and tireless in wrongdoing, apt to turn unkind and undutiful when they grew up, in spite of all one had done for them, or had tried to do: for small painful doubts rose in them now and again when they looked at their completed works. Nannie couldn't abide her new- fangled grandchildren. "Wuthless, shiftless lot, jes plain scum, Miss Sophia Jane; I cain't undahstand it aftah all the raisin' dey had."

The Grandmother defended them, and dispraised her own sec- ond generation—heartily, too, for she sincerely found grave faults in them—which Nannie defended in turn. "When they are little, they trample on your feet, and when they grow up they trample on your heart." This was about all there was to say about children in any generation, but the fascination of the theme was endless. They said it thoroughly over and over with thousands of small variations, with always an example among their own friends or family connections to prove it. They had enough material of their own. Grandmother had borne eleven children, Nannie thirteen. They boasted of it. Grandmother would say, "I am the mother of eleven children," in a faintly amazed tone, as if she hardly expected to be believed, or could even quite believe it herself. But she could still point to nine of them. Nannie had lost ten of hers. They were all buried in Kentucky. Nannie never doubted or expected anyone else to doubt she had children. Her boasting was of another order. "Thirteen of 'em," she would say, in an appalled voice, "yas, my Lawd and my Redeemah, thirteen!"

The friendship between the two old women had begun in early childhood, and was based on what seemed even to them almost mythical events. Miss Sophia Jane, a prissy, spoiled five-year-old, with tight black ringlets which were curled every day on a stick, with her stiffly pleated lawn pantalettes and tight bodice, had run to meet her returning father, who had been away buying horses and Negroes. Sitting on his arm, clasping him around the neck, she had watched the wagons filing past on the way to the barns and quarters. On the floor of the first wagon sat two blacks, male and female, holding between them a scrawny, half-naked black child, with a round nubbly head and fixed bright monkey eyes. The baby Negro had a potbelly and her arms were like sticks from wrist to shoulder. She clung with narrow, withered, black leather fingers to her parents, a hand on each.

"I want the little monkey," said Sophia Jane to her father, nuzzling his cheek and pointing. "I want that one to play with."

Behind each wagon came two horses in lead, but in the second wagon there was a small shaggy pony with a thatch of mane over his eyes, a long tail like a brush, a round, hard barrel of a body. He was standing in straw to the knees, braced firmly in a padded stall with a Negro holding his bridle. "Do you see that?" asked her father. "That's for you. High time you learned to ride."

Sophia Jane almost leaped from his arm for joy. She hardly recognized her pony or her monkey the next day, the one clipped and sleek, the other clean in new blue cotton. For a while she could not decide which she loved more, Nannie or Fiddler. But Fiddler did not wear well. She outgrew him in a year, saw him pass without regret to a small brother, though she refused to allow him to be called Fiddler any longer. That name she reserved for a long series of saddle horses. She had named the first in honor of Fiddler Gay, an old Negro who made the music for dances and parties. There was only one Nannie and she outwore Sophia Jane. During all their lives together it was not so much a question of affection between them as a simple matter of being unable to imagine getting on without each other.

Nannie remembered well being on a shallow platform out in front of a great building in a large busy place, the first town she had ever seen. Her father and mother were with her, and there was a thick crowd around them. There were several other small groups of Negroes huddled together with white men bustling them about now and then. She had never seen any of these faces before, and she never saw but one of them again. She remembered it must have been summer, because she was not shivering with cold in her cotton shift. For one thing, her bottom was still burning from a spanking someone (it might have been her mother) had given her just before they got on the platform, to remind her to keep still.

Her mother and father were field hands, and had never lived in white folks' houses. A tall gentleman with a long narrow face and very high curved nose, wearing a great-collared blue coat and immensely long light-colored trousers (Nannie could close her eyes and see him again, clearly, as he looked that day) stepped up near them suddenly, while a great hubbub rose. The red-faced man standing on a stump beside them shouted and droned, waving his arms and pointing at Nannie's father and mother. Now and then the tall gentleman raised a finger, without looking at the black people on the platform. Suddenly the shouting died down, the tall gentleman walked over and said to Nannie's father and mother, "Well, Eph! Well, Steeny! Mister Jimmerson comin' to get you in a minute." He poked Nannie in the stomach with a thickly gloved forefinger. "Regular crowbait," he said to the auctioneer. "I should have had lagniappe with this one."

"A pretty worthless article right now, sir, I agree with you," said the auctioneer, "but it'll grow out of it. As for the team, you won't find a better, I swear."

"I've had an eye on 'em for years," said the tall gentleman, and walked away, motioning as he went to a fat man sitting on a wagon tongue, spitting quantities of tobacco juice. The fat man rose and came over to Nannie and her parents.

Nannie had been sold for twenty dollars: a gift, you might say, hardly sold at all. She learned that a really choice slave sometimes cost more than a thousand dollars. She lived to hear slaves brag about how much they had cost. She had not known how little she fetched on the block until her own mother taunted her with it. This was after Nannie had gone to live for good at the big house, and her mother and father were still in the fields. They lived and worked and died there. A good worming had cured Nannie's pot-belly, she thrived on plentiful food and a species of kindness not so indulgent, maybe, as that given to the puppies; still it more than fulfilled her notions of good fortune.

The old women often talked about how strangely things come out in this life. The first owner of Nannie and her parents had gone, Sophia Jane's father said, hog-wild about Texas. It was a new Land of Promise, in 1832. He had sold out his farm and four slaves in Kentucky to raise the money to take a great twenty-mile stretch of land in southwest Texas. He had taken his wife and two young children and set out, and there had been no more news of him for many years. When Grandmother arrived in Texas forty years later,

she found him a prosperous ranchman and district judge. Much
later, her youngest son met his granddaughter, fell in love with
her, and married her—all in three months.

The judge, by then eighty-five years old, was uproarious and
festive at the wedding. He reeked of corn liquor, swore by God
every other breath, and was rearing to talk about the good old
times in Kentucky. The Grandmother showed Nannie to him.
"Would you recognize her?" "For God Almighty's sake!" bawled
the judge, "is that the strip of crowbait I sold to your father for
twenty dollars? Twenty dollars seemed like a fortune to me in
those days!"

While they were jolting home down the steep rocky road on the
long journey from San Marcos to Austin, Nannie finally spoke out
about her grievance. "Look lak a jedge might had better raisin',"
she said, gloomily, "look lak he didn't keer how much he hurt a
body's feelins."

The Grandmother, muffled down in the back seat in the corner
of the old carryall, in her worn sealskin pelisse, showing coffee-
brown at the edges, her eyes closed, her hands wrung together,
had been occupied once more in reconciling herself to losing a
son, and, as ever, to a girl and a family of which she could not
altogether approve. It was not that there was anything seriously
damaging to be said against any of them; only—well, she wondered
at her sons' tastes. What had each of them in turn found in the
wife he had chosen? The Grandmother had always had in mind
the kind of wife each of her sons needed; she had tried to bring
about better marriages for them than they had made for themselves. They had merely resented her interference in what they
considered strictly their personal affairs. She did not realize that
she had spoiled and pampered her youngest son until he was in
all probability unfit to be any kind of a husband, much less a good
one. And there was something about her new daughter-in-law, a
tall, handsome, firm-looking young woman, with a direct way of
speaking, walking, talking, that seemed to promise that the spoiled
Baby's days of clover were ended. The Grandmother was annoyed
deeply at seeing how self-possessed the bride had been, how she
had had her way about the wedding arrangements down to the last
detail, how she glanced now and then at her new husband with
calm, humorous, level eyes, as if she had already got him sized
up. She had even suggested at the wedding dinner that her idea
of a honeymoon would be to follow the chuck-wagon on the round-
up, and help in the cattle-branding on her father's ranch. Of course
she may have been joking. But she was altogether too Western,
too modern, something like the "new" woman who was beginning

to run wild, asking for the vote, leaving her home and going out in the world to earn her own living . . .

The Grandmother's narrow body shuddered to the bone at the thought of women so unsexing themselves; she emerged with a start from the dark reverie of foreboding thoughts which left a bitter taste in her throat. "Never mind, Nannie. The judge just wasn't thinking. He's very fond of his good cheer."

Nannie had slept in a bed and had been playmate and work-fellow with her mistress; they fought on almost equal terms, Sophia Jane defending Nannie fiercely against any discipline but her own. When they were both seventeen years old, Miss Sophia Jane was married off in a very gay wedding. The house was jammed to the roof and everybody present was at least fourth cousin to everybody else. There were forty carriages and more than two hundred horses to look after for two days. When the last wheel disappeared down the lane (a number of the guests lingered on for two weeks), the larders and bins were half empty and the place looked as if a troop of cavalry had been over it. A few days later Nannie was married off to a boy she had known ever since she came to the family, and they were given as a wedding present to Miss Sophia Jane.

Miss Sophia Jane and Nannie had then started their grim and terrible race of procreation, a child every sixteen months or so, with Nannie nursing both, and Sophia Jane, in dreadful discomfort, suppressing her milk with bandages and spirits of wine. When they each had produced their fourth child, Nannie almost died of puerperal fever. Sophia Jane nursed both children. She named the black baby Charlie, and her own child Stephen, and she fed them justly turn about, not favoring the white over the black, as Nannie felt obliged to do. Her husband was shocked, tried to forbid her; her mother came to see her and reasoned with her. They found her very difficult and quite stubborn. She had already begun to develop her implicit character, which was altogether just, humane, proud, and simple. She had many small vanities and weaknesses on the surface: a love of luxury and a tendency to resent criticism. This tendency was based on her feeling of superiority in judgment and sensibility to almost everyone around her. It made her very hard to manage. She had a quiet way of holding her ground which convinced her antagonist that she would really die, not just threaten to, rather than give way. She had learned now that she was badly cheated in giving her children to another woman to feed; she resolved never again to be cheated in just that way. She sat nursing her child and her foster child, with a sensual warm pleasure she had not dreamed of, translating her natural physical relief into something holy, God-sent, amends from heaven for what she had suffered in childbed. Yes, and for what she missed in the marriage bed, for there also something had failed. She said to Nannie quite calmly, "From now on, you will nurse your children and I will nurse mine," and it was so. Charlie remained her special favorite among the Negro children. "I understand now," she said to her older sister Keziah, "why the black mammies love their foster children. I love mine." So Charlie was brought up in the house as playmate for her son Stephen, and exempted from hard work all his life.

Sophia Jane had been wooed at arm's length by a mysteriously attractive young man whom she remembered well as rather a snubby little boy with curls like her own, but shorter, a frilled white blouse and kilts of the Macdonald tartan. He was her second cousin and resembled her so closely they had been mistaken for brother and sister. Their grandparents had been first cousins, and sometimes Sophia Jane saw in him, years after they were married, all the faults she had most abhorred in her elder brother: lack of aim, failure to act at crises, a philosophic detachment from practical affairs, a tendency to set projects on foot and then leave them to perish or to be finished by someone else; and a profound conviction that everyone around him should be happy to wait upon him hand and foot. She had fought these fatal tendencies in her brother, within the bounds of wifely prudence she fought them in her husband, she was long after to fight them again in two of her sons and in several of her grandchildren. She gained no victory in any case, the selfish, careless, unloving creatures lived and ended as they had begun. But the Grandmother developed a character truly portentous under the discipline of trying to change the characters of others. Her husband shared with her the family sharpness of eye. He disliked and feared her deadly willfulness, her certainty that her ways were not only right but beyond criticism, that her feelings were important, even in the lightest matter, and must not be tampered with or treated casually. He had disappeared at the critical moment when they were growing up, had gone to college and then for travel; she forgot him for a long time, and when she saw him again forgot him as he had been once for all. She was gay and sweet and decorous, full of vanity and incredibly exalted daydreams which threatened now and again to cast her over the edge of some mysterious forbidden frenzy. She dreamed recurrently that she had lost her virginity (her virtue, she called it), her sole claim to regard, consideration, even to existence, and after frightful moral suffering which masked altogether her physical experience she would wake in a cold sweat, disordered and terrified. She had heard that her cousin Stephen was a little "wild," but that was to be expected. He was leading, no doubt, a dashing life full of manly indulgences, the sweet dark life of the knowledge of evil which caused her hair to crinkle on her scalp when she thought of it. Ah, the delicious, the free, the wonderful, the mysterious and terrible life of men! She thought about it a great deal. "Little daydreamer," her mother or father would say to her, surprising her in a brown study, eyes moist, lips smiling vaguely over her embroidery or her book, or with hands fallen on her lap, her face turned away to a blank wall. She memorized and saved for these moments scraps of high-minded poetry, which she instantly quoted at them when they offered her a penny for her thoughts; or she broke into a melancholy little song of some kind, a song she knew they liked. She would run to the piano and tinkle the tune out with one hand, saying, "I love this part best," leaving no doubt in their minds as to what her own had been occupied with. She lived her whole youth so, without once giving herself away; not until she was in middle age, her husband dead, her property dispersed, and she found herself with a houseful of children, making a new life for them in another place, with all the responsibilities of a man but with none of the privileges, did she finally emerge into something like an honest life: and yet, she was passionately honest. She had never been anything else.

Sitting under the trees with Nannie, both of them old and their long battle with life almost finished, she said, fingering a scrap of satin, "It was not fair that Sister Keziah should have had this ivory brocade for her wedding dress, and I had only dotted swiss . . ."

"Times was harder when you got married, Missy," said Nannie. "Dat was de yeah all de crops failed."

"And they failed ever afterward, it seems to me," said Grandmother.

"Seems to me like," said Nannie, "dotted swiss was all the style when you got married."

"I never cared for it," said Grandmother.

Nannie, born in slavery, was pleased to think she would not die in it. She was wounded not so much by her state of being as by the word describing it. Emancipation was a sweet word to her. It had not changed her way of living in a single particular, but she was proud of having been able to say to her mistress, "I aim to stay wid you as long as you'll have me." Still, Emancipation had seemed to set right a wrong that stuck in her heart like a thorn. She could not understand why God, Whom she loved, had seen fit to be so hard on a whole race because they had got a certain kind of skin. She talked it over with Miss Sophia Jane. Many times. Miss Sophia Jane was always brisk and opinionated about it: "Nonsense! I tell you, God does not know whether a skin is black or white. He sees only souls. Don't be getting notions, Nannie—of course you're going to Heaven."

Nannie showed the rudiments of logic in a mind altogether untutored. She wondered, simply and without resentment, whether God, Who had been so cruel to black people on earth, might not continue His severity in the next world. Miss Sophia Jane took pleasure in reassuring her; as if she, who had been responsible for Nannie, body and soul in this life, might also be her sponsor before the judgment seat.

Miss Sophia Jane had taken upon herself all the responsibilities of her tangled world, half white, half black, mingling steadily and the confusion growing ever deeper. There were so many young men about the place, always, younger brothers-in-law, first cousins, second cousins, nephews. They came visiting and they stayed, and there was no accounting for them nor any way of controlling their quietly headstrong habits. She learned early to keep silent and give no sign of uneasiness, but whenever a child was born in the Negro quarters, pink, worm-like, she held her breath for three days, she told her eldest granddaughter, years later, to see whether the newly born would turn black after the proper interval . . . It was a strain that told on her, and ended by giving her a deeply grounded contempt for men. She could not help it, she despised men. She despised them and was ruled by them. Her husband threw away her dowry and her property in wild investments in strange territories: Louisiana, Texas; and without protest she watched him play away her substance like a gambler. She felt that she could have managed her affairs profitably. But her natural activities lay elsewhere, it was the business of a man to make all decisions and dispose of all financial matters. Yet when she got the reins in her hands, her sons could persuade her to this and that enterprise or investment; against her will and judgment she accepted their advice, and among them they managed to break up once more the stronghold she had built for the future of her family. They got from her their own start in life, came back for fresh help when they needed it, and were divided against each other. She saw it as her natural duty to provide for her household, after her husband had fought stubbornly through the War, along with every other man of military age in the connection; had been wounded, had lingered helpless, and had died of his wound long after the great fervor and excitement had faded in hopeless defeat, when to be a man wounded and ruined in the War was merely to have proved oneself, perhaps, more heroic than wise. Left so, she drew her family together and set out for Louisiana, where her husband, with her money, had bought a sugar refinery. There was going to be a fortune in sugar, he said; not in raising the raw material, but in manufacturing it. He had schemes in his head for operating cotton gins, flour mills, refineries. Had he lived . . . but he did not live, and Sophia Jane had hardly repaired the house she bought and got the orchard planted when she saw that, in her hands, the sugar refinery was going to be a failure.

She sold out at a loss, and went on to Texas, where her husband had bought cheaply, some years before, a large tract of fertile black land in an almost unsettled part of the country. She had with her nine children, the youngest about two, the eldest about seventeen years old; Nannie and her three sons, Uncle Jimbilly, and two other Negroes, all in good health, full of hope and greatly desiring to live. Her husband's ghost persisted in her, she was bitterly outraged by his death almost as if he had willfully deserted her. She mourned for him at first with dry eyes, angrily. Twenty years later, seeing after a long absence the eldest son of her favorite daughter, who had died early, she recognized the very features and look of the husband of her youth, and she wept.

During the terrible second year in Texas, two of her younger sons, Harry and Robert, suddenly ran away. They chose good weather for it, in mid-May, and they were almost seven miles from home when a neighboring farmer saw them, wondered and asked questions, and ended by persuading them into his gig, and so brought them back.

Miss Sophia Jane went through the dreary ritual of discipline she thought appropriate to the occasion. She whipped them with her riding whip. Then she made them kneel down with her while she prayed for them, asking God to help them mend their ways and not be undutiful to their mother; her duty performed, she broke down and wept with her arms around them. They had endured their punishment stoically, because it would have been disgraceful to cry when a woman hit them, and besides, she did not hit very hard; they had knelt with her in a shamefaced gloom, because religious feeling was a female mystery which embarrassed them, but when they saw her tears they burst into loud bellows of repentance. They were only nine and eleven years old. She said in a voice of mourning, so despairing it frightened them: "Why did you run away from me? What do you think I brought you here for?" as if they were grown men who could realize how terrible the situation was. All the answer they could make, as they wept too, was that they had wanted to go back to Louisiana to eat sugar cane. They had been thinking about sugar cane all winter . . . Their mother was stunned. She had built a house large enough to shelter them all, of hand-sawed lumber dragged by ox-cart for forty miles, she had got the fields fenced in and the crops planted, she had, she believed, fed and clothed her children; and now she realized they were hungry. These two had worked like men; she felt their growing bones through their thin flesh, and remembered how mercilessly she had driven them, as she had driven herself, as she had driven the Negroes and the horses, because there was no choice in the matter. They must labor beyond their strength or perish. Sitting there with her arms around them, she felt her heart break in her breast. She had thought it was a silly phrase. It happened to her. It was not that she was incapable of feeling afterward, for in a way she was more emotional, more quick, but griefs never again lasted with her so long as they had before. This day was the beginning of her spoiling her children and being afraid of them. She said to them after a long dazed silence, when they began to grow restless under her arms: "We'll grow fine ribbon cane here. The soil is perfect for it. We'll have all the sugar we want. But we must be patient."

By the time her children began to marry, she was able to give them each a good strip of land and a little money, she was able to help them buy more land in places they preferred by selling her own, tract by tract, and she saw them all begin well, though not all of them ended so. They went about their own affairs, scattering out and seeming to lose all that sense of family unity so precious to the Grandmother. They bore with her infrequent visits and her advice and her tremendous rightness, and they were impatient of her tenderness. When Harry's wife died—she had never approved of Harry's wife, who was delicate and hopelessly inadequate at housekeeping, and who could not even bear children successfully, since she died when her third was born—the Grandmother took the children and began life again, with almost the same zest, and with more indulgence. She had just got them brought up to the point where she felt she could begin to work the faults out of them—faults inherited, she admitted fairly, from both sides of the house—when she died. It happened quite suddenly one afternoon in early October, after a day spent in helping the Mexican gardener of her third daughter-in-law to put the garden to rights. She was on a visit in far western Texas and enjoying it. The daughter-in-law was exasperated but apparently so docile, the Grandmother, who looked upon her as a child, did not notice her little moods at all. The son had long ago learned not to oppose his mother. She wore him down with patient, just, and reasonable argument. She was careful never to venture to command him in anything. He consoled his wife by saying that everything Mother was doing could be changed back after she was gone. As this change included moving a fifty-foot adobe wall, the wife was not much consoled. The Grandmother came into the house quite flushed and exhilarated, saying how well she felt in the bracing mountain air—and dropped dead over the doorsill.

Elizabeth Madox Roberts

(1881–1941)

*Born in Perryville, Kentucky, Elizabeth Roberts grew up in Spring-
field, Kentucky, a small rural town where her father ran a store,
worked for the railroad, and farmed. Never strong physically, she
attended local schools and went to high school in nearby Covington,
where she lived with her grandmother. With the exception of a few
visits to Colorado for her health, she continued to live with her
family in Springfield until she entered the University of Chicago at
the age of 35. As a published poet, she became good friends with
a group of younger poets and writers including Yvor Winters, Glen-
way Wescott, Monroe Wheeler, and Janet Lewis. After graduating
from the University of Chicago in 1921, she published a book of
poetry, her second, entitled* Under the Tree *(1922), and returned
to Springfield. There she began work on* The Time of Man *(1926),
a lyrical novel that Ford Madox Ford praised, a bit overemphatically, as was his generous custom, as "the most beautiful individual
piece of writing that has yet come out of America." With* The Time
of Man, *Roberts introduced the characteristic blending of poetic
prose, mythic correspondence, and deep rural attachment that she
continued to develop in her subsequent writing. Roberts had been
able to finish* The Time of Man *when her friends from Chicago
collected a fund to send her to the Riggs Foundation in Stockbridge,
Massachusetts. In 1930, she published her second major novel,* The
Great Meadow, *set at the time of the American Revolution, when
the western movement from Virginia to Kentucky penetrates deeper
and deeper into the primitive landscapes and forests. A major theme
in that book, and in much of her work, involves an extremely personal meditation on the working of the collective regional past on
the individual present. In 1932, after having returned to Springfield,
she published a collection of short stories,* The Haunted Mirror. *In
the late 1930s, her chronic fragile health deteriorated critically.
After a traumatic throat operation, she was discovered to have Hodg-*

kin's disease. She lived long enough to complete her final novel,
Black Is My True Love's Hair *(1938), and a book of poems,* Song
in the Meadow *(1940). Shortly after her death, in 1941, her second
collection of stories,* Not by Strange Gods, *was published. Among
her other works are* My Heart and My Flesh *(1927),* Jingling in the
Wind *(1928),* A Buried Treasure *(1931), and* He Sent Forth a
Raven *(1935). "The Haunted Palace," from* Not by Strange Gods,
first appeared in Harper's Monthly Magazine *(July 1937).*

THE HAUNTED PALACE

✿

The House stood at the head of a valley where the hollow melted
away into the rolling uplands. The high trees about the place so
confined the songs of the birds that on a spring morning the jar-
goning seemed to emerge from the walls. The birds seemed to be
indoors or within the very bricks of the masonry. In winter the
winds blew up the hollow from the valley and lashed at the old
house that stood square before the storms. The place was called
Wickwood. It had been the abode of a family, Wickley, a group
that had once clustered about the hearths there or had tramped
over the courtyard or ridden through the pastures.

From a road that ran along the top of a ridge two miles to the
east, the House could be seen as a succession of rhomboids and
squares that flowed together beneath the vague misty reds of the
mass. Or from the valley road to the west, looking up the hollow
into the melting hills, in winter one could see it as a distant brick
wall set with long windows, beneath a gray sloping roof. Sometimes
a traveler, allured by the name of the place or by the aloof splendor
of the walls as seen vaguely from one or the other of these high-
ways, would cross the farmlands by the way of the uneven roads.
He would trundle over the crooked ways and mount through the
broken woodland to come at last to the House. Leaving his conveyance, he would cross the wide courtyard on the smooth flagstones, and he would hear the strange report his footfalls made as
they disturbed the air that had, but for the birds and the wind,
been quiet for so great a length of time that it had assumed stillness.
He would wonder at the beauty of the doorways and deplore the
waste that let the House stand unused and untended. He would

venture up the stone steps at the west front and peer through the glass of the side lights. The strange quality of the familiar fall of his own shoe on stone would trouble his sense of all that he had discovered, so that he would at last come swiftly away.

The country rolled in changing curves and lines and spread toward the river valleys, where it dropped suddenly into a basin. The farms were owned by men and women who had labored to win them. But among these were younger men who worked for hire or as share-owners in the yield.

One of these last, Hubert, lived with Jess, his wife, in a small whitewashed shelter behind a cornfield. Jess spoke more frequently than the man and thus she had more memory. She had been here two years, but before that time she had lived beside a creek, and before that again in another place, while farther back the vista was run together in a fog of forgetting. She had courted Hubert in a cabin close beside a roadway. She remembered another place where there was a plum tree that bore large pink-red fruits, and a place where her father had cut his foot with an ax. Now, as a marker, her own children ran a little way into a cornfield to play. Beyond these peaks in memory, going backward, the life there rested in a formless level out of which only self emerged. She met any demand upon this void with a contempt in which self was sheltered.

Hubert was a share-laborer, but he wanted to be able to rent some land. He wanted to use land as if he were the owner, and yet to be free to go to fresh acres when he had exhausted a tract as he willed. After the first child, Albert, was born, he said to Jess:

"If a person could have ahead, say, four hundred dollars, and against the Dean land might come idle . . ."

His fervor had the power of a threat. He was knotty and bony and his muscles were dry and lean. He had learned at school to write his name and to make a few slow marks that signified numbers or quantities, but later he had used this knowledge so infrequently that most of it was lost to him. He wrote his name painfully and, writing, he drew his fingers together about the pen. His breath would flow hard and fast under the strain, his hand trembling. If there were other men standing about he would, if he were asked to write his name, sometimes say that he could not, preferring to claim complete illiteracy rather than to undergo the ordeal.

"Against the Dean land might come idle . . ." He had a plan over which he brooded, wanting to get a power over some good land that he might drain money out of it. He was careful, moving forward through the soil, taking from it.

When the second child came they lived at the Dean land, behind the cornfield. Jess would fling a great handful of grain toward her hens and they would come with reaching bills and outthrust necks, their wings spread. She would throw ears of corn to the sow and it would chew away the grains while the sucklings would drag milk, the essence of the corn, from the dark udders.

"We ought, it seems, to build the sow a little shed against winter comes," Jess said to Hubert.

"We might eat the sow. I might fatten up the sow and get me another."

"She always was a no-account sow. Has only five or six to a litter. It's hardly worth while to pester yourself with a lazy hog."

"Fannie Burt asked me what was the name of the sow or to name what kind or breed she was. 'Name?' I says. As if folks would name the food they eat!"

Hubert laughed at the thought of naming the food. Names for the swine, either mother or species, gave him laughter. To write with one's hand the name of a sow in a book seemed useless labor. Instead of giving her a name he fastened her into a closed pen and gave her all the food he could find. When she was sufficiently fat he stuck her throat with a knife and prepared her body for his own eating.

Jess yielded to the decision Hubert made, being glad to have decisions made for her, and thus she accepted the flesh of the brood sow. Of this she ate heavily. She was large and often of a placid temper, sitting in unbrooding inattention, but often she flamed to sudden anger and thrust about her then with her hands or her fists. She did not sing about the house or the dooryard. Singing came to her from a wooden box that was charged by a small battery. She adjusted the needle of this to a near sending station and let the sound pour over the cabin. Out of the abundant jargon that flowed from the box she did not learn, and before it she did not remember. . . .

Jess had a few friends who came sometimes to see her. They were much like herself in what they knew and in what they liked. She would look curiously at their new clothing.

But one of them, named Fannie Burt, would come shouting to the children as she drove up the lane in a small cart, and her coming filled the day with remembered sayings and finer arrangements. When Fannie came Jess would call Albert, the oldest child, and send him on his hands and knees under the house to rob the hen's nest if there were not enough eggs in the basket, for the day called for a richer pudding. Fannie had no children as yet and she could be light and outflowing. She went here and there and she knew many of the people.

"Miss Anne mended the cover to the big black sofa in the parlor . . ." She would tell of many things—of tapestry on a wall, blue and gold. Words seemed light when she talked, as being easily made to tell of strange and light matters. Jess was not sure that Fannie knew more of these things than she knew herself, since the words conveyed but an undefined sense. The lightness of bubbles floated about Fannie, things for which Jess had no meanings. Fannie had lived the year before at a farm where the owner had been as a neighbor to her. She often went back to call there, staying all day as a friend.

"Miss Anne mended the cover to the sofa where it was worn." Jess laughed with Fannie, and she scarcely knew whether she laughed at the sofa or at the mended place. She herself could not sew, and thus she could not mend any broken fabric of any kind. She laughed, however, Fannie's call being just begun. She was not yet hostile to it. She tried for the moment to stretch her imaginings to see something desired or some such thing as grace or beauty in the person who leaned over the ancient tapestry to mend it. The effort was spent in wonder and finally in anger. Fannie laughed at the sullenness that came to Jess. The sofa had come from Wickwood, she said. It had been given to Miss Anne at her marriage, for she was somehow related to the Wickleys. Laughing, Fannie tossed the least child and settled to tell again. Her tales would be, all together, a myth of houses and families, of people marrying and settling into new abodes. She was gay and sharp, and her face was often pointed with smiles. Or she would be talking now with the children and telling them the one story she had from a book.

"Then a great ogre lived in the place . . . a Thing that threatens to get you . . . a great Thing . . . destroys . . . eats up Life itself. Drinks the blood out of Life. It came with a club in its hand. . . . It was a fine place, but had a Thing inside it. . . . That would be when little Blue Wing went to the woods to play. She found this place in the woods . . ."

"What was that?" Jess asked suddenly. "What kind was that you named?"

"A giant. Ogry or ogre. A Thing. Comes to eat up a man and to eat Life itself. . . ."

Fannie would be gone and Jess would be glad to have an end of her. As if too much had been asked of her she would sit now in vague delight, and she would forget to run her radio instrument while she saw Fannie's bright pointed face as something slipping past her. The stories that had been told had become a blend of indistinct mental colorings that would drop out of memory at length, as a spent pleasure no longer wanted. She would reject the visit completely and turn to anger, thrusting Fannie out. Then, complete hostility to the visitor having come to her, she would set roughly upon her tasks. If the children spoke of the stories that had been told she would order them to be quiet.

Some of the farms had lost their former owners. A house here and there was shut and still while the acres were farmed by the shifting men who lived in the cabins or in the town. A man came searching for Hubert at the end of the harvest to offer him a part of the Wickley place to farm.

"It's said fine people once lived there," Hubert said when he told Jess of his offer.

"If they're gone now I wouldn't care."

"It's not like any place ever you saw in life. It's good land, howsoever."

Other tenants would be scattered over the acres, laborers who would farm by sharing the crops. Hubert would rent the acres about the house and he would live there.

"Is there a good well of water?"

"Two wells there are," he answered her.

"I never heard of two wells."

"One has got a little fancy house up over it."

"What would I do with a little fancy house built up over a well? I can't use such a house." As if more might be required of her than she could perform, Jess was uneasy in thinking of the new place to which they would go. She did not want to go there. "It's a place made for some other," she said. She could not see the women of the place going about their labors. She could not discover what they might carry in their hands and what their voices might call from the doorways, or how they would sleep or dress themselves or find themselves food. In her troubled thought, while she came and went about the cabin room where the least child lay, shapes without outline, the women of the Wickleys, went into vague distances where doors that were not defined were opened and closed into an uncomprehended space.

But the next day Fannie Burt came and there was something further to know. The Wickley farm was called Wickwood, she said. Miss Anne's father had gone there in old Wickley's lifetime. Together these two men had made experiments in the growing of fine animals. Sometimes it would be a horse old Wickley wanted.

"Egad!" he would say, or, "I'm not dead yet!" Another story running into a comic ending, "A good colt she is, but a leetle matter of interference. Look at her hind feet." Fannie had something that Miss Anne had in mind. It was told imperfectly, thrown out in a hint and retained in a gesture, put back upon Miss Anne, who could tell with fluent words and meaning gestures. She would be sitting over the last of the dessert in the old, faded dining room. She would be telling for the pure joy of talking, laughing with the past. "Pappy went over to Wickwood. . . . It was Tuesday. . . . Came Sunday then and we all said, 'Where's Pappy?' Came to find out and he's still over to Wickwood with Cousin Bob. All that time to get the brown mare rightly in foal. And all still on paper."

Fannie would seem to be talking fast, and one thing would seem to be entangled with another, although she spoke with Miss Anne's quiet, slow cadence. In her telling men would be sitting together in a library. One would be making a drawing of a horse, such a horse as he would be devising. A horse would be sketched on paper before it was so much as foaled. This would be old Robert Wickley, a pen between his thumb and his fingers. "What we want after all is a good Kentucky saddle horse, fifteen hands high and two inches over. Take Danbury II, say, over at Newmarket . . ."

"You take Danbury and you'll plumb get a jackass."

"Pappy laughed over a thing once for a week before he told us," Miss Anne's speaking through Fannie's speaking. "Pappy in a big tellen way one day and he let it be known what he was so amused about."

A man had come in at the door at Wickwood, a hurried man with money in cash saved by. He wanted the Wickley land on which to grow something. He wanted to buy, offering cash.

"Do you think you could live in my house and on my land?" old Wickley asked.

Fannie would be telling as Miss Anne had told and, beyond again, the father who had told in a moment of amusement. Men who came on business were let in at a side door. "Business was a Nobody then," Miss Anne said. Mollie would be off somewhere in the house singing. Carline had run off to get married. Old Wickley, father to Robert, rolling back his shirtsleeves because the day was hot, and walking barefoot out into the cool grass, or he would be standing under the shower in the bath house while somebody pumped the water that sprayed over him. Miss Sallie made the garden with her own hands and designed the sundial. They made things for themselves with their hands. Bob Wickley sketching for himself the horse he wanted on a large sheet of manila paper. His grandmother had, as a bride, set the house twelve feet back of the builder's specifications in order to save a fine oak tree that still grew before the front door. A man wanting to plow his pastures . . .

"Two hundred dollars an acre for the creek bottom, cash money."

Wickley had called him a hog and sent him away. "Pappy laughed over it for a week. ' "You think you could live in my house? Come back three generations from now." . . . And, egad, he couldn't,' Pappy said."

"Hogs want to root in my pasture," Bob Wickley said. He was angry. . . . Miss Anne speaking through Fannie's speaking, reports fluttering about, intermingled, right and wrong, the present and the past. Fannie could scarcely divide one Wickley from another. One had gathered the books. One had held a high public office. One had married a woman who pinned back her hair with a gold comb. Their children had read plentifully from the books. Justus, William, and Robert had been names among them. Miss Anne now owned the portrait of the lady of the golden comb. There had been farewells and greetings, dimly remembered gifts, trinkets, portraits to be made, children to be born. . . .

In this telling as it came from the telling of Miss Anne, there was one, a Robert, who danced along the great parlor floor with one named Mollie. Mollie was the wife of Andrew. She had come from a neighboring farm. When they danced the music from the piano had crashed and tinkled under the hands of Miss Lizette, Robert's mother, or of Tony Barr, a young man who came to visit at Wickwood. Down would fling the chords on the beat and at the same instant up would fling the dancers, stepping upward on the rhythm and treading the air. Mollie's long slim legs would flash from beneath her flying skirts, or one would lie for an instant outstretched while the pulse of the music beat, then off along the shining floor, gliding and swaying with the gliding of Robert, until it seemed as if the two of them were one, and as if they might float out the window together, locked into the rhythms, and thus dance away across the world.

"Where are they now?" Jess asked.

Fannie did not know. Miss Anne had not told her.

"Where would be Andrew, the one that was her husband?" She was angry and she wanted to settle blame somewhere.

He would be beside the wall. He would look at Mollie with delight. His head would move, or his hands, with the rhythm, and his eyes would be bright. Mollie loved him truly.

Sometimes it would be the old fast waltzes that were danced, and then Miss Lizette and old Bob would come into it. Then they would whirl swiftly about the floor and the music would be "Over the Waves." The young would try it, dizzy and laughing, or they would change the steps to their own.

"What did they do?" Jess asked. "I feel staggered to try to know about such a house."

"They had a wide scope of land," Fannie answered her. "They burned the bricks and made the house. They cut the timber for the beams of the house off their own fields."

The House had become an entity, as including the persons and the legends of it. All the Wickleys were blurred into one, were gathered into one report.

"There was a woman, Mollie Wickley. She was the mother of Andrew, or maybe she was his wife," Fannie said. "I don't recall. It's all one. There was a Sallie Wickley. I don't know whe'r she was his daughter or his wife."

"Iffen he couldn't keep it for his children," Jess called out, "why would he build such a place?"

"He lived in the house *himself*."

Jess and Hubert would be going to the place where these had been. All these were gone now. The land was still good. Hubert would be able to take money out of it. He would hold the plow into the soil and his tongue would hang from the side of his mouth in his fervor to plant more and to have a large yield. The people would be gone. Jess dismissed them with the clicking of her tongue. They seemed, nevertheless, to be coming nearer. In Fannie's presence, while she sat in the chair beside the door, they came nearer, to flit as shapes about her fluttering tongue while Jess fixed her gaze upon the mouth that was speaking or shifted to look at the familiar cups and plates on the table. Shapes fluttered then over the cups. Vague forms, having not the shapes of defined bodies, but the ends of meanings, appeared and went. Fannie knew little beyond the myths she had made, and Jess knew much less, knew nothing beyond the bright tinkle of Fannie's chatter.

"It was the horse then," Fannie said, in part explaining. "Now nobody wants enough horses. . . . Now it's tobacco."

Hubert and Jess came to the place, Wickwood, at sundown of an early winter afternoon. Hubert talked of the land, of the fields, growing talkative as their small truck rolled slowly through the ruts of the old driveway. When they had passed through the woodland, which was now in part denuded of its former growth, they came near to the house. It seemed to Jess that there was a strange wideness about the place, as if space were spent outward without bounds. They went under some tall oaks and maples while Hubert muttered of his plans.

A great wall arose in the dusk. The trees stretched their boughs toward the high wall in the twilight. When it seemed that the truck would drive into the hard darkness of the wall that stood before them as if it went into the sky, Hubert turned toward the left and rounded among the trees. Other walls stood before them. Jess had never before seen a place like this. It seemed to her that it might be a town, but there were no people there. The children began to cry and Albert screamed, "I want to go away!" Jess herself was frightened.

"Hush your fuss," Hubert said. His words were rough. "Get out of the truck," he said to her. She attended to his short angry speech; it jerked her out of her fear and dispersed a part of her dread of the place. It made her know that they, themselves and their goods, their life and their ways of being, would somehow fit into the brick walls, would make over some part of the strangeness for their own use. He had climbed from the vehicle and he walked a little way among the buildings, stalking in the broad courtyard among the flagstones and over the grass. He looked about him. Then he went toward a wing of the largest house and entered a small porch that stood out from one of the walls.

"We'll live here," he said.

She did not know how he had discovered which part of the circle of buildings, of large houses and small rooms, would shelter them. He began to carry their household goods from the truck. Jess found her lantern among her things and she made a light. When the lantern was set on a shelf she could look about the room where they would live.

There were windows opposite the door through which they had entered. Outside, the rain dripped slowly through the great gnarled trees. The rain did not trouble her. A press built into the wall beside the chimney seemed ample to hold many things. Hubert set the cooking stove before the fireplace and fixed the stovepipe into the small opening above the mantel. The children cried at the strangeness, but when the lamp was lighted and food had been cooked they cried no more. When Jess set the food on the table they had begun to live in the new place.

Hubert went away across the courtyard and his step was hollow, amplified among the walls of the building. He came back later, the sound he made enlarged as he walked nearer over the flagstones.

"It's no such place as ever I saw before!" Jess cried out.

She had begun a longer speech but she was hushed by Hubert's hostile look. They would stay here, he said. It was the Wickley place. She closed the door to shut in the space she had claimed for their living, being afraid of the great empty walls that arose outside. The beds were hastily set up and the children fell asleep clutching the familiar pillows and quilts. Her life with Hubert, together with her children and her things for housekeeping, these she gathered mentally about her to protect herself from being obliged to know and to use the large house outside her walls. She began to comfort herself with thoughts of Hubert and to court him with a fine dish of food she had carefully saved.

The morning was clear after the rain. Hubert had gone to bring the fowls from their former abode. Albert had found a sunny nook in which to play and with the second child he was busy there.

"What manner of place is this?" Jess asked herself again and again. Outside the windows toward the south were the great gnarled trees. Outside to the north was the courtyard round which were arranged the buildings, all of them built of red, weathered brick. Toward the west, joined to the small wing in which Hubert had set up their home, arose the great house. There were four rows of windows here, one row above the other.

The buildings about the court were empty. A large bell hung in the middle of the court on the top of a high pole. There was a deep well at the back of the court where the water was drawn by a bucket lifted by a winch. Jess had a great delight in the well, for it seemed to hold water sufficient to last through any drought. Not far from the well stood a large corncrib, holding only a little corn now, but ready for Hubert's filling. She went cautiously about in the strange air.

She had no names for all the buildings that lay about her. She was frightened of the things for which she had no use, as if she might be called upon to know and to use beyond her understanding. She walked toward the west beneath the great wall of the tallest house.

There were birds in the high trees and echoes among the high walls. The singing winter wren was somewhere about, and the cry of the bird was spread widely and repeated in a shadowy call again and again. Jess rounded the wall and looked cautiously at the west side. There were closed shutters at some of the windows, but some of the shutters were opened. In the middle of the great western wall there were steps of stone. They were cut evenly and laid smoothly, one above another, reaching toward a great doorway about which was spread bright glass in straight patterns at the sides, in a high fan-shape above.

Jess went cautiously up the steps, watching for Hubert to come with the fowls, delaying, looking out over the woodland and the fields. Hubert had said again and again that this would be the Wickley place, Wickwood, that they would live there, tilling the soil, renting the land. Jess saw before her, on the great left-hand door, a knocker. She lifted it and tapped heavily, listening to the sound she made, waiting.

There was no sound to answer her rap but a light echo that seemed to come from the trees. Her own hate of the place forbade her and she dared not tap again. Standing half fearfully, she waited, laying her hands on the smooth door frame, on the fluted pillars and the leading of the glass. A cord hung near her hand and, obeying the suggestion it offered, she closed her fingers about it and pulled it stiffly down. A sound cut the still air where no sound had been for so long a time that every vibration had been stilled. The tone broke the air. The first tone came in unearthly purity, but later the notes joined and overflowed one another.

She waited, not daring to touch the cord again. The stillness that followed after the peal of the bell seemed to float out from the house itself and to hush the birds. She could not think what kind of place this might be or see any use that one might make of the great doorway, of the cord, of the bell. A strange thing stood before her. Strangeness gathered to her own being until it seemed strange that she should be here, on the top of a stair of stone before a great door, waiting for Hubert to come with her hens. It was as if he might never come. As if hens might be gone from the earth.

She saw then that the doors were not locked together, that one throbbed lightly on the other when she touched it with her hand. She pushed the knob and the door spread open wide.

Inside, a great hall reached to a height that was three or four times her own stature. Tall white doors were opened into other great rooms and far back before her a stairway began. She could not comprehend the stair. It lifted, depending from the rail that spread upward like a great ribbon in the air. Her eyes followed it, her breath coming quick and hard. It rose as a light ribbon spreading toward a great window through which came the morning sun. But leaving the window in the air, it arose again and wound back, forward and up, lost from view for a space, to appear again, higher up, at a mythical distance before another great window where the sun spread a broad yellow glow. It went at last into nothingness, and the ceiling and the walls melted together in shadows.

When she had thus, in mind, ascended, her eyes closed and a faint sickness went over her, delight mingled with fear and hate. She was afraid of being called upon to know this strange ribbon of ascent that began as a stair with rail and tread and went up into unbelievable heights, step after step. She opened her eyes to look again, ready to reject the wonder as being past all belief and, therefore, having no reality.

"What place is this?" she asked, speaking in anger. Her voice rang through the empty hall, angry words, her own, crying, "What place is this?"

At one side of the floor there were grains of wheat in streaks, as if someone might have stored sacks of wheat there. Jess thought of her hens, seeing the scattered grain, and she knew that they would pick up the remaining part of it. They would hop from stone to stone, coming cautiously up the steps, and they would stretch their long necks cautiously in at the doorway, seeing the corn. They would not see the great stairway.

A light dust lay on the window ledges. A few old cobwebs hung in fragments from the ceiling. The dust, the webs, and the wheat were a link between things known and unknown, and, seeing them, she walked a little way from the hall, listening, going farther, looking into the rooms, right and left. She was angry and afraid. What she could not bring to her use she wanted to destroy. In the room to her right a large fireplace stood far at the end of a patterned floor. There were shelves set into the white wall beside the large chimney. She left this room quickly and turned toward the room at the left. Here two large rooms melted together and tall doors opened wide. There were white shapes carved beneath the windows and oblong shapes carved again on the wood of the doors, on the pillars that held the mantel. Before her a long mirror was set into a wall. In it were reflected the boughs of the trees outside against a crisscross of the window opposite.

She was confused after she had looked into the mirror, and she looked about hastily to find the door through which she had come. It was a curious, beautiful, fearful place. She wanted to destroy it. Her feet slipped too lightly on the smooth wood of the floor. There was no piece of furniture anywhere, but the spaces seemed full, as filled with their wide dimensions and the carvings on the wood. In the hall she looked again toward the stair and she stood near the doorway looking back. Then suddenly without plan, scarcely knowing that her own lips spoke, she flung out an angry cry, half screaming, "Mollie Wickley! Mollie! Where's she at?" The harsh echoes pattered and knocked among the upper walls

after her own voice was done. Turning her back on the place, she
went quickly out of the doorway.

In the open air she looked back toward the steps she had ascended, seeing dimly into the vista of the hall and the upward-
lifting ribbon of the stair. A sadness lay heavily upon her because
she could not know what people might live in the house, what
shapes of women and men might fit into the doorway. She hated
her sadness and she turned it to anger. She went from the west
front and entered the courtyard. Hubert came soon after with the
fowls and there was work to do in housing them and getting them
corn.

On a cold day in January when his ewes were about to lamb,
Hubert brought them into the large house, driving them up the
stone steps at the west front, and he prepared to stable them in
the rooms there. The sheep cried and their bleating ran up the
long ribbon of the stair. They were about thirty in number, and
thus the wailing was incessant. Hubert and Jess went among them
with lanterns. The ewes turned and drifted about among the large
rooms; but as they began to bear their lambs Hubert bedded them
here and there, one beneath the stairway and three others in the
room to the right where the empty bookshelves spread wide beside
the tall fireplace. The night came, dark and cold.

"They are a slow set," Jess said. She wanted to be done and
she was out of patience with delaying sheep.

"Whoop, here! Shut fast the door!" Hubert called.

Jess was wrapped in a heavy coat and hooded in a shawl. She
went among the sheep and she held a lantern high to search out
each beast. If a ewe gave birth to three lambs she took one up
quickly and dropped it beside a stout young beast that was giving
life to but one and she thus induced it to take the second as her
own. She flung out sharp commands and she brought the animals
here and there. The halls were filled with the crying of the sheep.
Threats came back upon her from her own voice, so that she was
displeased with what she did and her displeasure made her voice
more high-pitched and angry. Anger spoke again and again
through the room. She wanted the lambing to be easily done, but
the days had been very cold and the sheep delayed.

"It was a good place to come to lamb the sheep," she called to
Hubert. "I say, a good place." She had a delight in seeing that
the necessities of lambing polluted the wide halls. "A good place
to lamb. . . ."

"Whoop! Bring here the old nanny as soon as you pick up the dead lamb!" Hubert was shouting above the incessant crying of the sheep.

The ewes in labor excited her anew so that she wanted to be using her strength and to be moving swiftly forward, but she had no plan beyond Hubert's. "Whoop, rouse up the young nanny! Don't let the bitches sleep! Whoop, there!"

He was everywhere with his commands. When the task was more than half done he called to Jess that he must go to the barn for more straw for bedding. "Whoop! Shut the door tight after me. Keep the old ewe there up on her legs." He went away, carrying his lantern.

Jess fastened the outer door and she turned back into the parlors. Then she saw a dim light at the other end of the long dark space that lay before her. She saw another shape, a shrouded figure, moving far down the long way. The apparition, the Thing, seemed to be drifting forward out of the gloom, and it seemed to be coming toward her where she stood among the sheep. Jess drove the laboring mothers here and there, arranging their places and assisting their travail with her club. She would not believe that she saw anything among the sheep at the farther end of the rooms, but as she worked she glanced now and then toward the way in which she had glimpsed it. It was there or it was gone entirely. The sheep and the lambs made a great noise with their crying. Jess went to and fro, and she forgot that she had seen anything beyond the sheep far down the room in the moving dusk of white and gray which flowed in the moving light of her lantern.

All at once, looking up suddenly as she walked forward, she saw that an apparition was certainly moving there and that it was coming toward her. It carried something in its upraised hand. There was a dark covering over the head and shoulders that were sunk into the upper darkening gloom. The whole body came forward as a dark thing illuminated by a light the creature carried low at the left side. The creature or the Thing moved among the sheep. It came forward slowly and became a threatening figure, a being holding a club and a light in its hands. Jess screamed at it, a great oath flung high above the crying of the sheep. Fright had seized her and with it came a great strength to curse with her voice and to hurl forward her body.

"God curse you!" she yelled in a scream that went low in scale and cracked in her throat. "God's curse on you!" She lunged forward and lifted her lantern high to see her way among the sheep. "God's damn on you!"

The curse gave strength to her hands and to her limbs. As she hurled forward with uplifted stick the other came forward toward her, lunging and threatening. She herself moved faster. The creature's mouth was open to cry words but no sound came from it.

She dropped the lantern and flung herself upon the approaching figure, and she beat at the creature with her club while it beat at her with identical blows. Herself and the creature then were one. Anger continued, shared, and hurled against a crash of falling glass and plaster. She and the creature had beaten at the mirror from opposite sides.

The din arose above the noise of the sheep, and for an instant the beasts were quiet while the glass continued to fall. Jess stood back from the wreckage to try to understand it. Then slowly she knew that she had broken the great mirror that hung on the rear wall of the room. She took the lamp again into her hand and peered at the breakage on the floor and at the fragments that hung, cracked and crazed, at the sides of the frame.

"God's own curse on you!" She breathed her oath heavily, backing away from the dust that floated in the air.

Hubert was entering with a load of straw on his back. He had not heard the crash of glass nor had he noticed the momentary quiet of the sheep. These were soon at their bleating again, and Jess returned from the farther room where the dust of the plaster still lay on the air. Hubert poured water into deep pans he had placed here and there through the rooms. He directed Jess to make beds of the straw in each room. Their feet slipped in the wet that ran over the polished boards of the floor.

It was near midnight. Jess felt accustomed to the place now and more at ease there, she and Hubert being in possession of it. They walked about through the monstrous defilement. Hubert was muttering the count of the sheep with delight. There were two lambs beside each of the ewes but five and there were but two lambs dead and flung to the cold fireplace where they were out of the way. There were thirty-two ewes, they said, and their fingers pointed to assist and the mouths held to the sums, repeating numbers and counting profits.

Lamb by lamb, they were counted. There were two to each mother but the three in the farther room and the two under the staircase. These had but one each. "Twice thirty-two makes sixty-four," they said to assist themselves, and from this they subtracted one for each of the deficient ewes, but they became confused in this and counted all one by one. Counting with lantern and club, Jess went again through the halls, but she made thus but forty lambs, for she lost the sums and became addled among the words Hubert muttered. At last by taking one from sixty-four and then another, four times more, in the reckoning they counted themselves thirty-two ewes and fifty-nine lambs. The sheep were becoming quiet. Each lamb had nursed milk before they left it. At length they fastened the great front door with a rope tied to a nail in the door frame, and they left the sheep stabled there, being pleased with the number they had counted.

William Gilmore Simms

(1806–1870)

The most prominent and prolific Southern writer of the antebellum period, Simms published over 80 volumes during his lifetime as a novelist, essayist, editor, poet, popular historian, and Southern apologist. His extremely versatile talents ranged back through the whole history of the South, and touched on almost every fashionable Southern theme. He was born in Charleston, South Carolina, and lived there, or nearby, all his life. His mother, a native Charlestonian, died when he was two, and his father, an Irish tradesman, left Charleston after her death and settled on a plantation in Mississippi. Simms was raised in Charleston by his maternal grandmother. In 1824, after several years as a druggist's apprentice, he visited his father in Mississippi. He and his father made long trips on horseback deep into the Southern frontier (border) country, and Simms later drew on these memories in his various "Border Romances." When he returned to Charleston, he read law, and became a lawyer in 1827. His first wife died in 1832, and in 1836 he married Chevillette Roach. They settled at Woodlands, a plantation belonging to the Roach family, and Simms wholeheartedly embraced his new life as a Southern planter. His first publications were several volumes of youthful, derivative, florid verse. He continued to write poetry all his life, but seldom with any degree of originality or lasting success. His first book of prose fiction was Martin Faber (1833), a criminal-confession story later praised by Poe. During the 1830s he wrote perhaps his best novel, The Yemassee (1835), a tale of the Indian uprising in colonial Carolina. He also published Guy Rivers (1834), the first of his Border Romances, and The Partisan (1835), the first of his Revolutionary War novels. During the 1840s and '50s he served in the South Carolina legislature (1844–46), edited several important Southern journals, including The Southern Quarterly Review (1849–55), and continued to turn out historical romances, biographies, popular histories of the South, and, increasingly, out-

spoken propaganda in favor of Southern interests. His last novel, and one of his best, The Cassique of Kiawah, *a satire of colonial Charleston, was published just before the Civil War in 1859. During the war, his house at Woodlands was burned, his library destroyed, and his fortune lost. Within a few years of one another, his wife and four children had died. In a desperate effort to provide for the rest of his family, he continued writing and planning new books up until the day he died. Though much of his fiction was composed according to the formulaic conventions of the heroic romance, he was capable of creating, especially in his tales and short stories, powerful portraits in a vigorous, emphatic narrative prose. "How Sharp Snaffles Got His Capital and Wife," based on an 1847 camping trip with professional Appalachian hunters, is a case in point, and one of the best dialect stories written in the "Southern humorist" tradition. Among his many other works are* Border Beagles *(1840),* Donna Florida *(1843),* The Life of Francis Marion *(1844),* The Wigwam and the Cabin *(1845), and* The Golden Christmas *(1852). "How Sharp Snaffles Got His Capital and Wife" first appeared in* Harper's New Monthly Magazine *(October 1870).*

HOW SHARP SNAFFLES
GOT HIS CAPITAL
AND WIFE

❁

1

The day's work was done, and a good day's work it was. We had bagged a couple of fine bucks and a fat doe; and now we lay camped at the foot of the "Balsam Range" of mountains in North Carolina, preparing for our supper. We were a right merry group of seven; four professional hunters, and three amateurs—myself among the latter. There was Jim Fisher, Aleck Wood, Sam or Sharp Snaffles, *alias* "Yaou," and Nathan Langford, *alias* the "Pious."

These were our *professional* hunters. Our *amateurs* may well continue nameless, as their achievements do not call for any present record. Enough that we had gotten up the "camp hunt," and provided all the creature comforts except the fresh meat. For this we were to look to the mountain ranges and the skill of our hunters.

These were all famous fellows with the rifle—moving at a trot along the hill-sides, and with noses quite as keen of scent as those of their hounds in rousing deer and bear from their deep recesses among the mountain laurels.

A week had passed with us among these mountain ranges, some sixty miles beyond what the conceited world calls "civilization."

Saturday night had come; and, this Saturday night closing a week of exciting labors, we were to carouse.

We were prepared for it. There stood our tent pitched at the foot of the mountains, with a beautiful cascade leaping headlong toward us, and subsiding into a mountain runnel, and finally into a little lakelet, the waters of which, edged with perpetual foam, were as clear as crystal.

Our baggage wagon, which had been sent round to meet us by trail routes through the gorges, stood near the tent, which was of stout army canvas.

That baggage wagon held a variety of luxuries. There was a barrel of the best bolted wheat flour. There were a dozen choice hams, a sack of coffee, a keg of sugar, a few thousand of cigars, and last, not least, a corpulent barrel of Western uisquebaugh,* vulgarly, "whisky"; to say nothing of a pair of demijohns of equal dimensions, one containing peach brandy of mountain manufacture, the other the luscious honey from the mountain hives.

Well, we had reached Saturday night. We had hunted day by day from the preceding Monday with considerable success—bagging some game daily, and camping nightly at the foot of the mountains. The season was a fine one. It was early winter, October, and the long ascent to the top of the mountains was through vast fields of green, the bushes still hanging heavy with their huckleberries.

From the summits we had looked over into Tennessee, Virginia, Georgia, North and South Carolina. In brief, to use the language of Natty Bumppo, we beheld "Creation." We had crossed the "Blue Ridge;" and the descending water-courses, no longer seeking the Atlantic, were now gushing headlong down the western slopes, and hurrying to lose themselves in the Gulf Stream and the Mississippi.

From the eyes of fountains within a few feet of each other we

---

* "Uisquebaugh," or the "water of life," is Irish. From the word we have dropped the last syllable. Hence we have "uisque," or, as it is commonly written, "whisky"— a very able-bodied man-servant, but terrible as a mistress or housekeeper.

had blended our *eau de vie* with limpid waters which were about to part company forever—the one leaping to the rising, the other to the setting of the sun.

And buoyant, full of fun, with hearts of ease, limbs of health and strength, plenty of venison, and a wagon full of good things, we welcomed the coming of Saturday night as a season not simply of rest, but of a royal carouse. We were decreed to make a night of it.

But first let us see after our venison.

The deer, once slain, is, as soon after as possible, clapped upon the fire. All the professional hunters are good butchers and admirable cooks—of bear and deer meat at least. I doubt if they could spread a table to satisfy Delmonico; but even Delmonico might take some lessons from them in the preparation for the table of the peculiar game which they pursue, and the meats on which they feed. We, at least, rejoice at the supper prospect before us. Great collops hiss in the frying-pan, and finely cut steaks redden beautifully upon the flaming coals. Other portions of the meat are subdued to the stew, and make a very delightful dish. The head of the deer, including the brains, is put upon a flat rock in place of gridiron, and thus baked before the fire—being carefully watched and turned until every portion has duly imbibed the necessary heat, and assumed the essential hue which it should take to satisfy the eye of appetite. This portion of the deer is greatly esteemed by the hunters themselves; and the epicure of genuine stomach for the *haut goût* takes to it as an eagle to a fat mutton, and a hawk to a young turkey.

The rest of the deer—such portions of it as are not presently consumed or needed for immediate use—is cured for future sale or consumption; being smoked upon a scaffolding raised about four feet above the ground, under which, for ten or twelve hours, a moderate fire will be kept up.

Meanwhile the hounds are sniffing and snuffing around, or crouched in groups, with noses pointed at the roast and broil and bake; while their great liquid eyes dilate momently while watching for the huge gobbets which they expect to be thrown to them from time to time from the hands of the hunters.

Supper over, and it is Saturday night. It is the night dedicated among the professional hunters to what is called "The Lying Camp!"

"The Lying Camp!" quoth Columbus Mills, one of our party, a wealthy mountaineer, of large estates, of whom I have been for some time the guest.

"What do you mean by the 'Lying Camp,' Columbus?"

The explanation soon followed.

Saturday night is devoted by the mountaineers engaged in a camp hunt, which sometimes contemplates a course of several weeks, to stories of their adventures—"long yarns"—chiefly relating to the objects of their chase, and the wild experiences of their professional life. The hunter who actually inclines to exaggeration is, at such a period, privileged to deal in all the extravagances of invention; nay, he is *required* to do so! To be literal, or confine himself to the bald and naked truth, is not only discreditable, but a *finable* offense! He is, in such a case, made to swallow a long, strong, and difficult potation! He can not be too extravagant in his incidents; but he is also required to exhibit a certain degree of *art,* in their use; and he thus frequently rises into a certain realm of fiction, the ingenuities of which are made to compensate for the exaggerations, as they do in the "Arabian Nights," and other Oriental romances.

This will suffice for explanation.

Nearly all our professional hunters assembled on the present occasion were tolerable *raconteurs*. They complimented Jim Fisher, by throwing the raw deer-skin over his shoulders; tying the antlers of the buck with a red handkerchief over his forehead; seating him on the biggest boulder which lay at hand; and, sprinkling him with a stoup of whisky, they christened him "The Big Lie," for the occasion. And in this character he complacently presided during the rest of the evening, till the company prepared for sleep, which was not till midnight. He was king of the feast.

It was the duty of the "Big Lie" to regulate proceedings, keep order, appoint the *raconteurs* severally, and admonish them when he found them foregoing their privileges, and narrating bald, naked, and uninteresting truth. They must deal in fiction.

Jim Fisher was seventy years old, and a veteran hunter, the most famous in all the country. He *looked* authority, and promptly began to assert it, which he did in a single word:

"Yaou!"

2

"Yaou" was the *nom de nique* of one of the hunters, whose proper name was Sam Snaffles, but who, from his special smartness, had obtained the farther sobriquet of "*Sharp* Snaffles."

Columbus Mills whispered me that he was called "Yaou" from his frequent use of that word, which, in the Choctaw dialect, simply means "Yes." Snaffles had rambled considerably among the Choctaws, and picked up a variety of their words, which he was fond of using in preference to the vulgar English; and his common use of *"Yaou,"* for the affirmative, had prompted the substitution of it for his own name. He answered to the name.

"Ay—yee, Yaou," was the response of Sam. "I was *afeard,* 'Big Lie,' that you'd be hitching me up the very first in your team."

"And what was you afeard of? You knows as well how to take up a crooked trail as the very best man among us; so you go ahead and spin your thread a'ter the best fashion."

"What shill it be?" asked Snaffles, as he mixed a calabash full of peach and honey, preparing evidently for a long yarn.

"Give 's the history of how you got your capital, Yaou!" was the cry from two or more.

"O Lawd! I've tell'd that so often, fellows, that I'm afeard you'll sleep on it; and then agin, I've tell'd it so often I've clean forgot how it goes. Somehow it changes a leetle every time I tells it."

"Never you mind! The Jedge never haird it, I reckon, for one; and I'm not sure that Columbus Mills ever did."

So the "Big Lie."

The "Jedge" was the *nom de guerre* which the hunters had conferred upon me; looking, no doubt, to my venerable aspect— for I had traveled considerably beyond my teens—and the general dignity of my bearing.

"Yaou," like other bashful beauties in oratory and singing, was disposed to hem and haw, and affect modesty and indifference, when he was brought up suddenly by the stern command of the "Big Lie," who cried out:

"Don't make yourself an etarnal fool, Sam Snaffles, by twisting your mouth out of shape, making all sorts of redickilous ixcuses. Open upon the trail at onst and give tongue, or, dern your digestion, but I'll fine you to hafe a gallon at a single swallow!"

Nearly equivalent to what Hamlet says to the conceited player:

> "Leave off your damnable faces and begin."

Thus adjured with a threat, Sam Snaffles swallowed his peach and honey at a gulp, hemmed thrice lustily, put himself into an attitude, and began as follows. I shall adopt his language as closely as possible; but it is not possible, in any degree, to convey any adequate idea of his *manner,* which was admirably appropriate to the subject matter. Indeed, the fellow was a born actor.

3

"You see, Jedge," addressing me especially as the distinguished stranger, "I'm a telling this hyar history of mine jest to please *you*, and I'll try to please you ef I kin. These fellows hyar have hearn it so often that they knows all about it jest as well as I do my own self, and they knows the truth of it all, and would swear to it afore any hunters' court in all the county, ef so be the affidavy was to be tooken in camp and on a Saturday night.

"You see then, Jedge, it's about a dozen or fourteen years ago, when I was a young fellow without much beard on my chin, though I was full grown as I am now—strong as a horse, ef not quite so big as a buffalo. I was then jest a-beginning my 'prenticeship to the hunting business, and looking to sich persons as the 'Big Lie' thar to show me how to take the track of b'ar, buck, and painther.

"But I confess I weren't a-doing much. I hed a great deal to l'arn, and I reckon I miss'd many more bucks than I ever hit—that is, jest up to that time—"

"Look you, Yaou," said "Big Lie," interrupting him, "you're gitting too close upon the etarnal stupid truth! All you've been a-saying is jest nothing but the naked truth as I knows it. Jest crook your trail!"

"And how's a man to lie decently onless you lets him hev a bit of truth to go upon? The truth's nothing but a peg in the wall that I hangs the lie upon. A'ter a while I promise that you sha'n't see the peg."

"Worm along, Yaou!"

"Well, Jedge, I warn't a-doing much among the *bucks* yit—jest for the reason that I was quite too eager in the scent a'ter a sartin *doe!* Now, Jedge, you never seed my wife—my Merry Ann, as I calls her; and ef you was to see her *now*—though she's prime grit yit—you would never believe that, of all the womankind in all these mountains, she was the very yaller flower of the forest; with the reddest rose cheeks you ever did see, and sich a mouth, and sich bright curly hair, and so tall, and so slender, and so all over beautiful! O Lawd! when I thinks of it and them times, I don't see how 'twas possible to think of buck-hunting when thar was sich a doe, with sich eyes shining me on!

"Well, Jedge, Merry Ann was the only da'ter of Jeff Hopson and Keziah Hopson, his wife, who was the da'ter of Squire Claypole, whose wife was Margery Clough, that lived down upon Pacolet River—"

"Look you, Yaou, ain't you gitting into them derned facts agin, eh?"

"I reckon I em, 'Big Lie!' Scuse me: I'll kiver the pegs *direct-lie,* one a'ter t'other. Whar was I? Ah! Oh! Well, Jedge, poor hunter and poor man—jest, you see, a squatter on the side of a leetle bit of a mountain close on to Columbus Mills, at Mount Tryon, I was all the time on a hot trail a'ter Merry Ann Hopson. I went thar to see her a'most every night; and sometimes I carried a buck for the old people, and sometimes a doe-skin for the gal, and I do think, bad hunter as I then was, I pretty much kept the fambly in deer meat through the whole winter."

"Good for you, Yaou! You're a-coming to it! That's the only fair trail of a lie that you've struck yit!"

So the "Big Lie," from the chair.

"Glad to hyar you say so," was the answer. "I'll git on in time! Well, Jedge, though Jeff Hopson was glad enough to git my meat always, he didn't affection me, as I did his da'ter. He was a sharp, close, money-loving old fellow, who was always considerate of the main chaince; and the old lady, his wife, who hairdly dare say her soul was her own, she jest looked both ways, as I may say, for Sunday, never giving a fair look to me or my chainces, when his eyes were sot on *her.* But 'twa'n't so with my Merry Ann. She hed the eyes for me from the beginning, and soon she hed the feelings; and, you see, Jedge, we sometimes did git a chaince, when old Jeff was gone from home, to come to a sort of onderstanding about our feelings; and the long and the short of it was that Merry Ann confessed to me that she'd like nothing better than to be my wife. She liked no other man but me. Now, Jedge, a'ter that, what was a young fellow to do? That, I say, was the proper kind of incourage-ment. So I said, 'I'll ax your daddy.' Then she got scary, and said, 'Oh, don't; for somehow, Sam, I'm a-thinking daddy don't like you enough *yit.* Jest hold on a bit, and come often, and bring him venison, and try to make him laugh, which you kin do, you know, and a'ter a time you kin try him.' And so I did—or rether I didn't. I put off the axing. I come constant. I brought venison all the time, and b'ar meat a plenty, a'most three days in every week."

"That's it, Yaou. You're on trail. That's as derned a lie as you've tell'd yit; for all your hunting, in them days, didn't git more meat than you could eat your one self."

"Thank you, 'Big Lie.' I hopes I'll come up in time to the right measure of the camp.

"Well, Jedge, this went on for a long time, a'most the whole winter, and spring, and summer, till the winter begun to come in agin. I carried 'em the venison, and Merry Ann meets me in the woods, and we hes sich a pleasant time when we meets on them little odd chainces that I gits hot as thunder to bring the business to a sweet honey finish.

"But Merry Ann keeps on scary, and she puts me off; ontil, one day, one a'ternoon, about sundown, she meets me in the woods, and she's all in a flusteration. And she ups and tells me how old John Grimstead, the old bachelor (a fellow about forty years old, and the dear gal not yet twenty), how he's a'ter her, and bekaise he's got a good fairm, and mules and horses, how her daddy's giving him the open mouth incouragement.

"Then I says to Merry Ann:

" 'You sees, I kain't put off no longer. I must out with it, and ax your daddy at onst.' And then her scary fit come on again, and she begs me not to—not *jist yit*. But I swears by all the Hokies that I won't put off another day; and so, as I haird the old man was in the house that very hour, I left Merry Ann in the woods, all in a trimbling, and I jist went ahead, determined to have the figure made straight, whether odd or even.

"And Merry Ann, poor gal, she wrings her hainds, and cries a smart bit, and she wouldn't go to the house, but said she'd wait for me out thar. So I gin her a kiss into her very mouth—and did it over more than onst—and I left her, and pushed headlong for the house.

"I was jubous; I was mighty oncertain, and a leetle bit scary myself; for, you see, old Jeff was a fellow of tough grit, and with big grinders; but I was so oneasy, and so tired out waiting, and so desperate, and so fearsome that old bachelor Grimstead would get the start on me, that nothing could stop me now, and I jist bolted into the house, as free and easy and bold as ef I was the very best customer that the old man wanted to see."

Here Yaou paused to renew his draught of peach and honey.

4

"Well, Jedge, as I tell you, I put a bold face on the business, though my hairt was gitting up into my throat, and I was almost a-gasping for my breath, when I was fairly in the big room, and standing up before the old Squire. He was a-setting in his big squar hide-bottom'd arm-chair, looking like a jedge upon the bench, jist about to send a poor fellow to the gallows. As he seed me come in, looking queer enough, I reckon, his mouth put on a sort of grin, which showed all his grinders, and he looked for all the world as ef he guessed the business I come about. But he said, good-natured enough:

" 'Well, Sam Snaffles, how goes it?'

"Says I:

" 'Pretty squar, considerin'. The winter's coming on fast, and I reckon the mountains will be full of meat before long.'

"Then says he, with another ugly grin, 'Ef 'twas your smoke-house that had it all, Sam Snaffles, 'stead of the mountains, 'twould be better for you, I reckon.'

" 'I 'grees with you,' says I. 'But I rether reckon I'll git my full shar' of it afore the spring of the leaf agin.'

" 'Well, Sam,' says he, 'I hopes, for your sake, 'twill be a big shar'. I'm afeard you're not the pusson to go for a big shar', Sam Snaffles. Seems to me you're too easy satisfied with a small shar'; sich as the fence-squarrel carries onder his two airms, calkilating only on a small corn-crib in the chestnut-tree.'

" 'Don't you be afeard, Squaire. I'll come out right. My cabin sha'n't want for nothing that a strong man with a stout hairt kin git, with good working—enough and more for himself, and perhaps another pusson.'

" 'What other pusson?' says he, with another of his great grins, and showing of his grinders.

" 'Well,' says I, 'Squaire Hopson, that's jest what I come to talk to you about this blessed Friday night.'

"You see 'twas Friday!

" 'Well,' says he, 'go ahead, Sam Snaffles, and empty your brain-basket as soon as you kin, and I'll light my pipe while I'm a-hearing you.'

"So he lighted his pipe, and laid himself back in his chair, shet his eyes, and begin to puff like blazes.

"By this time my blood was beginning to bile in all my veins, for I seed that he was jest in the humor to tread on all my toes, and then ax a'ter my feelings. I said to myself:

" 'It's jest as well to git the worst at onst, and then thar'll be an eend of the oneasiness.' So I up and told him, in pretty soft, smooth sort of speechifying, as how I was mighty fond of Merry Ann, and she, I was a-thinking, of me; and that I jest come to ax ef I might hev Merry Ann for my wife.

"Then he opened his eyes wide, as ef he never ixpected to hear sich a proposal from me.

" 'What!' says he. 'You?'

" 'Jest so, Squaire,' says I. 'Ef it pleases you to believe me, and to consider it reasonable, the axing.'

"He sot quiet for a minit or more, then he gits up, knocks all the fire out of his pipe on the chimney, fills it, and lights it agin, and then comes straight up to me, whar I was a-setting on the chair in front of him, and without a word he takes the collar of my coat betwixt the thumb and forefinger of his left hand, and he says:

" 'Git up, Sam Snaffles. Git up, ef you please.'

"Well, I gits up, and he says:

" 'Hyar! Come! Hyar!'

"And with that he leads me right across the room to a big looking-glass that hung agin the partition wall, and thar he stops before the glass, facing it and holding me by the collar all the time.

"Now that looking-glass, Jedge, was about the biggest I ever did see! It was a'most three feet high, and a'most two feet wide, and it had a bright, broad frame, shiny like gold, with a heap of leetle figgers worked all round it. I reckon thar's no sich glass now in all the mountain country. I 'member when first that glass come home. It was a great thing, and the old Squaire was mighty proud of it. He bought it at the sale of some rich man's furniter, down at Greenville, and he was jest as fond of looking into it as a young gal, and whenever he lighted his pipe, he'd walk up and down the room, seeing himself in the glass.

"Well, thar he hed me up, both on us standing in front of this glass, whar we could a'most see the whole of our full figgers, from head to foot.

"And when we hed stood thar for a minit or so, he says, quite solemn like:

" 'Look in the glass, Sam Snaffles.'

"So I looked.

" 'Well,' says I. 'I sees you, Squaire Hopson, and myself, Sam Snaffles.'

" 'Look good,' says he, '*obzarve* well.'

" 'Well,' says I, 'I'm a-looking with all my eyes. I only sees what I tells you.'

" 'But you don't *obzarve*,' says he. 'Looking and seeing's one thing,' says he, 'but obzarving's another. Now *obzarve*.'

"By this time, Jedge, I was getting sort o' riled, for I could see that somehow he was jest a-trying to make me feel redickilous. So I says:

" 'Look you, Squaire Hopson, ef you thinks I never seed myself in a glass afore this, you're mighty mistaken. I've got my own glass at home, and though it's but a leetle sort of a small, mean consarn, it shows me as much of my own face and figger as I cares to see at any time. I never cares to look in it 'cept when I'm brushing, and combing, and clipping off the straggling beard when it's too long for my eating.'

" 'Very well,' says he; 'now obzarve! You sees your own figger, and your face, and you air obzarving as well as you know how. Now, Mr. Sam Snaffles—now that you've hed a fair look at yourself—jest now answer me, from your honest conscience, a'ter all you've seed, ef you honestly thinks you're the sort of pusson to hev *my* da'ter!'

"And with that he gin me a twist, and when I wheeled round he hed wheeled round too, and thar we stood, full facing one another.

"Lawd! how I was riled! But I answered, quick:

" 'And why not, I'd like to know, Squaire Hopson? I ain't the handsomest man in the world, but I'm not the ugliest; and folks don't generally consider me at all among the uglies. I'm as tall a man as you, and as stout and strong, and as good a man o' my inches as ever stepped in shoe-leather. And it's enough to tell you, Squaire, whatever *you* may think, that Merry Ann believes in me, and she's a way of thinking that I'm jest about the very pusson that ought to hev her.'

" 'Merry Ann's thinking,' says he, 'don't run all fours with her fayther's thinking. I axed you, Sam Snaffles, to *obzarve* yourself in the glass. I told you that seeing warn't edzactly obzarving. You seed only the inches; you seed that you hed eyes and mouth and nose and the airms and legs of the man. But eyes and mouth and legs and airms don't make a man!'

" 'Oh, they don't!' says I.

" 'No, indeed,' says he. 'I seed that you hed all them; but then I seed thar was one thing that you hedn't got.'

" 'Jimini!' says I, mighty conflustered. 'What thing's a-wanting to me to make me a man?'

" '*Capital!*' says he, and he lifted himself up and looked mighty grand.

" 'Capital!' says I; 'and what's that?'

" 'Thar air many kinds of capital,' says he. 'Money's capital, for it kin buy every thing. House and lands is capital; cattle and horses and sheep—when thar's enough on 'em—is capital. And as I obzarved you in the glass, Sam Snaffles, I seed that *capital* was the very thing that you wanted to make a man of you! Now I don't mean that any da'ter of mine shall marry a pusson that's not a *parfect* man. I obzarved you long ago, and seed whar you was wanting. I axed about you. I axed your horse.'

" 'Axed my horse!' says I, pretty nigh dumfoundered.

" 'Yes; I axed your horse, and he said to me: "Look at me! I hain't got an ounce of spar' flesh on my bones. You kin count all my ribs. You kin lay the whole length of your airm betwixt any two on 'em, and it'll lie thar as snug as a black snake betwixt two poles of a log-house." Says he, "Sam's got *no capital!* He ain't got, any time, five bushels of corn in his crib; and he's such a monstrous feeder himself that he'll eat out four bushels, and think it mighty hard upon him to give *me* the other one." Thar, now, was your horse's testimony, Sam, agin you. Then I axed about your cabin, and your way of living. I was curious, and went to see you one day when I knowed you waur at home. You hed but one chair, which you gin me to set on, and you sot on the eend of a barrel for yourself. You gin me a rasher of bacon what hedn't a streak of fat in it. You hed a poor quarter of a poor doe hanging from the rafters—a poor beast that somebody hed disabled—'

" 'I shot it myself,' says I.

" 'Well, it was a-dying when you shot it; and all the hunters say you was a poor shooter at any thing. You cooked our dinner yourself, and the hoe-cake was all dough, not hafe done, and the meat was all done as tough as ef you had dried it for a month of Sundays in a Flurriday sun! Your cabin had but one room, and that you slept in and ate in; and the floor was six inches deep in dirt! Then, when I looked into your garden, I found seven stalks of long collards only, every one seven foot high, with all the leaves stript off it, as ef you wanted 'em for broth; till thar waur only three top leaves left on every stalk. You hedn't a stalk of corn growing, and when I scratched at your turnip-bed I found nothing bigger than a chestnut. Then, Sam, I begun to ask about your fairm, and I found that you was nothing but a squatter on land of Columbus Mills, who let you have an old nigger pole-house, and an acre or two of land. Says I to myself, says I, "This poor fellow's got *no capital*; and he hasn't the head to git *capital*"; and from that moment, Sam Snaffles, the more I obzarved you, the more sartin 'twas that you never could be a man, ef you waur to live a thousand years. You may think, in your vanity, that you air a man; but you ain't, and never will be, onless you kin find a way to git *capital*; and I loves my gal child too much to let her marry any pusson whom I don't altogether consider a man!'

"A'ter that long speechifying, Jedge, you might ha' ground me up in a mill, biled me down in a pot, and scattered me over a manure heap, and I wouldn't ha' been able to say a word!

"I cotched up my hat, and was a-gwine, when he said to me, with his derned infernal big grin:

" 'Take another look in the glass, Sam Snaffles, and obzarve well, and you'll see jest whar it is I thinks that you're wanting.'

"I didn't stop for any more. I jest bolted, like a hot shot out of a shovel, and didn't know my own self, or whatever steps I tuk, tell I got into the thick and met Merry Ann coming towards me.

"I must liquor now!"

5

"Well, Jedge, it was a hard meeting betwixt me and Merry Ann. The poor gal come to me in a sort of run, and hairdly drawing her breath, she cried out:

" 'Oh, Sam! What does he say?'

"What could I say? How tell her? I jest wrapped her up in my airms, and I cries out, making some violent remarks about the old Squaire.

"Then she screamed, and I hed to squeeze her up, more close than ever, and kiss her, I reckon, more than a dozen times, jest to keep her from gwine into historical fits. I telled her all, from beginning to eend.

"I telled her that thar waur some truth in what the old man said: that I hedn't been keerful to do the thing as I ought; that the house *was* mean and dirty; that the horse was mean and poor; that I hed been thinking too much about her own self to think about other things; but that I would do better, would see to things, put things right, git corn in the crib, git 'capital,' ef I could, and make a good, comfortable home for *her*.

" 'Look at me,' says I, 'Merry Ann. Does I look like a man?'

" 'You're are all the man I wants,' says she.

" 'That's enough,' says I. 'You shall see what I kin do, and what I *will* do! That's ef you air true to me.'

" 'I'll be true to you, Sam,' says she.

" 'And you won't think of nobody else?'

" 'Never,' says she.

" 'Well, you'll see what I kin do, and what I *will* do. You'll see that I *em* a man; and ef thar's capital to be got in all the country, by working and hunting, and fighting, ef that's needful, we shill hev it. Only you be true to me, Merry Ann.'

"And she throwed herself upon my buzzom, and cried out:

" 'I'll be true to you, Sam. I loves nobody in all the world so much as I loves you.'

" 'And you won't marry any other man, Merry Ann, no matter what your daddy says?'

" 'Never,' she says.

" 'And you won't listen to this old bachelor fellow, Grimstead, that's got the "capital" already, no matter how they spurs you?'

" 'Never!' she says.

" 'Sw'ar it!' says I—'sw'ar it, Merry Ann—that you will be my wife, and never marry Grimstead!'

" 'I sw'ars it,' she says, kissing *me,* bekaize we had no book.

" 'Now,' says I, 'Merry Ann, that's not enough. Cuss him for my sake, and to make it sartin. Cuss that fellow Grimstead.'

" 'Oh, Sam, I kain't cuss,' says she; 'that's wicked.'

" 'Cuss him on my account,' says I—'to my credit.'

" 'Oh,' says she, 'don't ax me. I kain't do that.'

"Says I, 'Merry Ann, if you don't cuss that fellow, some way, I do believe you'll go over to him a'ter all. Jest you cuss him, now. Any small cuss will do, ef you're in airnest.'

" 'Well,' says she, 'ef that's your idee, then I says, "*Drot his skin,** and drot *my* skin, too, ef ever I marries any body but Sam Snaffles." '

" 'That'll do, Merry Ann,' says I. 'And now I'm easy in my soul and conscience. And now, Merry Ann, I'm gwine off to try my best, and git the "capital." Ef it's the "capital" that's needful to make a man of me, I'll git it, by all the Holy Hokies, if I kin.'

"And so, after a million of squeezes and kisses, we parted; and she slipt along through the woods, the back way to the house, and I mounted my horse to go to my cabin. But, afore I mounted the beast, I gin him a dozen kicks in his ribs, jest for bearing his testimony agin me, and telling the old Squire that I hedn't 'capital' enough for a corn crib."

6

"I was mightily let down, as you may think, by old Squire Hopson; but I was mightily lifted up by Merry Ann.

"But when I got to my cabin, and seed how mean every thing was there, and thought how true it was, all that old Squire Hopson had said, I felt overkim, and I said to myself, 'It's all true! How

---

*"Drot," or "Drat," has been called an American vulgarism, but it is genuine old English, as ancient as the days of Ben Jonson. Originally the oath was, "God rot it;" but Puritanism, which was unwilling to take the name of God in vain, was yet not prepared to abandon the oath, so the pious preserved it in an abridged form, omitting the G from God, and using, "Od rot it." It reached its final contraction, "Drot," before it came to America. "Drot it," "Drat it," "Drot your eyes," or "Drot his skin," are so many modes of using it among the uneducated classes.

kin I bring that beautiful yaller flower of the forest to live in sich a mean cabin, and with sich poor accommydations? She that had every thing comforting and nice about her.'

"Then I considered all about 'capital'; and it growed on me, ontil I begin to see that a man might hev good legs and arms and thighs, and a good face of his own, and yit not be a parfect and proper man a'ter all! I hed lived, you see, Jedge, to be twenty-three years of age, and was living no better than a three-old-year b'ar, in a sort of cave, sleeping on shuck and straw, and never looking after to-morrow.

"I couldn't sleep all that night for the thinking, and obzarvations. That impudent talking of old Hopson put me on a new track. I couldn't give up hunting. I knowed no other business, and I didn't hafe know that.

"I thought to myself, 'I must l'arn my business so as to work like a master.'

"But then, when I considered how hard it was, how slow I was to git the deers and the b'ar, and what a small chaince of money it brought me, I said to myself:

" 'Whar's the "capital" to come from?'

"Lawd save us! I ate up the meat pretty much as fast as I got it!

"Well, Jedge, as I said, I had a most miserable night of consideration and obzarvation and concatenation accordingly. I felt all over mean, 'cept now and then, when I thought of dear Merry Ann, and her felicities and cordialities and fidelities; and then, the cuss which she gin, onder the kiver of 'Drot,' to that dried up old bachelor Grimstead. But I got to sleep at last. And I hed a dream. And I thought I seed the prettiest woman critter in the world, next to Merry Ann, standing close by my bedside; and, at first, I thought 'twas Merry Ann, and I was gwine to kiss her agin; but she drawed back and said:

" 'Scuse me! I'm not Merry Ann; but I'm her friend and your friend; so don't you be down in the mouth, but keep a good hairt, and you'll hev help, and git the "capital" whar you don't look for it now. It's only needful that you be detarmined on good works and making a man of yourself.'

"A'ter that dream I slept like a top, woke at day-peep, took my rifle, called up my dog, mounted my horse, and put out for the laurel hollows.

"Well, I hunted all day, made several *starts*, but got nothing; my dog ran off, the rascally pup, and, I reckon, ef Squire Hopson had met him he'd ha' said 'twas bekaise I starved him! Fact is, we hedn't any on us much to eat that day, and the old mar's ribs stood out bigger than ever.

"All day I rode and followed the track and got nothing.

"Well, jest about sunset I come to a hollow of the hills that I hed never seed before; and in the middle of it was a great pond of water, what you call a lake; and it showed like so much purple glass in the sunset, and 'twas jest as smooth as the big looking-glass of Squaire Hopson's. Thar wa'n't a breath of wind stirring.

"I was mighty tired, so I eased down from the mar', tied up the bridle and check, and let her pick about, and laid myself down onder a tree, jest about twenty yards from the lake, and thought to rest myself ontil the moon riz, which I knowed would be about seven o'clock.

"I didn't mean to fall asleep, but I did it; and I reckon I must ha' slept a good hour, for when I woke the dark hed set in, and I could only see one or two bright stars hyar and thar, shooting out from the dark of the heavens. But, ef I seed nothing, I haird; and jest sich a sound and noise as I hed never haird before.

"Thar was a rushing and a roaring and a screaming and a plashing, in the air and in the water, as made you think the univarsal world was coming to an eend!

"All that set me up. I was waked up out of sleep and dream, and my eyes opened to every thing that eye could see; and sich another sight I never seed before! I tell you, Jedge, ef there was one wild-goose settling down in that lake, thar was one hundred thousand of 'em! I couldn't see the eend of 'em. They come every minit, swarm a'ter swarm, in tens and twenties and fifties and hundreds; and sich a fuss as they did make! sich a gabbling, sich a splashing, sich a confusion, that I was fairly conflusterated; and I jest lay whar I was, a-watching 'em.

"You never seed beasts so happy! How they flapped their wings; how they gabbled to one another; how they swam hyar and thar, to the very middle of the lake and to the very edge of it, jest a fifty yards from whar I lay squat, never moving leg or arm! It was wonderful to see! I wondered how they could find room, for I reckon thar waur forty thousand on 'em, all scuffling in that leetle lake together!

"Well, as I watched 'em, I said to myself:

" 'Now, if a fellow could only captivate all them wild-geese—fresh from Canniday, I reckon—what would they bring in the market at Spartanburg and Greenville? Walker, I knowed, would buy 'em up quick at fifty cents a head. Forty thousand geese at fifty cents a head. Thar was "capital!" '

"I could ha' fired in among 'em with my rifle, never taking aim, and killed a dozen or more, at a single shot; but what was a poor dozen geese, when thar waur forty thousand to captivate?

"What a haul 'twould be, ef a man could only get 'em all in one net! Kiver 'em all at a fling!

"The idee worked like so much fire in my brain.

"How kin it be done?

"That was the question!

" 'Kin it be done?' I axed myself.

" 'It kin,' I said to myself; 'and I'm the very man to do it!' Then I begun to work away in the thinking. I thought over all the traps and nets and snares that I hed ever seen or haird of; and the leetle eends of the idee begun to come together in my head; and, watching all the time how the geese flopped and splashed and played and swum, I said to myself:

" 'Oh! most beautiful critters! ef I don't make some "capital" out of you, then I'm not dezarving sich a beautiful yaller flower of the forest as my Merry Ann!'

"Well, I watched a long time, ontil dark night, and the stars begun to peep down upon me over the high hill-tops. Then I got up and tuk to my horse and rode home.

"And thar, when I hed swallowed my bit of hoe-cake and bacon and a good strong cup of coffee, and got into bed, I couldn't sleep for a long time, thinking how I was to git them geese.

"But I kept nearing the right idee every minit, and when I was fast asleep it come to me in my dream.

"I seed the same beautifulest young woman agin that hed given me the incouragement before to go ahead, and she helped me out with the idee.

"So, in the morning, I went to work. I rode off to Spartanburg, and bought all the twine and cord and hafe the plow-lines in town; and I got a lot of great fishhooks, all to help make the tanglement parfect; and I got lead for sinkers, and I got cork-wood for floaters; and I pushed for home jist as fast as my poor mar' could streak it.

"I was at work day and night, for nigh on to a week, making my net; and when 'twas done I borrowed a mule and cart from Columbus Mills, thar;—he'll tell you all about it—he kin make his affidavy to the truth of it.

"Well, off I driv with my great net, and got to the lake about noonday. I knowed 'twould take me some hours to make my fixings parfect, and git the net fairly stretched across the lake, and jest deep enough to do the tangling of every leg of the birds in the very midst of their swimming and snorting and splashing and cavorting! When I hed fixed it all fine, and jest as I wanted it, I brought the eends of my plow-lines up to where I was gwine to hide myself. This was onder a strong sapling, and my calkilation was when I hed got the beasts all hooked, forty thousand, more or less—and I could tell how that was from feeling on the line— why, then, I'd whip the line round the sapling, hitch it fast, and draw in my birds at my own ease, without axing much about their comfort.

" 'Twas a most beautiful and parfect plan, and all would ha' worked beautiful well but for one leetle oversight of mine. But I won't tell you about that part of the business yit, the more pre- tickilarly as it all turned out for the very best, as you'll see in the eend.

"I hedn't long finished my fixings when the sun suddenly tumbled down the heights, and the dark begun to creep in upon me, and a pretty cold dark it waur! I remember it well! My teeth begun to chatter in my head, though I was boiling over with inward heat, all jest coming out of my hot eagerness to be captivating the birds.

"Well, Jedge, I hedn't to wait overlong. Soon I haird them coming, screaming fur away, and then I seed them pouring, jest like so many white clouds, straight down, I reckon, from the snow mountains off in Canniday.

"Down they come, millions upon millions, till I was sartin thar waur already pretty nigh on to forty thousand in the lake. It waur always a nice calkilation of mine that the lake could hold fully forty thousand, though onst, when I went round to measure it, stepping it off, I was jubous whether it could hold over thirty-nine thousand; but, as I tuk the measure in hot weather and in a dry spell, I concluded that some of the water along the edges hed dried up, and 'twa'n't so full as when I made my first calkilation. So I hev stuck to that first calkilation ever since.

"Well, thar they waur, forty thousand, we'll say, with, it mout be, a few millions and hundreds over. And Lawd! how they played and splashed and screamed and dived! I calkilated on hooking a good many of them divers, in pretickilar, and so I watched and waited, ontil I thought I'd feel of my lines; and I begun, leetle by leetle, to haul in, when, Lawd love you, Jedge, sich a ripping and raging, and bouncing and flouncing, and flopping and splashing, and kicking and screaming, you never did hear in all your born days!

"By this I knowed that I hed captivated the captains of the host, and a pretty smart chaince, I reckoned, of the rigilar army, ef 'twa'n't edzactly forty thousand; for I calkilated that some few would git away—run off, jest as the cowards always does in the army, jest when the shooting and confusion begins; still, I reason- ably calkilated on the main body of the rigiments; and so, gitting more and more hot and eager, and pulling and hauling, I made one big mistake, and, instid of wrapping the eends of my lines around the sapling that was standing jest behind me, what does I do but wraps 'em round my own thigh—the right thigh, you see—and some of the loops waur hitched round my left arm at the same time!

"All this come of my hurry and ixcitement, for it was burning like a hot fever in my brain, and I didn't know when or how I hed tied myself up, ontil suddently, with an all-fired scream, all together, them forty thousand geese rose like a great black cloud in the air, all tied up, tangled up—hooked about the legs, hooked about the gills, hooked and fast in some way in the beautiful leetle twistings of my net!

"Yes, Jedge, as I'm a living hunter to-night, hyar a-talking to you, they riz up all together, as ef they hed consulted upon it, like a mighty thunder-cloud, and off they went, screaming and flouncing, meaning, I reckon, to take the back track to Canniday, in spite of the freezing weather.

"Before I knowed whar I was, Jedge, I was twenty feet in the air, my right thigh up and my left arm, and the other thigh and arm a-dangling useless, and feeling every minit as ef they was gwine to drop off.

"You may be sure I pulled with all my might, but that waur mighty leetle in the fix I was in, and I jest hed to hold on, and see whar the infernal beasts would carry me. I couldn't loose myself, and ef I could I was by this time quite too fur up in the air, and darsn't do so, onless I was willing to hev my brains dashed out, and my whole body mashed to a mammock!

"Oh, Jedge, jest consider my sitivation! It's sich a ricollection, Jedge, that I must rest and liquor, in order to rekiver the necessary strength to tell you what happened next."

7

"Yes, Jedge," said Yaou, resuming his narrative, "jest stop whar you air, and consider my sitivation!

"Thar I was dangling, like a dead weight, at the tail of that all-fired cloud of wild-geese, head downward, and gwine, the Lawd knows whar!—to Canniday, or Jericho, or some other heathen territory beyond the Mississipp, and it mout be, over the great etarnal ocean!

"When I thought of *that*, and thought of the plow-lines giving way, and that on a suddent I should come down plump into the big sea, jest in the middle of a great gathering of shirks and whales, to be dewoured and tore to bits by their bloody grinders, I was ready to die of skeer outright. I thought over all my sinnings in a moment, and I thought of my poor dear Merry Ann, and I called out her name, loud as I could, jest as ef the poor gal could hyar me or help me.

"And jest then I could see we waur a drawing nigh a great thunder-cloud. I could see the red tongues running out of its black jaws; and 'Lawd!' says I, 'ef these all-fired infarnal wild beasts of birds should carry me into that cloud to be burned to a coal, fried, and roasted, and biled alive by them tongues of red fire!'

"But the geese fought shy of the cloud, though we passed mighty nigh on to it, and I could see one red streak of lightning run out of the cloud and give us chase for a full hafe a mile; but we waur too fast for it, and, in a tearing passion bekaise it couldn't ketch us, the red streak struck its horns into a great tree jest behind us, that we hed passed over, and tore it into flinders, in the twink of a musquito.

"But by this time I was beginning to feel quite stupid. I knowed that I waur fast gitting onsensible, and it did seem to me as ef my hour waur come, and I was gwine to die—and die by rope, and dangling in the air, a thousand miles from the airth!

"But jest then I was roused up. I felt something brush agin me; then my face was scratched; and, on a suddent, thar was a stop put to my travels by that conveyance. The geese had stopped flying, and waur in a mighty great conflusteration, flopping their wings, as well as they could, and screaming with all the tongues in their jaws. It was clar to me now that we hed run agin something that brought us all up with a short hitch.

"I was shook roughly agin the obstruction, and I put out my right arm and cotched a hold of a long arm of an almighty big tree; then my legs waur cotched betwixt two other branches, and I rekivered myself, so as to set up a leetle and rest. The geese was a tumbling and flopping among the branches. The net was hooked hyar and thar; and the birds waur all about me, swinging and splurging, but onable to break loose and git away.

"By leetle and leetle I come to my clar senses, and begun to feel my sitivation. The stiffness was passing out of my limbs. I could draw up my legs, and, after some hard work, I managed to onwrap the plow-lines from my right thigh and my left arm, and I hed the sense this time to tie the eends pretty tight to a great branch of the tree which stretched clar across and about a foot over my head.

"Then I begun to consider my sitivation. I hed hed a hard riding, that was sartin; and I felt sore enough. And I hed hed a horrid bad skear, enough to make a man's wool turn white afore the night was over. But now I felt easy, bekaise I considered myself safe. With day-peep I calkilated to let myself down from the tree by my plow-lines, and thar, below, tied fast, warn't thar my forty thousand captivated geese?

" 'Hurrah!' I sings out. 'Hurrah, Merry Ann; we'll hev the "capital" now, I reckon!'

"And singing out, I drawed up my legs and shifted my body so as to find an easier seat in the crutch of the tree, which was an almighty big chestnut oak, when, O Lawd! on a suddent the stump I hed been a-setting on give way onder me. 'Twas a rotten jint of the tree. It give way, Jedge, as I tell you, and down I went, my legs first and then my whole body—slipping down not on the outside, but into a great hollow of the tree, all the hairt of it being eat out by the rot; and afore I knowed whar I waur, I waur some twenty foot down, I reckon; and by the time I touched bottom, I was up to my neck in honey!

"It was an almighty big honey-tree, full of the sweet treacle; and the bees all gone and left it, I reckon, for a hundred years. And I in it up to my neck.

"I could smell it strong. I could taste it sweet. But I could see nothing.

"Lawd! Lawd! From bad to worse; buried alive in a hollow tree with never a chaince to git out! I would then ha' given all the world ef I was only sailing away with them bloody wild-geese to Canniday, and Jericho, even across the sea, with all its shirks and whales dewouring me.

"Buried alive! O Lawd! O Lawd! 'Lawd save me and help me!' I cried out from the depths. And 'Oh, my Merry Ann,' I cried, 'shill we never meet agin no more!' Scuse my weeping, Jedge, but I feels all over the sinsation, fresh as ever, of being buried alive in a beehive tree and presarved in honey. I must liquor, Jedge."

8

Yaou, after a great swallow of peach and honey, and a formidable groan after it, resumed his narrative as follows:

"Only think of me, Jedge, in my sitivation! Buried alive in the hollow of a mountain chestnut oak! Up to my neck in honey, with never no more an appetite to eat than ef it waur the very gall of bitterness that we reads of in the Holy Scripters!

"All dark, all silent as the grave; 'cept for the gabbling and the cackling of the wild-geese outside, that every now and then would make a great splurging and cavorting, trying to break away from their hitch, which was jist as fast fixed as my own.

"Who would git them geese that hed cost me so much to captivate? Who would inherit my 'capital?' and who would hev Merry Ann? and what will become of the mule and cart of Mills fastened in the woods by the leetle lake?

"I cussed the leetle lake, and the geese, and all the 'capital.'

"I cussed. I couldn't help it. I cussed from the bottom of my hairt, when I ought to ha' bin saying my prayers. And thar was my poor mar' in the stable with never a morsel of feed. She had told tales upon me to Squaire Hopson, it's true, but I forgin her, and thought of her feed, and nobody to give her none. Thar waur corn in the crib and fodder, but it warn't in the stable; and onless Columbus Mills should come looking a'ter me at the cabin, thar waur no hope for me or the mar'.

"Oh, Jedge, you couldn't jedge of my sitivation in that deep hollow, that cave, I may say, of mountain oak! My head waur jest above the honey, and ef I backed it to look up, my long ha'r at the back of the neck a'most stuck fast, so thick was the honey.

"But I couldn't help looking up. The hollow was a wide one at the top, and I could see when a star was passing over. Thar they shined, bright and beautiful, as ef they waur the very eyes of the angels; and, as I seed them come and go, looking smiling in upon me as they come, I cried out to 'em, one by one:

" 'Oh, sweet sperrits, blessed angels! ef so be thar's an angel sperrit, as they say, living in all them stars, come down and extricate me from this fix; for, so fur as I kin see, I've got no chaince of help from mortal man or woman. Hairdly onst a year does a human come this way; and ef they did come, how would they know I'm hyar? How could I make them hyar me? O Lawd! O blessed, beautiful angels in them stars! O give me help! Help me out!' I knowed I prayed like a heathen sinner, but I prayed as well as I knowed how; and thar warn't a star passing over me that I didn't pray to, soon as I seed them shining over the opening of the hollow; and I prayed fast and faster as I seed them passing away and gitting out of sight.

"Well, Jedge, suddently, in the midst of my praying, and jest after one bright, big star hed gone over me without seeing my sitivation, I hed a fresh skeer.

"Suddent I haird a monstrous fluttering among my geese—my 'capital.' Then I haird a great scraping and scratching on the outside of the tree, and, suddent, as I looked up, the mouth of the hollow was shet up.

"All was dark. The stars and sky waur all gone. Something black kivered the hollow, and, in a minit a'ter, I haird something slipping down into the hollow right upon me.

"I could hairdly draw my breath. I begun to fear that I was to be siffocated alive; and as I haird the strange critter slipping down, I shoved out my hands and felt ha'r—coarse wool—and with one hand I cotched hold of the ha'ry leg of a beast, and with t'other hand I cotched hold of his tail.

" 'Twas a great b'ar, one of the biggest, come to git his honey. He knowed the tree, Jedge, you see, and ef any beast in the world loves honey, 'tis a b'ar beast. He'll go his death on honey, though the hounds are tearing at his very haunches.

"You may be sure, when I onst knowed what he was, and onst got a good gripe on his hindquarters, I warn't gwine to let go in a hurry. I knowed that was my only chaince for gitting out of the hollow, and I do believe them blessed angels in the stars sent the beast, jest at the right time, to give me human help and assistance.

"Now, yer see, Jedge, thar was no chaince for him turning round upon me. He pretty much filled up the hollow. He knowed his way, and slipped down, eend foremost—the latter eend, you know. He could stand up on his hind-legs and eat all he wanted. Then, with his great sharp claws and his mighty muscle, he could work up, holding on to the sides of the tree, and git out a'most as easy as when he come down.

"Now, you see, ef he weighed five hundred pounds, and could climb like a cat, he could easy carry up a young fellow that hed no flesh to spar', and only weighed a hundred and twenty-five. So I laid my weight on him, eased him off as well as I could, but held on to tail and leg as ef all life and etarnity depended upon it.

"Now I reckon, Jedge, that b'ar was pretty much more skeered than I was. He couldn't turn in his shoes, and with something fastened to his ankles, and, as he thought, I reckon, some strange beast fastened to his tail, you never seed beast more eager to git away, and git upwards. He knowed the way, and stuck his claws in the rough sides of the hollow, hand over hand, jest as a sailor pulls a rope, and up we went. We hed, howsomdever, more than one slip back; but, Lawd bless you! I never let go. Up we went, I say, at last, and I stuck jest as close to his haunches as death sticks to a dead nigger. Up we went. I felt myself moving. My neck was out of the honey. My airms were free. I could feel the sticky thing slipping off from me, and a'ter a good quarter of an hour the b'ar was on the great mouth of the hollow; and as I felt that I let go his tail, still keeping fast hold of his leg, and with one hand I cotched hold of the outside rim of the hollow; I found it fast, held on to it; and jest then the b'ar sat squat on the very edge of the hollow, taking a sort of rest a'ter his labor.

"I don't know what 'twas, Jedge, that made me do it. I warn't a-thinking at all. I was only feeling and drawing a long breath. Jest then the b'ar sort o' looked round, as ef to see what varmint it was a-troubling him, when I gin him a mighty push, strong as I could, and he lost his balance and went over outside down cl'ar to the airth, and I could hyar his neck crack, almost as loud as a pistol.

"I drawed a long breath a'ter that, and prayed a short prayer; and feeling my way all the time, so as to be sure agin rotten branches, I got a safe seat among the limbs of the tree, and sot myself down, determined to wait tell broad daylight before I tuk another step in the business."

9

"And thar I sot. So fur as I could see, Jedge, I was safe. I hed got out of the tie of the flying geese, and thar they all waur, spread before me, flopping now and then and trying to ixtricate themselves; but they couldn't come it! Thar they waur, captivated, and so much 'capital' for Sam Snaffles.

"And I hed got out of the lion's den; that is, I hed got out of the honey-tree, and warn't in no present danger of being buried alive agin. Thanks to the b'ar, and to the blessed, beautiful angel sperrits in the stars, that hed sent him thar seeking honey, to be my deliverance from my captivation!

"And thar he lay, jest as quiet as ef he waur a-sleeping, though I knowed his neck was broke. And that b'ar, too, was so much 'capital.'

"And I sot in the tree making my calkilations. I could see now the meaning of that beautiful young critter that come to me in my dreams. I was to hev the 'capital,' but I was to git it through troubles and tribulations, and a mighty bad skeer for life. I never knowed the valley of 'capital' till now, and I seed the sense in all that Squaire Hopson told me, though he did tell it in a mighty spiteful sperrit.

"Well, I calkilated.

"It was cold weather, freezing, and though I had good warm clothes on, I felt monstrous like sleeping, from the cold only, though perhaps the tire and the skeer together hed something to do with it. But I was afeard to sleep. I didn't know what would happen, and a man has never his right courage ontil daylight. I fou't agin sleep by keeping on my calkilation.

"Forty thousand wild-geese!

"Thar wa'n't forty thousand, edzactly—very far from it—but thar they waur, pretty thick; and for every goose I could git from forty to sixty cents in all the villages in South Carolina.

"Thar was 'capital!'

"Then thar waur the b'ar.

"Jedging from his strength in pulling me up, and from his size and fat in filling up that great hollow in the tree, I calkilated that he couldn't weigh less than five hundred pounds. His hide, I knowed, was worth twenty dollars. Then thar was the fat and tallow, and the biled marrow out of his bones, what they makes b'ars grease out of, to make chicken whiskers grow big enough for game-cocks. Then thar waur the meat, skinned, cleaned, and all; thar couldn't be much onder four hundred and fifty pounds, and whether I sold him as fresh meat or cured, he'd bring me ten cents a pound at the least.

"Says I, 'Thar's capital!'

" 'Then,' says I, 'thar's my honey-tree! I reckon thar's a matter of ten thousand gallons in this hyar same honey-tree; and if I kint git fifty to seventy cents a gallon for it thar's no alligators in Flurriday!'

"And so I calkilated through the night, fighting agin sleep, and thinking of my 'capital' and Merry Ann together.

"By morning I had calkilated all I hed to do and all I hed to make.

"Soon as I got a peep of day I was bright on the look-out.

"Thar all around me were the captivated geese critters. The b'ar laid down parfectly easy and waiting for the knife; and the geese, I reckon they waur much more tired than me, for they didn't seem to hev the hairt for a single flutter, even when they seed me swing down from the tree among 'em, holding on to my plow-lines and letting myself down easy.

"But first I must tell you, Jedge, when I seed the first signs of daylight and looked around me, Lawd bless me, what should I see but old Tryon Mountain, with his great head lifting itself up in the east! And beyant I could see the house and fairm of Columbus Mills; and as I turned to look a leetle south of that, thar was my own poor leetle log-cabin standing quiet, but with never a smoke streaming out from the chimbley.

" 'God bless them good angel sperrits,' I said, 'I ain't two miles from home!' Before I come down from the tree I knowed edzactly whar I waur. 'Twas only four miles off from the lake and whar I hitched the mule of Columbus Mills close by the cart. Thar, too, I hed left my rifle. Yit in my miserable fix, carried through the air by them wild-geese, I did think I hed gone a'most a thousand miles towards Canniday.

"Soon as I got down from the tree I pushed off at a trot to git the mule and cart. I was pretty sure of my b'ar and geese when I come back. The cart stood quiet enough. But the mule, having nothing to eat, was sharping her teeth upon a boulder, thinking she'd hev a bite or so before long.

"I hitched her up, brought her to my bee-tree, tumbled the b'ar into the cart, wrung the necks of all the geese that waur thar—many hed got away—and counted some twenty-seven hundred that I piled away atop of the b'ar."

"Twenty-seven hundred!" cried the "Big Lie" and all the hunters at a breath. "Twenty-seven hundred! Why, Yaou, whenever you telled of this thing before you always counted them at 3150!"

"Well, ef I did, I reckon I was right. I was sartinly right then, it being all fresh in my 'membrance; and I'm not the man to go back agin his own words. No, fellows, I sticks to first words and first principles. I scorns to eat my own words. Ef I said 3150, then 3150 it waur, never a goose less. But you'll see how to 'count for all. I reckon 'twas only 2700 I fotched to market. Thar was 200 I gin to Columbus Mills. Then thar was 200 more I carried to Merry Ann; and then thar waur 50 at least, I reckon, I kep for myself. Jest you count up, Jedge, and you'll see how to squar' it on all sides. When I said 2700 I only counted what I sold in the villages, every head of 'em at fifty cents a head; and a'ter putting the money in my pocket I felt all over that I hed the 'capital.'

"Well, Jedge, next about the b'ar. Sold the hide and tallow for a fine market-price; sold the meat, got ten cents a pound for it fresh—'twas most beautiful meat; biled down the bones for the marrow; melted down the grease; sold fourteen pounds of it to the barbers and apothecaries; got a dollar a pound for that; sold the hide for twenty dollars; and got the cash for every thing.

"Thar warn't a fambly in all Greenville and Spartanburg and Asheville that didn't git fresh, green wild-geese from me that season, at fifty cents a head, and glad to git, too; the cheapest fresh meat they could buy; and, I reckon, the finest. And all the people of them villages, ef they hed gone to heaven that week, in the flesh, would have carried nothing better than goose-flesh for the risurrection! Every body ate goose for a month, I reckon, as the weather was freezing cold all the time, and the beasts kept week after week, ontil they waur eaten. From the b'ar only I made a matter of full one hundred dollars. First, thar waur the hide,

$20; then 450 pounds of meat, at 10 cents, was $45; then the grease, 14 pounds, $14; and the tallow, some $6 more; and the biled marrow, $11.

"Well, count up, Jedge; 2700 wild-geese, at 50 cents, you sees, must be more than $1350. I kin only say, that a'ter all the selling— and I driv at it day and night, with Columbus Mills's mule and cart, and went to every house in every street in all them villages. I hed a'most fifteen hundred dollars, safe stowed away onder the pillows of my bed, all in solid gould and silver.

"But I warn't done! Thar was my bee-tree. Don't you think I waur gwine to lose that honey! no, my darlint! I didn't beat the drum about nothing. I didn't let on to a soul what I was a-doing. They axed me about the wild-geese, but I sent 'em on a wild-goose chase; and 'twa'n't till I hed sold off all the b'ar meat and all the geese that I made ready to git at that honey. I reckon them bees must ha' been making that honey for a hundred years, and was then driv out by the b'ars.

"Columbus Mills will tell you; he axed me all about it; but, though he was always my good friend, I never even telled it to him. But he lent me his mule and cart, good fellow as he is, and never said nothing more; and, quiet enough, without beat of drum, I bought up all the tight-bound barrels that ever brought whisky to Spartanburg and Greenville, whar they hes the taste for that article strong; and day by day I went off carrying as many barrels as the cart could hold and the mule could draw. I tapped the old tree—which was one of the oldest and biggest chestnut oaks I ever did see—close to the bottom, and drawed off the beautiful treacle. I was more than sixteen days about it, and got something over two thousand gallons of the purest, sweetest, yellowest honey you ever did see. I could hairdly git barrels and jimmyjohns enough to hold it; and I sold it out at seventy cents a gallon, which was mighty cheap. So I got from the honey a matter of fourteen hundred dollars.

"Now, Jedge, all this time, though it went very much agin the grain, I kept away from Merry Ann and the old Squaire, her daddy. I sent him two hundred head of geese—some fresh, say one hundred, and another hundred that I hed cleaned and put in salt—and I sent him three jimmyjohns of honey, five gallons each. But I kept away and said nothing, beat no drum, and hed never a thinking but how to git in the 'capital.' And I did git it in!

"When I carried the mule and cart home to Columbus Mills I axed him about a sartin farm of one hundred and sixty acres that he hed to sell. It hed a good house on it. He selled it to me cheap.

I paid him down, and put the titles in my pocket. 'Thar's capital!' says I.

"*That* waur a fixed thing for ever and ever. And when I hed moved every thing from the old cabin to the new farm, Columbus let me hev a fine milch cow that gin eleven quarts a day, with a beautiful young caif. Jest about that time thar was a great sale of the furniter of the Ashmore family down at Spartanburg, and I remembered I hed no decent bedstead, or any thing rightly sarving for a young woman's chamber; so I went to the sale, and bought a fine strong mahogany bedstead, a dozen chairs, a chist of drawers, and some other things that ain't quite mentionable, Jedge, but all proper for a lady's chamber; and I soon hed the house fixed up ready for any thing. And up to this time I never let on to any body what I was a-thinking about or what I was a-doing, ontil I could stand up in my own doorway and look about me, and say to myself—this is my 'capital,' I reckon; and when I hed got all that I thought a needcessity to git, I took 'count of every thing.

"I spread the title-deeds of my fairm out on the table. I read 'em over three times to see ef 'twaur all right. Thar was my name several times in big letters, 'to hev and to hold.'

"Then I fixed the furniter. Then I brought out into the stable-yard the old mar'—you couldn't count her ribs *now,* and she was spry as ef she hed got a new conceit of herself.

"Then thar was my beautiful cow and caif, sealing fat, both on 'em, and sleek as a doe in autumn.

"Then thar waur a fine young mule that I bought in Spartanburg; my cart, and a strong second-hand buggy, that could carry two pussons convenient of two different sexes. And I felt big, like a man of consekence and capital.

"That warn't all.

"I had the shiners, Jedge, besides—all in gould and silver—none of your dirty rags and blotty spotty paper. That was the time of Old Hickory—General Jackson, you know—when he kicked over Nick Biddle's consarn, and gin us the beautiful Benton Mint Drops, in place of rotten paper. You could git the gould and silver jest for the axing, in them days, you know.

"I hed a grand count of my money, Jedge. I hed it in a dozen or twenty little bags of leather—the gould—and the silver I hed in shot-bags. It took me a whole morning to count it up and git the figgers right. Then I stuffed it in my pockets, hyar and thar, every whar, wherever I could stow a bag; and the silver I stuffed away in my saddle-bags, and clapped it on the mar'.

"Then I mounted myself, and sot the mar's nose straight in a bee-line for the fairm of Squaire Hopson.

"I was a-gwine, you see, to supprise him with my 'capital'; but, fust, I meant to give him a mighty grand skeer.

"You see, when I was a-trading with Columbus Mills about the fairm and cattle and other things, I ups and tells him about my courting of Merry Ann; and when I told him about Squire Hopson's talk about 'capital,' he says:

" 'The old skunk! What right hes he to be talking big so, when he kain't pay his own debts. He's been owing me three hundred and fifty dollars now gwine on three years, and I kain't git even the *intrust* out of him. I've got a mortgage on his fairm for the whole, and ef he won't let you hev his da'ter, jest you come to me, and I'll clap the screws to him in short order.'

"Says I, 'Columbus, won't you sell me that mortgage?'

" 'You shill hev it for the face of the debt,' says he, 'not considerin' the intrust.'

" 'It's a bargain,' says I; and I paid him down the money, and he signed the mortgage over to me for a vallyable consideration.

"I hed that beautiful paper in my breast pocket, and felt strong to face the Squire in his own house, knowing how I could turn him out of it! And I mustn't forget to tell you how I got myself a new rig of clothing, with a mighty fine over-coat, and a new fur cap; and as I looked in the glass I felt my consekence all over at every for'a'd step I tuk; and I felt my inches growing with every pace of the mar' on the high-road to Merry Ann and her beautiful daddy!"

10

"Well, Jedge, before I quite got to the Squire's farm, who should come out to meet me in the road but Merry Ann, her own self! She hed spied me, I reckon, as I crossed the bald ridge a quarter of a mile away. I do reckon the dear gal hed been looking out for me every day the whole eleven days in the week, counting in all the Sundays. In the mountains, you know, Jedge, that the weeks sometimes run to twelve, and even fourteen days, specially when we're on a long camp-hunt!

"Well, Merry Ann cried and laughed together, she was so tarnation glad to see me agin. Says she:

" 'Oh, Sam! I'm so glad to see you! I was afeard you had clean gin me up. And thar's that fusty old bachelor Grimstead, he's a-coming here a'most every day; and daddy, he sw'ars that I shill marry him, and nobody else; and mammy, she's at me too, all the time, telling me how fine a fairm he's got, and what a nice carriage, and all that; and mammy says as how daddy'll be sure to beat me ef I don't hev him. But I kain't bear to look at him, the old griesly!'

" 'Cuss him!' says I. 'Cuss him, Merry Ann!'

"And she did, but onder her breath—the old cuss.

" 'Drot him!' says she; and she said louder, 'and drot me, too, Sam, ef I ever marries any body but you.'

"By this time I hed got down and gin her a long strong hug, and a'most twenty or a dozen kisses, and I says:

" 'You sha'n't marry nobody but me, Merry Ann; and we'll hev the marriage this very night, ef you says so!'

" 'Oh! psho, Sam! How you does talk!'

" 'Ef I don't marry you to-night, Merry Ann, I'm a holy mortar, and a sinner not to be saved by any salting, though you puts the petre with the salt. I'm come for that very thing. Don't you see my new clothes?'

" 'Well, you hev got a beautiful coat, Sam; all so blue, and with sich shiny buttons.'

" 'Look at my waistcoat, Merry Ann! What do you think of that?'

" 'Why, it's a most beautiful blue welvet!'

" 'That's the very article,' says I. 'And see the breeches, Merry Ann; and the boots!'

" 'Well,' says she, 'I'm fair astonished, Sam! Why whar, Sam, did you find all the money for these fine things?'

" 'A beautiful young woman, a'most as beautiful as you, Merry Ann, come to me the very night of that day when your daddy driv me off with a flea in my ear. She come to me to my bed at midnight—'

" 'Oh, Sam! *ain't* you ashamed!'

" ' 'Twas in a dream, Merry Ann; and she tells me something to incourage me to go for'a'd, and I went for'a'd, bright and airly next morning, and I picked up three sarvants that hev been working for me ever sence.'

" 'What sarvants?' says she.

" 'One was a goose, one was a b'ar, and t'other was a bee!'

" 'Now you're a-fooling me, Sam.'

" 'You'll see! Only you git yourself ready, for, by the eternal Hokies, I marries you this very night, and takes you home to *my* fairm bright and airly to-morrow morning.'

" 'I do think, Sam, you must be downright crazy.'

" 'You'll see and believe! Do you go home and git yourself fixed up for the wedding. Old Parson Stovall lives only two miles from your daddy, and I'll hev him hyar by sundown. You'll see!'

" 'But ef I waur to b'lieve you, Sam—'

" 'I've got on my wedding-clothes o' purpose, Merry Ann.'

" 'But *I* hain't got no clothes fit for a gal to be married in,' says she.

" 'I'll marry you this very night, Merry Ann,' says I, 'though you hedn't a stitch of clothing at all!'

" 'Git out, you sassy Sam,' says she, slapping my face. Then I kissed her in her very mouth, and a'ter that we walked on together, I leading the mar'.

"Says she, as we neared the house, 'Sam, let me go before, or stay hyar in the thick, and you go in by yourself. Daddy's in the hall, smoking his pipe and reading the newspapers.'

" 'We'll walk in together,' says I, quite consekential.

"Says she, 'I'm so afeard.'

" 'Don't you be afeard, Merry Ann,' says I; 'you'll see that all will come out jest as I tells you. We'll be hitched to-night, ef Parson Stovall, or any other parson, kin be got to tie us up!'

"Says she, suddenly, 'Sam, you're a-walking lame, I'm a-thinking. What's the matter? Hev you hurt yourself any way?'

"Says I, 'It's only owing to my not balancing my accounts even in my pockets. You see I feel so much like flying in the air with the idee of marrying you to-night that I filled my pockets with rocks, jest to keep me down.'

" 'I do think, Sam, you're a leetle cracked in the upper story.'

" 'Well,' says I, 'ef so, the crack has let in a blessed chaince of the beautifulest sunlight! You'll see! Cracked, indeed! Ha, ha, ha! Wait till I've done with your daddy! I'm gwine to square accounts with *him*, and, I reckon, when I'm done with him, you'll guess that the crack's in *his* skull, and not in mine.'

" 'What! you wouldn't knock my father, Sam!' says she, drawing off from me and looking skeary.

" 'Don't you be afeard; but it's very sartin, ef our heads don't come together, Merry Ann, you won't hev me for your husband to-night. And that's what I've swore upon. Hyar we air!'

"When we got to the yard I led in the mar', and Merry Ann she ran away from me and dodged round the house. I hitched the mar' to the post, took off the saddle-bags, which was mighty heavy, and walked into the house stiff enough I tell you, though the gould in my pockets pretty much weighed me down as I walked.

"Well, in I walked, and thar sat the old Squire smoking his pipe and reading the newspaper. He looked at me through his specs over the newspaper, and when he seed who 'twas his mouth put on that same conceited sort of grin and smile that he ginerally hed when he spoke to me.

" 'Well,' says he, gruffly enough, 'it's you, Sam Snaffles, is it?'

Then he seems to diskiver my new clothes and boots, and he sings out, 'Heigh! you're tip-toe fine to-day! What fool of a shop-keeper in Spartanburg have you tuk in this time, Sam?'

"Says I, cool enough, 'I'll answer all them iligant questions a'ter a while, Squire; but would prefar to see to business fust.'

" 'Business!' says he; 'and what business kin you hev with me, I wants to know?'

" 'You shill know, Squire, soon enough; and I only hopes it will be to your liking a'ter you l'arn it.'

"So I laid my saddle-bags down at my feet and tuk a chair quite at my ease; and I could see that he was all astare in wonderment at what he thought my sassiness. As I felt I had my hook in his gills, though he didn't know it yit, I felt in the humor to tickle him and play him as we does a trout.

"Says I, 'Squire Hopson, you owes a sartin amount of money, say $350, with intrust on it for now three years, to Dr. Columbus Mills.'

"At this he squares round, looks me full in the face, and says:

" 'What the old Harry's that to you?'

"Says I, gwine on cool and straight, 'You gin him a mortgage on this fairm for security.'

" 'What's that to you?' says he.

" 'The mortgage is over-due by two years, Squire,' says I.

" 'What the old Harry's all that to you, I say?' he fairly roared out.

" 'Well, nothing much, I reckon. The $350, with three years' intrust at seven per cent., making it now—I've calkelated it all without compounding—something over $425—well, Squire, that's not much to *you*, I reckon, with your large capital. But it's something to me.'

" 'But I ask you again, Sir,' he says, 'what is all this to you?'

" 'Jist about what I tells you—say $425; and I've come hyar this morning, bright and airly, in hope you'll be able to square up and satisfy the mortgage. Hyar's the dockyment.'

"And I drawed the paper from my breast pocket.

" 'And you tell me that Dr. Mills sent you hyar,' says he, 'to collect this money?'

" 'No; I come myself on my own hook.'

" 'Well,' says he, 'you shill hev your answer at onst. Take that paper back to Dr. Mills and tell him that I'll take an airly opportunity to call and arrange the business with him. You hev your answer, Sir,' he says, quite grand, 'and the sooner you makes yourself scarce the better.'

" 'Much obleeged to you, Squire, for your ceveelity,' says I;

'but I ain't quite satisfied with that answer. I've come for the money due on this paper, and must hev it, Squaire, or thar will be what the lawyers call *four closures* upon it!'

" 'Enough! Tell Dr. Mills I will answer his demand in person.'

" 'You needn't trouble yourself, Squaire; for ef you'll jest look at the back of that paper, and read the 'signmeant, you'll see that you've got to settle with Sam Snaffles, and not with Columbus Mills!'

"Then he snatches up the dockyment, turns it over, and reads the rigilar 'signmeant, writ in Columbus Mills's own handwrite.

"Then the Squaire looks at me with a great stare, and he says, to himself like:

" 'It's a *bonny fodder* 'signmeant.'

" 'Yes,' says I, 'it's *bonny fodder*—rigilar in law—and the titles all made out complete to me, Sam Snaffles; signed, sealed, and delivered, as the lawyers says it.'

" 'And how the old Harry come you by this paper?' says he.

"I was gitting riled, and I was detarmined, this time, to gin my hook a pretty sharp jerk in his gills; so I says:

" 'What the old Harry's that to *you*, Squaire? Thar's but one question 'twixt us two—air you ready to pay that money down on the hub, at onst, to me, Sam Snaffles?'

" 'No, Sir, I am not.'

" 'How long a time will you ax from me, by way of marciful indulgence?'

" 'It must be some time yit,' says he, quite sulky; and then he goes on agin:

" 'I'd like to know how you come by that 'signmeant, Mr. Snaffles.'

"Mr. Snaffles! Ah! ha!

" 'I don't see any neecessity,' says I, 'for answering any questions. Thar's the dockyment to speak for itself. You see that Columbus Mills 'signs to me for full *con*sideration. That means I paid him!'

" 'And why did you buy this mortgage?'

" 'You might as well ax me how I come by the money to buy any thing,' says I.

" 'Well, I do ax you,' says he.

" 'And I answers you,' says I, 'in the very words from your own mouth, What the old Harry's that to you?'

" 'This is hardly 'spectful, Mr. Snaffles,' says he.

"Says I, ' 'Spectful gits only what 'spectful gives! Ef any man but you, Squaire, hed been so onrespectful in his talk to me as you hev been I'd ha' mashed his muzzle! But I don't wish to be onrespectful. All I axes is the civil answer. I wants to know when you kin pay this money?'

" 'I kain't say, Sir.'

" 'Well, you see, I thought as how you couldn't pay, spite of all your "capital," as you hedn't paid even the *intrust* on it for three years; and, to tell you the truth, I was in hopes you couldn't pay, as I hed a liking for this fairm always; and as I am jest about to git married, you see—'

" 'Who the old Harry air you gwine to marry?' says he.

" 'What the old Harry's that to you?' says I, giving him as good as he sent. But I went on:

" 'You may be sure it's one of the woman kind. I don't hanker a'ter a wife with a beard; and I expects—God willing, weather premitting, and the parson being sober—to be married this very night!'

" 'To-night!' says he, not knowing well what to say.

" 'Yes; you see I've got my wedding-breeches on. I'm to be married to-night, and I wants to take my wife to her own fairm as soon as I kin. Now, you see, Squaire, I all along set my hairt on this fairm of yourn, and I determined, ef ever I could git the "capital," to git hold of it; and that was the idee I hed when I bought the 'signmeant of the mortgage from Columbus Mills. So, you see, ef you kain't pay a'ter three years, you never kin pay, I reckon; and ef I don't git my money this day, why—I kain't help it—the lawyers will hev to see to the *four closures* to-morrow!'

" 'Great God, Sir!' says he, rising out of his chair, and crossing the room up and down, 'do you coolly propose to turn me and my family headlong out of my house?'

" 'Well now,' says I, 'Squaire, that's not edzactly the way to put it. As I reads this dockyment'—and I tuk up and put the mortgage in my pocket—'the house and fairm are *mine* by law. They onst was yourn; but it wants nothing now but the *four closures* to make 'em mine.'

" 'And would you force the sale of property worth $2000 and more for a miserable $400?'

" 'It must sell for what it'll bring, Squaire; and I stands ready to buy it for my wife, you see, ef it costs me twice as much as the mortgage.'

" 'Your wife!' says he; 'who the old Harry is she? You once pertended to have an affection for my da'ter.'

" 'So I hed; but you hedn't the proper affection for your da'ter that I hed. You prefar'd money to her affections, and you driv me off to git "capital!" Well, I tuk your advice, and I've got the capital.'

" 'And whar the old Harry,' said he, 'did you git it?'

" 'Well, I made good tairms with the old devil for a hundred years, and he found me in the money.'

" 'It must hev been so,' said he. 'You waur not the man to git capital in any other way.'

"Then he goes on: 'But what becomes of your pertended affection for my da'ter?'

" ' 'Twa'n't pertended; but you throwed yourself betwixt us with all your force, and broke the gal's hairt, and broke mine, so far as you could; and as I couldn't live without company, I hed to look out for myself and find a wife as I could. I tell you, as I'm to be married to-night, and as I've swore a most etarnal oath to hev this fairm, you'll hev to raise the wind to-day, and square off with me, or the lawyers will be at you with the *four closures* to-morrow, bright and airly.'

" 'Dod dern you!' he cries out. 'Does you want to drive me mad!'

" 'By no manner of means,' says I, jest about as cool and quiet as a cowcumber.

"But he was at biling heat. He was all over in a stew and a fever. He filled his pipe and lighted it, and then smashed it over the chimbly. Then he crammed the newspaper in the fire, and crushed it into the blaze with his boot. Then he turned to me, suddent, and said:

" 'Yes, you pertended to love my da'ter, and now you are pushing her father to desperation. Now ef you ever did love Merry Ann, honestly, raally, truly, and *bonny fodder,* you couldn't help loving her yit. And yit, hyar you're gwine to marry another woman, that, prehaps, you don't affection at all.'

" 'It's quite a sensible view you takes of the subject,' says I; 'the only pity is that you didn't take the same squint at it long ago, when I axed you to let me hev Merry Ann. *Then* you didn't valley her affections or mine. You hed no thought of nothing but the "capital" then, and the affections might all go to Jericho, for what you keered! I'd ha' married Merry Ann, and she me, and we'd ha' got on for a spell in a log cabin, for, though I was poor, I hed the genwine grit of a man, and would come to something, and we'd ha' got on; and yit, without any "capital" your own self, and kivered up with debt as with a winter over-coat, hyar, you waur positive that I shouldn't hev your da'ter, and you waur a-preparing to sell her hyar to an old sour-tempered bachelor, more than double her age. Dern the capital! A man's the best capital for any woman, ef so be he *is* a man. Bekaise, ef he be a man, he'll work out cl'ar, though he may hev a long straining for it through the sieve. Dern the capital! You've as good as sold that gal child to old Grimstead, jest from your love of money!'

" 'But she won't hev him,' says he.

" 'The wiser gal child,' says I. 'Ef you only hed onderstood me and that poor child, I hed it in me to make the "capital"—dern the capital!—and now you've ruined her, and yourself, and me, and all; and dern my buttons but I must be married to-night, and jest as soon a'ter as the lawyers kin fix it I must hev this fairm for my wife. My hairt's set on it, and I've swore it a dozen o' times on the Holy Hokies!'

"The poor old Squaire fairly sweated; but he couldn't say much. He'd come up to me and say:

" 'Ef you only did love Merry Ann!'

" 'Oh,' says I, 'what's the use of your talking that? Ef you only hed ha' loved your own da'ter!'

"Then the old chap begun to cry, and as I seed that I jest kicked over my saddle-bags lying at my feet, and the silver Mexicans rolled out—a bushel on 'em, I reckon—and, O Lawd! how the old fellow jumped, staring with all his eyes at me and the dollars!

" 'It's money!' says he.

" 'Yes,' says I, 'jest a few hundreds of thousands of *my* "capital." ' I didn't stop at the figgers, you see.

"Then he turns to me and says, 'Sam Snaffles, you're a most wonderful man. You're a mystery to me. Whar, in the name of God, hev you been? and what hev you been doing? and whar did you git all this power of capital?'

"I jest laughed, and went to the door and called Merry Ann. She come mighty quick. I reckon she was watching and waiting.

"Says I, 'Merry Ann, that's money. Pick it up and put it back in the saddle-bags, ef you please.'

"Then says I, turning to the old man, 'Thar's that whole bushel of Mexicans, I reckon. Thar monstrous heavy. My old mar'—ax her about her ribs now!—she fairly squelched onder the weight of me and that money. And I'm pretty heavy loaded myself. I must lighten; with your leave, Squaire.'

"And I pulled out a leetle doeskin bag of gould half eagles from my right-hand pocket and poured them out upon the table; then I emptied my left-hand pocket, then the side pockets of the coat, then the skairt pockets, and jist spread the shiners out upon the table.

"Merry Ann was fairly frightened, and run out of the room; then the old woman she come in, and as the old Squaire seed her, he tuk her by the shoulder and said:

" 'Jest you look at that thar.'

"And when she looked and seed, the poor old hypercritical scamp sinner turned round to me and flung her airms round my neck, and said:

" 'I always said you waur the only right man for Merry Ann.'

"The old spooney!

"Well, when I hed let 'em look enough, and wonder enough, I jest turned Merry Ann and her mother out of the room.

"The old Squire, he waur a-setting down agin in his airm-chair, not edzactly knowing what to say or what to do, but watching all my motions, jest as sharp as a cat watches a mouse when she is hafe hungry.

"Thar was all the Mexicans put back in the saddle-bags, but he hed seen 'em, and thar was all the leetle bags of gould spread upon the table; the gould—hafe and quarter eagles—jest lying out of the mouths of the leetle bags as ef wanting to creep back agin.

"And thar sot the old Squire, looking at 'em all as greedy as a fish-hawk down upon a pairch in the river. And, betwixt a whine and a cry and a talk, he says:

" 'Ah, Sam Snaffles, ef you ever did love my leetle Merry Ann, you would never marry any other woman.'

"Then you ought to ha' seed me. I felt myself sixteen feet high, and jest as solid as a chestnut oak. I walked up to the old man, and I tuk him quiet by the collar of his coat, with my thumb and forefinger, and I said:

" 'Git up, Squire, for a bit.'

"And up he got.

"Then I marched him to the big glass agin the wall, and I said to him: 'Look, ef you please.'

"And he said, 'I'm looking.'

"And I said, 'What does you see?'

"He answered, 'I sees you and me.'

"I says, 'Look agin, and tell me what you *obzarves*.'

" 'Well,' says he, 'I obzarves.'

"And says I, 'What does your *obzarving* amount to? That's the how.'

"And says he, 'I sees a man alongside of me, as good-looking and handsome a young man as ever I seed in all my life.'

" 'Well,' says I, 'that's a correct obzarvation. But,' says I, 'what does you see of *your own self?*'

" 'Well, I kain't edzackly say.'

" 'Look good!' says I. 'Obzarve.'

"Says he, 'Don't ax me.'

" 'Now,' says I, 'that won't edzactly do. I tell you now, look good, and ax yourself ef you're the sawt of looking man that hes any right to be a feyther-in-law to a fine, young, handsome-looking fellow like me, what's got the "capital?" '

"Then he laughed out at the humor of the sitivation; and he says, 'Well, Sam Snaffles, you've got me dead this time. You're a different man from what I thought you. But, Sam, you'll confess, I reckon, that ef I hedn't sent you off with a flea in your ear when I hed you up afore the looking-glass, you'd never ha' gone to work to git in the "capital." '

" 'I don't know *that*, Squaire,' says I. 'Sarcumstances sarve to make a man take one road when he mout take another; but when you meets a man what has the hairt to love a woman strong as a lion, and to fight an inimy big as a buffalo, he's got the raal grit in him. You knowed I was young, and I was poor, and you knowed the business of a hunter is a mighty poor business ef the man ain't born to it. Well, I didn't do much at it jest bekaise my hairt was so full of Merry Ann; and you should ha' made a calkilation and allowed for *that*. But you poked your fun at me and riled me consumedly; but I was determined that you shouldn't break *my* hairt or the hairt of Merry Ann. Well, you hed your humors, and I've tried to take the change out of you. And now, ef you raally thinks, a'ter that obzarvation in the glass, that you kin make a respectable feyther-in-law to sich a fine-looking fellow as me, what's got the "capital," jest say the word, and we'll call Merry Ann in to bind the bargin. And you must talk out quick, for the wedding's to take place this very night. I've swore it by the etarnal Hokies.'

" 'To-night!' says he.

" 'Look at the "capital" ' says I; and I pinted to the gould on the table and the silver in the saddle-bags.

" 'But, Lawd love you, Sam,' says he, 'it's so suddent, and we kain't make the preparations in time.'

"Says I, 'Look at the "capital," Squaire, and dern the preparations!'

" 'But,' says he, 'we hain't time to ax the company.'

" 'Dern the company!' says I; 'I don't b'lieve in company the very night a man gits married. His new wife's company enough for him ef he's sensible.'

" 'But, Sam,' says he, 'it's not possible to git up a supper by to-night.'

"Says I, 'Look you, Squaire, the very last thing a man wants on his wedding night is supper.'

"Then he said something about the old woman, his wife.

"Says I, 'Jest you call her in and show her the "capital." ' "

"So he called in the old woman, and then in come Merry Ann, and thar was great hemmings and hawings; and the old woman she said:

" 'I've only got the one da'ter, Sam, and we *must* hev a big wedding! We must spread ourselves. We've got a smart chaince of friends and acquaintances, you see, and 'twon't be decent onless we axes them, and they won't like it! We *must* make a big show for the honor and 'spectability of the family.'

"Says I, 'Look you, old lady! I've swore a most tremendous oath, by the Holy Hokies, that Merry Ann and me air to be married this very night, and I kain't break sich an oath as that! Merry Ann,' says I, 'you wouldn't hev me break sich a tremendous oath as that?'

"And, all in a trimble, she says, 'Never, Sam! No!'

" 'You hyar that, old lady!' says I. 'We marries to-night, by the Holy Hokies! and we'll hev no company but old Parson Stovall, to make the hitch; and Merry Ann and me go off by sunrise to-morrow morning—you hyar?—to my own fairm, whar thar's a great deal of furniter fixing for her to do. A'ter that you kin ad-vartise the whole county to come in, ef you please, and eat all the supper you kin spread! Now hurry up,' says I, 'and git as ready as you kin, for I'm gwine to ride over to Parson Stovall's this minit. I'll be back to dinner in hafe an hour. Merry Ann, you gether up that gould and silver, and lock it up. It's *our* "capital!" As for you, Squaire, thar's the mortgage on your fairm, which Merry Ann shill give you, to do as you please with it, as soon as the parson has done the hitch, and I kin call Merry Ann, Mrs. Snaffles— Madam Merry Ann Snaffles, and so forth, and aforesaid.'

"I laid down the law that time for all parties, and showed the old Squaire sich a picter of himself, and me standing aside him, looking seven foot high, at the least, that I jest worked the business 'cording to my own pleasure. When neither the daddy nor the mammy hed any thing more to say, I jumped on my mar' and rode over to old Parson Stovall.

"Says I, 'Parson, thar's to be a hitch to-night, and you're to see a'ter the right knot. You knows what I means. I wants you over at Squaire Hopson's. Me and Merry Ann, his da'ter, mean to hop the twig to-night, and you're to see that we hop squar', and that all's even, 'cording to the law, Moses, and the profits! I stand treat, Parson, and you won't be the worse for your riding. I pays in gould!'

"So he promised to come by dusk; and come he did. The old lady hed got some supper, and tried her best to do what she could at sich short notice. The venison ham was mighty fine, I reckon, for Parson Stovall played a great stick at it; and ef they hedn't cooked up four of my wild-geese, then the devil's an angel of light, and Sam Snaffles no better than a sinner! And thar was any quantity of jimmyjohns, peach and honey considered. Parson Stovall was a great feeder, and I begun to think he never would be done. But at last he wiped his mouth, swallowed his fifth cup of coffee, washed it down with a stiff dram of peach and honey, wiped his mouth agin, and pulled out his prayer-book, psalmody, and Holy Scrip —three volumes in all—and he hemmed three times, and begun to look out for the marriage text, but begun with giving out the 100th Psalm.

" 'With one consent, let's all unite—'

" 'No,' says I, 'Parson; not all! It's only Merry Ann and me what's to unite to-night!'

"Jest then, afore he could answer, who should pop in but old bachelor Grimstead! and he looked round 'bout him, specially upon me and the parson, as ef to say:

" 'What the old Harry's they doing hyar!'

"And I could see that the old Squaire was oneasy. But the blessed old Parson Stovall, he gin 'em no time for ixplanation or palaver; but he gits up, stands up squar', looks solemn as a meat-axe, and he says:

" 'Let the parties which I'm to bind together in the holy bonds of wedlock stand up before me!'

"And, Lawd bless you, as he says the words, what should that old skunk of a bachelor do, but he gits up, stately as an old buck in spring time, and he marches over to my Merry Ann! But I was too much and too spry for him. I puts in betwixt 'em, and I takes the old bachelor by his coat-collar, 'twixt my thumb and forefinger, and afore he knows whar he is, I marches him up to the big looking-glass, and I says:

" 'Look!'

" 'Well,' says he, 'what?'

" 'Look good,' says I.

" 'I'm looking,' says he. 'But what do you mean, Sir?'

"Says I, 'Obzarve! Do you see yourself? Obzarve!'

" 'I reckon I do,' says he.

" 'Then,' says I, 'ax yourself the question, ef you're the sawt of looking man to marry my Merry Ann.'

"Then the old Squaire burst out a-laughing. He couldn't help it.

" 'Capital!' says he.

" 'It's capital,' says I. 'But hyar we air, Parson. Put on the hitch, jest as quick as you kin clinch it; for thar's no telling how many slips thar may be 'twixt the cup and the lips when these hungry old bachelors air about.'

" 'Who gives away this young woman?' axes the parson; and the Squire stands up and does the thing needful. I hed the ring ready, and before the parson had quite got through, old Grimstead vamoosed.

"He waur a leetle slow in onderstanding that he warn't wanted, and warn't, nohow, any party to the business. But he and the Squire hed a mighty quarrel a'terwards, and ef 't hedn't been for me, he'd ha' licked the Squire. He was able to do it; but I jest cocked my cap at him one day, and, says I, in the Injin language:

"'Yaou!' And he didn't know what I meant; but I looked tom-ahawks at him, so he gin ground; and he's getting old so fast that you kin see him growing downwards all the time.

"All that, Jedge, is jest thirteen years ago; and me and Merry Ann git on famously, and thar's no eend to the capital! Gould breeds like the cows, and it's only needful to squeeze the bags now and then to make Merry Ann happy as a tomtit. Thirteen years of married life, and look at me! You see for yourself, Jedge, that I'm not much the worse for wear; and I kin answer for Merry Ann, too, though, Jedge, we hev hed thirty-six children."

"What!" says I, "thirty-six children in thirteen years!"

The "Big Lie" roared aloud.

"Hurrah, Sharp! Go it! You're making it spread! That last shot will make the Jedge know that you're a right truthful sinner, of a Saturday night, and in the 'Lying Camp.' "

"To be sure! You see, Merry Ann keeps on. But you've only got to do the ciphering for yourself. Here, now, Jedge, look at it. Count for yourself. First we had *three* gal children, you see. Very well! Put down three. Then we had *six* boys, one every year for four years; and then, the fifth year, Merry Ann throwed deuce. Now put down the six boys a'ter the three gals, and ef that don't make thirty-six, thar's no snakes in all Flurriday!

"Now, men," says Sam, "let's liquor all round, and drink the health of Mrs. Merry Ann Snaffles and the thirty-six children, all alive and kicking; and glad to see you, Jedge, and the rest of the company. We're doing right well; but I hes, every now and then, to put my thumb and forefinger on the Squire's collar, and show him his face in the big glass, and call on him for an *obzarvation*— for he's mighty fond of *going shar's* in my 'capital.' "

Madison Tensas, M.D.
(Henry Clay Lewis)
(1825–1850)

Madison Tensas was the pseudonym of Henry Clay Lewis, who was born in Charleston, South Carolina. His father was a native Frenchman who had come to the United States to fight in the Revolution. His mother was a native of Charleston and member of a prominent Charleston family. When Lewis was four years old, his family moved to Cincinnati, Ohio, where he lived for six years. After his mother's death in 1831, he stayed with a brother, but ran away and worked for a short time as a cabin boy on a steamboat. He was eventually taken in by another brother in Yazoo City, Mississippi. For five years he received little formal education, and worked mainly in the cotton fields. At the age of 16, however, he was apprenticed to a doctor, and he made up his mind to study medicine. He managed to enroll in the Louisville Medical Institute, and in 1846 received his medical degree. He moved to Louisiana to practice, and for the next five years enjoyed a prosperous, though difficult, career in the isolated bayous and on the remote plantations where his patients lived. Before moving to Louisiana, he had already begun writing sketches of his life, and had published some of them in William T. Porter's Spirit of the Times. *He continued writing as a doctor in Louisiana, and put together his only book, a half-autobiographical collection of tales and remembrances published in 1850 as* Odd Leaves from the Life of a Louisiana "Swamp Doctor". *It was published under the pseudonym Madison Tensas, M.D., a name Lewis took from the place where he first lived in Louisiana, Madison Parish, where the Tensas River joins Bayou Despair.* Odd Leaves *is divided into four sections, roughly following an autobiographical chronology: "Runaway," "Sawbones' Apprentice," "Grave Rat" (concerning his days as a medical student in Louisville), and "Swamp Doctor." Recognized as one of the most realistic writers in the Southwestern school of humorists, Lewis died in a drowning accident while returning home exhausted after battling a cholera epidemic. "The Indefatigable Bear-Hunter" first appeared in book form in* Odd Leaves from the Life of a Louisiana "Swamp Doctor" *(1850).*

THE INDEFATIGABLE
BEAR-HUNTER

✿

In my round of practice, I occasionally meet with men whose peculiarities stamp them as belonging to a class composed only of themselves. So different are they in appearance, habits, taste, from the majority of mankind, that it is impossible to classify them, and you have therefore to set them down as queer birds "of a feather," that none resemble sufficiently to associate with.

I had a patient once who was one of these queer ones; gigantic in stature, uneducated, fearless of real danger, yet timorous as a child of superstitious perils, born literally in the woods, never having been in a city in his life, and his idea of one being that it was a place where people met together to make whiskey, and form plans for swindling country folks. To view him at one time, you would think him only a whiskey-drinking, bear-fat-loving mortal; at other moments, he would give vent to ideas, proving that beneath his rough exterior there ran a fiery current of high enthusiastic ambition.

It is a favourite theory of mine, and one that I am fond of consoling myself with, for my own insignificance, that there is no man born who is not capable of attaining distinction, and no occupation that does not contain a path leading to fame. To bide our time is all that is necessary. I had expressed this view in the hearing of Mik-hoo-tah, for so was the subject of this sketch called, and it seemed to chime in with his feelings exactly. Born in the woods, and losing his parents early, he had forgotten his real name, and the bent of his genius inclining him to the slaying of bears, he had been given, even when a youth, the name of Mik-hoo-tah, signifying "the grave of bears," by his Indian associates and admirers.

To glance in and around his cabin, you would have thought that the place had been selected for ages past by the bear tribe to yield up their spirits in, so numerous were the relics. Little chance, I ween, had the cold air to whistle through that hut, so thickly was it tapestried with the soft, downy hides, the darkness of the surface relieved occasionally by the skin of a tender fawn, or the short-haired irascible panther. From the joists depended bear-hams and tongues innumerable, and the ground outside was literally white with bones. Ay, he was a bear-hunter, in its most comprehensive sense—the chief of that vigorous band, whose occupation is nearly gone—crushed beneath the advancing strides of romance-destroying civilization. When his horn sounded—so tradition ran—the bears began to draw lots to see who should die that day, for painful experience had told them the uselessness of all endeavouring to escape. The "Big Bear of Arkansas" would not have given him an hour's extra work, or raised a fresh wrinkle on his already care-corrugated brow. But, though almost daily imbruing his hands in the blood of Bruin, Mik-hoo-tah had not become an impious or cruel-hearted man. Such was his piety, that he never killed a bear without getting down on his knees—to skin it—and praying to be d—ned if it warn't a buster; and such his softness of heart, that he often wept, when he, by mistake, had killed a suckling bear—depriving her poor offspring of a mother's care—and found her too poor to be eaten. So indefatigable had he become in his pursuit, that the bears bid fair to disappear from the face of the swamp, and be known to posterity only through the one mentioned in Scripture, that assisted Elisha to punish the impertinent children, when an accident occurred to the hunter, which raised their hopes of not being entirely exterminated.

One day, Mik happened to come unfortunately in contact with a stray grizzly fellow, who, doubtless in the indulgence of an adventurous spirit, had wandered away from the Rocky Mountains, and formed a league for mutual protection with his black and more effeminate brethren of the swamp. Mik saluted him, as he approached, with an ounce ball in the forehead, to avenge half a dozen of his best dogs, who lay in fragments around; the bullet flattened upon his impenetrable skull, merely infuriating the monster; and before Mik could reload, it was upon him. Seizing him by the leg, it bore him to the ground, and ground the limb to atoms. But before it could attack a more vital part, the knife of the dauntless hunter had cloven its heart, and it dropped dead upon the bleeding form of its slayer, in which condition they were shortly found by Mik's comrades. Making a litter of branches, they placed Mik upon it, and proceeded with all haste to their camp, sending one of the company by a near cut for me, as I was the nearest physician. When I reached their temporary shelter I found

Mik doing better than I could have expected, with the exception of his wounded leg, and that, from its crushed and mutilated condition, I saw would have to be amputated immediately, of which I informed Mik. As I expected, he opposed it vehemently; but I convinced him of the impossibility of saving it, assuring him if it were not amputated, he would certainly die, and appealed to his good sense to grant permission, which he did at last. The next difficulty was to procure amputating instruments, the rarity of surgical operations, and the generally slender purse of the "Swamp Doctor," not justifying him in purchasing expensive instruments. A couple of bowie-knives, one ingeniously hacked and filed into a saw—a tourniquet made of a belt and piece of stick—a gun-screw converted for the time into a tenaculum—and some buckskin slips for ligatures, completed my case of instruments for amputation. The city physician may smile at this recital, but I assure him many a more difficult operation than the amputation of a leg has been performed by his humble brother in the "swamp," with far more simple means than those I have mentioned. The preparations being completed, Mik refused to have his arms bound, and commenced singing a bear song; and throughout the whole operation, which was necessarily tedious, he never uttered a groan, or missed a single stave. The next day, I had him conveyed by easy stages to his pre-emption; and tending assiduously, in the course of a few weeks, he had recovered sufficiently for me to cease attentions. I made him a wooden leg, which answered a good purpose; and with a sigh of regret for the spoiling of such a good hunter, I struck him from my list of patients.

A few months passed over and I heard nothing more of him. Newer, but not brighter, stars were in the ascendant, filling with their deeds the clanging trump of bear-killing fame, and, but for the quantity of bear-blankets in the neighbouring cabins, and the painful absence of his usual present of bear-hams, Mik-hoo-tah bid fair to suffer that fate most terrible to aspiring ambitionists—forgetfulness during life. The sun, in despair at the stern necessity which compelled him to yield up his tender offspring, day, to the gloomy grave of darkness, had stretched forth his long arms, and, with the tenacity of a drowning man clinging to a straw, had clutched the tender whispering straw-like topmost branches of the trees—in other words it was near sunset—when I arrived at home from a long wearisome semi-ride-and-swim through the swamp. Receiving a negative to my inquiry whether there were any new calls, I was felicitating myself upon a quiet night beside my tidy bachelor hearth, undisturbed by crying children, babbling women, or amorous cats—the usual accompaniments of married life—

when, like a poor henpecked Benedick crying for peace when there is no peace, I was doomed to disappointment. Hearing the splash of a paddle in the bayou running before the door, I turned my head towards the bank, and soon beheld, first the tail of a coon, next his body, a human face, and, the top of the bank being gained, a full-proportioned form clad in the garments which, better than any printed label, wrote him down raftsman, trapper, bear-hunter. He was a messenger from the indefatigable bear-hunter, Mik-hoo-tah. Asking him what was the matter, as soon as he could get the knots untied which two-thirds drunkenness had made in his tongue, he informed me, to my sincere regret, that Mik went out that morning on a bear-hunt, and in a fight with one had got his leg broke all to flinders, if possible worse than the other, and that he wanted me to come quickly. Getting into the canoe, which awaited me, I wrapped myself in my blanket, and yielding to my fatigue, was soon fast asleep. I did not awaken until the canoe striking against the bank, as it landed at Mik's pre-emption, nearly threw me in the bayou, and entirely succeeded with regard to my half-drunken paddler, who—like the sailor who circumnavigated the world and then was drowned in a puddle-hole in his own garden—had escaped all the perils of the tortuous bayou to be pitched overboard when there was nothing to do but step out and tie the dug-out. Assisting him out of the water, we proceeded to the house, when, to my indignation, I learnt that the drunken messenger had given me the long trip for nothing, Mik only wanting me to make him a new wooden leg, the old one having been completely demolished that morning.

Relieving myself by a satisfactory oath, I would have returned that night, but the distance was too great for one fatigued as I was, so I had to content myself with such accommodations as Mik's cabin afforded, which, to one blessed like myself with the happy faculty of ready adaptation to circumstances, was not a very difficult task.

I was surprised to perceive the change in Mik's appearance. From nearly a giant, he had wasted to a mere huge bony framework; the skin of his face clung tightly to the bones, and showed nothing of those laughter-moving features that were wont to adorn his visage; only his eye remained unchanged, and it had lost none of its brilliancy—the flint had lost none of its fire.

"What on earth is the matter with you, Mik? I have never seen any one fall off so fast; you have wasted to a skeleton—surely you must have the consumption."

"Do you think so, Doc? I'll soon show you whether the old bellows has lost any of its force!" and hopping to the door, which he threw wide open, he gave a death-hug rally to his dogs, in such a loud and piercing tone, that I imagined a steam whistle was being discharged in my ear, and for several moments could hear nothing distinctly.

"That will do! stop!" I yelled, as I saw Mik drawing in his breath preparatory to another effort of his vocal strength; "I am satisfied you have not got consumption; but what has wasted you so, Mik? Surely, you ain't in love?"

"Love! h–ll! you don't suppose, Doc, even if I was 'tarmined to make a cussed fool of myself, that there is any gal in the swamp that could stand that hug, do you?" and catching up a huge bull-dog, who lay basking himself by the fire, he gave him such a squeeze that the animal yelled with pain, and for a few moments appeared dead. "No, Doc, it's grief, pure sorrur, sorrur, Doc! when I looks at what I is now and what I used to be! Jes think, Doc, of the fust hunter in the swamp having his sport spilte, like bar-meat in summer without salt! Jes think of a man standin' up one day and blessing old Master for having put bar in creation, and the next cussing high heaven and low h–ll 'cause he couldn't 'sist in puttin' them out! Warn't it enough to bring tears to the eyes of an Injun tater, much less take the fat off a bar-hunter? Doc, I fell off like 'simmons arter frost, and folks as doubted me, needn't had asked whether I war 'ceitful or not, for they could have seed plum threw me! The bar and painter got so saucy that they'd cum to the tother side of the bayou and see which could talk the impudentest! 'Don't you want some bar-meat or painter blanket?' they'd ask; 'bars is monstrous fat, and painter's hide is mighty warm!' Oh! Doc, I was a miserable man! The sky warn't blue for me, the sun war always cloudy, and the shade-trees gin no shade for me. Even the dogs forgot me, and the little children quit coming and asking, 'Please, Mr. Bar-Grave, cotch me a young bar or a painter kitten.' Doc, the tears would cum in my eyes and the hot blood would cum biling up from my heart, when I'd hobble out of a sundown and hear the boys tell, as they went by, of the sport they'd had that day, and how the bar fit 'fore he was killed, and how fat he war arter he was slayed. Long arter they was gone, and the whip-poor-will had eat up their voices, I would sit out there on the old stump, and think of the things that used to hold the biggest place in my mind when I was a boy, and p'raps sense I've bin a man.

"I'd heard tell of distinction and fame, and people's names never dying, and how Washington and Franklin, and Clay and Jackson, and a heap of political dicshunary-folks, would live when their big hearts had crumbled down to a rifle-charge of dust; and I begun, too, to think, Doc, what a pleasant thing it would be to know folks a million years off would talk of me like them, and it made me 'tarmine to 'stinguish myself, and have my name put in a book with a yaller kiver. I warn't a genus, Doc, I nude that, nor I warn't dicshunary; so I determined to strike out in a new track for glory, and 'title myself to be called the 'bear-hunter of Ameriky.' Doc, my heart jump up, and I belted my hunting-shirt tighter for fear it would lepe out when I fust spoke them words out loud.

" 'The bar-hunter of Ameriky!' Doc, you know whether I war ernin' the name when I war ruined. There is not a child, white, black, Injun, or nigger, from the Arkansas line to Trinity, but what has heard of me, and I were happy when"—here a tremor of his voice and a tear glistening in the glare of the fire told the old fellow's emotion—"when—but les take a drink—Doc, I found I was dying—I war gettin' weaker and weaker—I nude your truck warn't what I needed, or I'd sent for you. A bar-hunt war the medsin that my systum required, a fust class bar-hunt, the music of the dogs, the fellers a screaming, the cane poppin', the rifles crackin', the bar growlin', the fight hand to hand, slap goes his paw, and a dog's hide hangs on one cane and his body on another, the knife glistenin' and then goin' plump up to the handle in his heart!—Oh! Doc, this was what I needed, and I swore, since death were huggin' me, anyhow, I mite as well feel his last grip in a bar-hunt.

"I seed the boys goin' long one day, and haled them to wait awhile, as I believed I would go along too. I war frade if I kept out of a hunt much longer I wood get outen practis. They laughed at me, thinkin' I war jokin'; for wat cood a sick, old, one-legged man do in a bar-hunt? how cood he get threw the swamp, and vines, and canes, and backwater? and s'pose he mist the bar, how war he to get outen the way?

"But I war 'tarmined on goin'; my dander was up, and I swore I wood go, tellin' them if I coodent travel 'bout much, I could take a stand. Seein' it war no use tryin' to 'swade me, they saddled my poney, and off we started. I felt better right off. I knew I cuddent do much in the chase, so I told the fellers I would go to the cross-path stand, and wate for the bar, as he would be sarten to cum by thar. You have never seed the cross-path stand, Doc. It's the singularest place in the swamp. It's rite in the middle of a cane-brake, thicker than har on a bar-hide, down in a deep sink, that looks like the devil had cummenst diggin' a skylite for his pre-emption. I knew it war a dangersome place for a well man to go in, much less a one-leg cripple; but I war 'tarmined that time to give a deal on the dead wood, and play my hand out. The boys gin me time to get to the stand, and then cummenst the drive. The

bar seemed 'tarmined on disappinting me, for the fust thing I heard
of the dogs and bar, they was outen hearing. Everything got quiet,
and I got so wrathy at not being able to foller up the chase, that
I cust till the trees cummenst shedding their leaves and small
branches, when I herd them lumbrin back, and I nude they war
makin' to me. I primed old 'bar death' fresh, and rubbed the frizin,
for it war no time for rifle to get to snappin'. Thinks I, if I happen
to miss, I'll try what virtue there is in a knife—when, Doc, my
knife war gone. H–ll! bar, for God's sake have a soft head, and
die easy, for I *can't* run!

"Doc, you've hearn a bar bustin' threw a cane-brake, and know
how near to a harrycane it is. I almost cummenst dodgin' the trees,
thinkin' it war the best in the shop one a comin', for it beat the
loudest thunder ever I heard; that ole bar did, comin' to get his
death from an ole, one-legged cripple, what had slayed more of
his brethren than his nigger foot had ever made trax in the mud.
Doc, he heerd a *monstrus long ways ahead of the dogs.* I warn't
skeered, but I must own, as I had but one shot, an' no knife, I
wud have prefurd they had been closer. But here he cum! he bar—
big as a bull—boys off h–llwards—dogs nowhar—no knife—but
one shot—*and only one leg that cood run!*

"The bar 'peered s'prised to see me standin' ready for him in
the openin'; for it war currently reported 'mong his brethren that
I war either dead, or no use for bar. I thought fust he war skeered;
and, Doc, I b'leve he war, till he cotch a sight of my wooden leg,
and that toch his pride, for he knew he would be hist outen every
she bear's company, ef he run from a poor, sickly, one-legged
cripple, so on he cum, a small river of slobber pourin from his
mouth, and the blue smoke curlin outen his ears. I tuck good aim
at his left, and let drive. The ball struck him on the eyebrow, and
glanced off, only stunnin' him for a moment, jes givin' me time to
club my rifle, an' on he kum, as fierce as old grizzly. As he got in
reach, I gin him a lick 'cross the temples, brakin' the stock in fifty
pieces, an' knockin' him senseless. I struv to foller up the lick,
when, Doc, I war fast—my timber toe had run inter the ground,
and I cuddent git out, though I jerked hard enuf almost to bring
my thigh out of joint. I stuped to unscrew the infurnal thing, when
the bar cum too, and cum at me agen. Vim! I tuck him over the
head, and, cochunk, he keeled over. H–ll! but I cavorted and
pitched. Thar war my wust enemy, watin' for me to giv him a
finisher, an' *I cuddent* git at him. I'd cummense unscrewin' leg—
here cum bar–vim–cochunk—he'd fall out of reach—and, Doc, *I
cuddent git to him.* I kept workin' my body round, so as to unscrew
the leg, and keep the bar off till I cood 'complish it, when jes as

I tuck the last turn, and got loose from the d——d thing, here cum bar, more venimous than ever, and I nude thar war death to one out, and comin' shortly. I let him get close, an' then cum down with a perfect tornado on his head, as I thought; but the old villin had learnt the dodge—the barrel jes struck him on the side of the head, and glanst off, slinging itself out of my hands bout twenty feet 'mongst the thick cane, and thar I war in a fix sure. Bar but little hurt—no gun—no knife—no dogs—no frens–no chance to climb—*an' only one leg that cood run.* Doc, I jes cummenst makin' 'pologies to ole Master, when an idee struck me. Doc, did you ever see a piney woods nigger pullin at a sassafras root? or a suckin' pig in a tater patch arter the big yams? You has! Well, you can 'magin how I jurkt at that wudden leg, for it war the last of pea-time with me, sure, if I didn't rise 'fore bar did. At last, they both cum up, bout the same time, and I braced myself for a death struggle.

"We fit all round that holler! Fust I'd foller bar, and then bar would chase me! I'd make a lick, he'd fend off, and showin' a set of teeth that no doctor, 'cept natur, had ever wurkt at, cum tearin' at me! We both 'gan to git tired, I heard the boys and dogs cumin', so did bar, and we were both anxshus to bring the thing to a close 'fore they cum up, though I wuddent thought they were intrudin' ef they had cum up some time afore.

"I'd worn the old leg pretty well off to the second jint, when, jest 'fore I made a lick, the noise of the boys and the dogs cummin' sorter confused bar, and he made a stumble, and bein' off his guard I got a fair lick! The way that bar's flesh giv in to the soft im-presshuns of that leg war an honor to the mederkal perfeshun for having invented sich a weepun! I hollered—but you have heered me holler an' I won't describe it—I had whipped a bar in a fair hand to hand fight—me, an old sickly one-legged bar-hunter! The boys cum up, and, when they seed the ground we had fit over, they swore they would hav thought, 'stead of a bar-fight, that I had been cuttin' cane and deadenin' timber for a corn-patch, the sile war so worked up, they then handed me a knife to finish the work.

"Doc, les licker, it's a dry talk—when will you make me another leg? for bar-meat is not over plenty in the cabin, and I feel like tryin' another!"

Thomas Bangs Thorpe

(1815–1878)

Born in Westfield, Massachusetts, Thorpe grew in up Albany, New York, and New York City after the death of his father in 1819. He received some formal training as an aspiring artist, but his family lacked the resources to allow him to continue his studies. In 1837, after two years at Wesleyan University, he left for the South and settled in the Felicianas near Baton Rouge. He first tried to support himself and his wife by painting portraits of the local planters, but soon turned to the newspaper business as a more reliable career. During his long stay in Louisiana, he published and edited several newspapers, including two in New Orleans, the Commercial Times *and the* Daily Tropic. *He also turned to writing sketches and tales of the frontier South, often illustrating his own work. His first published piece, "Tom Owen, the Bee Hunter," appeared in William T. Porter's New York magazine* Spirit of the Times, *in 1839, and launched his career as one of Porter's leading Southern humorists. Through the 1840s, Thorpe wrote many sketches and stories; the best-known was his masterpiece, "The Big Bear of Arkansas" (1841). In 1846, he published his first book, the collection of stories entitled* The Mysteries of the Backwoods; or Sketches of the Southwest. *During the Mexican War, Thorpe accompanied General Zachary Taylor as a newspaper correspondent, and later published his accounts of the campaign in three books, including* Our Army on the Rio Grande *(1846) and* Our Army at Monterey *(1847). After the war, and back in Louisiana, Thorpe continued his painting, writing, and newspaper work, but in 1854 he decided to return north, and he and his family moved to New York. Just before his move, he had published an essay, "Sugar and the Sugar Regions of Louisiana," in the prestigious* Harper's New Monthly Magazine. *It was the first of a long series he wrote for* Harper's *on life and society in the South. The year he moved he also published two major works, a thoroughly revised collection of his frontier sketches en-*

titled The Hive of "The Bee-Hunter" *(1854) and an antislavery novel,* The Master's House: A Tale of Southern Life *(1854), that nevertheless praised the South in an attempt to defend it against the charges contained in Stowe's* Uncle Tom's Cabin *(1852). During the Civil War, as a Unionist, Thorpe was commissioned as a colonel under the notorious General B. F. "Beast" Butler to supervise the occupation of New Orleans after its capture in 1862. After the war, Thorpe returned to New York, where his last years were lived prosperously, writing essays and newspaper articles. "The Big Bear of Arkansas" first appeared in* Spirit of the Times *in March 1841.*

THE BIG BEAR
OF ARKANSAS

❀

A steamboat on the Mississippi, frequently, in making her regular trips, carries between places varying from one to two thousand miles apart; and, as these boats advertise to land passengers and freight at "all intermediate landings," the heterogeneous character of the passengers of one of these up-country boats can scarcely be imagined by one who has never seen it with his own eyes.

Starting from New Orleans in one of these boats, you will find yourself associated with men from every State in the Union, and from every portion of the globe; and a man of observation need not lack for amusement or instruction in such a crowd, if he will take the trouble to read the great book of character so favorably opened before him.

Here may be seen, jostling together, the wealthy Southern planter and the pedler of tin-ware from New England—the Northern merchant and the Southern jockey—a venerable bishop, and a desperate gambler—the land speculator, and the honest farmer—professional men of all creeds and characters—Wolvereens, Suckers, Hoosiers, Buckeyes, and Corncrackers, beside a "plentiful sprinkling" of the half-horse and half-alligator species of men, who are peculiar to "old Mississippi," and who appear to gain a livelihood by simply going up and down the river. In the pursuit of pleasure or business, I have frequently found myself in such a crowd.

On one occasion, when in New Orleans, I had occasion to take a trip of a few miles up the Mississippi, and I hurried on board the well-known "high-pressure-and-beat-every-thing" steamboat "Invincible," just as the last note of the last bell was sounding; and when the confusion and bustle that is natural to a boat's getting under way had subsided, I discovered that I was associated in as heterogeneous a crowd as was ever got together. As my trip was to be of a few hours' duration only, I made no endeavors to become acquainted with my fellow-passengers, most of whom would be together many days. Instead of this, I took out of my pocket the "latest paper," and more critically than usual examined its contents; my fellow-passengers, at the same time, disposed of themselves in little groups.

While I was thus busily employed in reading, and my companions were more busily still employed, in discussing such subjects as suited their humors best, we were most unexpectedly startled by a loud Indian whoop, uttered in the "social hall," that part of the cabin fitted off for a bar; then was to be heard a loud crowing, which would not have continued to interest us—such sounds being quite common in that *place of spirits*—had not the hero of these windy accomplishments stuck his head into the cabin, and hallooed out, "Hurra for the Big Bear of Arkansaw!"

Then might be heard a confused hum of voices, unintelligible, save in such broken sentences as "horse," "screamer," "lightning is slow," &c.

As might have been expected, this continued interruption, attracted the attention of every one in the cabin; all conversation ceased, and in the midst of this surprise, the "Big Bear" walked into the cabin, took a chair, put his feet on the stove, and looking back over his shoulder, passed the general and familiar salute—"Strangers, how are you?"

He then expressed himself as much at home as if he had been at "the Forks of Cypress," and "prehaps a little more so."

Some of the company at this familiarity looked a little angry, and some astonished; but in a moment every face was wreathed in a smile. There was something about the intruder that won the heart on sight. He appeared to be a man enjoying perfect health and contentment; his eyes were as sparkling as diamonds, and good-natured to simplicity. Then his perfect confidence in himself was irresistibly droll.

"Prehaps," said he, "gentlemen," running on without a person interrupting, "prehaps you have been to New Orleans often; I never made *the first visit before,* and I don't intend to make another in a crow's life. I am thrown away in that ar place, and useless, that ar a fact. Some of the gentlemen thar called me *green*—well, prehaps I am, said I, *but I arn't so at home;* and if I aint off my trail much, the heads of them perlite chaps themselves wern't much the hardest; for according to my notion, they were *real know-nothings,* green as a pumpkin-vine—couldn't, in farming, I'll bet, raise a crop of turnips; and as for shooting, they'd miss a barn if the door was swinging, and that, too, with the best rifle in the country. And then they talked to me 'bout hunting, and laughed at my calling the principal game in Arkansaw poker, and high-low-jack.

" 'Prehaps,' said I, 'you prefer checkers and roulette;' at this they laughed harder than ever, and asked me if I lived in the woods, and didn't know what *game* was?

"At this, I rather think *I* laughed.

" 'Yes,' I roared, and says I, 'Strangers, if you'd asked me *how we got our meat* in Arkansaw, I'd a told you at once, and given you a list of varmints that would make a caravan, beginning with the bar, and ending off with the cat; that's *meat* though, not game.

"Game, indeed,—that's what city folks call it; and with them it means chippen-birds and shite-pokes; may be such trash live in my diggins, but I arn't noticed them yet: a bird anyway is too trifling. I never did shoot at but one, and I'd never forgiven myself for that, had it weighed less than forty pounds. I wouldn't draw a rifle on any thing less heavy than that; and when I meet with another wild turkey of the same size, I will drap him."

"A wild turkey weighing forty pounds!" exclaimed twenty voices in the cabin at once.

"Yes, strangers, and wasn't it a whopper? You see, the thing was so fat that it couldn't fly far; and when he fell out of the tree, after I shot him, on striking the ground he bust open behind, and the way the pound gobs of tallow rolled out of the opening was perfectly beautiful."

"Where did all that happen?" asked a cynical-looking Hoosier.

"Happen! happened in Arkansaw: where else could it have happened, but in the creation State, the finishing-up country—a State where the *sile* runs down to the centre of the 'arth, and government gives you a title to every inch of it? Then its airs—just breathe them, and they will make you snort like a horse. It's a State without a fault, it is."

"Excepting mosquitoes," cried the Hoosier.

"Well, stranger, except them; for it ar a fact that they are rather *enormous,* and do push themselves in somewhat troublesome. But, stranger, they never stick twice in the same place; and give them a fair chance for a few months, and you will get as much above noticing them as an alligator. They can't hurt my feelings, for they lay under the skin; and I never knew but one case of injury resulting from them, and that was to a Yankee: and they take worse to foreigners, any how, than they do to natives. But the way they used that fellow up! first they punched him until he swelled up and busted; then he sup-per-a-ted, as the doctor called it, until he was as raw as beef; then, owing to the warm weather, he tuck the ager, and finally he tuck a steamboat and left the country. He was the only man that ever tuck mosquitoes at heart that I knowd of.

"But mosquitoes is natur, and I never find fault with her. If they ar large, Arkansaw is large, her varmints ar large, her trees ar large, her rivers ar large, and a small mosquito would be of no more use in Arkansaw than preaching in a cane-brake."

This knock-down argument in favor of big mosquitoes used the Hoosier up, and the logician started on a new track, to explain how numerous bear were in his "diggins," where he represented them to be "about as plenty as blackberries, and a little plenti-fuller."

Upon the utterance of this assertion, a timid little man near me inquired, if the bear in Arkansaw ever attacked the settlers in numbers?

"No," said our hero, warming with the subject, "no, stranger, for you see it ain't the natur of bear to go in droves; but the way they squander about in pairs and single ones is edifying.

"And then the way I hunt them—the old black rascals know the crack of my gun as well as they know a pig's squealing. They grow thin in our parts, it frightens them so, and they do take the noise dreadfully, poor things. That gun of mine is a perfect *epidemic among bear*: if not watched closely, it will go off as quick on a warm scent as my dog Bowieknife will: and then that dog—whew! why the fellow thinks that the world is full of bear, he finds them so easy. It's lucky he don't talk as well as think; for with his natural modesty, if he should suddenly learn how much he is acknowledged to be ahead of all other dogs in the universe, he would be aston-ished to death in two minutes.

"Strangers, that dog knows a bear's way as well as a horse-jockey knows a woman's: he always barks at the right time, bites at the exact place, and whips without getting a scratch.

"I never could tell whether he was made expressly to hunt bear, or whether bear was made expressly for him to hunt; any way, I believe they were ordained to go together as naturally as Squire Jones says a man and woman is, when he moralizes in marrying a couple. In fact, Jones once said, said he, 'Marriage according to law is a civil contract of divine origin; it's common to all countries as well as Arkansaw, and people take to it as naturally as Jim Doggett's Bowieknife takes to bear.' "

"What season of the year do your hunts take place?" inquired a gentlemanly foreigner, who, from some peculiarities of his baggage, I suspected to be an Englishman, on some hunting expedition, probably at the foot of the Rocky Mountains.

"The season for bear hunting, stranger," said the man of Arkansaw, "is generally all the year round, and the hunts take place about as regular. I read in history that varmints have their fat season, and their lean season. That is not the case in Arkansaw, feeding as they do upon the *spontenacious* productions of the sile, they have one continued fat season the year round; though in winter things in this way is rather more greasy than in summer, I must admit. For that reason bear with us run in warm weather, but in winter they only waddle.

"Fat, fat! its an enemy to speed; it tames every thing that has plenty of it. I have seen wild turkeys, from its influence, as gentle as chickens. Run a bear in this fat condition, and the way it improves the critter for eating is amazing; it sort of mixes the ile up with the meat, until you can't tell t'other from which. I've done this often.

"I recollect one perty morning in particular, of putting an old he fellow on the stretch, and considering the weight he carried, he run well. But the dogs soon tired him down, and when I came up with him wasn't he in a beautiful sweat—I might say fever; and then to see his tongue sticking out of his mouth a feet, and his sides sinking and opening like a bellows, and his cheeks so fat that he couldn't look cross. In this fix I blazed at him, and pitch me naked into a briar patch, if the steam didn't come out of the bullet-hole ten foot in a straight line. The fellow, I reckon, was made on the high-pressure system, and the lead sort of bust his biler."

"That column of steam was rather curious, or else the bear must have been very *warm*," observed the foreigner, with a laugh.

"Stranger, as you observe, that bear was WARM, and the blowing off of the steam show'd it, and also how hard the varmint had been run. I have no doubt if he had kept on two miles farther his insides would have been stewed; and I expect to meet with a varmint yet of extra bottom, that will run himself into a skinfull of bear's grease: it is possible; much onlikelier things have happened."

"Whereabouts are these bears so abundant?" inquired the foreigner, with increasing interest.

"Why, stranger, they inhabit the neighborhood of my settlement, one of the prettiest places on old Mississipp—a perfect location, and no mistake; a place that had some defects until the river made the 'cut-off' at 'Shirt-tail bend,' and that remedied the evil, as it brought my cabin on the edge of the river—a great advantage in wet weather, I assure you, as you can now roll a barrel of whiskey into my yard in high water from a boat, as easy as falling off a log. It's a great improvement, as toting it by land in a jug, as I used to do, *evaporated* it too fast, and it became expensive.

"Just stop with me, stranger, a month or two, or a year, if you like, and you will appreciate my place. I can give you plenty to eat; for beside hog and hominy, you can have bear-ham, and bear-sausages, and a mattrass of bear-skins to sleep on, and a wildcat-skin, pulled off hull, stuffed with corn-shucks, for a pillow. That bed would put you to sleep if you had the rheumatics in every joint in your body. I call that ar bed, a *quietus*.

"Then look at my 'pre-emption'—the government aint got another like it to dispose of. Such timber, and such bottom land,—why you can't preserve any thing natural you plant in it unless you pick it young, things thar will grow out of shape so quick.

"I once planted in those diggins a few potatoes and beets; they took a fine start, and after that, an ox team couldn't have kept them from growing. About that time I went off to old Kaintuck on business, and did not hear from them things in three months, when I accidentally stumbled on a fellow who had drapped in at my place, with an idea of buying me out.

" 'How did you like things?' said I.

" 'Pretty well,' said he; 'the cabin is convenient, and the timber land is good; but that bottom land ain't worth the first red cent.' "

" 'Why?' said I.

" ' 'Cause,' said he.

" ' 'Cause what?' said I.

" ' 'Cause it's full of cedar stumps and Indian mounds, and *can't be cleared.*'

" 'Lord,' said I, 'them ar "cedar stumps" is beets, and them ar "Indian mounds" tater hills.'

"As I had expected, the crop was overgrown and useless: the sile is too rich, *and planting in Arkansaw is dangerous*.

"I had a good-sized sow killed in that same bottom land. The old thief stole an ear of corn, and took it down to eat where she slept at night. Well, she left a grain or two on the ground, and lay down on them: before morning the corn shot up, and the percussion killed her dead. I don't plant any more: natur intended Arkansaw for a hunting ground, and I go according to natur."

The questioner, who had thus elicited the description of our hero's settlement, seemed to be perfectly satisfied, and said no more; but the "Big Bear of Arkansaw" rambled on from one thing to another with a volubility perfectly astonishing, occasionally disputing with those around him, particularly with a "live Sucker" from Illinois, who had the daring to say that our Arkansaw friend's stories "smelt rather tall."

The evening was nearly spent by the incidents we have detailed; and conscious that my own association with so singular a personage would probably end before morning, I asked him if he would not give me a description of some particular bear hunt; adding, that I took great interest in such things, though I was no sportsman. The desire seemed to please him, and he squared himself round towards me, saying, that he could give me an idea of a bear hunt that was never beat in this world, or in any other. His manner was so singular, that half of his story consisted in his excellent way of telling it, the great peculiarity of which was, the happy manner he had of emphasizing the prominent parts of his conversation. As near as I can recollect, I have italicized the words, and given the story in his own way.

"Stranger," said he, "in bear hunts *I am numerous*, and which particular one, as you say, I shall tell, puzzles me.

"There was the old she devil I shot at the Hurricane last fall—then there was the old hog thief I popped over at the Bloody Crossing, and then—Yes, I have it! I will give you an idea of a hunt, in which the greatest bear was killed that ever lived, *none excepted*; about an old fellow that I hunted, more or less, for two or three years; and if that aint a *particular bear hunt*, I ain't got one to tell.

"But in the first place, stranger, let me say, I am pleased with you, because you ain't ashamed to gain information by asking and listening; and that's what I say to Countess's pups every day when I'm home; and I have got great hopes of them ar pups, because they are continually *nosing* about; and though they stick it sometimes in the wrong place, they gain experience any how, and may learn something useful to boot.

"Well, as I was saying about this big bear, you see when I and some more first settled in our region, we were drivin to hunting naturally; we soon liked it, and after that we found it an easy matter to make the thing our business. One old chap who had pioneered 'afore us, gave us to understand that we had settled in the right place. He dwelt upon its merits until it was affecting, and showed us, to prove his assertions, more scratches on the bark of the sassafras trees, than I ever saw chalk marks on a tavern door 'lection time.

" 'Who keeps that ar reckoning?' said I.

" 'The bear,' said he.

" 'What for?' said I.

" 'Can't tell,' said he; 'but so it is: the bear bite the bark and wood too, at the highest point from the ground they can reach, and you can tell, by the marks,' said he, 'the length of the bear to an inch.'

" 'Enough,' said I; 'I've learned something here a'ready, and I'll put it in practice.'

"Well, stranger, just one month from that time I killed a bar, and told its exact length before I measured it, by those very marks; and when I did that, I swelled up considerably—I've been a prouder man ever since.

"So I went on, larning something every day, until I was reckoned a buster, and allowed to be decidedly the best bear hunter in my district; and that is a reputation as much harder to earn than to be reckoned first man in Congress, as an iron ramrod is harder than a toadstool.

"Do the varmints grow over-cunning by being fooled with by green-horn hunters, and by this means get troublesome, they send for me, as a matter of course; and thus I do my own hunting, and most of my neighbors'. I walk into the varmints though, and it has become about as much the same to me as drinking. It is told in two sentences—

"A bear is started, and he is killed.

"The thing is somewhat monotonous now—I know just how much they will run, where they will tire, how much they will growl, and what a thundering time I will have in getting their meat home. I could give you the history of the chase with all the particulars at the commencement, I know the signs so well—*Stranger, I'm certain*. Once I met with a match, though, and I will tell you about it; for a common hunt would not be worth relating.

"On a fine fall day, long time ago, I was trailing about for bear, and what should I see but fresh marks on the sassafras trees, about eight inches above any in the forests that I knew of. Says I, 'Them marks is a hoax, or it indicates the d——t bear that was ever grown.' In fact, stranger, I couldn't believe it was real, and I went on. Again I saw the same marks, at the same height, and *I knew the thing lived*. That conviction came home to my soul like an earthquake.

"Says I, 'Here is something a-purpose for me: that bear is mine, or I give up the hunting business.' The very next morning, what should I see but a number of buzzards hovering over my cornfield. 'The rascal has been there,' said I, 'for that sign is certain': and, sure enough, on examining, I found the bones of what had been as beautiful a hog the day before, as was ever raised by a Buckeye. Then I tracked the critter out of the field to the woods, and all the marks he left behind, showed me that he was *the bear*.

"Well, stranger, the first fair chase I ever had with that big critter, I saw him no less than three distinct times at a distance: the dogs run him over eighteen miles and broke down, my horse gave out, and I was as nearly used up as a man can be, made on *my* principle, *which is patent.*

"Before this adventure, such things were unknown to me as possible; but, strange as it was, that bear got me used to it before I was done with him; for he got so at last, that he would leave me on a long chase *quite easy.* How he did it, I never could understand.

"That a bear runs at all, is puzzling; but how this one could tire down and bust up a pack of hounds and a horse, that were used to overhauling every thing they started after in no time, was past my understanding. Well, stranger, that bear finally got so sassy, that he used to help himself to a hog off my premises whenever he wanted one; the buzzards followed after what he left, and so, between *bear and buzzard,* I rather think I got *out of pork.*

"Well, missing that bear so often took hold of my vitals, and I wasted away. The thing had been carried too far, and it reduced me in flesh faster than an ager. I would see that bear in every thing I did: *he hunted me,* and that, too, like a devil, which I began to think he was.

"While in this shaky fix, I made preparations to give him a last brush, and be done with it. Having completed every thing to my satisfaction, I started at sunrise, and to my great joy, I discovered from the way the dogs run, that they were near him. Finding his trail was nothing, for that had become as plain to the pack as a turnpike road.

"On we went, and coming to an open country, what should I see but the bear very leisurely ascending a hill, and the dogs close at his heels, either a match for him this time in speed, or else he did not care to get out of their way—I don't know which. But wasn't he a beauty, though! I loved him like a brother.

"On he went, until he came to a tree, the limbs of which formed a crotch about six feet from the ground. Into this crotch he got and seated himself, the dogs yelling all around it; and there he sat eyeing them as quiet as a pond in low water.

"A greenhorn friend of mine, in company, reached shooting distance before me, and blazed away, hitting the critter in the centre of his forehead. The bear shook his head as the ball struck it, and then walked down from that tree, as gently as a lady would from a carriage.

" 'Twas a beautiful sight to see him do that—he was in such a rage, that he seemed to be as little afraid of the dogs as if they had been sucking pigs; and the dogs warn't slow in making a ring around him at a respectful distance, I tell you; even Bowieknife himself, stood off. Then the way his eyes flashed!—why the fire of them would have singed a cat's hair; in fact, that bear was in a *wrath all over*. Only one pup came near him, and he was brushed out so totally with the bear's left paw, that he entirely disappeared; and that made the old dogs more cautious still. In the mean time, I came up, and taking deliberate aim, as a man should do, at his side, just back of his foreleg, *if my gun did not snap*, call me a coward, and I won't take it personal.

"Yes, stranger, *it snapped*, and I could not find a cap about my person. While in this predicament, I turned round to my fool friend—'Bill,' says I, 'you're an ass—you're a fool—you might as well have tried to kill that bear by barking the tree under his belly, as to have done it by hitting him in the head. Your shot has made a tiger of him; and blast me, if a dog gets killed or wounded when they come to blows, I will stick my knife into your liver, I will ——.' My wrath was up. I had lost my caps, my gun had snapped, the fellow with me had fired at the bear's head, and I expected every moment to see him close in with the dogs and kill a dozen of them at least. In this thing I was mistaken; for the bear leaped over the ring formed by the dogs, and giving a fierce growl, was off—the pack, of course, in full cry after him. The run this time was short, for coming to the edge of a lake, the varmint jumped in, and swam to a little island in the lake, which it reached, just a moment before the dogs.

" 'I'll have him now,' said I, for I had found my caps in the *lining of my coat*—so, rolling a log into the lake, I paddled myself across to the island, just as the dogs had cornered the bear in a thicket. I rushed up and fired—at the same time the critter leaped over the dogs and came within three feet of me, running like mad; he jumped into the lake, and tried to mount the log I had just deserted, but every time he got half his body on it, it would roll over and send him under; the dogs, too, got around him, and pulled him about, and finally Bowieknife clenched with him, and they sunk into the lake together.

"Stranger, about this time I was excited, and I stripped off my coat, drew my knife, and intended to have taken a part with Bowieknife myself, when the bear rose to the surface. But the varmint staid under—Bowieknife came up alone, more dead than alive, and with the pack came ashore.

" 'Thank God!' said I, 'the old villain has got his deserts at last.'

"Determined to have the body, I cut a grape-vine for a rope, and dove down where I could see the bear in the water, fastened my rope to his leg, and fished him, with great difficulty, ashore. Stranger, may I be chawed to death by young alligators, if the thing I looked at wasn't a *she bear, and not the old critter after all*.

"The way matters got mixed on that island was onaccountably curious, and thinking of it made me more than ever convinced that I was hunting the devil himself. I went home that night and took to my bed—the thing was killing me. The entire team of Arkansaw in bear-hunting acknowledged himself used up, and the fact sunk into my feelings as a snagged boat will in the Mississippi. I grew as cross as a bear with two cubs and a sore tail. The thing got out 'mong my neighbors, and I was asked how come on that individ-u-al that never lost a bear when once started? and if that same individ-u-al didn't wear telescopes when he turned a she-bear, of ordinary size, into an old he one, a little larger than a horse?

" 'Prehaps,' said I, 'friends'—getting wrathy—'prehaps you want to call somebody a liar?'

" 'Oh, no,' said they, 'we only heard of such things being *rather common* of late, but we don't believe one word of it; oh, no,'— and then they would ride off, and laugh like so many hyenas over a dead nigger.

"It was too much, and I determined to catch that bear, go to Texas, or die,—and I made my preparations accordin'.

"I had the pack shut up and rested. I took my rifle to pieces, and iled it.

"I put caps in every pocket about my person, *for fear of the lining*.

"I then told my neighbors, that on Monday morning—naming the day—I would start THAT B(E)AR, and bring him home with me, or they might divide my settlement among them, the owner having disappeared.

"Well, stranger, on the morning previous to the great day of my hunting expedition, I went into the woods near my house, taking my gun and Bowieknife along, just *from habit,* and there sitting down, also from habit, what should I see, getting over my fence, but *the bear!* Yes, the old varmint was within a hundred yards of me, and the way he walked *over that fence*—stranger; he loomed up like a *black mist,* he seemed so large, and he walked right towards me.

"I raised myself, took deliberate aim, and fired. Instantly the varmint wheeled, gave a yell, and *walked through the fence,* as easy as a falling tree would through a cobweb.

"I started after, but was tripped up by my inexpressibles, which, either from habit or the excitement of the moment, were about my heels, and before I had really gathered myself up, I heard the old varmint groaning, like a thousand sinners, in a thicket near by, and, by the time I reached him, he was a corpse.

"Stranger, it took five niggers and myself to put that carcass on a mule's back, and old long-ears waddled under his load, as if he was foundered in every leg of his body; and with a common whopper of a bear, he would have trotted off, and enjoyed himself.

" 'Twould astonish you to know how big he was: I made a *bed-spread of his skin*, and the way it used to cover my bear mattress, and leave several feet on each side to tuck up, would have delighted you. It was, in fact, a creation bear, and if it had lived in Samson's time, and had met him in a fair fight, he would have licked him in the twinkling of a dice-box.

"But, stranger, I never liked the way I hunted him, *and missed him*. There is something curious about it, that I never could understand,—and I never was satisfied at his giving in so *easy at last*. Prehaps he had heard of my preparations to hunt him the next day, so he jist guv up, like Captain Scott's coon, to save his wind to grunt with in dying; but that ain't likely. My private opinion is, that that bear was an *unhuntable bear, and died when his time come*."

When this story was ended, our hero sat some minutes with his auditors, in a grave silence; I saw there was a mystery to him connected with the bear whose death he had just related, that had evidently made a strong impression on his mind. It was also evident that there was some superstitious awe connected with the affair,— a feeling common with all "children of the wood," when they meet with any thing out of their every-day experience.

He was the first one, however, to break the silence, and, jumping up, he asked all present to "liquor" before going to bed,—a thing which he did, with a number of companions, evidently to his heart's content.

Long before day, I was put ashore at my place of destination, and I can only follow with the reader, in imagination, our Arkansas friend, in his adventures at the "Forks of Cypress," on the Mississippi.

Jean Toomer

(1894–1967)

*Born in Washington, D.C., Toomer was raised by his maternal
grandfather, P. B. S. Pinchback, a mixed-blood "freeman of color"
who had been the lieutenant governor of Louisiana during Reconstruction. Toomer's father, also of mixed-blood origins, was from
Georgia, where he returned after deserting his family before Toomer
was a year old. His mother remarried, but when she died in 1909
Toomer returned to his grandfather's house in Washington. After
leaving Washington for the University of Wisconsin, Toomer began
a life of wandering and instability that ended only when he and his
second wife, a wealthy daughter of a New York broker, joined the
Society of Friends in the 1940s. He attended several universities,
but never graduated. In 1920, he decided to become a writer, and
spent three months teaching in Sparta, Georgia, an experience that
led to the writing of* Cane *(1923), his collection of unified stories
and poems that has rightly become a classic of modern fiction. In
1923, Toomer came under the influence of Gurdjieff, and spent time
at the Gurdjieff Institute in France. From then on, he published
very little, and devoted himself instead to a life of mysticism and
spiritual regeneration. Though Toomer maintained he was of seven
blood strains, including black and Indian,* Cane *is an undisguised
affirmation of Toomer's deeply felt affiliations with the black culture
of the rural South. There has been much speculation about the
reasons behind Toomer's decision to stop writing imaginative fiction. Langston Hughes suggested that Toomer's second wife, and
the financial security she brought to the marriage, may have been
the primary influence, but Toomer himself seems to have indepen-
dently judged literature of secondary importance, compared with
his determination to re-create a new spiritual selfhood. As he once
said of himself: "I am of no particular race, I am of the human
race, a man at large in the human world, preparing a new race."
Among his few works are several essays and poems, a collection of*

451

short sayings, Essentials *(1931), and a recent collection of various pieces edited by Darwin T. Turner,* The Wayward and the Seeking: A Collection of Writings *(1980). "Blood-Burning Moon," from* Cane, *first appeared in* Prairie 1 *(March–April 1923).*

BLOOD-BURNING MOON

❀

1

Up from the skeleton stone walls, up from the rotting floor boards and the solid hand-hewn beams of oak of the pre-war cotton factory, dusk came. Up from the dusk the full moon came. Glowing like a fired pine-knot, it illumined the great door and soft showered the Negro shanties aligned along the single street of factory town. The full moon in the great door was an omen. Negro women improvised songs against its spell.

Louisa sang as she came over the crest of the hill from the white folks' kitchen. Her skin was the color of oak leaves on young trees in fall. Her breasts, firm and up-pointed like ripe acorns. And her singing had the low murmur of winds in fig trees. Bob Stone, younger son of the people she worked for, loved her. By the way the world reckons things, he had won her. By measure of that warm glow which came into her mind at thought of him, he had won her. Tom Burwell, whom the whole town called Big Boy, also loved her. But working in the fields all day, and far away from her, gave him no chance to show it. Though often enough of evenings he had tried to. Somehow, he never got along. Strong as he was with hands upon the ax or plow, he found it difficult to hold her. Or so he thought. But the fact was that he held her to factory town more firmly than he thought for. His black balanced, and pulled against, the white of Stone, when she thought of them. And her mind was vaguely upon them as she came over the crest of the hill, coming from the white folks' kitchen. As she sang softly at the evil face of the full moon.

A strange stir was in her. Indolently, she tried to fix upon Bob or Tom as the cause of it. To meet Bob in the canebrake, as she was going to do an hour or so later, was nothing new. And Tom's proposal which she felt on its way to her could be indefinitely put off. Separately, there was no unusual significance to either one. But for some reason, they jumbled when her eyes gazed vacantly at the rising moon. And from the jumble came the stir that was strangely within her. Her lips trembled. The slow rhythm of her song grew agitant and restless. Rusty black and tan spotted hounds, lying in the dark corners of porches or prowling around back yards, put their noses in the air and caught its tremor. They began plaintively to yelp and howl. Chickens woke up and cackled. Intermittently, all over the countryside dogs barked and roosters crowed as if heralding a weird dawn or some ungodly awakening. The women sang lustily. Their songs were cotton-wads to stop their ears. Louisa came down into factory town and sank wearily upon the step before her home. The moon was rising towards a thick cloud-bank which soon would hide it.

> Red nigger moon. Sinner!
> Blood-burning moon. Sinner!
> Come out that fact'ry door.

2

Up from the deep dusk of a cleared spot on the edge of the forest a mellow glow arose and spread fan-wise into the low-hanging heavens. And all around the air was heavy with the scent of boiling cane. A large pile of cane-stalks lay like ribboned shadows upon the ground. A mule, harnessed to a pole, trudged lazily round and round the pivot of the grinder. Beneath a swaying oil lamp, a Negro alternately whipped out at the mule, and fed cane-stalks to the grinder. A fat boy waddled pails of fresh ground juice between the grinder and the boiling stove. Steam came from the copper boiling pan. The scent of cane came from the copper pan and drenched the forest and the hill that sloped to factory town, beneath its fragrance. It drenched the men in circle seated around the stove. Some of them chewed at the white pulp of stalks, but there was no need for them to, if all they wanted was to taste the cane. One tasted it in factory town. And from factory town one could see the soft haze thrown by the glowing stove upon the low-hanging heavens.

Old David Georgia stirred the thickening syrup with a long ladle, and ever so often drew it off. Old David Georgia tended his stove and told tales about the white folks, about moonshining and cotton picking, and about sweet nigger gals, to the men who sat there about his stove to listen to him. Tom Burwell chewed cane-stalk and laughed with the others till some one mentioned Louisa. Till some one said something about Louisa and Bob Stone, about the silk stockings she must have gotten from him. Blood ran up Tom's neck hotter than the glow that flooded from the stove. He sprang up. Glared at the men and said, "She's my gal." Will Manning laughed. Tom strode over to him. Yanked him up and knocked him to the ground. Several of Manning's friends got up to fight for him. Tom whipped out a long knife and would have cut them to shreds if they hadnt ducked into the woods. Tom had had enough. He nodded to Old David Georgia and swung down the path to factory town. Just then, the dogs started barking and the roosters began to crow. Tom felt funny. Away from the fight, away from the stove, chill got to him. He shivered. He shuddered when he saw the full moon rising towards the cloud-bank. He who didnt give a godam for the fears of old women. He forced his mind to fasten on Louisa. Bob Stone. Better not be. He turned into the street and saw Louisa sitting before her home. He went towards her, ambling, touched the brim of a marvelously shaped, spotted, felt hat, said he wanted to say something to her, and then found that he didnt know what he had to say, or if he did, that he couldnt say it. He shoved his big fists in his overalls, grinned, and started to move off.

"Youall want me, Tom?"

"Thats what us wants, sho, Louisa."

"Well, here I am—"

"An here I is, but that aint ahelpin none, all th same."

"You wanted to say something? . ."

"I did that, sho. But words is like th spots on dice: no matter how y fumbles em, there's times when they jes wont come. I dunno why. Seems like th love I feels fo yo done stole m tongue. I got it now. Whee! Louisa, honey, I oughtnt tell y, I feel I oughtnt cause yo is young an goes t church an I has had other gals, but Louisa I sho do love y. Lil gal, Ise watched y from them first days when youall sat right here befo yo door befo th well an sang sometimes in a way that like t broke m heart. Ise carried y with me into th fields, day after day, an after that, an I sho can plow when yo is there, an I can pick cotton. Yassur! Come near beatin Barlo yesterday. I sho did. Yassur! An next year if ole Stone'll trust me, I'll have a farm. My own. My bales will buy yo what y gets from white folks now. Silk stockings an purple dresses—course I dont believe what some folks been whisperin as t how y gets them things now. White folks always did do for niggers what they likes. An they jes cant help alikin yo, Louisa. Bob Stone likes y.

Course he does. But not th way folks is awhisperin. Does he, hon?"

"I dont know what you mean, Tom."

"Course y dont. Ise already cut two niggers. Had t hon, t tell em so. Niggers always tryin t make somethin out a nothin. An then besides, white folks aint up t them tricks so much nowadays. Godam better not be. Leastawise not with yo. Cause I wouldnt stand f it. Nassur."

"What would you do, Tom?"

"Cut him jes like I cut a nigger."

"No, Tom—"

"I said I would an there aint no mo to it. But that aint th talk f now. Sing, honey Louisa, an while I'm listenin t y I'll be makin love."

Tom took her hand in his. Against the tough thickness of his own, hers felt soft and small. His huge body slipped down to the step beside her. The full moon sank upward into the deep purple of the cloud-bank. An old woman brought a lighted lamp and hung it on the common well whose bulky shadow squatted in the middle of the road, opposite Tom and Louisa. The old woman lifted the well-lid, took hold the chain, and began drawing up the heavy bucket. As she did so, she sang. Figures shifted, restlesslike, between lamp and window in the front rooms of the shanties. Shadows of the figures fought each other on the gray dust of the road. Figures raised the windows and joined the old woman in song. Louisa and Tom, the whole street, singing:

> Red nigger moon. Sinner!
> Blood-burning moon. Sinner!
> Come out that fact'ry door.

3

Bob Stone sauntered from his veranda out into the gloom of fir trees and magnolias. The clear white of his skin paled, and the flush of his cheeks turned purple. As if to balance this outer change, his mind became consciously a white man's. He passed the house with its huge open hearth which, in the days of slavery, was the plantation cookery. He saw Louisa bent over that hearth. He went in as a master should and took her. Direct, honest, bold. None of this sneaking that he had to go through now. The contrast was repulsive to him. His family had lost ground. Hell no, his family still owned the niggers, practically. Damned if they did, or he wouldnt have to duck around so. What would they think if they knew? His mother? His sister? He shouldnt mention them, shouldnt think of them in this connection. There in the dusk he blushed at doing so. Fellows about town were all right, but how about his friends up North? He could see them incredible, repulsed. They didnt know. The thought first made him laugh. Then, with their eyes still upon him, he began to feel embarrassed. He felt the need of explaining things to them. Explain hell. They wouldnt understand, and moreover, who ever heard of a Southerner getting on his knees to any Yankee, or anyone. No sir. He was going to see Louisa to-night, and love her. She was lovely— in her way. Nigger way. What way was that? Damned if he knew. Must know. He'd known her long enough to know. Was there something about niggers that you couldnt know? Listening to them at church didnt tell you anything. Looking at them didnt tell you anything. Talking to them didnt tell you anything—unless it was gossip, unless they wanted to talk. Of course, about farming, and licker, and craps—but those werent nigger. Nigger was something more. How much more? Something to be afraid of, more? Hell no. Who ever heard of being afraid of a nigger? Tom Burwell. Cartwell had told him that Tom went with Louisa after she reached home. No sir. No nigger had ever been with his girl. He'd like to see one try. Some position for him to be in. Him, Bob Stone, of the old Stone family, in a scrap with a nigger over a nigger girl. In the good old days . . . Ha! Those were the days. His family had lost ground. Not so much, though. Enough for him to have to cut through old Lemon's canefield by way of the woods, that he might meet her. She was worth it. Beautiful nigger gal. Why nigger? Why not, just gal? No, it was because she was nigger that he went to her. Sweet . . . The scent of boiling cane came to him. Then he saw the rich glow of the stove. He heard the voices of the men circled around it. He was about to skirt the clearing when he heard his own name mentioned. He stopped. Quivering. Leaning against a tree, he listened.

"Bad nigger. Yassur, he sho is one bad nigger when he gets started."

"Tom Burwell's been on th gang three times fo cuttin men."

"What y think he's agwine t do t Bob Stone?"

"Dunno yet. He aint found out. When he does— Baby!"

"Aint no tellin."

"Young Stone aint no quitter an I ken tell y that. Blood of th old uns in his veins."

"Thats right. He'll scrap, sho."

"Be gettin too hot f niggers round this away."

"Shut up, nigger. Y dont know what y talkin bout."

Bob Stone's ears burned as though he had been holding them over the stove. Sizzling heat welled up within him. His feet felt as if they rested on red-hot coals. They stung him to quick movement. He circled the fringe of the glowing. Not a twig cracked beneath his feet. He reached the path that led to factory town. Plunged furiously down it. Halfway along, a blindness within him veered him aside. He crashed into the bordering canebrake. Cane leaves cut his face and lips. He tasted blood. He threw himself down and dug his fingers in the ground. The earth was cool. Cane-roots took the fever from his hands. After a long while, or so it seemed to him, the thought came to him that it must be time to see Louisa. He got to his feet and walked calmly to their meeting place. No Louisa. Tom Burwell had her. Veins in his forehead bulged and distended. Saliva moistened the dried blood on his lips. He bit down on his lips. He tasted blood. Not his own blood; Tom Burwell's blood. Bob drove through the cane and out again upon the road. A hound swung down the path before him towards factory town. Bob couldnt see it. The dog loped aside to let him pass. Bob's blind rushing made him stumble over it. He fell with a thud that dazed him. The hound yelped. Answering yelps came from all over the countryside. Chickens cackled. Roosters crowed, heralding the bloodshot eyes of southern awakening. Singers in the town were silenced. They shut their windows down. Palpitant between the rooster crows, a chill hush settled upon the huddled forms of Tom and Louisa. A figure rushed from the shadow and stood before them. Tom popped to his feet.

"Whats y want?"

"I'm Bob Stone."

"Yassur—an I'm Tom Burwell. Whats y want?"

Bob lunged at him. Tom side-stepped, caught him by the shoulder, and flung him to the ground. Straddled him.

"Let me up."

"Yassur—but watch yo doins, Bob Stone."

A few dark figures, drawn by the sound of scuffle, stood about them. Bob sprang to his feet.

"Fight like a man, Tom Burwell, an I'll lick y."

Again he lunged. Tom side-stepped and flung him to the ground. Straddled him.

"Get off me, you godam nigger you."

"Yo sho has started somethin now. Get up."

Tom yanked him up and began hammering at him. Each blow

sounded as if it smashed into a precious, irreplaceable soft something. Beneath them, Bob staggered back. He reached in his pocket
and whipped out a knife.

"Thats my game, sho."

Blue flash, a steel blade slashed across Bob Stone's throat. He
had a sweetish sick feeling. Blood began to flow. Then he felt a
sharp twitch of pain. He let his knife drop. He slapped one hand
against his neck. He pressed the other on top of his head as if to
hold it down. He groaned. He turned, and staggered towards the
crest of the hill in the direction of white town. Negroes who had
seen the fight slunk into their homes and blew the lamps out.
Louisa, dazed, hysterical, refused to go indoors. She slipped, crumbled, her body loosely propped against the woodwork of the well.
Tom Burwell leaned against it. He seemed rooted there.

Bob reached Broad Street. White men rushed up to him. He
collapsed in their arms.

"Tom Burwell. . . ."

White men like ants upon a forage rushed about. Except for the
taut hum of their moving, all was silent. Shotguns, revolvers, rope,
kerosene, torches. Two high-powered cars with glaring search-
lights. They came together. The taut hum rose to a low roar. Then
nothing could be heard but the flop of their feet in the thick dust
of the road. The moving body of their silence preceded them over
the crest of the hill into factory town. It flattened the Negroes
beneath it. It rolled to the wall of the factory, where it stopped.
Tom knew that they were coming. He couldnt move. And then
he saw the search-lights of the two cars glaring down on him. A
quick shock went through him. He stiffened. He started to run. A
yell went up from the mob. Tom wheeled about and faced them.
They poured down on him. They swarmed. A large man with dead-
white face and flabby cheeks came to him and almost jabbed a
gun-barrel through his guts.

"Hands behind y, nigger."

Tom's wrists were bound. The big man shoved him to the well.
Burn him over it, and when the woodwork caved in, his body
would drop to the bottom. Two deaths for a godam nigger. Louisa
was driven back. The mob pushed in. Its pressure, its momentum
was too great. Drag him to the factory. Wood and stakes already
there. Tom moved in the direction indicated. But they had to drag
him. They reached the great door. Too many to get in there. The
mob divided and flowed around the walls to either side. The big
man shoved him through the door. The mob pressed in from the
sides. Taut humming. No words. A stake was sunk into the ground.
Rotting floor boards piled around it. Kerosene poured on the

rotting floor boards. Tom bound to the stake. His breast was bare. Nails' scratches let little lines of blood trickle down and mat into the hair. His face, his eyes were set and stony. Except for irregular breathing, one would have thought him already dead. Torches were flung onto the pile. A great flare muffled in black smoke shot upward. The mob yelled. The mob was silent. Now Tom could be seen within the flames. Only his head, erect, lean, like a blackened stone. Stench of burning flesh soaked the air. Tom's eyes popped. His head settled downward. The mob yelled. Its yell echoed against the skeleton stone walls and sounded like a hundred yells. Like a hundred mobs yelling. Its yell thudded against the thick front wall and fell back. Ghost of a yell slipped through the flames and out the great door of the factory. It fluttered like a dying thing down the single street of factory town. Louisa, upon the step before her home, did not hear it, but her eyes opened slowly. They saw the full moon glowing in the great door. The full moon, an evil thing, an omen, soft showering the homes of folks she knew. Where were they, these people? She'd sing, and perhaps they'd come out and join her. Perhaps Tom Burwell would come. At any rate, the full moon in the great door was an omen which she must sing to:

> Red nigger moon. Sinner!
> Blood-burning moon. Sinner!
> Come out that fact'ry door.

Mark Twain
(Samuel Langhorne Clemens)
(1835–1910)

The major Southern writer of his age, Mark Twain was often linked with the Southern humorists and local colorists popular in his lifetime. His own best fiction, however, including his masterpiece, Adventures of Huckleberry Finn (1885), is the work of an original maverick, deeply divided in his attitude toward the real South, and skeptical of all popular myths and legends. Born Samuel Clemens, in Florida, Missouri, and raised in nearby Hannibal, on the Mississippi, Twain lived his youth in a slave state settled by migrating Southerners, but surrounded by the constant reminder that Southern certitudes were not shared by all Americans. His father was a Virginian and a lawyer, a prototypical purse-poor gentleman dreamer whose combination of high-minded principle and noble misman-agement of all practical affairs produced in his son a permanent distrust of all aristocratic pretense. His mother was born in Kentucky and, unlike her husband, possessed a warm sense of humor that Twain would praise, along with her Southern drawl and her sto-rytelling gifts, the rest of his life. When his father died in 1847, young Sam went to work as a printer's helper, but as he himself claimed later, his real life began when he signed on as an apprentice steamboat pilot in 1855. He received his pilot's license in 1857, and worked the Mississippi for four years, the "happiest of his life." The Civil War put a stop to his steamboating career, and he joined a volunteer troop of the Confederate army. He changed his mind almost at once, and taking rebelliousness one step further, left the war behind to go west with his brother Orion, secretary to the governor of the Nevada Territory. There he wrote journalistic pieces and humorous sketches, and gained a measure of local fame in San Francisco. After the Civil War, he returned east and joined a cultural tour of Europe and the Far East, hired by a newspaper to write his impressions of the voyage. A full-scale account, The Innocents

Abroad, *was published in 1869. In 1870, he married Olivia Langdon, daughter of a wealthy merchant in Elmira, New York. After a short stay in Buffalo, he and his wife moved to Hartford, Connecticut, their home for many years. In 1872, Twain published* Roughing It, *a fully engaging history of his time in Nevada and California, and, in 1875, with a series of articles for* The Atlantic Monthly, *"Old Times on the Mississippi," he launched his brilliant trilogy of the South:* The Adventures of Tom Sawyer *(1876), his "hymn to boyhood";* Life on the Mississippi *(1883); and* The Adventures of Huckleberry Finn *(1885), defined by Allan Tate as the "first modern Southern novel." During the last decades of his life, troubled by financial strains, personal tragedy that included the death of his favorite daughter, and a darkening pessimistic view of existence, Twain lashed out in a series of bitter satires against a multitude of human, and even divine, follies. A powerful work in this final period is his indictment of Belgium imperialism in the Congo,* King Leopold's Soliloquy *(1905). After his wife's death in 1904, his last years were spent dictating a vast, rambling autobiography that he never finished. Among his other works are* The Gilded Age *(1873, with Charles Dudley Warner),* A Connecticut Yankee in King Arthur's Court *(1889),* The Tragedy of Pudd'nhead Wilson, *and the* Comedy of Those Extraordinary Twins *(1894), and* The Mysterious Stranger *(1916). "The Private History of a Campaign That Failed" first appeared in* The Century Magazine *(December 1885).*

THE PRIVATE HISTORY
OF A CAMPAIGN
THAT FAILED

❈

You have heard from a great many people who did something in the war; is it not fair and right that you listen a little moment to one who started out to do something in it, but didn't? Thousands entered the war, got just a taste of it, and then stepped out again permanently. These, by their very numbers, are respectable, and are therefore entitled to a sort of voice—not a loud one, but a modest one; not a boastful one, but an apologetic one. They ought not to be allowed much space among better people—people who did something. I grant that; but they ought at least to be allowed to state why they didn't do anything, and also to explain the process by which they didn't do anything. Surely this kind of light must have a sort of value.

Out West there was a good deal of confusion in men's minds during the first months of the great trouble—a good deal of unsettledness, of leaning first this way, then that, then the other way. It was hard for us to get our bearings. I call to mind an instance of this. I was piloting on the Mississippi when the news came that South Carolina had gone out of the Union on the 20th of December, 1860. My pilot mate was a New Yorker. He was strong for the Union; so was I. But he would not listen to me with any patience; my loyalty was smirched, to his eye, because my father had owned slaves. I said, in palliation of this dark fact, that I had heard my father say, some years before he died, that slavery was a great wrong, and that he would free the solitary negro he then owned if he could think it right to give away the property of the family when he was so straitened in means. My mate retorted that a mere impulse was nothing—anybody could pretend to a good impulse; and went on decrying my Unionism and libeling my ancestry. A month later the secession atmosphere had considerably thickened on the Lower Mississippi, and I became a rebel; so did he. We were together in New Orleans the 26th of January, when Louisiana went out of the Union. He did his full share of the rebel shouting, but was bitterly opposed to letting me do mine. He said that I came of bad stock—of a father who had been willing to set slaves free. In the following summer he was piloting a Federal gunboat and shouting for the Union again, and I was in the Confederate army. I held his note for some borrowed money. He was one of the most upright men I ever knew, but he repudiated that note without hesitation because I was a rebel and the son of a man who owned slaves.

In that summer—of 1861—the first wash of the wave of war broke upon the shores of Missouri. Our State was invaded by the Union forces. They took possession of St. Louis, Jefferson Barracks, and some other points. The Governor, Claib Jackson, issued his proclamation calling out fifty thousand militia to repel the invader.

I was visiting in the small town where my boyhood had been spent—Hannibal, Marion County. Several of us got together in a secret place by night and formed ourselves into a military company.

One Tom Lyman, a young fellow of a good deal of spirit but of no military experience, was made captain; I was made second lieutenant. We had no first lieutenant; I do not know why; it was long ago. There were fifteen of us. By the advice of an innocent connected with the organization we called ourselves the Marion Rangers. I do not remember that any one found fault with the name. I did not; I thought it sounded quite well. The young fellow who proposed this title was perhaps a fair sample of the kind of stuff we were made of. He was young, ignorant, good-natured, well-meaning, trivial, full of romance, and given to reading chivalric novels and singing forlorn love-ditties. He had some pathetic little nickel-plated aristocratic instincts, and detested his name, which was Dunlap; detested it, partly because it was nearly as common in that region as Smith, but mainly because it had a plebeian sound to his ear. So he tried to ennoble it by writing it in this way: *d'Unlap*. That contented his eye, but left his ear unsatisfied, for people gave the new name the same old pronunciation—emphasis on the front end of it. He then did the bravest thing that can be imagined—a thing to make one shiver when one remembers how the world is given to resenting shams and affectations; he began to write his name so: *d'Un Lap*. And he waited patiently through the long storm of mud that was flung at this work of art, and he had his reward at last; for he lived to see that name accepted, and the emphasis put where he wanted it by people who had known him all his life, and to whom the tribe of Dunlaps had been as familiar as the rain and the sunshine for forty years. So sure of victory at last is the courage that can wait. He said he had found, by consulting some ancient French chronicles, that the name was rightly and originally written d'Un Lap; and said that if it were translated into English it would mean Peterson: *Lap,* Latin or Greek, he said, for stone or rock, same as the French *pierre,* that is to say, Peter; *d',* of or from; *un,* a or one; hence, d'Un Lap, of or from a stone or a Peter; that is to say, one who is the son of a stone, the son of a Peter—Peterson. Our militia company were not learned, and the explanation confused them; so they called him Peterson Dunlap. He proved useful to us in his way; he named our camps for us, and he generally struck a name that was "no slouch," as the boys said.

That is one sample of us. Another was Ed Stevens, son of the town jeweler—trim-built, handsome, graceful, neat as a cat; bright, educated, but given over entirely to fun. There was nothing serious in life to him. As far as he was concerned, this military expedition of ours was simply a holiday. I should say that about half of us looked upon it in the same way; not consciously perhaps, but unconsciously. We did not think; we were not capable of it. As for myself, I was full of unreasoning joy to be done with turning out of bed at midnight and four in the morning for a while; grateful to have a change, new scenes, new occupations, a new interest. In my thoughts that was as far as I went; I did not go into the details; as a rule, one doesn't at twenty-four.

Another sample was Smith, the blacksmith's apprentice. This vast donkey had some pluck, of a slow and sluggish nature, but a soft heart; at one time he would knock a horse down for some impropriety, and at another he would get homesick and cry. However, he had one ultimate credit to his account which some of us hadn't: he stuck to the war, and was killed in battle at last.

Jo Bowers, another sample, was a huge, good-natured, flax-headed lubber; lazy, sentimental, full of harmless brag, a grumbler by nature; an experienced, industrious, ambitious, and often quite picturesque liar, and yet not a successful one, for he had had no intelligent training, but was allowed to come up just any way. This life was serious enough to him, and seldom satisfactory. But he was a good fellow anyway, and the boys all liked him. He was made orderly sergeant; Stevens was made corporal.

These samples will answer—and they are quite fair ones. Well, this herd of cattle started for the war. What could you expect of them? They did as well as they knew how; but really what was justly to be expected of them? Nothing, I should say. That is what they did.

We waited for a dark night, for caution and secrecy were necessary; then, towards midnight, we stole in couples and from various directions to the Griffith place, beyond the town; from that point we set out together on foot. Hannibal lies at the extreme southeastern corner of Marion County, on the Mississippi River; our objective point was the hamlet of New London, ten miles away, in Ralls County.

The first hour was all fun, all idle nonsense and laughter. But that could not be kept up. The steady trudging came to be like work; the play had somehow oozed out of it; the stillness of the woods and the somberness of the night began to throw a depressing influence over the spirits of the boys, and presently the talking died out and each person shut himself up in his own thoughts. During the last half of the second hour nobody said a word.

Now we approached a log farmhouse where, according to report, there was a guard of five Union soldiers. Lyman called a halt; and there, in the deep gloom of the overhanging branches, he began to whisper a plan of assault upon that house, which made the gloom more depressing than it was before. It was a crucial moment; we realized, with a cold suddenness, that here was no jest—we were standing face to face with actual war. We were equal to the occasion. In our response there was no hesitation, no indecision: we said that if Lyman wanted to meddle with those soldiers, he could go ahead and do it; but if he waited for us to follow him, he would wait a long time.

Lyman urged, pleaded, tried to shame us, but it had no effect. Our course was plain, our minds were made up: we would flank the farmhouse—go out around. And that was what we did.

We struck into the woods and entered upon a rough time, stumbling over roots, getting tangled in vines, and torn by briers. At last we reached an open place in a safe region, and sat down, blown and hot, to cool off and nurse our scratches and bruises. Lyman was annoyed, but the rest of us were cheerful; we had flanked the farmhouse, we had made our first military movement, and it was a success; we had nothing to fret about, we were feeling just the other way. Horse-play and laughing began again; the expedition was become a holiday frolic once more.

Then we had two more hours of dull trudging and ultimate silence and depression; then, about dawn, we straggled into New London, soiled, heel-blistered, fagged with our little march, and all of us except Stevens in a sour and raspy humor and privately down on the war. We stacked our shabby old shotguns in Colonel Ralls's barn, and then went in a body and breakfasted with that veteran of the Mexican War. Afterwards he took us to a distant meadow, and there in the shade of a tree we listened to an old-fashioned speech from him, full of gunpowder and glory, full of that adjective-piling, mixed metaphor, and windy declamation which were regarded as eloquence in that ancient time and that remote region; and then he swore us on the Bible to be faithful to the State of Missouri and drive all invaders from her soil, no matter whence they might come or under what flag they might march. This mixed us considerably, and we could not make out just what service we were embarked in; but Colonel Ralls, the practiced politician and phrase-juggler, was not similarly in doubt; he knew quite clearly that he had invested us in the cause of the Southern Confederacy. He closed the solemnities by belting around me the sword which his neighbor, Colonel Brown, had worn at Buena Vista and Molino del Rey; and he accompanied this act with another impressive blast.

Then we formed in line of battle and marched four miles to a shady and pleasant piece of woods on the border of the far-reaching expanses of a flowery prairie. It was an enchanting region for war—our kind of war.

We pierced the forest about half a mile, and took up a strong position, with some low, rocky, and wooded hills behind us, and a purling, limpid creek in front. Straightway half the command were in swimming and the other half fishing. The ass with the French name gave this position a romantic title, but it was too long, so the boys shortened and simplified it to Camp Ralls.

We occupied an old maple sugar camp, whose half-rotted troughs were still propped against the trees. A long corn-crib served for sleeping quarters for the battalion. On our left, half a mile away, were Mason's farm and house; and he was a friend to the cause. Shortly after noon the farmers began to arrive from several directions, with mules and horses for our use, and these they lent us for as long as the war might last, which they judged would be about three months. The animals were of all sizes, all colors, and all breeds. They were mainly young and frisky, and nobody in the command could stay on them long at a time; for we were town boys, and ignorant of horsemanship. The creature that fell to my share was a very small mule, and yet so quick and active that it could throw me without difficulty; and it did this whenever I got on it. Then it would bray—stretching its neck out, laying its ears back, and spreading its jaws till you could see down to its works. It was a disagreeable animal in every way. If I took it by the bridle and tried to lead it off the grounds, it would sit down and brace back, and no one could budge it. However, I was not entirely destitute of military resources, and I did presently manage to spoil this game; for I had seen many a steamboat aground in my time, and knew a trick or two which even a grounded mule would be obliged to respect. There was a well by the corn-crib; so I substituted thirty fathom of rope for the bridle, and fetched him home with the windlass.

I will anticipate here sufficiently to say that we did learn to ride, after some days' practice, but never well. We could not learn to like our animals; they were not choice ones, and most of them had annoying peculiarities of one kind or another. Stevens's horse would carry him, when he was not noticing, under the huge excrescences which form on the trunks of oak trees, and wipe him out of the saddle; in this way Stevens got several bad hurts. Sergeant Bowers's horse was very large and tall, with slim, long legs, and looked like a railroad bridge. His size enabled him to reach all about, and as far as he wanted to, with his head; so he was always biting Bowers's legs. On the march, in the sun, Bowers slept a good deal; and as soon as the horse recognized that he was asleep he would reach around and bite him on the leg. His legs were black and blue with bites. This was the only thing that could ever make him swear, but this always did; whenever his horse bit him he always swore, and of course Stevens, who laughed at everything, laughed at this, and would even get into such convulsions over it as to lose his balance and fall off his horse; and then Bowers, already irritated by the pain of the horse-bite, would resent the laughter with hard language, and there would be a quarrel; so that horse made no end of trouble and bad blood in the command.

However I will get back to where I was—our first afternoon in the sugar-camp. The sugar-troughs came very handy as horse-troughs, and we had plenty of corn to fill them with. I ordered Sergeant Bowers to feed my mule; but he said that if I reckoned he went to war to be a dry-nurse to a mule, it wouldn't take me very long to find out my mistake. I believed that this was insubordination, but I was full of uncertainties about everything military, and so I let the thing pass, and went and ordered Smith, the blacksmith's apprentice, to feed the mule; but he merely gave me a large, cold, sarcastic grin, such as an ostensibly seven-year-old horse gives you when you lift his lip and find he is fourteen, and turned his back on me. I then went to the captain, and asked if it was not right and proper and military for me to have an orderly. He said it was, but as there was only one orderly in the corps, it was but right that he himself should have Bowers on his staff. Bowers said he wouldn't serve on anybody's staff; and if anybody thought he could make him, let him try it. So, of course, the thing had to be dropped; there was no other way.

Next, nobody would cook; it was considered a degradation; so we had no dinner. We lazied the rest of the pleasant afternoon away, some dozing under the trees, some smoking cob-pipes and talking sweethearts and war, some playing games. By late supper-time all hands were famished; and to meet the difficulty all hands turned to, on an equal footing, and gathered wood, built fires, and cooked the meal. Afterwards everything was smooth for a while; then trouble broke out between the corporal and the sergeant, each claiming to rank the other. Nobody knew which was the higher office; so Lyman had to settle the matter by making the rank of both officers equal. The commander of an ignorant crew like that has many troubles and vexations which probably do not occur in the regular army at all. However, with the song-singing and yarn-spinning around the camp-fire, everything presently became serene again; and by and by we raked the corn down level in one end of the crib, and all went to bed on it, tying a horse to the door, so that he would neigh if any one tried to get in.*

We had some horsemanship drill every forenoon; then, afternoons, we rode off here and there in squads a few miles, and visited the farmers' girls, and had a youthful good time, and got an honest good dinner or supper, and then home again to camp, happy and content.

For a time life was idly delicious, it was perfect; there was nothing to mar it. Then came some farmers with an alarm one day. They said it was rumored that the enemy were advancing in our direction from over Hyde's prairie. The result was a sharp stir among us, and general consternation. It was a rude awakening from our pleasant trance. The rumor was but a rumor—nothing definite about it; so, in the confusion, we did not know which way to retreat. Lyman was for not retreating at all in these uncertain circumstances; but he found that if he tried to maintain that attitude he would fare badly, for the command were in no humor to put up with insubordination. So he yielded the point and called a council of war—to consist of himself and the three other officers; but the privates made such a fuss about being left out that we had to allow them to remain, for they were already present, and doing the most of the talking too. The question was, which way to retreat; but all were so flurried that nobody seemed to have even a guess to offer. Except Lyman. He explained in a few calm words that, inasmuch as the enemy were approaching from over Hyde's prairie, our course was simple: all we had to do was not to retreat *towards* him; any other direction would answer our needs perfectly. Everybody saw in a moment how true this was, and how wise; so Lyman got a great many compliments. It was now decided that we should fall back on Mason's farm.

It was after dark by this time, and as we could not know how soon the enemy might arrive, it did not seem best to try to take the horses and things with us; so we only took the guns and am-

---

*It was always my impression that that was what the horse was there for, and I know that it was also the impression of at least one other of the command, for we talked about it at the time, and admired the military ingenuity of the device; but when I was out West, three years ago, I was told by Mr. A. G. Fuqua, a member of our company, that the horse was his; that the leaving him tied at the door was a matter of mere forgetfulness, and that to attribute it to intelligent invention was to give him quite too much credit. In support of his position he called my attention to the suggestive fact that the artifice was not employed again. I had not thought of that before.

munition, and started at once. The route was very rough and hilly and rocky, and presently the night grew very black and rain began to fall; so we had a troublesome time of it, struggling and stumbling along in the dark; and soon some person slipped and fell, and then the next person behind stumbled over him and fell, and so did the rest, one after the other; and then Bowers came with the keg of powder in his arms, while the command were all mixed together, arms and legs, on the muddy slope; and so he fell, of course, with the keg, and this started the whole detachment down the hill in a body, and they landed in the brook at the bottom in a pile, and each that was undermost pulling the hair and scratching and biting those that were on top of him; and those that were being scratched and bitten scratching and biting the rest in their turn, and all saying they would die before they would ever go to war again if they ever got out of this brook this time, and the invader might rot for all they cared, and the country along with him—and all such talk as that, which was dismal to hear and take part in, in such smothered, low voices, and such a grisly dark place and so wet, and the enemy, maybe, coming any moment.

The keg of powder was lost, and the guns, too; so the growling and complaining continued straight along while the brigade pawed around the pasty hillside and slopped around in the brook hunting for these things; consequently we lost considerable time at this; and then we heard a sound, and held our breath and listened, and it seemed to be the enemy coming, though it could have been a cow, for it had a cough like a cow; but we did not wait, but left a couple of guns behind and struck out for Mason's again as briskly as we could scramble along in the dark. But we got lost presently among the rugged little ravines, and wasted a deal of time finding the way again, so it was after nine when we reached Mason's stile at last; and then before we could open our mouths to give the countersign several dogs came bounding over the fence, with great riot and noise, and each of them took a soldier by the slack of his trousers and began to back away with him. We could not shoot the dogs without endangering the persons they were attached to; so we had to look on helpless, at what was perhaps the most mortifying spectacle of the Civil War. There was light enough, and to spare, for the Masons had now run out on the porch with candles in their hands. The old man and his son came and undid the dogs without difficulty, all but Bowers's; but they couldn't undo his dog, they didn't know his combination; he was of the bull kind, and seemed to be set with a Yale time-lock; but they got him loose at last with some scalding water, of which Bowers got his share and returned thanks. Peterson Dunlap afterwards made up a fine name for this engagement, and also for the night march which preceded it, but both have long ago faded out of my memory.

We now went into the house, and they began to ask us a world of questions, whereby it presently came out that we did not know anything concerning who or what we were running from; so the old gentleman made himself very frank, and said we were a curious breed of soldiers, and guessed we could be depended on to end up the war in time, because no government could stand the expense of the shoe-leather we should cost it trying to follow us around. "Marion *Rangers!* good name, b'gosh!" said he. And wanted to know why we hadn't had a picket-guard at the place where the road entered the prairie, and why we hadn't sent out a scouting party to spy out the enemy and bring us an account of his strength, and so on, before jumping up and stampeding out of a strong position upon a mere vague rumor—and so on, and so forth, till he made us all feel shabbier than the dogs had done, not half so enthusiastically welcome. So we went to bed shamed and low-spirited; except Stevens. Soon Stevens began to devise a garment for Bowers which could be made to automatically display his battle-scars to the grateful, or conceal them from the envious, according to his occasions; but Bowers was in no humor for this, so there was a fight, and when it was over Stevens had some battle-scars of his own to think about.

Then we got a little sleep. But after all we had gone through, our activities were not over for the night; for about two o'clock in the morning we heard a shout of warning from down the lane, accompanied by a chorus from all the dogs, and in a moment everybody was up and flying around to find out what the alarm was about. The alarmist was a horseman who gave notice that a detachment of Union soldiers was on its way from Hannibal with orders to capture and hang any bands like ours which it could find, and said we had no time to lose. Farmer Mason was in a flurry this time himself. He hurried us out of the house with all haste, and sent one of his negroes with us to show us where to hide ourselves and our telltale guns among the ravines half a mile away. It was raining heavily.

We struck down the lane, then across some rocky pasture-land which offered good advantages for stumbling; consequently we were down in the mud most of the time, and every time a man went down he black-guarded the war, and the people that started it, and everybody connected with it, and gave himself the master dose of all for being so foolish as to go into it. At last we reached the wooded mouth of a ravine, and there we huddled ourselves under the streaming trees, and sent the negro back home. It was a dismal and heart-breaking time. We were like to be drowned with the rain, deafened with the howling wind and the booming thunder, and blinded by the lightning. It was, indeed, a wild night. The drenching we were getting was misery enough, but a deeper misery still was the reflection that the halter might end us before we were a day older. A death of this shameful sort had not occurred to us as being among the possibilities of war. It took the romance all out of the campaign, and turned our dreams of glory into a repulsive nightmare. As for doubting that so barbarous an order had been given, not one of us did that.

The long night wore itself out at last, and then the negro came to us with the news that the alarm had manifestly been a false one, and that breakfast would soon be ready. Straightway we were light-hearted again, and the world was bright, and life as full of hope and promise as ever—for we were young then. How long ago that was! Twenty-four years.

The mongrel child of philology named the night's refuge Camp Devastation, and no soul objected. The Masons gave us a Missouri country breakfast, in Missourian abundance, and we needed it: hot biscuits; hot "wheat bread," prettily criss-crossed in a lattice pattern on top; hot corn pone; fried chicken; bacon, coffee, eggs, milk, buttermilk, etc.; and the world may be confidently challenged to furnish the equal of such a breakfast, as it is cooked in the South.

We stayed several days at Mason's; and after all these years the memory of the dullness, and stillness, and lifelessness of that slumberous farmhouse still oppresses my spirit as with a sense of the presence of death and mourning. There was nothing to do, nothing to think about; there was no interest in life. The male part of the household were away in the fields all day, the women were busy and out of our sight; there was no sound but the plaintive wailing of a spinning-wheel, forever moaning out from some distant room—the most lonesome sound in nature, a sound steeped and sodden with homesickness and the emptiness of life. The family went to bed about dark every night, and as we were not invited to intrude any new customs we naturally followed theirs. Those nights were a hundred years long to youths accustomed to being up till twelve. We lay awake and miserable till that hour every time, and grew old and decrepit waiting through the still eternities for the clock-strikes. This was no place for town boys. So at last it was with something very like joy that we received news that the enemy were on our track again. With a new birth of the old warrior spirit we sprang to our places in line of battle and fell back on Camp Ralls.

Captain Lyman had take a hint from Mason's talk, and he now gave orders that our camp should be guarded against surprise by the posting of pickets. I was ordered to place a picket at the forks of the road in Hyde's prairie. Night shut down black and threatening. I told Sergeant Bowers to go out to that place and stay till midnight; and, just as I was expecting, he said he wouldn't do it. I tried to get others to go, but all refused. Some excused themselves on account of the weather; but the rest were frank enough to say they wouldn't go in any kind of weather. This kind of thing sounds odd now, and impossible, but there was no surprise in it at the time. On the contrary, it seemed a perfectly natural thing to do. There were scores of little camps scattered over Missouri where the same thing was happening. These camps were composed of young men who had been born and reared to a sturdy independence, and who did not know what it meant to be ordered around by Tom, Dick, and Harry, whom they had known familiarly all their lives, in the village or on the farm. It is quite within the probabilities that this same thing was happening all over the South. James Redpath recognized the justice of this assumption, and furnished the following instance in support of it. During a short stay in East Tennessee he was in a citizen colonel's tent one day talking, when a big private appeared at the door, and, without salute or other circumlocution, said to the colonel:

"Say, Jim, I'm a-goin' home for a few days."

"What for?"

"Well, I hain't b'en there for a right smart while, and I'd like to see how things is comin' on."

"How long are you going to be gone?"

" 'Bout two weeks."

"Well, don't be gone longer than that; and get back sooner if you can."

That was all, and the citizen officer resumed his conversation where the private had broken it off. This was in the first months of the war, of course. The camps in our part of Missouri were under Brigadier-General Thomas H. Harris. He was a townsman of ours, a first-rate fellow, and well liked; but we had all familiarly known him as the sole and modest-salaried operator in our telegraph office, where he had to send about one dispatch a week in ordinary times, and two when there was a rush of business; consequently, when he appeared in our midst one day, on the wing, and delivered a military command of some sort, in a large military fashion, nobody was surprised at the response which he got from the assembled soldiery:

"Oh, now, what'll you take to *don't,* Tom Harris?"

It was quite the natural thing. One might justly imagine that we were hopeless material for war. And so we seemed, in our ignorant state; but there were those among us who afterwards learned the grim trade; learned to obey like machines; became valuable soldiers; fought all through the war, and came out at the end with excellent records. One of the very boys who refused to go out on picket duty that night, and called me an ass for thinking he would expose himself to danger in such a foolhardy way, had become distinguished for intrepidity before he was a year older.

I did secure my picket that night—not by authority, but by diplomacy. I got Bowers to go by agreeing to exchange ranks with him for the time being, and go along and stand the watch with him as his subordinate. We stayed out there a couple of dreary hours in the pitchy darkness and the rain, with nothing to modify the dreariness but Bower's monotonous growlings at the war and the weather; then we began to nod, and presently found it next to impossible to stay in the saddle; so we gave up the tedious job, and went back to the camp without waiting for the relief guard. We rode into camp without interruption or objection from anybody, and the enemy could have done the same, for there were no sentries. Everybody was asleep; at midnight there was nobody to send out another picket, so none was sent. We never tried to establish a watch at night again, as far as I remember, but we generally kept a picket out in the daytime.

In that camp the whole command slept on the corn in the big corn-crib; and there was usually a general row before morning, for the place was full of rats, and they would scramble over the boys' bodies and faces, annoying and irritating everybody; and now and then they would bite some one's toe, and the person who owned the toe would start up and magnify his English and begin to throw corn in the dark. The ears were half as heavy as bricks, and when they struck they hurt. The persons struck would respond, and inside of five minutes every man would be locked in a death-grip with his neighbor. There was a grievous deal of blood shed in the corn-crib, but this was all that was spilt while I was in the war. No, that is not quite true. But for one circumstance it would have been all. I will come to that now.

Our scares were frequent. Every few days rumors would come that the enemy were approaching. In these cases we always fell back on some other camp of ours; we never stayed where we were. But the rumors always turned out to be false; so at last even we

began to grow indifferent to them. One night a negro was sent to
our corn-crib with the same old warning: the enemy was hovering
in our neighborhood. We all said let him hover. We resolved to
stay still and be comfortable. It was a fine warlike resolution, and
no doubt we all felt the stir of it in our veins—for a moment. We
had been having a very jolly time, that was full of horse-play and
school-boy hilarity; but that cooled down now, and presently the
fast-waning fire of forced jokes and forced laughs died out altogether, and the company became silent. Silent and nervous. And
soon uneasy—worried—apprehensive. We had said we would stay,
and we were committed. We could have been persuaded to go,
but there was nobody brave enough to suggest it. An almost noiseless movement presently began in the dark by a general but un-
voiced impulse. When the movement was completed each man
knew that he was not the only person who had crept to the front
wall and had his eye at a crack between the logs. No, we were all
there; all there with our hearts in our throats, and staring out
towards the sugar-troughs where the forest footpath came through.
It was late, and there was a deep woodsy stillness everywhere.
There was a veiled moonlight, which was only just strong enough
to enable us to mark the general shape of objects. Presently a
muffled sound caught our ears, and we recognized it as the hoof-
beats of a horse or horses. And right away a figure appeared in
the forest path; it could have been made of smoke, its mass had
so little sharpness of outline. It was a man on horseback, and it
seemed to me that there were others behind him. I got hold of a
gun in the dark, and pushed it through a crack between the logs,
hardly knowing what I was doing, I was so dazed with fright.
Somebody said "Fire!" I pulled the trigger. I seemed to see a
hundred flashes and hear a hundred reports; then I saw the man
fall down out of the saddle. My first feeling was of surprised gratification; my first impulse was an apprentice-sportsman's impulse
to run and pick up his game. Somebody said, hardly audibly,
"Good—we've got him!—wait for the rest." But the rest did not
come. We waited—listened—still no more came. There was not a
sound, not the whisper of a leaf; just perfect stillness; an uncanny
kind of stillness, which was all the more uncanny on account of
the damp, earthy, late-night smells now rising and pervading it.
Then, wondering, we crept stealthily out, and approached the man.
When we got to him the moon revealed him distinctly. He was
lying on his back, with his arms abroad; his mouth was open and
his chest heaving with long gasps, and his white shirt-front was all
splashed with blood. The thought shot through me that I was a
murderer; that I had killed a man—a man who had never done

me any harm. That was the coldest sensation that ever went through my marrow. I was down by him in a moment, helplessly stroking his forehead; and I would have given anything then—my own life freely—to make him again what he had been five minutes before. And all the boys seemed to be feeling in the same way; they hung over him, full of pitying interest, and tried all they could to help him, and said all sorts of regretful things. They had forgotten all about the enemy; they thought only of this one forlorn unit of the foe. Once my imagination persuaded me that the dying man gave me a reproachful look out of his shadowy eyes, and it seemed to me that I could rather he had stabbed me than done that. He muttered and mumbled like a dreamer in his sleep about his wife and his child; and I thought with a new despair, "This thing that I have done does not end with him; it falls upon *them* too, and they never did me any harm, any more than he."

In a little while the man was dead. He was killed in war; killed in fair and legitimate war; killed in battle, as you may say; and yet he was as sincerely mourned by the opposing force as if he had been their brother. The boys stood there a half-hour sorrowing over him, and recalling the details of the tragedy, and wondering who he might be, and if he were a spy, and saying that if it were to do over again they would not hurt him unless he attacked them first. It soon came out that mine was not the only shot fired; there were five others—a division of the guilt which was a great relief to me, since it in some degree lightened and diminished the burden I was carrying. There were six shots fired at once; but I was not in my right mind at the time, and my heated imagination had magnified my one shot into a volley.

The man was not in uniform, and was not armed. He was a stranger in the country; that was all we ever found out about him. The thought of him got to preying upon me every night; I could not get rid of it. I could not drive it away, the taking of that unoffending life seemed such a wanton thing. And it seemed an epitome of war; that all war must be just that—the killing of strangers against whom you feel no personal animosity; strangers whom, in other circumstances, you would help if you found them in trouble, and who would help you if you needed it. My campaign was spoiled. It seemed to me that I was not rightly equipped for this awful business; that war was intended for men, and I for a child's nurse. I resolved to retire from this avocation of sham soldiership while I could save some remnant of my self-respect. These morbid thoughts clung to me against reason; for at bottom I did not believe I had touched that man. The law of probabilities decreed me guiltless of his blood; for in all my small experience with guns I had never hit anything I had tried to hit, and I knew I had done my best to hit him. Yet there was no solace in the thought. Against a diseased imagination demonstration goes for nothing.

The rest of my war experience was of a piece with what I have already told of it. We kept monotonously falling back upon one camp or another, and eating up the country. I marvel now at the patience of the farmers and their families. They ought to have shot us; on the contrary, they were as hospitably kind and courteous to us as if we had deserved it. In one of these camps we found Ab Grimes, an Upper Mississippi pilot, who afterwards became famous as a dare-devil rebel spy, whose career bristled with desperate adventures. The look and style of his comrades suggested that they had not come into the war to play, and their deeds made good the conjecture later. They were fine horsemen and good revolver shots; but their favorite arm was the lasso. Each had one at his pommel, and could snatch a man out of the saddle with it every time, on a full gallop, at any reasonable distance.

In another camp the chief was a fierce and profane old blacksmith of sixty, and he had furnished his twenty recruits with gigantic home-made bowie-knives, to be swung with two hands, like the *machetes* of the Isthmus. It was a grisly spectacle to see that earnest band practicing their murderous cuts and slashes under the eye of that remorseless old fanatic.

The last camp which we fell back upon was in a hollow near the village of Florida, where I was born—in Monroe County. Here we were warned one day that a Union colonel was sweeping down on us with a whole regiment at his heel. This looked decidedly serious. Our boys went apart and consulted; then we went back and told the other companies present that the war was a disappointment to us, and we were going to disband. They were getting ready themselves to fall back on some place or other, and were only waiting for General Tom Harris, who was expected to arrive at any moment; so they tried to persuade us to wait a little while, but the majority of us said no, we were accustomed to falling back, and didn't need any of Tom Harris's help; we could get along perfectly well without him—and save time, too. So about half of our fifteen, including myself, mounted and left on the instant; the others yielded to persuasion and stayed—stayed through the war.

An hour later we met General Harris on the road, with two or three people in his company—his staff, probably, but we could not tell; none of them were in uniform; uniforms had not come into vogue among us yet. Harris ordered us back; but we told him there was a Union colonel coming with a whole regiment in his wake, and it looked as if there was going to be a disturbance; so we had concluded to go home. He raged a little, but it was of no use; our minds were made up. We had done our share; had killed one man, exterminated one army, such as it was; let him go and kill the rest, and that would end the war. I did not see that brisk young general again until last year; then he was wearing white hair and whiskers.

In time I came to know that Union colonel whose coming frightened me out of the war and crippled the Southern cause to that extent—General Grant. I came within a few hours of seeing him when he was as unknown as I was myself; at a time when anybody could have said, "Grant?—Ulysses S. Grant? I do not remember hearing the name before." It seems difficult to realize that there was once a time when such a remark could be rationally made; but there *was,* and I was within a few miles of the place and the occasion, too, though proceeding in the other direction.

The thoughtful will not throw this war paper of mine lightly aside as being valueless. It has this value: it is a not unfair picture of what went on in many and many a militia camp in the first months of the rebellion, when the green recruits were without discipline, without the steadying and heartening influence of trained leaders; when all their circumstances were new and strange, and charged with exaggerated terrors, and before the invaluable experience of actual collision in the field had turned them from rabbits into soldiers. If this side of the picture of that early day has not before been put into history, then history has been to that degree incomplete, for it had and has its rightful place there. There was more Bull Run material scattered through the early camps of this country than exhibited itself at Bull Run. And yet it learned its trade presently, and helped to fight the great battles later. I could have become a soldier myself if I had waited. I had got part of it learned; I knew more about retreating than the man that invented retreating.

Eudora Welty
(1909–   )

Born in Jackson, Mississippi, where she has lived most of her life, Welty was the eldest of three children. Her mother was a schoolteacher from West Virginia with family ties in Virginia, and her father was a former schoolteacher from Ohio who settled in Jackson to work for, and later direct, the Lamar Life Insurance Company. After attending local schools in Jackson, Welty spent two years at the Mississippi State College for Women before transferring to the University of Wisconsin, where she graduated in 1929. After a year of studies at the Columbia University Graduate School of Business, she returned to Jackson, living in the family house after her father's death in 1931. She worked for a time with radio and with newspapers, and beginning in 1933 she worked for three years as a publicity agent with the W.P.A. (Works Progress Administration). She traveled all over Mississippi, storing up a local knowledge of Mississippi's past and present that only her contemporary, William Faulkner, could equal. A book of photographs she made during the W.P.A. years was later published as One Time, One Place: Mississippi in the Depression/ A Snapshot Album (1971). Her first published story, "Death of a Traveling Salesman," appeared in 1936, and from then on she steadily gained a reputation among critics and fellow writers as one of the leading, most original voices of her generation. She published several stories in The Southern Review, then edited by Robert Penn Warren and Cleanth Brooks, and in 1941, her first collection, A Curtain of Green, was published with an introduction by Katherine Anne Porter. The 1940s fully confirmed her reputation. She published two novels, The Robber Bridegroom (1942) and Delta Wedding (1946), and two of her most powerful and imaginative collections of stories, The Wide Net (1943) and The Golden Apples (1949). She also traveled in Europe, and drew on her travels for The Bride of the Innisfallen (1955), a collection that included several stories with European settings. During the 1960s, Welty continued writing, but was also deeply absorbed in taking care of her ill mother, who died in 1966. Two major novels appeared in the 1970s, Losing Battles (1970) and The Optimist's Daughter (1972). She has also written several important essays on the craft of writing, most of which are collected in The Eye of the Story (1978). Her Collected Stories were published in 1980, and four years later Harvard University Press brought out her best-selling autobiography, One Writer's Beginnings (1984). In a recent tribute to Welty, Cleanth Brooks said that she "has a quality that surpasses generosity and that I must call great-heartedness." "First Love," from The Wide Net, first appeared in Harper's Bazaar in February 1942.

FIRST LOVE

❀

Whatever happened, it happened in extraordinary times, in a season of dreams, and in Natchez it was the bitterest winter of them all. The north wind struck one January night in 1807 with an insistent penetration, as if it followed the settlers down by their own course, screaming down the river bends to drive them further still. Afterwards there was the strange drugged fall of snow. When the sun rose the air broke into a thousand prisms as close as the flash-and-turn of gulls' wings. For a long time afterwards it was so clear that in the evening the little companion-star to Sirius could be seen plainly in the heavens by travelers who took their way by night, and Venus shone in the daytime in all its course through the new transparency of the sky.

The Mississippi shuddered and lifted from its bed, reaching like a somnambulist driven to go in new places; the ice stretched far out over the waves. Flatboats and rafts continued to float downstream, but with unsignalling passengers submissive and huddled, mere bundles of sticks; bets were laid on shore as to whether they were alive or dead, but it was impossible to prove it either way.

The coated moss hung in blue and shining garlands over the trees along the changed streets in the morning. The town of little galleries was all laden roofs and silence. In the fastness of Natchez it began to seem then that the whole world, like itself, must be in a transfiguration. The only clamor came from the animals that suffered in their stalls, or from the wildcats that howled in closer rings each night from the frozen cane. The Indians could be heard from greater distances and in greater numbers than had been guessed, sending up placating but proud messages to the sun in continual ceremonies of dancing. The red percussion of their fires could be seen night and day by those waiting in the dark trance of the frozen town. Men were caught by the cold, they dropped in its snare-like silence. Bands of travelers moved closer together, with intenser caution, through the glassy tunnels of the Trace, for all proportion went away, and they followed one another like insects going at dawn through the heavy grass. Natchez people turned silently to look when a solitary man that no one had ever seen before was found and carried in through the streets, frozen the way he had crouched in a hollow tree, gray and huddled like a squirrel, with a little bundle of goods clasped to him.

Joel Mayes, a deaf boy twelve years old, saw the man brought in and knew it was a dead man, but his eyes were for something else, something wonderful. He saw the breaths coming out of people's mouths, and his dark face, losing just now a little of its softness, showed its secret desire. It was marvelous to him when the infinite designs of speech became visible in formations on the air, and he watched with awe that changed to tenderness whenever people met and passed in the road with an exchange of words. He walked alone, slowly through the silence, with the sturdy and yet dreamlike walk of the orphan, and let his own breath out through his lips, pushed it into the air, and whatever word it was it took the shape of a tower. He was as pleased as if he had had a little conversation with someone. At the end of the street, where he turned into the Inn, he always bent his head and walked faster, as if all frivolity were done, for he was boot-boy there.

He had come to Natchez some time in the summer. That was through great worlds of leaves, and the whole journey from Virginia had been to him a kind of childhood wandering in oblivion. He had remained to himself: always to himself at first, and afterwards too—with the company of Old Man McCaleb, who took him along when his parents vanished in the forest, were cut off from him, and in spite of his last backward look, dropped behind. Arms bent on destination dragged him forward through the sharp bushes, and leaves came toward his face which he finally put his hands out to stop. Now that he was a boot-boy, he had thought little, frugally, almost stonily, of that long time . . . until lately Old Man McCaleb had reappeared at the Inn, bound for no telling where, his tangled beard like the beards of old men in dreams; and in the act of cleaning his boots, which were uncommonly heavy and burdensome with mud, Joel came upon a little part of the old adventure, for there it was, dark and crusted . . . came back to it, and went over it again. . . .

He rubbed, and remembered the day after his parents had left him, the day when it was necessary to hide from the Indians. Old Man McCaleb, his stern face lighting in the most unexpected way, had herded them, the whole party alike, into the dense cane brake, deep down off the Trace—the densest part, where it grew as thick and locked as some kind of wild teeth. There they crouched, and each one of them, man, woman, and child, had looked at all the others from a hiding place that seemed the least safe of all, watching in an eager wild instinct for any movement or betrayal. Crouched by his bush, Joel had cried; all his understanding would desert him suddenly and because he could not hear he could not see or touch or find a familiar thing in the world. He wept, and Old Man McCaleb first felled the excited dog with the blunt end of his axe, and then he turned a fierce face toward him and lifted the blade in the air, in a kind of ecstasy of protecting the silence they were keeping. Joel had made a sound. . . . He gasped and put his mouth quicker than thought against the earth. He took the leaves in his mouth. . . . In that long time of lying motionless with the men and women in the cane brake he had learned what silence meant to other people. Through the danger he had felt acutely, even with horror, the nearness of his companions, a speechless embrace of which he had had no warning, a powerful, crushing unity. The Indians had then gone by, followed by an old woman—in solemn, single file, careless of the inflaming arrows they carried in their quivers, dangling in their hands a few strings of catfish. They passed in the length of the old woman's yawn. Then one by one McCaleb's charges had to rise up and come out of the hiding place. There was little talking together, but a kind of shame and shuffling. As soon as the party reached Natchez, their little cluster dissolved completely. The old man had given each of them one long, rather forlorn look for a farewell, and had gone away, no less preoccupied than he had ever been. To the man who had saved his life Joel lifted the gentle, almost indifferent face of the child who has asked for nothing. Now he remembered the white gulls flying across the sky behind the old man's head.

Joel had been deposited at the Inn, and there was nowhere else for him to go, for it stood there and marked the foot of the long Trace, with the river back of it. So he remained. It was a non-committal arrangement: he never paid them anything for his keep, and they never paid him anything for his work. Yet time passed, and he became a little part of the place where it passed over him. A small private room became his own; it was on the ground floor behind the saloon, a dark little room paved with stones with its ceiling rafters curved not higher than a man's head. There was a fireplace and one window, which opened on the courtyard filled always with the tremor of horses. He curled up every night on a highbacked bench, when the weather turned cold he was given a collection of old coats to sleep under, and the room was almost excessively his own, as it would have been a stray kitten's that came to the same spot every night. He began to keep his candlestick carefully polished, he set it in the center of the puncheon table, and at night when it was lighted all the messages of love carved into it with a knife in Spanish words, with a deep Spanish gouging, came out in black relief, for anyone to read who came knowing the language.

Late at night, nearer morning, after the travelers had all certainly pulled off their boots to fall into bed, he waked by habit and passed with the candle shielded up the stairs and through the halls and rooms, and gathered up the boots. When he had brought them all down to his table he would sit and take his own time cleaning them, while the firelight would come gently across the paving stones. It seemed then that his whole life was safely alighted, in the sleep of everyone else, like a bird on a bough, and he was alone in the way he liked to be. He did not despise boots at all— he had learned boots; under his hand they stood up and took a good shape. This was not a slave's work, or a child's either. It had dignity: it was dangerous to walk about among sleeping men. More than once he had been seized and the life half shaken out of him by a man waking up in a sweat of suspicion or nightmare, but he dealt nimbly as an animal with the violence and quick frenzy of dreamers. It might seem to him that the whole world was sleeping in the lightest of trances, which the least movement would surely wake; but he only walked softly, stepping around and over, and got back to his room. Once a rattlesnake had shoved its head from a boot as he stretched out his hand; but that was not likely to happen again in a thousand years.

It was in his own room, on the night of the first snowfall, that a new adventure began for him. Very late in the night, toward morning, Joel sat bolt upright in bed and opened his eyes to see the whole room shining brightly, like a brimming lake in the sun. Boots went completely out of his head, and he was left motionless.

The candle was lighted in its stick, the fire was high in the grate, and from the window a wild tossing illumination came, which he did not even identify at first as the falling of snow. Joel was left in the shadow of the room, and there before him, in the center of the strange multiplied light, were two men in black capes sitting at his table. They sat in profile to him, tall under the little arch of the rafters, facing each other across the good table he used for everything, and talking together. They were not of Natchez, and their names were not in the book. Each of them had a white glitter upon his boots—it was the snow; their capes were drawn together in front, and in the blackness of the folds, snowflakes were just beginning to melt.

Joel had never been able to hear the knocking at a door, and still he knew what that would be; and he surmised that these men had never knocked even lightly to enter his room. When he found that at some moment outside his knowledge or consent two men had seemingly fallen from the clouds onto the two stools at his table and had taken everything over for themselves, he did not keep the calm heart with which he had stood and regarded all men up to Old Man McCaleb, who snored upstairs.

He did not at once betray the violation that he felt. Instead, he simply sat, still bolt upright, and looked with the feasting the eyes do in secret—at their faces, the one eye of each that he could see, the cheeks, the half-hidden mouths—the faces each firelit, and strange with a common reminiscence or speculation. . . . Perhaps he was saved from giving a cry by knowing it could be heard. Then the gesture one of the men made in the air transfixed him where he waited.

One of the two men lifted his right arm—a tense, yet gentle and easy motion—and made the dark wet cloak fall back. To Joel it was like the first movement he had ever seen, as if the world had been up to that night inanimate. It was like the signal to open some heavy gate or paddock, and it did open to his complete astonishment upon a panorama in his own head, about which he knew first of all that he would never be able to speak—it was nothing but brightness, as full as the brightness on which he had opened his eyes. Inside his room was still another interior, this meeting upon which all the light was turned, and within that was one more mystery, all that was being said. The men's heads were inclined together against the blaze, their hair seemed light and floating. Their elbows rested on the boards, stirring the crumbs where Joel had eaten his biscuit. He had no idea of how long they had stayed when they got up and stretched their arms and walked out through the door, after blowing the candle out.

When Joel woke up again at daylight, his first thought was of Indians, his next of ghosts, and then the vision of what had happened came back into his head. He took a light beating for forgetting to clean the boots, but then he forgot the beating. He wondered for how long a time the men had been meeting in his room while he was asleep, and whether they had ever seen him, and what they might be going to do to him, whether they would take him each by the arm and drag him on further, through the leaves. He tried to remember everything of the night before, and he could, and then of the day before, and he rubbed belatedly at a boot in a long and deepening dream. His memory could work like the slinging of a noose to catch a wild pony. It reached back and hung trembling over the very moment of terror in which he had become separated from his parents, and then it turned and started in the opposite direction, and it would have discerned some shape, but he would not let it, of the future. In the meanwhile, all day long, everything in the passing moment and each little deed assumed the gravest importance. He divined every change in the house, in the angle of the doors, in the height of the fires, and whether the logs had been stirred by a boot or had only fallen in an empty room. He was seized and possessed by mystery. He waited for night. In his own room the candlestick now stood on the table covered with the wonder of having been touched by unknown hands in his absence and seen in his sleep.

It was while he was cleaning boots again that the identity of the men came to him all at once. Like part of his meditations, the names came into his mind. He ran out into the street with this knowledge rocking in his head, remembering then the tremor of a great arrival which had shaken Natchez, caught fast in the grip of the cold, and shaken it through the lethargy of the snow, and it was clear now why the floors swayed with running feet and unsteady hands shoved him aside at the bar. There was no one to inform him that the men were Aaron Burr and Harman Blennerhassett, but he knew. No one had pointed out to him any way that he might know which was which, but he knew that: it was Burr who had made the gesture.

They came to his room every night, and indeed Joel had not expected that the one visit would be the end. It never occurred to him that the first meeting did not mark a beginning. It took a little time always for the snow to melt from their capes—for it continued all this time to snow. Joel sat up with his eyes wide open in the shadows and looked out like the lone watcher of a conflagration. The room grew warm, burning with the heat from the little grate, but there was something of fire in all that happened. It was from

Aaron Burr that the flame was springing, and it seemed to pass across the table with certain words and through the sudden nobleness of the gesture, and touch Blennerhassett. Yet the breath of their speech was no simple thing like the candle's gleam between them. Joel saw them still only in profile, but he could see that the secret was endlessly complex, for in two nights it was apparent that it could never be all told. All that they said never finished their conversation. They would always have to meet again. The ring Burr wore caught the firelight repeatedly and started it up again in the intricate whirlpool of a signet. Quicker and fuller still was his eye, darting its look about, but never at Joel. Their eyes had never really seen his room. . . . the fine polish he had given the candlestick, the clean boards from which he had scraped the crumbs, the wooden bench where he was himself, from which he put outward—just a little, carelessly—his hand. . . . Everything in the room was conquest, all was a dream of delights and powers beyond its walls. . . . The light-filled hair fell over Burr's sharp forehead, his cheek grew taut, his smile was sudden, his lips drove the breath through. The other man's face, with its quiet mouth, for he was the listener, changed from ardor to gloom and back to ardor. . . . Joel sat still and looked from one man to the other.

At first he believed that he had not been discovered. Then he knew that they had learned somehow of his presence, and that it had not stopped them. Somehow that appalled him. . . . They were aware that if it were only before him, they could talk forever in his room. Then he put it that they accepted him. One night, in his first realization of this, his defect seemed to him a kind of hospitality. A joy came over him, he was moved to gaiety, he felt wit stirring in his mind, and he came out of his hiding place and took a few steps toward them. Finally, it was too much: he broke in upon the circle of their talk, and set food and drink from the kitchen on the table between them. His hands were shaking, and they looked at him as if from great distances, but they were not surprised, and he could smell the familiar black wetness of travelers' clothes steaming up from them in the firelight. Afterwards he sat on the floor perfectly still, with Burr's cloak hanging just beside his own shoulder. At such moments he felt a dizziness as if the cape swung him about in a great arc of wonder, but Aaron Burr turned his full face and looked down at him only with gravity, the high margin of his brows lifted above tireless eyes.

There was a kind of dominion promised in his gentlest glance. When he first would come and throw himself down to talk and the fire would flame up and the reflections of the snowy world grew bright, even the clumsy table seemed to change its substance and to become a part of a ceremony. He might have talked in another language, in which there was nothing but evocation. When he was seen so plainly, all his movements and his looks seemed part of a devotion that was curiously patient and had the illusion of wisdom all about it. Lights shone in his eyes like travelers' fires seen far out on the river. Always he talked, his talking was his appearance, as if there were no eyes, nose, or mouth to remember; in his face there was every subtlety and eloquence, and no features, no kindness, for there was no awareness whatever of the present. Looking up from the floor at his speaking face, Joel knew all at once some secret of temptation and an anguish that would reach out after it like a closing hand. He would allow Burr to take him with him wherever it was that he meant to go.

Sometimes in the nights Joel would feel himself surely under their eyes, and think they must have come; but that would be a dream, and when he sat up on his bench he often saw nothing more than the dormant firelight stretched on the empty floor, and he would have a strange feeling of having been deserted and lost, not quite like anything he had ever felt in his life. It was likely to be early dawn before they came.

When they were there, he sat restored, though they paid no more attention to him than they paid the presence of the firelight. He brought all the food he could manage to give them; he saved a little out of his own suppers, and one night he stole a turkey pie. He might have been their safety, for the way he sat up so still and looked at them at moments like a father at his playing children. He never for an instant wished for them to leave, though he would so long for sleep that he would stare at them finally in bewilderment and without a single flicker of the eyelid. Often they would talk all night. Blennerhassett's wide vague face would grow out of devotion into exhaustion. But Burr's hand would always reach across and take him by the shoulder as if to rouse him from a dull sleep, and the radiance of his own face would heighten always with the passing of time. Joel sat quietly, waiting for the full revelation of the meetings. All his love went out to the talkers. He would not have known how to hold it back.

In the idle mornings, in some morning need to go looking at the world, he wandered down to the Esplanade and stood under the trees which bent heavily over his head. He frowned out across the ice-covered racetrack and out upon the river. There was one hour when the river was the color of smoke, as if it were more a thing of the woods than an element and a power in itself. It seemed to belong to the woods, to be gentle and watched over, a tethered and grazing pet of the forest, and then when the light spread higher and color stained the world, the river would leap suddenly out of the shining ice around, into its full-grown torrent of life, and its strength and its churning passage held Joel watching over it like the spell unfolding by night in his room. If he could not speak to the river, and he could not, still he would try to read in the river's blue and violet skeins a working of the momentous event. It was hard to understand. Was any scheme a man had, however secret and intact, always broken upon by the very current of its working? One day, in anguish, he saw a raft torn apart in midstream and the men scattered from it. Then all that he felt move in his heart at the sight of the inscrutable river went out in hope for the two men and their genius that he sheltered.

It was when he returned to the Inn that he was given a notice to paste on the saloon mirror saying that the trial of Aaron Burr for treason would be held at the end of the month at Washington, capital of Mississippi Territory, on the campus of Jefferson College, where the crowds might be amply accommodated. In the meanwhile, the arrival of the full, armed flotilla was being awaited, and the price of whisky would not be advanced in this tavern, but there would be a slight increase in the tariff on a bed upstairs, depending on how many slept in it.

The month wore on, and now it was full moonlight. Late at night the whole sky was lunar, like the surface of the moon brought as close as a cheek. The luminous ranges of all the clouds stretched one beyond the other in heavenly order. They seemed to be the streets where Joel was walking through the town. People now lighted their houses in entertainments as if they copied after the sky, with Burr in the center of them always, dancing with the women, talking with the men. They followed and formed cotillion figures about the one who threatened or lured them, and their minuets skimmed across the nights like a pebble expertly skipped across water. Joel would watch them take sides, and watch the arguments, all the frilled motions and the toasts, and he thought they were to decide whether Burr was good or evil. But all the time, Joel believed, when he saw Burr go dancing by, that did not touch him at all. Joel knew his eyes saw nothing there and went always beyond the room, although usually the most beautiful woman there was somehow in his arms when the set was over. Sometimes they drove him in their carriages down to the Esplanade and pointed out the moon to him, to end the evening. There they sat showing everything to Aaron Burr, nodding with a magnificence that approached fatigue toward the reaches of the ice that stretched

over the river like an impossible bridge, some extension to the
west of the Natchez Trace; and a radiance as soft and near as rain
fell on their hands and faces, and on the plumes of the breaths
from the horses' nostrils, and they were as gracious and as grand
as Burr.

Each day that drew the trial closer, men talked more hotly on
the corners and the saloon at the Inn shook with debate; every
night Burr was invited to a finer and later ball; and Joel waited.
He knew that Burr was being allotted, by an almost specific consent, this free and unmolested time till dawn, to meet in conspiracy,
for the sake of continuing and perfecting the secret. This knowledge Joel gathered to himself by being, himself, everywhere; it
decreed his own suffering and made it secret and filled with private
omens.

One day he was driven to know everything. It was the morning
he was given a little fur cap, and he set it on his head and started
out. He walked through the dark trodden snow all the way up the
Trace to the Bayou Pierre. The great trees began to break that
day. The pounding of their explosions filled the subdued air; to
Joel it was as if a great foot had stamped on the ground. And at
first he thought he saw the fulfillment of all the rumor and
promise—the flotilla coming around the bend, and he did not know
whether he felt terror or pride. But then he saw that what covered
the river over was a chain of great perfect trees floating down,
lying on their sides in postures like slain giants and heroes of battle,
black cedars and stone-white sycamores, magnolias with their
heavy leaves shining as if they were in bloom, a long procession.
Then it was terror that he felt.

He went on. He was not the only one who had made the pil-
grimage to see what the original flotilla was like, that had been
taken from Burr. There were many others: there was Old Man
McCaleb, at a little distance. . . . In care not to show any excitement
of expectation, Joel made his way through successive little groups
that seemed to meditate there above the encampment of militia
on the snowy bluff, and looked down at the water.

There was no galley there. There were nine small flatboats tied
to the shore. They seemed so small and delicate that he was
shocked and distressed, and looked around at the faces of the
others, who looked coolly back at him. There was no sign of a
weapon about the boats or anywhere, except in the hands of the
men on guard. There were barrels of molasses and whisky, rolling
and knocking each other like drowned men, and stowed to one
side of one of the boats, in a dark place, a strange little collection
of blankets, a silver bridle with bells, a book swollen with water,

and a little flute with a narrow ridge of snow along it. Where Joel stood looking down upon them, the boats floated in clusters of three, as small as water-lilies on a still bayou. A canoe filled with crazily wrapped-up Indians passed at a little distance, and with severe open mouths the Indians all laughed.

But the soldiers were sullen with cold, and very grave or angry, and Old Man McCaleb was there with his beard flying and his finger pointing prophetically in the direction of upstream. Some of the soldiers and all the women nodded their heads, as though they were the easiest believers, and one woman drew her child tightly to her. Joel shivered. Two of the young men hanging over the edge of the bluff flung their arms in sudden exhilaration about each other's shoulders, and a look of wildness came over their faces.

Back in the streets of Natchez, Joel met part of the militia marching and stood with his heart racing, back out of the way of the line coming with bright guns tilted up in the sharp air. Behind them, two of the soldiers dragged along a young dandy whose eyes glared at everything. There where they held him he was trying over and over again to make Aaron Burr's gesture, and he never convinced anybody.

Joel went, in all, three times to the militia's encampment on the Bayou Pierre, the last time on the day before the trial was to begin. Then out beyond a willow point a rowboat with one soldier in it kept laconic watch upon the north.

Joel returned on the frozen path to the Inn, and stumbled into his room, and waited for Burr and Blennerhassett to come and talk together. His head ached. . . . All his walking about was no use. Where did people learn things? Where did they go to find them? How far?

Burr and Blennerhassett talked across the table, and it was growing late on the last night. Then there in the doorway with a fiddle in her hand stood Blennerhassett's wife, wearing breeches, come to fetch him home. The fiddle she had simply picked up in the Inn parlor as she came through, and Joel did not think she bothered now to speak at all. But she waited there before the fire, still a child and so clearly related to her husband that their sudden movements at the encounter were alike and made at the same time. They stood looking at each other there in the firelight like creatures balancing together on a raft, and then she lifted the bow and began to play.

Joel gazed at the girl, not much older than himself. She leaned her cheek against the fiddle. He had never examined a fiddle at all, and when she began to play it she frightened and dismayed him by her almost insect-like motions, the pensive antennae of her arms, her mask of a countenance. When she played she never blinked an eye. Her legs, fantastic in breeches, were separated slightly, and from her bent knees she swayed back and forth as if she were weaving the tunes with her body. The sharp odor of whisky moved with her. The slits of her eyes were milky. The songs she played seemed to him to have no beginnings and no endings, but to be about many hills and valleys, and chains of lakes. She, like the men, knew of a place. . . . All of them spoke of a country.

And quite clearly, and altogether to his surprise, Joel saw a sight that he had nearly forgotten. Instead of the fire on the hearth, there was a mimosa tree in flower. It was in the little back field at his home in Virginia and his mother was leading him by the hand. Fragile, delicate, cloud-like it rose on its pale trunk and spread its long level arms. His mother pointed to it. Among the trembling leaves the feathery puffs of sweet bloom filled the tree like thousands of paradisical birds all alighted at an instant. He had known then the story of the Princess Labam, for his mother had told it to him, how she was so radiant that she sat on the roof-top at night and lighted the city. It seemed to be the mimosa tree that lighted the garden, for its brightness and fragrance overlaid all the rest. Out of its graciousness this tree suffered their presence and shed its splendor upon him and his mother. His mother pointed again, and its scent swayed like the Asiatic princess moving up and down the pink steps of its branches. Then the vision was gone. Aaron Burr sat in front of the fire, Blennerhassett faced him, and Blennerhassett's wife played on the violin.

There was no compassion in what this woman was doing, he knew that—there was only a frightening thing, a stern allurement. Try as he might, he could not comprehend it, though it was so calculated. He had instead a sensation of pain, the ends of his fingers were stinging. At first he did not realize that he had heard the sounds of her song, the only thing he had ever heard. Then all at once as she held the lifted bow still for a moment he gasped for breath at the interruption, and he did not care to learn her purpose or to wonder any longer, but bent his head and listened for the note that she would fling down upon them. And it was so gentle then, it touched him with surprise; it made him think of animals sleeping on their cushioned paws.

For a moment his love went like sound into a myriad life and was divided among all the people in his room. While they listened, Burr's radiance was somehow quenched, or theirs was raised to equal it, and they were all alike. There was one thing that shone in all their faces, and that was how far they were from home, how far from everywhere that they knew. Joel put his hand to his own face, and hid his pity from them while they listened to the endless tunes.

But she ended them. Sleep all at once seemed to overcome her whole body. She put down the fiddle and took Blennerhassett by both hands. He seemed tired too, more tired than talking could ever make him. He went out when she led him, They went wrapped under one cloak, his arm about her.

Burr did not go away immediately. First he walked up and down before the fire. He turned each time with diminishing violence, and light and shadow seemed to stream more softly with his turning cloak. Then he stood still. The firelight threw its changes over his face. He had no one to talk to. His boots smelled of the fire's closeness. Of course he had forgotten Joel, he seemed quite alone. At last, with a strange naturalness, almost with a limp, he went to the table and stretched himself full length upon it.

He lay on his back. Joel was astonished. That was the way they laid out the men killed in duels in the Inn yard; and that was the table they laid them on.

Burr fell asleep instantly, so quickly that Joel felt he should never be left alone. He looked at the sleeping face of Burr, and the time and the place left him, and all that Burr had said that he had tried to guess left him too—he knew nothing in the world except the sleeping face. It was quiet. The eyes were almost closed, only dark slits lay beneath the lids. There was a small scar on the cheek. The lips were parted. Joel thought, I could speak if I would, or I could hear. Once I did each thing. . . . Still he listened . . . and it seemed that all that would speak, in this world, was listening. Burr was silent; he demanded nothing, nothing. . . . A boy or a man could be so alone in his heart that he could not even ask a question. In such silence as falls over a lonely man there is child-like supplication, and all arms might wish to open to him, but there is no speech. This was Burr's last night: Joel knew that. This was the moment before he would ride away. Why would the heart break so at absence? Joel knew that it was because nothing had been told. The heart is secret even when the moment it dreamed of has come, a moment when there might have been a revelation. . . . Joel stood motionless; he lifted his gaze from Burr's face and stared at nothing. . . . If love does a secret thing always, it is to reach backward, to a time that could not be known—for it makes a history of the sorrow and the dream it has contemplated in some instant of recognition. What Joel saw before him he had a terrible wish to speak out loud, but he would have had to find names for the places of the heart and the times for its shadowy and tragic events, and they seemed of great magnitude, heroic and terrible and splendid, like the legends of the mind. But for lack of a way to tell how much was known, the boundaries would lie between him and the others, all the others, until he died.

Presently Burr began to toss his head and to cry out. He talked, his face drew into a dreadful set of grimaces, which it followed over and over. He could never stop talking. Joel was afraid of these words, and afraid that eavesdroppers might listen to them. Whatever words they were, they were being taken by some force out of his dream. In horror, Joel put out his hand. He could never in his life have laid it across the mouth of Aaron Burr, but he thrust it into Burr's spread-out fingers. The fingers closed and did not yield; the clasp grew so fierce that it hurt his hand, but he saw that the words had stopped.

As if a silent love had shown him whatever new thing he would ever be able to learn, Joel had some wisdom in his fingers now which only this long month could have brought. He knew with what gentleness to hold the burning hand. With the gravity of his very soul he received the furious pressure of this man's dream. At last Burr drew his arm back beside his quiet head, and his hand hung like a child's in sleep, released in oblivion.

The next morning, Joel was given a notice to paste on the saloon mirror that conveyances might be rented at the Inn daily for the excursion to Washington for the trial of Mr. Burr, payment to be made in advance. Joel went out and stood on a corner, and joined with a group of young boys walking behind the militia.

It was warm—a "false spring" day. The little procession from Natchez, decorated and smiling in all they owned or whatever they borrowed or chartered or rented, moved grandly through the streets and on up the Trace. To Joel, somewhere in the line, the blue air that seemed to lie between the high banks held it all in a mist, softly colored, the fringe waving from a carriage top, a few flags waving, a sword shining when some gentleman made a flourish. High up on their horses a number of the men were wearing their Revolutionary War uniforms, as if to reiterate that Aaron Burr fought once at their sides as a hero.

Under the spreading live-oaks at Washington, the trial opened like a festival. There was a theatre of benches, and a promenade; stalls were set out under the trees, and glasses of whisky, and colored ribbons, were sold. Joel sat somewhere among the crowds.

Breezes touched the yellow and violet of dresses and stirred them, horses pawed the ground, and the people pressed upon him and seemed more real than those in dreams, and yet their pantomime was like those choruses and companies whose movements are like the waves running together. A hammer was then pounded, there was sudden attention from all the spectators, and Joel felt the great solidifying of their silence.

He had dreaded the sight of Burr. He had thought there might be some mark or disfigurement that would come from his panic. But all his grace was back upon him, and he was smiling to greet the studious faces which regarded him. Before their bright façade others rose first, declaiming men in turn, and then Burr.

In a moment he was walking up and down with his shadow on the grass and the patches of snow. He was talking again, talking now in great courtesy to everybody. There was a flickering light of sun and shadow on his face.

Then Joel understood. Burr was explaining away, smoothing over all that he had held great enough to have dreaded once. He walked back and forth elegantly in the sun, turning his wrist ever so airily in its frill, making light of his dream that had terrified him. And it was the deed they had all come to see. All around Joel they gasped, smiled, pressed one another's arms, nodded their heads; there were tender smiles on the women's faces. They were at Aaron Burr's feet at last, learning their superiority. They loved him now, in their condescension. They leaned forward in delight at the parading spectacle he was making. And when it was over for the day, they shook each other's hands, and Old Man McCaleb could be seen spitting on the ground, in the anticipation of another day as good as this one.

Blennerhassett did not come that night.

Burr came very late. He walked in the door, looked down at Joel where he sat among his boots, and suddenly stooped and took the dirty cloth out of his hand. He put his face quickly into it and pressed and rubbed it against his skin. Joel saw that all his clothes were dirty and ragged. The last thing he did was to set a little cap of turkey feathers on his head. Then he went out.

Joel followed him along behind the dark houses and through a ravine. Burr turned toward the Halfway Hill. Joel turned too, and he saw Burr walk slowly up and open the great heavy gate.

He saw him stop beside a tall camellia bush as solid as a tower and pick up one of the frozen buds which were shed all around it on the ground. For a moment he held it in the palm of his hand,

and then he went on. Joel, following behind, did the same. He held the bud, and studied the burned edges of its folds by the pale half-light of the East. The bud came apart in his hand, its layers like small velvet shells, still iridescent, the shriveled flower inside. He held it tenderly and yet timidly, in a kind of shame, as though all disaster lay pitifully disclosed now to the eyes.

He knew the girl Burr had often danced with under the rings of tapers when she came out in a cloak across the shadowy hill. Burr stood, quiet and graceful as he had always been as her partner at the balls. Joel felt a pain like a sting while she first merged with the dark figure and then drew back. The moon, late-risen and waning, came out of the clouds. Aaron Burr made the gesture there in the distance, toward the West, where the clouds hung still and red, and when Joel looked at him in the light he saw as she must have seen the absurdity he was dressed in, the feathers on his head. With a curious feeling of revenge upon her, he watched her turn, draw smaller within her own cape, and go away.

Burr came walking down the hill, and passed close to the camellia bush where Joel was standing. He walked stiffly in his mock Indian dress with the boot polish on his face. The youngest child in Natchez would have known that this was a remarkable and wonderful figure that had humiliated itself by disguise.

Pausing in an open space, Burr lifted his hand once more and a slave led out from the shadows a majestic horse with silver trappings shining in the light of the moon. Burr mounted from the slave's hand in all the clarity of his true elegance, and sat for a moment motionless in the saddle. Then he cut his whip through the air, and rode away.

Joel followed him on foot toward the Liberty Road. As he walked through the streets of Natchez he felt a strange mourning to know that Burr would never come again by that way. If he had left in disguise, the thirst that was in his face was the same as it had ever been. He had eluded judgment, that was all he had done, and Joel was glad while he still trembled. Joel would never know now the true course, or the true outcome of any dream: this was all he felt. But he walked on, in the frozen path into the wilderness, on and on. He did not see how he could ever go back and still be the boot-boy at the Inn.

He did not know how far he had gone on the Liberty Road when the posse came riding up behind and passed him. He walked on. He saw that the bodies of the frozen birds had fallen out of the trees, and he fell down and wept for his father and mother, to whom he had not said good-bye.

Thomas Wolfe

(1900–1938)

Born in Asheville, North Carolina, Wolfe was the youngest of seven children. His mother was a native of North Carolina and his father a mason and stonecutter who had moved to Asheville from Pennsylvania. When Wolfe was six years old, his mother opened a boardinghouse and from then on had little time for her son. He received a good education, however, at a local school where he was taken under the wing of a teacher, Margaret Roberts, whose love of literature made a deep impression on him. At the age of 16, Wolfe enrolled in the University of North Carolina at Chapel Hill. He studied under the well-known Renaissance scholar Edwin Greenlaw, played an active role in student affairs, and began his literary career. Two of his undergraduate plays were staged by the Carolina Playmakers. On graduating, he went to Harvard, where he continued writing as one of the leading students in George Pierce Baker's drama workshop. In 1923, he received an M.A. in English literature, and for the next six years he taught at New York University. During this period, he was unable to place his plays, including a long Civil War drama, Mannerhouse (1948), and consequently turned to prose fiction. Aided by Maxwell Perkins, an editor with Charles Scribner's Sons, he managed to reduce a long autobiographical novel to publishable size. It appeared, as Look Homeward, Angel, in 1929, and Wolfe was widely praised as one of the most promising novelists of his generation. Possessed of tremendous energy, and remarkably prolific, Wolfe was not usually able to channel and control his narrative flow, and almost all his novels benefited from varying degrees of editorial assistance and reshaping. Perkins closely guided Wolfe's work on his second novel, Of Time and the River (1935), which centered, like Look Homeward, Angel, on the autobiographical character Eugene Gant. After two more books published with Scribner's Sons, From Death to Morning (1935) and The Story of a Novel (1936), Wolfe broke with Perkins and changed publishers.

*He had written over a million words of a new novel, based on
another highly autobiographical character, George Webber, when
he died of complications following an attack of pneumonia in 1938.
Edward C. Aswell, his editor with his new publishers, Harper &
Brothers, cut and rearranged the sprawling manuscript into three
separate volumes:* The Web and the Rock *(1939),* You Can't Go
Home Again *(1940), and* The Hills Beyond *(1941). It has been
argued that Wolfe's tendency toward digressive excess was restrained
by the natural strictures of the short story, and that some of his best
work was done in short narratives, and in the self-contained episodes
of his long novels. Certainly much of his most powerful writing can
be found in the recent* The Complete Short Stories of Thomas Wolfe
*(1987), edited by Francis E. Skipp. "The Bell Remembered" first
appeared as a "Work in Progress" in* The American Mercury *(August 1936).*

THE BELL REMEMBERED

❀

1

It sometimes seems to me my whole life has been haunted by the
ringing of the courthouse bell. The courthouse bell gets into almost
every memory I have of youth; it beats wildly with receding and
advancing waves of sound through stormy autumn days; and in
the sharp burst suddenness of spring, the blade of April, and the
green of May, the courthouse bell is also there with its first stroke,
giving a brazen pulse to haunting solitudes of June, getting into
the rustling of a leaf, cloud shadows passing on the hills near home,
speaking to morning with its wake-o-day of come-to-court; jarring
the drowsy torpor of the afternoon with "court again."

It was a rapid and full-throated cry; a fast stroke beating on the
heels of sound; its brazen tongue, its fast hard beat was always
just the same, I knew, and yet the constant rhythm of its stroke
beat through my heart and brain and soul and through the pulses
of my blood with all the passionate and mad excitements of man's
fate and error.

I never heard it—as a boy—without a faster beating of the pulse, a sharp dry tightening of the throat, the numb aerial buoyancy of deep excitement, even though I did not always know the cause. And yet, at morning, shining morning, in the spring, it would seem to speak to me of work-a-day, to tell me the world was up-and-doing, advancing to the rattling traffics of full noon. And then, in afternoon, it spoke with still another tongue; it broke the drowsy hush of somnolent repose with its demand for action; it spoke to bodies drowsing in the mid-day warmth, and it told us we must rudely break our languorous siesta, it spoke to stomachs drugged with heavy food, crammed full of turnip greens and corn, string beans and pork, hot biscuit and hot apple pie, and it told us it was time to gird our swollen loins for labor, that man's will and character must rise above his belly, that work was doing, and that night was not yet come.

Again, in morning it would speak of civil action; of men at law and the contention of a suit; its tone was full of writs and summonses or appearances and pleading; sometimes its hard fast tongue would now cry out, "Appear!"

"Appear, appear, appear appear appear appear appear, appear appear appear!"

Or, "Your property is mine—is mine—is mine—is mine!"

Or, again, harsh and peremptory, unyielding, unexplained:

"You must come to court—to court—to court—to court—to court—to court—to court."

Or, more brutal still and more peremptory, just:

"Court—court—court—court—court—court—court—court—court—"

In afternoon, the courthouse bell spoke of more fatal punishment: murder on trial, death through the heated air, a dull, slow-witted mountain wretch who sat there in the box, with a hundred pairs of greedy eyes upon him, and still half unaware of what he did, the killer's sudden sob, itself like blood and choking in the throat, the sun gone blood-smeared in the eyes, the feel and taste of blood throughout, upon the hot air, on the tongue and in the mouth, across the visage of the sun, with all the brightness of the day gone out—and then the sudden stroke, and the gold-bright sun of day returning, a cloud shape that passes on the massed green of a mountain flank, bird-thrumming wood-notes everywhere, swift and secret, bullet-wise within the wilderness, the drowsy stitch and drone of three o'clock through coarse wet grasses of the daisied fields, and the life-blood of a murdered man soaking quietly before him down into an unsuspected hand's breadth of familiar earth on mountain meadow—all as sudden, swift, and casual as this, all swiftly done as the swift thrummings in a wood—

and all unknowing of the reason why he did it; now the prisoner's box, two hundred greedy eyes upon him, a stunned animal caught in the steel traps of law, and the courthouse bell that pounds upon the torpor of hot afternoon the brutal imperative of its inflexible command:

"To kill to kill to kill to kill to kill to kill—" and then, simply: "Kill kill kill kill kill kill kill kill kill—"

2

I sometimes wonder if the people of a younger and more urban generation realize the way the courthouse bell, the country courthouse, shaped life and destiny through America some sixty years ago. For us in Libya Hill, at any rate, it was the center of the life of the entire community, the center of the community itself—for Libya Hill was first a country courthouse, then a town—a town that grew up round the courthouse, made a Square, and straggled out along the roads that led to the four quarters of the earth.

And for the country people round about, even more than for the people who lived in the town, the courthouse was the center of their life, and of more interest to them than it was to us. They came to town to trade and barter—they came to town to buy and sell, but when their work was over, it was always to the courthouse that they turned.

When court was being held, one could always find them here. Here were their mules, their horses, ox-teams, and their covered wagons; here their social converse, their communal life; here were their trials, suits, and punishments; here their drawling talk of rape and lust and murder—the whole shape and pattern of their life, the look of it, its feel, its taste, its smell.

Here was, in sum, it seems to me, the framework of America; the abysmal gap between our preachment and performance, our grain of righteousness and our hill of wrong. Not only in the lives and voices and persons of these country people, these rude mountaineers, who sat and spat and loitered on the courthouse steps, but in the very design and shape and structure of the courthouse building itself did the framework of this life of ours appear. Here in the pseudo-Greek facade with its front of swelling plaster columns trying to resemble stone, as well as in the high square dimensions of the trial courtroom, the judge's bench, the prisoner's box, the witness stand, the lawyer's table, the railed-off area for participants, the benches for spectators behind, the crossed flags of the State and of the nation, and the steel engraving of George

Washington—in all these furnishings of office, there was some effort to maintain the pomp of high authority, the dignified impartial execution of the law.

But, alas, the impartial execution of the law was, like the design and structure of the courthouse itself, not free from error, and not always sound. The imposing Doric and Corinthian columns were often found, upon inspection, to be just lath and brick and plaster trying to be stone. And no matter what pretensions to a classic austerity the courtroom itself would try to make, the tall gloomy-looking windows were generally unwashed; no matter what effect of Attic grace the grand facade could make upon the slow mind of the country man, the wide dark corridors were full of drafts and ventilations, darkness, creaking boards, and squeaking stairways, the ominous dripping of an unseen tap.

And the courthouse smell was also like the smell of terror, crime, and justice in America—a certain essence of our life, a certain sweat out of ourselves, a certain substance that is ours alone and unmistakable—the smell of courthouse justice in this land.

It was—to get down to its basic chemistries—first of all a smell of sweat, tobacco-juice, and urine—a smell of sour flesh, feet, clogged urinals, and broken-down latrines. It was, mixed in and subtly interposed with these, a smell of tarry disinfectant, a kind of lime and alum, a strong ammoniac smell. It was a smell of old dark hallways and old used floors, a cool, dark, dank, and musty cellar-smell. It was a smell of old used chairs with creaking bottoms; a smell of sweated woods and grimy surfaces; a smell of rubbed-off arm-rests, bench-rests, chair-rests, counter-, desk-, and table-rests; a smell as if every inch of woodwork in the building had been oiled, stewed, sweated, grimed, and polished by man's flesh.

In addition to all these, it was a smell of rump-worn leathers, a smell of thumb-worn calfskin, yellowed papers and black ink; it was a smell of brogans, shirtsleeves, overalls, and sweat and hay and butter; and it was a kind of exciting smell of chalk, starched cuffs that rattled, the incessant rattling of dry papers, the crackling of dry knuckles and parched fingers, the dry rubbing of white chalky hands; a country lawyer smell of starch and broadcloth.

And oh, much more than these—and all of these—it was a smell of fascination and terror, a smell of throbbing pulse and beating heart and the tight and dry constriction of the throat; it was a smell made up of all the hate, the horror, the fear, the chicanery, and the loathing that the world could know, a smell made up of the intolerable anguish of men's nerve and heart and brain and sinew; the sweat and madness of man's perjured soul enmeshed in trick-

ery—a whole huge smell of violence and crime and murder, of
shyster trickeries and broken faith—it was one small smell of justice, fairness, truth, and hope in one high mountainous stench of
error, passion, guilt, and graft, and wrong.

It was, in short, America—the wilderness America, the sprawling, huge, chaotic criminal America; it was murderous America
soaked with murdered blood, tortured and purposeless America;
savage, blind, and mad America, exploding, through its puny laws,
its pitiful pretense; America with all its almost hopeless hopes, its
almost faithless faiths; America with the huge blight on her of her
own error, the broken promise of her lost dream and her un-
achieved desire; and it was America as well with her unspoken
prophecies, her unfound language, her unuttered song; and just
for all these reasons it was for us all our own America, with all
her horror, beauty, tenderness, and terror, with all we know of
her that never has been proved, that never yet was uttered—the
only one we know, the only one there is.

3

I suppose my interest in the courthouse and the courthouse bell
was a double one; the sound of that great brazen bell not only
punctuated almost every experience of my youth, but it also punctuated almost every memory I have of my father. He had been
made a Judge of the Circuit Court some years after the War, and
the whole record of his life about this period might have been
chronicled in the ringing of the bell. When the bell rang, court
was in session and my father was in town; when the bell did not
ring, court was not in session, and my father was holding court in
some other town.

Moreover, when the bell began to ring, my father was at home;
and before the bell had finished ringing, he was on his way to
court. The ceremony of his going was always the same; I suppose
I watched him do it a thousand times, and it never changed or
varied by a fraction. He would get home at one o'clock, would
eat dinner in a pre-occupied silence, speaking rarely, and probably
thinking of the case that he was trying at the moment. After dinner,
he would go into his study, stretch himself out on his old leather
sofa, and nap for three-quarters of an hour. I often watched him
while he took this brief siesta; he slept with a handkerchief spread
out across his face, and with only the top of his bald head visible.
Often, these naps produced snores of very formidable proportions,

and the big handkerchief would blow up beneath the blast like a sail that catches a full wind.

But no matter how profound these slumbers seemed to be, he would always rouse himself at the first stroke of the courthouse bell, snatch the handkerchief from his face, and sit bolt upright with an expression of intense and almost startled surprise on his red face and in his round blue eyes:

"There's the *bell!*" he would cry, as if this was the last thing on earth he had expected. Then he would get up, limp over to his desk, thrust papers, briefs, and documents into his old brief case, jam a battered old slouch hat upon his head, and limp heavily down the hall where my mother would be busy with her sewing in the sitting room.

"I'm going now!" he would announce in a tone that seemed to convey a kind of abrupt and startled warning. To this my mother would make no answer whatever, but would continue placidly at her knitting, as if she had been expecting this surprising information all the time.

Then my father, after staring at her for a minute in a puzzled and undecided manner, would limp off down the hall, pause halfway, limp back to the open door, and fairly shout:

"I say, I'm *going!*"

"Yes, Edward," my mother would answer placidly, still busy with her needles. "I heard you."

Whereupon Father would glare at her again, in a surprised and baffled manner, and finally blurt out:

"Is there anything you want from town?"

To which my mother would say nothing for a moment, but would lift the needle to the light, and squinting, thread it.

"I say," my father would shout, as if he were yelling to someone on top of a mountain, "*is—there—anything—you—want—from town?*"

"No, Edward," Mother would presently reply, with the same maddening placidity. "I think not. We have everything we need."

At these words, Father would stare at her fixedly, breathing heavily, with a look of baffled indecision and surprise. Then he would turn abruptly, grunting, "Well, good-bye, then," and limp down the hall toward the steps, and heavily and rapidly away across the yard—and that would be the last I would see of my father until evening came: a stocky, red-faced man, with a bald head and a battered-up old brief case underneath his arm, limping away up the straggling street of a little town down South some sixty years ago, while the courthouse bell beat out its hard and rapid stroke.

I have heard my father say that, outside of a battlefield, a courtroom could be the most exciting place on earth, and that the greatest opportunity for observing life and character was in a courtroom; and I think that he was right. When an interesting case was being tried, he sometimes took me with him; I saw and heard a great many wonderful and fascinating things, a great many brutal and revolting things, as well; but by the time I was fifteen I was not only pretty familiar with courtroom procedure, but I had seen men on trial for their lives; the thrilling and terrible adventure of pursuit and capture; the cunning efforts of the hounds of law to break down evidence, to compel confession, to entrap and snare—hounds running, and the fox at bay; and I had heard trials for every other thing on earth as well—for theft, assault, and robbery; for blackmail, arson, rape, and greed, and petty larceny; for deep-dyed guilt or perjured innocence—all of the passion, guilt, and cunning, all of the humor, love, and faithfulness, all of the filth and ignorance, the triumph or defeat, the pain or the fulfillment, that the earth can know, or of which a man's life is capable.

Although my father's house on College Street was just a few blocks from the courthouse on the Square—so near, in fact, that he could be in court before the bell had finished its brazen ringing—in those days we could pass a large part of the whole town's population in the course of that short journey. It certainly seemed to me, every time I went along with him, that we *spoke* to the whole town; every step of our way was punctuated by someone greeting him with "Hello, General," or "Good morning, General," or "Good afternoon"—(outside the courtroom everybody called him General)—and my father's brief, grunted-out replies as he limped along:

" 'Lo, Ed," "Morning, Jim," " 'Day, Tom."

He was a good walker in spite of his limp and, when in a hurry, could cover ground fast—so fast indeed that I had to stir my stumps to keep ahead of him.

Arrived at the courthouse, we were greeted by the usual nondescript conglomeration of drawling country folk, tobacco-chewing mountaineers, and just plain loafers who made the porch, the steps, and walls of the old brick courthouse their club, their prop, their stay, their fixed abode, and almost, so it seemed to me, their final resting place—certainly some of them were, in Father's phrase, "as old as God," and had been sitting on the courthouse steps or leaning against the courthouse walls longer than most of us could remember.

Chief among these ancient sons of leisure—I think he was, by tacit consent, generally considered chief of them—was the venerable old reprobate who was generally referred to, when his back was turned, as Looky Thar. My father had given him that title, and it stuck forever after, chiefly because of its exceeding fitness. Old Looky Thar's real name was Old Man Slagle; although he called himself Major Slagle, and was generally addressed as Major by his familiars, friends, and acquaintances, the title was self-bestowed, and had no other basis in fact or actuality.

Old Looky Thar had been a soldier in the War and in addition to the loss of a leg, he had suffered a remarkable injury which had earned him the irreverent and flippant name of Looky Thar. This injury was a hole in the roof of his mouth, "big enough to stick your hull fist through," in Looky Thar's own description of its dimensions, the result of an extraordinary shrapnel wound which had miraculously spared his life, but had unfortunately not impaired his powers of speech. I think he was about the lewdest, profanest, dirtiest-minded old man I ever saw or heard, and furthermore, his obscenities were published in a high cracked falsetto and accompanied by a high cracked cackle, publishable for blocks, and easily heard by people a hundred yards away.

He was, if anything, prouder of that great hole in his mouth than he was of his wooden leg; he was more pleased about it than he would have been over election to the Legion of Honor, the bestowal of the Victoria Cross, or the winning of a famous victory. That hole in the roof of his mouth not only became the be-all and the sufficient reason for his right to live; it became the be-all for his right to loaf. Moreover, the hole not only justified him in everything he thought or felt or did; but he also felt apparently that it gave to all his acts and utterances a kind of holy and inspired authority, a divine and undebatable correctness. And if anyone had the effrontery—was upstart enough—to question any one of Looky Thar's opinions (and his opinions were incessant and embraced the universe), whether on history, politics, religion, mathematics, hog-raising, peanut-growing, or astrology, he might look forward to being promptly, ruthlessly, and utterly subdued—discomfited—annihilated—put in his place at once by the instant and infallible authority of old Looky Thar's chief "frame of reference"—the huge hole in the roof of his mouth.

It did not matter what was the subject, what was the occasion, what the debate; old Looky Thar might argue black was white, or top was bottom, that the earth was flat instead of round—but whatever his position, no matter what he said was right, was right because he said it, because a man who had a big hole in the roof of his mouth could never *possibly* be wrong about anything.

On these occasions, whenever he was questioned or opposed in anything, his whole demeanor would change in the wink of an eye.

In spite of his wooden leg, he would leap up out of his old splint-bottomed chair as quick as a monkey, and so angry that he punctuated every word by digging his wooden peg into the earth with vicious emphasis. Then, opening his horrible old mouth so wide that one wondered how he would ever get it closed again, exposing a few old yellow fangs of teeth, he would point a palsied finger at the big hole, and in a high cracked voice that shook with passion, scream:

"Looky thar!"

"I know, Major, but—"

"*You* know?" old Looky Thar would sneer. "Whut do *you* know, sir? A miserable little upstart that don't know *nothin'* tryin' to talk back to a man that fit all up an' down Virginny an' that's got a hole in the roof of his mouth big enough to stick your hull fist through. . . . *You* know!" he screamed, "*Whut* do you know? . . . Looky thar!"

"All right, I can see the hole, all right, but the argument was whether the earth was round or flat, and *I* say it's round!"

"*You* say it's round," Looky Thar would sneer. "What do *you* know about it, sir—a pore little two-by-fo' upstart that *don't know nothin'*? . . . How do *you* know whether it's round or flat? . . . When you ain't *been* nowhere yet . . . and ain't *seen* nothin' yet . . . an' never been five miles from home in your hull *life!* . . . talkin' back to a man that's fit all up an' down Virginny an' that's got a hole in the roof of his mouth you could stick your hull fist through—Looky thar!" and he would dig viciously into the earth with his wooden peg, crack his jaws wide open, and point to the all-justifying hole with a palsied and triumphant hand.

Otherwise, if not opposed in any way, old Looky Thar was amiable enough, and would talk endlessly and incessantly to anyone within hearing distance, who might have leisure or the inclination to listen to unending anecdotes about old Looky Thar's experiences in war, in peace, with horses, liquor, niggers, men and women—especially with women, his alleged relations with the female sex being lecherously recounted in a high cracked voice, punctuated by high-cracked bursts of bawdy laughter, all audible for several hundred yards.

My father loathed him; he represented everything my father hated most—shiftlessness, ignorance, filth, lechery, and professional veteranism; but hate, love, loathing, anger or contempt were not sufficient to prevail above old Looky Thar; he was a curse, a burden, and a cause of untold agony, but he was there in his splint-bottomed chair against the courthouse porch, and there to stay—a burden to be suffered and endured.

Although old Looky Thar could pop up from his chair as quick and nimble as a monkey when he was mad, and someone had opposed him, when he greeted my father he became the aged and enfeebled veteran, crippled from his wounds, but resolved to make a proper and respectful greeting to his honored chief.

At Father's approach, old Looky Thar, who would have been regaling his tobacco-chewing audience with tall tales of "how we fit 'em—we fit 'em up an' down Virginny"—he would cease talking suddenly, tilt his chair forward to the ground, place his palsied hands upon the arms of the chair, and claw frantically and futilely at the floor with his wooden stump, all the time grunting and groaning, and almost sobbing for breath, like a man at the last gasp of his strength, but resolved to do or die at any cost.

Then he would pause, and still panting heavily for breath, gasp out in a voice mealy with hypocrisy and assumed humility:

"Boys, I'm ashamed to have to ask fer help, but I'm afraid I got to! Here comes the General an' I *got* to get up on my feet; will one of you fellers lend a hand?"

Of course, a dozen lending, sympathetic hands were instantly available; they would pull and hoist old Looky Thar erect. He would stagger about drunkenly and claw frantically at the floor with his wooden peg in an effort to get his balance, catch hold of numerous shoulders in an effort to regain his balance—and then, slowly, and with a noble effort, come up to the salute—the most florid and magnificent salute you ever saw, the salute of a veteran of the Old Guard saluting the Emperor at Waterloo.

There were times when I was afraid my father was going to strangle him. Father's face would redden to the hue of a large and very ripe tomato, the veins in his thick neck and forehead would swell up like whipcording, his big fingers would work convulsively for a moment into his palms while he glared at Looky Thar; then without another word he would turn and limp away into the court.

To me, however, his comment on one occasion, while brief, was violent and descriptively explosive.

"There's another of your famous veterans," he growled. "Four years in war and forty years on your hind-end. There's a fine old veteran for you."

"Well," I protested, "the man *has* got a wooden leg."

Father stopped abruptly, faced me, his square face reddened painfully as he fixed me with the earnest, strangely youthful look of his blue eyes:

"Listen to me, boy," he said very quietly, and tapped me on the shoulder with a peculiar and extraordinarily intense quality of conviction. "Listen to me; a wooden leg is no excuse for *anything!*"

I stared at him, too astonished to say anything; and not knowing what reply to make to what seemed to me one of the most extraordinary and meaningless remarks I had ever heard.

"Just remember what I tell you," he said. "A wooden leg is no excuse for anything!"

Then, his face very red, he turned and limped heavily and rapidly into the court, leaving me still staring in gape-mouthed astonishment at his broad back.

4

One day, about six months after this conversation with my father, I was in his study reading an account of the Battle of Spottsylvania by one of the generals in Hancock's command who had been present at the fight. I had finished reading his description of the first two movements of that bloody battle—namely, Hancock's charge upon the Confederate position and the thrilling counter-charge of our own troops—and was now reading the passages that described the final movement—the hand-to-hand fighting that was waged by forces of both armies over the earth embankment—a struggle so savage and prolonged that, in the words of this officer, "almost every foot of earth over which they fought was red with blood." Suddenly I came upon this passage:

> There have been other battles of the War in which more troops were engaged, where the losses were greater, and the operations carried on on a more extensive scale, but in my own estimation, there has been no fighting in modern times that was as savage and destructive as was the hand-to-hand fighting that was waged back and forth over the earth embankment there at Spottsylvania in the final hours of the battle. The men of both armies fought hand to hand and toe to toe; the troops of both sides stood on top of the embankment firing pointblank in the faces of the enemy, getting fresh muskets constantly from their comrades down below. When one man fell, another sprang up to take his place. No one was spared—from private soldier up to captain, from captain to brigade commander; I saw general officers fighting in the thick of it shoulder to shoulder with the men of their own ranks; among others, I saw Mason among his mountaineers, firing and loading until he was himself shot down and borne away by his own men, his

right leg so shattered by a Minie ball that amputation was imperative—

Something blurred and passed across my eyes, and suddenly all the gold and singing had gone out of the day. I got up and walked out of the study, and down the hallway, holding the book open in my hand.

When I got to the sitting room, I looked in and saw my mother there; she looked up placidly, and then looked at me quickly, startled, and got up, putting her sewing things down upon the table as she did.

"What is it? What's the matter with you?"

I walked over to her, very steadily, I think.

"This book," I said, and held the page up to her, pointing at the place—"Read what it says here—"

She took it quickly, and read. In a moment she handed it back to me; her fingers shook a little, but she spoke calmly:

"Well?"

"What the book says—is that Father?"

"Yes," she said.

"Then," I said, staring slowly at her and swallowing hard—"does that mean that Father—"

Then I saw that she was crying; she put her arms around my shoulders and said:

"Your father is so proud—he wouldn't tell you. He couldn't bear to have his son think he was a cripple."

Then I knew what he had meant.

A cripple! Fifty years and more have passed since then, but every time the memory returns, my vision blurs, and something tightens in my throat, and the gold and singing passes from the sun as it did on that lost day in spring, long, long ago. A cripple—he a cripple!

I see his bald head and red face, his stocky figure limping heavily away to court . . . and hear the hard fast ringing of the bell . . . and remember Looky Thar, the courthouse loafers and the people passing . . . the trials, the lawyers, and the men accused . . . the generals coming to our house the way they did all through the 'eighties . . . the things they talked of and the magic that they brought . . . and my heart boy-drunk with dreams of war and glory . . . the splendid generals and my father, who was so un-warlike as I thought . . . and the unworthiness of my romantic unbelief . . . to see that burly and prosaic figure as it *limped* away toward court . . . and tried to vision him with Gordon in the Wilderness . . . or charging through the shot-torn fields and woods at Gettysburg . . . or wounded, sinking to his knees at Sharpsburg, by Antietam Creek . . . and failing miserably to see him so; and, boy-like, failing to envisage how much of madness or of magic even brick-red faces and bald heads may be familiar with . . . down the Valley of Virginia, long years ago. . . .

But a cripple!—No! He was no cripple, but the strongest, straightest, plainest, most uncrippled man I ever knew! . . . And fifty years have gone by since then, but when I think of that lost day, it all comes back . . . the memory of each blade, each leaf, each flower . . . the rustling of each leaf and every light and shade that came and went against the sun . . . the dusty Square, the hitching posts, the mules, the ox-teams, and the horses, the hay-sweet bedding of the country wagons and the smell of bedded melons . . . the courthouse loafers . . . and old Looky Thar—and Spangler's mule teams trotting by across the Square . . . each door that opened . . . and each gate that slammed . . . and everything that passed throughout the town that day . . . the women sitting on the latticed porches of their brothels at the edge of Niggertown . . . the whores respiring in warm afternoon, and certain only of one thing—that night would come! . . . all things known or un-seen—a part of my whole consciousness . . . a little mountain town down South one afternoon in May some fifty years ago . . . and time passing like the humming of a bee, time passing like the thrumming in a wood, time passing as cloud shadows pass above the hill-flanks of the mountain meadows or like the hard fast pounding of the courthouse bell . . . a man long dead and long since buried who limped his way to court and who had been at Gettysburg . . . and time passing . . . passing like a leaf . . . time passing like a river flowing . . . time passing . . . and remembered suddenly as here, like the forgotten hoof and wheel of sixty years ago . . . time passing as men pass who never will come back again . . . and leaving us, Great God, with only this . . . knowing that this earth, this time, this life are stranger than a dream.

Richard Wright

(1908–1960)

*Born on a cotton plantation near Natchez, Mississippi, Wright suf-
fered through a painful childhood of poverty, insecurity, and home-
lessness. His father was an illiterate mill worker who deserted the
family when Wright was five years old. His mother was a schoolteacher who was forced to place her two sons in an orphanage in
Memphis until she earned enough to move her family to her sister's
house in Elaine, Arkansas. When Wright's uncle was killed by a
white mob, and after his mother was stricken by a series of paralytic
strokes, Wright moved to Jackson, Mississippi, where he lived with
his maternal grandmother, and finally received a taste of stability
and regular education. He left school after the ninth grade and went
to Memphis, where he worked as a delivery boy for a year. In 1927,
he moved to Chicago, where eventually his mother, brother, and
grandmother joined him. He held a variety of jobs, and began
writing stories, poems, and essays in journals of the political left.
He joined the Communist Party in 1933, and in 1937 moved to New
York as Harlem editor of the* Daily Worker. *In New York, he
published his first book, a collection of stories dealing with poor
blacks victimized by racism in the rural South:* Uncle Tom's Children *(1938). Two years later, his best novel, and one of the major
black novels of the century,* Native Son, *appeared. It was a huge
critical and popular success, and with the publication of his autobiographical narrative,* Black Boy, *in 1945, Wright became the most
famous living black writer in the world. In 1947, he moved to Paris
with his second wife, Ellen Poplar, and he remained there for the
rest of his life. Though he continued writing, after he moved to Paris
his reputation declined in the United States, and he never regained
the popularity or critical esteem accorded his first books. He remained politically active, writing a large number of essays and books
documenting his travels throughout Europe, Africa, and Asia. In
1959, his daughter Julia was admitted to Cambridge, but the British*

authorities refused him permission to live in England. He died the following year, and was buried in Paris. Among his other books are The Outsider *(1953),* Black Power: A Record of Reactions in a Land of Pathos *(1954),* Pagan Spain *(1957),* The Long Dream *(1958),* Eight Men *(1961), and* Lawd Today *(1963). "Silt" first appeared in* New Masses *in August 1937. It was later included in his posthumous collection of stories,* Eight Men, *under the title of "The Man Who Saw the Flood."*

SILT

⌘

When the Flood Waters Recede, the Poor Folk Along the River Start from Scratch

At last the flood waters had receded. A black father, a black mother, and a black child tramped through muddy fields, leading a tired cow by a thin bit of rope. They stopped on a hilltop and shifted the bundles on their shoulders. As far as they could see the ground was covered with flood-silt. The little girl lifted a skinny finger and pointed to a mud-caked cabin.

"Look, Pa! Ain' that our home?"

The man, round-shouldered, clad in blue, ragged overalls, looked with bewildered eyes. Without moving a muscle, scarcely moving his lips, he said: "Yeah."

For five minutes they did not speak or move. The flood waters had been more than eight feet high here. Every tree, blade of grass, and stray stick had its flood-mark: caky, yellow mud. It clung to the ground, cracking thinly here and there in spider-web fashion. Over the stark fields came a gusty spring wind. The sky was high, blue, full of white clouds and sunshine. Over all hung a first-day strangeness.

"The hen house is gone," sighed the woman.

"N the pig pen," sighed the man.

They spoke without bitterness.

"Ah reckon them chickens is all done drowned."

"Yeah."

"Miz Flora's house is gone, too," said the little girl.

They looked at a clump of trees where their neighbor's house had stood.

"Lawd!"

"Yuh reckon anybody knows where they is?"

"Hard t' tell."

The man walked down the slope and stood uncertainly.

"There wuz a road erlong here somewheres," he said.

But there was no road now. Just a wide sweep of yellow, scalloped silt.

"Look, Tom!" called the woman. "Here's a piece of our gate!"

The gate-post was half buried in the ground. A rusty hinge stood stiff, like a lonely finger. Tom pried it loose and caught it firmly in his hand. There was nothing in particular he wanted to do with it; he just stood holding it firmly. Finally he dropped it, looked up, and said:

"C'mon. Le's go down n see whut we kin do."

Because it sat in a slight depression, the ground about the cabin was soft and slimy.

"Gimme tha' bag o' lime, May," he said.

With his shoes sucking in mud, he went slowly around the cabin, spreading the white lime with thick fingers. When he reached the front again he had a little left; he shook the bag out on the porch. The fine grains of floating lime flickered in the sunlight.

"Tha' oughta hep some," he said.

"Now, yuh be careful, Sal!" said May. "Don' yuh go n fall down in all this mud, yuh hear?"

"Yessum."

The steps were gone. Tom lifted May and Sally to the porch. They stood a moment looking at the half-opened door. He had shut it when he left, but somehow it seemed natural that he should find it open. The planks in the porch floor were swollen and warped. The cabin had two colors: near the bottom it was a solid yellow; at the top it was the familiar grey. It looked weird, as though its ghost were standing beside it.

The cow lowed.

"Tie Pat t' the pos' on the en' of the porch, May."

May tied the rope slowly, listlessly. When they attempted to open the front door, it would not budge. It was not until Tom had placed his shoulder against it and gave it a stout shove that it scraped back jerkily. The front room was dark and silent. The damp smell of flood-silt came fresh and sharp to their nostrils. Only one-half of the upper window was clear, and through it fell a rectangle of dingy light. The floors swam in ooze. Like a mute warning, a wavering flood-mark went high around the walls of the room. A dresser sat cater-cornered, its drawers and sides bulging like a bloated corpse. The bed, with the mattress still on it, was like a casket forged of mud. Two smashed chairs lay in a corner, as though huddled together for protection.

"Le's see the kitchen," said Tom.

The stove-pipe was gone. But the stove stood in the same place.

"The stove's still good. We kin clean it."

"Yeah."

"But where's the table?"

"Lawd knows."

"It must've washed erway wid the rest of the stuff, Ah reckon."

They opened the back door and looked out. They missed the barn, the hen house, and the pig pen.

"Tom, yuh bettah try tha ol' pump 'n see ef any watah's there."

The pump was stiff. Tom threw his weight on the handle and carried it up and down. No water came. He pumped on. There was a dry, hollow cough. Then yellow water trickled. He caught his breath and kept pumping. The water flowed white.

"Thank Gawd! We's got some watah."

"Yuh bettah boil it fo yuh use it," he said.

"Yeah. Ah know."

"Look, Pa! Here's yo ax," called Sally.

Tom took the ax from her. "Yeah. Ah'll need this."

"N here's somethin else," called Sally, digging spoons out of the mud.

"Waal, Ahma git a bucket n start cleanin," said May. "Ain no use in waitin, cause we's gotta sleep on them floors tonight."

When she was filling the bucket from the pump, Tom called from around the cabin. "May, look! Ah done foun mah plow!" Proudly he dragged the silt-caked plow to the pump. "Ah'll wash it n it'll be awright."

"Ah'm hongry," said Sally.

"Now, yuh jus wait! Yuh et this mawnin," said May. She turned to Tom. "Now, whutcha gonna do, Tom?"

He stood looking at the mud-filled fields.

"Yuh goin back t Burgess?"

"Ah reckon Ah have to."

"Whut else kin yuh do?"

"Nothin," he said. "Lawd, but Ah sho hate t start all over wid tha white man. Ah'd leave here ef Ah could. Ah owes im nigh eight hundred dollahs. N we needs a hoss, grub, seed, n a lot mo other things. Ef we keeps on like this tha white man'll own us body n soul. . . ."

"But, Tom, there ain nothin else t do," she said.

"Ef we try t run erway they'll put us in jail."

"It coulda been worse," she said.

Sally came running from the kitchen. "Pa!"

"Hunh?"

"There's a shelf in the kitchen the flood didn't git!"

"Where?"

"Right up over the stove."

"But, chile, ain nothin up there," said May.

"But there's somethin on it," said Sally.

"C'mon. Le's see."

High and dry, untouched by the flood-water, was a box of matches. And beside it a half-full sack of Bull Durham tobacco. He took a match from the box and scratched it on his overalls. It burned to his fingers before he dropped it.

"May!"

"Hunh?"

"Look! Here's muh 'bacco n some matches!"

She stared unbelievingly. "Lawd!" she breathed.

Tom rolled a cigarette clumsily.

May washed the stove, gathered some sticks, and after some difficulty, made a fire. The kitchen stove smoked, and their eyes smarted. May put water on to heat and went into the front room. It was getting dark. From the bundles they took a kerosene lamp and lit it. Outside Pat lowed longingly into the thickening gloam and tinkled her cowbell.

"Tha old cow's hongry," said May.

"Ah reckon Ah'll have t be gitting erlong t Burgess."

They stood on the front porch.

"Yuh bettah git on, Tom, fo it gits too dark."

"Yeah."

The wind had stopped blowing. In the east a cluster of stars hung.

"Yuh goin, Tom?"

"Ah reckon Ah have t."

"Ma, Ah'm hongry," said Sally.

"Wait erwhile, honey. Ma knows yuh's hongry."

Tom threw his cigarette away and sighed.

"Look! Here comes somebody!"

"Tha's Mistah Burgess now!"

A mud-caked buggy rolled up. The shaggy horse was splattered all over. Burgess leaned his white face out of the buggy and spat.

"Well, I see you're back."

"Yessuh."

"How things look?"

"They don look so good, Mistah."

"What seems to be the trouble?"

"Waal, Ah ain got no hoss, no grub, nothing. . . . The only thing Ah is got is tha ol cow there. . . ."

"You owe eight hundred dollahs down at the store, Tom."

"Yessuh, Ah know. But, Mistah Burgess, can't yuh knock somethin off of tha, seein as how Ahm down n out now?"

"You ate that grub, and I got to pay for it, Tom."

"Yessuh, Ah know."

"It's going to be a little tough, Tom. But you got to go through with it. Two of the boys tried to run away this morning and dodge their debts, and I had to have the sheriff pick em up. I wasn't looking for no trouble out of you, Tom. . . . The rest of the families are going back."

Leaning out of the buggy, Burgess waited. In the surrounding stillness the cowbell tinkled again. Tom stood with his back against a post.

"Yuh got t go on, Tom. We ain't got nothin here," said May.

Tom looked at Burgess.

"Mistah Burgess, Ah don wanna make no trouble. But this is jus *too* hard. Ahm worse off now than befo. Ah got to start from scratch. . . ."

"Get in the buggy and come with me. I'll stake you with grub. We can talk over how you can pay it back." Tom said nothing. He rested his back against the post and looked at the mud-filled fields.

"Well," asked Burgess. "You coming?" Tom said nothing. He got slowly to the ground and pulled himself into the buggy. May watched them drive off.

"Hurry back, Tom!"

"Awright."

"Ma, tell Pa t bring me some 'lasses," begged Sally.

"Oh, Tom!"

Tom's head came out of the side of the buggy.

"Hunh?"

"Bring some 'lasses!"

"Hunh?"

"Bring some 'lasses fer Sal!"

"Awright!"

She watched the buggy disappear over the crest of the muddy hill. Then she sighed, caught Sally's hand, and turned back into the cabin.

FOR THE BEST IN PAPERBACKS, LOOK FOR THE

In every corner of the world, on every subject under the sun, Penguin represents quality and variety—the very best in publishing today.

For complete information about books available from Penguin—including Pelicans, Puffins, Peregrines, and Penguin Classics—and how to order them, write to us at the appropriate address below. Please note that for copyright reasons the selection of books varies from country to country.

In the United Kingdom: For a complete list of books available from Penguin in the U.K., please write to *Dept E.P., Penguin Books Ltd, Harmondsworth, Middlesex, UB7 0DA.*

In the United States: For a complete list of books available from Penguin in the U.S., please write to *Dept BA, Penguin*, Box 120, Bergenfield, New Jersey 07621-0120.

In Canada: For a complete list of books available from Penguin in Canada, please write to *Penguin Books Ltd, 2801 John Street, Markham, Ontario L3R 1B4*.

In Australia: For a complete list of books available from Penguin in Australia, please write to the *Marketing Department, Penguin Books Ltd, P.O. Box 257, Ringwood, Victoria 3134*.

In New Zealand: For a complete list of books available from Penguin in New Zealand, please write to the *Marketing Department, Penguin Books (NZ) Ltd, Private Bag, Takapuna, Auckland 9.*

In India: For a complete list of books available from Penguin, please write to *Penguin Overseas Ltd, 706 Eros Apartments, 56 Nehru Place, New Delhi, 110019.*

In Holland: For a complete list of books available from Penguin in Holland, please write to *Penguin Books Nederland B.V., Postbus 195, NL-1380AD Weesp, Netherlands.*

In Germany: For a complete list of books available from Penguin, please write to *Penguin Books Ltd, Friedrichstrasse 10-12, D-6000 Frankfurt Main 1, Federal Republic of Germany.*

In Spain: For a complete list of books available from Penguin in Spain, please write to *Longman, Penguin España, Calle San Nicolas 15, E-28013 Madrid, Spain.*

In Japan: For a complete list of books available from Penguin in Japan, please write to *Longman Penguin Japan Co Ltd, Yamaguchi Building, 2-12-9 Kanda Jimbocho, Chiyoda-Ku, Tokyo 101, Japan.*